D1572161

# Bociany

*Other titles in the Library of Modern Jewish Literature*

*Anna in Chains.* Merrill Joan Gerber
*At the Center.* Norma Rosen
*Bloodshed and Three Novellas.* Cynthia Ozick
*The Cannibal Galaxy.* Cynthia Ozick
*The Empire of Kalman the Cripple.* Yehuda Elberg
*Focus.* Arthur Miller
*God's Ear.* Rhoda Lerman
*The Island Within.* Ludwig Lewisohn
*The Jewish War.* Tova Reich
*John and Anzia: An American Romance.* Norma Rosen
*Lazar Malkin Enters Heaven.* Steve Stern
*Leah's Journey.* Gloria Goldreich
*Levitation: Five Fictions.* Cynthia Ozick
*My Own Ground.* Hugh Nissenson
*Of Lodz and Love.* Chava Rosenfarb
*O My America!* Johanna Kaplan
*The Pagan Rabbi and Other Stories.* Cynthia Ozick
*Plague of Dreamers.* Steve Stern
*The Rose Rabbi.* Daniel Stern
*Ship of the Hunted.* Yehuda Elberg
*Shira.* S. Y. Agnon
*The Suicide Academy.* Daniel Stern
*While the Messiah Tarries.* Melvin Jules Bukiet

# *Bociany*

Chava Rosenfarb

*Translated from the Yiddish by the Author*

Syracuse University Press

First Edition 2000
00 01 02 03 04 05 6 5 4 3 2 1

The paper used in this publication meets the minimum requirements of American National Standard for Information Sciences—Permanence of Paper for Printed Library Materials, ANSI Z39.48-1984. ∞™

**Library of Congress Cataloging-in-Publication Data**
Rosenfarb, Chawa, 1923-
[Botshani. 2. teyl. English]
Bociany / by Chava Rosenfarb.
p. cm.—(The library of modern Jewish literature)
ISBN 0-8156-0576-5 (cloth : alk. paper)
I. Title. II. Series.
PJ5129.R597B5813 1999
839'. 134—DC21 98-54858

Manufactured in the United States of America

For my children, Goldie and Abraham

*The end of reality is the beginning of legend . . .*

**Chava Rosenfarb** was born in Lodz, Poland. She is a survivor of the Lodz Ghetto as well as the Auschwitz and Bergen-Belsen concentration camps. She is the recipient of numerous literary prizes. In 1979 she was awarded the Manger Prize—the highest award for Yiddish literature—for her trilogy *The Tree of Life, (Der boim fun lebn).* She now resides in Canada.

# Bociany

# 1

THROUGH THE WINDOW OF THE GARRET, the first gray of dawn crowded in. It was late summer, and the sky outside was very deep and slightly hazy, as if filled with transparent cotton. In the east its color turned to a pale orange. A cock began to crow, then another. A few birds responded. The crickets had been singing all night, and now, with the oncoming day, their tunes became louder, sawing through the stillness with a gnawing, irritating monotony.

Hindele Polin, the scribe's wife, was fully dressed. She adjusted the wig on her head, wrapped herself in her plaid shawl, and picked up an empty jug from the shelf where the kitchen utensils were stored. She faced the room. Although its corners were still steeped in darkness, the familiar contours of everything in it were outlined quite discernibly by the gray light coming in through the window. What a cheerless, dingy dwelling it was! The crooked floor was cracked, and it swayed under the slightest step. The slanted roof descended almost to Hindele's head. It was only in the middle, where the table stood, that it was possible to raise a hand and not touch the beams. In the summer it was suffocatingly hot, in the winter freezing cold, and the roof leaked. Yet Hindele liked this home of hers very much, despite its dreariness and the misfortunes it seemed to attract.

She turned her puffy eyes to the bed where the two sick ones lay, her husband, Hamele the Scribe, and her eldest son, Itchele. Itchele was an *ile,* a genius, whose name was renowned not only in Bociany, but even in the town of Chwosty. He had been stricken with consumption just when it had been decided that after his bar mitzvah he would leave for the yeshiva in Sielce. His father had contracted the same disease two years earlier.

Both father and son breathed with difficulty, emitting heavy, labored sighs. Each sigh cut into Hindele's heart like the blade of a sharp knife, causing a fresh wave of tears to come to her eyes. The tears seemed to pour directly from the wounds of pain within her. The whites of her enormous black eyes were red, her eyelids were puffed like bluish boils, her cheeks were swollen. She no longer had any strength to cry, and yet whenever she was alone, the tears refused to stop, as if her entire body were made of weeping, and the tears issued from a bottomless well. She could no longer feel her tears, nor did she wipe them away. They would go their way undammed, and she would go hers. In spite of them, she did all that she had to do. There was no time to devote herself, even for a moment, solely to the luxury of crying.

She turned her overflowing eyes to the rumpled bed at the opposite side of the room. There she made out the empty space that still held the imprint of her body. Close to the wall, at the foot of the bed, slept her two youngest, the girls. From there, her gaze wandered toward the straw mattress on the floor under the window, where the other two sons slept entangled in a feather quilt, their limbs braided together.

Yacov, the younger of the two, stirred as she looked at him, as if he had felt his mother's glance in his sleep. Quickly she turned away, afraid that her eyes might awaken him. But as soon as she moved toward the door, she heard his voice, "I'm coming too, Mameshie!"

Afraid that he might start crying, she went back to the table and cut him a slice of bread from the quarter loaf she had placed there. "Hurry then," she whispered. "Wash and say the benediction." She wiped her face quickly with the edge of her plaid shawl. As soon as the boy had disengaged himself from the feather quilt and slipped out, she went over to cover his brother. Then she leaned out through the open window and inhaled deeply as she continued to dry her face with the palms of her hands.

The storks on the roofs were quiet. Only the crickets and a few birds, early risers, disturbed the stillness with their tuneful chattering. Hindele's gaze wandered over the roofs of the shtetl and halted for a while on the church tower, which pierced the deep, hazy gray with its pale, shimmering cross. Then, as she leaned a little further out the window, her eyes fell on the garden of the neighboring cloister.

Two nuns, dressed in black, with spotless white wimples and bibs, were walking among the flower beds, holding little prayer books in their hands. They were already up and about, eager to enjoy a last summer's day in peace. It did not occur to Hindele to envy them. They were too alien to be envied. Yet the sight of them was soothing; they made her think of her own faith. She sighed and whispered, raising her eyes to the sky, "Father in Heaven, show me your kindness with this new day."

A tiny, hopeful smile appeared at the corners of her mouth, which harbored a salty aftertaste of tears. She knew that this day would differ little from any other, and she was far from considering herself fortunate, yet the arrival of a new day was uplifting, even if accompanied by tears. She did not hope for a miracle. The hope she nourished every morning fed on the power of her faith, the capacity to accept the judgment of the Almighty, to surrender to His will and not falter in her trust in Him. "God will help," she muttered. Yet the grief in her heart quickened as she inhaled the intoxicating fragrances that reached her from the nuns' garden, the perfume of roses, jasmine, and acacias. The crickets chirped stubbornly, pricking the mind like a million pins. Hindele turned back toward the room, where the scents of the flowers mingled with the stale inside air and shadows hovered like the outstretched wings of a monstrous bird of prey.

The slice of bread she had cut for Yacov had vanished. He was standing at the door, manipulating the bolt, which hung loosely on its screws. Hindele placed a pitcher of fresh water on the stool near the sickbed. Her eyes met the hot, glassy stare of her husband. "You feel better, don't you?" she asked in a tone that sounded more like a statement than a question.

"Blessed be the Almighty," he replied in a weak voice, his thin nose struggling for air, the wings of his nostrils fluttering. "Move the stool with the books closer, too," he muttered.

She frowned, then moved the stool laden with heavy tomes closer to the bed. Her voice was soft. "It's still dark in here. Why don't you sleep some more?" She turned towards Yacov. "Have you said the prayer?"

He nodded. She picked up the empty jug, which she had deposited on the table, and they left the room, carefully finding their way down the flight of stairs in the dark. The wooden stairs were winding and shaky. Some boards were partially broken off, while others were missing completely. The banister shook and groaned with the stairs as she and the boy descended. In the dark, they felt with the soles of their shoes for the strong spots that would support their weight, so that they might descend without mishap. On the landing they came eye-to-eye with Manka the Washerwoman's cow, which occupied the ruined room on the ground floor.

In the yard, Hindele noticed that Manka, who did the laundry for the lessee and a few other wealthy families, was already at work in front of her house. Her arms and legs bare, she was standing over a steaming washtub, her thick torso swaying energetically back and forth over the scrubbing board. At the sight of Hindele, she stopped for a moment to wipe the sweat off her face with her bare arm, and asked, "How are they?"

"God will help," Hindele replied hurriedly, dragging Yacov with her by the hand. When she had passed Manka, she turned her head, adding as an afterthought, "You can kindle the stove in an hour and put the pot on to warm up."

"Shall be done," Manka replied without looking up, again engrossed in her work.

As she walked on, Hindele thought about Manka, whose luck was similar to hers. Manka was a widow, and nearly three years earlier, her house, which had stood across the street, burned to the ground. If not for the heroic exertions of her cousin, the fire chief Vaslav Spokojny, the whole street, and perhaps all of Bociany as well, would have gone up in flames. Now Manka lived in a hut that bordered on Hindele's backyard.

Hindele and Manka had always been civil to one another, but until the time of her misfortunes, Hindele had never allowed herself to establish a close personal contact with the gentile woman. Now that every day at dawn she had to hurry to Reb Faivele the Miller's farm on the Blue Mountain in order to get a jug of fresh goat milk for her sick men—this being one of Reb Faivele's charitable gestures—Hindele had accepted Manka's offer to keep an eye on her window. At the slightest sound from upstairs, Manka would go up, kindle the stove, and put the breakfast pot on the fire to warm.

"How strange," Hindele shook her head in amazement as she plodded with Yacov through the wheel-rutted alley. "If not for our misfortunes, we would never have come in contact with one another like human beings."

As the road grew wider, Hindele marched with more energy, holding on to the boy's hand. She did not mind taking him along. True, he needed those few hours of sleep in the morning, yet she was certain that this walk with her compensated for it somehow. Although he said nothing—her boys were not overly given to talking—she could feel that he enjoyed walking beside her as much as she enjoyed having him do so. To her it was a consolation to hold his tiny hand, rest her eyes on his dreamy, delicate face, and see there a contented smile. That little smile was very precious to her, especially since he had recently become such a crybaby. Well, not quite a crybaby. He did not cry at all like a child, but rather like herself, silently, letting the tears roll down his cheeks.

If she asked him why he was crying, he would reply, "I'm not crying, Mameshie. My eyes are sweating."

"Why are your eyes sweating?"

"Because I'm scared."

"What are you scared of, Yacov?"

"I don't know, Mameshie."

She would not insist that he tell her. Her little girls would often cry as well, but as children do, noisily, with a persistent urgency that often tested her patience. But when Yacov cried, her heart would fill with such dread and premonition that she could hardly bear it.

A few men with prayer bags under their arms went by on their way to the synagogue. As Hindele and Yacov passed the beautiful wooden structure, they could see through the open door a number of praying men wrapped in prayer shawls. Other men were standing on the threshold, arguing about something. The street was dotted with peasants. The field boys and serving men of the landowner hurried in the opposite direction, toward the Narrow Poplar Road, which led to the manor. A sleepy shepherd boy was herding some cows to the nearby pasture.

As Hindele and Yacov came out onto the Wide Poplar Road and the sky brightened, they noticed Reb Senderl the Cabalist approaching them from the distance. Yesterday, when she was sitting in front of her shop on the roofed market, which was known as the Potcheyov, Hindele had seen Reb Senderl lock up his store and set out in the direction of this road. Now he was on his way back, with a sack of herbs slung over his shoulder. She knew that he had spent the night near the marshes, bathing in the lake. Perhaps he had even seen the face of the moon on the past moonless night. He had once told her about the moon representing the face of the Divine Emanation, the *Shkhina*, her eyes blinded from crying over the exile she shared with the children of Israel. For even when the moon shone, it was not with its own light, but with the dull light of a blind person's eyes. As Reb Senderl passed them, Hindele greeted him from the side of the road with heartfelt reverence.

"What's new?" he called from the distance.

"Blessed be His holy Name. God will help," she replied, moving on, but allowing her eyes to rest on him a while longer. The sight of this small, elderly man with his magnificent gray beard was soothing. She could feel a healing kindness radiate from his figure. She had no doubt that on his way from his nocturnal escapade he had visited Yoel the Blacksmith, who lived alone in a hut near his smithy on the Wide Poplar Road, far beyond the Blue Mountain. For many years no one in Bociany would have anything to do with Yoel, who was a drunkard and was suspected of ugly deeds. Only wagon drivers and Hasidim on their way to the Rabbi of Chwosty would stop at his place to shoe their horses. Reb Senderl was the only one who befriended the man.

Reb Senderl had once explained this to Hindele. "The Rabbi Reb Mayer," Reb Senderl had said, "carried on a friendship with Elisha Ben Abuya, the sinful infidel. When he was asked why he carried on with such a despicable person, Rabbi Mayer answered, 'I liken Elisha Ben Abuya to a pomegranate. So I throw away its outer husk and take delight in the fruit.'"

This Hindele had learned from Reb Senderl, and she followed his example in her relationships with her women friends, such as Nechele the Pockmarked, the sexton's wife, and even with Manka the Washerwoman. But she followed it particularly with Nechele the Pockmarked, because Nechele was closer to her heart, almost like a relative, and therefore her shortcomings were all the more irritating.

Nechele was so strictly observant of the religious laws that she could not bear to hear Hindele say a single good word about Manka the Washerwoman, because Manka was a devout Christian. Had Nechele known that Hindele did not scold her children for playing with Manka's children, she would have broken off all contact with her. Nechele sat in judgment on everyone's words and deeds, proclaiming her opinion on what people did or said, without taking into account any mitigating circumstances. Nonetheless, Hindele loved Nechele the Pockmarked, despite her rigidity. Nechele's soul was full of yearning. She loved Hasidic and cantorial song, and she was lonesome, without even a child to console her. Moreover, Nechele was goodhearted. More than once had she cooked a soup from her own supplies for Hindele's sick, and she shared with Hindele the bargains that she bought on market days, as Hindele had neither the time nor the patience to go looking for bargains herself.

In the huts people were waking. Barefoot peasant women in white fustian nightshirts were feeding the animals. The cocks started to crow more energetically, while the birds prattled feverishly. The sun came out. Its rays shot through the poplar boughs onto the road, greeting Hindele and Yacov with sudden dazzling light. The world was transformed into a lumi nous, cheerful place. A passing cart seemed to be rolling straight into the sun's beams. Hindele called after the driver. She knew him, as she knew most of the peasants of the region, from dealings with them in her shop on the Potcheyov. Soon mother and son had clambered into the cart and seated themselves on top of a sweet-smelling stack of hay.

Yacov was engrossed in watching his mother, observing her face as it was washed by the sun's rays. His legs, which had begun to hurt during the long walk, were now nestled deep in the hay under Hindele's skirt. He shut his sleepy eyes but opened them again, so as not to miss his mother's hidden smile or the sight of her delicate stooped body outlined by the sun's quivering rays. His mother was small and thin. Although she worked hard and he could not remember a day when he had seen her lying in bed sick, except when his youngest sister was born, he still trembled for her safety, as if she were so weak the slightest breeze might blow her away. It seemed to him that she was a rare creature, almost holy, made of precious, fragile matter, which had to be handled with care and protected. Yet in her fragility she was his rock of support. He helped her as much as he could, but it was to her that he ran for attention and comfort whenever he needed it. Now the plaid shawl on her shoulders, which before had seemed to him like a mourning hood or the cowl of a ghost, looked like the folded wings of a stork at rest.

"You see the sunflowers?" She sniffled and pointed with her chin in the direction of a plot of land covered with high-stemmed sunflowers.

Yacov turned his head, following her gaze with his eyes. The plot of land looked like an island of suns in a sea of green and gave off a cheerful light of its own. He smiled. "They look funny."

She knew that by "funny" he meant fun, delightful to look at. She nodded and enveloped him in her shawl. She observed him from the corner of her eye. "Between him and me there is a kind of fiddle music playing," she said to herself. "I wonder whether he is aware of it, too." She wiped her nose with the corner of her shawl and adjusted her wig, which had the habit of sitting askew on her head. It was her only wig and, in truth, she should be saving it for the Sabbath and the holidays and wear just a kerchief or a bonnet, as many of the other married women did. But she stood all day in the Potcheyov, exposed to the public and, after all, she was Reb Hamele the Scribe's wife and herself a descendant of the Rabbi from Wurke. Besides, she felt somehow safer in the wig.

They arrived at the foot of the Blue Mountain. Hindele and the boy disembarked and thanked the peasant. She and Yacov began to climb up the hill. After a while, she let go of his hand and left him behind as she darted ahead to leave the jug on the step of the miller's verandah. By the time Yacov reached the top of the hill, his mother was already waiting for him in front of the fence that surrounded the miller's yard.

They sat down beside a cluster of heather in the tussocky grass over which Hindele had spread the edge of her plaid. She fondled the heather with her hand as she and Yacov looked at its tiny flowering heads. Then they watched the revolving sails of the mill and listened to their pleasant squeaking. The air glistened with crystalline brightness, its fragrance sharp and intoxicating. Yacov cradled his head in Hindele's lap, shut his eyes to protect them from the sun's glare, and before long drifted into slumber. She looked down at his delicate, pale face. A curly brown sidelock trembled on his cheek as he breathed deeply, calmly. She put her hand over his head as if to cover it with an additional skullcap and turned her eyes to the distance.

Far in the valley Hindele saw Bociany wreathed by the two poplar roads, the Narrow and the Wide. It had been by the nearer one, the Wide Poplar Road, that she had arrived in the shtetl to marry Reb Hamele. She had always liked the shtetl's name. Storks built their nests on its rooftops. The Polish word for storks is "bociany," so the name of the shtetl was Bociany.

As she gazed down upon it, she saw Bociany nestled between the Blue Mountain and the White Mountain, itself looking like a stork's nest. The pointed, dark-yellow straw roofs and brick-colored shingle roofs peeked out like the bills of young fowl. It was a remote, forgotten shtetl, where time seemed to arrive very slowly. News, when it reached Bociany through the Wide Poplar Road that led from Chwosty, the closest town, was so old that it had already grown a beard.

The valley in which Bociany lay was an offshoot of the larger Vistula Valley. With the exception of a swampy ring surrounding the shtetl, the region was blessed with good, rich soil. Hindele's eyes wandered over the fields of rye and wheat, oats and potatoes, interspersed by green pastures and orchards, which stretched mile upon mile into the distance. Here and there, like islands dotting the gold and green, were the stark shadows of forest land or the glimmering mirror of a lake or a pond.

The Blue Mountain was blue, and the White Mountain white, because during the summer, the former wore a hood of bluebells and the latter a hood of white daisies. On a day as bright and sunny as this one, the bluebottles and daisies, together with the red poppies and yellow buttercups in the pastures and on the hills, along with the lilies-of-the-valley, the forget-me-nots in the marshes, the water lilies in the lake, and the sunflowers near the huts, joined with the golden fields and green pastures, with the bright birch wood and the shadowy pine wood, to create a lively and colorful carpet. The carpet was not only reflected in the sky, but it infused the very air with its shimmer. So crystal clear was the air in that region that one was never sure whether the clouds on the horizon were really clouds, or the outlines of the distant Tatra Mountains. These mountains belonged to the Austrian Empire, whereas the shtetl, located on this side of the mountains, belonged to Russia and Tsar Nicholas II.

Aside from the fact that the noise of the world reached it even later than other Polish shtetlekh, Bociany differed very little from Hindele's home shtetl or the shtetlekh she knew. That is to say, Bociany was something between a little town and a village, and its official representative was not a burgomaster but a county officer. As in the other shtetlekh, Bociany's life centered around the cobblestone marketplace, where the peasants from the countryside gathered to sell their wares on Tuesday market days. The marketplace was surrounded only by a few brick or stone buildings. From where she now sat, Hindele could see the buildings protruding from the density of wooden huts like a half-circle of uneven teeth, the tallest and pointiest being the Church of All Saints.

And yet Hindele considered Bociany an exceptional shtetl. This fact had struck her as soon as she had approached it for the first time and its rooftops had come into sight. It was amazing. Each one of the roofs, whether it covered a proud brick house or a moldy sunken shack, whether it belonged to a Jewish or to a gentile family, displayed an old wheel attached to its front like a box of phylacteries. On these wheels pairs of storks would build their nests every year, lay their eggs, and sit on them until they hatched, then bring up their young and stay on for the rest of the summer.

The storks of Bociany were majestic white birds, three, sometimes four feet in height, with black flight feathers, dark-red bills, and spindly reddish legs. They were inclined to stand motionless on one foot and meditate and would have devoted entire days to this activity—were it not for the prosaic problems of sustenance, which, in comparison to the problems of the hosts on whose roofs they lived, were not inordinately severe.

The storks derived their livelihood from the swamps surrounding the shtetl, which swarmed with frogs, tadpoles, snails, and earthworms. The human habit of storing away supplies against a "black hour" was alien to them. They could fill themselves and their offspring so far and no more, yet the thought of their treasures in the swamps gave them no peace of mind. Several times a day they felt compelled to check on their "gold mines," if only to fish for a snack for their little ones, or merely to survey the marshes by cruising above them. Because of this, the air above the shtetl always resounded with their bustling cries and the clatter of their bills, sounds that expressed with urgency the grave state of stork affairs.

It is therefore no wonder that a wandering band of beggars, which regularly descended on Bociany for the Tuesday market day, had coined the term "a Bociany fair" for any racket loud enough to reach the sky. Every Tuesday, the clamor from the humans below, and the cacophony from the birds above, threatened to deafen the unprepared ears of a stranger, before he even realized that he was actually caught between two towns, a Bociany on earth and a Bociany in the heavens, both towns preoccupied in dead seriousness with practical problems, one with having too much, the other with having too little.

For the earthly Bociany fared not so "heavenly." The land around the shtetl was indeed generous and fertile, but it belonged to a landowner and to his heirs, who lived in a manor house at the foot of the White Mountain. Most of the peasants owned little more than a small piece of swampy land. They labored as field hands on the landlord's property. And as the Gentiles fared, so fared the Jews. The shtetl of Bociany was distinguished by its poverty.

It could not be helped. The pauper could neither escape his home nor his fate. What he could do was wait with iron fortitude, the Christian for the Kingdom of Heaven and the Jew for the coming of the Messiah, and in the meantime be consoled with whatever solace he could find. And the storks were a solace for the shtetl.

When the Polish autumn began to dip leaves in a pallet of sunset colors, when the sheaves of grain appeared on the scythed fields like figures embracing in a melancholy dance, and the time for blowing the ram's horn for the High Holy Days was passed, a peculiar restlessness entered the hearts of the people of Bociany and mixed with the usual autumnal sadness. That was the time when the storks, as if by a prearranged signal, rose from the rooftops, fluttered their wings as if waving good-bye, and soared toward the sky. For a while, they circled the region, as if to fix the familiar panorama in their memory. Then, as if on command, they formed themselves into long lines and, with majestic dignity, flew off toward distant lands.

"Who knows if they'll return," Manka the Washerwoman and the other peasant women would sigh, crossing themselves in awe.

A bird was not like a human being, who died where he was born. A bird was born free, soared high, and could see what was behind and what was ahead. So perhaps the storks could foresee that the abundant swamps would become arid, and they would seek out new homes for future summers. The peasant women blinked their moist eyes toward the sky, until the last quivering string of storks wound itself into the horizon and vanished.

Every year before spring arrived, even before the snow had melted, both the gentile boys and the heder boys ran through the muddy roads to await the arrival of the storks. The gentile boys headed toward the White Mountain and the Jewish boys toward the Blue Mountain, where the windmill stood, and where Hindele now sat. From here, they could see all of Bociany, see the lake where the demons bathed and Kailele the Bride had drowned herself, and see the fields and the woods across the lake. They could also discern, at a great distance, what they believed to be the Mountains of Darkness, which stood on the border of this world and the next. There, at the mysterious Sabbath River, the Sambation, lived the dragons that guarded the land of the eternally happy little red Jews, who knew nothing of exile. It was to the marshes of that happy land, the boys were convinced, that the storks flew every winter, and it was from there that they returned.

These same little boys brought the news to Bociany. "The storks are coming!"

The adults received this information with pretended indifference, as if to say, "May more important tidings be brought to us." But secretly, they sighed with relief. The return of the storks was a good omen. And out of gratitude to the storks for their devotion, the shtetl refused to mark the seasons by the calendar. Instead, the day on which the storks returned was considered the first day of summer, and the day they left, the first day of winter.

As far as the Jewish boys were concerned, most were convinced that one fine day the Messiah Ben David himself would arrive in the shtetl along with the storks. He would ride his donkey through the Wide Poplar

Road, and the storks would soar above his head. Together they would pass first the gentile cemetery and afterwards the Jewish. The storks' clucking would help the Messiah waken the dead, so that this particular day would be not only the first day of summer, but also the Day of Resurrection and Deliverance.

All generations of Jewish boys had been preoccupied with the same problem: What would the Messiah do when he rode past the gentile cemetery? Would the gentile dead also profit from the resurrection, or would the Messiah leave them rotting in the ground? And what would he do with the living goyim? Would he redeem them, too—not, of course, for their good deeds to the Jews, but perhaps because of their kindness to the storks? And since they could never make out the answers, the boys themselves would decide the issue, depending whether or not they were involved in a war with the gentile boys at the time.

The favorite pastime for the people of Bociany was to observe with a feeling of kinship how the storks built their nests on the roofs, and to philosophize on the similarity between human family life and that of the birds. This subject was of particular interest to the women, both Jew and gentile, some of whom kept prepared a bundle of good straw and sticks in order to save the storks the trouble of going too far in their search for building materials. And when the "she" became pregnant and was about to lay her eggs, these housewives would send their children to the nearest swamp for frogs, tadpoles, snails, or rain worms, which they offered to the female in a gesture of solidarity. They did not believe that a male bird had any more understanding of a female in such a condition than did the human male. The women would carry on this special attention both when the "she" was laying the eggs and during the entire month when the pair were sitting on the eggs. That the male sat on the eggs along with the female was regarded as further proof of male laziness. It was no great trick to join in the act of life-giving, if the wife bore all the pains of labor.

The women would watch the young storks set out for their first flight with their parents. They would smile wistfully, and then remind themselves that they had more important business to see to. The storks once again became a part of day-to-day life and were paid no more attention, unless danger threatened the shtetl, in the form of a fire or a storm.

The Jewish and gentile fire brigades, each of which had its own horses and wagons, its own water barrels and equipment, usually worked together. They had even worked out a special technique for saving the storks in dangerous situations. At such moments they were supposed to resort to a long pole with hooks. That was what they were supposed to do; in practice they hardly ever did so. There were more important things to remember during a fire than the pole with the hooks, or the storks. The houses of Bociany, except for those few brick or stone structures surrounding the marketplace, were made entirely of wood, the roofs were straw, and it took no more than a spark and a little breeze for the fire to spread. The only advantage in this situation was that since the pogrom after the death of Tsar Alexander II, when half the shtetl had gone up in flames, the Gentiles did not dare set fire to any Jewish house during an attack on the Jews. In this violent way they had learned that fire does not discriminate.

As far as the storks were concerned, they managed better without the fire brigades than their hosts did with the fire brigades. They usually escaped with their families intact, before the firemen even discovered where the fire was.

On the whole, thanks to the storks, harbingers of good fortune for humans—provided one behaved humanely to them in turn—the shtetl of Bociany, except in matters of livelihood, was a fortunate place for both Jew and Gentile. Since the storks, like nature in general, took no notice of the racial differences among their hosts, they saw to it that the wombs of both the kosher Jewish matrons and those of their gentile neighbors were never empty. Moreover, for the most part, Jew and Gentile lived quite peacefully together. Mutual needs called forth mutual support, in spite of mutual distrust. Although the two communities were worlds apart in their way of life, there was a certain civil contact between them; there were even friendships formed, although of a casual character. Friendships like the one between Hindele and Manka the Washerwoman were rather the exception than the rule.

Jewish peddlers who wandered through the villages, Jewish butcher boys and wagon drivers would drink with the peasants at the Jewish inn. Gentiles bought merchandise on credit in the Jewish stores on the Potcheyov. Often Jewish shopkeepers received bags of potatoes, cabbage, onions, or fruits as gifts from "their" peasants. If the bailiffs from the district office arrived to mark down a peasant's belongings as security against unpaid taxes, his Jewish acquaintances would organize a collection, just as if it were a Jewish cause, and help to save the threatened household. By the same token, through the intercession of a peasant, a Jewish father could influence the county officer to register his newborn son in the army recruitment books as having been born much later than he was, thus giving the Messiah a chance to arrive and cancel the recuitment altogether. And during a drought, or a plague among the cattle, if the Hasidim were on their way to visit the Rabbi of Chwosty and were in their wagons passing the peasant huts along the Wide Poplar Road, the peasants would call after them, "Don't forget, in God's name, to ask the *tsadik* for rain. Ask for a miracle for us, too!"

And yet, although the gentiles and Jews got along well, they became strangers, even enemies, as soon as Sunday or any other Christian holiday arrived. On Christian holy days, the Jews disappeared like mice into their holes, while the goyim took over Bociany. As a rule, Jewish fears ran wild automatically—for through the ages, the Jews had developed to perfection the art of worrying ahead of time, and their worries had seldom proved unfounded. True, in Bociany there was a great probability that they were worrying for nothing; still, they allowed their hearts to toll with alarm as soon as they heard the church bells toll for prayer.

Small wonder. On Christian holy days, the Gentiles of the shtetl, as well as those from the surrounding villages, and the nuns from the cloister, which was located on the border of the gentile district where Hindele lived, filled all the streets as they moved toward the market place, carrying holy pictures. Choir songs and incense made the familiar atmosphere seem alien, especially as the day wore on and the gaily dressed crowd began to pour out of the church door, overflowing into the town square, the marketplace, and the sidewalks around the Potcheyov. Soon bottles of the vodka known as *monopolka* appeared from behind the Sunday camisoles. The peasants would begin with a dance and end with a fight. A Jew would have had to be out of his mind not to lock the doors and windows and secure them with iron or wooden bars; he would have to be crazy not to tighten the wires that fastened the shutters, especially if he lived in one of the unfortunate houses that bordered directly on the areas where the Gentiles congregated.

With the exception of a few attacks on the Jews, however, everything had been quiet since Hindele had first arrived in Bociany. One of these attacks had been inspired by the unexplained death of a gentile boy; another had occurred after a too passionate sermon by the priest, a third after a baptism. There had also been one after a wedding and another after a funeral, when the intoxicated crowd had required more than the usual distraction.

After all, the heart of the shtetl was not inhabited by the Gentiles. True, the church stood at the shtetl's very center, in the marketplace, flanked by the parsonage on its right and by the county officer's stone house on its left. Adjoining the county officer's house stood the house where the gendarmes lived, which also contained the jail. But aside from these gentile structures, the marketplace was surrounded by Jewish houses, a few fashionably built with brick, the rest of wood, decrepit, mildewed, and rotting. All these houses were inhabited by the elite of the Jewish congregation. The brick houses were occupied by the families of such important people as the lessee, the wood merchant, or the landlord's Jewish bookkeeper, who was known as "the writer"; the other houses were occupied by the members of the Jewish clergy, the barber-surgeon, and Fishele the Butcher. As for the Potcheyov, it contained only Jewish shops.

From the marketplace, the crooked, muddy streets and alleys extended like the sun's rays in all directions. The nearer to the center they were, the more likely they were to be occupied by Jews. The further toward the countryside, the more likely they were to be inhabited by Gentiles. The distribution of the Jewish population was such that the more money one had, or the greater one's say in public affairs, the closer one lived to the heart of the shtetl. The view from the windows of these houses may have been unfortunate, but within them, life was good, or almost so.

As she looked now down on Bociany, Hindele asked herself how long it had actually been since that day when she had arrived there to marry Reb Hamele. She could hardly count the number of years that had passed, although the day of her arrival and her wedding day stood out in her memory very vividly. How long was it since she had seen her family? She missed her sisters, but more than anyone else, she missed her deceased mother. "Even very old people," Hindele thought, "still feel the need for their mothers, especially during hard times."

It was strange how she was prone to misfortune. The wise saying, "A change of place, a change of luck," could not be applied to her. Her distinguished lineage of descent in a straight line from King David's house had done nothing to alter her bad luck, even after she had moved to Bociany. Her more recent parentage, which derived from the house of the Rabbi of Wurke, also had no bearing on it, nor did her husband's descent from the very cream of the rabbinical world.

She tried to recall the features of her father's face, but she could see them only vaguely. She barely knew him, barely remembered him. He had been a fanatically devout Hasid who had lived with the Rabbi and for the Rabbi. His real home had been the Rabbi's court. Her mother however . . . Hindele could recall her mother's face down to the smallest detail; she saw her stooped figure, the way she had walked, talked, and gestured. Proud as her mother had been of her social position and of her pious husband, and joyful as she had always tried to be, in keeping with Hasidic tradition, she hardly ever had time to catch her breath. Not only did she have a house full of children and a husband to support, but she also had to receive and lodge visiting Hasidim from other towns whom her husband brought home as guests. She had to make ends meet as well as she could by taking on all kinds of business, especially peddling, and leaving the care of the household to Hindele, her eldest daughter. Only when her mother grew weaker and Hindele grew older was the procedure reversed. The mother stayed home, while the daughter went out to earn the daily bread for the family.

Hindele could not recall a single day when she had sat idle, even on the Sabbath, except when she was obliged to go to the synagogue with her family. To go for a walk with no purpose but pleasure in mind was an unheard-of thing. She was the first-born, a second mother to her siblings, privileged by nature to carry most of the family's burden on her shoulders. More than once, while still a very young girl, she had to remind her preoccupied mother to suckle her youngest brother, Zishele. Zishele later returned the favor in kind, when he taught Hindele all that he himself had learned in heder. Later still, when Zishele had begun studying the *Mishne,* they would go over the text together, in secret, because Zishele thought it was not proper for him to be seen studying with his sister, not even when she was occupied with mending socks while they studied. Yet those hours were so precious to them both that they were reluctant to give them up even when Zishele became a bar mitzvah boy. Then fate intervened, and Zishele died of an unknown disease.

Because of these studies with her brother, Hindele developed a love of reading. Before her husband's and son's illnesses, she was always doing business with the book peddler who visited Bociany a couple of times a year, his cart laden with phylacteries, mezuzahs, amulets, talismans for women in labor, and stacks and stacks of books, sacred and profane, hard and soft-covered, at the sight of which Hindele's head always began to swim. For a few kopecks a month, she would borrow whatever she saw:

morality books, books of verse and wise sayings, books of Hasidic lore, or interesting stories in Yiddish. But her favorites were stories from the Jewish past, tales woven around the heroes whom she had read about in the women's Bible. Such books fortified and sustained her in her daily life.

She had married very late, at eighteen. This was not because there had been a lack of matchmakers with interesting proposals, but because her mother had fallen ill, and Hindele had to wait for the next sister to grow experienced enough to take over the household duties. Only then did Hindele get the kind of groom she deserved. Oh, the time between her engagement and her wedding! It was then that Hindele had heard for the first time that she was "not an ugly" girl. When she came to Bociany to marry, she had long chestnut hair, which she wore braided in a huge bun at the nape of her neck. True, she was slight of build and seemed fragile, but in reality she was well developed, sturdy and healthy at the same time that she was slender, supple, and light-footed. At that time, she had moments when she worried about being pleasing to the eye and rejoiced when she discovered that she was.

Now this fussing over herself seemed like plain vanity. It was so alien to her present nature that she thought of herself in those times as if she had been living a dream. Now her life belonged exclusively to her husband and her children. It had become entirely dissolved in their lives, while she continued to try to make her "selfishness" vanish even more completely. Even her love of reading was not entirely linked to seeking self-gratification. In the back of her mind there was always the hope that in this manner she could more closely approach her husband's inner world and understand him better, so that she might serve him better. Or she memorized the stories that she read, in order to be able one day to recount them to her children. It seemed to her that only her body bore the traces of hardship and suffering, while her soul, enriched, continued to grow like a fertile tree, thanks to her life with her dear ones.

Hindele had followed in her mother's footsteps by supporting her family. She had opened a shop of odds and ends on the Potcheyov. She saw to it that the pipe leading from the stove in her garret to the neighboring shed should always be warm, so that her husband could do all his work in peace and comfort at the table inside. She made sure that he did not lack oil for his lamp, bread for his herring, an onion or a few potatoes, and that there should even be a leg of chicken on his plate for the Sabbath meal. Her husband was not just anybody, and what he was doing was no small thing. He had to invest all of his being in his work. He had once quoted the saying of Rabbi Reb Mayer to her. "I am a scribe," Rabbi Reb Mayer had said, "so I must pay attention to my work, for it is sacred. It is God's work. And if one leaves out a single letter, or adds one letter too many, one can, Heaven forbid, destroy the whole world."

Hindele's husband, Hamele the Scribe, was a Talmudic scholar whose name was well known throughout the province of Sielce. Not only did he occupy himself with the sacred task of writing Torah Scrolls for the surrounding communities, but he was also the author of a number of books devoted to close examination of the Scriptures, as well as question-and-answer books and a small volume of his own sharp thoughts about Jewish faith. His whole life had been one struggle to deserve this good fortune of being a scholar among Jews. But Hindele was aware that the greatest difficulty in that struggle lay in his daily life with his own family. He always felt that he owed his family a debt, owed his wife on account of her hard work, owed his little daughters because he rarely noticed them and when he did, he mixed up their names, and owed his sons because he devoted too little time to them. So he tried to pay them back, to reward them through the diligence of his work, through the effort he invested in his writings, and through his modesty and self-composure.

As she sat on the grass, waiting for Reb Faivele the Miller's goats to be milked, Hindele felt the night creep back into her heart along with thoughts about her husband. She tried to concentrate on Yacov, who was sleeping with his head cradled in her lap. She marveled at the boy's finely drawn eyebrows and his thin, almost transparent eyelids fringed with glistening brown lashes. She loved his eyes. They seemed like two dishes of honey, full of brown sweetness. She loved his mouth as well, so delicately red and shiny. She loved his chin, his ears, the shape of his entire face, and the form of his thin body, which made her think of a small, swaying tree. And he had a good mind as well. Of course, neither he nor Shalom, his elder brother, could compare with her eldest, Itchele, who was a genius; none of her sons resembled their father as much as Itchele did. Yet she was proud of her other sons just as much as she was of Itchele. She was proud of her two little girls as well, although no one saw any exceptional qualities in them. But Itchele—he was the most important of them all, not because of his gifts, but because he was so very ill.

The tears welled up and burst from Hindele's eyes, causing her body to convulse with spasms, as if it were nothing but a vessel filled to the brim with bitter, salty water. At that moment she heard Fredka, the miller's housekeeper, calling her. With the tears still lying fresh on her face, she lifted Yacov's head from her lap and made him sit up. She jumped to her feet and dashed into the yard, trying to control her sobs so as not to wake the miller's family, which slept on obliviously in the silent whitewashed house.

Fredka was waiting on the verandah. "Have they gotten worse?" she asked.

"God will help," Hindele stammered, choking on the words and the tears. She took the jug from Fredka's hand and bowed deeply, as if Fredka were the mistress of the house. "May God bless you," she added and turned around. She let her gaze drop into the jug, and her tears dripped into the white foam. The sight of the warm, bubbly milk calmed her. She stopped for a while outside the fence to regain her composure, then walked swiftly over to Yacov and took him by the hand, and they walked down the path in the direction of the Wide Poplar Road.

## 2

IT WAS FRIDAY, the day that Bociany looked forward to all week. The shtetl was busy with preparations for the Sabbath. The marketplace, the stalls, and the shops of the Potcheyov teemed with people.

Hindele stood beside the stool in front of her shop, surrounded by her children and a few customers. The boys, Shalom and Yacov, had returned early from the heder, and after she had fed them some bread, Hindele had left them to mind the shop and had run home to feed her husband and son. She had done the housecleaning and prepared the Sabbath meal for that evening, as well as the *cholnt* for the next day. The *cholnt* was customarily prepared in Bociany as a *yaptzok* consisting of a hash of potatoes and beans, with bones or meat or *kishka* if one could afford them. She had taken the *cholnt* to the baker's to be kept in his oven until noon the next day, then had returned to her shop and made the boys run some errands for her and take her contributions to charity. She had also paid a few kopecks of what she owed to the *melamed* of the *heder,* to the grocery man and the butcher. Her two little girls, Gitele and Shaindele, had remained beside her all the while, playing in the gutter.

Now, hours later, the children were hungry again. They clung to her, impatiently waiting for her to be finished with the customers, so that she might give them some food. Hindele pretended not to notice. The children could wait; the customers could not. For the time being, she had to concentrate on her shop.

She called it a shop for lack of a better word to describe her place of business. In fact, she owned nothing more than a "blind" window with shelves in the wall of the Potcheyov. On these shelves she kept the boxes with her merchandise, "vanities" she called them: shoelaces, buttons, combs, hand mirrors, safety pins, hairpins, foot swaddles, kerchiefs, socks, gloves, colored ribbons, rolls of lace, and countless similar items. When there were no customers to attend to, she usually sat nearby on a little stool, and if it rained or snowed, she protected her head from the elements by covering it with the cardboard lid of a box. If it was very cold and wet, she draped an oilcloth over her merchandise, herself, and her children when they were around.

She also kept house here in front of the shelves, especially recently, because she wanted her healthy children to keep away from home as much as possible, so that they would not catch the disease of their father and brother. She would bring along a loaf of bread as well as a jar with schmaltz herring, some onions, and a pot of oatmeal, which she kept warm on a fire pot filled with charcoal.

Business was sluggish all week, except for Tuesday market days and Fridays. On the other days of the week, Hindele might sit idle for hours, sometimes from morning until night, without even earning the few kopecks she needed for a loaf of bread. That might happen on the busy days as well, but then as soon as one customer appeared—as had just that moment occurred—she was immediately surrounded by others. Her hands nervously pulled out boxes. She climbed on her stool to reach for the boxes on the upper shelves. She bent down to pull out other boxes from the bottom shelves. She almost knocked over the fire pot as she tried to balance by holding on to the middle shelf that served as her counter. Her loose wig turned sideways, and her forehead and nose dripped with perspiration, as box covers flew open, and socks, ribbons, combs, and buttons piled up in front of her in a messy pile, although she always managed to keep count of everything.

Most customers decided after a while that she did not have what they needed. But she detained them, trying to convince them that if she did not have what they needed at the moment, then she had what they might need later on, even if they themselves were not yet aware of the need. Kopecks piled up in her fist. She thrust them into her pocket as one customer left with a few buttons, another with a couple of hairpins, a third with a bobbin of sewing thread, and their places were taken by others.

Her impatient daughters pulled at the folds of Hindele's skirt, whining, "Mameshie, bread and herring!"

She pretended that she did not hear them and did not feel the tug at her skirt. This moment was precious; she had to concentrate on what she was doing. The proper use of her vocabulary of polite words and servile expressions could be decisive in the conclusion of a deal. And she did know how to talk to the peasants. She treated them with deference, bowing, humbly suggesting this or that item, complimenting them on their looks, while addressing them as *Prosze Pani* or *Prosze Pana,* as if they were the masters of the manor and not its servants. This was no pretense; she did feel humble. She did feel like a beggar before them. Whether or not her children would have bread and herring to eat depended on them.

At last she was left with only one customer, but he was the most difficult one. He had come, heaven preserve her, to chat with her on this day of all days; buying something had been only an excuse that he quickly forgot. She had no idea what he meant by paying her these frequent visits, nor why he always stared at her with the bulging, bloodshot eyes of a drunkard while he questioned her about personal matters that were none of his business. She needed the strength of Samson to remain composed despite her heavy heart and her fatigue, and to answer his questions correctly and honestly. It was not in her nature to put off anyone, especially him, a Gentile. And he was, after all, the fire chief, Pan Vaslav Spokojny. Because of his bravery, her family had been evacuated and her home saved from the fire that had broken out at his cousin Manka's house nearly three years earlier.

"Why are your eyes redder today than they were the last time I saw you?" he asked as soon as the other customers had left. He fingered the merchandise, which lay strewn over the middle shelf, and looked straight into her face. He shook his head in amazement and grinned. "You look like the Holy Mary after Pan Jesus' crucifixion!"

"Why should my eyes be redder?" Hindele mumbled, averting her eyes while she held up a pair of socks for him. "Does Pan Fire Chief want to take these socks, or should I put them away?"

He took the socks from her hand and placed them on top of the heap on the counter shelf. "It's too bad about your eyes, Hindele," he said, and moved closer to her. He was a corpulent man with an enormous belly, which bulged over the pants of his paramilitary uniform. He wore the tails of his navy blue jacket thrust to the side, with the brass buttons undone. His bulk filled the entire front of the shop, so that Hindele and the two girls clinging to her skirts were forced to retreat to the wall. "Such huge black eyes . . . " Pan Vaslav simpered. He stepped closer to her, and his thick alcoholic breath blew in her face. "They say that the devil has black eyes. While yours . . . I swear there is an angel looking out from your black eyes. It's the Angel of Mercy. Do you know, Hindele, that the Angel of Mercy is looking at me from your eyes?"

She had heard this remark from him many times before. "Why should the Angel of Mercy be looking out of my eyes?" she mumbled. In her heart she called on the Angel of Mercy, or at least on Yossele Abedale, her neighbor at the chalk shop, to come and rescue her. She unclenched the two little girls' fists from her skirt, plucked up her courage, and took a decisive step back to her shelves. "So if Pan Fire Chief doesn't want the socks, then perhaps some of this ribbon for his daughter Wanda?" She extracted a roll of red ribbon from the heap and showed it to him. She was not really afraid of him. He had never done her any harm. He just took up her time with his senseless and disturbing chatter, for which she had neither the nerves nor the patience today. If only he would at least make it worth her while by buying something, she thought, unrolling the ribbon and tying it into a luxurious bow with her fingers. "It would suit her, with her long blond hair. I saw her last week. She'll be a beauty one day."

He smiled a sudden desperate smile. "Do you have mercy on me?"

"I? Why, no . . . yes," she stuttered, waving the red bow distractedly. "What does Pan Fire Chief need my mercy for?"

"Because I am a miserable creature."

"Good heavens, Panie Fire Chief. Don't sin before the Almighty. I hope my enemies are never as fortunate as you."

"Oh, Hindele, don't say that. It is you who are fortunate. You are really fortunate."

Hindele bit her lips. How strange it was that this drunkard's words could penetrate her heart and touch some sensitive cord within it. She composed herself and nodded. "Perhaps you're right, Panie Fire Chief. I thank the Almighty every day for my good fortune. So, should I cut a yard of this ribbon for you, Panie Fire Chief?"

"Cut it, yes," he sighed. "Cut my heart, too, Hindele. I would allow you to cut my heart, too."

Her hands shook as she cut the ribbon and rolled it up. "And what about the socks, Panie Fire Chief?" she muttered coaxingly. "Will you take them?"

"Yes, I'll take them. I'll take anything from you, Hindele."

She quickly handed him the socks, which she had wrapped around the roll of ribbon. "That makes a quarter of a ruble, Panie Fire Chief."

The fire chief's eyes welled up with tears. "I'm such a miserable creature . . . " he sniffled.

"A quarter of a ruble," she repeated, pointing at the roll of socks and ribbon in his hand. She followed his other hand with her eyes as he reached into his pocket, but he brought out no more than ten kopecks. She waited for him to try the other pocket, but instead, he shrugged his shoulders. "So I'll put it down on your account, Panie Fire Chief," she said, reaching into her skirt pocket for a stub of pencil.

"Yes, Hindele, put it all down on my account." He nodded gravely and tottered off before she had managed to scribble down what he owed her on the top of one of the boxes.

"Bread and herring!" the children exclaimed, surrounding her, smiling relieved.

Hindele unwrapped the linen cloth in which she kept the food for the children. They seated themselves on the wooden box where she kept her stock of merchandise, which she had pulled out from under the bottom shelf. She doled out a slice of bread for each, filled four bowls with oatmeal, and gave them each a wooden spoon. She reminded them to bless the food before eating, told the boys to mind the shop, and slipped away toward the store of Reb Senderl the Cabalist. She absolutely had to see him, if only for a few minutes.

The shopkeepers and customers in the Potcheyov noticed her, in spite of her effort to pass by unobserved, and if they were not too busy, they stopped her. They questioned her, told her of the latest remedies for consumption, gave her advice, and tried to fortify her faith in the kindness of the Almighty. She nodded in agreement, gave her pat response that "God will help," wished them a good Sabbath, and moved on, scanning the crowded marketplace with her eyes.

Carts and wagons moved to and fro. People stood about in knots, making islands and eddies, bargaining, disputing, and gesticulating energetically. Girls with live chickens under their arms were running to the house of the ritual slaughterer. Some women rushed by on their way to the bakery with pots of *yaptzok-cholnt.* Others, baskets dangling from their arms, did some last-minute shopping, looking in the baskets of the peasant women for bargain fruits for the Sabbath; the peasant women had brought the fruits to the market to sell at the same time as they did some shopping for Sunday. Two pairs of Jews, the tails of their black gabardines and the tassels of their ritual undergarments flying in the air, carried two benches to the synagogue. The tailor and the cobbler were on their way back from delivering their work for the Sabbath. They quarreled heatedly as they stood between two horses that lashed them with their tails, while the wagon drivers amused themselves by gathering on top of their wagons and urging the two to have it out in a fistfight. A few tethered horses fed at the manger in the middle of the marketplace. From the water pump nearby walked Hatzkele the Water-Carrier, balancing two pails of water suspended from a wooden yoke on his shoulders. Flocks of stray chickens and geese accompanied by a couple of stray pigs promenaded between the carts, searching for their "lost yesterdays," as the shtetl people said. A sudden gust of wind arriving from behind the church blew the skullcaps off the heads of two elderly Jews on their way to the bathhouse.

The clamor of voices, animal and human, mingled with the monotonous sing-song of the young men studying the Talmud at the small study house, the *besmedresh;* it mingled with the deafening shrieks of the little boys free from heder and with the chatter of the storks that circled in the sky above, as if they, too, were preparing for the Sabbath.

Hindele saw everything, heard everything, but it all seemed muffled, blurred by the heavy cloud smothering her heart. Absentmindedly, she walked straight into the little bagel vendor who had positioned himself in front of the shops, yelling at the top of his voice, "Fresh hot bagels! Six for ten!" She almost knocked the basket of bagels out of his hand. Then she bumped into a porter with ropes around his waist, who almost knocked her over. Finally, she chased away the goat that was nibbling at the cord by which the door shutter of Reb Senderl's shop was fastened to the wall, and went in.

She stopped reverently a little distance from the cabalist, who was seated deep inside the dark, damp cubicle, illuminated by the light of a naphtha lamp. She was in awe of the man. In her opinion, he was a holy *Bal-Shem,* a man who knew the secret of the Almighty's ineffable name. She was not surprised that some men of Bociany, even some of the erudites who swam in the sea of Talmudic knowledge, would visit Reb Senderl to watch how his soul joined with the soul of Rabbi Isaac Luria, the holiest of the cabalists, who had lived in the town of Safed, in the Holy Land, hundreds of years ago. Whenever these men had the premonition that danger threatened the shtetl, they would lock themselves in with Reb Senderl in his shop. People said that once inside, they invoked the name of Shabriri, the demon of blindness, and by giving him the appropriate directions, forced him to foretell the nature of the approaching peril. They said exorcisms together, exchanged amulets, and, in order to transform the anticipated evil into a good, they would do everything inside the shop in reverse, put their clothes on inside out, walk backwards, and read excerpts from the Scriptures from the end to the beginning.

Hindele frequently paid visits to Reb Senderl to ask for amulets and for prayers that would transform the danger approaching her doorstep into a good. She would also buy some broth, which he concocted from herbs, for the sick ones at home, and would mix it into their food so that her husband would not notice, because he maintained that Reb Senderl did more harm than good. Although she respected her husband to the point of reverence and never questioned his judgment, when it came to Reb Senderl, Hindele considered herself entitled to her own opinion. After all, she was nothing but a silly uneducated woman, and silly and uneducated women had the right to silly and uneducated beliefs of their own.

As soon as Reb Senderl noticed Hindele in the light of the doorway, he pulled out a hair from his magnificent gray beard and placed it on the page of the volume that he was in the middle of studying. He then pushed the volume away and beckoned to her with a small, pale finger. Feeling guilty for disturbing him, Hindele approached the table, mumbling apologetically.

Reb Senderl reached for his pipe, tapped out the dottle, and refilled the bowl with fresh tobacco, which lay in a heap on a dirty piece of rag on the table. He lit the pipe and smiled at Hindele with his childlike eyes, which were of such a startling blue that they seemed to light up the entire windowless shop.

"The Holy Books," he replied to her apologies between puffs, as if he were slowly drawing the words from the stem of the pipe, "were given for the benefit of the human being, and not the reverse. From that I infer that a human being is more important than all the Holy Books put together."

"Even a sinful woman?" Hindele asked deferentially.

His thin, dark-blue lips parted and spread into a guileless smile, which revealed the tip of the pipe between his brown teeth. "The more sinful, the closer one ought to come . . . "

Although Reb Senderl dealt in the most sacred matters, he was an openhearted man, and made no distinction in his treatment of man, woman, and child. When asked a question, he replied in a soft, clear voice, which seemed to flow directly from his pure soul. Hindele considered him a *Bal-Shem* not because of his ability to cure with incantations, magic formulas, or herbs, but because of what he was capable of achieving without them.

She could not now tell him that she had dropped in only to have a cry in his presence, so that she might have a peaceful Sabbath. Crying in front of Reb Senderl did not compare to crying at night or in the morning, secretly, in solitude. Crying in front of Reb Senderl was comparable only to the most purifying, most soothing kind of prayer. So she asked him for a piece of kosher soap because he sold soap in his shop, and it was only when he handed it to her, asking, "Your heart is heavy, isn't it?" that she burst into tears.

"I have a well of tears instead of a heart, Reb Senderl," she sobbed, looking at him through the mist of tears in her eyes. He looked back at her without averting his gaze, unlike other Jewish males, who always avoided looking directly at a woman. The blue of his eyes became dark and hazy, filled with infinite sadness, while his eyebrows grew sharply pointed, as if something had begun to pain him. When he removed the pipe from his mouth, his lower lip pouted like that of a forlorn child on the verge of tears. Every wrinkle in his face expressed such torment and sorrow that even while she was weeping, Hindele felt that he had absorbed part of her grief and that it was she who had to console him. She did not expect him to say anything, not even the pious consolations that any Jew might utter at such a moment; and in fact, he remained silent. Instead, it was she who spoke as if to cheer him, "May the Almighty protect us. Have a good Sabbath, Reb Senderl." She gazed at the piece of soap in her hand as she left his shop. She knew that the soap Reb Senderl sold was an allusion to the balm of compassion he offered to cleanse a person's heavy heart of total despair.

She felt remarkably calm and composed. Suddenly she remembered that her husband and Itchele always felt better on the Sabbath and that tonight they would dress and sit down at the table. Her whole family would sit around the table, and the white tablecloth and lit candles would make the room look festive; the children would sing table songs. All day tomorrow people would come in to sit with the sick, to pray and study with them. Then, as she walked back to her shop, she remembered that all her preparations for the holy day were completed. All that remained was to wait for the closing of the shops, to take her children home, to wash and dress them, and to attend to herself as well.

She noticed that her neighbor, the chalk-and-lime merchant, Yossele Abedale, was standing on the threshold of his chalk shop. Beside him, Abele, the town fool, sat slouched on the ground, leaning against the wall as he smiled his broad idiot's smile at the bustling world around him. He stretched out his hand to Hindele, and she put a kopeck into his huge palm. Yossele Abedale, who towered over Abele, pretended not to see her. Walking by, she glanced at his face, trying to read his frame of mind from its expression.

As he stood there leaning against the door post, his hands folded behind his back, and his large torso swaying from side to side, Yossele Abedale looked like a caged animal. His body barely fit into the door frame of his tiny store; his head almost touched the upper beam of the door. During the night of the fire at Manka the Washerwoman's house, nearly three years before, he had lost his wife in childbirth, and ever since, Hindele had tried to show the man a bit of neighborly friendliness. But he, a silent sulky man, given to outbursts of anger when shown too much kindness, never acknowledged Hindele's attentions, nor ever returned them. He and Hindele greeted each other in the morning, he inquiring about her sick husband and son, she about his children. But apart from this, and nodding to one another after closing their shops, they rarely exchanged a word.

At Hindele's shop, the children were finishing their food, scratching at the bowls with the wooden spoons, which they polished clean with their tongues. It grew windy in the marketplace and suddenly it became quite cool. In general the weather had been pleasant. Sometimes it was even hot during the day, but as soon as the sun began its descent, one was reminded that the storks would be leaving soon and that the summer was practically over. Now clouds gathered overhead and Hindele felt a few drops of rain on her face. She pulled out the oilcloth, covered her merchandise, sank down on her stool, and pulled the oilcloth over the children's heads and her own. There she sat with them, huddled like a mother hen with her chicks.

"Let's put the fire pot in the middle," proposed her elder daughter, Gitele.

Hindele added some charcoal to the fire pot and placed it in the middle of the children's legs on a small iron tripod. The children put their hands on the fire pot. Afraid that the boys would become restless and run off into the cold and rain, she decided to tell them a tale about the Bal-Shem Tov, in order to put them in the proper Sabbath mood. Then she told them about the Rabbi from Wurke, whose descendants they were. While she spoke, she placed a pot with chicory coffee on the fire pot. Toybe-Kraindele, the women's bathhouse assistant, passed by with the "bobe" beans that she sold on the Potcheyov for additional income, carrying the pot of cooked beans suspended from her neck on a cord. Hindele had done exceptionally well at the shop today, so she bought a full quart of the large hot beans for her children, asking Toybe-Kraindele to pour the beans into the bowls the children had just emptied. Since Hatzkele the Water-Carrier was passing by at that moment, she called him over and offered him a mug of chicory coffee and some beans.

She whispered to her children in her story-telling tone, "Who knows if Hatzkele is not one of the *Lamed Vov,* the thirty-six righteous men on whose merits the world is founded."

Hatzkele the Water-Carrier had already buried three wives and four children, and when the remaining children had run off, leaving him alone, he had lost the faculty of speech. People said that he had taken the oath of silence on himself as a punishment for being such a *schlimazel.* But Hindele was rather of the opinion that Hatzkele the Water-Carrier was not what he appeared to be, but was really a holy man in disguise, who carried pails full of water as an allusion to the pails full of the tears of the people of Israel. While she was busy feeding him, her children leaned over the full pails he had put down, and saw their faces reflected in the "water-tears."

Abele, the town fool, who was still sitting in front of Yossele Abedale's chalk shop, had noticed Hindele handing the coffee and beans to the water carrier, and after Hatzkele had moved away and Hindele had called "Have a good Sabbath!" after him, he approached her with his hand outstretched. Hindele doled him out some beans and handed him a mug of coffee, which he gulped down noisily. Then he bent down, slipped under the oilcloth sheet and sat down on the ground. He put his huge hands on those of the children who started to converse with him in his "language."

As Abele stared at them, smiling and drooling, Hindele explained to her children that in truth Abele was not always smiling; the shape of his mouth just made it seem as if he were. She also told them not to make fun of Abele. She discerned a hidden meaning in his prattle and sensed something mystical concealed in him, in his appearance, his unusual height, and his unknown origin. She even had a vague suspicion, which she shared with Reb Senderl the Cabalist, that Abele the Fool was a kind of golem created by a holy *tsadik* through the ineffable name of God, and that he had been planted in Bociany for the purpose of fulfilling a sacred mission, which was perhaps related to the end of the exile and the coming of the Messiah. Had she not been present in Reb Senderl's shop when a man had come in to ask whether Abele could be permitted as the tenth in the quorum required for services, and Reb Senderl had replied, "It depends . . . "?

Hindele's words about the golem fired Yacov's imagination, and he began to ply her with all kinds of questions. So Hindele told her children what she knew about golems, although the children were still too young to understand, and she herself was no expert on such matters. But she wished to kindle the first sparks of wonderment within them, the sense of awe at things concealed and mysterious, and she especially wanted to do so now, a few hours before the arrival of the Sabbath.

"You ask why Adam, the first man, was also a golem?" her voice took on the particular lilt that it acquired when she was telling a story. "It is because the Lord created Adam in the same way that a *tsadik* creates a golem. He kneaded him out of clay, out of the soil. That's why he was called Adam, because the Hebrew word for earth is *adamah.* And into this clump of earth the Almighty blew His own breath, giving Adam a soul, and so made him human. But before Adam received God's breath inside him, he was a golem."

"So a golem has no soul, Mameshie?" Yacov asked.

"Perhaps he has, but another kind."

"What kind?"

"I don't know. Perhaps the kind that Abele has. Because the holy *tsadik* who creates the golem using God's name is no more than a man, a human being. So his creation cannot be the same as the Almighty's creation. It is as if the Almighty and the holy *tsadik* were standing on a ladder, but the Almighty was on the topmost rung while the *tsadik* was on the lowest."

"So Abele the Fool has the lowest kind of soul," concluded Hindele's elder daughter, Gitele.

Abele, aware that they were talking about him, but understanding nothing, considered himself entitled to participate in the conversation. "No!" he exclaimed, shaking his head. "Abele a *tsadik!*"

"No," Hindele repeated after him, smiling, but somehow ill-at-ease. Was she confusing the minds of her children? Perhaps, but no doubt she stimulated them as well. She continued more emphatically, "Abele's soul is just different, as are the souls of many other creatures and things. There is nothing in this world that doesn't bear a trace of God's imprint. True, we don't understand Abele, but who knows what kind of mission he was designated to fulfill? Because before the real Messiah, the Messiah Ben David, comes, there will be another one, the Messiah Ben Joseph, and this messiah will be a kind of golem who will clear the way for our true savior. Therefore, only if you yourself are a fool, would you call Abele the Fool, a fool. But some people are like that. If they don't understand something, they say it is stupid. If they don't understand someone, they say that he is a fool, a golem. You understand, it is not easy to know who is the wise man and who the fool."

"But why is Abele so big?" Gitele pretended that she understood every word that her mother was saying, and that she was just as interested in the story as Yacov or her older brother, Shalom, who was listening silently.

"I don't know why," Hindele admitted. "When it comes to these hidden matters, grown-ups are just as ignorant as children. I only know that Adam was also big, as big as from one end of the world to the other. That's why we have the saying that every human being is an entire world. Only later, when Adam began to sin, did he shrink. But apparently with the golems the reverse happens. They keep growing."

"So Abele will be a bigger fool still!" Gitele exclaimed.

"No, Abele a *tsadik,*" Abele insisted, shaking his head and drooling.

Again Hindele smiled uncomfortably, but continued, looking at her sons searchingly. "We don't see it, but on the golem's forehead the word *emes* is written, which means truth. And when a golem grows too big and strong and the *tsadik* who created him becomes frightened of him, he erases the first letter of the word on the golem's forehead, and the word *mes* remains, which means dead. Then the golem collapses and turns into a heap of dust again."

"And what happens to his mission?" Yacov interrupted.

"It all comes to naught," she replied. "Because the things that a human being creates, even if he is a *tsadik,* he often spoils or destroys himself. Just like the cow that gives a full bucket of milk, but then kicks and spills it. It once happened that a golem grew so big that his creator, the holy *tsadik,* could no longer reach his forehead to erase the first letter of the word *emes* and turn it into *mes* when he wanted to get rid of the golem. So what did he do? The *tsadik* asked the golem, who worked for him as a servant, to bend down and take the shoes off his feet, which the golem did. Then the *tsadik* quickly erased the first letter of the word *emes* on the golem's forehead, and the golem collapsed, turning into a mound of clay. But what should happen then? He turned into such a heavy mound of clay, that while collapsing, he fell on the *tsadik* and, may God preserve us, crushed him to death. Which goes to teach the people that even if one is a holy *tsadik* creating important things, one should not become conceited, because one's end is the same as that of every golem."

Hindele folded her hands in her lap and scrutinized the faces of her children. If her words were not completely clear to them, so what? Let them know that in this world nothing is completely clear, while the things that seem the clearest are the most complicated and misleading. She also believed that one should speak to children in the same way as to adults. What they were mature enough to grasp, they would, and the rest would not impress them one way or another.

As they watched Abele the Fool resume his place beside Yossele Abedale in front of the neighboring shop, they noticed the Eretz-Israel Jew arriving from the town of Chwosty, to collect money on the Potcheyov for the Holy Land. Although the man looked like any other Jew in the shtetl, he always seemed to be enveloped in desert dust and to be carrying the smell of oriental spices with him.

So Hindele began to tell her children a new tale, this time about Eretz Israel and the holy city of Jerusalem, about the forefathers of Israel and how they had lived. Before long, the story turned into a game. As soon as they noticed an interesting figure in the crowd on the Potcheyov, like the tailor or the cobbler, who had been quarreling before but were now heading in peace toward their respective shops; or the tin man; or Fishele the Butcher; or Reb Laibele Yaptzok-Fresser, the sexton of the synagogue, the children and Hindele would transport them in their fancy to the sand-and-stone marketplaces of ancient Israel, trying to imagine what each of them might be doing there, how each would look and how and where they would live.

Shalom, Hindele's elder boy, spoke for the first time, pointing to Yossele Abedale, who still stood in the entrance of his shop. "Him . . . I would not allow him into Eretz Israel at all."

"Why?" Hindele looked at Shalom with astonishment.

"Because I can't stand him. He has a mean face and he never says a word to you."

"I'm a woman, silly," she said mildly.

"But if you say good morning to him, he can answer you like a human being, no? So why does he grumble?"

"Because he is a *roshe-merushe,* the meanest of the mean!" Gitele nodded in agreement with her elder brother, although while he frowned, she was giggling.

"Heaven forbid!" Hindele, too, had to smile, although she did not quite know why. "There are some very miserable people who give the impression of being *roshe-merushes.*"

Gitele did not stop giggling. "That big bear, Yossele Abedale, you call miserable people? He makes other people miserable by shouting at them. You know that, Mameshie."

"And what do you think, Mameshie, that Yossele Abedale would do in Eretz Israel?" Yacov inquired.

"Yossele Abedale?" Hindele grew thoughtful. "I think that he would be a prophet."

"A prophet!" the children gasped, attempting to conceal their laughter by muffling their mouths with their hands, as they threw sidelong glances at Yossele to check whether or not he had guessed that they were talking about him.

"Yes, a prophet," Hindele concluded more emphatically. "He looks like one, too."

The children continued tittering. Gitele adjusted Hindele's wig, which was again lying askew on her head. Shalom looked at his mother with mocking reproach in his eyes. "Have you ever heard of a prophet who doesn't speak to anyone?"

"Yes, who's ever heard of a mute prophet?" Gitele gaily seconded her brother.

"Who says that he is mute?" Hindele was determined to treat her children's arguments seriously. "He is a silent man. So what? He's raising seven children without a mother, don't forget that, and don't worry, inside, in his mind, he talks a great deal." She looked inquisitively at her older son. "I'm surprised at you, Shalom. You're not one of the great talkers either. So you should know . . . "

She began to explain to her children about people, Jews and Gentiles, about human nature, about the world in general and their shtetl, Bociany, in particular. She used simple words but tried to make them reflect her views and attitudes, her ideas about life and its illusory nature. According to her, the shtetl of Bociany, for instance, was not, in its entirety, a real place; instead, it was a kind of mask that lay superimposed on another arcane locality. The simplest events that occurred in Bociany were rife with concealed symbolic meaning.

As she spun out her train of thought about everything that is real and unreal, illusion and not illusion in this concrete and yet marvelously unconcrete world, Yacov raised his eyes to her, and asked, "You mean to say, Mameshie, that I myself, am also not really real?"

"Who knows?" Hindele smiled secretively. "It is quite possible that the Almighty has something special in mind for you, something of which you are not yet aware. Perhaps you have come into this world to fulfill an unusually important mission, as a man, not a golem, and He will reveal it to you bit by bit, as you grow older, and you will realize that you have another self."

"But you, Mameshie!" Yacov exclaimed with a note of exasperation in his voice. He felt more like crying than rejoicing at the prospect of having another self. "You must be real! All real!"

"Of course I am." She put her hand reassuringly on his knee. She grinned broadly at her children, a grin such as they had not seen in a long time, and concluded, "There is one thing which is all real and not the least bit unreal."

"What's that?" Gitele exclaimed.

After a suspenseful pause, Hindele replied, "That I love you all."

She hugged each one of them as they held their shining eyes fastened on her. She was grateful to them for having joined her in these calm moments of expectation of the arrival of the Sabbath. In fact, the special beadle was already walking from shop to shop, knocking at the doors with his wooden mallet and calling, "Closing time! Prepare yourselves for the Sabbath!" The neighbors were locking up their shops. The wind seemed to let up, and the rain turned into a soft drizzle. Although there was a great commotion everywhere, the noise seemed subdued, as if the whole earth were preparing to receive Queen Sabbath, whose silken slippers would soon be heard approaching. Hindele left the children under the oilcloth, while she busied herself with closing the shop.

Yacov followed his mother's movements with his eyes. He thought about the storks. He envied them their wings and their ability to rise high in the air. During the winter, when the earth was clamped under an icy sheet of frost, they did not have to sit in their nests like the people of Bociany, but could fly off to the lands where it was warm. Now it occurred to him that his mother was like a mother stork, and that he and his siblings were like baby storks whom she was teaching that although they had to spend the winter in the mud and dirt of Bociany, they could rise with her and fly off in their imagination to where it was warm.

"Have a good Sabbath, neighbor!" he heard Yossele Abedale call to his mother as he left the Potcheyov.

"A good Sabbath, a good year!" Hindele and her children replied in unison.

Yacov thought a great deal about all the things that his mother told him. As long as it was still warm outside and the window of the loft was kept open at night, he would lie beside his brother Shalom on the straw mattress beneath the window, and his mother's words would sparkle and glimmer about him like fireflies. Intoxicating fragrances wafted into the room from the nuns' garden. Sometimes the moon shone through the window's upper corner straight into his eyes. Little fragments of cloud like white threads of smoke curled across the piece of navy-blue sky that could be seen through the window. "They're trying to write the letters of a secret alphabet," he would say to himself. He looked beyond the swimming letters, and it seemed to him that the sky opened like a curtain, and behind it there was another curtain, and behind that one, still another. A vague yearning gnawed at his heart, a desire to reach the very last curtain, to see it open up and allow him to look into the awesome depth of the Creator's ultimate secret.

When the nights grew colder, however, his mother's words acquired a different meaning. The cold brought to mind both the past winter and the winter that would soon be coming. Yacov remembered the frost and snow of the previous year, which had given the world a new face. Everything had looked transformed, icy, and strangely beautiful. He recalled jumping onto the sleigh of the *melamed's* helper, along with the other heder boys, and how they had sat with lighted lanterns in their laps, while the darkness around them helped to create a picture that confirmed his mother's words. Everything in this world had faces behind faces, masks behind masks. Probably every human face was equally veiled, one veil on top of another.

On such cold nights Yacov would cuddle up to Shalom's warm body and stare at the cold moon shining with frosty rays through the window pane. Its reflection would sneak over to the pail of water in the corner of the room, covering it with a silvery sheet, a thin layer of ice, as if trying to keep it warm with its iciness. A mouse under the floor would chew frantically at the boards, trying to carve out an escape route for itself from the frosty solitude that smothered it. Yacov shuddered under the feather quilt, his face covered up to his eyes. He stared at the objects in the room. They too had lost their everyday appearance in the moon-washed night and were dressed in new faces. The furniture looked like otherworldly creatures who possessed souls with which to entice him, and who spoke in an alien yet comprehensible language, saying, "Even these are not our true faces."

In order to calm himself, he would follow the instructions of his friends from heder on how to conquer fear, and imagined God's ineffable name in fiery letters, although his friends had warned him that it was forbidden to do this in bed. But it would not help. Thus very quietly, so as not to wake anyone, especially his father, Yacov would slip out of his sleeping place and sneak himself into the bed where his mother slept with his two little sisters at her feet. She covered him with her feather quilt, and it suddenly seemed strange to him that he had become so frightened. What was there to be afraid of, if his mother was nearby? He would fall asleep and, in his sleep, hear his mother's words, which again acquired another meaning.

That night it was pouring outside. Rain dripped in through the ceiling. Hindele had put the four healthy children in her bed, the boys at the head, the girls at the foot, a basin to catch the rain in the middle, and she herself lay down on the boys' straw mattress beneath the window, with a tin container on her belly to catch the rain.

The rain clinked against the shingles of the roof, against the furniture, the table, the floor, and the pots and basins placed on the featherbeds near the bodies of the sleeping. It seemed to Yacov that a thousand ghosts were rapping at the room with skeletal fingers, ready to break in. He no longer knew whether he was asleep or awake, or whether he was a dream in someone else's sleep, so utterly confused was he about what was real and what was not.

He kept his eyes tightly shut. When he opened them for one moment, however, he saw his father sitting on a low stool near the stove, beside a bench on which there stood a lit candle in a roasting pot. The chalk white of his father's face contrasted so sharply with his sparse black beard that the beard appeared to be glued on. Ashes covered his head. He sobbed along with the rain as he swayed over the open volume in his lap. His tears clinked against the roof, the pots, the pans, the basins, while the ghosts answered him with the knocks of their cadaverous fingers. His father was weeping over the destruction of the Temple, over the *Shkhina,* the Almighty's emanation, which was in exile, and over the sorrow and woe of the People of Israel.

Yacov could no longer restrain himself. He cried, with the edge of the pillow stuck in his mouth to smother the sounds. "Have pity on my Tateshie," he implored the ghosts. "Don't harm my Tateshie," he begged them.

When, through his tears, he looked again in the direction of the stove, he saw that it was not his father swaying over the open book in his lap, but the Angel of Death himself, looking into the Book of Names and searching for the ones to cross out. Yacov sobbed even more, until Hindele, who also was lying awake, heard him. She came over to the bed, took him up in her arms, and carried him over to the straw mattress. She let him cuddle up against the wall where it was dry and stretched herself out beside him, putting the tin container back in position on her belly.

"Hush, don't cry," she calmed him with a barely audible whisper. "Your father is crying for all of us."

Yacov, soothed, lay there beside her and pondered how strange it was that the idea had never entered his head to go over to his father, or for that matter to his eldest brother, the *ile,* to sit by their bedside, and ask them about all the things that were tormenting him. He had never asked them to explain the riddles that he encountered at every step as he grew older. His father and Itchele were somehow like saints whose bodies alone dwelt with the family; they themselves were like visitors from another world, a world apart, whom one could only worship and serve. It even appeared normal to Yacov that they should die, that the Almighty had sent them down to earth for a short time, in order to let people see to what heights they could raise themselves. He had also sent them down, Yacov thought, to honor Hindele and her remaining children by allowing them to live in the presence of these two *tsadikim,* who bestowed upon them a fortifying light to illuminate the rest of their lives.

Usually, Yacov took his questions to Reb Senderl the Cabalist. Reb Senderl liked children and always received him with a broad smile. The problem was, however, that although Reb Senderl treated Yacov's questions very seriously, he would answer the questions by telling stories that, while fascinating, were both more disturbing and more confusing than his mother's stories.

The best solution seemed to be to approach his *melamed* in the heder. Yacov had a warm feeling in his heart for the *melamed.* True, he often scolded the *heder* boys, but the worst punishment that he ever inflicted was a tiny slap over the fingers, or a pull of the ears or nose, which did not really hurt. The most opportune time to ask him anything was during the holiday of Lagbomer, in the spring, when the *melamed* took the boys to the fields belonging to the wood merchant. Then the *melamed* would be in an excellent frame of mind and could be asked the wildest questions without risk of arousing his anger. And the *melamed* certainly knew what was written in the Holy Books, black on white, about all things real and unreal that occurred in the world.

But spring was still far away. It was fall. The days after Tishebov, the ninth day of the month of Ab, had been exceptionally cold. The ears were still full of the sounds of lamentation over the destruction of the Temple in Jerusalem, and the other catastrophes of the Jewish past, when the Days of Awe arrived. New Year's was celebrated. All the neighbors who had quarreled during the past year made peace with one another, wishing each other a good and happy New Year, saying, "May you be inscribed and sealed for a good year." The blowing of the ram's horn was heard in the synagogue. People wept and chanted, "How many will pass away, how many come into being . . . Who will live and who will die . . . " Cries of lamentation issued from the cemetery, the *besmedresh,* and the private houses. Women were saying the *tkhines* and did not cease weeping. Soon white cocks were carried through the marketplace toward the house of the ritual slaughterer. These were the *kapores.* To these cocks had been transferred all the suffering and sins of humanity. The wind scattered a snow-white cloud of feathers from out of the ritual slaughterer's house.

It was the eve of Yom Kippur. Yacov's father and Itchele got out of bed and dressed in their baggy clothes. With the exception of the two little girls, the entire family went to the synagogue. Inside the synagogue, the lamps and candelabras were lit. The many burning candles everywhere shed an eerie light. The doors of the Holy Ark stood open. Like the other men, Yacov's father wore a white linen robe over his garments, and his head was covered with his prayer shawl. Yacov's heart was heavy, filled with anxious expectation. It was during Yom Kippur that people's fates were sealed.

Very quietly the cantor began to chant the Kol Nidre. His tremulous voice was soaked in such painful yearning that it took one's breath away; like the point of a vibrating pin, it penetrated the heart. From the throats of the congregation there erupted an explosion of sobs, of shouts of woe, grief-laden, yet soothed by the sweetness of hope and faith.

Yacov stood near his father, whose prayer shawl waved like a sail in a pitiless wind, and whose body shook like the dislodged mast of a boat. One more minute and the cantor's voice would catch him and carry him off into the depths of a blinding hurricane. Yacov's pale eldest brother, Itchele, stood nearby, trembling, his shaking legs barely supporting his thin body. With his open mouth he gulped at the air, while his eyes stared up at the hanging chandelier. Tears ran silently down his face. Shalom, strong and healthy, tried to support Itchele, but he was also sobbing. All the Jews of Bociany were drowning in a sea of tears, while Yacov's mother was far away. She was upstairs, in the women's gallery. Mortified, Yacov wept, calling not "God!" but "Mother!"

Yacov's father and Itchele began to feel worse, and a group of men had to carry them home. There, the father and Itchele returned to bed. They refused to touch the food that everyone implored them to eat, even though they were permitted to do so, as it was a question of preserving life. Yacov talked his two little sisters into fasting, too, although all three children were exempt, being too young. The three of them announced their decision to their mother, explaining that they were fasting "so that Tateshie and Itchele will get better."

Hindele wiped the tears from her eyes and said, "If you insist, so be it. It won't, heaven forbid, harm you. And who knows, a child's fast might melt the Almighty's heart."

So the entire household fasted. Yacov was ashamed because of his fierce hunger. He swallowed saliva to calm his rumbling stomach as he watched Gitele and little Shaindele sipping curds from a jug all of the next day. "This is not called eating," they explained to Hindele.

"Certainly not," she concurred, offering each a raw egg to drink. "This is not called eating either," she assured them.

Yacov would not touch a thing and fasted like the grownups. Then, when his hunger had grown so strong that he had practically ceased to feel it, and when Yom Kippur was drawing toward Ne'ilah, the last prayer recited on this most sacred of all sacred days, and the gates of the Al-mighty's mercy were about to close—his father suddenly gave up his soul.

## 3

LIKE HINDELE THE SCRIBE'S WIDOW, Yossele Abedale, the chalk vendor, also lived on the border of the gentile district. But Hindele lived to the south, near the Wide Poplar Road, whereas Yossele lived to the north, near the Narrow Poplar Road. Nor was Yossele a wealthy man, although the cottage that he lived in was his own and had been built with his own two hands right after his wedding. He was not overly proud of this piece of property and called his house the *bude,* by which he meant that it was fit for a dog.

Yossele Abedale came from generations of Jews who had derived their livelihood from the forests near the tributaries of the Vistula, not as wood merchants or lessees, but as lumberjacks, barge and raft builders, and carpenters. Yossele would say of himself that he had been a carpenter while still in his mother's belly. He had come into this world with a love for wood, for its smell and its feel; he took delight in the way a piece of wood submitted to his hands and to his will. There was nothing Yossele was not capable of fashioning out of wood, and he fixed furniture in such a way that it lasted forever, massive and sturdy like himself.

But he had two problems. In Bociany people rarely acquired new things. They made do with what they had, and either they fixed things by themselves or did not fix them at all, allowing the broken pieces of furniture to wait for the Messiah to make them—along with their owners—whole again. For with the exception of two or three wealthy families, the difference between rich and poor was minimal in Bociany. Where in other regions a person with Yossele's "golden hands" might have accumulated a fortune on account of the frequent fires and the consequent need for new dwellings, in Bociany he could accumulate only "good deeds." After a fire, those who had been burned out would move into the community's poorhouse, while those who had been saved from the fire would contribute boards and logs and a helping hand in the construction of new huts. Yossele himself did more than lend a hand. He was the head of these undertakings. That had nothing to do with making a living, however. That was charity.

This, however, was not Yossele's main problem. His real problem was that he had had trouble with his eyes from a very early age. When he was outdoors, he could see quite well, but doing a precise job indoors became increasingly difficult for him. So he had had no choice but to give up his true vocation and take whatever bread-earning occupation was available; and he had had to do it when he was at the peak of his manhood. His wife, Miriam, whom he called Mariml, once she had begun to have children had given birth to a houseful of them, six girls and one boy. And as this was evidently all that she had been destined to achieve in the world, she left it, while still it in the prime of her life, after giving birth to the youngest girl, Binele.

As long as Mariml was healthy and well, and performed to perfection the duties of wife and mother, Yossele had made no fuss over her. But as soon as the Angel of Death had placed himself at her headboard, Yossele had set out to wrestle with him by all the means that were at a Jew's disposal.

He had contributed dozens of candles to the synagogue and had run to pray at the graves of her deceased relatives. He had sent out the neighbors to measure the wall of the cemetery and had brought all kinds of amulets and exorcisms from Reb Senderl the Cabalist. He had seen to it that the sexton gave Mariml the keys to the synagogue to hold in her hand, that the community book of records was put under her pillow, that a circle of chalk was drawn around her bed, and that the knots of all her dresses were opened. The walls of her room had been covered with slips of paper containing the necessary sayings and prayers, from a cord stretched across the ceiling had hung innumerable *shir-hamales* letters, and Yossele himself had taken the *mezuzah* off the doorpost and rushed to the scribe to check it. But despite these efforts and the fact that all of Bociany had prayed for her, Mariml had given up her soul, while bringing another female into the world. She had left Yossele all alone to struggle and earn bread for his children—from chalk, because he took over the chalk-and-lime shop that she had inherited from her parents.

This particular day was the third anniversary of Mariml's death. Yossele had lit a *yortsait* candle in honor of her memory, and had gone at dawn to pray for her soul in the synagogue. Then he had visited her grave at the cemetery. Otherwise this day differed little from any other day that had elapsed since her death. Every day was a day of mourning for him.

Mariml had died the night of the fire at the washerwoman Manka's house. The memory of that night still burned in Yossele's heart, and no lapse of time could ever put out that flame. Every detail of it, every moment, was so vividly etched in his memory that even now, as he stood in front of his shop, swaying to and fro, hands locked behind his back, his mind returned without effort to the hellish flaming darkness of that night.

He could see himself standing dazed in the corner of the room full of praying men, full of women. His eyes were glued to the curtain of white sheets in the opposite corner, behind which Mariml lay in agony. Her screams had long since subsided to be replaced by feeble moans, which were drowned out by the sound of praying voices. Then, suddenly, a voice had yelled from behind the door: "Fire! Fire!" The crowd in the room shuddered, swayed. Bewildered faces. Women shrieking, "The children!"

And so, as the women ran out from behind the curtain, Yossele saw Mariml for the last time, on her bed near the window. The tongues of flame sent up by the fire were reflected in the pane, giving him the impression that her bed stood atop a burning pyre. For a moment he saw himself as a young boy, lost in another fire, during the pogrom, screaming for help. But now he was no longer a boy. He was a man, the partner of Mariml's agony. He had to act! His children had been taken in by the neighbors, so that they would not witness their mother's flesh-tearing moments of giving birth. The neighbors would surely take care of them. But where was the fire? Should he carry Mariml outside on her bed? Not all of the men present in the room had run out; a few scholars had stayed on. He would send none of them to find out where the fire was. They and their prayers were more important here than he, Mariml's ignorant husband.

So he had run out himself. The night was chilly. "Thank Heaven for the cold," Yossele thought, racing through the crowded street. His neighbors were taking no chances. Their bundled-up children stood outside, huddled together, bewildered, frightened. Through the open doors and windows men and women threw their hastily packed belongings, or carried pieces of furniture. When he passed the house of his neighbor, Brontchele the Professional Mourner, Yossele had seen his own children standing with hers. He had quickly counted their heads, so he had one thing less to worry about.

He ran more quickly as he saw the flames coming nearer. They leaped toward the sky like yellow and red claws, as if they aimed to scratch the stars out of the navy-blue expanse. He crossed the marketplace, which swarmed with the shadows of villagers lamenting, and headed for the street of the cloister, where the fire raged in all its horrifying splendor. From that direction people were running with children in their arms or grasped by the hand, or they were holding packs and bundles. The flashing flames revealed the throng's dark contours. There were some men, like Yossele, who tried to plow through the oncoming mass, to get closer to the fire, so as to help the firemen. His way was blocked by wagons filled with barrels of water belonging both to the Jewish and gentile fire brigades. Shouts of "Water! Water!" came from all sides, mixing with the cracking and groaning of the collapsing smoke-spewing roof and beams of the burning house. Peasant boys and *besmedresh* boys hurried with empty pails to the nearest pumps and wells.

There had never been a fire in Bociany at which Yossele had not been present. He understood how the flames behaved, and he now grasped the situation immediately. The house was burning to the ground, while the firemen were trying to protect the neighboring houses by keeping them as wet as possible. Yossele struggled on, until he reached Fishele the Butcher, the Jewish fire chief. His face glistening with perspiration and splotched with soot, Fishele was maneuvering the hose and commanding his men in a self-assured voice that contained a tremor of delight.

"How is it going?" Yossele shouted at him.

"The street is saved!" Fishele shouted back. Yossele heaved a sigh of relief. He could relax and catch his breath, if only for a moment. Fishele came closer to him as he directed the hose at the very heart of the blaze. "Vaslav, may the cholera take him, was almost crushed by the falling beams!" Fishele bellowed excitedly. "The devil has gotten into him tonight. It's his cousin Manka's house. And do you know what else? He brought Hamele the Scribe down on his back. Can you imagine that?" Childhood memories of the days when he had lived close to Vaslav Spokojny, the gentile fire chief, and played with him, returned to Yossele, memories that had been blotted from his mind for many years.

"Look there, Yossele!" Fishele roared into Yossele's ear. "Those fat flames there," he pointed the hose in the direction of the flames. "Don't they look like a bunch of naked females? They make me think sinful thoughts, so help me God, Yossele. If you only knew how I would like to jump inside, grab those blazing forms by the throats and strangle the hell out of them with these two hands!"

Fishele went half crazy when he worked at extinguishing a fire. That was why he was such a good fireman. To do something well, Yossele thought, one had to be partly possessed. But Yossele had had enough of Fishele and turned away from him, heading back in the direction of his own street. He did not run. His legs felt lame and it was an effort to move them. He was stiff with anguish and wished that he might never reach the house. When he did reach it—and the birth of a daughter and the death of his wife were announced to him—he seemed neither moved nor shaken. He had known all along that Mariml was doomed. From the moment that he had seen her on her bed, with the tongues of flame reflected in the window pane, lying as if she were on a burning pyre, he had known that the Almighty had forsaken both her and him. This was the real reason why he had run out of the house, why he had procrastinated and delayed his return. He was unable to face her death, to face his own helplessness. There were no firemen capable of extinguishing the flames of the Almighty's wrath.

Yossele had never liked his shop. After Mariml's death he loathed it. Today, on the anniversary of her death, the obligatory vigil at the door, waiting for customers, was almost more than he could bear; almost, for he had no choice but to bear it. A Jew was supposed to accept whatever was given to him, with love. So he accepted it, with tight lips—but not with love. Today in particular, a seething rage had taken hold of him.

While he stood leaning against the doorpost of his shop, his thoughts had turned to the entire complicated business of loving, and he had arrived at such impious conclusions that he himself was frightened of them. He had begun to think that in reality there was no such thing as love; that even the biblical command, "Thou shalt love . . . " seemed ridiculous and childish, like a piece of candy inserted here and there to sweeten the Holy Scripture. He no longer understood how an adult Jew could even pretend to grasp the whole issue or feel the "Thou shalt love," as it was written, "with all thy heart and with all thy soul." How could a downtrodden human being, a mere trampled speck of existence, accomplish this feat, especially when it was given as a command? And how could He, who could smite with burning whips, who could crush a human being, even when the latter served Him with all the devotion of his heart, how could He demand, "Love me!" even if He was the Creator of the world Himself?

Yossele knew that the fear of God and the love of God were the two wings of a Jew's soul, the two wings of his prayers and deeds. But he could not help thinking that one of his wings was burnt, and that all he had left was the other: the fear of God.

Nor did Yossele delude himself now that he had loved his deceased wife, Mariml, although he could not put her out of his mind. He felt exactly as it had been written of a man who lost his wife—like someone who had personally lived through the destruction of the Holy Temple. He felt this, he told himself, because Mariml was simply his match; it had been decreed in Heaven. There the two of them had been paired and fused into one, and for this reason he now felt that he was only half a person. As for his attitude toward his children, it was not a question of love there either. He was their father, therefore it was his sacred duty to keep them alive and care for them as the storks on the roofs cared for their young. Every animal cared for its young. The species had to be perpetuated. It was a basic principle of life.

Duty existed, obligation existed, but not love, neither between man and man, nor between man and God. There was only one thing that was beyond doubt: the Almighty was the Master and the human being His servant. The latter was therefore required to obey the former like a serf his landlord. Consequently, the commandment, "Thou shalt love the Lord thy God," could mean only one thing, "Fulfill your obligation, do your duty." Every man had his function to perform. For this purpose he was placed on earth, and no one asked him whether he found the task pleasing or not.

As he stood there in front of his shop, steeped in thought, Yossele caught himself observing his neighbor, Hindele the Scribe's Widow, bargaining with a customer in front of her shelves of "vanities." Hindele, he recalled, was a descendant of the Rabbi of Wurke, and so Yossele's thoughts turned to the teachings of the Wurker Rabbi. The Wurker Rabbi had believed that the primal source of the universe was great love, that every human being could return to this source and, through it, be united with all of humanity as well as with his Maker.

What could have inspired that meek *tsadik* to come to such a conclusion, Yossele asked himself in amazement. Was it the fact that one human being was always ready to devour another? Was it the "kind-heartedness" of the tsar and his assistants, or of the Gentiles in general? How could he preach love to such a man as Yossele, who had to struggle all alone, not only for bread to feed his children, but for peace in his own heart, to struggle every day with his sense of futility, his helplessness, with the rage and hostility that devoured him as they devoured every human being? Perhaps the holy rabbi had known the trick of shedding his own pitiful humanity, of jumping out of his own skin? Or perhaps he had had the Nazarene in mind, who with his "great love" had caused Jewish blood to flow like water?

Yossele was now more than ever attracted to the teachings of another rabbi, the Rabbi of Kotzk, whose school of thought had always appealed to him. The Kotzker Rabbi had known that the world was nothing but a mass of matter and the human being no more than a speck of dust; that in whatever direction man turned, or even if he stood on his head, he would never be free of his earthliness and of all the soul-trimmings that went with it. True, the Rabbi of Kotzk also believed that a few exceptional individuals could rise above themselves. But on this point Yossele remained skeptical. The main thing was that the Rabbi of Kotzk seemed to express Yossele's own bitterness and rage, his frustration and sense of futility. The Kotzker had practiced seclusion and had fiercely cursed his Hasidic followers. There was power to his bitterness, the power of despair known to those individuals who were unable to find what these Jews, who "walked around in the Heavens with their boots on," claimed existed.

Yossele belonged to a Hasidic brotherhood that gathered to study in a room called a *shtibl,* of which there were a few in Bociany. The trouble was that Yossele did not fit in there, just as he did not fit into his chalk-and-lime business. He followed the Hasidic ways mechanically, without any particular enthusiasm, like an adult participating in a child's game, like an outsider. The day-to-day life of the *shtibl* failed to involve him, not because he did not want to be involved, but because this was his nature. Yet he firmly believed that a man must have not only a *shtib,* a room of his own, but also a *shtibl* of his own.

In general, Yossele did not fit in with many things, including his name. His real name was Yosef, which had been changed to Yossele, in the diminutive, as an endearment. The name suited Yossele, who was a tall burly man, like a baby's shirt suited a giant. It did not however occur to anyone, least of all to Yossele himself, to fight a tradition that the shtetl practiced for generations, that of making endearments out of people's names and then adding nicknames to them. Whenever his neighbors had a grudge against Yossele, and this was a frequent occurrence, they would shake their heads, raise their hands to the sky and exclaim, "Do we ever have a Yossele, may he live in good health!" Then the endearment sounded precisely as it should.

In appearance Yossele cut rather an imposing figure. He almost looked majestic. Not only was he tall and well-built, but he was also handsome, with thick blond eyebrows and a rich blond beard with long blond sidelocks. By his manner of moving and walking, by his sharp, tight-lipped way of conversing, by his behavior, living with the community and yet apart from it, he gave the impression of a figure lifted from the pages of the Bible and transposed to Bociany, as if for a trial: that he should struggle with the petty details of daily life without appearing ridiculous, yet remain a man who commanded respect. It was Yossele who was capable of making other people feel ridiculous, merely by his looking at them. His gaze was sharp and stern, perhaps because his eyes had no strength; in order to see better, he had to strain them badly, to arch his eyebrows, wrinkle his forehead and lean slightly forward. Yet in his sharp glance people detected the shadow of wise resignation, as if he were asking them with his eyes, "Why do you make such a hue and a cry over trivial matters, when making a fuss over essentials won't even help?"

Yossele's neighbors on the street, or on the Potcheyov, never really knew what attitude to adopt toward him. They respected him greatly, in spite of the fact that he was not a scholar. They revered his wisdom, his piety, and his honesty, and they often called upon him to arbitrate a discussion or squabble, instead of going to the *rov,* the official leader of the congregation, or the *dian,* who settled minor disputes. On the other hand, Yossele was also looked upon with a measure of contempt, because he was a wretched pauper and a ne'er-do-well to boot. "If Yossele took to selling candles," people would say, "the sun would never set." And he was a sullen person, never indulging in spontaneous conversation with his neighbors. This aloofness, suitable for a very wealthy man or a famous scholar, appeared ridiculous in one of Yossele's low standing.

Yet no one poked fun at him, not even behind his back. They dared accost him only when it was for his own good. And then they achieved nothing. Not only did Yossele arrogantly guard his honor, he was also fanatically stubborn. Mixing into Yossele's affairs did, however, somewhat calm the general conscience, so that people could assure themselves, "We did not look on indifferently; at least we tried what we could."

On a mild Wednesday after sunset, not long after the third anniversary of Mariml's death, Yossele was coming out of the synagogue, shoulder to shoulder with the two wealthiest members of the congregation, the lessee and the wood merchant. The two important men shook the hands, or rather the fingertips, of the men around them, including Yossele, uttered the customary wishes, and moved ahead in the direction of their brick houses on the marketplace. Yossele's hostile glance followed them as they moved away. In their clean, well-fitted black frocks made of expensive satin, with silk belts ringing their waists, in their spotless white socks and their shiny pantofles, they looked more elegant and more festively clad on this weekday than many a Jew on the Sabbath.

As long as he saw them in the prayer house occupying honorable seats at the eastern wall near the Holy Ark, Yossele did not mind their presence. But in the street, these two separated themselves from the rest of the congregation and became a world unto themselves—but not in the way that

Yossele was a world unto himself. Yossele lived with the people, was a part of them, and their troubles were his own. At the sight of the two men in the street, anger and bitterness swelled in his heart.

He became even more incensed when he saw the two men stop and shake hands with two other men who approached them at a leisurely pace. These men were the most detested inhabitants of Bociany. One of them was the bald "writer," Pan Henryk Faifer, whom the people called Pumpkinhead, and who dressed like a big-city Gentile, in shirts with stiff collars and neckties. His "writing" consisted of keeping the landowner's accounts. He also wrote up all kinds of transactions; did the yearly bookkeeping for the miller, the lessee, and the wood merchant; and twice a week, between two and three in the afternoon, he wrote out all kinds of petitions to the authorities, in Russian, for the local peasants and Jews. He was completely assimilated into gentile culture and made no secret of it. On the contrary, he often behaved as if he wanted to spite his fellow Jews with his un-Jewish conduct. Because of this, the congregation refused to have anything to do with him, except when it needed his assistance.

The other man was even more dangerous. This was the barber-surgeon, Shmulikl the Doctor. He was more dangerous because he was one of the shtetl's own, a son of a son of the town's paupers. He treated everyone like a brother, and it was not easy to get rid of him. Particularly annoying was his irritating habit of telling people off before they had a chance to tell him off. He was a total nonbeliever, and listening to Shmulikl expound his philosophies of life and his theories about the People of Israel—which he did regularly to anyone who would listen—was a pure abomination for a God-fearing person.

Only the lessee and the wood merchant had the nerve to break the general boycott against the two Jewish *goyim.* "So this is how sincere they are in their faith and in their brotherhood with the community," Yossele thought and spat three times, as he headed toward his street. He remembered that another important Jew, Reb Faivele the Miller, also broke the boycott against the two infidels, but that was another story altogether. The miller was a Galizianer and did not know any better. Moreover, he was the most kindhearted man anyone could imagine, and his actions compensated a million times for his shortcomings and his lax ways in observing religious tradition. He was a man who served the Almighty and His people better than many a more rigorous observer of The Law.

Yossele marched on with an energetic gait. Once the four shtetl bigshots were out of sight, he put them out of his mind as well. Night was falling, and he became aware of the shtetl through which he was walking. He liked Bociany at twilight, when it was enveloped by the blue light of dusk. Viewed through his weak eyes, it seemed suspended in its melancholy somewhere between the earth and the sky, lulled to sleep by the lilting voices of the men, young and old, studying in the *besmedresh,* in the *shtiblekh,* or in their homes. The melodic, monotonous chants mixed with the noises from the gentile homes, with the barking of the dogs, the singing of the frogs, and the solitary drawn-out complaint of a country fiddle.

Heder boys were cavorting in the empty marketplace. Several women were heading in the direction of the ritual slaughterer's house to visit the slaughterer's wife, Sore-Leyele, who was a formidable story teller. Other women stood chatting in front of their houses, or sat peeling potatoes in the doorways of their homes, so as not to miss the evening happenings in the street. Artisans in their work clothes, their thumbs tucked into the breast pockets of their threadbare vests, promenaded back and forth on the Potcheyov in front of their workshops, which doubled as their dwellings. Yossele could hear the sounds of a heated political dispute. Butcher boys and wagon drivers wearing high boots, with lighted cigarettes dangling from between their fingers, marched in clusters toward the tavern in the Jewish inn on the Wide Poplar Road, in order to drown their sadness and restlessness in drink.

Unnoticed, like a slow-moving cloud, cows from the landlord's herds began to wander into the marketplace from the fields to the north of the shtetl. Dreamy barefoot cowherds walked behind them. The *heder* boys gamboling in the marketplace escaped into the square called the Garden to continue with their games. The lank young men who had sauntered out from the *besmedresh* for a breath of fresh air and had been strolling about with their hands locked behind their backs, humming a Gemara tune, their heads far in the clouds, were suddenly caught in the sea of cows like flotsam on the waves of the ocean. They flung their long arms into the air, struggling for a way out. The church bells began to chime for the Angelus, and the air turned a deeper blue.

The prenocturnal serenity that had settled on Yossele was interrupted by two of his neighbors, their prayer bags tucked under their arms, who suddenly came abreast of him. One of them was Reb Gedaliele, whose wife, Peshele the Slob, made a living by teaching girls to read from the prayer book. Reb Gedaliele gave Yossele a certain respectful look and ingratiating smile, which immediately led Yossele to guess what his two neighbors were going to bother him about. Of late, they and the rest of Bociany had been knocking their brains out, trying to get him married, so that his children would not be left to grow up on the street. In fact, there was no lack of eager candidates. But Yossele, who had married his Mariml when she was barely fourteen years old, was determined to remain faithful to her even after her death.

"Yossele . . . " Reb Gedaliele began meekly.

Yossele did not give him time to catch his breath, but burst out indignantly, shaking his head, "No, never! My children will have no stepmother, not even if you stand on your heads!"

"But Yossele," interposed the other man, Reb Zorechl, whose wife, Toybe-Kraindele, was assistant at the women's ritual bath. "It's a sin . . . "

Yossele quickened his steps and barked back, "Giving my children a stepmother is a greater sin!"

The two men ran after him. Reb Zorechl was not giving up so easily. "Remember, Yossele," he warned him, "the best horse needs a whip, the wisest man needs advice, and even the most pious man needs a wife!"

"Will you let me be?" Yossele turned a stern face on them.

"No! We will not let you be!" Reb Gedaliele exclaimed courageously. "We are your friends and neighbors. We have your good at heart!"

The two men now began to speak simultaneously, but Yossele no longer heard them as he strode ahead, leaving them to lag behind. When Yossele broke into his marching pace, it was not easy to keep up with him.

The two good men, however, were not defeated for long, nor was the rest of Bociany. That same evening, the two wives of the two men came to Yossele's house to talk things over. These two women were taking care of his orphaned children and knew what arguments to use. But Yossele did not even give them a chance to open their mouths. He sent them away before they had managed to cross his threshold.

The neighbors pretended hurt indifference, and after that evening, Yossele had a couple of weeks respite, during which time his determined neighbors secretly sought the right person to help the community conquer Yossele's stubbornness. That was when Fishele the Butcher, the Jewish fire chief, entered their minds.

Fishele was the most suitable person for this particular mission because he had a powerful personality and a powerful build, with such muscles as were almost unbecoming in a Jew. In addition, he was a dogged pursuer of justice, never able to look on passively in the face of a wrongdoing. It was no secret that Fishele would give false weights to his wealthy customers, so that a poor woman might leave his shop with the bargain of a fine piece of meat for her children. And Fishele was a merrymaker, a wit, with a talent for infecting people with his optimism. A woman might come out of his butcher shop with only a few bones in her hand, but there was unfailingly a smile on her face.

Fishele was also a very devout man. He would drag his apprentices to the synagogue or *besmedresh* by the ears if necessary. And although he was as ignorant as his apprentices and could only read from the prayer book, he still spent all his free time in the *rov's* chambers or in the ritual slaughterer's kitchen. It was through listening to the words of the Torah there that he had almost acquired the language of a scholar, which he liked to show off whenever he came in touch with learned men. They might make fun of him behind his back, but they loved him for his effort. Moreover, Fishele was the type of person who "had the entire town on his head." He was intimately involved in everyone's business, like a brother. Not only did he know what was cooking in his neighbors' pots, but he also knew what was going on in their souls.

Fishele the Butcher claimed personal acquaintance with all the ghosts and demons that took over Bociany at night, especially Wednesday or Saturday night, when the female demon Igereth Bat Machelet went gamboling about the town with her eighteen million demon-familiars. When Sore-Leyele, the ritual slaughterer's wife, who specialized in interpreting dreams, had trouble making sense of a difficult dream, to whom should she turn but to Fishele? Fishele had a habit of seeing evil spirits at work in his own dreams, and what he saw them doing was mixing up the dreams of his neighbors in such a way as to make interpretation impossible. As soon as Fishele awoke in the morning and said his prayers, before he even took a bite of food—and a man like Fishele has a fine appetite—he would dash over to the about-to-be-stricken neighbor and warn him that a complicated dream was being prepared for him, but that he should not worry.

"Jews," Fishele asserted, "have enough worries about what happens to them in the daytime. They need the worry about what happens to them at night like a hole in the head." This was another reason why Fishele was regarded as a man of great kindness, a man without gall.

In addition to all this, Fishele was considered a suitable person to talk to Yossele, because he was Yossele's friend from the *heder* years, and he was the Jewish fire chief, while Yossele was in charge of rebuilding those houses that the fire had demolished. So the two men could talk as equals, as one general to another, and Yossele would be forced to hear his colleague out.

Autumn was almost gone. The days were still dry and sunny, but the air was chilly and the nights were cold. It was the end of another quiet weekday on the Potcheyov. Despite the people milling about, business was dead. Yossele stood on the threshold of his shop, leaning against the doorpost. His twin daughters, Mashele and Faigele, who had been hanging around all day, had now wandered out of sight, into the yard of the Potcheyov.

Yossele's black gabardine was stained with white flecks of chalk, his beard and sidelocks were grizzled with chalk, and there were chalk marks on his face and lime dust on the hairs inside his nostrils. He looked into the distance with an angry, dissatisfied gaze. To remain like this an entire day with nothing to do, to watch the sun's pale rays wander up to his feet and then slowly ebb away, while he stood motionless, glued to the same spot, was the greatest test of his patience.

The sharp smell of the bare fields attacked his nostrils. A mischievous, cold breeze danced into the shop, blew apart the tails of Yossele's gabardine, and aggravated his feeling of being a doomed prisoner chained to a chalk-and-lime fate. His limbs ached with such a wild craving to move that he felt like screaming, like blaspheming, like bawling out the Almighty for arranging His world so clumsily. Yossele was certain that this would give him relief. Why should he bridle his thoughts and not let *them* at least run free? The more the body was restricted, the more one felt compelled to give the mind free reign. But he checked himself.

"What will come of it," he asked himself, "if I indulge in blasphemy? Will the Almighty take my curses seriously? Doesn't He know that such a devoted servant as Yossele Abedale is not to be found again so soon? So perhaps I should be cursing myself instead of cursing Him? But how does one curse oneself, if one is already cursed? And what would be the point if I cursed both of us even with the strongest curse? Would it really help me? Sure, it would ease my heart, but since when did it become a problem for Yossele Abedale to carry around a heavy heart?" Angry with himself, he locked his hands behind his back, and leaning against the doorpost, began to sway to and fro.

He looked about. Not only was there a woman, Hindele the Scribe's Widow, to his right, but there was also a woman in the shop to his left. In fact there were mostly women in the shops on this side of the Potcheyov, for the artisans had their shops on the rear side.

"Of course," Yossele shook his head resentfully. "The men have more important things to do. They study the Scriptures and serve the Almighty; they are served by women and leave such trifles as earning a living to them. Why not? Is it wrong to feel that you carry the world on your shoulders? After all, the *Toyre* is the light and the glory; it's filled with wisdom, it cleanses the soul, uplifts the spirit. Could there be anything better than to sit day and night, drinking from The Source, as if there were nothing in the world to worry about?" Yossele shrugged. "If I wanted, I could bring along a Holy Book to the shop, too. What does Reb Senderl the Cabalist do? He sits in his shop studying all day long. So which book should I bring along? The Bible and the commentaries by Rashi I know by heart, the book of prayers as well. But it takes me ages to plow through a paragraph of the Mishnah, and a person needs the proper frame of mind for such things. I would have to forget that terrible day when I was a bar mitzvah boy, studying the *Gemore,* and Bociany was drowned in blood."

A swarm of bad memories threatened to attack Yossele, and he shooed them quickly away. He forced his mind back to his original thoughts, telling himself that in truth he was not envious of the learned men. He was not one to spend a lifetime poring over huge tomes containing hundreds of pages, without having the slightest idea of what went on in the world. The world, with its beauty and ugliness had, after all, been created for Man, and for this reason the entire *Toyre* had been bequeathed to mankind. The question was, when did these scholars find the time to apply the wisdom that they acquired through their studies to their day-to-day lives?

Yossele, swaying from side to side, asked himself for the hundredth time whether the scholars' manner of studying the Scriptures brought them any closer to understanding the will of God. An unworthy thought popped into his head. "Perhaps their way of studying the *Toyre* is nothing but a fool's game played by Satan? For does not the pilpulistic hair-splitting that goes into the close examination of the Scriptures appear at times like a mockery? Had not Moses made everything as simple as adding one and one? Precisely because The Law is so simple, it is also so powerful that it can crush mountains. So what do I need with all the squabbling over a word, if I can surround myself with sacred rules as if they were impenetrable walls? The Law must be guarded, observed to the minutest detail, because the slightest neglect drills a hole in the fortress, which can, heaven forbid, destroy it entirely. Yet within this fortress I am allowed to feel free. I must not copy anyone else. A man is not an ape, and a Jew especially not."

With less bitterness and more relish, Yossele inhaled the smells coming from the fields. His eyes fell on the neighboring shop, where Hindele sat beside her shelves laden with "vanities." A Tzenerene, the women's Yiddish Bible, rested on her lap. Mashele and Faigele were playing with pebbles in the gutter, while Hindele's two little daughters kept them company. Next to Hindele stood the gentile fire chief, Pan Vaslav Spokojny.

Yossele blinked in astonishment. When had Vaslav managed to come over? How strange that Yossele should have been so deeply immersed in himself that although he had been looking in that direction, he had noticed nothing. What business did Vaslav have to come over to that miserable woman so often, seldom bothering to buy anything, but offering candy to the children, which she, of course, made them refuse? No doubt, Vaslav was drunk. Then why did she allow him to stand so close to her? And why did she answer his questions? If she kept silent and did not react to his talk, he would go away and stop bothering her.

The sight of Vaslav standing beside Hindele irritated Yossele, and made him feel restless again. "What business is it of mine?" He tried to calm himself. "As long as I have nothing to do with him . . . As long as I've warned her to beware of him . . . "

No sooner had Yossele finished his thought than Vaslav moved away from Hindele and approached him. "What's doing, Yossele?" the fire chief inquired in a drunken voice, focusing his watery eyes on Yossele. Vaslav was sad and despondent when he was drunk. He put his hand on Yossele's shoulder as if he wanted to prevent him from continually swaying from side to side. "If you only knew, brother . . . " Vaslav sighed, "if you only knew how much I want to repair our shattered friendship."

After an uneasy silence, Yossele replied grimly, "A shattered friendship can never be mended." He turned sharply and entered the shop, where he pretended to be occupied. Vaslav walked away from the door, in the direction of the marketplace to await the approach of his brother, the priest, who was crossing the street. Yossele ran over to Hindele to warn her, yet again, in his harsh, reproachful voice, not to engage in any conversation with the goy and certainly never to answer him.

Hindele raised her tear-stained eyes from the Bible and stared at Yossele, a silly half-smile on her lips. "Believe me, Reb Yossele, it's not that I want to chat with him. Do you think he means any harm?"

The sight of her sorrowful face made Yossele ill-at-ease. He understood what she was going through. Nevertheless, he barked back, "But what business do you have talking to him?"

She gaped at him almost indecently. "What else can I do? A person comes over to exchange a few words, how can I not answer him?"

"How? By keeping your mouth shut, that's how!" he snapped, inwardly dissatisfied with himself. "Can't you see he's as drunk as Lot?"

"So he is," she nodded. "You can smell it a mile away. He finds it easier to speak of the things that make his heart heavy when he's drunk." Yossele was not in the habit of getting into long conversations with his neighbor or with any woman, and he only growled as he resumed his customary place at the door of his shop. But she moved her stool closer to him, the open Bible still in her lap, and continued, "He's upset about his brother." She motioned with her chin in the direction of the priest who was passing through the marketplace. "The priest doesn't want to have anything to do with him. And do you know, Reb Yossele, what Vaslav said to me? He said, 'Your religion is the true Christian religion. To you, all Jews are brothers, while my own blood brother doesn't even know how to behave like one. He preaches 'Love one another' while he hates his own flesh and blood.' Do you know, Reb Yossele, what I told him?" Hindele's face lit up with the expression of a little girl who expects to be praised by her parent. "I told him that for him his religion is more suitable, while for us ours is more suitable. I consoled him. I told him that his brother did love him. If he didn't, then he wouldn't mind so much Vaslav's trespasses or his heavy drinking, since other good Christians do the same, and he forgives them."

She did not mention to Yossele the other thing that Vaslav, who had probably been too drunk to realize what he was saying, had told her. He said that whenever he thought of her sad black eyes, from which the Angel of Mercy peered, he did a better job of extinguishing a fire.

The priest, a skinny, tubercular man who was at least half a head taller than his brother, was on his way back from administering extreme unction to a dying soul. He was wearing his white robes and he carried the viaticum with him. Behind him followed the altar boys with the censer. One of them shook a little bell, as the peasants who passed the priest genuflected. Vaslav stood a few steps away, staring as his brother passed by without acknowledging his presence.

As Yossele watched the two brothers, the memories, which he had so persistently tried to ward off, returned. Against his will, he saw himself as a child, saw Vaslav and his older brother, Stanislav, the priest, as little boys of his own age. He saw the tents and shacks near the swamps where all three of them had romped together. The father of the two boys, as well as Yossele's father and his relatives, had helped hide Polish freedom fighters in the nearby forests after the defeat of the Polish uprising of 1863. Ten years after the event, the freedom fighters still sought to escape the long arm of the tsar's police force, whose spies were reputed to be lurking in the vicinity of Bociany.

The men of Yossele's family had built the rafts that Vaslav and Stanislav's father had used to paddle the rebels across the water into the dense forests between the marshes. The rebels were not just anybody. They were the sons of noblemen and of rich city dwellers. Some of them were friends and relatives of the landowner who lived in the manor near Bociany. And there were among the Legionaires also some Jews from Russian and Austro-Prussian Poland. At that time, Yossele's entire family had lived in wooden shacks situated between a shallow river and a swamp. Even now, Yossele could vividly recall the sad, pale faces of the noble young men who had hid in the shacks while they waited for transportation across the water. Some of them would say the evening prayer with Yossele's father. At night they were put on his mother's cot and given his mother's eiderdown as a blanket. The four-year-old Yossele, his brothers, and his mother had often spent the night shivering in another shack where the wind whistled through the cracks in the boards.

Then came the night when a raft fell into the trap the tsarist hunters had set up, and the father of Vaslav and Stanislav was killed. The landlord from Bociany took the little boys' widowed mother under his wing and sent Stanislav, her firstborn, to Czestochowa, to prepare him for the priesthood, which had always been Stanislav's dream.

Stanislav had been a very serious little boy who had acted out his dream of becoming a priest even in the games he played with the other children. Stanislav would try to baptize Yossele in the shallow pond where they all bathed, and he would drill both Yossele and Vaslav in the proper way to march in procession. Yossele went along with this game on condition that they all sang the Sabbath song *Lechu Dodi,* ending with the *Shma-Isroel!* That was as much Judaism as Yossele had known at the time. He had not yet started to go to heder.

After Stanislav had left for Czestochowa, his mother saw to it that the landlord should send Vaslav as well. But Vaslav had more pleasurable ambitions for his future, and after about a year he ran away from the cloister. Vaslav was the exact opposite of his ascetic older brother, who looked as if he had been born in his priest's robes. Vaslav was fleshy, greedy for earthly delights, full of inner fire and unquenched passions. In later years Yossele avoided him like the plague. Or perhaps it was not so much Vaslav whom he avoided, as the memory of the carefree first years of his life, as well as of his entire childhood, a paradise lost, drowned in a river of blood during the pogrom that had broken out after the death of Tsar Alexander II, the year of Yossele's bar mitzvah.

During a fire, however, it was impossible not to notice Vaslav, and Yossele would observe him stealthily. He noticed how Vaslav's red face was illuminated by the flames while he ground his teeth with both animal joy and fierce rage. It seemed that Vaslav would rather enlarge the flames than extinguish them. Yossele suspected that the heroism of Vaslav's father ate away at the son's heart like a *dybbuk*. Then Yossele would become more aware of how much he himself envied his own father's free, adventurous life, and he would shake off such thoughts as fast as he could. There could be no comparison between Vaslav's cravings or desires and his own. Vaslav was a slave to his cravings and desires, while Yossele was the master of his. Vaslav was a Gentile, and he was a Jew. An abyss yawned between them.

For many years Vaslav had enjoyed the respect of the Gentiles of Bociany, both because of his heroic father and because of his brother, the priest. Unable to swallow this undeserved respect, he had finally decided to earn prestige through his own unquestionable merits, and so had assumed the post of fire chief. He moved heaven and earth to prove his heroism, but all he succeeded in proving was his stupidity. A few times he had almost paid for it with his life. During a fire he was both drunk and fearless, moving among the flames as if he were strolling in a garden. And when it came to boasting, he had no equal. He would parade about in his special navy-blue uniform, the brass buttons undone, the coat-tails splayed, as if he were busy saving the world at every moment of the day. His swollen belly ballooning like a bagpipe over his thick leather belt, he was constantly on the lookout for someone to invite to the Jewish inn, where he could have a drink and, winding his wet hetman-like mustache around his finger, tell tall tales of his heroic feats. His actual bravery was never enough. He had to embellish it with fantastic details that no one believed, but that were never contradicted, partly because of the fear that Vaslav inspired, and partly because the stories were amusing.

Nor were Vaslav's achievements in the beds of the peasant women any less heroic. While the peasants spent their days working in the landlord's fields or in the gardens and orchards surrounding the manor house, Vaslav slept with their wives and kept order in the villages, because no one trusted the county officer, who was suspected of being in league with the tsarist police. In this way, Vaslav had in fact assumed the role of leader of the community. People addressed him by the title Pan Komendant, and only behind his back did they dare to call him Pan Komediant, as a joke.

Yossele grew tired of staring at Vaslav, who remained fixed in his spot in the marketplace like a telegraph pole, even though his brother's cortege had long since passed by. A hazy veil fell over Yossele's weak eyes. As if through a mist, he saw Fishele the Butcher leave his shop and head in his direction. He watched him as one would a bird or an animal, without really seeing it. Yossele kept on swaying, clutching the doorpost with his hands against his back, his eyes staring into the distance.

Fishele stopped in front of Yossele, lifted the hem of his blood-stained butcher's apron, and loudly blew his nose so as to wake Yossele from his reverie and to make his own head lighter. Although Fishele fancied himself a merrymaker and a wit, he took his role as a messenger from the congregation with great seriousness. This seriousness was now painted all over his fleshy, round face, down to the tip of his black beard. Exuding an air of self-importance, he smoothed the beard with a veined, hairy hand and aimed his now unclogged nose with flared nostrils at Yossele. Leaning against the opposite doorpost, Fishele, too, began to sway from side to side.

"Dead day today, isn't it Yossele?" Fishele began with great diplomacy, while across from him Yossele continued mutely swaying. Yossele wondered how to answer. Did Fishele need his confirmation that this day deserved to belong to the past year? For his part, Fishele was growing annoyed with Yossele's silence. In addition to discharging his obligation to the community, he had been looking for an opportunity to discuss some delicate private matters of his own with Yossele, and to ask for advice which only Yossele could give. But did he not know him, this stubborn mule, this brazen sulking bull, as stingy with speech as if every word he spoke was worth the price of gold? Fishele rearmed his heart and courageously asked another question, "How much do you charge for a sack of lime these days?"

Out of politeness Yossele finally grumbled back, "As much as I can." He even added a question of his own, "Do you want to whitewash your house?"

Fishele scratched the skull under his skullcap as if he were deliberating. "Well, I don't know. Maybe for next Passover, God willing."

"So come in before next Passover, God willing, and I'll tell you the price."

Fishele grew incensed. "Look at the reception he gives me! Have I sinned so greatly against you? I just came over to have a chat."

"I know what you've come over for, and I know who has sent you," Yossele retorted.

"If you know so much, perhaps you can tell me." Fishele looked like a man unjustly accused. "Am I not entitled to drop by? Don't the two of us have enough in common?"

"If we have something in common, then you should know that for those things worth talking about there are no words, while for those which are not worthwhile, even one word is too many."

"Oh, leave me alone. What do you have to be so huffy about? Did you win the lottery or something?"

"I would consider myself lucky enough just to have the money for a ticket." Yossele softened a little. "If you insist on talking, then why don't you talk?"

As joking with Yossele was impossible, and confiding in him was sheer madness, and even a normal human conversation required an effort, Fishele lost no more time, but launched into a frontal attack. "People are saying," he began, "that you've sent Reb Menashele the Matchmaker packing again. You almost, Heaven preserve us, split open his head, they say." It occurred to Fishele that his aggressive tone of voice might not be suitable. To soften it, he added a dash of flattery. "Do you want me to believe that you are violent by nature? No, brother, you won't talk me into believing that. But what you've done is the best proof that you're already well and proper in the hands of the Evil One. This is precisely what Satan wants, isn't it, that instead of marrying, Jews should sleep with his female demons? The best way to crush the People of Israel, isn't it?"

Yossele stepped back into his shop, picked up the ax, sat down on a chalk-stained stool, and with great anger began to split a lump of lime into pieces. So he had guessed right. Fishele had not come just as a friend to ease the heavy thoughts that attacked a man's mind during such a long day. The shtetl had sent him to torture Yossele once again. With an abrupt swing of the arm, Yossele swept the crushed pieces of lime away from him and turned his head sharply to the visitor.

"My children will not have a stepmother! Never!" He reached out for another lump of lime.

Seeing Yossele split the lime with his ax, Fishele overcame the momentary fear that had befallen him, and took half a step into the shop towards Yossele. "May I have as many good years as there are good stepmothers in the world. Some might be even better than one's own mother." He said this with much heart, having his own mother in mind. How many times during his childhood had he prayed that his own mother, the witch, should vanish from the face of the earth, and be replaced by a stepmother?

Yossele stretched out the ax to Fishele. "Here, better cut off your tongue than bring such words to your lips!" He shook the ax threateningly. "May my enemies have stepmothers!"

"And mine too," Fishele agreed, unsure of himself.

He tried to shake off the image of his mother that had suddenly come to his mind. The woman had tortured him to such an extent that he was certain that the worst stepmother would have been an angel in comparison. Not a single kind word had ever escaped her lips, just curses and blows. She had called him by the worst names she could invent, whenever she had caught him daydreaming. As a child, Fishele had had the habit of forgetting where he was, seeing himself instead amidst wild forests, or trekking across endless deserts, valiantly wrestling with tigers, elephants, and lions, and vanquishing them with his two bare hands. In reality, he was forever shaking with fear of his mother, who was more terrible than the worst female demon who ever appeared in his dreams. Although he now had the muscles of a wrestler, made his living as a butcher, and had earned a reputation as a brave fireman, loved and respected by all of Bociany, inwardly he still felt like a piece of dirt. In his imagination he was constantly taking revenge on his female progenitor. Of course, he knew that a Jew had to honor his parents no matter what, and he felt guilty for breaking this commandment, but he accepted his guilt as the price that he had to pay for the delight his murderous thoughts gave him.

"So you'd better not bother me." Yossele's words broke into Fishele's train of thought.

Fishele shook his head as if to shake off his private reflections and, disregarding Yossele's warning, proceeded with the issue at hand. "Honestly, Yossele, I don't begin to understand you," he resumed in his hearty tone of voice. "What kind of Jew are you? On the one hand, you're more pious and strict in observing The Law than any of us. On the other, you're not a *mentsh* at all. Why can't you be like Hersh-Berele the Baker? For how long did he remain a single widower? Or Mendele the Coachman? He barely had the patience to wait out the mourning period."

Yossele, who had been diligently splitting lumps of lime, shrugged his shoulders. "If I should be like this one or that one, then who would be like me?"

"Don't try to talk smart," Fishele waved his hand disparagingly. "If you cannot have the good of the People of Israel in mind, then at least have some pity on yourself. And what about the children and the fact that you need someone to help you out in the business? And apart from all that, you're a male, may you be protected from an evil eye, and . . . " Having his own problem on his mind, Fishele bent slightly towards Yossele, his voice now a grating whisper. "I sincerely confess to you, that I myself, although I'm married . . . "

He was overcome by a strong urge to tell Yossele about those dreams that he did not dare to even hint at to the shtetl's dream interpreter, Sore-Layele. No one but Yossele, owing to his wisdom and his own situation in life, could have some understanding, if only he were not such a hard nut to crack. Only to Yossele could Fishele tell of the naked women he saw night after night in his sleep, spread out on his chopping block, arms and legs dangling down. Desiring them, he would slice them into pieces with his long butcher's knife, as if they were chunks of kosher meat.

Fishele swallowed a few times to suppress the words that were sliding to the tip of his tongue and continued, "So why do you want to walk around with sinful thoughts in your head? Don't you know that Lilith flies around every night and clings to men who sleep alone? Do you want her to choke you with her hair? Don't you know that each strand of her hair is a snake capable of poisoning a platoon of soldiers? Is this what you need to add to your miserable luck? Sinful thoughts may destroy you in no time. Then, in the Next World, you'll be hung by your tongue. Even in the best event, you go straight to purgatory and are lost between heaven and earth." Carried away by the visions dancing in his head, Fishele shuddered. This was precisely the point he himself had reached.

Yossele spat out the lime dust that had collected in his mouth. "You'd better worry about your own sinful thoughts," he replied between spits. "Don't give yourself a headache about mine."

Fishele squirmed. "How do you know I have sinful thoughts?"

"Don't you? What are you, an angel?"

Fishele might as well have been beating his head against a brick wall. Of course, Yossele knew that all his faithful observations of The Law and all his religious devotion could never compensate for the sin of not getting married. But who was Fishele to come and preach to him? All of Bociany might consider Fishele to be a man without a trace of bile, a saint worthy of the highest praise, but Yossele did not trust him. A man who stole from his customers, even if they were rich, even if he did so in order to do a good deed, was still capable of stealing from anyone and finding proper justification. The greatest criminal was, after all, not a criminal in his own eyes, and the more sinful he was, the more adept he became at finding some loophole in the moral law with which to whitewash his deeds.

"It's because I'm not an angel," Fishele said, "that I think about the Almighty's judgment in the Other World. And you should give it some thought, too."

"For the time being I'm not done with the Almighty's judgment in this world," Yossele replied dryly.

"You say that because you haven't got a clue about what goes on in Gehenna! Aren't you scared?"

"What if I am? But my children will have no stepmother, not even if you stand on your head!"

Fishele stepped back, and shook his fist at Yossele from the doorway. "Remember, Yossele! The entire town wants to save you, and you won't let them!"

"Thanks for the favor!" Yossele snapped. "I can survive without it!"

"You can't!"

"It's not the community's business whether I get married or not."

"It is the community's business and the community is your business. The man who goes against the community always loses, don't forget that, Yossele!" Fishele slowly lowered his fist, waiting to see if Yossele would dare to deny his statement.

Yossele did not dare and did not contradict him. He also believed that every Jew constituted a limb of the body called the Jewish People and that if even one Jew sinned, it was a wound inflicted on the entire nation. On the other hand, he resented the fact that every townsman considered himself entitled to tell him how to behave. He waved his fist back at Fishele, "If you ever poke your nose into my business again . . . "

Fishele, angered and unhappy at the failure of his mission, clutched both doorposts and, like Samson, thrust his body forward, "You! You, Yossele, do more harm to your children than the worst stepfather! You're a cold-blooded bastard, that's what you are!" With that he disappeared.

Yossele remained sitting motionless with the ax in his hand. Fishele's last words rang like thunder in his ears. Could Fishele be right? Was he really like a cold-blooded stepfather to his children? Yossele stood up, letting the pieces of lime drop from his whitened lap. He stepped out of his shop and resumed his habitual place by the doorpost. The shopkeepers on the Potcheyov were already beginning to lock up their shops. His neighbor, Hindele, was winding the strings of loose ribbon around her fingers. Her two little girls clung to the folds of her skirt, while his own twin daughters watched from the side.

"There will be no more business today, Reb Yossele," Hindele said as though she wanted to console him. She had probably heard Fishele's outburst.

This woman, Hindele, had an odd, irritating voice, always tearful, melting, as if she were about to stroke the head of whoever she was speaking to. She was also most unpleasant to look at, not that Yossele cared particularly to look at her. She was small, except for her black eyes, which were the size of two large plums. The Rabbi-of-Wurke smile seemed always to wait hidden at the corners of her perpetually wet lips, a smile that Yossele thought silly. On top of that, her matron's wig always sat at an angle on her head. On cold days her nose ran. And she talked to her customers as if she were ready to lick their boots.

Fortunately, she left him alone, and did not bother him much during the long days they spent side by side waiting for customers. Often she would get the neighbor from the shop on her other side to mind the merchandise for her, while she ran home to look after her sick son. Or she would sit hunched over the *Tsenerene,* or read her prayer book in a whining whisper. He would inquire after her sick son, exchange a few words with her during the day, but that was all. It was only recently, since the cold weather had arrived, that she would invite Yossele's daughters, if they were around, to warm their hands on her firepot, and sometimes she would give them a bowl of warm soup. She would also take over a bowl of oatmeal for Yossele, hand him a wooden spoon and plead with him not to refuse and shame her. Barely containing his impatience, he would end by complying, if only to be rid of her as quickly as possible. He could not stand her, he could not abide these "Wurker" people. And he did not care whether or not she had heard Fishele's exclamation. He did not need her to console him.

Yet, in spite of himself, he began to think about Hindele. He remembered the first time he had seen her, newly arrived in Bociany to become the bride of Hamele the Scribe. The Hasidim had been overjoyed with the match, yet Yossele had been unable to appreciate the great "treasure" that Hamele was getting. Only the honor of her Wurker lineage was worth anything, otherwise she had no dowry to speak of and no looks worth discussing even then. Everything about her was insignificant, except perhaps her enormous plum-shaped eyes, or her bosom and her rounded hips. When she walked, it was as if she were afraid to touch the ground with her feet, so unlike his Mariml, who moved with the pride and self-assurance of the Queen of Sheba. Mariml's body had been massive, strong, as if hewn out of marble. It had been in the days when Hamele the Scribe was occupied with writing the new Torah Scroll for the synagogue that Mariml had gotten pregnant with their only son, Hershele. The scroll had been completed not long after Hershele's circumcision. It was like a wedding day when the scroll was carried to the synagogue to the accompaniment of song and dance. And Yossele had danced then perhaps for the last time in his life.

Rather than reply to Hindele's remark about the lack of business, Yossele reentered the shop. A ridiculous thought popped into his head, "If Fishele had mentioned her as a match for me, I would have split his head open with this ax." He put the ax away, swept up the chips of lime and locked the door.

## 4

YOSSELE REMAINED FIRM in his resolve not to remarry. When the neighbors saw him pass, they shook their heads, saying, "Do we ever have a Yossele, may he live in good health! He's not a man but a piece of iron, that's what he is!" Yet in spite of their resentment, they respected this iron quality in him. They thought that if such a respectable man, such a devout Hasid as Yossele, could put his foot down so hard, then perhaps the Almighty Himself had a hand in it. This did not, however, mean that they decided to leave Yossele alone and stop nagging him to get married. His obstinacy might, after all, not be due to the Almighty's approval, but to a dirty trick of the Evil One who had planted such an un-Jewish idea in Yossele's head. So, in order to be on the safe side and not to have to reproach themselves for having looked on and done nothing, they continued to nag at him.

What worried Yossele's neighbors most was that he was not becoming any more efficient as a mother substitute for his children than he had been from the start. His children wandered about in rags and tatters, perpetually dirty, perpetually hungry. On very cold winter days they stayed in their cottage. When it was warmer, the older ones hung around the street or wandered onto the Potcheyov, eating whatever some kindhearted shopkeeper might offer them, or helping themselves to whatever food they could find. The younger ones played in the mud in front of their home, or fell asleep in the entranceway, sucking on a finger or on a crust of bread that Yossele had asked a neighbor to provide. Their noses were runny, their faces smeared with dirt, their yellowish blond hair was entangled in snarls and full of scabs and lice. Peshele the Slob, Brontchele the Professional Mourner, and Toybe-Kraindele, the women's assistant at the ritual bath, had all sworn at Mariml's open grave that they would be like mothers to her children. And Peshele did indeed wash their hair every Friday, but without soap, which was the way she washed the hair of her own children. The soap had to be saved for more important holidays.

As soon as Yossele's older girls began to understand what was being said to them, the women who had nourished and cared for them began to send them on errands, to give them their own small children to carry around, or to order them to take out the slop bucket and sweep the floors of their cottages, so that the girls might learn to take care of themselves. But this occurred only on weekdays, and weekdays did not count. They were nothing but the passageway for the holy Sabbath, and on that day Yossele's house was a home again.

Some time after his conversation with Fishele the Butcher, Yossele became aware of two things at once. The first was that he could not bear his daily vigils at the doorpost and his imprisonment in the shop any longer; and second, that it was high time to initiate his two eldest girls into the secrets of the chalk-and-lime trade.

Not only was Yossele as strongly built a man as Fishele the Butcher or any other member of the Jewish fire brigade, which was made up of the strongest men of the shtetl, but he also compared favorably with any Gentile. And for a man to possess both physical strength and wisdom was a rarity in Bociany, just as it is in the rest of the world. Consequently, the members of the Jewish fire brigade, who also acted as an unofficial militia, would call on Yossele to smooth over squabbles and misunderstandings with the Gentiles. In spite of generally friendly relations between the two communities, arguments and fisticuffs often occurred, especially on market days. The Gentiles, too, acknowledged Yossele's rare qualities, and they respected him. Moreover, they understood his Yiddish better than that of the other Jews. He did not indulge in long arguments, but patiently heard out both parties, allowed neither to interrupt the other, and let each have his say until both were talked out. Then Yossele would say, "Hm . . . " and

"Nu . . . nu . . . ," pluck a couple of hairs from his beard and point at the guilty party.

If it were a trivial matter, the culprit so designated was invariably the Jew. Yossele would then say to the man in Yiddish, "Believe me, it's better like this, because when a Jew is right, then he is really in trouble." To the Gentile, he would say in Polish, "*Aby dalej, aby handel szedl,*" which roughly meant, "Let's carry on, let good commerce continue." He would then oblige the satisfied Gentile to shake the hand of his Jewish opponent, and peace would return to the shtetl. This was how Yossele acquired the nickname "Abedale," which was a slur of his usual Polish phrase "*Aby dalej*."

On the day after he had become aware of the two important facts already mentioned, Yossele left his elder girls, Raisele and Rochele, in charge of the shop, while he, with a sack of chalk and lime slung over his shoulder, set out for the surrounding countryside. The peasants received him respectfully, and he earned a few kopecks by selling them whatever they needed in the way of lime and chalk. He also spent some time at Reb Faivele the Miller's on the Blue Mountain. He fixed the porch and then wandered off to the village behind the mountain, where he spent the night in a barn.

At dawn, having said his morning prayers amid the fragrant hay, he left the barn to go peddling in the village. He even knocked at the door of Vaslav Spokojny, although he wanted to have nothing to do with him. Still, business was business, and Vaslav immediately showed him the way to his backyard, where he had a crooked outhouse which needed fixing. Yossele laid down his sack, asked for Vaslav's tools, and set to work.

The outhouse was located at the very end of the yard, between two pear trees. A few overripe, red-cheeked pears still clung to the topmost branches. To be able to work in the vicinity of such trees was a delight. The air was permeated with the smell of ripe fruit; and the day was bright, one of those last golden autumn days. From Vaslav's house came the sound of the sweet singing voice of Vaslav's eldest daughter, Wanda. True, a Jew was forbidden to hear female voices singing because that might lead to lewdness, but Wanda's voice filled the air, and Yossele accepted it as he accepted the chirping of the birds. He was concentrating on his job.

When the outhouse was fixed, Vaslav, who was already quite intoxicated, inspected it, twisted his mustache, and called his children to come out from the house. He commanded them one after the other to enter the outhouse and "baptize" it for good luck. Then he ordered them to form a straight military line like a guard of honor. Once more he twisted his mustache, then puffed out his body, stitched his fingers together to form a steeple, and imitating his brother, the priest, ceremoniously, with slow strutting steps, made his way to the outhouse, in order to "baptize" it as well. At that very moment, the church bells in distant Bociany began to toll for the Angelus prayers.

Vaslav's wife crossed herself, and hurried toward the porch of her house. She lifted the trussed-up chicken that had been lying on the porch with bound legs, its wings fluttering, and thrust it into Yossele's sack. Then she brought out a dozen eggs from the house and placed them in a rag whose corners she tied together to form a kind of basket. She counted out seven large red apples for each of Yossele's children and handed them to him, thus completing the payment on which they had previously agreed. Instead of thanking her, Yossele nodded, shoved away the shaggy dog who had been jumping at him, and turned toward the gate.

Vaslav had just stepped out of the outhouse. Walking uncertainly on his wobbly legs, he hurried along the path after Yossele. "Hey, Yossele!" he called after him. "Where are you running, may the Beelzebub take your mother's mother!" Buttoning his fly with one hand, he pulled a bottle out of his pocket with the other, and waved it across the distance at Yossele. "Wait, you horse, now we must 'baptize' the privy in the old Polish fashion!" As he rushed toward Yossele, he slipped the neck of the bottle between his mustached lips and took a long sip of *monopolka.*

Yossele shook his head and turned to walk off. But he had not managed to take more than a few steps before Vaslav slammed into him, grabbed his arm, and blinking his bloodshot eyes, waved the bottle in front of Yossele's nose. Vaslav's brood came running after him, clapping their hands, their dirty faces smiling from ear to ear. When Vaslav was drunk and stayed at home, they all had a holiday. Usually it meant that he was eaten by remorse and was repentful. He was kind to his wife, practiced boxing with his boys, and took care of his property. While doing this, he would sometimes burst into sobs, and indeed, it was while sobbing that he had constructed this new outhouse that stood so crookedly, shook on its foundations, and was such a *shpimba-degimba,* as Yossele put it, that one of Vaslav's sons had fallen through the hole because of the loose boards. It was this piece of handiwork that Yossele had been called upon to fix.

Vaslav stood glued to Yossele, urging the bottle into his mouth. "Here, have a swig!"

Yossele felt very much like toasting the occasion. It was an important day in his life. For the first time in years, he knew what it felt like to be free again. He felt festive in mind and body. In the outdoors, his eyes still served him well. He had fixed an outhouse and made it so solid that it would probably outlast Vaslav himself. Yossele cast a proud glance in the direction of the privy, but he pushed Vaslav's hand away and again shook his head. "No, I'm on my way."

He was determined not to give in to Vaslav, nor to himself. If a man felt good about himself, it was not difficult to overcome the strongest temptation. Today was Friday. Yossele needed a sober frame of mind to prepare himself and his home for the Sabbath. He promised himself to take double pleasure in the glass of cherry wine he would use for making kiddush that evening, at the Sabbath table. In addition, the sack on his back contained a squirming chicken, and the rag in his hand held a dozen freshly laid eggs. His children would at last get the taste of a real Sabbath. He was impatient to return. It was the first time that he had ever left them alone at night.

Vaslav was half a head shorter than Yossele, but he made up in width and bulk what he lacked in height. He held on to Yossele by wrapping his muscular arm around his neck. His mustache against Yossele's beard, he tried to force the bottle into the latter's mouth, but without success. "What the devil! Let's drink to friendship," he sputtered in his whining pleading voice, sending a spray of spittle into Yossele's face.

"No drinking!" Yossele turned his head away, stretching his shoulders and neck in an effort to extricate himself from Vaslav's embrace.

"And I say yes! You will drink to friendship!" Vaslav bleated, while his head bobbed unsteadily.

Yossele wrestled with him, trying to protect the rag containing the eggs, which he held in his hand. "I won't drink now. Another time I will."

"Sure, another time we'll drink again." Vaslav clung to Yossele, belly pressed against belly. Anger had already begun to boil within him. "So take a swig, plague take you! Here, brother, suck it in!"

Yossele could stand no more. Unable to use his hands, he pushed Vaslav away through the force of his chest and thighs. Vaslav swayed and aimed the bottle at Yossele as if it were a rock.

"Will you drink, you bleeding mongrel?" he roared and planted himself, arms and legs spread apart, so as to bar Yossele's exit through the gate.

Yossele required all his patience to control himself. In a calm voice he said, "Watch out, you'll break the bottle."

"Then take it and drink, you dog!"

Vaslav's wife ran up to them. "Drink, Yossele, take a sip," she pleaded. "Do it for him, the poor wretch. He's had another quarrel with his brother. Stanislav threw him out of the church. So *you* be a brother to him."

"No! I'm on my way!" Yossele looked around for a way to evade Vaslav.

"You're on your way all right. To the life everlasting! But first you'll empty this bottle to the last drop, until you choke!" Vaslav broke into loud guffaws and kicked the rag with the dozen eggs out of Yossele's hand.

A yellow glutinous stream dripped from the rag and formed a puddle on the ground near Yossele's feet. Vaslav's wife and children began to shriek. With his free hand, Vaslav grabbed the rake which hung on the fence and aimed it at Yossele, who snatched at its other end and gave it such a forceful tug that Vaslav began to hop in a kind of dancing step before falling over in a somersault, the liquor-spouting bottle still in his hand.

"Dear Jesus!" the woman raised her arms toward the heavens at the sight of her husband prostrate in the grass. Wanda, her eldest daughter, who had remained in the house the entire time, came running out.

Yossele removed the sack from his shoulder and helped the woman and her children carry the moaning Vaslav into the house. When Yossele came back outside, he cast a quick glance at the dozen eggs frying in the sun. He combed his beard through with his fingers, slung the sack with the squawking chicken over his shoulder, and stepped out onto the field path leading to the Wide Poplar Road.

As Yossele passed Yoel the Blacksmith's yard, he tried to look straight ahead, as if he had not even noticed the blacksmith. Strange stories circulated in Bociany about Yoel, and Yossele wanted nothing to do with that outcast. But although he was upset about the loss of the eggs, Yossele was feeling so good about himself in general that when the blacksmith's heavy bass voice called out after him, "Have a good Sabbath, Reb Yossele!" he could not resist waving his hand, and without turning his head, he called back, "A good Sabbath, a good year!"

The agitated chicken in the sack over his back seemed to be reproaching him for his procrastination, for not quickening his steps in order to bring it sooner to the ritual slaughterer, as if it were impatient to adorn Yossele's Sabbath table. So he complied and marched briskly, taking large, energetic steps. A gust of wind shook the stems of the slender poplar trees and raised the dust of the road. Dry yellow leaves mixed with kernels of dust flew against Yossele's face, as he breathed in the sharp, refreshing smell of the fields. The ends of his dust-covered beard whipped at his cheeks. He spat out the hair along with the grains of sand that had gotten into his mouth, and with long powerful breaths, he expelled the air tickling the insides of his nostrils.

The sails of the windmill perched high on top of the Blue Mountain turned in the wind. Peasant women squatted in the fields, digging herbs. On the other side of the road sat a woman by an open door, cranking the wheel of her spindle, spinning flax. Higher up, past the field with the sunflowers, walked another woman, a younger one, on her way toward the field shrine, a plaid shawl billowing from her shoulders like a pair of wings. Yossele thought of Mariml. He blinked his eyes and saw her in the cloud drifting above his head. She had emerged from beyond the horizon in the west, where the sun would soon set, and she would follow him to Bociany, to hover above his Sabbath table.

"Almighty of the Heavens!" he murmured as he faced the sky. "So You see, I do have the strength not to curse You when I am miserable. And You see, I bless You and praise You when I feel good. Yes, blessed art Thou, O Lord our God, King of the Universe, by whose word all things exist. But do me a favor, Father of the World, allow me to feel that I am my own man. You are indeed the cause of everything and I serve You in accordance with Your Laws, observing them as You commanded, down to the slightest detail. But truly, Almighty God, it is better to serve You without having to crawl on all fours. It is better to serve You while marching on one's own two feet, as I do now. Yes, just as I do now."

Composed and in good spirits, Yossele arrived at the shtetl. His agreeable frame of mind was not reflected in a smile on his face, yet it was evident in the smoothness of his brow and in the calm of his facial muscles, which were knotted when he was tense. It expressed itself in the proud flare of his nostrils, in the swing of his rich yellow beard, in his energetic buoyant stride, even in the manner in which his coattails flew up. And in order to treat himself to a richly deserved moment of pleasure, he stopped to catch his breath on the steps of the new synagogue, which had been built near the place where the old one had burnt down during the pogrom that followed the death of Tsar Alexander II.

In those days Yossele had been a bar-mitzvah boy. His family was already living in the shtetl proper, and Yossele had been studying with the Gemara *melamed.* The *melamed,* like many of the other Jews of Bociany, had thought that the arrival of the Messiah was imminent. It was only a matter of days. Yossele had expected him as well. With all his being he awaited the Savior. Along with the other heder boys, he had run out every day on the Wide Poplar Road and climbed the Blue Mountain, where the ruin of the windmill stood, the windmill that Reb Faivele the Miller had later rebuilt. From there the boys would look with trepidation into the distance. It seemed to them that soon, at any moment, they would hear the sound of the ram's horn. But all they really heard were the trumpets of death, just as in that other year of bloodshed and destruction, when the Cossacks led by Bogdan Chmielnicki had laid waste Jewish existence. That year, too, people had expected to hear the trumpet of the Messiah.

How such a tragedy should have come to Bociany was a mystery. Both the Gentiles and the Jews were upset by the murder of the tsar. The Jews never liked to pray for a new ruler because he might always be worse than the old. As for the Gentiles, the serfdom that had only been recently abolished was still fresh in their minds. Then the news arrived from the shtetl of Chwosty that there had been a three-day orgy of Jew-killing in Warsaw and a pogrom in Kiev. The inhabitants of Bociany consoled themselves with the belief that these were only rumors. Ever since Yossele could remember, there had been talk of pogroms and blood baths, either in one town or in another. People talked, repeating tales that hardly seemed to have any connection with Bociany. Then a rumor began to spread among the local peasants that the Jews had murdered the tsar and that the new tsar's minister, Graff Ignatief, had ordered the beating of Jews. Such was the new law, and the tsar's law had to be obeyed.

It was then that half of Bociany, along with the synagogue, had gone up in flames. Among the victims were Yossele's grandparents, an aunt, and her newborn baby; and Yossele's young sister-in-law, the wife of his newly married eldest brother, had been violated. Thus it could not be said that risking their lives to save Polish freedom fighters from the hands of the tsarist police had stood the members of Yossele's family in good stead.

The storm was over as soon as the fire had spread to engulf the peasant huts in flames. After that, almost overnight, Bociany was rebuilt. But Yossele had not gone back to studying the Talmud. He had avoided his *melamed* and the *besmedresh.* He had entirely lost the will to study, and what he had learned from the Gemara was now completely erased from his memory, leaving no trace.

Then they had built this new synagogue. It was not just a synagogue; for Bociany it was a solace, a jewel, a crown on the head of a trampled community. Even a large, rich city could have taken pride in such a house of prayer. And it had been built, of course, by Yossele's father and uncles. With the wounds in their hearts still bleeding, they had built it, out of stubbornness and spitefulness, and yet with great enthusiasm. Calling on their greatest talents, they had decorated the synagogue inside and out. Yossele's family were raft-builders and house-builders by trade, but their hearts lay in wood carving, at which they excelled. It was then, while working on the synagogue, that they had initiated Yossele into the secrets of carpentry.

The synagogue was made entirely of wood, with carved balconies for the women and winding stairs leading up to them. The handrails, the dais, the pulpit, the ceiling and the chandeliers, the massive entrance door and the small side door were all adorned with the carvings of small stags, lions, and clusters of grapes. Even the Gentiles respected the synagogue and helped to protect it against fire. Nevertheless, splendid though the synagogue was, it had a slight defect; it stood somewhat bent to one side like a hunchback, because of the swampy ground beneath it, and it was slowly beginning to sink. That, however, was in the hands of the Almighty. The shtetl pretended not to notice. It loved its synagogue with a proud and tender love, and it entrusted this house of worship with its soul.

Yossele's heart, for reasons of its own, was tied to the synagogue with a thousand threads of familiarity, pride of kin, and self-respect. He could never pass it without stopping on the threshold for a moment, just to inhale its odor, an odor not simply of wood, but of something inexplicably fortifying and elating. It was then that he felt with his whole being that only the walls of the Holy Temple in Jerusalem had been destroyed, that its spirit still dwelled within the wooden ramparts of the synagogue in Bociany, which his relatives had built. When he touched the fine carvings on the door, his own father's work, it seemed to him that his father, now long dead, greeted him with a "shalom" from the Other World. It was a powerful feeling.

So, although Yossele was in a great hurry, he lingered for a while on the steps of the synagogue, stroking his father's door with his hand. The synagogue's sexton, Reb Laibele Yaptzok-Fresser, had seen Yossele approach through the little window in the antechamber. Supporting his potbelly by linking his hands beneath it, Reb Laibele came out to greet Yossele.

Reb Laibele was a short, skinny man, hollow-cheeked and sour-faced. A pair of curious, greedy eyes peered out from under his protruding bony eyebrows. The fat red nose was the only fleshy part of his entire face. Reb Laibele had a potbelly as if he were nine months pregnant, a *yaptzok* belly. For him the *yaptzok-cholnt* which his wife, Nechele the Pockmarked, prepared for the Sabbath was never enough, and he was not particularly shy about walking over to the most prominent and wealthy homes and asking for a bowlful of what he called the "real thing." The "real thing" was a thick *cholnt,* a hash of fat, meat, potatoes, and peas and with kishka. This revived Rab Laibele and gave him just the right taste of the Sabbath; this and a good shot of schnapps were his undisguised passions.

"Spent the night in the village, eh?" Reb Laibele, for whom there were no secrets, asked in his grating voice. "Had a bit of schnapps too, eh?" he grinned.

"Heaven forbid!" Yossele shrugged with satisfaction, remembering how close he had in fact come to having that bit of schnapps. But Reb Laibele, whom he could not abide, had spoiled his moment of calm on the threshold of the synagogue, so he waved to the man and walked off in the direction of the ritual slaughterer's house.

All around him the shtetl was feverishly preparing for the Sabbath. Women were frenziedly cleaning their houses, sweeping the garbage away from the front of their doors, and piling the dust into little heaps in the middle of the street. Others were rushing to the synagogue to light candles for the deceased. The men, tasseled undergarments flying in the breeze, milled about, trying to finish off the business of the week before the Sabbath set in. At the sight of the beggars scampering from house to house collecting alms, Yossele grimaced with contempt.

"Do-nothings!" he mumbled to himself. "Such arrogance! Running around as if they were collecting debts!" But he put his hand into his pocket and distributed some of the kopecks he had earned to whichever beggar happened to pass him by. Nor did he forget to leave some money with his son's *melamed* as he passed the latter's house. He also left a contribution for the hostel of the poor. Finally, with a light heart and a lighter pocket and the slaughtered chicken on his back, Yossele headed toward his shop on the Potcheyov to see what his daughters had been up to in his absence, and to lock up for the Sabbath.

After he had heard his daughters' report that all had gone well and that they had even earned ten kopecks, Yossele gave each of them a slap in the face for not having swept the dirt away from the front of the shop. Then, as he bolted the door, he called out to Hindele the Scribe's Widow, "Have a good Sabbath, neighbor!"

"A good Sabbath, a good year!" she replied in her soft voice.

On his way home, Yossele stepped into the house of his neighbor Brontchele the Professional Mourner and handed her the chicken from his bag and the bit of flour that Reb Faivele the Miller had given him the day before for fixing his porch. Yossele asked Brontchele to cook a chicken soup with noodles for his family. Brontchele nodded matter-of-factly, preoccupied with her housework. She was a busy but kindhearted woman who spent her days at the "gates of life and death." She and the group of women under her command, who were adept at weeping, were always in demand to assist at difficult childbirths or deaths. In this manner she was able to support her husband and her many young sons, because nothing of any meaning happened in Bociany without the presence of Brontchele and her weeping women. To keep in practice, Brontchele would often cry while she did her housework, but not today, on the eve of the Sabbath. Today she had neither the time nor the mood for it. She even managed to call out a cheerful "Have a good Sabbath!" to Yossele as he left.

Yossele entered his own house and set about tidying it up with the help of the eldest girls. Then, after he had rushed over to the bathhouse, he dressed in his faded Sabbath gabardine with the torn silk belt, and put on his threadbare fur-edged hat, which he wore on the Sabbath and holidays. His face warm and rosy, the beard clean and combed, he took his son, Hershele, by the hand and together they joined the procession of men streaming toward the synagogue, all of them dressed in clean black frock coats, with white shirts and socks. Yossele himself looked as if he had just stepped out of a page in the Bible.

In order that the Sabbath be even more festive, the members of the congregation invited home any stranger or homeless pauper as a visitor to adorn the Sabbath table. Yossele too brought home a house guest—Abele the Fool.

One look at Abele was enough to bring a smile to the most serious face. He was the tallest man in Bociany, with huge hands and feet. His potato nose was red and always running, his protruding lips, which dripped with spittle, smiled the wet smile of a moron. His hair was neither blond nor gray, just white, as were the lashes of his bulging eyes, which were continually blinking. But the funniest things about him were the eyebrows. They were as black as coal, two thick black stripes, which instead of descending downward at the edges, like normal eyebrows, rose upward, giving the impression of two brush-like boats swaying up and down on the forehead, tossed on the wrinkles as if on the waves of a sea. Using his eyebrows, Abele made faces to delight Yossele's children.

Abele was meek and in his own way, lovable. The innocence of a four year old had remained with him, and it was at that very age, it seemed, that his mind had ceased to develop. Only his body was that of an adult, still young but already hunched over and dried out. The people of Bociany both liked and distrusted him. He did not seem to have the looks, mannerisms, or characteristics of a Jewish fool, although when pressed, no one could say exactly what these characteristics were supposed to be. It seemed to be more a question of sensing, of smelling out the unfamiliar.

Abele did not resemble a gentile fool either. One thing was sure. The shtetl had thoroughly investigated the matter—he was circumcised. But exactly where he had come from no one knew. One snowy morning many winters before, Hatzkele the Water-Carrier—this was before he had taken the vow of silence—had noticed a strange creature sleeping near the oven on a bench in the *besmedresh,* and this was how Abele had come to the shtetl.

When asked, "Abele, where do you come from?" Abele would reply, "From Moreso."

No one knew if he meant Warsaw, or if there was not in fact such a place as Moreso. So they asked him again, "Where is Moreso, Abele?"

And he replied, "There, by the cherries."

"Which cherries?"

"Behind the cemeteries."

So people were reluctant to take him into their houses, especially because it meant another mouth to feed. But Yossele took pity on him and let him live in the shed where he stocked his merchandise behind his chalk-and-lime shop on the Potcheyov. And that was how Abele had acquired his name. When people asked what his name was or where he lived, Abele would reply with a childish smile, the saliva dribbling from his mouth, "Abe . . . Abe . . . " as if it were too difficult for him to pronounce the entire word "Abedale."

Abele was devoted to Yossele Abedale, as a dog is to his master. He accepted without complaint Yossele's tempers and irritations and understood his moods at a glance. During the week, he fed himself by grabbing from here and there the food sold in the Potcheyov, or regaled himself on the scraps handed to him by the shopkeepers. But every Friday night and Saturday he was a guest at Yossele's table, where his presence was enough to brighten the atmosphere. Yossele did not, of course, participate in the general merriment—none of his children had ever seen him smile—but the air around him seemed easier to breathe, owing mainly to the Sabbath, but also to Abele's presence, which was of course also due to the Sabbath.

On this particular Sabbath eve, Yossele was in an unusually cheerful frame of mind. He had started a new chapter in his life; he had ventured out into the countryside. Now, as they were sitting at the table, after they had finished the chicken soup with noodles and had consumed the chicken, an unusual thing happened. Yossele's son, Hershele, made bold by his father's pleasant disposition, managed to work up enough courage to ask Yossele the question that had been bothering him for a very long time.

"Tateshie," Hershele raised his dark, slightly slanted eyes at Yossele. "Why do you never laugh or even smile?"

Yossele was not angered by his son's daring question. He replied in a warm, guttural voice, "Because only children and fools laugh. A sane adult Jew doesn't laugh."

"Why, Tateshie? In the *besmedresh* I often see Jews laughing." Hershele grew braver in the face of his father's docility.

"They laugh because they're stupid," Yossele answered calmly.

"Is my *melamed,* Reb Shapsele, also stupid?" True, Hershele's *melamed,* Reb Shapsele, did not laugh with exactly the kind of laughter that Hershele had in mind. The *melamed* smirked and grinned as he mocked the heder boys who did not know the assigned passage from the Scripture, but it was a kind of laughter nonetheless.

Yossele explained, "Reb Shapsele uses his laughter as a means of teaching."

"And the Hasidim? They really laugh and are merry and they dance and enjoy themselves."

"If you observed them a little closer, you'd notice that they laugh the loudest when they feel like crying."

"And the *Rov?* I've seen him myself. He was laughing together with a few of the men while they were walking from the synagogue."

"The *rov* doesn't want to shame the others, so he laughs along. Believe me, inside, in his heart, he is far from laughing."

"Why is it so?"

"Because so it is. Because the truth is that there is nothing to laugh about. The Almighty is involved in a war of life and death with the Evil One, and there is no end in sight. In the meantime, the Holy Temple has been destroyed, and the Jewish people are in exile. So, when a man laughs, he is really mocking the Almighty's shortcomings, His failures. He's laughing at the fault in God's world, in his works. To laugh means to mock the Creator. And do you think it is right to mock the Father of the Universe, the Heavenly Master whose children we all are?"

"But Tateshie," Hershele's cheeks were aflame. So awed was he by his father's approachability that he did not notice himself plucking single threads of hair from his flaxen sidelocks. "But, Tateshie, the Messiah will come one day after all, and the Almighty Father in the Heavens wants His children, the Jews, to be merry and not to lose hope."

"That's true. Without their hope, the Jews would not be Jews. But laughter is as much related to merriment and hope as a dog is related to a ritual undergarment."

"But the *melamed* says . . . "

"How does the *melamed* know?"

"It's clearly written . . . "

"Even if it's clearly written . . . " Yossele interrupted his son. He did not mind at all that Hershele knew that it was written, while he himself did not know, nor for that matter was he overly proud of his son's superiority in scriptural matters. That was how he wanted it to be. He continued on, "One needs to be as wise as the Almighty to know precisely the meaning of every word written in the Holy Scriptures." Yossele realized that such words might easily lead his son astray. The cherry wine had probably gone to his head. So he added quickly, "One thing you must know: that laughing and being merry are not one and the same thing. Neither are laughing and hoping the same thing. For instance, take Abele the Fool. What is there to laugh about with such a miserable idiot, eh, tell me?"

Hershele, confused by his father's speech, pretended to have understood. "So why does Tateshie not get angry when we laugh at Abele?" he asked.

"At whom should I get angry, silly head?" Yossele retorted almost tenderly. "Aren't you all on Abele's level? I just told you, as far as children and fools are concerned, all such things as laughter, merriment, and hope are one and the same thing."

"And you, Tateshie, you aren't a child or a fool, but in any case, you are merry tonight, aren't you, even if you don't laugh?"

"Of course I am, silly head. First of all, it is the Sabbath tonight. Secondly, with such an interrogator as you, my *kaddish,* I consider myself fortunate enough to rejoice doubly."

Something stirred within Yossele's heart. He looked at the boy ruefully, then transferred the gaze to his other children, who were engaged in climbing on Abele's lap and playing games with him. Their faces shone in the darkness of the room, illuminated by the glittering light of the Sabbath candles on the table. A powerful yearning overcame Yossele as he looked at the radiant, freckled face of his youngest, little Binele, whose hair had a reddish sheen. Her eyes responded to his gaze with a sharp, biting sparkle.

Humming a table song, he stood up and stepped over to the window. Through the darkness outside he could see the brightly lit windows across the street as the candles flickered on his neighbors' tables. Through the panes he could make out the families, the man on one side of the table, the woman on the other. "A king and a queen," he thought wistfully. "The symbolic union of the Almighty with the Sabbath Queen, with the *shkhina* who has returned to Him tonight so that they might be one." Yossele forced himself to sing the Sabbath song louder, more defiantly, so as to drive away the edge of sadness that laced his thoughts. Tonight was the Sabbath, and there was no room for despondency in a man's heart. And why should he be despondent? His Mariml was with him and would come to be with him in the night as well.

On his cot, at night, before he fell asleep, strange tangled thoughts entered Yossele's mind. He remembered the events of the past two days that he had spent in the villages and could not fall asleep. His brain mulled over exactly those matters which he was not supposed to think about on the eve of the Sabbath, matters of livelihood, worries about his children, his distrust of Vaslav and the other goyim. Then, when his wakefulness grew hazy, he became troubled by weird images he had no power to chase away. They dragged him down into the pits of a hellish underworld.

"Perhaps this is a preparation for what awaits me," he thought. "There is no doubt that for a man without a wife the heavens are locked tight. He goes straight to Gehenna . . . " He accepted this judgment with cold-blooded courage.

But when he finally drifted into sleep and began dreaming, he started to tremble with fright. Now he was really in hell, fully awake in his nightmare. His body went limp, shuddering, squirming as it surrendered to the horror. He saw himself during the night of the pogrom, walking through it again as a boy, saw the corpses of the grandparents, saw the blood-covered monster throw himself on his sister-in-law with his pants down. Then he saw himself. He was the monster mounting the girl. No, he was a mannequin, a rag doll. The pendulous-breasted, long-haired female demons of hell attacked him from all sides, manacling his hands, dragging him somewhere by the rings of a chain. They laid him down on a bed of nails and fire, howling, "Marry me, Yossele! Marry me!" Each woman tugged him in another direction, while the bed of nails and fire skinned him alive. There was hellish female laughter, flashes of milk-white teeth that were not teeth but short white pipes from which oozed and hissed the milk-white oil to add fuel to the flames. The red-tongued blaze set fire to his body. His glowing limbs cracked. Beads of sweat popped from his face and body, as if he were a piece of firewood, the trunk of an oak, its sap oozing through the bark.

Then he saw Lilith's eyes cutting through the dark like torches. She was approaching him, coming closer, falling upon him. She wound her hair around him, each strand like a snake, like the poisonous burning ivy that climbs the stem of a tree. "I am your Mariml . . . your Mariml . . . " she whispered in a sweet, biting voice, while her breath pierced him with fiery needles. "I am still your wife. You are still my husband. Promise me . . . promise me . . . forever and ever . . . and ever!"

Although Yossele knew even in his dream that this was a lie, that his Mariml could be nowhere but in heavenly paradise, he called out, carried away by his pain, "I promise! For ever and ever and ever!" He made love to her and he, Yossele Abedale, whose eyes had grown dim, but had never been veiled by tears, cried in his sleep.

As he cried, he saw himself lying all alone, arms and legs spread apart, on a raft that he himself had built, drifting on the stormy river of his own tears. The current swept him along, carrying him down cascading waterfalls, and he had no power to resist. As he drifted on, he saw his naked children emerge from the forest that grew along the marshes by the shore. Their faces were pale, their limbs thin. He exploded into such sobs that the raft beneath him began to dissolve and disintegrate. He began to sink, he was drowning, while his children—not seven, but hundreds—soared above his head. They were a flock of black-winged storks. They swept down upon him, burrowing into his flesh with their bills, with the nails of their claws, picking at his wounds, pressing him deeper and deeper into the bottomless pit. He was falling, rolling into a swirling whirlpool when, from his mouth, a final scream escaped.

The scream woke him. He looked about the room, where the gray of the morning shed a faint light upon the heaps of rags beneath which his children slept on their wooden cots. He looked at the walls, the whitewash long since peeled off, revealing the rotten corrosion of the wood. He saw the moldy water bench, the slanting cupboards with their meager array of dishes, black pots, and dirty basins. He felt an ache in his entire body, a bitter taste in his mouth, and with an emptiness in the pit of his stomach, he consoled himself, "Thank heaven, another night has passed."

Then he saw the table that stood crookedly on the clay floor, saw the burnt-out candles on the torn white tablecloth. A light went on in his head that was so bright and overwhelming that it made him throw his legs to the floor, sit up, and place his hands delightedly on his knees. "Sabbath today!" As if the word itself were a magic formula, his mood brightened. Of the night just past he remembered nothing. It had only left him with a feeling of unpleasant, gnawing emptiness. Now this emptiness was filled with a sweet soothing calm.

Soon the children were awake. With mock severity, he chased them out from under the covers, "It's the Sabbath today!"

They were just as delighted as he was. Father was home. Today they could be like all the other children in the street. With slices of challah in their hands, they darted toward the window in their tattered undershirts. The day was gray and cold. The wind swept the street, raising clouds of dried leaves, dirt, and dust. But a subdued commotion could already be heard outside. The shutters of all the windows in the street flew open. The beadle was knocking on the shutters with his mallet, calling the congregation to prayer.

Yossele's children dressed in a hurry. Yossele himself donned his faded Sabbath gabardine, put the threadbare fur-trimmed hat on his head and threw the prayer shawl over his shoulders. Soon they were all in the street. Yossele held Hershele's hand, while Hershele carried his father's prayer book in his other hand. Behind them walked the four older girls and the neighbors' daughters, carrying the matrons' prayer books tied in white handkerchiefs. In the marketplace, festively dressed people greeted each other with warm whispers. "Good Sabbath, good year" rustled through the air, echoed by the falling leaves. These were not the same people, not the same greetings, as those of the workaday week. Today there was something unearthly about them, as there was about the marketplace, the silent Potcheyov, the entire shtetl. The very air seemed different, with its particular Sabbath breath. It smelled of loftier worlds.

At the synagogue, the cantor showed off his voice. The congregation delighted in the sweetness of the melodies, which poured into its heart like the pure water of a river's source. Yossele became so engrossed in his prayer, in his Sabbath joy, that he lost all sense of time and place.

When they came out of the synagogue, the world was transformed even further, and Bociany was no longer Bociany. Only the externals, the skeleton of streets and alleys, were the same. Now, as the people headed toward home for the Sabbath meal for which they had waited all week, they did not hurry as if urged on by empty stomachs, but walked slowly, proudly, serenely, taking time to look about them. The aura of sanctity seemed to hover over the distant fields and mountains. Colors, the shimmer of objects, every reflection of tangible reality grew transparent, endowed with a soulful, awesome beauty. The silence of the surroundings was so clear, so complete, that one could both hear and not hear the echoes of the peasant voices coming from the huts, one could hear and not hear the sound of one's own footsteps. So lightly suspended in the harmonious balance of the universe did one feel.

Yossele's two eldest daughters rushed along with their girlfriends to the baker's to fetch the *cholnt* Peshele had prepared for them. As usual, Yossele brought Abele the Fool home for the meal. They were sitting around the table, tin cutlery chiming as their lips slurped delightedly at the piping-hot *yaptzok-cholnt,* when Toybe Kraindele's daughter appeared in the doorway with a plate covered by an embroidered serviette. "Mother sent a piece of noodle *kugl,*" she said shyly as she slowly approached the table and put down the dish; her ribbons dangled sloppily from her kinky hair. A little later, another girl came in carrying a plate of honey cookies.

Like every good father after the Sabbath meal, Yossele tested his son to see how well he had studied that week's chapter from the Holy Book. He asked Hershele questions, pretending that he knew the answers. In reality, he was learning from his son, learning better than he had learned from his own *melamed* as a boy. This was how it was supposed to be, how he wanted it to be. Nor did he overdo the examination. He grew very sleepy, which was a sign to him of the Almighty's benevolence.

Yossele would not indulge in analyzing problems of faith. Reading all kinds of meaning into the holy words and speculating over them was not his way. Such deliberations made him think sometimes of a Jew's weakness of faith, of his doubts, rather than of his strength. He himself had tied his soul to God's law; it was an armor that held him together, and everything in the world fell automatically into place. Take this moment, for instance, for which he had waited all week long. It was a good deed to free one's mind of earthly thoughts on the Sabbath, so he freed it. It was forbidden to worry about profane matters on the Sabbath, so he did not, not even if the world turned upside down. He had no intention of outsmarting the Almighty. True, he had not slept well the night before. The profanity of the previous week had probably lingered in his mind a little too long. But there was not the slightest doubt that this afternoon he would sleep better than he had during the rest of the week put together, for the Sabbath had taken possession of his whole being.

In order that the children should not disturb him while he slept, he sent them out of the house in the company of Abele the Fool, forbade them to return until called, and bolted the door.

With a contented sigh, he unbuttoned his clothes and threw himself on the ragged dirty heap of bedding with such heavy abandon that the red cover of the eiderdown burst in a few more places, and a snow of feathers was released into the air. Then he grew aware that one of the beams supporting his cot had slipped out of place. The cots had not been fixed since the day he first constructed them. Now he was forced to get up and put the beam back into place. He stood up but was too sleepy to bother fixing anything, so he threw himself down again on a pile of rags that had been pushed into a corner of the room when the rest of the clay floor had been sprinkled with yellow sand in honor of the Sabbath.

An unpleasant thought crossed his mind. "I," he said to himself, "build for others things that can last for all eternity, but for myself I could only build this *shpimbe-degimbe* doghouse of a home, with *shpimbe-degimbe* furniture that doesn't even deserve the name, shaking and rocking as if it were made of straw, not wood. I deal in chalk and lime, yet I have never managed to find the time to whitewash the walls; I let them rot and grow over with mold and fungus. And it doesn't even once enter my mind to call in the glass peddler, at least to ask the price of replacing the broken window panes. I just leave them to clank in the wind and replace the missing pieces with knots of rags or old pillows."

He recalled with guilt that whenever he found a nail, rather than putting it to good use in repairing his house, he would instead straighten it out and save it for building the *suke* for the Holiday of Tabernacles. Since the days of the pogrom, he had felt that whatever he built for himself would not last.

Suddenly he remembered: "It's Sabbath! Sabbath today!" He locked away the grim thoughts in his mind and unlocked the Holy of Holies in his heart, where he kept the image of Mariml. He saw her soaring toward him in a white Sabbath dress she had acquired in the Heavens, for her earthly Sabbath dress had been black. In her white dress she looked like a bride again. She was the *Shkhina,* the Queen Sabbath. The touch of her hand was healing, soothing, holy. And healing, soothing and holy was the peace that poured into him through her fingers.

He slept well, deeply. Even the chattering of the storks, Mendl and Gnendl, as the children called them, did not wake him. On the contrary, his thunderous snore, which reached the storks through the opening in the chimney, mixed with the rhythm of their own chatter, creating a drumming effect. It joined the snores and the chattering sing-songs issuing from all the neighboring huts, rising toward the sky as if to let the

Almighty know that Bociany was having its Saturday after-*cholnt* rest. For had not He, the Creator of the Universe, so prescribed it?

Between the peacefully sleeping houses, the children gamboled. Those few hours when the watchful eyes of the grownups were not upon them were used to indulge in all the tricks and games they could not allow themselves the rest of the week. But if they played *palent,* with a stick serving as a ball, or waged war, Jews against Canaanites, they did so with hushed voices, so as not to wake the adults and spoil the fun.

Yossele's children were more careful and quiet than the others. First of all, not counting Hershele, they were all girls, and second, from the time their minds had sprung into consciousness, they had ceased to regard themselves as children. Children's games did not tempt them. Mostly the girls sat on the doorstep wrapped in their rags and plaids, the smaller ones in the laps of the older ones, repeating stories to one another that they had heard from the women in the street. The only game they indulged in was *strulkes,* a pebble game.

Nor did their brother, Hershele, venture far from the house. He sat nearby on a rock, huddled over a volume of the Scripture, which shook with the knocking of his knees against each other. He was cold. He studied or stared at the storks, the harbingers of good fortune, who were late in leaving Bociany that year. Curious about the young in their nest, he was aching to climb onto the roof and have a good look at them. But his father had strictly forbidden this, and Hershele, like his sisters, was more afraid of his father than of the Almighty Himself.

The children had not the slightest doubt that although their father was deep in his Sabbath sleep, he knew precisely what they were doing and where they were at that very moment. The very thought of this made Hershele divert his eyes guiltily from the storks and bury his nose in the Book resting on his shaking knees. Nor did he merely keep his eyes glued to the tiny print; he resumed his studies with diligence. He loved studying. The Holy Book was the best avenue of escape from this harsh world without running the risk of punishment. And although his street friends tried to inveigle him into joining their games and scoffed at him when he declined, he did not budge from his place. With even greater fervor he swayed over the Book, humming the words quietly to the appropriate tune, as he plucked hairs from his flaxen sidelocks and shivered with cold.

How, after all, could the children move from the house, when inside rested he who held all the threads of their lives in his hands?

## 5

THE WINTER AFTER HIS FATHER'S DEATH, Yacov, the youngest son of Hindele the Scribe's Widow, was hardly aware that he himself was alive. Icy death, hard and impenetrable, had formed a shroud of freezing white and wrapped the entire world with it. Yacov found himself somewhere beneath it; he felt as though he had fallen into a dark pit. There, his days and nights had joined to become one stagnant, frosty emptiness that dulled his senses. It sometimes seemed to him that it was he, Yacov, who had been extinguished, who was gone.

Then the fog of his mourning thinned. Little by little, the pit of darkness was flooded with light, and his soul rose to the surface for a breath of fresh air. The grief in his garret home became bearable.

It was not long after that the *melamed* announced the good news to Hindele that Yacov was ready to study the Talmud, and he started to attend the heder with his new *melamed,* Reb Shapsele. This event marked the first time that Yacov failed to understand his mother. Was it not she who had always insisted that the Torah was sweet? How was it then that its taste had begun to acquire the bitterness of poison? With tears in his eyes, he would swallow the printed words of the sage Rabbi Abba, and with fear in his heart he mumbled the words of the other sage, Rabbi Rabba.

Reb Shapsele was a hunchbacked little man whose nose continuously ran and whose tiny eyes continuously watered. He sat with his heder boys at a long, corroded table, a red handkerchief in one hand, the disciplinary whip in the other. The greatest praise for a student was when the *melamed* did not mock him or shame him in front of the others, or did not give him a going-over with the whip. The heder itself was located in a moldy, dingy cottage, where the *melamed's* wife and daughters, their faces powdered with coal dust, busied themselves around the black sacks of coal that they were selling. Everything and everyone was smeared with the coal dust, including the boys' clothes and faces. Here in this dark room, its mildewed walls covered with dark blotches, the students spent their days. The *melamed's* wife and daughters ordered them around or made them do household chores, scolded them, and checked to make sure that they did not play cards under the table.

Reb Shapsele had a very good name in Bociany, respected by scholars, parents, and former students alike. He was a truly learned man, capable of breathing life into every commentary, every *medresh,* every *aggadah.* He took his mission, forming young minds, very seriously and devoted all his talents and knowledge to the practice of his vocation. He did not allow himself a minute's respite and, needless to say, allowed his students none as well. The usual tricks and pranks of heder boys were dearly paid for. The fact that he was an impatient man, and that his students had to recite the lesson as smoothly "as water" in order to avoid a whipping, only added to his renown in Bociany, although it was not common for a Gemara *melamed* to resort to the whip so often. But Reb Shapsele was no ordinary *melamed.* Even Reb Laibele Yaptzok-Fresser, the synagogue's sexton, who never said a good word about anyone, had to admit that not counting himself, Reb Shapsele was the greatest treasure that Bociany had ever possessed.

The heder boys studied quite diligently and even enjoyed some of their lessons. But the hours at the heder were long, and not a single day passed that, in addition to the usual slaps with the handle of the whip, the *melamed* did not call on one of the boys to "put himself down." From this experience, Yacov learned the true character of his friends and formed some idea of what to expect from them.

Some boys, when called to "put themselves down," would whine and flutter like leaves. Others would cry, tremble like fish in the water on the Day of Atonement, but would also kiss the *melamed's* hand, beg his forgiveness, and implore him to forget the punishment just this time, this one time. They would shower the *melamed* with impassioned promises about how good and obedient they would be in the future, how they would recite the chapter of the week "like water," and how in the future they would behave like angels. Then there were those who would grind their teeth and stare at the *melamed* with daggers in their eyes. Some would even stick out their tongues at him and put up a struggle, showing no fear at all of the double portion of blows that awaited them. And then there were those who accepted the punishment as something that they rightly deserved. They did not cry or kick, but let their shoulders sag, and then, indifferent to their fate, they would unbutton their pants and put themselves down on the chair or the table or wherever the *melamed* ordered. On their own, they rolled up their undershirts and bared their behinds.

The *melamed* then blew his nose and took his time wiping it thoroughly with his red handkerchief. In order not to shame the boys, the women would withdraw to a little shed adjacent to the room, but they usually left the door open, and the boys had no doubt that the women were watching from there, impatient to go back to their coal business. This ordeal, to lower one's pants, roll up one's undershirt and personally prepare one's behind for the *melamed's* whip, while the women looked on, was the worst. It hurt more than the thrashing itself. Then one really felt like a worm, on which any adult felt free to trample. And out of shame and humiliation, one's heart burst out with a scream to the Master of the Universe, calling on him to look down and see how the children of His people studied His Torah, precisely as they should, with trepidation.

During the first few weeks, Reb Shapsele spared Yacov. Now and then he struck him a blow with the handle of the whip, but he did not call him to "put himself down." He was a newly orphaned boy, after all. But this indulgence did not even last until a newer orphan showed up. Yacov was in any case nothing special to Reb Shapsele or to his friends. Orphans were not lacking at the heder. And so one day Yacov's turn arrived, and he came face to face with his own character.

Yacov had tried to prepare himself for the ordeal from the day when he had first come to study with Reb Shapsele. He had decided to behave like the two bravest boys, Ariele, Fishele the Butcher's son, and Hershele, Yossele Abedale's son, who was already an advanced student.

Ariele was the most brilliant student at the heder, but he was also a robust, fun-loving boy who was not afraid of anyone and would allow no one to boss him around. He led the boys in all kinds of street fights for "justice," and was not afraid to pick a quarrel with the gentile boys. He was known as a great democrat because he befriended even the most unpopular boys, such as Yacov himself, who was considered a sissy, a mama's boy, and was nicknamed Soft Mirl, a girl's name, because he avoided all fights. In spite of, or perhaps because of that, Ariele had taken Yacov under his wing and had become his most beloved friend. This new friend of Yacov's would struggle with Reb Shapsele like a lion, kicking, biting, calling him all kinds of dirty butcher names, until Reb Shapsele, exasperated, would blow his nose and call in his studious eldest son from the other room. Together, they would force Ariele to "put himself down," and Ariele, the hero of the heder, would receive the fiercest blows from the *melamed's* whip.

On the other hand, Hershele, Yossele Abedale's son, was a direct contrast to Ariele. He did not beg the *melamed* for forgiveness. In fact, he never said a word. Like an experienced soldier, he would swiftly pull down his pants, lay himself across the chair, and hastily roll up his undershirt, revealing the marks of the licking he had received from his father a day or two previously. Unlike the others, he did not emit so much as a sigh as the whip came swishing down on his behind. He kept his hands folded into tight fists pressed against his thighs. When it was over and he stood up, his lower lip and part of his chin bore deep traces of the teeth he had buried in them to prevent any sound from escaping his mouth. His eyes were filled to the brim with tears, but none rolled down his cheeks.

When the *melamed,* in his matter-of-fact tone, repeated the invitation to Yacov to "put himself down," Yacov cast a swift stealthy look at the door, and before he himself knew what was happening, he found himself outside in the street. He started off at a wild gallop, heading straight for the Potcheyov and his mother. But before he arrived there, a sudden thought forced him to change direction. "No," he decided. "I will not run to Mother. I'm no longer a little boy. I'm a *Gemore* student and should have the strength to deal with my shame on my own. And then, Mother cries day and night lately. I'm not going to cause her to cry more. And suppose Mother had the bright idea of coming along to the heder tomorrow to plead special indulgence for me?"

At the mere thought of this possibility, Yacov squirmed. He did not care for his mother as much as he used to. How could she have made him feel that he was something special? How could she have given him that proud glance, that smile through tears, on the first day when he had set out for the Gemara *melamed's* heder? Had she not known what was waiting for him? And how was it that neither Shalom nor Itchele, his brothers, had made much fuss about the beatings they received at the heder? How had they taken them so matter-of-factly? How had they born the shame?

Why had they not warned him ahead of time of how important and how shattering were the experiences that he would have to go through?

He found himself running along the Wide Poplar Road. Some carts and sleighs passed him by. He also came abreast of small groups of older boys whose mothers held their belongings for them. These were the post–Bar Mitzvah boys, belatedly heading for the yeshiva in Chwosty. The mothers hailed the carts and seated their sons on them amid a profusion of hugs and kisses. This sight made jealousy grip Yacov's throat. How he wished to have advanced this far, and to be able to ride off! Running, he turned his head away as he passed them. He was sweaty. His clothes clung to him. He grew tired and had to slacken his pace. Slowly he began to feel the wintry cold.

There had been a heavy snowfall a few days previously. The fields were covered with snowy featherbeds, while the road itself was full of patches of ice and snow drifts. He had left the heder without the winter caftan that he had inherited from Shalom. He had not even remembered to grab the woolen scarf his mother had knitted especially for him. Fine thing it would be if he came home ill, like Itchele! It occurred to him that his mother would not survive his becoming sick or his running away from home. He hesitated for a moment. Then he made an about-face and raced back in the direction of the heder. All the while in his head the same thought repeated itself, "Yacov is running to be sacrificed . . . " He dashed back into the heder and straight up to Reb Shapsele. Out of the corner of his eye, he caught the mocking glances of the other boys.

He heard them hissing, "Coward! Soft Mirl!"

The *melamed* pointed Yacov to his seat as if nothing had happened and went on with the lesson. Yacov, squeezed into his bench between two boys, sat as if on hot coals. With terror he met the stealthy reproving glances of the other boys. No encouragement from anywhere, except perhaps from Ariele, the butcher's son, who looked at him as if to say, "You can still be my friend, if . . . "

At last the *melamed* turned to Yacov and asked him to "put himself down." Yacov's shame was doubled by the lack of compassion from his friends. And he did cry when the whip descended on his backside. He screamed "Mameshie!" which amused his friends even more.

On the way home, in the slush and cold, his body bruised, his heart sore, Yacov stumbled in the dark, blinded by his tears. The lit lantern he held in his hand did not prevent him from getting lost in the maze of narrow, muddy alleys. "I've lost my way home and I don't care," he mumbled to himself, wiping away the tears that washed down his face. "I want to die. I'll put myself to bed with Itchele and never get up. How can I live with this shame all alone in the world?" Of course he was alone. His mother did not count; she had betrayed him. She was a stupid old woman who nursed the crazy notion that there were no *roshe-merushes,* no evil people in this world. How could she have dared to say that, knowing Reb Shapsele? He, Yacov, would never believe a word of hers again. Unless . . . Unless she had something else in mind. Unless Reb Shapsele was not really a human being but was the spawn of Asmodeus hiding behind the face of a human being.

When he finally entered the loft, he saw his mother sitting with a bowl of soup in her hand, spoon-feeding Itchele. She turned her sorrowful eyes to Yacov and scrutinized his wet face smeared with coal dust, his crookedly buttoned caftan, and the tasseled undergarment sticking out from it. Her eyes questioned him, but she said nothing and turned her head back to Itchele.

"I had a fight with the boys," Yacov felt obliged to say by way of explanation. His voice was still hoarse with tears. She gave him another searching look. He could see immediately that she did not believe him.

As he sat down at the table to wait for his bowl of soup, she turned to him again. "Why did the *melamed* whip you?" she finally asked.

Of course she had guessed. Should he tell her now that the *melamed* had whipped him because he was daydreaming and had lost sight of the paragraph they were studying? Yacov had fancied, just at that moment, that he was walking along the Narrow Poplar Road near the landlord's manor and had suddenly found a jewel the size of a loaf of bread. Although this extraordinary jewel was of such exquisite beauty that parting with it was heartbreaking, he had given it back to the landlord to whom it belonged. And for his honesty and for resisting the temptation of stealing, the landlord had rewarded him with one hundred million rubles. Yacov was on his way home to tell his mother the good news. From now on she need no longer slave at the shop or at home. His little sisters would get the prettiest dresses in the world, and his mother would get a better-fitting wig for use on the Sabbath. And most important, Itchele would be sent to the best hospital in the world and be cured. Yacov was almost upstairs, at the loft's door, about to see the delighted faces of his family, when he heard the *melamed's* voice asking, "Where are we, Yacov?"

"Almost at home!" he had called out excitedly, still immersed in his daydream. Then he heard the giggles of his friends and realized where he was.

Should he tell his mother why the *melamed* had whipped him? Did it matter now? No, only one thing mattered: never to allow such a humiliation to happen to him again, ever! So he resolutely announced to Hindele, "I'm not going back to heder!" She said nothing, as if she had not heard him. But he knew that she had. Did she take it lightly then? Most likely so. She considered him a weakling, just like everyone else did. "I said I'm not going back to the heder!" he repeated more loudly.

"I heard you," she replied. "Until tomorrow morning you're not going back."

Of course. That was what he had expected her to say. But then she stood up, put the bowl away, and approached him, wrapping him in her arms so tenderly that he almost melted in her embrace. "Don't be silly, little son," she said warmly. "What do you mean you're not going back to heder? Is such a thing possible? Go wash and have your supper." She made him get up from the table and wanted to accompany him to the basin of water, but although he needed her closeness more than ever now, and it hurt to break away from her, he gave a violent jerk of the arms and broke free from her embrace.

"I'm not going back!" he cried out. Although his stomach rumbled, and both body and soul craved a bit of hot potato soup, he grabbed his caftan and dashed out of the room.

Morning came. The stove was heated but the room was cold. Wind and frost blew in through the cracks in the walls and roof. The window panes looked like ice cubes glued together. Yacov had slept badly. He had again dreamed about finding the treasure, but this time the jewel, although it sparkled like a diamond, was like a chunk of ice, freezing his fingers. And there was a nightmarish figure, either Reb Shapsele or the Devil himself, pursuing him as he ran down the slippery road. As soon as he opened his eyes, he remembered the incidents of the day before. "I'm not going to the heder!" he called out loudly to Hindele, who was handing a mug of chicory coffee to Itchele.

"A Jewish boy must go to heder," she replied. "There is nothing in this world for a Jew if he refuses to study God's *Toyre*."

It did not help, nor did her pleas that he not break her already broken heart. Yacov remained adamant in his decision. She enlisted the help of her other sons in her argument with her youngest. Itchele rasped out some wise words through his dull cough, his chest working like a rusty machine, and added that he wished nothing better than to be able to join his brother in his Talmudic studies. The *melamed's* blows were nothing compared to what he was ready to bear just to be able to sit down at the Gemara with his friends at the *besmedresh*. When even this was of no avail, Hindele, who had passed the night worrying about her eldest son and in making tearful prayers, lost her patience.

"You will go!" she lashed out. "Never mind, the *melamed* will not kill you. A boy can survive a few well-deserved blows. All boys do! It will teach you a lesson! The main thing is to study and serve the Almighty. For that a person should be able to take what comes and survive!" Finally, when she realized that her words were falling on deaf ears, she wrapped herself in her plaid shawl, forced Yacov to put on his caftan, grabbed him by the hand, and dragged him out of the room. They almost fell down the slippery stairs. She pulled him through the yard, weeping and panting. "Fine son that you are," she reproached him, "shaming me in front of all Bociany. That's how much heart you have for me now, after your father's death, with a sick brother at home yet!"

He did indeed have no "heart" for her. He had never seen her like this before. She was transformed in front of his eyes into a wicked Jezebel. She did not love him, and she was no longer his mother. He was all alone in this world and nothing really mattered. But it did matter not to go back to the heder, ever!

As he struggled with her, people passing in the street looked on and smiled. No one had any pity on him, so he would have pity on no one either; certainly not on this woman with the power of a giant and the face of a monster. At the same time, he knew inwardly that he would not tear himself away from her or even try to use all his force to escape, that it would be in vain, and that sooner or later he would allow her to bring him back to the heder and to Reb Shapsele. He felt like a worm.

The long, cold winter after her husband's death had passed in a haze for Hindele as well. It was not that the world seemed unreal to her. It was that its reality had stunned and blinded her, leaving her aware of only the sick child whom she had to save and the healthy children whom she had to protect. On the surface, she went through the motions of a living person; her mind was present, alert. At the same time, her soul was joined to that of her mysterious, beloved mate, who was now gone.

Spring arrived. The storks returned. Against her will, Hindele's senses gradually began to awaken. Her heart, slowly emerging from the pit of dullness and darkness, began to expand with hope. She would save her child with her love and with the help of the Almighty's love.

She neglected the shop, leaving the boys to attend to it after they came home from the heder. Sometimes she would ask the woman in the adjoining shop to mind the merchandise for her, and she would hurry home to be with Itchele. She spent her evenings in the garret, preparing food for the next day, mending the children's clothes, ceaselessly talking to her firstborn, trying to cheer him. The other children kept their distance from her, as if they were protecting themselves against her anxiety and the gloom of their home. She was glad. She did not want them at home lest they, too, catch the disease. And she was glad that they were struggling to shake the sorrow from their hearts. Time was a merciful healer and accomplished this feat much more quickly with children than with adults, in particular when the lightness of spring assisted in the cure. And then, their absence gave her a chance, when Itchele was asleep, to deal with her own grief.

Her bereavement and her worry took up so much of her strength that she had barely any energy left for all the things that she had to do, and it took her more time to get them done. She had also started to eat poorly. She simply forgot about it, and when she did remember, she was glad that she felt no hunger. She was earning very little in the shop. There were days when she had to borrow the few kopecks for a loaf of bread from Nechele the Pockmarked. Whatever she did earn went for dairy products for Itchele, which were considered the only remedy for his illness. She still continued with her predawn walks to Reb Faivele the Miller's farm to be offered a jugful of fresh goat milk.

It was a Sunday evening. Hindele's two little girls were still playing in the yard. Shalom and Yacov had gone to a neighbor's house. After Itchele had fallen asleep, Hindele slumped into a chair near the open window. She sat motionless, inhaling deeply, her mind blank. Then, at a certain moment, she became aware of the smell of lilac reaching her nostrils from the nuns' garden. Her mind stirred, and so did her stomach. She was famished. The pangs of hunger surprised and angered her. She had only single slices of bread and herring left for the children to eat before they went to bed. She inhaled the lilac scent with a sigh, hoping it would fill her stomach. It made her head swim. A thought struck her: she had no right to be going on like this. What would happen if she were to collapse? Was it her fault that she was only human and a human being needed nourishment in order to function? She would have to force herself to take care of her miserable body. Her children needed a healthy mother.

She went over to the jar with the schmaltz herring, cut a piece of it for herself, brought a mug of chicory coffee over to the window, and sat down to her feast. After she had washed down the salty herring with another mug of coffee, she felt satisfied, cheered. A dim longing to open one of her long-neglected books stirred in her, but she dismissed it. She would not be able to understand what she was reading anyway. The letters would obscure her sight like black pepper and transport her into reveries of the past when her family had been intact, a past which was in any case still alive in her.

She moved closer to the window to look into the nuns' garden, at the blossoming lilac trees that she liked so much. It was quite late, but the days had grown longer. She could see the trees and shrubs, their blossoms having acquired a particular softness of color in the after-sunset light. She watched the nuns strolling among the flower beds, puttering around the bushes, pruning and working the soil. She thought of those moments, not so long ago, when, beside herself with grief and bereavement, she had envied these silent creatures their relaxed movements, their peace, and the serenity on their faces, as if pain had never been part of their lives.

She did not envy them now. She knew that she could never lead such a life. She could see nothing in it. To her, the awesome splendor of God's world could be truly appreciated only through the prism of the life on this side of the cloister's fence. It seemed to her that the salt of man's tears made the taste of existence palatable—of course only if it were not oversalted, like the herring that she had just eaten on an empty stomach and that now burned her insides. Naturally, she longed for serenity, but not at the expense of oblivion, of turning her back on ugliness, fear, suffering, and pain. She wanted to accept the negative, too, as a gift from the Almighty, to submit to it humbly, and yet to weather its embrace with fortitude and, with calm in her heart, praise the Creator nonetheless.

The people whom she really envied were the Jewish men. They were capable of a close bond with their Maker, so that when they said, "The Lord is right and His judgment is right," they felt it with all their hearts. She envied her own husband who, with so much trust and serenity, had drifted into the long tunnel of silence, as if it were not filled with darkness but with soothing light.

That kind of serenity she could not achieve. Although all her life she had had to claw her way out of one misfortune after another, and she had even learned to make peace with the loss of her husband, she knew that she was not prepared, nor would she ever be, for the loss of her child. She shuddered at the mere thought and tried to drive it away by continuing to inhale deeply the scents from the nuns' garden. These were not suitable thoughts for such a beautiful evening, when all the world was permeated with hope and promise. She must allow hope to fill her heart as well, allow it to become so powerful as to embrace the screaming wound inside her. She smiled faintly, a salty, tearful smile, as she felt the salt herring bite at the pit of her stomach.

She noticed Manka the Washerwoman sitting in the yard, resting in front of her house, while her children and a few others, including Hindele's own two girls, played in the grass-covered ruin of Manka's former dwelling across the lane. Because it was Sunday evening, Manka was dressed in her Sunday best. Hindele thought of her friend Nechele the Pockmarked and the other women who often dropped in to see her in the evening. They would chat with her or weep with her, trying to ease her burdened heart. She was grateful to them. It was a blessing to live in a community of her own, among people as close as her family, sharing the same joys and sorrows. She felt so much less alone in the world. Yet she was glad that none of them had come by that evening. For some reason, however, she felt inclined to go and sit with Manka, who never wept over Hindele's misfortunes because she never wept over her own.

Hindele stood up and wrapped herself in her plaid shawl. She listened for a while to Itchele breathing in his sleep and then went down to the yard. Manka made room for her on the doorstep. They exchanged a few words about the weather. Hindele described the nuns' garden to Manka, how it looked when everything was in bloom; from Manka's house one could only see the enclosure. Then the two women sank into silence.

Manka was a quiet, sad woman. Her vigor and strength were a strange contrast to her languid, melancholy moods. She had, however, a fine voice for singing, and when she was at home in her garret, Hindele would often hear her sing long Polish ballads and would admire the warmth and softness of the tunes and the voice that sang them. Yet if Hindele asked Manka to hum something, she refused.

Hindele thought of Manka's children, Marysia and Bronek, now playing with her own two girls. Both had big, bright-blue eyes, which were as sad as their mother's. Bronek, the younger, although he was Yacov's age, still sucked his thumb. Brother and sister moved as if in slow motion, never laughing too loud or shouting. Manka's heaviness of heart seemed to have taken root in their souls. Hindele prayed that her own grief should not have a similar effect on her own children.

"Why are you always so quiet, so downhearted, even on a Sunday?" Hindele finally asked, turning to face Manka. "After all, you have a house with a plot of land. You have an income from doing the laundry. Your children don't walk about barefoot in the cold, nor do they suffer from hunger."

"I'm not sad," Manka shrugged. "Life is sad."

"Even on an evening like this?"

"Especially on such an evening." Manka frowned, fingering the cross that was suspended from her neck on a string of beads. "The more beautiful the world, the sadder the soul."

Hindele cringed. It was as if Manka had read her own mind. Still she asked, "But why? You Gentiles have it good in this world. Mother earth feeds you. We Jews have to get our crust of bread practically from the air. And then there is the children's *melamed* to pay and all kinds of charity to give to. We don't live only for ourselves, precisely because we are suspended in the air."

"We don't live only for ourselves either," Manka shook her head.

"I know, but there is a difference."

"Not as much difference as you think."

"But you don't live in fear as we do."

"Have you looked into our hearts? How can a human being live without fear? And what if the crop goes bad? If the taxes for the tsar go up? And what if a fire breaks out, or there is a flood, or someone gets sick?"

"But you are on your plot of land, at home. No one in the world will beat you up or chase you out, just because they feel like it. You must remember the pogrom, Manka."

Manka shrugged. "I don't remember a thing. Anyway, our people fight among themselves, too, and not for fun, believe me. Life is not a bed of roses. People fight out of despair, instead of supporting each other in their despair. That's precisely what is so sad."

Manka loved her sadness and seemed to cling to it with passionate stubbornness. In truth, Hindele liked her for this; through Manka's melancholy and gloom, she felt her vitality, her love of life, and her strength. She did not expect Manka to understand how the Jews differed in their fears from the Gentiles, yet she took seriously what Manka told her.

In Hindele's view of the world, the Gentiles had their part to play in the scheme of things. They were a part of the magnificent symbolic reality superimposed on the true, concealed universe. She knew the Polish language well; she had learned it as a girl peddling in the villages. She liked to repeat the peasants' sayings, their proverbs and tales, seeing in them meaningful signs and portents. She learned their songs, not only from Manka or from Manka's niece Wanda, who had a beautiful voice, but also whenever an opportunity presented itself. She would hum the songs to herself or to her children, while giving the tunes her own Hasidic twist. In them, too, she found some secret significance. And before the tragedies had befallen her, she could, when in the mood, adapt her own Yiddish lyrics to the tunes. When she met with Nechele the Pockmarked, who loved music and songs so very much, she would hum them to her. From Nechele, Hindele learned many Hasidic melodies, and when she met Manka, she would hum those to her. Before long, one could hear the Hasidic melodies resound through the fields, sung by Wanda and her girlfriends with a rhythm permeated with the lightness of the wind and with youthful femininity.

Hindele sat with Manka for an hour or so, their long silences sparsely interwoven with short exchanges of opinion. Then she stood up, called her daughters, and nodded to Manka, "Time for them to go to bed." She noticed Yacov and Shalom scuttling through the alley on their way home from a neighbor's house. At the same time she caught sight of the bulky figure of the fire chief, Pan Vaslav Spokojny, as he came up the road, surrounded by his brood, to pay Manka a visit.

In the loft, Hindele doled out a slice of bread and some herring to each of her children. She saw to it that they washed, said their prayers, and undressed. Itchele woke up, and she fed him some curds, fixed his pillow, and wiped his face with a damp piece of rag. She gulped down a full mug of cold water because the herring was still alive in her stomach. Stroking Itchele soothingly, she sat at his bedside until he fell asleep again. She remained sitting there a while longer, her hand on his forehead. It seemed that his fever had gone down, and she heaved a sigh of relief.

Outside, the aquamarine sky grew darker. Hindele could hear the mooing of the cows, the barking of the dogs, intermingled with snatches of conversation and children's laughter. Wanda's visits were the only times when Manka's children became cheerful and noisy.

Hindele sat down at the window beside the mattress of her other two sons. She listened to the boys' deep, regular breathing and shook her head in disbelief. Young people passed from wakefulness into sleep in no time. She blessed them in her mind. "Let the Almighty allow me to keep them all. May I be worthy to bring them up for the *Toyre,* the wedding canopy, and for good deeds." The noise downstairs increased. She could make out no faces in the dark but realized that other gentile neighbors had joined the company in front of Manka's house. She could hear glasses clinking and loud voices. Then all was quiet. Wanda sang. She was the only one capable of making Manka join her in song. Someone was softly accompanying them on a harmonica. The tune was silken and thin, full of nocturnal yearning. Hindele's eyes filled with tears. "Oh, God, dear God," she whispered. "Be blessed for Thy work. In spite of my sorrow, be a thousand times blessed for Thy kindness and mercy."

She leaned out of the window so as not to miss the thin, soft sounds, and noticed a shadow approaching her house, directly across from her. She saw a white face raised toward her in the dark and heard a voice calling in a harsh whisper. "Hindele, are you there?" She recognized the fire chief, Vaslav Spokojny, and withdrew her head into the room. He continued calling her name with increasing loudness.

Frightened, she could not say of what, she leaned out, lest he wake the children, and asked with a stammer, "What is it you want, Panie Fire Chief?"

"Come down and sit with us!" She saw him raise a bottle at her.

"Thank you, Panie Fire Chief, " she mumbled. "Thank you."

"What are you thanking me for? Come down. You'll hear my Wanda sing."

"I can hear her from here, too."

"Aye, don't refuse an old friend. Why should you sit alone?"

"I'm not alone."

"Shall I come up and bring you down?"

"Heaven forbid!" She jumped to her feet and looked desperately at her sleeping children. She covered Itchele tighter with the feather quilt and, wrapping herself in her plaid shawl, once again trotted down the stairs to the yard.

Once in the yard, she managed to avoid the fire chief and approached the gathering hesitantly from the other side, halting forlornly at the back, until Manka beckoned to her. She made her way through the singing group toward Manka, who pointed to a seat beside her. The fire chief followed right behind. Hindele kept her eyes on her window, and he kept his eyes on her. His wife was sitting nearby. She was an ashen-faced, ashen-haired woman, healthy-looking but for her dried, wrinkled skin; her arms and hands were roped with prominent veins. Vaslav patted her on the shoulder affectionately, as if to make her keep her peace, and made his way through to Hindele with the bottle still raised in his hand. He sat himself down at her feet and said, panting, "So, now I can look at your Jewish eyes to my heart's delight!"

"Quiet, you old sot!" his wife scolded him. "People are singing, aren't they?"

Hindele pulled the shawl tighter around her. She tried to stare at her window, but could not help noticing the uneasy grins of the people around her. Vaslav held out the bottle of *monopolka* to her. "Here, have a swig, little trembling sparrow," he whispered hoarsely. "It'll warm you on the spot."

"Will you take the bloody bottle away from her?" Vaslav's wife spoke again. She turned to Hindele. "Don't pay any attention to him. He's been drinking all day."

"Your Wanda has the loveliest voice I've ever heard," Hindele replied gratefully, trying to compose herself.

"And you have the loveliest eyes I've ever seen!" Vaslav exclaimed to Hindele, "and the loveliest soul, too!"

The company erupted into loud, artificial laughter. The singing broke off. Wanda stared at her father with disgust. She was still in her midteens, a fiery, temperamental creature with a full bosom and swaying hips. She liked to dress in flashy full skirts and wear earrings like a mature woman, to show off her beauty. But more than that she liked to show off her voice. Wherever she went, her voice preceded her, announcing her arrival like the clear, delicate sound of a flute. Now, interrupted by her father, she turned from the gathering at Manka's door, took hold of two girlfriends, and marched off, followed by the rest of the young people.

Now, instead of the bottle, Hindele beheld a dish full of pastries in front of her nose. Vaslav held it out to her, grinning, "At least take one of these, Hindele. Come on, don't be shy."

Manka took the plate from his hand. "Leave her alone! Don't you know that she's kosher?"

"To hell with you, Manka!" Vaslav boomed. "So I was right after all to offer her the bottle. *Monopolka* is kosher, isn't it, Hindele?"

"A woman has a weak mind as it is, Panie Fire Chief," Hindele attempted to respond humorously, although her teeth chattered. "Our women don't touch this."

"But you're not a woman!" Vaslav exclaimed. "You're an angel!"

Manka fidgeted in her seat. The only person who could tell Vaslav off was his wife, so she leaned over and whispered something in the woman's ear. The woman burst out at her husband. "Will you let people enjoy themselves a bit, you lout, devil take you! Or do you want us to leave right away?"

"I want you to leave right away!" Vaslav roared, but without malice. "I am letting you enjoy yourselves. It's you who don't let me!" Suddenly fired up, he jumped to his feet and called out to the gathering, "Yeah, why don't you go to hell, all of you, you bunch of filthy asses!" He aimed the bottle at the heads of Manka's visitors.

This brought Hindele's heart to her mouth and made her jump to her feet as well. "Good night . . . good night," she whispered in a flutter.

"You see, you've scared her off!" Vaslav fumed. He grabbed Hindele's arm and screamed at the gathering, "You filthy lot of flaming pigs! Back to your sties!" He shook the bottle threateningly and pushed Hindele into her seat. "Sit down!"

She sat down, swaying, her head reeling, trying all the while to keep her eyes on her window. The other visitors got up to leave, prodded by Manka. Vaslav's wife slowly accompanied them to the alley. There she stopped and turned her head. "Come on, you wretched sot. Stop making a nuisance of yourself!" she called in Vaslav's direction.

"You go by yourself, you old hag, may the cholera take you into life everlasting!" Vaslav barked back cheerfully, satisfied with himself. He sat down on his previous place on the ground, very close to Hindele, and glared at Manka. "You better get inside too!" he bellowed at her. "You can see that I want to talk to her, can't you?" He laid his hand on Hindele's shoulder.

Manka gathered her courage. "This is my place," she barked back at him, "and I'll do as I please. You better go home and leave the woman alone."

Vaslav glanced at Hindele. Then, composed and relaxed, suddenly quite sober, he asked, "What are you afraid of, Manka? I won't do Hindele any harm. You can rely on me. All I want is to talk to her like a human being."

"When you drink you're anything but a human being," Manka replied with a vigorous shake of her head.

"But I was pretending, silly Manka. How else could I get rid of that pack of mongrels? And you, dear cousin, be a friend and go inside." Vaslav motioned her toward the house with a polite nod.

Manka cast an uncertain glance at Hindele, then turned and disappeared inside the house, reappearing the next moment in the dark shadow of the door. In her hand she held a pail of water, which she was prepared to fling at her cousin's head should the need arise.

"What do you want to talk to me about, Panie Fire Chief?" Hindele asked with a terrified giggle.

He replied in a heavily charged voice, "About everything!"

"I'm a stupid old woman, Panie Fire Chief. I am . . . I'm nothing but a speck of dust."

"You are the Angel of Mercy," he whispered back. "You look like the Virgin Mary on the day of the crucifixion. You do, I swear. The Virgin Mary was a Jewess, wasn't she? She didn't sit all dressed up in a church, did she? She sat on the Potcheyov, selling trinkets, and she saw through hypocrites like my brother, the priest. She cried for miserable creatures like me . . . " Vaslav began to sob.

Hindele strained to see Manka in the entrance of the house but could not make her out from where she sat. She tried to stand up, but Vaslav grabbed her plaid shawl with both hands and pulled her down again to her seat. Suddenly she saw him kneeling before her. "Stay. Stay a little while longer," he implored. "Have mercy on me, Hindele." She made another attempt to get up, but he held her back. "Sit, I said." He wept. "You make me feel good, clean . . . "

She gained possession of herself and replied in a surer tone of voice, "But if you want to be good, Panie Fire Chief, then you should not frighten me so and keep me from going to my children. You know that I have a sick son."

"I frighten you? I am not good to you?"

It occurred to her how ridiculous the two of them must look, but she could hardly smile at the thought. "You're frightening me out of my wits."

"How? Tell me how? Because I want to look at your kind face and warm my frozen heart a bit? Because I want to be near the light that you shed?"

"But, Panie Fire Chief, you don't know what you're saying. I'm full of darkness."

"You're my good light."

"There is no good light in me," she shook her head as if she, too, were intoxicated. "I am a broken-hearted woman, a shard, a speck of dust, a poor ugly Jewess whom you could trample at your will."

"You are the most beautiful Holy Mary."

" You abuse her . . . and me too, by comparing us to one another."

"You are so pure and saintly that it makes me cry. I would give my life for you right now. Just ask me, just help me, Holy Maria. Save me."

"You're ridiculous, Panie Fire Chief. I can't save anyone, not even my own child, not even myself. Can't you see that I'm in your hands? So please, have mercy on me and leave me alone. Please, Panie Fire Chief, don't torture me so."

He let go of her. When she stood up, she was trembling. He did not restrain her this time but, with an effort, raised himself up as well. "Can't you stay a little longer?" He looked at her imploringly, his face distorted by an odd grimace, his hetman mustache twisted in awkward disarray around his mouth.

"I have been here far too long already," she said, wiping her face with a corner of her plaid shawl. "Don't drink so much, Panie Fire Chief. When you sober up, you'll see how things really are, and you'll laugh at yourself for having said the words you've said to me tonight."

"That's not so, Hindele," he shook his head gravely, keeping pace with her as she essayed the few hesitant steps in the direction of her house. "I drink myself into sobriety—understand, little woman—into sobriety! Then I see how things really are. It's not the Devil inside me that's so thirsty, but . . . " He wiped his face with the corner of his undone fire chief's jacket, but the tears went on rolling down his cheeks. "I'm such a miserable creature, such a cursed, godforsaken bastard." He turned and hobbled off, lurching from side to side until he disappeared into the darkness of the alley.

Manka came out and placed the pail of water near the door. "This pail would have sobered him," she said, shaking with rage and indignation.

Hindele could not answer. She only waved feebly with her hand, entered her doorway, and climbed up the stairs. Once inside the loft, she locked the door securely and barricaded it by pushing the table across the door. "I must do something," she mumbled to herself frenziedly. She felt weak. The salt herring burned her stomach. She went over to the window and fanned her face with the edge of her plaid shawl, trying without success to pull herself together. What was she to do? Where could she and her children hide from the impending danger? She had a sick child. There was nowhere she could go. Moreover, weak woman that she was, she had to keep quiet about the whole affair. It had all been her own fault. She had spent too much time talking to Vaslav. She had befriended him, even though Yossele Abedale had warned her against him. Perhaps she should talk to Yossele, who was a wise and strong man? Many people asked his advice when it came to dealing with the Gentiles. The Gentiles liked him. The problem was that he did not seem to be on good terms with Vaslav. Besides, it was difficult to talk to Yossele, especially for a woman.

No, she decided, she would not talk to Yossele nor to anyone else. There was nothing to talk about, nothing to tell. After all, Vaslav had done nothing more sinister than chat with her. She was exaggerating the whole thing because she was made hysterical by her exhaustion. She would surely handle herself better the next time she met Vaslav. She would get rid of him, and the Almighty would help her. Whose help was equal to His, after all? In whose hands was she, if not in His? She had nothing to fear. She had only to be hopeful. And surely the Almighty would laugh at her for barring the door with a table. She would move the table back to its place, lest the children ask questions in the morning. She would not worry them needlessly.

Quietly she moved the table away, but Yacov awoke and sat up on the straw mattress, rubbing his eyes. "Is that you, Mameshie?" he asked.

"Of course it's me," she whispered. "Who else?"

"I dreamed that Asmodeus had come in through the window. He laughed so loudly that he woke me up."

"Asmodeus?" Her heart froze, but she made an effort to compose herself. "A dream is a silly thing. You know that."

"Too bad that I'm so big now that I can't come into your bed anymore," he said, lying down.

"Don't say too bad," she replied softly. "You're becoming a young man. What's so bad about that?"

It seemed strange to Yacov that summer and winter each lasted the same length of time, yet the summer always seemed to pass faster than the winter. This summer in particular had flown by like a short dream, while his soul was adjusting to the loss of his father. Before he knew it, a year had passed. The High Holidays had come and gone, and presently the feast of Tabernacles had brought with it the holiday of Simhath Torah. It was a day of rejoicing. The annual reading of the Torah had come to an end. It was a day that the heder boys looked forward to all year, as they were the major participants in the celebration.

The synagogue overflowed with people. Seven times, the Torah Scrolls were carried around the dais, and the women and girls were permitted to enter the main hall and kiss the Scrolls as they passed. Children and adults danced around while the elders carried the Scrolls. The boys held paper flags mounted on sticks, with red sugar-coated apples stuck on the tips, each apple holding a lighted candle. The miller, Reb Faivele, had arrived with a wagonload of sponge cakes, candies, and nuts for everyone, and with schnapps for those who could hold it and even for those who could not. The Hasidim grew tipsy, more from joy than from drink, but their legs buckled and they broke some glasses. Reb Laibele Yaptzok-Fresser, the sexton, whom only piety and poverty kept from habitual drunkenness, took a number of long, passionate swigs directly from the liquor bottle and became friendly with everyone, which was not normally his habit.

"He behaves as if he were the host at a private party," commented one of the older matrons, as she and her daughters watched the celebration.

Another nodded in agreement, "Yes, he's become so soothing that you could apply him to a boil and cure it."

Indeed, on this day all of Bociany seemed like one happy family, united around its greatest treasure, the Holy Scrolls, which alone gave meaning to life. All Jews were brothers, the Almighty's children, who lived according to the Torah, which supported them so that they had no reason to fear, for the Torah was their shield. All these feelings, all of this transported delight, was written on the faces of the crowd, but most clearly and beautifully on the face of the young *rov,* the leader of the congregation. Wrapped in his prayer shawl, he danced around with the Torah Scroll, looking as dignified as a High Priest and as elated and wistful as a heder boy.

Yacov and Shalom followed the others in the dance with the Torah Scrolls, which were dressed in mantles ornamented with silver. The boys joined in the enthusiastic clapping and sang along with the rest of the congregation, "Rejoice, rejoice in the celebration of Simhath Torah! Give praise and honor to the Torah!" The joy was great, the Torah was sweet, and all was well with God's world.

After a while, Yacov lost sight of Shalom in the crowd, but he ran into Ariele, Fishele the Butcher's son. Ariele was still Yacov's best friend, despite Yacov's despicable cowardice and his persistent avoidance of all kinds of fighting. Yacov still preferred the other games of the heder boys, such as acting out the story of Joseph and his brothers, or of David and King Saul, or of David and Jonathan.

Yacov and Ariele hopped along arm-in-arm after the dancing Hasidim, then, exhausted, slumped down on a bench not far from where Reb Senderl the Cabalist sat surrounded by a group of young men who studied on their own in the *besmedresh.* With the fingers of one of his small white hands, Reb Senderl combed his magnificent silvery beard; in the other hand he held a glass of schnapps. "The sky, *hashamaim,*" he said, pausing between one sip and another, "means *eysh* and *maim,* fire and water. The stars are made of fire, while the rest is water. And yet the sky is one perfect entity. The same you can say about the sky and the earth. They are likewise two contrasts, yet they keep together. Therefore Rabbi Simeon Bar Youchai said that the earth and the sky fit together like a pot and its lid."

Bells began to toll in Yacov's head. He had understood! He had grasped the meaning of Reb Senderl's words, which expressed a wonderful truth! Ariele had grasped it as well, but he accepted it as something he had known all his life. Yacov jumped to his feet. Fearful that he might forget the way Reb Senderl had formulated this important thought, he left Ariele. He had to run home straightaway to repeat this marvelous saying to his mother and his brother, who was so sick that it had been a very long time since he had taken part in celebrating Simhath Torah. Such a saying would surely cheer them both up!

In his hurry to leave, he bumped into a big girl who had just entered the antechamber of the synagogue, holding a smaller girl by the hand. The tiny child, really not much more than a bundle wrapped in layers of rags, was knocked down by the impact. She began to scream, and her older sister moved threateningly toward Yacov. "Where are your eyes? Are you blind?" she yelled at him.

Yacov recognized Raisele, Yossele Abedale's eldest daughter. "I didn't see you . . . " he mumbled apologetically.

"I can see that you didn't see us!" she shot back. "You could have killed her!" She bent down to inspect the little one, who had not yet stopped screaming.

For some reason Yacov could not turn away. He watched as Raisele deftly picked up her little sister and rocked her in her arms. "Is she badly hurt?" he inquired shyly.

"And what business is that of yours?"

"I made her fall."

"So you want a gold medal for it? Am I not late enough as it is?" Raisele snapped. The child in her arms took a sudden interest in one of Yacov's sidelocks and though still weeping, reached out to touch it. Her sister smacked her arm and removed her hand.

"Let her touch it. I don't mind," Yacov said. "What's her name?"

"Binele is her name, and better leave me alone. I knew we'd be late!" Herself near tears, the older girl dashed into the hall with her sister in her arms.

In the backyard of his house, Yacov noticed Manka the Washerwoman sitting on the front step of her house with her head and arms buried in her lap, as if she were weeping. Then he ran into Shalom, who came dashing down the stairway, calling in a broken voice, "Come quick!"

When Yacov entered the loft, Hindele was sitting on the floor. A thin, elongated form covered with a black cloth lay in front of her. Candles burned on both sides of the elongated heap. There were many weeping women in the room and some men as well. Among the wailing women sat Nechele the Pockmarked, Sore-Leyele, the wife of the ritual slaughterer, and Brontchele the Professional Mourner with a few of her companions. They huddled together on the straw mattress under the window.

Itchele was dead.

## 6

NO CHILDREN IN BOCIANY had their hearts so intently set on the forthcoming holidays as did Yossele Abedale's children. Their days dragged on, one as gray and dull as the next, as if each were a ring in a rusty chain, and were only made bearable by the fact that they led from one holiday to the next. Unfortunately, after *Simhath Torah* there were no more holidays for many weeks, not until the winter reached its icy peak and the holiday of Hanukkah came along, falling this year on a Sabbath. Hanukkah was the holiday Yossele Abedale's children enjoyed the most because they could light the Hanukkah candles and play spin-the-top to their hearts' content, and because they received Hanukkah money, two kopecks distributed to each of them by their father.

Yossele was away peddling in the villages. It had now become his routine to leave the eldest girls to mind the shop every Thursday and Friday, while he set out with his merchandise to wander the outskirts of Bociany. The children were restless, impatient for him to come home. Fortunately, the shops closed early on Fridays, so on this Friday before Hanukkah, the girls closed the shop even earlier still. The children decided to go out on the Wide Poplar Road to meet their father. A noisy, gaily chattering band they made, clothed in their winter tatters, torn hats over frost-bitten faces smeared with dirt, and their feet in formless remainders of what had once been shoes and were now rags. The older ones dragged the younger ones by the hands, and so, prattling, yelling, wiping their running noses on their sleeves, they partly walked, partly ran ahead, until, finally, Faigele, the liveliest and least patient of the lot, called out, "Tateshie's coming!"

They all grew silent and moved ahead shyly, until they came to a halt a few feet from Yossele. Yossele bent forward slightly in order to see them better with his weak eyes. Then he straightened himself and resumed his normal energetic stride, which caused the youngest, Binele, to trip, fall, get up, and fall again as she tried to keep up with the others.

After a few minutes of marching this way in complete silence, with the children's heads bashfully turned toward him, Yossele called out heartily, "So what have you been up to, pranksters, while your father was away?" His eyes rested first on Hershele.

Hershele blushed and plucked at his sidelocks. "I know the chapter of the week as smoothly as water, Tateshie." He pointed to his sisters. "And I told them the story of Hanukkah!"

"And I locked up the shop and swept the garbage away from the door," Raisele boasted.

"And I ran home to sweep the floor, and I swept Brontchele the Mourner's floor, too!" Rochele called out.

"And I took both ours and Peshele the Slob's *cholnt* to the baker's!" Faigele added.

"And I rocked her baby!" her twin sister, Mashele, put in.

"I too! I too!" called the two youngest, Dvorele and Binele.

First Yossele slapped Raisele and Rochele in the face, for having locked the shop so early. As for the other children, nothing that they had done impressed him. He nipped their cheeks and slapped them indiscriminately to the right and to the left. The children accepted the slaps cheerfully, even with a kind of gaiety and enthusiasm. It was clear as day that these slaps were meant to let them know how impatient their father had been to see them, how much he had missed them, that he knew that they loved him with their whole hearts, and that they could scarcely breathe because of their anticipation of his arrival. Thus instead of keeping a distance to avoid the slaps, they pushed and fought one another for the place nearest to him. When tears spilled from their eyes because of the cold and the smacks they received, they quickly wiped them, happy to have felt the touch of his hand, as if they had received not slaps, but the most tender caresses, and they thought of the holiday about to be celebrated.

They wrestled with each other, to see who would take a sack from their father's arms because there were not enough sacks to go around. Yossele slapped them again to quiet them. Obediently, they settled down and tried to guess how many potatoes he had brought for the potato pancakes. And perhaps he had brought two chickens, not one, in honor of the Sabbath and of Hanukkah and perhaps even some secondhand clothes as a Hanukkah gift for one or two of them?

Yossele was stirred deep in his heart by the eyes full of yearning and devotion that they turned toward him. He felt how they clung to him, accepting even the slaps as the meaningless price that they readily paid for the good feeling of being near him. But he was also aware that this feeling of closeness, which he reciprocated, was accompanied by uneasiness. It had always been that way between them and him. For some reason, neither he nor they ever felt completely at home in their own skins when they were together.

The Almighty was a strict Master, or rather a cynical Lord, who gave man a lame and mute tongue when it came to communicating with his own flesh and blood. It was difficult—no, all but impossible—to find a common language. Things were clear and simple between Yossele and his children only on the Sabbath or during a holiday, when Abele the Fool served as a kind of lightning rod and Yossele himself was in a positive frame of mind. Yet for some reason, things were even more simple and clear when Yossele was angry and dealt out blows. "If only the Almighty had sent me down at least another two sons," Yossele mused as he walked on with his brood, "instead of these six females, each one staring at me with Mariml's eyes. Come to think of it, doesn't Mariml look at me through my *kaddish* Hershele's eyes as well?"

With a nervous push, he shoved the children ahead of him, telling them to hurry, so he would not see them staring at him with those eyes. Tonight was both the Sabbath Eve and Hanukkah Eve. He missed Mariml more than ever. The thought of what things would have been like, had she been alive now, was unbearable.

They came into the shtetl. As they passed the synagogue, Yossele asked the children to stop and put their hands on the carved door, so that they might feel their grandfather greeting them with a "shalom" from the Other World. Reb Laibele Yaptzok-Fresser, the sexton, emerged from the antechamber, and the men shook the tips of each other's fingers and wished each other a good holiday, as if they were the best of friends.

As soon as they turned into their own street, Yossele's children sped ahead of him, calling out with glee to the other children of the neighborhood, "Our Tateshie is home already!"

It was a Sabbath and a Hanukkah to remember. Yossele had increased the amount of the children's Hanukkah money from two to four kopecks each, and they played spin-the-top to their hearts' delight. He had brought an old pair of wooden clogs for his eldest daughter Raisele, and two used dresses from Fredka, the miller's housekeeper, one for each of the twins. There was enough food to eat and Yossele had brought firewood to keep the oven going throughout the holiday.

However, as soon as Hanukkah was over, Yossele felt somewhat guilty for having broken his firm resolution not to spoil his children. A human being had to learn early in life how bitter the struggle for existence was, and how difficult it was to attain even the least significant goal. The harder things were for his children now, he thought, the easier they would be for them later, when he was no longer around to protect them. "Just as one hammers a piece of gold, so one must beat a child in order to make a *mentsh* out of it," he would say to himself. And he was glad that he could afford to "harden" them thus, because they took after him. They were strong and healthy and were content even with "the hole in the bagel." He had heard from the neighbors that children occasionally fall sick with children's diseases. Not his children. If they sometimes moaned or groaned, whined or whimpered, lay on the mattress or on the doorstep, had runny noses, a cough, or a rash, he pretended not to notice. It did not matter. He knew that nothing could ever happen to them.

So if Yossele beat up one of his children for no reason at all, he did so with all the more application when he had a reason. If one of his children did not behave the way he or she ought, Yossele felt an accusatory finger being pointed against him for neglecting his children's upbringing, and an even stronger sense of guilt worked its way into his heart. Then he would do a thorough job, meting out the justly deserved punishment to the child with the disciplinary whip, which hung in a prominent place in the house. If during the process feelings of compassion overcame him, either for himself or for his victim, he drowned them in his own shouts. Then, in his sleep, he would dream of the pogrom and see himself with the red marks of a lash all over his body.

Right after Hanukkah Yossele was presented with an opportunity to teach a lesson to his son. Twice in two days the *melamed,* Reb Shapsele, had given Hershele a whipping at the heder, and there was therefore no doubt in Yossele's mind that Hershele was slipping in his studies. The mere thought of such a situation was unbearable.

Yossele always punished Hershele with particular earnestness. He sincerely believed that he who spares his son does not deserve to have a son. For a son was a man's greatest blessing. Not only was a son the person who said the *kaddish* after a man's death, but a son assured the continuity of the family and therefore of the entire People of Israel.

Although Yossele had more than a few things with which to reproach the learned men, he was adamant in his decision that Hershele should grow up to become an important Talmudic scholar and attain the position of *rov.* He wanted this not only for spiritual reasons or reasons of prestige, but for practical reasons as well. He wanted Hershele to have an easier life than he had had. And scholars seemed to have both this world and the next in their pockets, so to speak. Having assured themselves a good life in Heaven, they lived in the meantime quite well on earth. Rich people sought them out as bridegrooms for their daughters, supported them, fed them all their lives, while they, the scholars, spent their days studying God's word. They were honored and respected, whether they came from respectable lineage or not. They had a say in community affairs and had the best opportunity to serve both the Almighty and His people.

Whenever he saw the handsome imposing young *rov* of Bociany, Yossele would wistfully think of his Hershele in the future. True, the young *rov* was perhaps a little too involved in matters of the spirit, which made him absentminded and forgetful in daily matters, but he cared for the community and was responsive to its needs, and he made a good living on top of it all. The community supported him, respected him, and loved him. Even his plump, pretty wife and his children were treated with reverence. His Hershele, Yossele mused, would have the same success with his congregation, only he would be more down-to-earth. For surely he had inherited not only his father's physical strength, but his practicality and will as well.

Hershele, for his part, wanted for himself exactly what his father wanted for him, but for different reasons. First, he wanted to please his father and wanted to make him proud. Second, he loved to study. He was a diligent heder boy, quiet and obedient. He never ran to the fields to play or fight with the gentile boys, never even went as far as the marshes to see the storks catch little frogs, and he certainly never went as far as the lake, although he was just as curious as the other boys to see the mysterious place where Kailele, the crazy bride, had drowned herself. It was said that Kailele's eyes could be seen swimming on the surface of the water, and that the lake's water lilies were really the lace trimmings of her bridal gown. Nor did Hershele ever wander off to the manor to look through the barred grating of the fence to see the landowner's sons parade about on their white horses.

He never picked a fight with other heder boys, nor did he wrestle with them just for the fun of it. Because he daily carried pails of water for the neighborhood women in return for a bowl of hot soup, he had developed muscular arms, despite his meager diet. He had grown stronger than the other boys his age. On the rare occasions when the other boys provoked Hershele into a fight, they would set up a hew and cry when they were defeated, and then run home to tell their fathers, who would tell Yossele, with the obvious consequences.

In addition, Hershele had inherited his father's aversion to devious ways, to playing tricks behind people's backs. He was direct, honest to a fault, stiff-necked, disciplined, and so stubborn that he could never be bent, only broken. But precisely because of this nature of his, it seemed both to his father and to his *melamed,* Reb Shapsele, that Hershele needed to be punished harder and more often than any other boy, in order to achieve the proper results. And although Hershele knew that he deserved to be spared, being an orphan, he agreed with them out of a perverse sense of pride. It seemed to him that with each set of blows his head grew clearer, more receptive to God's word, especially when his father's beating followed immediately on that of the *melamed.* And that was in fact what happened on one cold evening shortly after Hanukkah.

Although this time his father's blows had been fiercer than usual, Hershele took them, as usual, without a murmur. His body was entirely covered with welts after he had received the full portion, but, lips tightly pressed together, he had quickly buttoned up his pants. His eyes were filled with tears, but not a single one was allowed to slide down his cheeks. He knew that a Jew in exile had to be strong, that the sweetness of studying God's Torah, like any gift from God, had to be tempered with drops of suffering.

Yossele panted heavily after the session was over and concluded with his habitual question, "So, are you going to do that again, you good-for-nothing?"

Although Hershele had no clear idea what he had actually done, he replied in a dry, slightly hoarse voice, "I will never do it again, Tateshie."

Yossele wagged his finger at him, "And tonight, as punishment, you go to sleep without bread and herring, do you hear?"

"I hear, Tateshie!" Hershele replied like a soldier, kissed his father's hand and quickly opened the creased Book, which was all covered with coal dust. If it was true that blows and whipping sharpened a heder boy's mind, then he had to take advantage of the opportunity to get as much as he could into his head while the bruises were still fresh. But that night, after the fire in the oven had gone out and he was shivering with cold under his cover of rags, his sore back hurt him more than usual. Finally he gave in, and he prayed, "Come Messiah, come quickly, because it hurts to be beaten up. When you come no one will hurt me and we shall all be redeemed."

The following morning, Hershele could not budge from his cot when his father shook him by the shoulder. The stripes and welts from the combined whippings of his father and the *melamed* covered his body like red-and-blue netting. He felt as heavy as a stump of wood. Yossele had no choice but to pour a mug of cold water under the cover to help wake him up. When Hershele finally managed to drag himself from his cot, Yossele gave him a couple of smacks on the face, so loud that they woke up his daughters.

The girls sat up on their cots and huddled close together. They wrapped themselves in their blankets of rags and watched the snowstorm sweep past the windowpane. They looked on as Hershele, chewing on a crust of dry bread, filled his shoes with strips of paper to keep his toes warm. Their father lit the lantern for Hershele, as it was still pitch-dark outside. Then they watched their brother open the door and, like a tired bird, fly out to be swallowed by the gale and the snowy darkness. They watched as their father put on his phylacteries, said the morning prayer, kindled the oven, and then disappeared as well into the windy outdoors as soon as the church bell tolled for Angelus.

No sooner was their father gone than the girls picked up the slices of bread he had left for each of them and climbed onto the *piekelik,* the extension of the oven, where they could sit and be warm. Raisele held the youngest, Binele, in her lap, and Rochele held the second youngest, Dvorele, in hers. The sisters nibbled at their dry crusts of bread while pitying their father and brother for having to leave the coziness of the house in such weather.

Raisele, the eldest gave vent to a heavy sigh, the kind she had learned from Brontchele the Professional Mourner. "I cannot understand," she said, turning to Rochele, "why the Almighty is so angry with men, even though the men behave better toward Him than the women. The men have to suffer at the heder and then at the *besmedresh,* where they dry up and grow so pale that they go green. Then they get married and have to study even more and pray to God. And in addition, our Tateshie must still make a living. Brontchele the Mourner said the other day that Sore-Leyele the Slaughterer's Wife had said that men are like soldiers in the Almighty's army. That the Almighty is just like Tsar Nicholas, and the men have to serve in His army all their lives."

"Of course," Rochele agreed. She was a girl who could cry on command and who loved to follow all the funeral processions in the shtetl. Her favorite expression was *"olevesholem,"* which means "May he rest in peace." Ignorant of its meaning, she would often insert it in conversation where it made the least sense, yet she made it sound exceptionally clever. "The men shake over the Gemaras day and night, *olevesholem,*" she said. "They shake and study at the *besmekdesh* . . . "

"How many times must I tell you to say *besmedresh,* not *besmekdesh* ?" Raisele reproached her. "The *besmekdesh* is something else altogether. It's the Holy Temple that got destroyed."

"Yes," Rochele meekly agreed and, with the crust of bread in her hand, began mournfully to sway over little Dvorele in her lap. "The *besmekdesh* was destroyed and the men shake over the Gemaras in the *besmedresh,* and they move their mouths all the time, swallowing all the dust, *olevesholem.*"

Raisele nodded her approval and droned on in the same tone of voice, "Do the men know what it means to be alive? Of course not. And if they need to do something, even the slightest thing, they have to think a thousand times whether to do it or not. Because a Jew must always remember in his head what a Jew is allowed to do and what he is not allowed to do. And they must be afraid of the Almighty even more than the women must. I myself heard the *rov's* wife say to Sore-Leyele the Slaughterer's Wife how hard it is to be a Jew. That's what she said. Because whatever a Jew does, he takes a sin on himself."

"I'm glad that I'm not a Jew!" exclaimed their younger sister Faigele.

"You are a Jew, too," Raisele nodded emphatically. "You're a Jewish girl, Israel's daughter."

"You mean Yossele Abedale's daughter." Rochele hoped that she had finally found a point on which she could correct her older sister.

"No," Raisele shook her head authoritatively. "I mean Israel's daughter, a daughter of the People of Israel."

"So I am two daughters, not one?" Faigele laughed, amused by her elder sisters' battle for intellectual hegemony.

Raisele pulled Faigele toward her, placed her head on little Binele's lap, and began looking for lice in her hair. Rochele swallowed her confusion along with the last bite of bread and pulled Faigele's twin sister, Mashele, toward her. She put Mashele's head on Dvorele's lap, and she too began looking for lice in her sister's hair. Raisele and Rochele deloused their sisters diligently and in silence, spittle forming in the corners of their mouths.

Finally Rochele spoke, "Surely no one cares what a daughter of Israel does. The Almighty, *olevesholem,* probably doesn't care either."

"This I wouldn't say," Raisele paused thoughtfully with her fingers in Faigele's hair. "Sore-Leyele the Slaughterer's Wife says that we women are our husbands' footstools in Heavenly Paradise, may we live in good health."

"Is that what she said?" Faigele abruptly jerked her head out from under Raisele's hands. She jumped down from the *piekelik,* got down on all fours, and raised her head to Raisele. "Is this how a footstool looks? Look Raisele! Will we bend like this and the men will keep their feet on our backs?"

"Like this?" the two youngest giggled.

"Yes, more or less like that," Raisele declared, not entirely sure of herself.

"You mean this is how we'll have to kneel the whole day?" Faigele was flabbergasted.

"And the whole night, too," Raisele was forced to admit.

"Why?" Rochele too could not understand. "Don't people go to sleep in the Heavenly Paradise, *olevesholem*?"

"No. There is no day or night there," Raisele explained.

"What is there, then?" Rochele asked.

"Nothing. Eternity."

"Eternity means that there is nothing?"

"Eternity means that everything is there and you need nothing."

"But we need to be footstools and kneel on all fours all the time?"

Faigele grew tired of her position and began rubbing her knees. "But my knees will hurt and my back, too."

"In Heavenly Paradise nothing hurts, *olevesholem.*" Rochele now saw her way clear to an explanation.

"But I won't be able to stand straight, and I will get a hump on my back!" Faigele cried.

Raisele smiled wisely. "Don't worry, you won't get a hump. In the Heavenly Paradise all the humps are taken away even from the real humpbacks and are sent to hell for the goyim and the sinners, the *roshe-merushes.*"

"But I won't be able to stay on my knees for all maternity!" Faigele insisted and jumped to her feet.

"You mean eternity," Rochele hastened to correct her, and in the process almost dropped Dvorele from her lap. She gave Faigele the look of a stern disciplinarian. "Would you prefer to go to hell, so that the Devil might roast and burn you, *olevesholem?*"

"I don't want to go anywhere!" Faigele cried.

"You're not going yet," Raisele smiled her wise, maternal smile.

"Of course not," Rochele confirmed. "In order to get into Heavenly Paradise, you have to be one hundred and twenty years old first, *olevesholem.*"

"That's not so." Raisele gave her a supercilious look and sighed. "First one must die, and before that one must get married."

"That I want!" Faigele clapped her hands. "I want to get married!"

"Of course, for us women it's good to get married." Rochele also cheered up and forgot to add her customary *olevesholem.* "We can be mothers, and the men can't."

"I want to be a mother!" Faigele, who liked talking about mothers, picked up her rag doll and climbed back onto the *piekelik.*

"I want to be a mother, too," said her twin sister, Mashele.

"Me too!" the two youngest called out.

Raisele heaved a sigh in the style of Brontchele the Mourner. "Who says it's bad to be a mother? What would our own Mameshie have to complain about, if she were alive?"

"Keep quiet," Rochele begged her. "Let's not talk about our Mameshie."

"I want to hear about her! Tell us, Raisele!" Faigele urged.

Rochele laid her hand against Raisele's mouth. "Don't," she said. "Do you want me to cry?"

"You won't cry," Faigele assured her. "When Raisele tells about our Mameshie, it's very nice."

But Raisele agreed with Rochele. She removed Rochele's hand from her mouth and gave her a long, mournful look. Embracing Binele and rocking her in her lap, she whispered in a voice that began to break, "When I forget that Mameshie is dead, it is very nice . . . " She burst into sobs. Rochele, who cried easily, now also began to sob.

"Don't cry, please don't," Faigele whispered. "All right, you don't have to tell about Mameshie, Raisele." She, too, burst into tears and flung her doll away. Her twin sister, Mashele, a sad, silent little girl, and the two youngest grew frightened, and before long all were crying. The weeping went on for a long time while the snowstorm whirled madly outside the window panes.

The storm was still raging in the late afternoon. The girls had eaten up the other slices of bread their father had left them for lunch. Then Hershele came home, ate his portion, and hurried outside again to carry water for the neighbors. On such days he had to carry more pails than usual, for the women were glad to stay indoors if they could.

Then Yacov, the son of Hindele the Scribe's Widow, arrived, warmly wrapped in a brightly colored wool scarf. He was carrying a pot of steaming soup. "Mother sent this for you," he handed Raisele the pot.

Raisele took the pot without a word, and gave each of her sisters a wooden spoon. She placed the pot in a pile of rags in the corner and she and her sisters sat down around it and ate with gusto. In truth, it was more for sipping than for eating. The soup was no more than liquid thickened with oats, but it was hot and delicious. The spoons of the two youngest girls lost most of their contents on the way from pot to mouth. Raisele and Rochele made up for the loss by now and then spoon-feeding the two. Yacov joined them in the corner. Little Binele caught his attention. He watched with amusement as she clutched her sisters' wrists and eagerly guided the spoons in their hands to her own mouth.

Warmed as they were by the soup, the girls ignored the boy. Their eyes twinkled; their lips smiled as they wiped their mouths on their sleeves. When the pot was empty, Raisele matter-of-factly handed it back to Yacov. But before he could manage to stand up, little Binele jumped to her feet, climbed onto his back, and wrapped her arms around his neck. "Take me piggyback!" she insisted.

Yacov left the pot on the floor, stood up, and took off his wet coat and scarf. He put Binele on a chair, and from there carried her piggyback around the room. The sisters followed him with their eyes. They had no respect for him, even though he had recently lost his eldest brother, and his father not long before that. He had the reputation of a Soft Mirl, a sissy, whom their own brother could beat up with one hand. They watched him as a while later he sat Binele down on a cot, produced a piece of string from his pocket, and began teaching her to play cat's cradle.

"Phew," Raisele said. The haughty expression on her face was accompanied by a gesture of revulsion. "Such a big boy playing with girls, and such small ones at that! No wonder they call you Soft Mirl."

The boy did not seem offended, but he stopped playing with Binele. He put the piece of string back into his pocket, jerked his coat on, and wrapped the bright scarf around his neck. Then he took the pot and left.

Yossele's daughters never complained of their lot. Their lives had a certain routine, of which going without food for long periods of time was an integral part. Sooner or later their need for food was satisfied either by their neighbors, their father, or their own resourcefulness. They were accustomed to the cold and to going about in rags. They had stable relationships with their women neighbors, who substituted as best they could for their missing mother; and then, once a week, Sabbath descended upon earth.

Yossele's experiment in allowing his eldest daughters to take care of the shop had been a success. Raisele and Rochele learned to count on their fingers and were learning to memorize numbers a little. So at length Yossele decided to ignore the advice of his women neighbors, who insisted that the girls might profit more by continuing to help them with their housekeeping chores, and decided to let the two girls take care of the shop on a permanent basis as soon as the winter was gone. He initiated them into the secrets of the trade and, with the help of slaps liberally administered, they quickly became expert at computing the price of lime and chalk. They learned the value of a kopeck, when to raise the price, when to lower it, when to bargain, when to allow the customer to walk away, and when to call him back for lack of an alternative.

From then on, Raisele and Rochele, quickly followed by Faigele and Mashele, helped out their neighbors on the street only after the shops closed. In addition to that, the entire weight of their own housekeeping now fell on them because Yossele, seeing that they were reliable, began to spend most of his time on the road, or in the villages. So the girls left behind their childhood slippers, which they had in any case never worn, and fully began "to live."

Thanks to his newly won freedom, Yossele too began to live fully. He again took joy in the use of his body, of his limbs, and in the delightful fatigue that he felt after having been in motion for hours on end.

With his sack of chalk and lime slung over his back, he walked from village to village. The peasants greeted him with familiarity and respect. He sold his merchandise, and if an opportunity presented itself, he lent a hand in repairing a roof or a stable, a shed or an outhouse. He did not waste too much time on bargaining, but stated his price, lowered it a bit, waved his hand, sighed an *"Aby dalej,"* and took whatever he was offered. In only one thing did he refuse to give in to the peasants. He adamantly rejected their pleas that he arbitrate their conflicts.

Because he was now on the road all the time, Yossele treated himself to the luxury of stepping off the road and into the redolent birch wood, in order to say his prayers at the lakeside among the clusters of oaks that fringed the lake. He placed himself facing an oak tree—and then his praying acquired an additional dimension. Yossele felt more at home among the oak trees than in his *bude* of a home. He knew the oaks inside out. In his youth, he had worked with oakwood and was familiar with its smell and texture, its most intimate nature, as it were. As he stood among the oaks, he felt himself becoming one with their simplicity, their honesty, their massiveness; the oaklike qualities within him felt supported by them. It seemed to him that the oaks assimilated a part of him in return and said the eighteen blessings along with him.

As soon as he was on his way home again, his eyes scanned the shtetl on the horizon, waiting for the roof of the synagogue to come into sight. He intended, as usual, to stop by it and say "shalom" to his father, as he put it to himself. However, when Yossele finally reached the synagogue, Reb Laibele Yaptzok-Fresser came out to greet him, an honor Yossele could have done without.

Reb Laibele would unbraid his hands, with which he supported his "pregnant" belly, and stretch out his right hand toward Yossele, greeting him with a hearty *"Sholem-aleykhem!"* As he only came up to Yossele's shoulder, he had to raise himself on tiptoe in order to give Yossele a good sniff. "Had a good stiff one, eh, Yossele?" he would giggle as his sharp mousy eyes lit up with his own craving for a sip of *monopolka.*

Before Yossele could begin to remonstrate, swearing by his beard and sidelocks that he had not set foot in the inn, Reb Laibele patted Yossele's pockets. Yossele responded to this intrusion with a vigorous prod of the elbow and a growl, "Check your own pockets first, Reb Laibele."

Actually, Reb Laibele was not a real Hasid. "My *shtibl* is all of Israel," he would say of himself. He believed that it was high time, as he put it in his fire-and-brimstone pronouncements, for the squabbles between the followers of the various rabbis to stop, so that all could unite against the real danger to the shtetl of Bociany, namely this new plague of "enlightenment" and "modernism," which were simply new words for heathenism.

A decade or so earlier, this malaise called "enlightenment" had appeared on the face of Bociany like a little blister. It had been limited to a few wealthy homes and had had no influence on the shtetl's life. But ever since Shmulikl the Doctor had opened his shop, where he practiced as a barber-surgeon, and had begun to speak of his "enlightened" thoughts in private and in public, the blister had festered to the point where it urgently needed treatment.

"This yoctor," Reb Laibele deliberately mispronounced the word "doctor," as he raised his little fist at whoever might be listening to him, "we need him here like a hole in the head! We should all unite and drive him out of Bociany to where the black pepper grows!"

Yossele actually agreed with this, although he could not see how there could be unity among the followers of different rabbis, if there was none among the followers of the same rabbi. He also suspected that Reb Laibele, who loved petty intrigues, had something else in mind, namely, that he nurtured the ambition of himself becoming a leader of the community.

On the surface, it seemed that Reb Laibele could easily satisfy this ambition. First, he was the sexton of the synagogue, and second, he dealt out *malkes,* the public punishment of those who came to the synagogue to confess their sins and to ask the community to help them repent. Also, Bociany was unable to support a truly learned clergy. If they were learned, then there was something else wrong with them. The former *rov,* for instance, had been sick for a long time before he died, and after his death Bociany had been left without a *rov* for years. When the new *rov* finally arrived, it immediately became obvious that he was too young and inexperienced to command respect, at least in Reb Laibele's opinion. On the other hand, the *dian,* who settled minor disputes and decided on questions of ritual cleanliness, did have the legitimate qualifications to be a *rov.* He was so refined and kindhearted a person that even Reb Laibele could find no blemish in his character. The *dian,* however, was old and weak, with one foot in the grave. As for Reb Laibele himself, he was a man in the prime of life, energetic, outspoken, erudite as a scholar, and knowledgeable in all the minutiae of shtetl life. His only problem was that he had no luck. The people of Bociany were not overly fond of him, and so he carried a chip on his shoulder and was jealous of anyone who seemed to enjoy a position of prestige in the community.

Against Yossele Abedale, Reb Laibele had always had a particular grudge, although the reason was no clearer to Reb Laibele than it was to Yossele. Perhaps it was because Reb Laibele was childless, which in his own eyes placed him not far above the level of a criminal—while Yossele was the father of seven. In addition to that, Reb Laibele was a man of insignificant stature, if one overlooked his belly, whereas Yossele was tall and handsome and looked as if he had just stepped out of the pages of the Bible. So maybe it seemed to Reb Laibele that Yossele, the ignoramus, even though he was a widower, possessed everything that Laibele himself did not have, and that he commanded undeserved respect. Reb Laibele could find nothing in Yossele's character to account for this respect. So, although he knew that he made a fool of himself, he could not resist spreading stories about Yossele, hinting that the real reasons for Yossele's frequent forays into the villages were alcohol and gentile women, that Yossele had become a heretic, an apostate ripe for conversion, and so on. After repeating these things, Reb Laibele would spit three times.

It had been a day like any other. Yossele had returned from the villages and had stopped on the threshold of the synagogue. Reb Laibele had been in a gloomy mood, his spirits low, and Yossele had responded gruffly to his friendly greeting. So Reb Laibele decided then and there to take more drastic action than he ever had before. He went to see the young *rov,* despite the fact that the young *rov* was not to his taste and was not a figure of authority as far as he was concerned. After all, what kind of *rov* could such a miserable shtetl as Bociany acquire, except an insignificant creature like this, a lanky absentminded dreamer who knew nothing about anything? Late into the night, a candle could be seen burning in the *rov*'s window while he allegedly studied the Scriptures. He bathed in cold water and, long before sunrise, rushed to the synagogue for morning prayers. He always had a golem-like grin on his face and he never made a move without first consulting the *dian,* a man so old and weak that not even a mouse could make out what he was saying.

Reb Laibele was not surprised that the shtetl was so enthusiastic about the young *rov,* that it was so proud of him and loved him so much. "Of course," Reb Laibele would say to himself. "Where there are no fish, even a herring can become an important dish."

Yet Reb Laibele did have to admit that the *rov* had a talent for leading the congregation in prayer, and that he was also expert at finding the synthesis between two diametrically opposed and seemingly inconsistent arguments. He could pair quotes from Maimonides with those from the Gemara, ask questions and answer them, argue the pros and cons, back and forth, until his listeners grew dizzy. Then he could bring his thoughts together so that everything made perfect sense and was in logical order. It was true that more than once even Reb Laibele had found himself enchanted with the *rov's* sharpness of mind. But the shtetl did not know what Reb Laibele suspected, namely, that the sharpness of the young *rov's* mind was due to the fact that the mind belonged not to him, but to the *dybbuk* of some sinful rabbi who inhabited his lean body. Reb Laibele suspected this because, in his opinion, the young *rov* behaved like a man possessed. Why else was he such a passionate chess player? What else could make him so adept at cabalistic calculations and put him on such friendly terms with Reb Senderl the Cabalist? He even visited Reb Senderl so as to read the passage of the week in the *Zohar* with him. And if all this were not enough, he was a wizard at Hebrew grammar.

And what did the *rov* say to Reb Laibele's accusations against Yossele? "Send for him at once! There is a subject on which I must ask his advice," was what he said.

Reb Laibele's heart winced at this display of the *rov's* chutzpah. "Why ask advice from him?" he mumbled.

"Why not?" The *rov* seemed to be mocking the tone of Reb Laibele's voice. "He is the right person to ask about the problem that I need solved. If I had a problem regarding the synagogue, I'd ask for your advice, Reb Laibele."

"I've told you why you shouldn't ask anything of him, Rov dear. Yossele has lately become unsuitable for kosher things, that's why."

"Not quite," the *rov* laughed in his resonant, youthful voice. "Gossiping and speaking ill of someone behind his back is also not very kosher, Reb Laibele."

"You call this gossip? You call this speaking ill of someone behind his back?"

"That's what I call it. And don't forget to send Reb Yossele in to me. The sooner the better."

Curiosity got the upper hand of Reb Laibele's wounded heart. "The sooner the better?" he asked, pretending to have forgotten the hurt that the *rov* had inflicted on him. "And what problem is it, dear Rov, if I may ask? Or is it a secret?"

The *rov* motioned with his slender finger for Reb Laibele to approach. "For the Gentiles it is a secret," he said in a half whisper. "The thing is that Reb Gershon Sheres, the lessee, has just been here. He had gone to see the landowner about some business this morning and there, at the mansion, he caught sight of a gazette, where he read a story about demonstrations and strikes taking place throughout Russia. Exactly what all this means I have no idea yet, but we need no one to point a finger for us, do we, Reb Laibele? Whatever happens, it's the Jews' fault. That being the case, I've decided to put on a night watch. We'll let on that we're doing it to guard against fires. And as far as I can see, Yossele Abedale would be the most suitable man to be put in charge of such project. Don't you think so, too, Reb Laibele?"

Reb Laibele motioned with his head in such a fashion that it could be interpreted as either yes or no. He left the *rov's* chambers deeply shaken and frightened. It was certain that the lessee had not invented this story. Perhaps it had even been he who had suggested the idea of organizing a night watch to the *rov,* who in Reb Laibele's opinion was not a very smart individual, in spite of his talent for scholarly argument. A threat was hovering over Jewish heads again. Who knew what danger might be approaching Bociany?

For a week or so, Reb Laibele did not mention Yossele or the other sinful members of the congregation in his conversations with people. He kept an eye on the night watch that Yossele organized, and a few times went outside in the middle of the night to see whether the guards were at their posts.

Purim fell on a mild, sunny day. The snow had melted. The roads around Bociany, the fields, the Blue Mountain, and the White Mountain were full of mud. The shtetl basked in the sun and drowned in the mud as it enjoyed the holiday. Purim players acted out the story of the wicked Haman, who had tried to destroy the Jews in the kingdom of the stupid Syrian King Ahasuerus, and of the Jewish queen Esther, his wife, who had saved her people. The streets resounded with the sounds of children's laughter, the rattle of noisemakers, and the shouts of exuberant and tipsy adults.

On this day Reb Laibele the Sexton could drink legally because it was considered a good deed to get happily drunk. Because he was a luckless person, however, his happiness was marred by the attitude of his own wife, Nechele the Pockmarked, who had decided to act out a Purim play of her own invention in front of her husband.

All year round Nechele lived resigned to the fact that she would never have any children. She had had time to get used to her tragedy and to care for Reb Laibele as if he were all of her children rolled into one. She looked after him with true motherly devotion. Yet she was basically a fun-loving person to whom the joy of Purim was no joy at all if one had no children, and it was at Purim that she found it most difficult to forgive her husband her childless state.

Reb Laibele actually agreed with his wife. He had spent every spare kopeck on traveling to the various *tsadikim* and wonder rabbis in the province of Sielce. He had visited all the places where it was said that there lived a *Bal-shem* capable of performing miracles. He could not forgive Bociany's own *Bal-shem,* Reb Senderl the Cabalist, for being unable to come up with a remedy for him, and counted him as a personal enemy for that very reason. Pious though he was, Reb Laibele had even visited a gentile quack and a doctor in Chwosty. There was only one thing that he could not bring himself to do. He could not divorce his Nechele, although ten years of their barren marriage had elapsed and, according to The Law, he was entitled to leave her. He could not even do it for her sake, so that she might bring children into the world by another man, in case the gentile doctor was right and the barrenness of their marriage was entirely his fault. He could not imagine life without Nechele, and he felt guilty, sinful, and downtrodden.

Today Nechele, as was her habit during Purim, was doing her best to ruin her husband's day, the one day in the year when, high on alcohol, he had the opportunity to forget himself and feel like a full-fledged human being. As soon as he had staggered into their house, lightheartedly humming a Purim tune, the storm broke out. He had brought in a sea of mud from outdoors, and the newly scrubbed floor was now covered with the imprint of Reb Laibele's steps. Nechele, who would have been in seventh heaven, had the damage been done by a gang of little mischiefs of her own, jumped to her feet as if she herself had been splashed with the mud, and in her helplessness and sorrow began throwing whatever came to her hand at her husband.

Reb Laibele dashed out of the house as if he had been attacked by a werewolf. As he was tipsy and not in control of his legs, one of his feet immediately got tangled with the other, and he toppled over. As he lay there, in the middle of the mud puddle in the marketplace, he caught sight of Fishele the Butcher and Reb Dovtchele the Badkhan, who entertained at weddings, leading the people in the merrymaking. As soon as they noticed him struggling to get back on his feet, they, the clowns, the Purim players, the Hasidim, and the *besmedresh* boys, all of them tipsy and wearing their gabardines inside out, burst into applause and laughter, while the children twirled their rattles gleefully. If it had not been Purim day, when one was commanded to be joyful even if one's heart was shredded with woe, Reb Laibele would have burst into tears.

As it was Purim, and as he was drunk, Reb Laibele began laughing louder than all the others, so as to make it appear that he had fallen into the puddle on purpose, to amuse the crowd. Once back on his feet, he scraped off the mud as best he could, and although his knees hurt and his white socks now squeaked muddily in his shoes, he threw himself into a dance to the band music that reached him from the Hasidic *shtibl*.

As he skipped, holding on to the belts of two young *besmedresh* men, Reb Laibele noticed Yossele Abedale arrive in the marketplace with his raggedly dressed offspring, who needed no costumes or face paint to look like Purim players. Yossele loosed his gang upon the crowd as if he were releasing a pack of young dogs, and removing himself to the side, leaned against a wall, tall and stiff as a telegraph pole, his yellow beard spread over his chest. There was not the slightest trace of a smile on his face. He looked completely sober, without a speck of enthusiasm, dutifully clapping his hands in rhythm to the lively tunes. Although Yossele kept his head tilted upwards, as if he preferred watching the arrival of the storks and their celebrations in the sky to what was going on below, to Reb Laibele it seemed that Yossele was watching him and gloating at his misery.

Reb Laibele stopped dancing. He waited for a moment for his head to stop spinning, feeling lost amid the laughing and singing crowd. Then, with his pain and torment raging like fire within him, he started to run, nearly falling over himself again, in the direction of the *rov's* dwelling, which was located in the house belonging to the ritual slaughterer.

On this day the doors of that house on the marketplace stood open. The *rov* was celebrating in the company of a gathering of prominent Hasidim. His wife, the *rebetsin,* a plump, black-wigged woman, was busy in the kitchen with a battalion of women helpers. She was dressed in a black dress augmented by yellowish pearl earrings, a string of yellowish pearls around her neck, and a band decorated with lace and more yellow pearls around her graceful head.

The women saw Reb Laibele enter the vestibule and burst into laughter at the sight of his creased, mud-spattered capote, which clung to his body, and his face, freckled all over with mud spots. The young *rebetsin,* who in Reb Laibele's opinion was even less intelligent than her husband, restrained her laughter between puckered lips. "Pfui, Reb Laibele," she managed to say. "A person like you shouldn't make such a fool of himself."

The yellow pearl earrings dangling from her ears swayed like little bells as she shook her head and put her hands on her shapely hips to suppress another fit of laughter. On no account would she allow him to enter the *rov's* courtroom dressed like that, but handed him an old caftan that had once belonged to her husband, and sent him out to the shed to change. Before he had even managed to get to the door, Reb Laibele could hear her and the other women explode in loud giggles.

Dressed in the *rov's* too tight and too long caftan, which made him look like a real Purim player, Reb Laibele entered the *rov's* chamber. He expected that there, too, he would be received with an outburst of mockery, so he set his mind on playing the fool, in the hope that this might warm their hearts to him. But no one noticed him enter.

The *rov* was delivering a Purim speech. His listeners sat at the tables, squeezed together like herring in a barrel. They listened transfixed, their gazes glued to the *rov's* princely figure, to his pale, almost transparent face, to his eyes, which burned like two torches in black skies. The *rov,* as was his habit, was gesticulating, modulating his melodic voice, causing it to sound at times heavy and rich like velvet, or thin and soft like silk. The voice really did seem to issue from his long neck like that of a *dybbuk* slithering around in his skeletal body. He appeared to be feverish with ecstasy and fluttered like a leaf. The crowd of listeners, mesmerized, shook and fluttered with him. It was as if all those present were trying to shake off their actual surroundings in order to rise into the realm of a perfect otherworldly festivity.

After the *rov's* speech, song and food acquired the particular quality of mundane things inextricably blended with spiritual ones. Then, in the very middle of the meal, Reb Senderl the Cabalist put his head down on the white tablecloth and stretched his two small hands over the table. His gray head, buried between his arms, looked like a sleeping bird. A deep silence descended on the room. The people sat open-mouthed, the food remained unswallowed in their mouths. No one moved. People scarcely allowed themselves to breathe.

Reb Laibele sat as if thunderstruck. Granted, he considered the cabala to be the teaching of Satan, not only full of contradictions but full of obscenities that might, Heaven forbid, bring forth another false messiah, and he had personal reasons for disliking Reb Senderl as well. Still, the atmosphere of mystery created by the old man was overwhelming.

Reb Senderl's small hands slowly began to lock into fists and a sidelock moved on his sunken cheek. The *rov* made a sign to the gathering, and the silence gave way to noisy jubilation. Hands began to clap and the room resounded again with Purim song. In the meantime, Reb Senderl recovered, straightened himself, and raised his radiant face to those around him. Love and enchantment peered out from his bright blue, childlike eyes and caressed the faces of the others. The *rov* pounded on the table with his hand and called for attention. The crowd fell silent and Reb Senderl, like a grandfather surrounded by children eager for a story, began to recount what he had just seen as he accompanied the Heavenly Chariot in his vision.

Reb Laibele only partly listened to Reb Senderl's story. He had recovered from the mysterious fear that had come over him during the silence in the room; frequent attacks of such inexplicable fear were nothing new to him. Now he watched the room full of Hasidim, including the *rov,* rise like an airship to the highest realms of mystic beatitude, while he remained below, anchored by his heartache to the cold ground.

When the *rov* seemed to have recovered somewhat from his flight on the wings of Reb Senderl's tale, Reb Laibele made an attempt to approach him. He finally succeeded in squeezing himself into a spot on the bench between the *rov* and a talkative Hasid, and greeted the *rov* with a "Good *yontev!*" shaking the tips of the latter's fingers. He gave the *rov* a report of the merrymaking going on in the marketplace, and as if in passing, put in a remark about Yossele Abedale's unbecoming conduct.

The *rov's* head was still partly in the clouds. If he had heard about Yossele's unbecoming conduct one time, he had heard about it a dozen times. So he continued clapping his hands in rhythm to the tune that was being sung around them. "Don't worry, Reb Laibele," he remarked absentmindedly, and added, "Send him to see me." He took a piece of traditional Haman cake and washed it down with raspberry juice. He then challenged the cantor to a singing competition.

The cantor, a stranger whom the *rov* had brought to Bociany from God alone knew where, had the voice of a nightingale, Reb Laibele had to admit. But otherwise he could not abide the man, who behaved as if he owned the entire synagogue. As to the *rov's* voice, it might have been spun from silk and velvet; this, too, Reb Laibele had to admit. He and his wife, Nechele, were connoisseurs when it came to music and singing; their mutual love of singing was one of the bonds that kept them together. They especially enjoyed and appreciated cantorial singing. More than once, the singing of either the cantor or the *rov* had taken their breath away. Reb Laibele also had to admit that with the advent of the *rov* and the cantor in Bociany, even the women had come to know entire treasuries of cantorial melodies by heart and often sang them as lullabies to their children.

As soon as the *rov* and the cantor began the display of their vocal art, the people from the marketplace started to crowd around the ritual slaughterer's house. The *rebetsin,* with her entourage of women, stood in the corridor, near the open door of the *rov's* chamber; her eyes glistened as she listened to the singing. When she grew aware of the commotion outside, she whispered into the room that the window should be opened inside, so that the people gathering in front might also enjoy the singing. Her message reached those Hasidim who sat closest to the window. They opened it as far as it would go, so that the outside and the inside became one.

The musicians who had been playing in the marketplace also moved closer to the house. The fiddler's bow glided ever so lightly over the strings of his instrument, so as not to drown out the sweetness of the singing coming through the open window. In this way Bociany allowed itself to be carried to such heights and to such depths—this time carrying Reb Laibele along—that he could no longer bear it. He felt himself choking on his Adam's apple, and he sneaked out of the room.

Unnoticed, he dashed to the shed in the yard, changed back into his own gabardine, and scuttled quickly away toward his house. There he saw Nechele, wrapped in her festive shawl, sitting all alone near the open window of their room, listening to the melodies that emanated from the *rov's* house. Tears the size of beans rolled down the pockmarks on her face.

"For Heaven's sake, what's the matter?" she asked softly, seeing her husband standing lost and forlorn in the middle of the room. "You've lost a ship of sour milk on such a glorious Purim day? Look at the funeral face you have!" She wiped her own face with both hands and added, as her eyes fell on his muddy capote, "Go, take some Haman cake, and may all the Hamans in the world take over your misery." Instead of doing as she suggested, Reb Laibele took the broom and, swaying, tried to sweep up all the mud he had again tracked in over the spotless floor. His distressed look made Nechele stand up. She took the broom from his hands and swiftly cleaned the floor. Then she gave him some Haman cake and a mug of chicory coffee. She opened the other window and placed a chair next to it. "Sit here!" she commanded. "You can hear the singing very well from here, too!" And together they listened to the singing of the *rov* and the cantor.

The next day was an ordinary weekday. As soon as the shopkeepers started locking up their shops on the Potcheyov, Reb Laibele rushed over to Yossele Abedale, who usually made it back from the villages in time to close his shop, and told him that the *rov* wanted to see him. Yossele, his face, hands, and gabardine covered with chalk-and-lime dust, bolted his shop, dismissed his daughters, and without once looking at Reb Laibele, crossed the marketplace to the *rov's* dwelling.

Before Yossele could enter the house, Reb Laibele managed to get in ahead of him, and as soon as they walked into the *rov's* courtroom, he called out, "Here he is!"

The *rov,* whose eyes wore an absent, far-off expression, glanced up at the intruders from over the pages of the large book he had been studying, as if he did not recognize the two men. Slowly he recovered himself, smiled absentmindedly, and stretched out his long, pale-fingered hand. "Welcome, people," he greeted them. "What's new?"

"You asked me yesterday to call him in to see you, Rov dear." Reb Laibele motioned with his chin at Yossele. The *rov* seemed not to hear. His eyes were again buried in the Book. He swayed over it, silently mouthing the words with his lips. "You asked me to send him in to see you," Reb Laibele repeated, stepping closer to the *rov.* Startled, the *rov* raised his head again. Reb Laibele prompted him, "You know, Rov, about the rumors . . . "

"Rumors? What rumors?" The *rov* continued swaying, keeping one eye on the Book.

"I don't know," Reb Laibele was growing desperate. "People in the street are talking. Some say . . . I heard from someone that . . . "

"Heard what?" Yossele demanded impatiently.

"Heard what?" Reb Laibele could no longer contain himself. "That you've become a heathen! They say you've become a complete unbeliever, a willful sinner, ever since you started dragging yourself around in the villages."

"An unbeliever? Who?" The *rov* disengaged himself from the book at last.

"He! That's who!" Reb Laibele pointed an accusing finger at Yossele.

The *rov's* eyes cleared. "He? You mean Reb Yossele here is a complete unbeliever?"

"And what an unbeliever, Rov dear!" Reb Laibele braided the fingers of both hands under his belly, as if he were trying to lift it and thereby lighten the load of all the charges that he had to bring against his enemy. "If only half of what people are saying about him is true, he deserves to be chained to the entrance of the synagogue and do penance. Take, for example, such a simple fact as what took place yesterday, dear Rov. A day like Purim, when people ought to be enjoying themselves . . . I myself saw him standing in the marketplace among the goyim, looking at us with a mocking sour expression on his face, as if to spite us all. It was, you should forgive my saying so, like seeing someone eating pork in public."

Yossele gave Reb Laibele an icy stare. How true it was, he thought, that jealousy and hatred could turn the wisest man into a babbling idiot. He looked at the *rov.* The latter smiled at him like a mischievous child and beckoned him to sit down at his side. Yossele obeyed. As he sat there, his rich yellow beard falling over his chest, his straight broad shoulders twice the size of the *rov's*, it seemed to Reb Laibele that Yossele was the *rov,* while the *rov* was one of Yossele's students.

"Here, let's go over this passage," the *rov* said to Yossele, pointing to a spot on the page of the open volume in front of him.

Yossele plucked at his beard and gave the *rov* the same icy glance he had given Reb Laibele. "I've told you a million times, Rov, that I'm not fluent in these things."

"What do you mean you're not fluent?" the *rov* blinked in amusement, and, under the table, he lightly pressed on the tip of Yossele's foot with his pantofle.

"I'm ignorant of the Talmud is what I mean!" Yossele burst out, not comprehending the game that the *rov* was playing with him.

The *rov* clapped his hands with delight, laughed into his beard, and called out to Reb Laibele as if he had at that moment mated him in a game of chess. "Now explain, Reb Laibele! How can Reb Yossele be an unbeliever if he is an ignoramus? Well, I'm asking you. To be a true unbeliever a man must be a scholar, an expert on the Talmud. He must be able to defend his atheistic thoughts against the sharp expositions of our sages!" As far as the *rov* was concerned the problem was solved. He held his hand out to his visitors and shook the tips of their fingers lightly, before returning to the tome in front of him.

Yossele looked scornfully in Reb Laibele's direction and said, "The ass went to get himself a pair of horns and came back without his ears, eh?"

"Is that so?" Reb Laibele squirmed as if he had been pricked by a spear. He darted toward the *rov* and shook him by the arm. "Then ask him, dear Rov, please, why he doesn't get married, if he's such a saint. Ask him if it is in accordance with Jewish law to be a father of seven, may they be protected from an evil eye, and let them wander unwatched wherever they will, all over the town?"

Slowly the *rov* lifted his eyes to Yossele. "You really don't have a wife, Reb Yossele?"

"I've told you a thousand times, Rov, that I don't." Yossele was having difficulty controlling himself.

"Of course!" The *rov* slapped himself lightly on the forehead. "It had slipped from my memory. So why don't you get married, Reb Yossele?"

The blood ebbed from Yossele's face. He was seething with rage. What did these two want from his life, that they irritated him like a pair of annoying flies? "Because I don't want my children to have a stepmother!" he spat out the words and headed for the door.

The *rov* called after him, waving a finger cheerfully, "Don't worry, Reb Yossele. We shall, with the Almighty's help, find a good woman for you. Then you and your children will, with God's help, mend your broken lives and start afresh."

"Rov! I'm not getting married!" Yossele shook his head violently.

"Oh, you will, with God's help!" the *rov* laughed.

"I will not! Never in my life!" Yossele ran out in a rage.

Alone in the room with the *rov,* Reb Laibele wrapped the capote tightly around his belly and spoke in a consoling tone of voice. "You'll see, my dear Rov, it is as evident as oil on water that I'm right about Yossele, just as I'm right about Yoel the Blacksmith." The *rov* had resumed swaying over his book, all the while caressing his straight black beard with one hand. Reb Laibele realized that to speak now was literally to talk to the wall, and he made his way to the door. But before leaving, he added, "He will still get the whipping he deserves, so help me God, Rov dear!" Consoling himself with the image of himself whipping Yossele as a penance in the antechamber of the synagogue, Reb Laibele left.

An hour later the *rov* remembered why he had really sent for Yossele, and dispatched someone to bring him back. It was a question of checking the rumors of unrest among the Gentiles in the villages. Yossele promised the *rov* to keep his eyes and ears open.

As for Reb Laibele's denunciations, they did nothing to enhance Yossele's feelings of affection toward the sexton. But they also did not make much of an impression on him. He knew that only the miserable spread gossip about others who were seemingly more fortunate than they. There was a saying: "The greater the man, the greater his demons." In Yossele's opinion, it would have been more correct to say, "The smaller the man, the greater his demons." Because Yossele did not, as a rule, take too much to heart what people said about him, Reb Laibele's words, which others kept repeating back to Yossele, bothered him not much more than last year's snow.

Yossele worked on himself until he succeeded in not minding Reb Laibele's appearance on the threshold of the synagogue. He would not allow the sexton to spoil his pleasure in greeting his father's spirit with "shalom." If Reb Laibele blocked his way, Yossele would push him aside with one arm, as if the sexton were some insignificant object.

## 7

AS TIME MARCHED ON and Yossele's children grew older, they began to realize that the youngest, Binele, was somehow strange. She gave the impression that a demon lived within her, perhaps the demon of Kailele, the crazy bride who had drowned herself in the lake.

The apple of Yossele's eye was his only son, Hershele, his *kaddish*. For his sake, Yossele dreamed dreams and made plans for the future. In Hershele, Yossele wanted to see the best of himself and his forefathers. Hershele carried the destiny of his family and of the People of Israel into posterity. Hershele had to be a perfect human being.

Yet Yossele worried about Binele, his youngest, at whose birth he had lost his Mariml, even more than he did about Hershele. Binele awakened feelings in his heart for which he had no name. At the sight of her, his sorrowful yearnings ran wild. He felt a combination of such painful tenderness, nagging regret, and joy that he could barely pretend the usual matter-of-fact attitude with which he treated his other children. He spanked her more often and harder than he did the other girls, although, unlike them, she kept away from him as much as she could.

Binele resembled her mother more than the other siblings did. Her cheekbones were high, her eyes slanted slightly, and her yellow hair had a reddish sheen. But she was as stubborn as her father, quarreling and fighting with her sisters and brother even before there was any strength in her thin arms. And even before she could understand what was meant by the word "mother," she had heard from her siblings that she was the cause of their mother's leaving this world.

Binele found it impossible to grasp how her mother could have left this world on account of her. How was it possible for someone to leave this world at all? She was even less able to grasp how she could have been the cause of her mother's death when she found out that there existed a terrible angel, called the Angel of Death, who took away a person's breath, after which the person was considered "dead" and was buried in the cemetery, and that this was the real meaning of "leaving the world." True, she was born on the same day that her mother had died, but her sisters themselves had told her that Mendl and Gnendl, the two storks on the roof, had brought her from the Heavens. So what connection did she have to the Angel of Death? Why was it her fault that her mother had left the world at exactly the time she, Binele had arrived in it?

Unless her mother had left the world on account of Binele's ugliness. That she was ugly, Binele knew well. Her sisters and all the neighbors called her Marzepa, a word used to denote the ugliest and meanest person who could possibly exist. Binele thought that her mother had taken one good look at her, when she was brought down from Heaven, and fainted. Then the Angel of Death had snatched her away.

But if her mother had been so appalled at the sight of Binele's ugliness and refused to have her as a child, was not that her mother's problem? Binele had not the least intention of feeling guilty for her mother's behavior. And if Binele was such a Marzepa that everyone chased her away, saying, "Go! I can't bear to look at you!" then they all had the same choice as her mother and could leave this world. More than once had she wished that some of them would do so. That they refused to comply with her wish was their problem, too, but at least she could show them what she was capable of. If one was a Marzepa, it no longer made any difference whether one was good and obedient; nobody cared anyway. So Binele annoyed her sisters as much as she could. To spite them, she would not let them tell her what to do; or she would do just the opposite.

When Yossele spanked her until he gasped for breath, more upset than exhausted by the effort, and then asked, "Will you do it again, will you, snotnose?" she screamed but refused to answer. So he continued spanking and repeated, "Will you do it again?" She pretended not to hear and went on yelling without giving the reply that he expected. How could he, her clever father, ask such a stupid question? Of course she would do it again. She let him go on hitting her until Yossele, stubborn though he was, was forced to let go of her.

As Binele grew, so did the scabs on her head, until they spread all over her skull. Her sisters told her that the scabs were a punishment for her being the cause of her mother's leaving this world. But she was now old enough to stand up to them. "If I want to," she yelled at them, "I can make all of you leave this world, too!"

It was different with the children in the street, who called after her, "Hey, Marzepa-Scabby-Head! Lice are feasting in your bed!"

Mothers would not allow their children to play with her, but out of respect for Yossele and pity for Binele, they would place a slice of bread or a dish with a boiled potato outside their doors, calling as if to a dog, "Come, little Marzepa, have something to eat!"

When Binele turned six, she could no longer bear the itching, burning, scratching, and burrowing. Nor could she bear the shame and the ugliness. It made her feel that the scabs were a mark of Cain for a sin that she had, in fact, committed. She began to hate herself. The world seemed so unbearable that one day, after making sure that her sisters were at home preparing the evening meal, she ran to see her father in the shop. "I don't want to be called Marzepa-Scabby-Head!" she wailed.

"Who calls you Marzepa-Scabby-Head?" he asked.

"Everyone, that's who!"

"Why?"

"Because I have scabs!" She glared at him suspiciously through her tears, to see whether he was making fun of her. Could he possibly not know what all of Bociany knew? She stood frozen in one spot for a moment, then in desperation, bent her head down in front of him, "Here, look!"

He put his palms on her ears, bent down to see her head and squinted; the veins on his forehead swelled. He jumped to his feet and looked bewildered out on the Potcheyov. His first thought was to go with Binele to see Fraidele the Shoe-Stitcher's Wife. But Fraidele's method of curing scabs was a torture just to watch. He had seen her at work. Fraidele would paste a layer of pitch upon pieces of cotton, hold them over the fire, then apply the cotton pieces to the mangy head until they formed a kind of bonnet, a burning clown's wig. The next day, Fraidele would tear off the bonnet, tearing the skin off along with it, and apply hot pitch again on the bleeding skull. Day after day and week after week the procedure was repeated. Yossele knew that he would never be able to endure it if this hellish treatment were applied to Binele. But what solution was there?

Suddenly an idea struck him. Shmulikl the Doctor! Surely in such a case it was permissible to consult him; it was a question of saving a life after all, the life of a child. Shmulikl, the barber-surgeon, had seen the world. Perhaps he had learned another method of curing scabs. One had to try every alternative before delivering the child into Fraidele's hands. Yossele grabbed Binele's hand, asked his neighbor Hindele to look after the shop and ran with his daughter across the marketplace to the barber-surgeon's house.

Shmulikl the Doctor was a short, vivacious man in his late thirties, with a pointed goatee and a small barber's mustache that made his pointed nose seem shorter than it really was. He had left Bociany many years previously as a fervent yeshiva boy with one burning ambition—to come back an accomplished Talmudic scholar, entitled to take up the post of *rov* in Bociany. But when the winds of change had begun to blow over Russia, they blew away Shmulikl's ambition and carried him off as far as the city of Kiev, where he decided instead to take up the challenge of studying medicine.

The city of Kiev was prone to pogroms, and Shmulikl had witnessed quite a number of them. He collected his share of experiences in that field, as well as a diploma to practice barber-surgery. This last was a great enough achievement for a Jew from Poland who came from a long line of paupers. In Kiev he had also become a passionate adherent of the Lovers of Zion. Since it was fashionable among the Russian and Jewish intelligentsia of the time to "go among the people," Shmulikl decided to go among his own people in the shtetl of Bociany. And so he had returned, and brought with him a wife who did not wear the matron's wig, but rather kept her own hair on her head, and had a diploma of her own, as a midwife.

Their jointly held ambition of "going among their own people" was not an ideal that was easily realized, however. Their own people ridiculed them and continued consulting Reb Senderl the Cabalist for remedies and cures, while the shtetl's own female specialists who assisted with deliveries went on with their jobs as usual. Consequently, Shmulikl the Doctor and his wife had to content themselves with taking their "hygiene" to the homes of the rich and of those peasants who considered a Jewish barber-surgeon to be a better witch doctor than one of their own.

Shmulikl had worked as a barber during his student years, and this occupation had helped him survive and earn his diploma. It helped him again in his activities in Bociany. A barber shop made a good meeting place, the door being always open for anyone to drop in. Shmulikl considered himself fortunate in that his barbershop was located at the heart of the shtetl, on the marketplace, to the right of the Potcheyov. It gave him an ideal opportunity to disseminate his ideas and opinions by accosting those who gathered in front of his shop, or by reacting to what was going on right in front of his eyes.

When the Jewish yearning for Zion had found expression in the birth of a political movement, Shmulikl had become an ardent follower and propagandist. Bociany's attitude toward him did not frighten him. He had grown tired of all kinds of fear, and he had no intention of hiding his new way of life. Yet for legal reasons he did not declare himself a Zionist. Zionism, in any case, had little meaning for the "Jewish masses" of Bociany, who in contrast to the few well-off Jews, knew nothing of the movement. The name of Doctor Herzl, its founder, was unknown to them. Thus Shmulikl spoke his mind as he pleased, but he avoided modern terminology and used only the language familiar to "the masses," which served his purpose even better.

Shmulikl's barber shop was always crowded with peasants. When there was no need to cut their hair or pull their teeth, he would take them into his "kabinet," a small room that contained his desk surrounded by closets and shelves, all crammed with papers, magazines, books, flagons, and bottles of all sizes. There, beside the wall where his diploma hung beneath the portrait of Dr. Herzl, Shmulikl carried out his diagnostic examinations. If it proved necessary, he either sent the patient to consult the doctor in Chwosty or performed the medical operation himself in his shop.

It was mealtime and the barbershop was empty when Yossele arrived with Binele, except for a peasant whose arm was being attended to. The peasant had a dislocated elbow, and another peasant was helping Shmulikl pull at the arm, so as to set the elbow back into its joint. Shmulikl did not even stop to blink when he saw Yossele, but continued panting along with the two peasants. It was not easy work, and it looked as if there might be no end to it.

"Come here and lend a hand," Shmulikl panted at Yossele.

Yossele obeyed. He took hold of the moaning peasant's arm and pulled it with all his strength, until there was the sound of a crack, and the elbow was once again in place. Shmulikl wiped the sweat from his forehead and glasses with a large handkerchief and turned to quiz Yossele, asking for details of his life, as if he and Yossele were two relatives who had not seen each other for years. In the meantime, the patient's companion placed a head of cabbage and a large cheese wrapped in cheesecloth on the counter. It was Shmulikl's pay. The two peasants left, and Yossele tried to interrupt Shmulikl's questions about matters that were none of his business, and to tell him briskly and to the point the reason for his visit. But the interruptions had the same effect on Shmulikl as "cupping glasses might have had on a corpse," that is, they had no effect at all.

It was only when Shmulikl was satisfied that he had found out all there was to know that he took Binele's hand and led her into the "kabinet" behind the shop. He asked Yossele to stop at the door, as there was not much room inside. From that position Yossele was immediately struck by the sight of the portrait hanging opposite him on the wall, above Shmulikl's diploma. It showed a man with a full beard, but an uncovered head, obviously a freethinker, or rather a "free-stinker" as Yossele called those without God in their hearts. He guessed that this was this Hertzke, Shmulikl's professional colleague of sorts, also a doctor, whom the people of Bociany said Shmulikl worshiped like a god.

Shmulikl seated Binele on a chair near the crooked table laden with bottles, papers, and books. He scrutinized her head and moaned loudly to himself. He gave her an unexpectedly friendly pinch on the cheek, and taking her hand, suggested that they "get to work."

Binele's heart jumped with joy. "Let's get to work" could only mean that he would undertake to cure her. A warmth spread over her limbs at the touch of Shmulikl's hand. She would have followed him to the ends of the earth. But he only led her back out into the shop and lifted her into the barber's chair. He took his strange-looking tools, placed them in a container, and put them on the spirit burner to cook, as if he were about to make a soup of them. Then he picked up the head of cabbage and the cheese and disappeared through the door of his "kabinet." Binele's heart pounded louder than it ever had before, as she waited for him to return and listened to the water boil in the container. She sat stiffly, exactly as Shmulikl the Doctor had seated her. Not once did she turn her head to where her father stood behind her back.

Shmulikl returned and took his tools from the container. Briskly he warned her, "It will hurt a bit."

She looked at him with radiant eyes and answered encouragingly, "I won't cry."

"*Molodietz!* Brave girl!" he exclaimed, adding as if to amuse her, "You may cry, you may even scream, but don't turn your head, because I might drive the razor into your ear!" He began shaving her head and cutting away the strands of hair from around the scabs. Binele bit her lips, swallowing her tears without a word. Then, at the very peak of her suffering, the kindhearted Shmulikl suddenly began to abuse her father.

"You know the *Gemore* by heart, don't you?" Shmulikl snapped at Yossele. "But what the *Gemore* tells you, that you're deaf to, eh?" Shmulikl's breath was like a gust of hot wind in Binele's ear, as he fumed, "You're all a bunch of fanatic donkeyheads and purblind hypocrites, that's what you are!"

Yossele, who had not had the courage to watch the operation at close range, was still standing near the entrance of Shmulikl's "kabinet," staring at the portrait on the wall inside. He clenched his fists, trying to restrain the impulse to punch the infidel Shmulikl in the ribs. But Binele, his own flesh and blood, was now in the hands of this despicable monster who might wound her with his razor, God only knew how badly. With an effort, Yossele summoned his self-control and grumbled, "What is there in the *Gemore* that a shameless infidel like you follows, and a good Jew doesn't?"

"It's written in the *Gemore,*" Shmulikl continued scraping at Binele's head with the unpleasantly grating razor, "that a dirty head brings blindness, and a dirty body falls prey to scabs and other diseases." He stopped talking as the blade reached Binele's ear.

Yossele, seeing Binele twisting and wincing with pain, felt trapped. He would gladly have grabbed the child from this sacrificial altar and escaped. But it was too late. In order to shorten this helpless waiting, and to divert his own attention from Binele's head and the unpleasant subject Shmulikl had raised, he motioned with his chin at the portrait in the "kabinet" and asked, "A relative of yours . . . that bearded goy in the picture, wearing no skullcap on his head?"

Shmulikl's blade had emerged from behind Binele's ear without mishap, but he did not answer right away. He busied himself wiping the blood off her head and dabbing at the sores with an unpleasant-looking brown liquid. Every time he touched her, she squirmed in her seat, emitting a stifled cry. Shmulikl cried along with her, "Brave girl! *Molodietz!*" and reassuringly patted her shoulder. "Doctor Herzl is as much a relative of mine as he is of yours," he finally answered Yossele.

"What do you mean by that?" Yossele asked, not because he was curious, but to keep his impatience at bay.

"By that I mean that Doctor Herzl is our second Moses."

"Really? No more, no less?"

"No more, no less," Shmulikl replied with controlled passion. "He's the man who'll lead us back to Zion."

"He will, will he?" Yossele was now certain that he had entrusted his child to the hands of the Evil One himself.

"It's not going to be easy," Shmulikl earnestly shook his head. "But never mind. Rely on Doctor Herzl. We'll buy back our land from the strangers' hands. Besides, he's carrying on negotiations with the Turkish Sultan, and the English are also more inclined to understand the issue. We'll negotiate with other countries, too."

"And are you also going to conduct negotiations with the Almighty?"

"The Almighty inspires the Jews to come to Zion to die. We want to live in Zion."

"Is that so?" Yossele pursed his lips as if ready to spit at Shmulikl. "Who are you," he lashed out with vehemence, "to shorten the time of our exile, you free-stinkers, without the help of the Almighty? You don't need a Messiah at all, do you? Do you know what you'll end up achieving, brains that you are? Only one thing! You'll turn the Holy Land into another exile, that's what you'll do!"

Shmulikl smeared an ointment over Binele's blue-red skull and did not allow himself to look fully at Yossele. "And what have we achieved by sitting with folded hands and waiting for the Messiah, pray tell me that, if you're so smart? He requires a few thousand more years of Jewish persecution and slaughter. He takes his time, the Redeemer, doesn't he? What do another few pogroms like the one in Kisheniev matter to him? What's the hurry? After all, Jewish blood is cheaper than water."

Yossele felt like blocking his ears so as not to hear Shmulikl's sacrilegious words. In this case, Reb Laibele the Sexton was undoubtedly right. A man like Shmulikl had to be driven out of Bociany. Yossele stepped closer to the barber's chair to see if he could grab Binele's arm and run out with her. But Shmulikl was still rubbing ointment on her skull. So Yossele locked his thumbs behind his back and started pacing up and down the barber shop. He chewed on his underlip, having decided to keep his mouth shut, so that Shmulikl might do the same. Yet in spite of himself he turned toward Shmulikl. He did not want to owe him an answer.

"You may stand on your head until doomsday, Shmulikl," he said in a resolute voice, "and you will not bring about redemption, do you hear me? The only thing you'll bring about is a pathway straight to hell for yourselves. That's all. Because the Almighty is with us believers, not with you. The *Shkhina* is in exile just as we are, so the sanctity of the people is here, not there. And it suits me fine to be here, too! You hear? It suits me fine!" He wiped his mouth and beard, adding, "You'll restore neither the Holy Land nor yourselves. All you really want is to run away, because you're afraid of the goy. But what can cowards achieve if they don't even have a Father in Heaven?"

Yossele was so engrossed in his own words that although he saw Shmulikl lift Binele off the barber's chair, he did not really notice it. Shmulikl gave her the jar of ointment to apply to her head and patted her shoulder. As he went to the basin to wash his hands, he told both father and daughter to apply the ointment twice a day, and to Yossele he added, "Come in another time and we'll finish the discussion. The door is always open and, as you see, I don't bite."

"May the dogs bite you!" Yossele almost exclaimed. But he had caught sight of Binele's tearful face and her grateful gaze beaming first at Shmulikl, then at himself, then back again. So he said not another word, but pulled the little girl by the sleeve, and they hurriedly left.

Outside, in the marketplace and on the Potcheyov, people followed Yossele and his daughter with eyes full of suspicion. Yossele had taken Binele and her scabs to Shmulikl the Doctor? Why was Fraidele the Shoe-Stitcher's Wife, who cured scabs without a trace, suddenly not good enough? The devout Yossele had certainly changed recently. Reb Laibele the Sexton had obviously not sucked his stories entirely out of his finger. But if the Evil One had indeed succeeded in working on the iron-willed Yossele, then the rest of Bociany was in even greater danger. So the men secretly checked the tassels of their undergarments, while the women whispered exorcisms and spat three times.

That night, Binele lay on her cot with her sisters Mashele and Dvorele, unable to sleep because of her burning scalp and because she was shaken by what had happened. Yet, although her scalp burned and pricked, she was happy. She could still feel Shmulikl's touch, feel his hand on her shoulder and around her fingers. A soft touch was such a nice thing! She heard Shmulikl's encouraging voice. He had praised her, called her "*Molodietz!* Brave girl!" She had no doubt that she would be rid of the scabs. When she finally fell asleep, there was a smile on her lips.

Yossele quickly forgot about Binele's scabs, but she lived with the reality of her shaven head day after day and week after week. She fashioned a kind of head cover for herself from a rag and held it together with a safety pin, which she had stolen from Toybe-Kraindele, the women's bathhouse attendant. Whenever she caught sight of her reflection in a window pane, she consoled herself with the thought that this headgear made her look like a grown-up woman. Every night after Mashele and Dvorele were asleep and all the others in the hut were on their cots, Binele would take off the head covering, bring out the ointment from under the cot and spread it over her head.

The scab wounds disappeared, but her hair seemed in no hurry to grow back. Weeks passed. Every day, when there was no one at home, Binele would remove the head cover, checking to see if perhaps today her skull would not feel so smooth. Finally, the smoothness was replaced by a bristly feeling. Drunk with victory, barely able to keep her secret to herself, she hid in a corner ten times a day and caressed the tiny bristles of hair beginning to grow on her skull. She measured them with the tips of her nails, and kept up her courage by recalling that grown women had similar bristles of hair under their matron's wigs after they married. She promised herself that she would never cut her hair, but would have long tresses for her wedding, so long that they would reach the floor.

Her sores were gone, her hair grew, and still the children called her Marzepa-Scabby-Head. She raced after them, tore the cover from her head, and called, "Look! I don't have scabs! I'm a *molodietz!* A brave girl!"

They laughed at her shaven head and called back, "Marzepa-Scabby-Head! Lice are feasting in your bed!"

Now, however, Binele had the children's mothers on her side. The women neighbors scolded their children and spanked their behinds for running after Binele, yet they too called her Marzepa. It seemed that all of Bociany had forgotten her real name—with the exception of one big boy, Yacov, the son of Hindele the Scribe's Widow. For some reason he remembered her real name, and as if to spite the others, called her Binele whenever he ran into her on the Potcheyov.

## 8

AFTER THE DEATH OF HIS FATHER AND BROTHER, Yacov's mother had become more important to him than ever before. When he stepped into the loft, she would come forward to greet him, take his hands between her palms, and blow on them in order to warm them. She set a bowl of potato soup before him and watched him eat. It was then that he felt that his mother was the only constant element in the world, that she was unchangeable and eternal. He felt that no matter how many faces the world assumed, nor how much he himself should change, her face would always remain the same, and the threads that bound her to him would remain unbreakable.

At the same time, however, she had begun to irritate him. Once, for example, she had slipped on the muddy stairs while carrying a pail of water. When Yacov came home from heder, she was sitting on the bench by the table, putting compresses on her swollen foot.

Yacov grew angry at the sight. "Why don't you wait for Shalom or me to bring the water?" he shouted dashing toward her. He could not forgive her weakness, was unable to watch her awkwardness as she hopped around the room on her good foot, serving the evening meal. He tried to push her away from the stove, insisting, "We'll get it ourselves!"

But she was strong in her lameness and shook her head adamantly, "It doesn't hurt, silly, go and wash."

When they sat down at the table, she served herself chicory coffee and no soup. This time it was Shalom who inquired, "Where is your soup?"

"I've eaten already," she said, waving her hand. "You came home late. I'm just sipping this to keep you company." Neither Shalom nor Yacov believed her. They understood that she had not erned a kopeck from the shop that day.

When Yacov lay beside Shalom on the mattress they shared, he saw his mother sitting by the stove, reading by the light of the oil lamp that stood above it. He drifted off to sleep to the sound of her whispering to herself. Both anger and sadness gnawed at his heart.

More and more often, Yacov's thoughts turned to issues of justice, human and divine. These problems had begun to nag at him so much that he ran the risk of boring himself. He could hardly wait to come to those parts in the Scriptures that dealt with these matters, so that he could understand why the Almighty was so brutal to his mother, the best and most charitable soul in the world. Why did He allow her to work so hard? Why, when it came to easing her lot, had He done it in such a terrible manner, by making her a widow and depriving her of her eldest son? Indeed, things were easier for his mother now that his father and Itchele were gone, but what kind of divine charity was that? If she was paying for the sins of Adam and Eve and was supposed to earn her slice of bread "by the sweat of her brow," why then was she always putting the bread aside for her children to eat?

Impatience and restlessness drummed at his heart, calling for action. He wanted to grow up as soon as possible and study on his own at the *besmedresh.* He wanted to be rid of his *melamed,* Reb Shapsele, the spawn of Asmodeus, who, with his "put yourself down" treatments, confounded any concept of justice. He wanted to find the answers to the questions that bothered him by himself. Then he would know what to do.

In the meantime, he could not resist sharing his thoughts with his mother, who had taken to inquiring about his studies. Shalom was now too big for Hindele to ask to sit down with her and teach her, but she could still ask Yacov to do so. One day, as he was going over the chapter of the week with her, he led the discussion into his dissatisfaction with the world order.

Hindele scolded him. "Heaven forbid such words, Yacov! Don't ever bring them to your lips again."

"I will bring them to my lips!" he shot back at her. "The Almighty is unfair to you, that's what He is!"

"Goodness alive! How can you say that? I'm the most fortunate woman in the world. I've had the honor of having your father for a husband and Itchele for a son, may they rest in peace. And what do I lack if I have you, my good and devoted children, may you all be well and healthy? Don't you know that all of Bociany envies me?" She pressed Yacov to her bosom, forgetting that a mother must refrain from doing this after her son has become a Gemara student. Then she added, "Your father used to quote from the Scriptures, saying, 'If what you possess is not yours, then why should you covet the things which you don't possess?' That makes sense, don't you think?"

She seemed very beautiful to him at that moment. In fact, Yacov carried two images of her in his heart. One was of an old, stooped, worry-worn woman about to collapse under the burden she carried; the other was of a magnificent radiant goddess, strong, cheerful, with warm eyes and a voice of eiderdown softness. She elaborated on the thought, "And if we really had all the good things that we need, who is to say whether we could enjoy them, if everyone around us went hungry and barefoot?"

This question enraged Yacov. "The lessee enjoys them quite well! So does the wood merchant and Reb Faivele the Miller!"

"How do you know? I've told you more than once, Yacov, that what you see and what seems to you to be true is not necessarily correct."

Yacov bit his lips. His mother and her talk of things only seeming to be true confused and irritated him.

Friday was a good day at the heder. On Friday the *melamed,* Reb Shapsele, put a suitable expression on his face in honor of the Sabbath Eve, and as Passover drew nearer, he made his students study the Song of Songs. For their part, the students understood not one word because Reb Shapsele zipped through the text without bothering to stop for explanation. Nonetheless the boys took delight in the melodic rhythms and the enticing mysterious sound of the words, which put the mind in a pre-Sabbath mood without lulling it to sleep. On the contrary, the Song awakened a wistful curiosity in their minds and made their hearts await something that was out of this world.

The *melamed* let the boys out early on Fridays, and this time, on his way to his mother's shop on the Potcheyov, Yacov decided instead to pay a visit to Reb Senderl the Cabalist, although normally he visited him on the Sabbath after the meal, to be tested.

Although Reb Senderl loved children and welcomed them with open arms, they usually made a point of visiting him in secret, so that their parents would not know. The people of Bociany, although viewing Reb Senderl with some awe, nevertheless thought it best to keep their distance from him. They ran to him for cures and amulets to fight disease, but they feared him, even though he looked harmless enough, and his voice never rose above a whisper. Mostly people were afraid that Reb Senderl might weaken the impressionable minds of their offspring with the magic of the cabala. The memories of the false messiahs, Sabbatai Zevi and Jacob Frank, lingered over the swamps of Bociany much longer than over the other shtetlekh of Poland. The suspicion remained that Reb Senderl was one of those who would not allow these painful memories to evaporate. Bociany awaited the Messiah with such longing! Just a spark, just one word from Reb Senderl, and the belief in a fake messiah might once again envelop Bociany, might set fire to the hearts of the young and sweep along the old, and again the people would be deceived and betrayed.

Hindele Polin did not share the misgivings of the others. To her, Reb Senderl's presence was a cure for the soul. Whenever it seemed to her that she had not adequately answered her children's questions, she advised them to go and ask Reb Senderl. She had even asked the old man to agree to test her sons every Saturday after the Sabbath meal. She did not fear his cabalistic magic. She knew that Reb Senderl would never study cabala with children; and she believed that a child could only understand what he was ready for.

Besides this, the truth was that deep in her heart Hindele was herself strangely attracted to the secrets of the cabala. Often she thought that they might calm her own yearnings toward the unknown, the concealed, the eternal mystery of existence. In her loft she kept the *Book of Creation* stashed away with her late husband's manuscripts and the genealogical book that traced her lineage back to the house of King David. She only kept it as a talisman, but when she was alone in the room, she would occasionally take the book into her hands and flip through its pages with awe. How very much she wanted to understand it, and yet she could not! Despite herself, she found herself yearning to have a rabbi, a teacher, a guide such as a man might have, so that she would not be condemned to stray through this forest of riddles alone.

Whenever the voice of the Torah, coming from the heders, the *besmedresh,* the synagogue or the open windows of the homes, reached Hindele's ears, she had the feeling that all Jewish men were priests in the service of the Almighty, each of them supporting God's world like a pillar. She viewed the wives and mothers as fulfilling a sacred function as well, by supporting their husbands and sons and serving them. In this way the women saw to it that the holy work of the Creator was fully accomplished. Consequently, the petty, day-to-day drudgery of a woman's life had to be accepted with equanimity, as it was part and parcel of her important role. Still, envy pricked Hindele's heart. She, too, wanted to study the sacred books, to fill her mind with the light of wisdom, at least for half a day, at least for an hour a day. Because this privilege had not been granted her, she wished to drink from all these sources through her sons.

The lit naphtha lamp in Reb Senderl's shop seemed to light up with a brighter flame when Reb Senderl noticed Yacov appear on the threshold of his shop. He motioned the boy to approach. His voice was soft and rustling, as he said playfully, "Welcome, Reb Yacov!" He stretched out a pale hand, and when the boy grasped it, he pulled him around the table where he sat, until Yacov stood by his knees. "And what questions have you brought along to disturb me with this time?" he asked, plucking a gray hair from his beard and placing it as a marker on the page which he had been studying. He then pushed the heavy tome away from him and lit his pipe.

From Reb Senderl, Yacov had learned that this pipe was not just a pipe, that inside, it contained magic secrets. In the dark of the shop, with only the dirty naphtha lamp flickering, the pipe did seem to emit a peculiar glow every time Reb Senderl puffed at it. "I can see the sparks!" Yacov called out, putting his finger close to the glowing tobacco in the pipe's bowl.

"Careful!" Reb Senderl caught his wrist. "When you want to save a spark, you must take care not to burn yourself, especially when it is a question of a spark as sacred as this one." Reb Senderl smiled a mischievous smile. The pipe was always their first topic of conversation.

"And tell me, please, Reb Senderl, how can you make sacred sparks come out of stinking tobacco?" Yacov sang the question to the lilt of the Gemara. Reb Senderl was about to reply, but Yacov stole the words from his mouth. "I know! I know! The sparks of holiness can come from the least clean things and still be saved. But what I want to know is how they got there in the first place."

"And this is precisely what I refuse to tell you, isn't it?" Reb Senderl purred with delight.

"Yes, but you promised to tell me after my bar mitzvah."

"Correct. The question is only when after . . . "

"Right after!"

Reb Senderl stirred the tobacco in the bowl of the pipe with a rusty nail, puffed at it, and exhaled the smoke with a sigh of satisfaction. "Aye, how good it tastes!"

"I know what you mean to say by that, too, Reb Senderl. The stinking tobacco that tastes so good," Yacov remarked earnestly. "The other day the gentile boys in my lane caught a rat, skinned it, and left it in the middle of the lane, in the snow. I was on my way home, and suddenly I saw a flower, a withered rose in the snow. It looked very pretty, Reb Senderl. But when I came closer, I saw that it was the skinned red rat. Another time just the opposite happened. I was sitting with my mother on the Potcheyov, and I looked, and there was a dead mouse lying near the wall. I went up close to it and what do you think it was? It was a newborn bird that had fallen out of its nest in the eaves."

They looked at one another in silent understanding. It was time for Yacov to ask his real questions. He knew that Reb Senderl would answer even the most daring questions without anger or mockery, unlike Reb Shapsele at the heder. Sometimes Reb Senderl answered with a fable, sometimes with a quote from the Scriptures. More often than not, Yacov could not make out what Reb Senderl was driving at with his enigmatic replies. But Reb Senderl showed him respect. That fact alone made it seem to Yacov that he had grasped the meaning of Reb Senderl's words, even when the meaning did not entirely penetrate his reason, and the chaos in his head would subside for a while.

Reb Senderl's shop was small and narrow. At the back lay the straw pallet on which the old man slept. In front stood the counter, made of raw boards so worn and used that they seemed polished. On the counter stood the naphtha lamp beside a pile of well-worn books, while yellow stacks of soap bricks covered the rest of the table. Weakly illuminated by the light of the lamp, the bricks of soap, like Reb Senderl's face, seemed to glow like lamps of gold. The firm's inscription, engraved into every brick in Roman letters, looked like a magic formula. Reb Senderl kept his kosher soap in a box near the straw pallet.

"Reb Senderl," Yacov at length gathered his courage for the main question. "Is it fair that my mother should suffer so much?"

Reb Senderl tapped the bowl of his pipe with his thumb as he considered his answer. With his free hand he smoothed the silvery wisps of hair at the tip of his beard. "Good Heavens, of course not," he said, removing the pipe from his mouth. Squinting, he looked into Yacov's troubled eyes.

"So why does the Almighty do nothing about it?"

"Who says He does nothing about it? He gave her a son like you. You call that nothing?"

"My mother says the same, but that's just talk."

"Why just talk? The Almighty knows and your mother knows that they can rely on you."

"On me? How can they rely on me? What can I do?"

"You are doing, Yacov."

"I'm doing what, Reb Senderl?"

"You are beside her. And you are not indifferent. That's the beginning of doing."

"But I have to study and so does Shalom. And she works like a mule, running between the home and the shop ten times a day and barely earning a few kopecks. Then she falls and hurts herself. Then she doesn't have any food for herself. Then she cries. She thinks that if she pretends to smile, I'll believe that she hasn't been crying. But I know. I can tell right away if someone has been crying, even if her eyes are dry."

"And I tell you that your mother is very fortunate and that she knows she is, even if she does cry."

"I cannot abide such a way of being fortunate! What should I do?"

"Be patient, that's what you should do. When the time comes, you'll know what to do. Sooner or later you'll know, because you're not indifferent."

"I want to know sooner, not later!"

"You may want to know, but are you capable of knowing? When the right moment comes, you'll have double power, a double soul. I have no doubt that when you were born, the soul of a good *tsadik,* who had not completed his task on earth, entered into you in order to assist you when the time comes." Reb Senderl waved his hand. "Eh, you're making me talk too much."

"What do you mean 'too much,' Reb Senderl? You've told me nothing." Then Yacov asked, utterly confounded, "And what has the Almighty done to help you? You have no son."

"He helps me all the time," Reb Senderl replied.

"How? This place is terribly cold. I can see the sky through the hole in the ceiling, and you don't even have enough straw in your mattress. You're practically sleeping on the bare floor."

"So what? First of all, there are a few boards spread underneath. Second, I can't very well fall off the ground, can I? But it is possible, with the Almighty's help, for me to rise from the ground. And as for the holes and cracks in the roof, it is cheerier like this, and it keeps me from shutting myself off from the world. One must always leave a crack open. Nor is it really so cold in here. If I do get a bit chilly, I saddle my thoughts and my heart and ride off to the Creator's concealed vineyards. It's warm there, sometimes even too hot for a weak human being, and I am forced to return to earth in haste."

"So you get even colder when you come back?" Yacov was trying to grasp the sense of Reb Senderl's words.

"It takes me some time before I get cold again. When I do, then off I go once more."

"That doesn't answer my question."

"What's your question?"

"My question is, how can a human being conquer the Evil One, if the Almighty Himself is unable to?"

"How do you know that He is unable?"

"That's what I see."

"You see nothing."

"You mean He is able, but doesn't want to? Then he's as mean as Asmodeus himself and there is no difference between the two." Yacov blushed. He expected Reb Senderl to be angry with him.

Reb Senderl only grew sad. He puffed at his pipe, exhaling the smoke with heavy sighs. He said in a whisper, "You see, Yacov, the issue of evil rests at the core of things since the days of creation. The question of why the evil man fares so well, while the good man suffers, is difficult to grasp with reason alone. Because a *mentsh* is no more than a *mentsh,* and when a human being is steeped in suffering, there are two possibilities. Either that person becomes completely dulled and his spirit dies, or his spirit becomes as clear as a mirror. In that mirror he sees everything as it really is, and then he no longer suffers pain, nor does he need an explanation any longer. From such a person one might learn the source of good and evil. But who is capable of understanding someone like that? Only another like himself. But he who suffers average pain, bearable misfortunes, cannot understand. He asks questions and gets no answers."

"I don't want to suffer pain!" Yacov exclaimed. "I don't want my mother to suffer any. She has suffered enough!"

Reb Senderl sank into silence. Yacov began absentmindedly to play with the bricks of soap on the table, arranging them into convoluted edifices. Suddenly, he had a brilliant idea. He would help his mother by selling cigarettes to the young men at the *besmedresh!* He stared at Reb Senderl with wide-eyed amazement. He had no doubt that the wise old man had planted this wonderful idea in his head. He sighed with relief, enthusiastically thanked Reb Senderl by pumping his hand vigorously, and darted out of the shop in an excellent frame of mind for the oncoming Sabbath.

Yacov spent the entire Sabbath day planning how to organize his business. Finally he could no longer keep the secret to himself and although it was forbidden to discuss business on the Sabbath, he confided his plans to his mother.

It being the Sabbath, it was also forbidden to grow upset. Hindele grew agitated nevertheless. "Heaven forbid!" she exclaimed. "God protect us, if I let you do such a thing. You are not even bar mitzvah yet. You sit on your behind and study! That's what you must do! Don't forget that you're still a child and you need as much play and enjoyment as you can get, because later . . . later in life it isn't so easy." She broke into sobs, and Yacov felt guilty for having made her cry on the Sabbath.

Of late, Hindele had been not merely sad but painfully sore at heart. Her bereavement at the loss of Itchele had only now grown to its full expanse, and her mind was racked with a thousand memories of her firstborn. Only occasionally were there days when she was cheerful and seemed to enjoy the wonderful pre-spring weather. To add to her grief, Reb Menashele the Matchmaker had begun bothering her. Her relatives, too, refused to leave her alone, writing to her and to the matchmaker with requests that she remarry. This was, after all, the way of the world. A man could be his own master and do as he pleased, but a sinful woman had to obey her family, something that Hindele was not the least inclined to do. There was no room in her heart for a new husband; her children took up all the space that she had left in that heart; every thought, every feeling, every moment of her day was devoted to them. She did not even allow herself the pleasure of joining Nechele the Pockmarked on her visits to the ritual slaughterer's wife, Sore-Leyele, who was a formidable storyteller. Spending time with her children was more important to her.

Hindele was on reasonably good terms with Reb Menashele the Matchmaker. He was a dignified-looking man who took his profession very seriously, almost as if it were a sacred mission. Matches between men and women were made in Heaven, and he was their practical executor here on earth. He was convinced that in the practice of bringing two people together to make one, he was guided by the Heavenly Hand. With great deliberation, he took into account the good qualities, and ignored the bad, of the marriageable candidates whose names he listed in alphabetical order in his bulging black notebook. In meticulous detail, he calculated which two people's good qualities would best harmonize to create a successful couple. Then he figured in more mundane problems, such as lineage and "pocket." Once these matters were taken into account, he believed that even a crooked union of a crooked pair could result in straight offspring.

Reb Menashele's dress was prim, almost elegant. Around his neck he wore a spotless red scarf under a topcoat that was buttoned all the way down to his ankles. This coat he wore both summer and winter, as if he were ready at any moment to take to the road to arrange a very important match. He did in fact set up matches between Bociany and Chwosty, or between Bociany and the other shtetlekh in the province of Sielce. The ubiquitous matchmaker's umbrella looked in Reb Menashele's hand like the staff of a heavenly emissary. Yet despite his great piety, Reb Menashele spoke the language of a worldly man who had both feet firmly planted on the ground.

He had this in common with Hindele: he, too, was a regular customer of the book merchant's and passionately devoured profane Yiddish story books. If the bookseller was a little slow in coming to Bociany, Reb

Menashele would exchange reading matter with Hindele. He made a point, however, of letting her know that he read these worthless books for professional reasons only, in order to better understand the youth of today. But a problem had arisen in his relationship with Hindele, namely, that whenever he tried to talk to her, she wept.

This time Hindele did not take her troubled heart to Reb Senderl. She needed female company, although Manka the Washerwoman would not do, either. Hindele had recently grown wary of sitting with Manka for too long. She felt so ill at ease with Vaslav Spokojny that she began to worry whether even the slightest contact with the Gentiles might lead to dangerous ends. She liked Manka as much as ever, but worry was worry. And then, only a Jewish woman could fully understand the heart of another Jewish woman. Nechele the Pockmarked was the kindred soul that Hindele needed.

Among her many good qualities, Nechele also possessed the ability to easily adapt herself to any kind of trouble. She was not a worrier or a brooder like some of the other women. But she was temperamental and had a low boiling point. If something or someone annoyed her, she reacted quickly, and she did not mince words. A moment later, however, she forgot the matter entirely. Nechele seldom wept. The exceptions were Purim, when the rest of the world was cheerful, or when she was moved by the melody of a song.

Nechele told Hindele exactly what Hindele wanted to hear. "If you're blessed with children, may they live in good health," she said, "then what do you need a husband on your head for? Of course you'll have to marry eventually, but what's the hurry? Postpone it. Tell Reb Menashele to come next time with a better proposal. After all, you're not just anybody. What's the use of being descended from the cream of the rabbinical world, if you don't get something out of it? Be choosy."

So Hindele pretended to be choosy when the matchmaker came to see her, and still she went on weeping. Reb Menashele explained to her that the longer she waited, the worse the marriage proposals would become. "Time doesn't stand still," he argued. A not-so-old widow like Hindele, he said, could more easily find a suitable bridegroom sooner than later, but a not-so-old widow with four children was already a less promising match than a middle-aged widow without children. And while it was true that an honorable lineage was important, it was also true that without a kopeck for a dowry, lineage in these practical times was not much taken into consideration. Reb Menashele added that he would not be making such an effort on Hindele's behalf if her family had not been inundating him with urgent letters, and if she herself were not a good friend of his. He wanted to see her happily married, making a good home for herself, her children, and the widower so-and-so and his children. The widower, her future husband, would not be just anybody, but an honorable Hasid of whom Hindele's family was sure to be proud.

In the meantime, it did not escape the notice of Hindele's children that whenever their mother's good friend Reb Menashele the Matchmaker paid her a visit in the loft, and they were sent out, it was with a swollen tear-washed face that she greeted them on their return. Finally Shalom put two and two together and whispered to Yacov, "He wants Mameshie to marry and she doesn't want to."

Astounded, Yacov gaped at his brother. "I don't want her to, either!" he exclaimed.

"She must," said Shalom, who was not a great talker.

"What do you mean, 'she must'? Who can force her if you and I don't allow it?"

"What can we do?"

"We'll go to Reb Menashele and warn him not to set foot in our house again. If he does, he'll have to deal with us."

"And you think that he's afraid of us? The Law is with him. The Law exists for Mameshie's good and for ours, too."

"That's a lie! The Law is a calamity!"

"Stop blaspheming," Shalom retorted, unusually agitated.

"I'll throw a rock through his window! I'll make him trip in the street! I'll empty a pot of boiling water on his head!" Yacov fumed.

Shalom shook his head. "It won't help much." But finally he gave in to Yacov. "All right," he said. "Let's try and put it off. We'll stand guard. We must tell Gitele and Shaindele too, so that if you're at the heder and I'm at the *besmedresh,* they will watch the house. Reb Menashele won't approach Mameshie on the Potcheyov, so if we see him enter the yard, we'll tell him that she's not at home and there's no need for him to climb the stairs. In the meantime, we'll take out the loose boards of the stairs just in case he decides to go up anyway and check. He would not dare call her through the window. Mameshie wouldn't like it."

As the spring progressed, Hindele often wondered why Reb Menashele had suddenly given up his regular visits. Once he had attempted to approach her on the Potcheyov, but she had rushed up to him, blushing, imploring him not to speak to her there, with all of Bociany looking on, but rather to come to her house. What exacerbated her crying was the fact that her two little girls, Gitele and Shaindele, seemed to know the reason for her tears and shouted at the matchmaker to "get away from our Mameshie!"

It was then that Hindele discovered that she had another supporter in her neighbor, Yossele Abedale. One day, when he noticed Reb Menashele walking toward Hindele, he grabbed him by the lapels and exclaimed threateningly, "You're here again!"

Reb Menashele spread open his arms innocently. "Don't get so excited. It's not you I've come to see. It's her." He pointed toward Hindele. "Her family wants her to get married, but she turns up her nose. What her dowry consists of, you can see for yourself." He indicated Hindele's two girls.

When Reb Menashele had gone, Yossele was confronted by a weeping Hindele. "You must understand, Reb Yossele," she sniffled. "You don't want your children to have a stepmother, and that's that. But I am a miserable woman who has no say over her own life, although . . . although my heart is not in it . . . "

"You can rely on me," Yossele said shortly. "He won't dare come near you here on the Potcheyov."

Hindele grew more optimistic, hoping that the Almighty would have pity on her and see to it that she never married again. In the meantime, she enjoyed a respite from that particular worry, and her face began to brighten. She was able to concentrate on her reading, until a word or a sentence triggered a memory of Itchele and she was again plunged into despair; or until Vaslav Spokojny paid her a sudden visit on the Potcheyov and her heart became a whirlpool of dread and fear.

When Nechele the Pockmarked visited her at home, the two women hummed their favorite tunes, told each other Hasidic stories, or talked about wonder rabbis, until the children fell asleep. Then they philosophized about life and people and exchanged thoughts on their own fates and those of women in general.

Most of the time during Nechele's visits, Yacov only pretended to be asleep. He was curious about the things that his mother and Nechele talked about. Sometimes Nechele repeated stories she had heard from Sore-Leyele, the ritual slaughterer's wife. Yacov would listen to his mother argue with Nechele. Her opinion of ghosts differed from that of both Nechele and Sore-Leyele.

One particular night he heard his mother say to Nechele, "If it is true that demons are like people, both in appearance and behavior, then we would be bumping into them at every turn. The thing is that they have no bodies. That's why, although the world is full of them, we don't bump into them. If a person saw a real demon, he would never be able to survive it."

"But you do believe, don't you, that every ghost has four fingers rather than five and that their thumbs are missing?" Nechele asked.

"I told you," Hindele softly insisted. "We don't see them because they're completely invisible."

"Are you trying to tell me," Nechele was flabbergasted, "that they don't leave any traces on the snow or on the bare ground? May I have as many good years as I've seen them in front of my very own door!"

"The footprints you saw were those of a cock, not a demon, Nechele."

"But surely you believe that you must not leave any food under the bed, or that it is dangerous to drink unboiled water on Wednesday or Saturday night?" Nechele, a fanatically clean and punctilious housekeeper, boiled water every day of the week, to be on the safe side. She was convinced that ghosts were slobs who hated cleanliness.

"We must not leave food under our beds," Hindele responded, determined to hold fast to her own convictions, "because it attracts mice. And besides, there are all kinds of worms in the water, so it's healthier to boil it. Shmulikl the Doctor said exactly that to Manka downstairs."

"Do you believe what Shmulikl the Doctor says?"

"What difference does it make if I believe it or not? It's a fact that he cured Manka's children of diarrhea."

"Well, but at least you believe that it's dangerous to do things in pairs, don't you? Sore-Leyele has explicitly stated that a person must not drink two glasses of coffee, or four glasses, one after another. Nor should a person take two lumps of sugar, or eat two potatoes or four potatoes, because it attracts demons. The only exceptions are the four glasses of wine that are drunk at the Passover seder, she said."

"That seems silly to me," Hindele countered. "The limbs of a human being come in pairs. We have a pair of hands, a pair of legs, and also a pair of eyes and a pair of ears. Demons and ghosts are not what children imagine. Their world makes up only one face of the universe, which has thousands upon thousands of faces, one on top of the other. If these worlds were all as tangible as our own tangible world, they could not all be in the same place at the same time, could they, Nechele?"

"God's wonders are great," Nechele sighed. This reaction was the best proof of her devotion to Hindele; Nechele liked her so much that she forgave all her silly notions.

Hindele was a greater riddle to Nechele than even Sore-Leyele was. Hindele was a dreamer just like Sore-Leyele, who was also steeped in other worlds. Hindele herself had told her that when she was busy doing something with her hands, like scrubbing the floor or kneading the dough for the Sabbath noodles, her head was always somewhere else. Little wonder that she did not always notice that her wig was lying askew on her head or that her nose was running. However, unlike Sore-Leyele, who sometimes ruined her own housework, by creating *kashrut* problems while preparing a meal, Hindele was fully aware of what went on around her. It was as if Hindele had two minds; one was off, flying about, while the other was concentrating on the task at hand. She managed very well about getting supplies for her shop, and she could calculate like a man. Sore-Leyele, on the other hand, was either steeped in morbid presentiments or was exulting and joyous. Hindele took the middle road; she liked both to cry and to laugh, but without exaggeration. Nor was she shy about asking for sympathy when she wanted to be consoled, yet she herself could console others just as well as a loving mother. Nechele, who usually said exactly what she thought, pretended to respect Hindele's outrageous opinions about demons, although in truth they made her worry about Hindele's sanity. She kept her peace in order to preserve their friendship.

Yacov, as he lay on his mattress and listened, naturally agreed with his mother's opinions. Nonetheless he could see some truth in what Nechele the Pockmarked said, too. He was convinced that demons were invisible, yet sometimes they were very visible, staring out of the faces of people whom he met every day. This added another perplexity to his general confusion about matters of good and evil.

Just as Hindele had a devoted friend in Nechele, so Yacov had a bosom friend in Ariele, Fishele the Butcher's son. That year, Yacov often visited

Ariele and was coming to like this sturdy, round-faced boy more and more. Ariele was straightforward, proud of his good mind but not conceited, and he was also fun-loving. He resembled his father in his robust delight in all things sensual, and in glorying in his own courage and strength.

Yacov grew even more attached to Ariele when he discovered that Ariele was just as confused about important matters as he was. Whenever they met for walks, during the increasingly longer and brighter evenings of spring, and wandered through the alleys where the bud-laden trees stared down at them from over the fences on both sides, Yacov and Ariele speculated on the issue of justice. If they were caught in a spring shower, they set off at a gallop, deliberately jumping in all the deepest water puddles. Soaking wet, they would arrive at Ariele's house, which was still being heated because Ariele's mother suffered from the disease of the rich: she was rheumatic. The boys would shut themselves up in a tiny alcove, lay their clothes out to dry on the oven pipes, and settle down to "study," by which they meant continue their endless discussions.

Ariele was Reb Shapsele the Melamed's most brilliant student, and he was treated like a god by his family. Nobody ever dared to shout at him. His father pinned all his hopes on him, convinced that his gifted son was his best "trump card," and that, thanks to Ariele, a large chunk of his own sins would be taken off the scale during the final reckoning before his Maker. Ariele was whipped by his father only if the *melamed* complained that he was neglecting his studies. If Ariele strayed from the road, Fishele would be doomed, and the gates of Gehenna would open up to receive him. But Reb Shapsele could rarely substantiate his charges with proof that Ariele neglected his studies, since Ariele always knew much more than was required of him, despite his mischief-making. Fishele and all the members of the household walked around on tiptoe when Ariele was studying. Ariele was given the best parts of all the food, as if he were a prince. Whatever Ariele said was not just "wise" and "learned," it was sacred, almost divine, and both his parents listened to him reverently.

This particular evening the boys were sitting in Ariele's little room, studying a Gemara by the light of a spotlessly clean naphtha lamp. Yacov noticed that Ariele was oddly nervous and was not concentrating at all. He looked as if he were listening to the sound of someone pacing in the other room. Yacov did not dare to say anything.

Then Ariele whispered, "Can you hear him pacing up and down?"

"Yes, I can hear someone pacing," Yacov admitted.

"That's my father's visitor. He brought him home last night from Chwosty, very secretly."

"Why secretly?"

"He's supposed to be a holy man who has severed all ties with this world. Only his followers have the right to see him. My father takes food in to him. Last night they sat together and talked and talked. I think that my father sold his soul to the Devil the day he became a butcher. And do you know what else I think? I think that the man in that room is not a holy man at all but Asmodeus himself. I peeked in at him last night through the crack in the wall. He has no horns or anything like that, but he is all black and his evil eyes burn like torches. And what I heard was . . . Well, I don't know why, but I feel I must save my father from him. Father doesn't know the Scriptures, but he's a good man. The Devil is taking advantage of his ignorance. That stranger talks so that I myself almost begin to believe him. But at least I know that it is wrong, terribly wrong."

A shudder rippled over Yacov's skin. "Whatever you decide to do, I'll help you," he whispered.

"You will? Then let's listen to him together. We'll figure out what he's after. If we discover that he wants to take Father away with him, we'll set fire to his clothes and burn him."

"How can we do that?"

"We'll sneak inside his room. Last night he went out to the outhouse like a normal human being. I heard him. I didn't follow him because I wasn't suspicious yet. It was only when Father refused to introduce me and went in to see him alone that I became suspicious. So the next time this visitor goes to the outhouse, we'll sneak into his room, hide under the bed, and when we both decide that I'm right about him, we'll signal to each other, light a match and set fire to his gabardine."

"But if he is Asmodeus, then he'll know that we're there, and Asmodeus is not afraid of fire," Yacov whispered, his teeth chattering.

"True, but he pretends not to be Asmodeus, but a holy *tsadik*. If he shows his real face, he'll lose Father's soul. And he won't be able to lay a hand on us, because we'll say *kri-shma* and bring along a holy book, and you'll bring along an amulet from Reb Senderl."

"But it will be late at night. What will my mother say?"

"Tell her that you're sleeping over at my house, that we are going to study until very late."

Yacov's throat constricted with fear, but he nodded his agreement. It was high time he proved himself to Ariele; and then there was the problem of saving a soul from the Devil's hands. Granted, it seemed unlikely that two boys who were not even bar mitzvah yet could conquer the Devil by themselves, thereby erasing the source of all evil just by lighting a match. Granted, the clever Ariele was being unreasonable. But perhaps this strange visitor had already confused his mind, making him say and do unreasonable things? Yacov felt that for him at least there was no dilemma. His duty was to follow his friend to the gates of hell, if need be.

The following night everything went as Ariele had said it would. The two boys pretended to be studying in Ariele's room, where they chanted the Gemara text very loudly. Then the house grew silent and the beds in the other rooms squeaked. The two boys peered through the crack in the wall into the neighboring room, which was steeped in darkness. Someone inside was pacing. Then the door cracked, and they could hear the footsteps of someone leaving the adjoining room and walking into the vestibule. Then they heard steps squeaking in the mud outside.

"Now!" Ariele whispered, pulling Yacov with him by the sleeve.

They tiptoed across the vestibule, entered the visitor's room, quickly scrambled under the bed and, with bated breath, waited. Within a few minutes, Fishele the Butcher entered the room with something white gleaming in his hands—a plate. He placed it on the table and sat down slowly in a chair as if he were trying not to wake someone. A black figure of a man entered the room, humming. He wiped his hands on a white cloth.

"Rabbi . . . " the boys heard Fishele's voice implore with desperation, as if he were pleading to be saved from drowning. A chair squeaked lightly. "Do me a favor, Rabbi, and eat something. At least take a bite of the brisket or of the potato dumplings . . . "

"I have not come here to eat and be surfeited," a voice answered in a heavy whisper. "I have come to save your soul and the souls of an entire community. To make you whole and holy, have I come."

"Yes, Rabbi," Fishele whimpered. "But do me at least this small honor, and let me share my food with you. I am so sinful, so infested with the cravings of the flesh, so devoured by the lust for evil . . . Rabbi, please lift me up."

"I can lift no one up. This you must do by yourself. It is your responsibility."

"But you suffer so much for my sake, Rabbi."

"It is not for your sake that I suffer, but for the sake of the Eternal One, blessed be His name. And this is what you must learn, too. To suffer for Him. It is to teach you how to bear suffering that I have come, so that you may deserve His forgiveness. I must speak to you of suffering over and over again, until it becomes as much a part of you as your lust and the cravings of the flesh that are the tools of your salvation."

"Oh yes, Rabbi. You can speak to me of it, but first take a bite of food, I beg you."

"Very well then, if you insist. I will swallow your food, in order that you may, in return, swallow my words."

"I will. Speak to me, Rabbi, and eat in good health."

The boys heard the benediction over the food, then a voice speaking through a mouth still partly full, saying, "You must remember that this world of ours was not created by the Eternal One, but by the Evil One." A series of noisy smacks followed as though someone were being loudly kissed. "That is why there is suffering and death in the world. It is only by learning how to conquer suffering and death, integrating them into our lives so that we no longer fear them, that we can save this fallen world. You must believe this with all your heart and all your soul. In order to save man, to save the People of Israel, we must pass untarnished through the gates of evil and impurity. We must seek them out, not run away from them. We must dance with joy as we surrender to sin, so that we may conquer it. Do you believe in this with all your being? Answer me."

"I do, I do," Fishele mumbled eagerly.

"The world will never be saved and there will be no redemption, if the bravest of us lack the courage to descend into the very bowels of evil, in order to salvage the sparks of holiness that fell into the darkness when the vessels were broken at the Creation, and Adam, instead of saving them, allowed them to sink even deeper. Will you remember that?"

"I will, I will," Fishele stammered.

"The Messiah himself will have the hardest burden," the voice went on. "He will be prevented from observing the Torah as he lowers himself down deeper than the deepest depths. He needs the brave and the righteous to stand by him, to believe in him even when he takes on the face of the Devil himself. Will you remember that everlasting goodness can be achieved through sin, that the Commandments can be observed by not observing them, and that all these acts must be accomplished with the greatest secrecy? Answer me!"

"I will," Fishele answered, choking on his voice.

"Will you also believe that the Messiah can take on the shape of a woman, a maiden, a beautiful *Matronitha* who has no eyes, who can and will violate the *Toyre,* who will abandon the faith and, steeped in dirt, go whoring—all this in order to save us? Will you serve her, love her, covet her, and sin with her, in order that holiness be saved and the world redeemed?"

"I will," Fishele whispered passionately.

Ariele squeezed Yacov's arm. It was time to carry through their plan, for there could no longer be any doubt about who this *"tsadik"* was. But Yacov shook his head violently and held on to Ariele's arm with all his strength. Ariele tried frantically to free himself, and Yacov just as frantically wrestled with him. They were in danger of drawing attention to their presence. Realizing this, they grew quiet and lay where they were, listening further, mesmerized by the visitor's voice, his words, by the air of mystery and magic pervading the room.

Fishele, apparently growing drowsy, was still repeating, "I will," to each of the visitor's urgent questions, but his words were increasingly accompanied by yawns. The visitor finally dismissed him.

The boards of the bed under which the boys were lying began to creak. Above their heads the stranger lay stretched out, groaning heavily, mumbling words to himself that gradually turned into a loud, healthy snore, followed by a wheezing whistle. The room became full of these sounds, as if a machine were working away in it. Under cover of the snores, the boys managed to wriggle themselves out from under the bed and leave the room without a sound. They slipped back into Ariele's room and slumped down on his cot.

Ariele burst into sobs. "I knew that you were a coward! May I lose my tongue for ever, having confided in you! May I burn on the stake of Gehenna!"

"Don't say that." Yacov had never seen Ariele cry before. A wave of despair swept over him. Now, just when he had been prepared to be brave and to prove his devotion to Ariele—what inner obstacle had prevented him from doing so? "I just didn't hate him enough to want to burn him," he whispered guiltily.

"Of course!" Ariele fumed, still sobbing. "It's not your father he's got in his hands, it's mine! Your father has a secure place in the Garden of Eden!"

"Please, Ariele. It's not that. It's that I agree with him . . . a little."

"You do?"

"I think so."

There was a long silence. "So do I," Ariele confessed after a long pause. "Oh, dear God! I hoped he wouldn't trap you in his nets, too."

"I think he is right when he says that the world could not have been created by the Heavenly Father. And he is right when he says that even pure evil still possesses a spark of . . . But do you agree with committing sins, too, Ariele?"

Ariele sniffled for a while, then answered, "If it means saving the world . . ."

"Could you kill and murder? Could you . . . Could you go and sleep with a gentile woman?"

"To save the world . . . "

"But how can you save the world with blood on your hands? How can you save the world if you stink? That's what I don't understand."

"You said yourself that the world is not good."

"So you want to make it even worse by adding evil to it?"

"Yes . . . No . . . Oh, Yacov, he confused us. He trapped us with his smooth words, don't you see? He is the Evil One himself. I feel it in my bones. Don't you?"

"No," Yacov whispered. "An ordinary human being could have said the same things if his mind were tormented, gone crazy with all the horrors and suffering he has been through."

The boys continued whispering and weeping together, engulfed in their despair, pitying themselves and all of humanity. They stared with dread at the dark windows, until the spring dawn brightened the room and the chirping birds lulled them to sleep.

## 9

THE STORKS HAD RETURNED along with the profusion of colors and fragrances. The fields and forests were all covered with a fresh, delicate green. Young leaves fluttered and rustled like the wings of swarming birds. Clusters of blooms covered the lilac trees, and soon the cherry and apple trees were similarly graced. The soil steamed, seeming ready to rise like yeast bread. The shtetl of Bociany was all smiles.

Suddenly, just before Passover, a chilling wind brought a late-winter snowstorm on its tail. It was as though the spring had regretted its premature arrival and had withdrawn its arsenal of cheer and sunshine, just to spite the Jews. For the worst of the storm raged through the shtetl on the morning of the day of the first seder. It was heartbreaking to watch the storks shiver in confusion.

But the people of Bociany went on excitedly with the last preparations for the holiday. Homes were thoroughly inspected and swept clean of every trace of *hometz*. People koshered utensils, scrubbed pieces of furniture in the snowy outdoors, and attended to the last bits of business that remained to be cleared up before the holiday.

When the storm finally abated at noontime—as if it were conquered by the shtetl's sunny disposition—Hindele sent Yacov over to Reb Senderl the Cabalist's shop, to remind him that he had accepted her invitation to lead the Passover seder at her home.

Yacov disregarded his mother's pleas to put on his winter coat, but otherwise carried out her instructions. The moment he entered Reb Senderl's shop, he repeated her invitation word-for-word. But then it occurred to him to take advantage of the opportunity to "press Reb Senderl to the wall" by asking him a few questions. He had been burning to tell the old man about Fishele the Butcher's visitor, who had disappeared the following day, and about Fishele's wife's two silver candlesticks, which had disappeared along with him. Evidently the stranger practiced what he preached, namely, dishonesty and theft. Or maybe he was just an ordinary thief who had wormed his way into Fishele's house and had taken advantage of Fishele's ignorance. And yet there had been something to what this stranger had said; his words lingered in Yacov's mind, and he craved an explanation. But he was bound by the oath of silence that he had given Ariele.

So all he could do was to repeat his usual set of questions and conclude by asking Reb Senderl, "If all human experiences were also experienced by the Almighty, then surely He also experiences poverty and hunger. But how could the One who possesses everything, at the same time suffer from want and be poor and hungry as well?"

Reb Senderl replied by telling Yacov a story by the Bal-shem Tov, a story of a mighty king who lived in a palace of four hundred chambers, full of crystal, gold, silver, and jewels. The king sat on a throne of gopher wood and precious stone. All around him his treasures sparkled with a light that was impossible to describe. There the king sat, ready to receive the visitors who had spent all their lives trying to get a glimpse of the king's face.

"You understand?" Reb Senderl's eyes lit up like two blue lanterns. "When the visitors entered the king's palace, they didn't know where to look first, they were so dazzled. There was so much treasure lying around that they completely forgot what they had come for, but rushed from one room to the other, filling their bags with gold and silver and precious stones. The riches were unguarded, and everyone could take as much as he wanted. There was so much to take, so many chambers to go through, that they never got to see the king's face, although this had been their original desire. Only a few of the visitors, so few that you could count them on the fingers of one hand, behaved differently. They were the ones who had no sooner entered the palace than they raced through the chambers, looking neither to the right nor to the left, until they saw the face of the king in all its glory. Then they looked about them and realized that there was no palace, no chambers, no treasures; that poor was not poor and rich was not rich; that there were no divisions. For the king was as close as one's breath, closer still, for the king and the visitor shared the same breath. And this is my answer to your question."

Yacov stood with his head turned away from Reb Senderl, gazing through the open door, as he let the old man's words sink in. Oh yes, he had understood the story all right. He was just sick and tired of it, as he was of his mother's stories. They never answered his questions, they only dulled the acuteness of his craving for the truth. He preferred the words of Fishele's strange visitor. The latter had at least called for action, vile and horrible though it was. At least he had hinted at the possibility of change.

Yacov was considering how best to slip out of the shop without offending the old man, when he heard a strange commotion. He moved closer to the door and saw the gendarmes leading an echelon of prisoners, each chained to the other, through the marketplace. "Look, Reb Senderl!" he called out.

He stared at the shackles around the prisoners' ankles, at the long chain that attached one prisoner to the other, and at the bayonets fixed to the rifles in the hands of the gendarmes who followed behind. As the prisoners passed in front of the shop, Yacov could see the haggard faces of the men, the snow on their bare heads, on their eyebrows, and in the folds of their clothing. Yacov tried to imagine himself being one of them, to wear their threadbare clothes and walk in their shapeless boots, which were wrapped in rags up to the knees and were caked with snow and mud. A shudder went through his body.

The next moment a feeling of gratitude and relief overpowered him, and he felt a lump in his throat. He and his mother, his sisters, and his brother wore no chains. They were not chased through the snow and cold by gendarmes with bayonets. Tonight he would sit with them at the Passover table, read the Haggadah, and eat matzo-ball soup. Now he understood why Reb Senderl had said that his mother was fortunate. So she was—miserable, yet fortunate. And so was he, Yacov. They had a corner of the world they called their own, where they were all together.

"Where are they taking them?" he asked Reb Senderl, who had joined him at the door.

"To the Wide Poplar Road," the old man answered sadly.

"And from there?"

"Siberia, most probably. It's the fourth echelon this week. I've heard that there are Jews among them."

"What did they do to deserve this punishment?"

"They rebelled against the tsar. For us Jews, God is our emperor, but to the Gentiles the emperor is like a god and to rebel against him is the greatest crime. That is how the world takes revenge on those who try to destroy its established order. And . . . " Reb Senderl sighed deeply. "People tell me that this madness has infected thousands upon thousands. May Heaven preserve us from what might still happen."

Yacov did not hear him. He was still tense from watching the group of prisoners as they dragged themselves up the Wide Poplar Road. He could still hear the rusty clanking of the chains and see the forward slant of the men's bodies pushing against the mud. On both sides, the colorful snow-covered clusters of cherry and lilac blossoms bent low before them in the wind. From the distance, the gendarmes who held the ends of the chains looked like convicts themselves, tied to the fate of the captives whom they led. Yacov pitied them too.

He noticed that one of the prisoners at the end of the column suddenly tripped over the shackles of the man in front of him. Both fell over, dragging the rest of the group down, as well as one of the guards in the rear. The guard was on his feet again in an instant. He poked the two men between the shoulders with his bayonet. The two stood up, but the rest became even more entangled and again pulled down the two who had made it to their feet. The guard in the rear whacked the heap of entangled bodies with the butt of his rifle and kicked them with his boot.

"I will become a rebel too!" Yacov cried and ran out of Reb Senderl's shop.

With the tails of his caftan flying and his tasseled undergarment waving in the air like a flag, he raced in the direction of the prisoners. Several times the cap and skullcap fell from his head, and he was forced to turn back, retrieve them, and wet and muddy though they were, put them back on his head as he sped on. The prisoners at the bottom of the heap needed help, a hand to hold on to, in order to get up; then the entire group would be back on its feet. It was unbearable to watch the gendarme in the rear kick with his heavy boot at the helpless bodies.

Yacov halted by the side of the road, a dozen footsteps from the prisoners. Gentile boys had come running in a great rush from the yards and fields, stopping in front of the ditch that bordered the road. Yacov knew them all and moved closer to his friend Bronek, Manka the Washerwoman's son, who sucked on a twig while he stared at the sight before him with his blue eyes wide open.

"Come on, let's help them get up!" Yacov called to the boys.

They grinned uneasily at him. Long Stefek, the eldest among them, a lank boy with a face full of pimples, replied with a whistle through the hole of his two missing front teeth, "The soldiers will kill us."

Yacov, frozen in one place, stared at the boys searchingly. "Then I'll do it myself," he stammered, taking a deep breath. A voice within him called him to retreat. He had to hurry to his mother, to help her prepare for the Passover. He had to free himself of the horrible sight before him. "So I'll do it myself," he repeated. Again he inhaled deeply and returned a courageous glance to the mocking, disbelieving stares of the boys around him.

He turned quickly and rushed straight toward the heap of bodies still wriggling in the mud, entangled in chains and coats, still cringing under the blows of the gendarme's boot.

As he ran, Yacov pictured himself in his mind falling on his knees beside the men and helping those on the very bottom to stand up. But he stopped just behind the gendarme's back. He stood paralyzed, unable to make his legs take another step. A moment later, he was speeding breathlessly home, his chest struggling for air. He burst into loud sobs. It seemed to him that he heard the boys' laughter behind his back mingled with the guards' guffaws, and those of the prisoners as well. The prisoners! What had happened to them? Despite his shame, he had to stop and turn to look back—he had to know. Through his tears he saw that all the prisoners were back on their feet. "Thank Heaven!" he sighed with relief, rubbing his face with both hands. He did not move until he saw the chains disentangled and the prisoners beginning to march off. The guard was again attached to the chain as if he, too, were one of the doomed.

The gentile boys ran toward Yacov. He noticed them talking with great animation among themselves. His first impulse was to escape, but he controlled himself, steeled by the memory of his cowardice just a moment before. He began marching home at a fast pace, but he did not run, although he expected to be hit at any minute. The boys drew abreast of him, still whispering among themselves and shaking their heads gravely. Soon they had surrounded Yacov and were staring at him as if at an apparition, less with mockery than with admiration.

"He's crying real tears!" they pointed at him.

A girl who had joined the group whispered in awe, "He has a real Christian soul."

Yacov wiped his face on a sleeve. "I'm not crying anymore," he said, trying to advance.

He managed to walk only a few steps more before the entire group of children blocked his way. They called to others in the fields and yards. An ever larger crowd surrounded Yacov and kept him from moving on. They whispered among themselves with great earnestness, giving him looks full of compassion and pity as they trooped around him. Stupefied, he stared back at them questioningly. They responded with grave nods, expressions akin to those of affection on their faces, their eyes alight with curiosity and awe mixed with a kind of playful excitement.

"Would you like an entire head of cabbage for free?" Long Stefek asked Yacov whistling through the hole in his missing teeth.

"Of course I would," Yacov replied.

"And I will give you such a big piece of coal," another boy said, spreading his arms to show Yacov the size of the coal.

"And I will give you a scarf for your mother, for your holiday," a little girl squealed.

"I will give you something, too," added Bronek, Yacov's friend.

"Me too!" cried his elder sister, Marysia, in a friendly tone of voice.

The other children yelped, "Me too! Me too!"

In his imagination Yacov saw himself displaying for his mother the piece of coal, the head of cabbage, and the other gifts that he would receive from his gentile friends for the holidays. He allowed them to lead him back in the direction of the village. Instead of taking the side path, however, they continued along the Wide Poplar Road. Yacov did not understand this. "Where are we going?" he asked Long Stefek, who was walking beside him.

"We have a treasure buried in the birch wood." Long Stefek gave the others a meaningful look as he waited for them to nod their heads in confirmation, which after some hesitation they did. "There we'll give you all the good things we promised and more."

Yacov was growing suspicious and regretted his decision to follow them. "I must turn back," he mumbled. But curiosity got the better of him and he continued following them. "Today is Passover eve," he explained. "I have a lot to do."

"Our Passover is coming, too," Stefek replied dryly. "We, too, must prepare ourselves."

The children were still whispering among themselves. Stefek said something in the ear of the boy next to him, and a few of the children made off in the direction of the village huts. After a while, they came racing back and caught up with the rest of the crowd. In their hands they held ropes and rags.

Yacov pushed over to his friend Bronek, "What did they bring the ropes and the rags for?" he asked.

"That's for you." Long Stefek had overheard the question and delivered the explanation with a gap-toothed grin. "To wrap all the goodies and tie them up into a parcel."

When Stefek's head was turned, Bronek's sad blue eyes lit up warmly as he put his hand on Yacov's shoulder. "It's for you, but . . . " He wanted to say more but Stefek was looking, so he covered his mouth with the twig.

Stefek yelled that they should hurry, and the band of children accelerated their pace. They were breathing heavily as the procession advanced in tense silence, all eyes riveted on Yacov, who was feeling more and more frightened. A cold breeze blew through the poplar trees. He wrapped his caftan tightly around his body. His mind endlessly repeated a line from the Torah, "Here is the fire and here is the altar, but where is the lamb for the sacrifice?"

Were the gentile children going to kill him? Probably. Why else would they be walking so quietly, whispering among themselves? They had tricked him, cheated him. They were on their way to the birch wood to slaughter him. Slaughter him? Would Bronek, walking beside him so sadly, frantically sucking on the twig, slaughter his good friend and neighbor, Yacov? "Yes, he would," the voice within Yacov replied. He was stunned by the thought. How could he be so sure? How could it be that he should suspect a friend of wanting to do such a thing? For the unforgivable sin of thinking badly about a friend, Yacov decided that he deserved to be killed.

One way or another, he knew that he had to save himself, if only to spare his mother the sorrow. But there were hands restraining him now. He was trapped. He had recently taken to practicing his running, but he was still no match for Long Stefek. He could always scream or wrestle with them, but what difference would that make? All the huts along the road belonged to Gentiles. And just as the children, with Yacov trapped in their midst, drew nearer to the Jewish inn and the stables of the Jewish horse dealer, Yacov was led off the road into the field. In the distance was the Blue Mountain; at its top stood the windmill of Reb Faivele the Miller, its sails spinning, like arms rising toward the Heavens and coming down in silent surrender. No one would hear Yacov's scream from where he was. The howling wind made it difficult for the children even to hear each other. The gusts swallowed their words, and Yacov could understand nothing of what they were saying.

No one would have any idea where his bones lay. The children would probably throw his corpse into the lake. Nor would his eyes surface to swim on the face of thc water like those of Kailele the Bride, for the ice floes had completely melted and he would drown, immediately sinking to the very bottom of the lake. It was all because he was a coward, afraid even to escape death, just as before he had been afraid of helping the convicts who had fallen in the mud. Sometimes there was heroism in escaping and sometimes cowardice. If Yacov escaped, it would only be out of cowardice. So he would lie at the bottom of the lake as the summer arrived in Bociany. The trees would be heavy with fruit and the scent of the jasmine and acacia would rise from the nuns' garden and fill the garret. But he would not be there to smell them anymore. He would never smell or feel anything again.

He glanced sideways at Bronek. "You have no coal or cabbage hidden in the woods, do you?" he asked in a whisper. Bronek, still sucking on the twig, shook his head. "You're going to kill me in the woods, aren't you?"

Bronek looked questioningly at Long Stefek, who was listening. The latter thought for a while, then blinked at Bronek as though giving him permission to speak. Slowly Bronek removed the twig from his mouth and replied in a hoarse whisper. "We're not really going to kill you, only to play at killing."

"Why? What have I done to you?" Yacov stammered, his eyes fixed on Bronek's plump, sad face. Bronek was his only hope. "We're good friends," he reminded him.

"And that's why . . . " Bronek was so moved that he could barely speak. He blinked his sad blue eyes, which had turned misty, and when he spoke, his voice had a tremor in it. "That's why they say that I must be Judas, although I'm not a Jew. But that's what I must be."

"What do I have to do with Judas?" Yacov felt sick to his stomach.

"You do," another boy replied, also very moved. "You'll be our beloved Pan Jesus, because you're a Jew with a Christian soul. Not a single one of us cried when the convicts fell in the mud. You were the only one who wanted to help them, and we laughed at you."

"I don't want to be your Jesus!" Yacov called out in exasperation, as a chill passed through him.

"You must. You're a Jew," a boy laughed uneasily.

"Our poor, poor Pan Jesus," a girl sniffled.

Yacov made a frantic attempt to tear himself free of the arms that were holding him. But Long Stefek's hand was like a manacle clamped around his arm. Yacov continued struggling, twisting his arm in all directions and pulling backwards with all his strength. Stefek kicked him from behind.

"What are you kicking me for?" Yacov roared with pain.

"Pan Jesus was also kicked and spat at on his way," Stefek said calmly and spat into Yacov's face. "And you are not allowed to try to free yourself from my hands."

"Yes . . . Now you're on the way . . . " Bronek whispered in Yacov's ear in a soft voice. He bit into his twig and turned back his head to see if he could find his sister Marysia. "How was it called, the road that Pan Jesus Christ took?" he shouted at her.

Marysia came closer and wiped a tear from her cheek. "The Road to Golgotha, that's what they called it."

"Golgotha! Golgotha!" the children chanted.

"Then we must make a cross for him right away. He must carry it on his back!" one of the children called out.

A little girl pulled at Stefek's sleeve, "He must wear a crown of thorns! And he must fall and stand up again and then again."

"Burrs and thistles!" Stefek commanded, pulling both the cap and the skullcap from Yacov's head.

The children darted into the bushes, then tossed burrs on Yacov's head, where they stuck in his hair. The procession halted amid great noise. A girl insisted on covering Yacov's head with a perfectly round wreath made of burrs and thistles, but he was twisting so much that his head rolled in every direction and refused to stay still. In the meantime, a few boys climbed the pine tree that stood in the middle of the field and broke off two large boughs. Then they cleaned them of the needles and smaller shoots. Other boys busied themselves untying the cords and smoothing out the rags they had brought along. With most of the children busy preparing the Jesus costume, Yacov gathered his strength for yet another attempt at escape. But Stefek held him firmly, and two other strong boys helped to restrain him. Yacov, filled with the dread of dying, began to wail. Some of the children, themselves moved to tears, surrounded him and gave him sympathetic pats on the shoulder.

He felt the hand of Bronek on his shoulder. "You must not cry," Bronek whispered, barely restraining his own tears. "Pan Jesus must have pity on others, not on himself. He did not cry when he was on the road to . . . You must pray for us and for me too. Don't forget, I am your friend, and . . . " Bronek turned toward his sister. "What did Pan Jesus say to the people who tortured him?" he asked.

Marysia approached Yacov and stroked his back, "'Forgive them, God, for they know not what they do.' That's what Pan Jesus said."

The boys tied the partly peeled branches into a cross, which they tried to place on Yacov's shoulder. Yacov howled and squirmed so much that again and again he shook the cross off his back. "Tie it to him, quick! Tie the cross to him! Here's some rope!" An excited boy spread a piece of rope over the cross.

They threw Yacov to the wet, muddy ground, face down, and tied his wrists back. Then they fastened the cross to his shoulders.

They made him stand up again, and then the girls covered him with the rags they had brought along. Stefek pushed him forward. Yacov stumbled, picked himself up, fell, and rolled over in the grass again and again. The children stared wide-eyed and held their breath. They were all weeping now. Even Long Stefek was deeply touched; his pimples had turned a fiery red.

"Pray for us, dearest Pan Jesus!" The girls circled around Yacov, falling on their knees into the mud before him, crossing themselves and wringing their hands. The younger ones were wailing with increased fear in their voices, as Yacov almost toppled over on top of them.

"Don't cry. You mustn't cry." Bronek chased after Yacov until he was abreast of him. He whispered heatedly in his ear, "You do forgive us, don't you, Yacov? You do forgive us?"

"No!" Yacov shook his head violently.

"Please forgive us!" the others echoed, also falling to their knees and raising their folded hands to Yacov.

"No! No!" he roared like a wounded animal.

Long Stefek was growing impatient. He poked Yacov between the shoulders, pushing him forward with a powerful punch of his fist. "You must forgive us! Didn't you hear what Marysia said? You must forgive us, because we don't know what we're doing." He planted a kick on Yacov's rear.

"You do know!" Yacov screamed hoarsely. "You're kicking me!"

"Then forgive us!" Stefek kicked him again.

"I don't want to!" Yacov screeched, his throat hoarse. "You can kill me and still I won't forgive you!" Suddenly, he stopped and planted himself firmly in the muddy ground. The entire awe-stricken band of children stopped with him. For some inexplicable reason, they no longer pushed him on. "Good!" he exclaimed in the same shrill voice. "Come on, all of you! Come to the woods and kill me!" And with the cross still tied to his back, he slipped out of the bewildered Stefek's grasp and raced ahead alone, running with all his strength and at full speed. He could no longer cry because he had no tears left, but from his throat there emerged a wheezing sound. He kept on running over the grassy puddles without daring to stop, hands still tied behind his back, the cross shaking like a threatening whip over his head, the rags flying in all directions. He headed straight for the birch wood.

The crowd of children stood transfixed in the middle of the field, gaping after him, as if they were witnessing a miracle. But then a few recovered from their bewilderment and shouted angrily, "He's not a good Jesus! Pan Jesus is not supposed to run away with the cross!"

"Let's go and get him back!" Stefek ordered. "We'll soon catch him and he'll have to be a good Jesus."

"Catch him! Catch him!" the children yelled, dashing across the field at a gallop.

Yacov did not stop running. Now it was just a matter of moving his legs. They performed as if they were detached from his body. The tears on his face had dried, but now the sweat was pouring down his forehead into his eyebrows, burning his eyes. His clothes were glued to his body. He felt ready for anything. A part of him was coldly curious about what would happen. Now he understood not just what the prisoners in their chains had felt, but more, much more. Then he felt himself aflame with rage. Why did this need to happen? Whatever the reason, he was determined not to surrender. With the last ounce of strength left in his legs, he continued to run. He would not give up! They would not do to him what Stefek wanted . . .

He looked over his shoulder and saw with amazement that there was a distance between himself and the advancing mob. Even Stefek and a few others, although they were the nearest, were still separated from him by a good stretch of field. This renewed the supply of energy to his limbs. "I must be brave! I mustn't be a Soft Mirl!" he said to himself, panting, as he turned in the direction of the barns near the Wide Poplar Road. There his mother had once pointed out a patch of beautiful sunflowers to him. He noticed them in spite of his rush. They were still very young and fragile. He looked back once more and saw Stefek with the others following like a swarm of locusts, moving toward the road on the other side of the barns. Yacov came out on the road at the same time as the children also emerged there behind him. He sped ahead, scanning the distance for the sight of another human figure. "There is nothing to dying, nothing at all," he tried to reassure himself, his heart throbbing wildly.

He heard the sound of a horse's hooves. A four-wheeler softly appeared from the distance ahead. "Help! Help!" Yacov yelled, and without thinking, dashed straight toward the oncoming horse. The wagon slowed down. Yacov jumped to the side, raising his head toward the black-bearded, broad-shouldered man who drove the wagon.

The man jerked at the reins, stopped the horse and called out in Yiddish, "Good Heavens! A Jewish boy with his head uncovered!" With one pull of his strong arm, he helped Yacov into the four-wheeler. "And what's that?" He quickly broke some twigs off Yacov's back and untied his hands. "You looked like a Jesus from afar with this . . . this cross on your back and this gear on your head. What in Heaven's name were you up to?"

Yacov could not answer. A lump in his throat took his breath away. Shaking violently, he pointed to the mob of children who were now only a few steps away from the wagon. "Hurry! Hurry!" he moaned.

"Hoo-sha!" the man called, swishing the whip in the direction of the children so that they would come no closer. He elbowed Yacov away. "Just a minute! You'll end up by pricking my eyes out with these sticks and thorns. "

"They're coming again! Here they are! They'll kill me!" Yacov screamed frantically, while raising his free hand to his head to get the thistles and burrs out of his hair.

"Who'll kill you? What'll kill you?" The man threw the ropes and the rest of the broken branches into the ditch in front of the poplar trees. The whip swished through the air again, in the direction of the children, who still stood by the side of the road. "Hoo-sha! Hoo-sha!" he called at them gaily, then gave a yank at the reins. Yacov turned his head, wiped his face, and stuck his tongue out at Stefek and the others who remained behind. Before long, he felt composed enough to tell the man, slowly and between deep sighs, as he continued plucking thistles from his hair, what the children had wanted to do to him.

The man's face clouded over. "Had their God been living amongst them today, they would crucify him every Monday and Thursday." He turned to Yacov. "Whose son are you?"

"Hindele the Scribe's Widow's," Yacov replied. "And you are Reb Faivele the Miller, of course."

"Clear as the day! And now I'd better take you home or your mother will be so sick with worry that she won't have time to get into a good mood for the seder."

Yacov kept looking back in order to measure the distance dividing him from the gentile children. He said gratefully to Reb Faivele, "If you hadn't appeared on the road, my mother's seder would really have been spoiled. The Gentiles would have killed me if I had played Jesus the way they wanted me to, or even if I hadn't. Do you understand, Reb Faivele?"

Reb Faivele gave him an appraising glance. "If you're aware of that at your age, then you must be carrying an old head on your young shoulders. How is it you're so clever, tell me?" He handed Yacov a handkerchief to cover his head.

"Clever, Reb Faivele?" Yacov was suddenly so joyful that he could not keep from talking. "When somebody finds himself in a situation like the one I was just in, he can't be clever, believe me. And the worst of it is that in just such a situation one must be at one's most clever." He quickly made four knots in each corner of the large white handkerchief and slipped it on his head.

"What do you mean?" Reb Faivele stared intently at Yacov.

"I mean that when one is in danger, one needs to keep one's head on one's shoulders. The problem is that at precisely such a moment, one loses one's head completely. In general, Reb Faivele, it is high time to find a solution. The Jews must find a solution."

"What do you mean by a solution?"

"We must do something. The world is not good the way it is."

Reb Faivele nodded, talking as if to himself, "Well, there are those who are in fact doing something. They are doing so much that soon the world will stand upside down. But whether it'll do any good for us Jews, now that is the great question."

"Who's doing, Reb Faivele? You're not, by any chance, thinking of the convicts who were being driven to Siberia?"

"Actually, my friend, it's all been done already. The ball's over. But no one can ever know what tomorrow will bring."

"What's done? Please tell me, Reb Faivele. I'll be bar mitzvah soon. I'll understand."

"Revolution. Do you know the meaning of that?"

Yacov gaped at Reb Faivele at the sound of the unknown word. "What?"

"A chicken in the pot!" Reb Faivele exclaimed, jesting. They had arrived at the marketplace. With his whip handle, Reb Faivele pointed at the shops on the Potcheyov. "You see, your mother has closed up already. She must be busy preparing the seder. I'll let you off here." Yacov had to swallow his questions. He was still very curious, but there was no time now. He jumped down from the four-wheeler and thanked Reb Faivele profusely, wishing him a happy Passover. "Wait!" Reb Faivele called after him. "I almost forgot the main thing. A gift for your mother for the holidays!" He leaned forward and threw open a white sack which sat in the front corner of the wagon.

Yacov raised his hands to Reb Faivele as if to ward off a blow. "I've already received a holiday gift from you today."

"Don't be such a smart aleck." Reb Faivele pretended to be angry. "What's the matter with you? You don't want a bag of matzo meal?"

"Matzo meal?" Yacov turned red in the face. "By all means, Reb Faivele," he muttered. "Mother will be in seventh heaven!" He smiled at the people who had gathered around the wagon.

From beneath the front seat, Reb Faivele pulled out a pile of creased paper bags and scooped a heap of matzo meal into one of them. "Here, and have a happy Passover, you and your family!" He handed Yacov the bag, then began distributing bags of matzo meal to the poor people who surrounded the wagon, calling each one by name. Yacov watched, mesmerized, until he saw Reb Faivele clean his hands and coattails, straighten up, and take the reins and the whip in his hands.

Yacov dashed home with such speed that he could hardly catch his breath. Nothing hurt him anymore. All the wounds and bruises of his body were now singing with joy. He had lived to bring something home to contribute to the Passover meal. It seemed to him that his hours of torment and tears had bought this gift for his mother. It was from her that he had learned that a man like Reb Faivele could be both a miller and a messenger from heaven who had delivered and rewarded him. As he passed the house of Manka the Washerwoman, he swore never to speak to her children again.

He raced into the loft, where Hindele was spreading sack cloth over the freshly scrubbed floor. Before she could open her mouth, he called out to her, "Look what I have, Mameshie! Matzo meal! A full bag! A gift for you from Reb Faivele the Miller for Passover!" He pushed the bag into her hands. When his eyes met hers, he smiled lamely, "The wind carried off my cap and skullcap, so Reb Faivele gave me his handkerchief to cover my head."

"Go out with Shalom later on and find them." Hindele wiped the sweat from her face with the edge of her apron. She undid the knots of Reb Faivele's handkerchief, and said with a sigh of relief, "It has to be washed and ironed before we return it. Thank Heavens you're safe. Gitele and Shaindele are looking for you all over Bociany. My heart was trembling all day in case something should spoil the seder. A mother's heart is so foolish."

"A mother's heart is not foolish." The words almost slipped out of Yacov's mouth as he covered his head with another skullcap. He was anxious to tell her what had really happened, but how could he? The slightest thing might spoil his mother's Passover mood.

And that was, in fact, what happened. Hindele's Passover mood was spoiled by a trifle. She quarreled with her friend Nechele the Pockmarked. Ironically, this quarrel made it easier for her to bear the beauty of the holiday.

On the first day of the holiday, right after the snowy eve, the weather turned mild and pleasant. It grew so warm as the day progressed that the damp evaporated and the snow vanished like a bad dream. The ground grew dry and firm. The sun did not hide behind a cloud for one moment, and everything that its rays touched was fringed with gold. The lilac, the cherry and apple blossoms looked so fresh that they seemed to have been polished by yesterday's snow. The odor of the fertilized fields dissipated, and intoxicating fragrances permeated the air. The storks circled high overhead out of sheer pleasure, taking their cue from the festively dressed Jews who attempted to soar with their minds above all their worries as they strolled through the streets, cheerful and talkative.

All of Bociany was outdoors, enjoying the glorious day. Those who did not walk sat in their doorways on pillows. The square near the marketplace, called the Garden, teemed with Hasidim dressed in black holiday gabardines, standing around in groups, chatting, gesticulating, and laughing at each other's pleasantries. Yacov and Shalom mingled with them and with the young men from the *besmedresh,* or they listened to the deliberations of the most distinguished elderly men of Bociany, who were seated on benches under the chestnut trees.

Hindele held her two daughters by the hand and strolled in the direction of the house belonging to Nechele the Pockmarked, whose door and windows gave out on the marketplace. Both of Hindele's daughters were dressed in new linen dresses, which she had herself sewn for them for Passover. Their hair was decorated with bows made of fresh taffeta ribbons cut from the rolls she sold in her shop. As soon as they all arrived at Nechele's door, the two girls rushed off to show their new dresses to their girlfriends in the newly cleaned marketplace. Nechele the Pockmarked brought out a long pillow and placed it along the outside step of her house. The two women sat down to enjoy the fresh air and to watch the people strolling by.

Hindele and Nechele observed the men from the wealthier homes, who kept to themselves as they sauntered slowly by, exuding an air of self-importance. Their black satin caftans, tied with silken cords around the waists, sparkled in the sunlight. Behind them promenaded their wives, dressed in ruffles and lace. The matrons wore bonnets or fancy head scarves decorated with all manner of sparkling pins. The younger ones wore thin nets studded with pearls over their attractive wigs.

The wives and daughters of the lessee and the wood merchant attracted the most attention. These women strolled together in a bright, colorful group. Their dresses, made of Persian fabrics, swayed and rustled alluringly; pinched in at the waist, the dresses spread in rich, loose folds to the rims of their elegant pantofles. The dresses were topped by stiff bodices, on which the women displayed the pieces of jewelry that they had received at their marriages, or on other important occasions. Although they were dressed traditionally, so as not to offend the people of the shtetl, they still had an aura of worldliness about them. Behind them, there followed a long procession of admiring and envious young shtetl women and girls in cheap new dresses they had sewn themselves, who now felt considerably less elegant than they had felt when they first stepped out from their homes.

"Do you see the way those pompous turkeys have decked themselves out?" Nechele nudged Hindele, motioning toward the lessee's and the wood merchant's wives and their entourage. "Did you see that jewelry? Those are the kinds of pins that pierce out the eyes of poor people."

Hindele stroked Nechele's lap, smiling. "If you wear a piece of jewelry like that on your chest, you can't see the beauty of it anyway. We at least can feast our eyes on their pins and brooches. In my opinion, the only ornament a person really possesses is her face."

Nechele wiped her face with the palms of her hands. "Then my pockmarked ornament would make a horse laugh."

Hindele peered affectionately into Nechele's eyes, which were baggy and surrounded by nets of wrinkles. "You make too much of your pockmarks. There is a light that illuminates people's faces. Your good deeds, your noble thoughts, even your dreams illuminate yours. The Gentiles see the same light emanating from the saints, whom they paint with white plates around their heads. The truth is that everyone wears such a plate of light or shadow around his or her head. Take the face of Reb Senderl the Cabalist. It shines brighter than a thousand jewels. Or the *rov's* face. If a person is attuned to it, she can sense the kind of light another person gives off. To my eyes, Nechele, your face is very beautiful." She pressed Nechele's rough wrinkled hand warmly.

Nechele was pleased, yet she doubted Hindele's sincerity. "You mean to say," she asked, "that you don't envy the lessee's wife at all?"

"Of course I do," Hindele said. "But I won't allow my envy to eat at me. Mind you, the lessee's wife is not entirely free from envy either. She envies the landlord's wife, who in turn probably envies someone else. There's never an end to envy, which goes hand-in-hand with the fear of losing what one possesses. There is an advantage to being a pauper, too. You don't need to fear becoming one. And then, riches have the ugly habit of hardening the heart . . . " She pointed to the storks flying high above the marketplace. "All I ask of the Almighty is that He take care of me as He does of them. That's not too arrogant a demand, is it?"

At that moment, both women saw Yossele Abedale arriving from his street, his son, Hershele, at his side. Nechele prodded Hindele with her elbow and groaned ironically. "Do you see that *tsadik* over there and the fancy clothes he's wearing for the holiday? He can't even clean his gabardine of chalk and lime in honor of Passover."

Hindele bit her lips. Nechele's words had stung her. A long while passed before she could speak again. "That's neither chalk nor lime. Constant wear has worn the fabric of his caftan so thin that you can see through it. And why do you call him *tsadik* with such sarcasm?"

Nechele stirred in her seat and moved slightly away from Hindele. "Why do you pretend not to know what all of Bociany is saying about him? And I have a personal account to settle with him, too. He's shortening my husband's life. He sucks his blood like a leech, and he has shaken his fist at him more than once."

"Reb Yossele? But why? What does he have against your husband?" Hindele wondered why she was taking Nechele's accusations against Yossele so personally.

"Go and ask him," Nechele shot back. "You're his neighbor on the Potcheyov, aren't you? Have you ever heard a good word from that sulking good-for-nothing? He demands justice from others, but he himself has broken more than one law. Spending nights in the villages! And with all that he considers himself the owner of the synagogue. No small thing that honorable lineage of his, of raft-builders and carpenters!" Nechele gave Hindele a sharp, angry look. "You say you know me, Hindele? Then surely you know that whatever else I am, I'm not a gossip. Everything I say I got firsthand, from my husband, may he be well and healthy. And whatever else you may say about my husband, you cannot say that he doesn't know what he's talking about, or that he isn't an honest man. But you surprise me. How can someone who knows people as well as you do, not have the slightest idea what kind of a man her neighbor really is? You should know better than anyone else that something is not kosher with this '*tsadik*'."

"What's not kosher?" Hindele asked with effort. "He's a good and long-time neighbor of mine. "

"A good neighbor!" Nechele grinned bitterly. "You know, Hindele, sometimes it seems to me that you are false, that you, too, are nothing but a hypocrite."

Hindele gaped at her. What wrong could Yossele Abedale possibly have done to Nechele and her husband, that Nechele's hatred for him made her so venomous? How could all this poison have found room in Nechele's noble, unhappy heart? "You're hurting my feelings, Nechele," she whispered, her eyes starting to fill with tears.

"It's you who are hurting mine!" Nechele retorted. "If you are my friend, then you should be the friend of my husband, too, and not be defending his enemies. But you're only pretending to be my friend. That's what it is! What obligations have you got toward that chalk-smeared lout, tell me? But to me you do have certain obligations. From this I gather that, in truth, you don't care a hoot about me!" Nechele's eyes also filled with tears, although she rarely cried.

"Don't talk like that, Nechele," Hindele pleaded, her voice trembling.

"Why not? I'm allowed to speak the truth, aren't I?" Nechele fumed.

"But it's not the truth."

"So you're calling me a liar!" Nechele jumped to her feet and with an effort, Hindele stood up as well. Nechele grabbed the pillow on which they had both been sitting and ran into the house, slamming the door behind her. Hindele waited until she could compose herself, then called her daughters to her and, taking hold of their hands, turned in the direction of her own street.

Yacov noticed from the distance that his mother and sisters were heading home, and he pulled at Shalom's sleeve. Perhaps mealtime was approaching? His constant craving for food bothered him a great deal that Passover.

Keeping their distance, the brothers followed their mother home. Yacov's head was buzzing with all the things that he had heard from the Hasidim in the square. He was beginning to grasp the finer differences between one school of Hasidic thought and another, between the teachings of one rabbi and another. Never before had he felt such pride in being descended from the Wurker Rabbi. On a day like today it was impossible to believe that the Wurker had not been right, that Man's soul was basically a sacred vessel full of love. It was such a perfect Passover. Bociany was so peacefully nestled in God's lap that it made one forget all the sharp edges, all the dark corners of life. In his mind, Yacov was still running from the Christian boys who had been after him the day before. But today he refused to recognize the importance of the experience.

On their way home, he plied Shalom with questions. Shalom, true to his nature, answered with clear, short answers. As they passed the marketplace where Reb Faivele the Miller had dropped Yacov off the day before, Yacov remembered the strange word he had heard from the miller. "And tell me, Shalom," he turned toward his brother. "What is the meaning of the word 'vervolution'?"

Shalom looked at him out of the corner of his eye. "What did you say?"

"'Vervolution.' Reb Faivele the Miller said it. He said that something was going on in the world—a vervolution."

Shalom thought for a while and said, "He probably meant the slaughters in Kisheniev, or Shitomir, or Bialistok and Siedlec, or all those other places."

"What do you mean slaughters? What was slaughtered?"

"Better ask who was slaughtered. Jews, who else? They call it a pogrom. It probably means the same as . . . What did you say the word was?"

Yacov did not reply. Gruesome images mixed in his imagination with the memory—suddenly sharp and biting—of his experience with the gentile children the day before.

## 10

SOME TIME AFTER BINELE had recovered from her scabs, her neighbors Brontchele the Mourner, Peshele the Slob, and Toybe-Kraindele the Women's Bath Assistant began to whisper among themselves that Binele was smarter and shrewder than many an older girl. Busy as these women were, with the babies, the care of the household, and business, Binele gradually became more of a treasure to them than her older sisters had ever been.

They put Binele to work and began to love her "with all their hearts." But as soon as she sensed their need for her services, Binele began to lay down conditions. "If I hold the baby," she asked, "will you give me a big slice of challah?" "If I take out the slop pail for you, will you let me try on Sorele's shoes?"

She was jealous of the other children, who sometimes got new clothes for Passover, and she was especially jealous of their shoes. She herself had never yet owned a pair of shoes. During the summer, she went about barefoot, and in the winter, she wound rags around her feet for walking in the house. If she had to go outside, one or another of her sisters would lend her a pair of their own disintegrating shoes. But she was obliged to return that favor by being good and obedient, even when she did not feel like it, and this she deeply resented.

The neighborhood women gave in to her demands. They took her seriously and spoke to her as if she were an equal. This attitude was not unusual. There was no other way to talk to Yossele's children; their age did not matter. Among themselves they might behave like any other children, but to the outside world, to the neighbors, they were full-fledged little adults. What difference did it make whether Binele was seven years old or twenty, so long as she could be relied upon to carry out whatever errand she was sent on, mind whatever baby was entrusted to her care, or scrub whatever pot was placed in her hands? And she never dilly-dallied like the other children did, but concentrated on her work and did it quickly, smartly, and thoroughly, just like an adult would have, sometimes even better.

So if she occasionally helped herself to some food from the table or grabbed a hot potato from the pot, the women made no fuss over it. They scolded her, but did not report the matter to Yossele, unless the situation was exceptional, as when Peshele the Slob quarreled with Brontchele the Mourner over Binele. Each of them considered herself more entitled than the other to claim Binele's services. So finally, Brontchele had run to see Yossele.

"Believe me, Reb Yossele," she said. "Peshele the Slob is not at all the right kind of person to keep an eye on your little girl, poor thing, may she live in good health." Brontchele let out a deep professional sigh. "A child doesn't know how to behave and must be guided so that it can grow into a *mentsh.* If your little one, Reb Yossele, doesn't bless the bread before eating it, do you think that Peshele, the great *'rebetsin,'* makes an issue of it? Not on your life! Even if you paid me, I would never entrust a daughter of mine, if I had one, to Peshele, to teach her to read from the *sider.* Thank Heaven I've only got boys, may they live in good health." Then Binele got spanked by her father for not having blessed the bread.

But as much as the women loved her, Binele loathed them. First of all, she disliked mothers on principle. Second, Brontchele sometimes hit her. And then one and all preached endlessly to her, reminding her that she was an orphan and therefore had to behave like an angel to please her mother in heaven. As far as Binele was concerned, the women had no right to do or say such things to her. She did not like her father hitting her or telling her how to behave, either, but at least he was her father. Her big brother, Hershele, had told her that until the Messiah arrived, fathers had to behave like that. More than once, Binele had felt a strong urge to throw herself at Brontchele the Mourner, or any other woman who mistreated her, and bite their fingers off, or kick them in the stomach, or prick their eyes out, or tear the wigs off their heads. She resisted the impulse because she was afraid that they would tell her father. And after all, they did give her cooked food when they had enough left over after feeding their own children.

And then one day she discovered a way to manage without the women neighbors.

It was Tuesday, and Binele was wandering around the crowded marketplace. It was market day. She noticed a big-bellied woman moving among the peasants' carts not far from the water pump. The woman had a round face with red cheeks. Her two long blond braids reached below her waist, and they danced to and fro with every movement that she made. The braids, tied at the ends with wide red ribbons, shone in the sun like golden challahs, hypnotizing Binele and drawing her closer. Binele had never seen such a perfect creature in all her life. It immediately struck her that the only mother worth having was a mother who looked like this woman. Dazzled, she approached the woman and, tugging at a fold of her skirt, burst out, "Do you want to be my mother? I can scrub the floors, clean the pots, and . . . "

Before Binele could finish enumerating all her domestic talents, the woman slapped her hand and brushed her aside as if she were an unwanted kitten. She continued busying herself with the horse and cart. It appeared that she had just arrived at the market. The woman took the harness off the horse and tethered the animal to the post, hanging a sack of oats around its neck. Then she began sorting the crates and baskets of goods she had brought to sell.

Binele stood transfixed. This gorgeous woman sold butter, cream, curds, and cottage cheese. All these dairy products were as white as the lime and chalk in her father's shop. Occasionally, when she had been very hungry, Binele had gorged herself on the lime and chalk. But lime and chalk were far from tasty, while cream, curds, and cottage cheese tasted heavenly. She knew this because on market days she would sneak over to the peasants' carts and lick at some of the spilled curds and cream. Or she would lick clean the green leaves in which the peasants had wrapped their butter and then discarded for fresh ones.

As Binele stood enchanted, staring at the woman and her cart, she saw her turn her head toward the water pump and heard her tuneful voice call out in peasant language, "Yadwiga, the cholera take you, what are you doing there?"

A girl emerged from behind the water pump, carrying a jug of water. She had thin blond braids also tied with a red ribbon. Around her neck she wore a string of tiny red beads and a small wooden cross, which made her coarse linen dress look very elegant. The woman warned the girl not to get her dress messy if she wanted to come along to the market the next time. Then she set about calling out her wares in peasant language mixed with Yiddish words, and accosting those people who were hurrying by, hunting for bargains.

A new wave of ecstasy swept over Binele. What good luck this girl had! A beautiful mother and a cart full of dairy goods! There was no one to stop Binele from at least looking at the dairy products to her heart's content; no one would think to slap her for it. Binele decided that she would stay there all day and not take her eyes off the breathtaking sight. And if the woman and the girl left, she would follow them. She would find out where they lived, and they would be hers. Then she thought that if it were impossible to make contact with the splendid mother, she could at least try to make friends with the little girl. In any case, it was worth a try, even if she did risk another slap from the woman. Perhaps a drop of the other girl's good fortune might even fall on her.

She stepped up to Yadwiga and said, "Those are nice beads you're wearing."

Yadwiga did not understand a word of Yiddish, so she thought that Binele was asking for a sip of water, and she offered her the jug. Binele was not thirsty, but she gulped down as much water as she could. This gave her some time to recover from the excitement that throbbed through her limbs and drummed at her heart. She drank so avidly that she spilled half of the water in the jug over her chin and neck and onto her dress, so that it became soaking wet. Only when she heard Yadwiga giggle did she tear her mouth from the jug, and then she burst into laughter as well. She wiped her mouth on her sleeve and made a face so that Yadwiga would laugh even more. Jug in hand, she ran toward the pump, Yadwiga after her, and refilled the jug with water. And so she managed to spend the rest of the day with Yadwiga.

They wandered about the Potcheyov, peering into the shops. It is a different kind of looking, of seeing, when one walks in company. The spices in the spice shop had new aromas, the food in the food shops spoke a new language to the eyes and nostrils. The clay pots, the frying pans, the baking dishes, even the wooden spoons seemed to have acquired new forms, a livelier aspect. As for the shops with candles for sale, or those that dealt in tobacco and cigarettes, even Reb Senderl the Cabalist's shop, they were all transformed into mysterious hideaways. The bakery with bread and challah, or the pastry shop with Binele's favorite egg cookies, all looked like miniature Gardens of Eden. And then there were the shops displaying layers upon layers of fabrics in all kinds of textures, colors, and patterns. There were also the shops of ready-to-wear clothes for people of all sizes and ages, and shops that sold underwear or hats or gloves. There was the shop of Hindele the Scribe's Widow with its colorful ribbons, small hand mirrors, beads, and all sorts of combs, hairpins, buttons, scarves, and a hundred other enchanting knickknacks.

Then there was the other side of the Potcheyov, where the tailor sat over his eternally humming sewing machine called "Singer," and the shoemaker sat on a low stool, his mouth full of nails, which he extracted one by one to hammer into the sole of the shoe in his lap. There, too, were the workshops of the hatmaker, the tinker, the carpenter. Only Fishele the Butcher's shop was sad and uninteresting, with its rows of plucked chickens suspended from hooks in the entrance. It was more fun to watch the live pigs, goats, chickens, and geese that strayed all over the place, carrying on a never-ending war with the shopkeepers whose merchandise they ate or knocked over.

It was as though Binele and Yadwiga had arrived in an enchanted foreign country and did not know where to look first. They could not stop talking, each in her own language, communicating their mutual excitement with their eyes, or with giggles.

Binele took a large piece of chalk from her father's shop, and she and Yadwiga made all kinds of drawings on the sidewalk. It was not easy because they were constantly being knocked over by people hurrying back and forth. Their efforts to remain upright gave rise to a new wave of laughter. When they grew tired of the chalk game, they raced between the carts and wagons, chasing the stray animals and pointing out funny people and things to each other.

Binele purposely kept the two of them at a distance from Yadwiga's mother and the dairy cart. She did not want Yadwiga to know how attracted she was to that spot in the marketplace near the water pump, nor how much she wished to be near the beautiful woman with the braids like golden challahs, or to stand near that cart, which was full of the tastiest food in the world. Even while she was engrossed in playing with her new friend, she constantly had Yadwiga's mother before her eyes, imagining that the woman stroked her hair or offered her some cottage cheese, or curds, or cream, or gave her an egg to drink raw from the shell.

When the market day came to an end, Binele followed the dairy cart, the woman, and the girl. She felt irresistibly drawn to them, as if she were bound to them by an invisible cord. A few times, she considered running ahead and approaching the woman, asking to be allowed to walk near the cart or even to be allowed to lick clean the empty pots and cans. She knew that Yadwiga's mother could understand her language; she had heard her speak quite a passable Yiddish to her Jewish customers. But Binele did not trust herself when it came to begging. Whenever in the past she had asked someone for something, the answer had always been, "No!" That was why she found it easier to take things when no one was looking. But she could not take such a chance now. What would she do if Yadwiga or her mother chased her away? She was attached to them by a powerful bond of devotion that she felt would last forever.

As Yadwiga and her mother drew nearer to the village, Binele lengthened the distance between her and them. It was wiser not to be noticed by Yadwiga's mother. After all, she had learned a long time ago that mothers did not like other people's children when they did not need them.

Binele saw Yadwiga and her mother disappear through a gate. She ran forward, approached the gate, and peered into the yard through the cracks between the boards. She saw Yadwiga running around with some other children amidst chickens, pigs, geese, a cow, and a dog. Her mother was unharnessing the horse and tying it to the barn door. She then began emptying the cart of baskets, crates, pots, and cans from which a milk-white liquid still dripped. Binele's mouth watered. The image of the woman, whose long braids with the loosely tied ribbons slid over her back as she moved, danced before her eyes. A terrible sadness overwhelmed her, and she ran home.

The following day, first thing in the morning, she was back at her post by the gate of Yadwiga's house. She had missed Yadwiga so much that as soon as she saw her come out into the yard, she could not keep herself from calling her. Yadwiga came over, skipping rope. She grabbed hold of Binele's sleeve and pulled her inside the yard, showing her around while chattering nonstop in her peasant language. Binele nodded, not understanding a word. For a while they rolled around in the piles of hay stacked in the barn, along with Yadwiga's brothers and sisters. Then their mother shouted a command at them, and they all set out across the field to the pine wood, where they stole some fire wood and quickly returned. The older children disappeared again, in response to their mother's orders, but Yadwiga remained in the yard and taught Binele to jump rope.

The dog insisted on trying to jump along with Binele. She scolded him, mimicking Yadwiga by shouting, *"Pashol vont!"* as if she had been dealing with dogs all her life. The truth was that her sisters and brother and all the children on her street were terrified of dogs. Only goyim owned dogs in Bociany. But Binele, when she was with Yadwiga, tried to let on that nothing surprised or mystified her, and that she was very much at home with the things that she was seeing close up for the first time. Yadwiga offered her some spoiled sour milk to sip from a bottle. As she drank, Binele felt the cool liquid caress her insides, quenching her thirst and calming her tension. Then she followed Yadwiga and the cow out to the pasture.

Binele became a frequent visitor at the home of Yankova, Yadwiga's mother. She communicated with Yadwiga and the gentile children of the village in pantomime, each speaking her own language to the accompaniment of gestures that were sometimes so funny that they could not stop laughing. Binele tried to laugh louder than the other children, to show how much she liked them, but she made sure not to beat them in running, climbing, and jumping, so as not to make them hate her. But her heart was only partly in the games. She was continually trying to think of ways to spend some time in Yankova's presence, or if that was not possible, scheming about how to get the children to run into the house and bring back a piece of bread or a cucumber to share with her. At the same time, she looked about for opportunities to take something unnoticed and stuff it into her mouth.

She began learning new words and expressions in the peasant language and did not notice that she had to resort to pantomime less and less frequently. Now when she wanted to be near Yadwiga's mother for a while, she would pretend that she could not make herself understood and would get so upset about it that Yadwiga had to take her into the house in order to ask her mother to serve as translator.

Those were wonderful moments, although Yadwiga's mother was often too busy with her work and too nervous to hear Binele out properly. But her dumb act did give Binele the opportunity to stand close to Yankova, so close that she could smell the odor of the woman's body. She could see Yankova's big belly move as she talked directly to her. Eventually, with and without the help of Yankova, the girls created a kind of mixed language that finally removed the last barriers between them. They became best friends—forever.

Although Binele's help was not needed at Yankova's house, there being enough children of all sizes for various chores, she began to sneak away from the children's games and, of her own free will, help out their big-bellied mother. She peeled potatoes for her, washed the dishes, swept the floor, and cleared things away, just as she had done for the neighbor women on her street, but with much more enthusiasm and a greater will to please. When Yankova asked Yadwiga or one of the other children to do something, Binele volunteered to take their place.

"I will do it right away!" she assured the woman, thereby killing two birds with one stone, since Yankova praised her for it, and the children were grateful to her. She did not understand why it gave her so much pleasure to be close to this woman and to work in her presence. All she knew was that the smell of Yankova and the protective, soothing warmth that radiated from her large body attracted her with tremendous power. Finally Binele's heart was so full of affection for Yankova that she could no longer refrain from confiding in Yadwiga. One day, as they sat in the pasture, with the cow grazing nearby, Binele said, "You know, I like your mother very much."

Yadwiga casually tossed her thin braids to her back. "I don't like her so much when she carries."

Binele did not understand. "Carries? What does she carry?"

A mischievous smile appeared on Yadwiga's lips, and she glanced meaningfully at Binele. "Are you blind? Can't you see that she's carrying a belly?"

Binele blinked back at her and burst out laughing. "Everybody carries a belly!"

"Everybody carries a belly!" Yadwiga responded with laughter so loud and sharp that it echoed over the pasture. She greatly enjoyed Binele's joke. "Do you know what my father carries in his belly?" she asked, still choking with laughter. "A barrel of vodka, that's what he carries!"

Binele went on laughing along with Yadwiga, although inwardly she felt ill-at-ease. "And what does your mother carry in her belly?" she asked as if it were still a joke.

"Why, she's carrying a bastard!" Yadwiga burst out, throwing herself onto the grass. Still in a fit of giggles, she rolled about, looking like a soft pillow.

Binele rolled along with her, but she was determined to investigate the puzzle. Carefully she questioned Yadwiga, until she began to understand that Yankova was carrying a baby in her belly, and that she would be carrying it nine months, and that the cow also carried calves in its belly as the cat did kittens and the bitch puppies.

This was an extraordinary discovery, a fact that all of Bociany, including her father, sisters, and brother had concealed from her. Of course, she had seen the women of Bociany walk around with swollen bellies. Sometimes she had even heard them say to each other, "She carries well," or "She carries badly." But Binele had never connected the big bellies with the coming of babies into the world. When she had heard screams coming from a house, and the people gathered in front commented that the woman inside was "having a bad time of it"—and all women in Bociany had a bad time of it—she could not understand what they might possibly mean. How could these women be having such a bad time, when they lay in bed like queens, and the storks living on their roof did all the work, secretly dragging the babies down from the heavens for them. Yes, the storks did so even in wintertime, flying in from the warm lands, unnoticed by anyone, in order to fulfill their mission.

Now it dawned upon Binele that her family did not want her to know that her own mother had carried her inside her belly for nine months. Now she also understood why having a baby gave a woman such a hard time. Yadwiga had explained to her that even animals suffered pain when the babies came out of their bodies and that with people it was even worse. The midwife had to make a hole in the mother's belly and pull the baby out through it, whereas the animals needed no midwife, since they had a ready-made hole through which the baby animals came out by themselves.

"And also because people are born lazy," Yadwiga elaborated. "Even as babies, they are too lazy to come out by themselves. Only after communion do they begin to understand that they must do things by themselves. And when they grow older, they're forced to work hard, because people are not like animals, for whom Pan Jesus prepares food in the pastures."

A storm raged in Binele's heart as she sat listening to Yadwiga. She realized that other mothers recovered after having babies. Her own mother had also recovered after giving birth to her sisters and brother. But perhaps Binele had kicked too hard right from the beginning and had caused her mother too much suffering. Had she not come into this world a mean, naughty girl? Her sisters were right, then. She had killed her own mother. Guilt gnawed at her heart at the same time that she felt a tremendous craving to fill this blank spot in her mind, where an image was missing, with the features of the woman whom she had never seen and who had given her life.

From that day on Binele followed Yankova with even more awe than before, helping her, and serving her, as if she wanted to make up for the troubles she had caused her own mother.

It was a hazy summer's day after sunset. Binele was helping Yadwiga clear the table after supper at Yankova's, when Yanek, Yadwiga's father, began arguing with his wife. Yanek was not entirely sober. He never returned straight home after his day's work in the landlord's fields. His first stop was always the Jewish tavern on the Wide Poplar Road. It was not long before Yanek stood up from the table, grabbed his pregnant wife by a braid, and started beating her with his fists and then with the dog's leash.

For a moment Binele stood dumb, shocked by the scene taking place before her eyes. Then she began to scream, feeling Yanek's blows as if they were falling on her own back. She was about to dash forward and try to tear Yanek away from his wife, when the children, all tittering, restrained her by grabbing her arms and dress. They covered her mouth with their hands and dragged her outside. She shook them off and ran away into the field. She threw herself in the grass and wept bitterly, full of ungovernable despair. What was the sense of living in a world in which someone could hurt the beautiful Yankova?

Yadwiga joined her in the field and sat down next to her. The sky was turning dark, covered with layers of heavy cloud. To Binele it seemed that darkness was invading the earth and would smother it forever. She did not want to look at Yadwiga. She felt betrayed by her; they were no longer friends. To make matters worse, Yadwiga was smiling. Knees drawn to her chin, she rocked herself back and forth as if to tease Binele, who turned to her with wet eyes full of resentment. "Your father beats up your mother and you sit here laughing!" she burst out. "Go away and leave me alone!"

Yadwiga laughed even louder. "Why are you crying, stupid cow? It's fun when Father beats up Mother. Go into the house and you'll see how happy Mother is."

"I don't believe you! Are you happy when they beat you up?"

"No, but I will be when I have a husband and he beats me up."

"You don't know what you're talking about. Is that what you need a husband for, so that he can beat you up?"

"No, I need a husband so that I can have bastards. Our priest, Father Stanislav, won't allow us to have bastards without a husband. And I need a husband so that I can be happy every Sunday and go to church, or go dancing with him. Mother says that Father beats her up because he still loves her. When he stops loving her, then he'll stop beating her, and this will be very bad for the house and the whole family. I pray all the time to Pan Jesus, who said 'Love one another,' that my father doesn't stop loving my mother."

"But he could have killed the baby in her belly!" Binele stared at her in wide-eyed confusion, wiping the tears off her cheeks with the edge of her dress.

Yadwiga shrugged. "Who needs the baby in her belly? Doesn't she have enough bastards with me and my brothers and sisters? The baby will only mean more work for her and for us. It's a punishment from Pan Jesus, I think, that she's carrying another bastard. But there's still hope that if she doesn't get rid of it now, it will die after it's born. Maybe they'll be able to do something about it."

Despite the fact that he beat his wife, Binele could not help rather liking Yanek, Yadwiga's father. He had a funny, big mustache which was straight on one side, but ended in an upward turn on the other. And he was cheerful and approachable. His children were not only not afraid of him, but quite familiar, almost chummy with him. From dawn to dusk he worked the landlord's fields, and when he returned home, even if he was only half sober, he worked his own piece of land and took care of the farm. This was especially true now that Yankova's condition prevented her from doing much work outside the house. He would troop out with the children to his section of the field, where the children helped him dig potatoes, or he would join them in stealing turf or firewood from the redolent pine forest. Binele followed wherever they went, grateful to Yanek for not chasing her away.

Yanek's family and Binele herself took it for granted that she should sit down at the table to eat supper with them. And they sat down at the table every night, not like in her home, where they all seated themselves around the table only on the Sabbath. Binele was given huge chunks of bread, fresh and homemade, with a crackling brown crust, thickly spread with butter. Then there was always a bowl of cabbage soup to go with it. With her yellow hair, which she could already tie over her ears with a string, and which were the beginning of the braids that she dreamed of having, with her cheeks generously freckled, and with her short, broad nose, Binele looked little different from the other children. In fact, when he was half-drunk, Yanek would often forget who she was and remind her to say grace before the meal. She learned it quickly, folding her hands and lowering her head. She would cross herself like all the others at the table.

When it chanced that Yanek was required to work in the landlord's courtyard and gardens instead of the fields, he would wait until after the evening meal at his hut—the meal was a silent affair during which everyone was totally absorbed in the food—to regale the whole family with his tales of the wonders he had seen at the mansion. He described how the old master and mistress took their breakfast on the terrace among the roses at a table set for royalty, how they ate, what they ate, what they wore, and what they said. He told of the master's sons and daughters playing on the garden lawn with small white balls, which they hit back and forth all day, as did their guests. Or how they rode their princely white horses, and how one of them played the "pianino" inside, by the open window, while the rest danced the most stately dances. How they read books in the middle of the day or the gazettes and how this was all they did.

Enchanted, open-mouthed, Yanek's family listened. When he had finished his stories, they bombarded him with questions about this or that member of the master's court. Like the other peasants, they knew everything about everyone living at the manor, not only their names and nicknames, but also their personalities, their life stories, and their always-passionate love affairs, full of sad details. Although Yanek more often than not fabricated his stories, he had to make certain that the new "facts" matched the other "facts" that were already well known to the family.

Thus, along with learning the prayers at Yanek's house, Binele learned the intricate family relationships that reigned at the manor. During these moments of lively chatter around the table, she felt herself a part of Yanek's home, accepted into the circle of its members' confidence. She was, however, a little jealous of Yadwiga, who had begun to boast that she was in love with the handsome young master, the landlord's son.

It was during a hot, sun-drenched afternoon that Yadwiga decided to show her "lover" to Binele. She took her along for a "date." They walked ßbarefoot along the Narrow Poplar Road, the boiling hot sand burning the soles of their feet. Having reached the fence of the courtyard, they stood for many hours in the baking heat, the sweat dripping down their faces, as they peered through the railing, watching for the "lover." They hoped that he would appear before them suddenly, book in hand, as he strolled between the shady trees in the garden, wearing his elegant outfit; as he approached them, his heart would tell him to raise his sad eyes and look straight into Yadwiga's sad eyes.

Luck was with them; they had the good fortune of seeing him. He passed them on the road after sunset, riding not in a fancy diligence as they had expected, but in a surrey. When he saw the two girls standing on the concrete base of the fence and holding on to the bars, he swished his whip in their direction.

Yadwiga's voice was choked with emotion as she asked Binele, "Did you see how he looked at me?"

"At me too," Binele replied. "I think he wanted to shoo us away."

"Not me he didn't. You maybe," Yadwiga whispered starry-eyed. "He looked at me. It was at you that he waved the whip."

"Why only at me?"

"Because he is mine, and you are a *Zydoweczka*."

"What's a *Zydoweczka?*"

"I'm not sure, but my brother Mietek once asked Mother if he could marry you, because you helped him scrub the floor, and Mother said no, because you are a *Zydoweczka,* and *Zydoweczkas* and our people can't marry each other."

"But how would the young master know that I am a *Zydoweczka?*"

"The young master knows everything," Yadwiga asserted gravely. She noticed that Binele was pouting downheartedly, and she threw her arms around her, giving her a loud kiss on the cheek. "You needn't cry right away," she consoled her. "Mother says that you're almost like one of us, that when you're a bit older, the priest, Father Stanislav, will make you completely as we are, and you'll be able to marry Mietek."

"I don't want to marry Mietek!" Binele was growing irritable. "I want to fall in love with the young master!"

"All right. You can fall in love with him, too," Yadwiga finally conceded. "You are my best friend, so you're allowed to fall in love with him. We'll have him together. But we won't allow anyone else." Again she kissed Binele loudly on the cheek.

It was not long before Binele grew taller and stronger than her sister Dvorele and almost caught up with Faigele. The only problem was that the women neighbors could seldom find her when they needed her, so they set out to investigate the matter.

Brontchele the Mourner had no time to devote to such an investigation in person, busy as she was all day long with her profession; there was no lack of homes that required someone to help them weep. In addition, she had recently taken on the job of plucking chickens and geese for the wealthy houses, and aside from that, she had a houseful of boys to contend with, one of them still at the breast. She could, however, already rely on her eldest son, whose name was Berele, but whom the children in the street called the Moonwalker because of his somnambulistic inclinations. While fast asleep, he would climb out of bed on moonlit nights and wander about his backyard. Berele was otherwise said to have an adult's head on his shoulders. On his mother's orders, he began spying on Binele and soon found out where she disappeared to, which he reported to his mother.

When she heard the news, Brontchele had an attack of funeral spasms. Despite all her energy and bravura, she was a sickly looking woman, although her face still bore traces of her faded beauty. Once her legs had probably been strong and shapely, but now they were weak and spindly. On these legs she carried a body made up of three round parts, namely, the head, the bosom, and the belly, all covered by layers of shawls tied under her chin and around her waist, and knotted in back with thick knots. The knots seemed to keep her secured to the ground, lest the slightest breeze, or worse, the least bit of bad news, carry her off.

In order to recover from the shock of the news about Binele, Brontchele straightaway dropped what she was doing and rushed out to find Toybe-Kraindele, the women's bath attendant. Toybe-Kraindele was earning a few extra kopecks selling hot "bobe" beans on the Potcheyov. When she heard the news from Brontchele, she almost collapsed from heartache. She went to the corner of the Potcheyov and waited for Peshele the Slob, who was scheduled to pass by at any moment with her prayer book and pointer, on her way home from teaching the girls of marriageable age to read. Peshele the Slob grabbed hold of her wig when she heard the news. So did all the other women on the street. Had they not all promised Mariml at her open grave that they would take care of her children, especially Binele, and treat them as if they were their own?

As they did in fact feel like Mariml's representatives on earth, they decided together that things could no longer go on the way they had been going. And from then on, whenever Berele or anybody else noticed the "Marzepa" sneaking around barns and fences, they caught her and took her to the women neighbors. The neighbors, although too tired even to catch their breath, would grab Binele by one of her braids and beat her, out of the fullness of their hearts, although neither Toybe-Kraindele nor Peshele the Slob had ever beaten her before. Even Brontchele had never before been so fierce as she was now. In truth, the women neighbors were all affectionate creatures who meant better than well. Who knew what might have happened to Yossele's children, or to the other motherless youngsters on the street, if it had not been for their vigilance. But they were desperate now in the very serious case of Binele. Their desperation was clearly reflected in the moralizing and the tears that accompanied their blows.

In this way the good neighbors sacrificed themselves for Yossele, protecting him against the heartbreak that Binele's behavior would have caused him. Certainly there was no reason to envy Yossele, not even with his good luck in the villages. Rumors were spreading that undermined people's respect for him. Things were being implied that were not at all nice. But Yossele's neighbors, although fully informed of the details, bravely defended him and did not believe a word of all the gossip. Now, as if things were not bad enough, Yossele had a daughter who was growing up among the goyim.

The good intentions of the neighbor women accomplished little. Binele found other ways of sneaking in and out of the house unnoticed. The neighbors again came to the conclusion that "things could not go on like this any longer," that their efforts to save Yossele from heartbreak might lead to his getting an attack of apoplexy if he should accidentally chance to find out the truth. It was no longer a question of child's play; the women felt that they could not go on shouldering such a responsibility. Because, alas, the air around Binele was smelling more and more of conversion, they came to the conclusion that they had better inform Yossele.

Yossele was having one of his bad days. He had slept badly the night before, tormented by dreams of which, as usual, he remembered nothing. But their dark shadows hovered over his waking hours and made his heart heavy for reasons he did not quite understand. He had not gone to the villages that day but had sent his eldest daughters home to take care of the housework and cook a meal. Ever since he had begun peddling in the villages, he had brought home enough vegetables to make a soup every day.

So Yossele was all alone in the chalk-and-lime store, taking advantage of the opportunity afforded by solitude to mull over his opinions on various matters. As usual he was standing in the doorway of his shop, leaning against the doorpost and swaying to and fro while waiting for customers, when suddenly Fishele the Butcher appeared before him. Fishele looked extremely serious, almost morbidly so. He had come to see Yossele this time for strictly personal reasons. His problems had become unbearable now that they had been stirred up by the strange visit of the "rabbi-thief." The man's philosophy had so touched Fishele's most secret emotions, and had justified so beautifully his own evil passions, that had it not been for the missing silver candlesticks, Fishele would no longer have felt any qualms about following the path of sin.

Fishele was convinced that no one but Yossele would understand his plight. Like everyone else, he had heard of Yossele's suspicious activities in the villages, and like everyone else, he did not believe a word of it. But he had become more and more curious as to how Yossele managed without a woman. No doubt Yossele had his own problems in that domain. So Fishele had decided to confess all to Yossele. Yossele might be a cold fish, stingy with words and stingy in expressions of friendship, but he was the only person whom Fishele knew who was capable of keeping a secret. Yossele knew how a man must behave with himself and with others, and because of his own situation, he might be able to offer advice. In any case, Fishele was incapable of keeping it all inside any longer. If he did not unburden himself, he felt that he would burst.

He pretended not to notice the stony expression on Yossele's face. After a moment of silence, he took up his position at the doorpost opposite Yossele and slowly, in a whisper, began to unravel his horrible dreams before Yossele, confessing, in uncontrolled chaotic phrases, the torment of his morbid cravings and murderous impulses.

"Believe me, Yossele," he pounded his fist against the blood-stained apron that covered his chest. "I have no peace day or night. And I so badly want to be a good Jew, a good man. It's true that I like to crack a joke now and then, that I like to let myself go on Purim or Simches-Toyre, but I'm not, after all, like my butcher boys, with their cheap tricks and foul language. And you know that my Ariele, may he live in good health, will one day be a jewel in the crown of Israel. That's what the *rov* told me after he tested him last Sabbath. So, Yossele, if only for Ariele's sake . . ." Fishele blew his nose loudly into the edge of his apron. His eyes grew red and misty. "But the more good deeds I do, the more time I spend in the *rov's* chambers listening to learned discussions, or in the ritual slaughterer's kitchen, listening to Sore-Leyele's moral stories, the worse I feel." Fishele did not mention his strange visitor. He had forbidden everyone in his house to say anything about the missing candlesticks, lest he become the laughingstock of Bociany.

"So things have gotten to the point," he continued, "that when I'm busy putting out a fire, my temptations, my evil inclinations flare up even more. And would you believe it? I see the fires of the pogrom. Oh yes, only during a fire do I feel alive, only then does life become dear to me.

But otherwise I feel dead inside, a corpse with a storm raging in his head. Tell me, Yossele, you're a friend after all, aren't you? How could I have sinned so badly to be so smitten by horror? I don't want to shame my son or my family, and I do love my wife, I swear. May I live to hear the sound of the Messiah's *shofar,* I do love her. Yet I'm driven by this desire for female flesh, Yossele, and I don't want to go to hell for it, I don't want to roast on the stakes of the Evil One. There, in hell, there is no fire brigade." This was Fishele's attempt at comic relief. "If you burn there, you burn." He smiled a desperate smile. "I no longer know what's what, believe me. Maybe I'm sick, may God protect me."

"You're healthy as an ox," Yossele said at last. "That's your tragedy." Then, as an afterthought, he added in a hoarse whisper, more to himself than to Fishele, "and mine too."

Fishele's words had stirred something in Yossele. Flashes of his own dreams started coming back to him, causing cold beads of sweat to pop out on his forehead. He believed Fishele was a tormented man. In his mind he compared him to Vaslav Spokojny. It was amazing how the two resembled each other and how each had been led to do things according to his nature. Then he compared them both to himself, and a suspicion entered his mind. Perhaps he did frequent the villages for reasons other than the ones that were obvious to him? Perhaps he was driven there by the dark forces that held him in their grip during the night? But he would not allow such thoughts to overwhelm him. He, Yossele, was the master of his actions; that was the main thing.

"The stronger the body, the more power the mind needs to rid itself of evil temptations," he said, looking straight into Fishele's eyes.

"Yes," Fishele sighed. "It's a curse to have a strong body."

"No, it's a curse to have a weak mind."

"But you have a strong mind, Yossele, yet you say that your strong body is your tragedy too. I suspected it . . . And you are right, Yossele, marriage is no solution, although a Jew must have a wife." The beads of sweat on Yossele's forehead bore witness that Reb Laibele the Sexton had not sucked his stories about Yossele out of his finger. Fishele's heart was suddenly filled with the courage of a fire chief. "I'm trapped," he burst out. "I need a way out! I need a woman . . . a *shikse!*"

Yossele raised his eyebrows as if to widen the scope of his vision. "So you've come to me? Do I deal in *shikses,* for Heaven's sake?" Scolding Fishele was not Yossele's business, nor did he feel like doing so, out of pity for the man. Still, Fishele was ridiculous. Not so long ago this same *"tsadik"* had come in to him to preach Jewishness. Now he came with his tragicomic confession. One really had to be made of iron, as was Yossele himself, not to hold one's sides with laughter—or explode with anger.

Fishele was too busy with his own thoughts to wonder what Yossele was thinking. Encouraged by Yossele's silence, he continued in a heated whisper, "You see, it's not so much female flesh that I crave, as—I don't know myself what—perhaps just sin. I could have found myself a decent *shikse* long ago. I'm not conceited, Yossele, but you can't deny that I have quite a build, and I can crack jokes and make a woman laugh. You know I'm not boasting when I say that my female customers are crazy about me. So I think that even the best *shikse* would not be able to resist me. But . . . but my problem is that I'm scared to death of them. Scared of all of them, especially *goyish* females, the very ones who tempt me most. You wouldn't think it, to look at me, would you? But that's what it is. I look like some kind of bigshot afraid of nothing, don't I? But . . . " He put his hand on Yossele's shoulder. "You see, Yossele, things are so bad with me that I'm confessing to you what no man in his right mind would confess. I am not ashamed to open my heart to you, so that you might understand me."

"I understand you," Yossele said, shrugging free of Fishele's heavy hand.

Tears filled Fishele's eyes. "So I would like to get myself someone who . . . the fewer brains in the head, the better. Just as long as she's a piece of flesh. And an unmarried one would be the best of all." For a moment his own frankness frightened him, and he lowered his voice, adding as if to console his listener, "Believe me, Yossele, there are no saints in this world."

The air around Fishele was becoming repellent to Yossele. He turned his torso to the side. He noticed Hindele the Scribe's Widow struggling with a cardboard box she was trying to squeeze in beside all the other boxes on the top shelf of her window shop. "Silly woman," he thought. "Why doesn't she ask me to help? At least it would give me a chance to get away from Fishele." He would have walked over to help her, but a man like Fishele might suppose God only knew what. So he let his eyes wander back to Fishele, wondering at himself. "Since when do I care what people think of me? Oh God, You must be having a ball, watching two idiots like us. But we do deserve a little of Your pity, nevertheless." Yes, man was a ridiculous creature, struggling so hard with the darkness in his soul, while it was all nothing but a joke played by Fate, for heaven knew what purpose.

"This scream inside you," Yossele heard himself saying, "this great scream is nothing more than a mouse's squeak. You only imagine that it is so strong and will last God knows how long. In fact, it is nothing but a peep. Before you turn around, it will be over and done with. This of course won't satisfy you now. But it is good to remember that the cry of your body comes from your mind. The evil thoughts are here." He pointed to his temple. "So that's where you must struggle with them and overcome them. Because if you give in to the call of the flesh, you are doomed."

Fishele had no idea what Yossele was talking about. Was it not precisely his mind that complicated this call of the flesh, which would otherwise be so simple to answer? Yossele's words irritated him, and his eyes lit up with mocking irony. "Have you conquered your own evil thoughts in here?" He imitated Yossele's gesture and put a finger to his temple. "Or perhaps you would like me to believe that you haven't broken the commandment against covetousness? You think I didn't see you watching that neighbor of yours a minute ago? So I can imagine how you behave when there is no one around to see."

Yossele waved his arm in disgust. "Your problem is that you imagine too much. Why have you come to me with these matters, eh?"

"To whom else should I have gone? You're supposed to be a friend, damn it!" Fishele's voice grew imploring again. "You wouldn't refuse to do me a favor, would you?"

"What kind of a favor do you want? When it comes to these things, I am no Solomon. Go and see the *rov.*"

Fishele burst into hysterical guffaws. "Have you lost your senses, Yossele? Granted, he has a pretty wife, but whether he knows what to do with her is another story. That thin, dried out stick, that ascetic? All I have to do is hint at the women I see in my dreams and he would get apoplexy."

Yossele was thoroughly fed up with Fishele's sordid talk. "So do something about it yourself. I have more important things to worry about!" He waved Fishele away but not before adding in a calmer tone, "Everyone must do battle with his own demons. There is nothing I can do for you."

"But you can, Yossele," Fishele whispered urgently.

"What do you mean I can?"

"Get me a *shikse*."

Yossele took his hands off the doorpost and walked over to help Hindele, who was still struggling to get her cardboard box up on the top shelf. Without a word, he took the box from her hands and put it exactly in the spot where she wanted it. Before she had a chance to thank him, he was on his way to the water pump. He pumped vigorously, then put his mouth under the spout, allowing the stream of water to flow down into his beard. He felt dirty inside.

As he straightened up, he saw that Fishele was now speaking to someone inside the shop. A small man was standing there, waving his hands. Yossele hurried back. As he approached, he recognized Reb Laibele the Sexton and had an immediate impulse to run off again. Both Fishele and Reb Laibele came out of the shop to meet him.

"Yossele!" Reb Laibele grabbed him by the lapels with his small hands. There was not a trace of the customary distaste on his face. His tiny eyes looked frightened and he shook like a fish. "Yossele," he muttered, "we must do something. I've just told Fishele. Our lives are in grave danger, may God protect us."

Yossele slowly freed himself of the two small fists clutching his lapels. He looked from one man to the other. "What happened?" he asked.

"Don't ask, Yossele!" Reb Laibele lifted his belly with both hands in a quick panicky jerk. "Reb Gershon Sheres, the lessee, has just visited the *rov.* There has been a massacre of Jews in Chestochowa. Chestochowa, Yossele, not somewhere in Hotzeplotz, understand? You must start doing something right away!"

"I'll do what the *rov* decides," Yossele replied curtly.

"For Heaven's sake, Yossele! The *rov* is too young and absent-minded, a weakling, a dry, feeble stick. And he has never lived through a pogrom as we have."

"What difference does that make? Did our pogrom make us any wiser, Reb Laibele? Let's wait and see what the *rov* decides." Yossele pushed both the sexton and Fishele out on the sidewalk, but he still managed to lean over to Fishele and ask in a sarcastic tone of voice, "Do you feel a bit better? Fear is a good remedy for your complaint."

No sooner had Yossele rid himself of his visitors than Father Stanislav came up to him. The priest was wearing his black soutane; a large silver cross hung on his chest. His hair and eyes, his entire face seemed to be of the same silver color. Rosary beads dangled from a ring on his belt, as did another small wooden cross. Before entering Yossele's shop, he made a point of calling out in front of all the Potcheyov a loud "Good day to you, Yossele, my brother!" He stepped into the shop, and Yossele followed him in. They faced each other, and the priest peered at Yossele through watery eyes lined with red where the eyelashes should have been. From those eyes there shone the silvery light of love for his childhood friend.

"For some strange reason," the priest spoke in his smooth, flowing voice, "I was recalling bygone times today, Yossele." His dark-blue lips spread in a guileless smile. He seemed not to have noticed that Yossele had lost the power of speech, so shocked was he by this unexpected encounter. Yossele's face turned dark under the chalk blotches. The priest was thoroughly at ease, although weak. He gave the impression of being an ascetic, but a very sick ascetic at that, kept on his feet merely by the strength of his spirit. "So I decided to come over and give you the good news personally, because good things should be told more eagerly than bad. Do you remember how I used to baptize you in the river during those carefree, idyllic days of our childhood?"

Yossele gathered his strength, spat three times, and turned to face the wall. "I will not talk with you," he said.

The priest did not sound surprised. "Please, don't turn away from me, Yossele. I have come to you in the name of love and peace. We are all God's children, haven't you realized that yet? Is it not time to put an end to our differences and to our hatred?"

Yossele had not spoken so much as a word to the priest for many years. Whenever the priest accosted him, he pretended not to hear and walked away. He had no intention of speaking to him now. But with the wall in front of him, he was unable to breathe. He turned abruptly to the priest. "What do you want of me, for heaven's sake?" he asked in a voice that did not sound like his own.

The priest's pale, hollow-cheeked face grew increasingly softer. His voice was thin and smooth like a silver thread. "We have been strangers for too long, Yossele." He wet one bloodless lip with the other, smiling humbly. "So I am not surprised by your reaction. But we can become friends again. As the saying goes, 'Old wine and old friendships improve with time.'"

Yossele took a step toward the door, intending to run out, but the priest managed to hold on to the sleeve of his gabardine. Their eyes met on the same level because the priest, although thin and dried-up, was Yossele's height. The smile had vanished from his delicate face, which was now veiled in a melancholy sadness.

"I have come, as I told you, Yossele," he said, "out of the love that I bear for you, to tell you the good news that was announced to me this morning." Yossele's weak eyes grew large. He could run out now, for the priest had suddenly let go of him, but he stood frozen in place, his heart pounding in icy expectation. The priest nodded solemnly and said, "Tsar Nicholas is preparing a decree that all Jews must convert to Christianity. All of them. So I've come to see you. And in the name of our fathers' great sacrifice on the altar of a free fatherland, our beloved Polish Earth, I want to ask you, to appeal to you. The Jews of Bociany hold you in great esteem. So please, see to it that none of you convert to the Orthodox Church but accept instead the Polish Catholic faith. You Jews believe that you are God's chosen people. We Poles believe that we are the Christ of the nations, that's how much we have in common. You and we, two peoples crucified for His Glory."

The priest's words sent a chill down Yossele's spine. He shuddered. The priest made the sign of the cross over him, bowed deeply, and added humbly, "My door is always open to you, as are my arms. Glory be to His name!" He stood there in silence for another moment with his arms spread, ready to embrace Yossele. But Yossele was already out on the street.

While the priest slowly crossed the marketplace in the direction of the parsonage, Yossele was set upon by a horde of people. Everyone wanted to know what the priest had said to him. Beside himself with rage, he burst out, "Why don't you ask him yourselves?" He told Hindele to watch the store for him, and made straight for the *rov's* house.

The *rov* listened to Yossele attentively, asking him to repeat the priest's exact words over and over again. Then he called a meeting of his council and sent a messenger to the *rov* in Chwosty to find out what information the latter had on the issue. Then he sat down with all those present to recite the psalms.

When Yossele finally closed up his shop for the day and went home, he found the neighborhood women waiting for him. In Binele's presence, they told him of her escapades. They wrung their hands when they saw how he took the news to heart and his daughter "into his hands."

Binele was quite a big girl already, but her behavior was just the opposite of her brother's. While Hershele uttered not a single cry during his father's beatings, she screamed loudly enough to lift the roof. She was not ashamed to wail now so that all of Bociany might hear her and know what a brute she had for a father, a father who could beat the life out of his youngest child, an orphan with no mother to intercede for her. She hoped that his face would turn black with shame.

"Bad Father! Mean Father!" she yelled between one swoop of the whip and the next.

Yossele was, in fact, ashamed; ashamed not because all of Bociany might be listening, but ashamed for himself and for what he was doing before the Almighty. He was so ashamed that his heart pounded and his head reeled. Binele was right. He was a bad father, a monster. It was all his fault. The older his children grew, the less time he spent looking after them, when the opposite should have been the case. A young mind, newly awoken, was subject to strange, wild thoughts. And how could he possibly know what went on in the mind of a young girl? It was true that his other daughters behaved like little women, helping him both at home and in the shop. But Binele was different. Why? How could he possibly understand her? He was no woman. Flesh of his flesh and blood of his blood she might be, but he could not figure her out.

"Who is a bad father? Who?" He beat her out of anger at himself, while the words of Fishele and the priest rang in his head.

"You are!" She kicked and screamed but made certain that she gave each of his questions its proper answer.

Yossele's tired eyes looked down at the fragile, soft body squirming on the chair. How much could such a creature bear? How little strength it would take to crush it, to kill it. Suddenly, the sight before his eyes mixed in his imagination with the images of Chestochowa. He saw the town, the massacre, the blood of hundreds. Then he remembered the pogrom in his childhood in Bociany, a memory he had carried untarnished in his mind throughout his life. This memory returned to haunt him every time that he beat his children, but today the recollection of those hellish days was unbearable. In his head, he heard a voice teasing him with the question, "Are you the victim or the killer?" Yet instead of stopping him, the question goaded him on to greater violence, and the whip in his hand came down harder, until he lost all restraint. So what if Binele received blows that he himself deserved? So what if she was his dearest and most precious, the one that he worried about the most? So what if she was such a faithful reproduction of Mariml? So what if he was so pleased with her cleverness and her ability to manage so well on her own, pleased with her good height, charmed by her lively "Marzepa" face with the freckles on her cheeks, by her slanted eyes and knowing look? So what?

As he beat her, he remembered that the year before she had gotten hold of a pair of wooden clogs on her own, without waiting for him to bring her some worn-out shoes from the wealthier customers. Then, not long ago, she had come home in a dress without a single tear in it. He had never asked her where or how she had gotten it. What good would it have done to ask? She had been walking around in Mariml's old slip, which had lasted through the wearing of all the sisters before her; she had worn it pinned to one of Hershele's old worn caftans. Yes, he had good reason to be proud of her dexterity, her skill, her cleverness, her charm.

Why then did he increase the strength of his blows as all these thoughts flashed through his head? How could she have known of the danger to her soul that lay in wait for her in the gentile houses? He was certain that it was the Evil One who moved his hand. The Evil One was never too far away from him. He followed Yossele everywhere. Yes, Yossele deserved to be punished for the hell that he was going through in this world, with the hell that he had to look forward to in the next. There he stood, raising his arm again and again against an innocent, his own flesh and blood. And this was not the kind of discipline that a father was allowed. This raising of the arm was a frightening affair! Yossele was aware of the impulse he felt, to destroy this creature, to annihilate this most precious object of his feelings, the closest thing to his heart.

So was he not right when he said that there was no love in this world? That the only "love" that existed was the kind offered by Father Stanislav? Father Stanislav should have been there, in Yossele's shack, that very moment, to witness the scene and have his reward and take his revenge! There should be no pity for someone like Yossele Abedale! And the fact that all his life he had acted out of good intentions and that, despite his piety, it had all turned out bad, crooked, twisted and evil, was no excuse, no excuse at all!

As the whip continued whistling down on Binele, Yossele's rage, instead of abating, grew fiercer—not only against the girl, or against himself or the neighbor women who had told on her and were now standing around his *bude,* as if to make certain that he did not cheat in disciplining her—but against the entire world, against the cursed human race, against fate. And along with his rage grew his woe, his despondency, his sense of doom. How could he hold it against the Jews of Bociany that they looked at him with suspicion? Or against these women, his devoted neighbors? Danger lurked everywhere, and a Jewish child, his child, was being tempted by the Evil One right before his eyes. He had to do something to save his own flesh and blood and to save himself. But what, if the core of all existence was beyond salvation? Had he not been right in the belief he had held since childhood, that all was in vain? Within him, the heart of a thirteen-year-old cried to the heavens, while he stood there, whipping away at the soft, fragile body of his daughter.

For almost a week Binele could not move at all. Her back and buttocks were covered with red marks and blue blotches. Her sisters were good to her. Faigele tried to cheer her with funny stories. Raisele and Rochele applied rags dipped in cold water to her bruises. When Hershele came home and saw her lying face down on the cot, he sat down beside her and tried to console her.

"You'll see," he said one day. "Soon the Messiah will come and Tateshie won't hit you anymore."

She answered him calmly in a voice hoarse from crying, "Let him hit me. Let the Messiah hit me too. I don't care. I will play with Yadwiga anyway."

"Are you out of your mind?" He stared at her. "The Gentiles are nice to you because they want to convert you."

"So let them. Anyway, I don't want to be a *Zydovetchka.* I want to be Yankova's child. And Yadwiga kisses me, and Yanek never beats me up, although he beats up his wife."

"You're crazy! When our Messiah comes, the entire world will love one another. Then Tateshie will surely kiss you and all of us. Because Tateshie loves us more than anyone else does in the entire world."

Binele grew thoughtful. She had suddenly remembered that Yanek beat up Yankova because he loved her. She was beginning to wonder whether it would be worthwhile to convert in order to be loved by Yadwiga and her family. "I know . . . I know that he loves us," she said. "That's why he beats us up."

"That's right," Hershele nodded. "He has our good at heart. But when the Messiah comes, there will be no need to beat up anyone, because we will all be completely free of sin. And that's why it's good to be a Jew."

This reasoning eluded Binele. "Why?" she asked.

"Because we will bring the Messiah to the whole world," Hershele replied. "Without us, he will never come."

At dusk, Binele rose from her cot. Although she was still in great pain from the bruises on her back, she set out for the Wide Poplar Road. She wandered up to the inn, to see if by chance the Messiah had arrived yet. She called to him with all her heart as she looked down the stretch of road. When she returned—without the Messiah—it was already dark outside. Yossele, his children, and the neighbors had been looking for her all over Bociany. When they saw her appear down the street, they all gathered in front of the house. Yossele ran toward her, lifted her in his arms, and carried her inside.

"Where did you vanish to this time, you snotnose good-for-nothing? Where?" he bellowed. He repeated the question over and over again. She remained mute. He knew that she could barely move her bruised body, but what choice did he have? The other children were watching, the neighbors were peering in through the open door and windows. He began to beat her again.

It was then that she burst out in a scream, "I went to look for the Messiah, that's where I went! I wanted to tell on you! I wanted to tell him not to save you, because you're a bad father, a mean, mean father!"

## 11

THE SCYTHED FIELDS surrounding Bociany looked like freshly shaved blond heads, with the sheaves of rye gathered together like pigtails. The Days of Awe had come and gone, and now the Polish autumn was preceded by a sudden heat wave. The summer that had just passed had been the summer of Yacov's rebellion.

It had begun slowly at an unspecific time, at home, and now it announced its distinct arrival in the cooling of his affection for his mother. For reasons he could not explain, whatever she said or did irritated him. Even the sound of her soft voice grated on his ear. Sometimes he simply could not bear the sight of her. She was no longer beautiful in his eyes; she was downright ugly. It seemed to him that she, more than anyone else, had been an illusion. She was a liar. All her talk had only had one purpose—to muddle his mind and confuse him. She had confused him about everything, including man, God, and His world. She had wrapped the truth in the cotton of sweet words, had coated the bitter pill with candy so that he might swallow it more easily. She had made a sissy out of him. Just watching her speak to her customers, as if she were ready to kiss their hands and lick their boots, made him sick. Everything was her fault.

He still considered it his duty to help her out as much as he could. He carried pails of water for her, ran errands, and once in a while took over the shop for her. But he no longer cared whether she laughed or cried, and he stayed away from home as often as he could. What irritated him even more was her matter-of-fact attitude toward this change in his behavior. She appeared not to have noticed. True, she no longer kissed him or hugged him as she had used to, but this, he argued to himself, was due to her realizing how much he had grown.

At the same time, his relationship with his siblings also deteriorated. He had always looked up to his brother Shalom, who was a serious, taciturn boy, both a reliable son and a diligent student. He would answer Yacov's questions concerning a passage in the Mishnah so lucidly that there was no need for further questioning. Recently, however, Shalom's excellent qualities and irreproachable behavior had begun to make Yacov more aware of his own shortcomings and faults. Whatever Shalom said or did, Yacov took as a reproach to himself. And what he could bear the least was that Shalom was such a good son that he truly deserved their mother's love. So he now avoided Shalom as much as possible.

As for his sisters, Gitele and Shaindele, they had once been a source of amusement and delight to him. He had liked to chat and play with them whenever he had the time, despite the fact that doing so confirmed his heder friends' opinion of him as a sissy. Now, however, he considered himself at an age when it was sinful to look at girls at all, including his own sisters. Thus Gitele and Shaindele, too, had begun to annoy him. He refused to spend any time with them, he chased them away, and he yelled at them for no apparent reason.

He became obsessed with physical prowess. He felt the need to experience physical pain and master it, as well as to learn how to fight well. But his friends at the heder had outgrown their love of skirmishes and brawls. Even Ariele, the leader of the street gang, had quieted down considerably. So the only chance Yacov had of learning how to fight properly was to pick an argument with one of the gentile boys. His heart cried out for revenge against gap-toothed Stefek and his mob. But Stefek and the other gentile boys were working in the fields, helping out on the farms full time. His former friend Bronek, Manka the Washerwoman's son, with whom Yacov was no longer on speaking terms, had taken over all the physical chores at his mother's house and was learning to become a fireman. The only opportunity Yacov had for facing these boys was on a Sunday. But on Sundays, no Jew in his right mind ventured openly into the street. And then, Yacov had never been so frightened of Gentiles as he was now, having heard so much about the massacres taking place in the *shtetlekh* and towns.

He did not even have the chance to stand up against the *melamed,* Reb Shapsele, with his "put-yourself-downs," for they rarely occurred anymore. He was preparing for his bar mitzvah, and the *melamed* respected bar mitzvah boys. The only good thing was that Yacov would soon begin to study on his own in the *besmedresh,* or perhaps even leave for a yeshiva. Despite his preoccupation with physical prowess and practical, down-to-earth matters, he was incapable of neglecting his studies. He had the strange feeling that he had to dig through it all, know the Scriptures to perfection, in the same way that he had to know how to fight.

The only human being he loved now was Ariele. During the warm evenings, the two boys wandered through the streets and alleys. The air was full of the scents of late flowers and ripe fruit. The two friends, oblivious to their surroundings, discussed passages of the Scriptures, argued, digressed to subjects closer to their hearts, and always returned to the main topic: What to do?

Something, they agreed, had to be done to express their anger, to counteract their fears and change the general unsatisfactory order of things. Try as they might, they were no longer capable of delighting in simple mischief, and so could find no outlet in that. Although Ariele was brave and strong and had even learned from the butcher boys how to wield an ax, he now differed very little from Yacov. If they were going to be mischievous, it would have to be meaningful mischief. There had to be something more to it than just the fun to be had out of spite and destructiveness. The burden of responsibility already weighed on them. Although they both had yet to reach bar mitzvah, what they had learned at the heder, or from the Jews in the shtetl, had already sunk deeply into their souls.

The only daring thing that Yacov and Ariele could think to do was to stroll through the villages on just such warm evenings. The peasants and their families were either outside in front of their huts, resting, or could be seen through the open doors and windows, preparing for bed; they went to sleep "with the chickens," as the Jews said. Every so often, as the two boys wandered through the fields, they would see some stacks of sheaves that seemed to move as though animated, and they heard muffled sounds coming from inside. These sounds were either ghosts or couples making love. It took courage to hide behind those swaying monsters and listen.

Ariele knew a great deal about lovemaking, not only from the older heder boys, but also from listening to the butcher boys. With great relish he taught Yacov all the dirty words he knew and revealed the disturbing secrets of the lovemaking process to him. This feat required double courage. The excitement and fright of walking through the fields at night, listening to the couples fornicating, and then discussing sex with Ariele, was almost more than Yacov could bear. A chill would run down his spine, and his teeth would chatter. Ariele's presence was not much help. Imperceptibly, the time had passed when Yacov could be taken under Ariele's wing and made to feel safe. Now he felt that it was Ariele, despite his knowledge and prowess, who looked up to him, seeking support and counsel. Ariele's soul was in turmoil.

During one of these warm moonlit nights, as the two boys were walking along the Wide Poplar Road, a man suddenly jumped out of the ditch onto the field and began running in the direction of the village. Ariele stopped, stunned. "Did you see him?" he asked. "Didn't he look exactly like my father? The way he runs . . . "

"Not at all," Yacov whispered.

"I bet it's my father!" Ariele insisted.

"You're crazy! Where would your father be running to at this hour?"

"Come, let's go after him! He's in danger!"

"For heaven's sake, stop it, Ariele!" Yacov was shocked. "You're imagining things."

Ariele had already jumped the ditch, and Yacov had no choice but to follow. After all, he was Ariele's friend; he would stick with him through thick and thin. They raced through the fields after the figure of the man in the distance. To Yacov, it was like running in a dream. Could that large, dark figure heading toward the village really be Ariele's father, his own flesh and blood? One after another, the lights in the village flickered out. The boys were now in total darkness as they raced along the village path. In front of them, the man had stopped running. He was standing outside the hut of Magda the Widow, peering in through the window. As the man was about to vanish into the darkness of the hut, Ariele covered Yacov's eyes with his hand.

"Don't look! You saw nothing. That's not my father, you're right." Then he removed his hand, and he and Yacov stared into each other's eyes. Had it all been real? Had they really seen what they had seen? Ariele collapsed against a tree at the side of the path. "Oh God," he muttered. "What do I do now?"

Yacov squatted down beside him. "What do you mean? Let's go, that's what we should do."

"But Yacov, it was my father."

"How can you know for sure? And even if it was your father, perhaps he was only going to deliver some meat."

"Kosher meat? To Magda the Widow? Oh, Yacov, leave me alone." Ariele started crying. "You don't know what a wretched, miserable man I have for a father."

"I don't have a father at all," Yacov reminded him. He knew that Ariele was envious of his dead, respected father and his distinguished lineage, and that he was ashamed of his own father. "Come, Ariele," Yacov begged. "I'm sure that it wasn't your father."

"And I am sure that it was," Ariele sobbed. "He's a beast, not a man. But he wants so badly to be a good man, you know."

"He is a good man. Let's go!" Yacov tugged at his sleeve.

"No, I'm staying here. I must see him. Do you remember the visitor who came to my house the other night? He stole our silver candlesticks and in return left something dangerous in the house. Something terrible. You don't know, because Father doesn't show it, but he can't fool me. Oh God! I'm his son and I can't save him. I can't protect him from his own wicked nature. Yacov!" he grabbed his friend by the lapels. "I'm going out of my mind. Tell me what to do. You're the only friend I have in the world."

"That doesn't mean that I know what to do." Yacov stammered. "I think that you are mistaken. Your father would not do such a thing. All of Bociany loves and respects him."

"They don't know him." Ariele fixed his overflowing eyes on the dark window of Magda's hut.

"But you love him so much. How can you think what you think?"

"It's because I love him that I know. He is one way during the day and another at night. The greatest sins are committed at night."

His own experience with the gentile children came to Yacov's mind. "You're wrong," he said. "The greatest sins are committed in broad daylight."

Ariele waved his hand impatiently, annoyed with Yacov. "During the day he is in the butcher shop. After that, he sits in the ritual slaughterer's house. He would not do anything wrong during the day."

"Then let's go over to the ritual slaughterer's house to check."

Ariele suddenly jumped to his feet, and the two boys raced off in the direction of the shtetl. They peered into the kitchen window of the ritual slaughterer's house and then into the adjoining room. Inside, Sore-Leyele, the slaughterer's wife, was telling her stories, surrounded by a group of women. In the kitchen, which was similarly crowded, the men sat on benches around the table or stood leaning against furniture and walls. Some made a pretense of reading the open volumes of Gemara in front of them, but all were intently listening to Sore-Leyele's voice as it came to them from the next room. Fishele was not in sight.

Slowly the boys turned around, then quickly set out for Ariele's house. Perhaps Fishele was in bed, sound asleep? Ariele ran into the house, leaving Yacov outside to wait for him. Before long he reappeared in the yard. "I'm going to kill myself," he mumbled.

"Don't talk like that," Yacov begged, himself near tears. He pulled Ariele over to the water pump, which was located near a cherry tree. From the tree hung some overripe cherries that looked like small clots of dark, dry blood. He touched his friend's trembling shoulder. "Please, Ariele . . ."

"I've lost my father to the Evil One. My poor wretched father. I'll kill myself."

"Then I'll kill myself with you. This is not a world that deserves to be lived in anyway." The intoxicating smell of rotted fruit, wilting flowers, and fallen leaves, brought to him by a light breeze, penetrated Yacov deeply. He realized that his statement about the world was not entirely accurate. "Perhaps there is a reason for our being here, at this instant," he whispered. "Perhaps we are meant to accomplish something, and this is the way of making us aware of it."

"It's easy for you to talk like that. Your father has secured himself a safe place in heaven."

"What of it, if he's dead?"

"My father went inside . . . to Magda. That's worse than death."

"No, it isn't. As long as he's alive, he has the chance to repent, to mend his ways. You know that there are greater rewards awaiting those who have sinned and repented than those who are righteous by nature. Anyway, Ariele, if we are meant to save the world, that includes your father, too. Maybe this is our destiny, and even if it isn't our destiny, we could make it ours. Who is to prevent us?"

Ariele wiped his eyes and looked resentfully at Yacov. "You know who." He pointed to the sky.

"Why should He, if we are on His side?"

"How do you know which side is His?"

"Let's not blaspheme, Ariele."

That evening there was nothing that Yacov could do to cheer his friend. The two boys parted, rebounding onto themselves, like a thread snipped apart.

Because Yacov now spent all his free time with Ariele, who was beside himself with grief and needed him badly, he often returned home late in the evening. Inevitably, his mother would be sitting up, waiting for him while mending clothes. The girls and Shalom would already be asleep. Hindele would turn to face him as if to let him see how worried she had been. He would pretend that he had not noticed, as he prepared for bed.

One night, he burst out in spite of himself, "You don't have to wait up for me, you know. I'm not a child anymore."

"To me you'll always be a child," she whispered, also preparing for bed. "I worry when no one can find you and you don't come home at a decent hour."

"Then don't worry!" he shot back. "The devil won't carry me off!" He immediately regretted his words, aware that she was hurt. But he could not help it—he was furious. "Good for her," he thought. "She makes me sick with her constant worrying." Joining Shalom on the straw mattress beneath the window, he turned his thoughts to Ariele, trying to forget the guilt he felt towards his mother.

One splendid autumn day followed another. The leaves turned to shades of brown, yellow, red, and gold. Bociany basked in light, in the last precious embrace of sunshine. People spent their evenings outdoors, trying to make the most of these last gifts of pleasant air. The adults stood chatting in front of their doorways, the small children, still barefoot, ran about, kicking at the heaps of raked leaves, somersaulting into them, tunneling caves into their depths, or collecting the most beautiful leaves as if they were rare jewels.

Spending an entire day at the heder filled the heder boys' hearts with remorse for missing out on these last few moments of nature's bounty before the arrival of the winter's rain and snow. As soon as they were released from the heder, the boys would race out into the fields and marshes to celebrate spring in reverse, for now they could follow the first of the departing storks with their eyes. Some of the boys rushed along the Narrow Poplar Road to the manor house, to have a last glimpse of the courtyard through the railing and to watch the landlord's sons riding their graceful thoroughbreds. Others would take to the Wide Poplar Road, in the direction of the birch wood and the lake.

Yacov looked at the younger heder boys and realized how far behind he had left the playfulness of his own childhood. The more springlike the weather outside, the deeper the autumn in his heart, as with a strange detachment he observed the beauty of his shtetl. Doors and windows still stood open to the outdoors, the houses were still one with the gardens, the orchards, the earth, and the sky. God's world was still on holiday, the sun a kindly presence, embracing everything with maternal arms. But he was aware of nature's lie, and for him there was only the icy embrace of loneliness, not just his own, but also that of his friend Ariele, and of everything human. It was the loneliness of this painfully magnificent world that now, in its wilting, pretended to be smiling, pretended to forget the misery of winter that stood at its door. There was no one to lean on, no support, no solace—unless it could be found in that strange creature who was his mother, but with whom he no longer shared a common language.

Studying the Scriptures had finally lost its meaning for him. Yacov grew negligent and tried to avoid the heavy tomes whenever he could.

He slept badly, lying awake on his mattress beside the sleeping Shalom until late into the night. At times, when the moon stared down at him from the velvety sky studded with stars like jewels, he felt like weeping. He longed for his mother's embrace, and his guilt feelings nagged at him. Recently, he had not helped her with a single thing. "Doesn't she have enough problems as it is?" he thought. "Why do I add to them? Has some demon entered my heart? Perhaps it's been sitting there all along and only decided to surface now?"

He tried to call back the thoughts of the Passover when he had been so excited by the wisdom of the famous rabbis. But their words seemed stale to him now. Instead, he felt a revulsion against the rabbis and their teaching, a revulsion even against the Almighty Himself. He went over in his mind the familiar Talmudic arguments about judgment in the Other World, about reward and punishment there, and asked himself what worth or meaning this knowledge had against his own mother's tears, against human torment here on earth, in this world? He still could not forgive the Almighty the division into rich and poor, or into Jew and Christian. What was the Eternal One's purpose in mocking mankind, by creating the Jew Jesus, on whose account an abysmal hatred divided Jew from Gentile, with the Jew always the one who was beaten? How could this

Eternal One simply look on as His most devoted servants were slaughtered, they who carried His Torah through the world?

For the fun of it, Yacov would occasionally still visit Reb Senderl the Cabalist, to "press him to the wall" with questions that came into his mind on the spur of the moment. What would have happened, he would ask Reb Senderl, if Adam had not eaten from the Tree of Knowledge, but from the Tree of Life? And what was written on those tablets that Moses had smashed to bits? But Reb Senderl's answers found no path to Yacov's ears. This same autumn, he and Ariele had begun playing sinful little tricks, both to spite the Almighty and to test Him. In the evenings, they would walk along the village paths with their heads uncovered, or they would not wash their hands before eating or say the benediction over the food.

Hindele noticed Yacov's misbehavior, and when she reproached him, there was a note of exasperation in her voice. She was irritable, and he knew why. She had such a gift of worrying ahead of time that it sickened him. It was the time of recruitment for the army, and she was worrying about Shalom, who was due to be recruited in a very few years, if his true age were discovered. At Yacov's birth he had been registered in the county officer's book as Yacov's twin because twins were exempt from military service. Because of this worry, Hindele was already having trouble sleeping at night.

"I know, I know," she said in answer to Yacov's reproaches. "The army is child's play compared to vanishing for twenty-five years, or forever, with the Kantonists." And she would tell about the "catchers" who, until very recently, would hunt for young Jewish boys in the *shtetlekh* of the Russian Empire. They would drag the boys off for years and years, grooming them, through murderous treatment, to become the tsar's soldiers, and to forget their homes and their past. "But going into the army only for four years," she would add, "can't be taken lightly either, especially by a mother." She would smile apologetically through her tears. "Yes, small children, small worries; big children, big worries."

Hindele could not help it. Now, at this very time of year, the shtetl was full of young "corpses," young men of recruiting age who were supposed to stand up and face their fate. There were rumors spreading through Bociany that although Russia had been defeated by the Japanese, another war would soon break out. The poor young men of Bociany, and that was the overwhelming majority, were sure to be among the first recruited because the richer families could afford to bribe the authorities or grease the palms of the medical inspectors. A young man without wealth considered himself lucky if he had enough money just to pay a "fixer" in Chwosty, who would disable him, thereby making him unfit for military service. The "fixing" could take the form of anything from creating varicose veins on the legs to removing a toe or two, or pulling out all the teeth. Those who could not afford this luxury resorted to castor oil and fasting, which was the cheapest way of disabling oneself. And it did not help much. Most of these young people were in any case drafted into the tsar's army. People said that if war broke out, they would be sent to the front line, "to face the first fire."

The sight of these young men made Hindele's heart ache. It was no good trying to talk her out of her fears, especially as Yacov did it with angry reproaches in a hateful tone of voice. He wanted very much to speak to her softly and tenderly, but the curtain dividing them had become a wall. He felt that he had to shout if he wanted to get through, so that she might hear him; but the shouting seemed likewise in vain.

When the recruitment campaign was over for the year, Hindele recovered somewhat, and now it was Yacov that she began to worry about seriously. She felt his confusion, his inner disquietude, but considered it beyond her power to help him. She clung to the hope that her own past influence and that of his late father, as well as the influence of his *melamed,* and life in Bociany in general, would help him regain his equilibrium, so that he would find himself again. But she could not be a passive bystander. She tried to approach him, to breach from her side the invisible wall that separated them.

"Yacov," she said one day, a sad smile hiding in the corners of her mouth. "It's been days since I've seen you with a volume of Scripture in your hands. I know the days are still pleasant, but you could sit by the open window and study. That is a pleasure in itself."

He found himself wilting under the look of sad reproach she gave him. For a moment he was at a loss for words and did not reply. Then he averted his eyes and answered, "I'm studying enough with Reb Shapsele, don't worry."

"Yes, but you used to sit down with your Gemara at the window. You would even explain some passages to me." Her eyes, black and deep, lit up with a wistful light as she recalled the intimacy they used to share. "Do you remember how I used to tell you about the Heavenly Chariot?" she asked. "How the Almighty's Chariot is harnessed to the twenty-two letters of the alphabet, and that along with the ten *sefirot,* His emanations, they form the thirty-two ways of wisdom by which the universe was created?

Well, I don't know precisely how this is presented in the Holy Books; I've just picked up these stories from here and there. But I wanted you to know that these twenty-two letters are not only sacred, they are also healing; you must hold on to them, in order to overcome the hurdles of day-to-day life. The twenty-two letters are the hooks at the end of the bright threads to which our souls must attach themselves, so that, from our distance, we may come along on the heavenly ride. By the way, Reb Senderl told me that there is still a twenty-third letter, which we don't see, just as we don't see the letters hidden in the white spaces between the words. Only when the Messiah comes will we see all that. Then the entire Torah will read differently; the letters will be connected differently. But they will still be the same letters, Yacov my love."

Yacov would gladly have blocked his ears, so as not to hear the voice that forced him to remember the sweetness of her presence during the times when he had listened to her stories. Now every word she uttered hurt him.

The following day she saw him sitting with an open Gemara by the window. He was chanting the phrases to the appropriate cadence, although the letters remained on the paper and the words formed by his mouth did not penetrate his mind. Every now and again he raised his eyes and looked down into the nuns' garden and into the distance beyond. He watched the storks that still remained on the roofs, and the cows as they were being herded back from the pasture. From somewhere in the village the sound of a harmonica reached his ears. All the sights and sounds blended together as he looked at the horizon. All questions shrunk into one: What meaning was there to all this? That question was immediately followed by another: What meaning does my life have? The two questions in turn merged into a concrete single one: What must I do?

He heard Hindele's soft voice behind his back, "Why do you spend all evening in the house, Yacov?" she asked. "The air is so sticky in here. Go down and take a walk. You look pale." She came over and leaned out the window, inhaling deeply and with delight. "Do you have any idea how beautiful it smells outside? The crickets are singing like mad. Tomorrow will be another splendid day."

Yacov could not bear her closeness, yet he managed to say with a smile, "I honestly don't know what you want of me, Mameshie. If I spend time outside, you tell me to sit at home and study. If I sit at home and study, you tell me to go out."

The balmy days were gone and forgotten. The rains and winds of autumn took over the world in earnest. Yacov was again sitting at home, this time on account of the holes in his shoes, as Hindele had not yet saved enough money to get them repaired. He sat with a volume of the Scripture, which he leaned against the closed window. His sisters were playing on the landing outside the loft, while Hindele sat at the table darning socks.

Shalom entered, and after hanging his wet gabardine on a doornail, he, too, took up a book of Scripture and seated himself opposite Hindele. He stared at the book for a while. His face, illuminated on only one side by the naphtha lamp that stood near Hindele, seemed dark and shadowy. "Mameshie," he finally spoke in a voice unusually hesitant for him, "perhaps it would be a good idea for me to get married?"

Yacov felt as if he had been pierced in the heart. He was jealous of Shalom's courage and wisdom. Shalom was proposing to take a definite step. He would become someone's son-in-law and thereby be provided with room and board while he continued his studies. That way, he would no longer be a burden to his mother and would not have a worry in the world. Yacov mentally counted the years he had to wait before he could do the same.

Hindele raised her eyes from the sock she was mending and blinked in surprise. "If you insist, I can look around," she said, smiling broadly. "Reb Menashele the Matchmaker is still a good friend of mine."

Shalom opened his mouth to say something, then closed it again. He bit his lips as his face turned purple. He waved his hand. "No hurry," he said.

With regard to her children, Hindele needed few hints. She immediately realized that marriage had been on Shalom's mind for some time. Therefore, the first thing to do was to seek out Reb Menashele the Matchmaker and discuss the matter with him. She was confident that Reb Menashele would have the decency not to propose any marriage candidates for herself if she went to him on behalf of her son. In any case, she was convinced that Reb Menashele no longer had even a remotely suitable candidate for her because she was an old woman now with a marriageable son. She dismissed the fact that neither her face nor her body were yet badly wrinkled, and only her hands were rough and coarse, as owing to the fact that she had a dark olive complexion and skin of exceptionally good quality. Nor did it matter that she was still given to dreaming, musing, yearning, and that she still liked to laugh once in a while, to sing, and even to play the fool by composing rhyming stanzas to the tunes she picked up. What really mattered was that her day-to-day moods were doubtless those of an old woman, her heart heavy as a rock, loaded down with worries and fears.

She paid Reb Menashele a visit at his home, and before he had a chance to ask her to sit down, and before his wife had a chance to offer her the habitual glass of tea, she began the conversation with regard to her elder son. True, he was still relatively young, she said, but he was a *mentsh* before God and people, with a good head on his shoulders, not lazy nor a blabbermouth, but quiet, kind, modest, and on his word one could build a fortress. Once she had finally gotten around to sitting down, she continued, saying that of course there was no need to tell Reb Menashele of her son's distinguished lineage, or how charming and handsome her son was, or that all of Bociany envied her her children.

"You surely know better than any one else, Reb Menashele," she said, "that I'm not stressing all of my Shalom's good qualities as something I sucked out from my finger. I'm not inventing things simply because I am his mother."

Reb Menashele listened to Hindele with great patience even though he was in a hurry to leave for Chwosty, where he had to arrange an important marriage. He registered Shalom's name in his bulky black notebook and promised to do everything in his power to find him a bride the likes of whom Bociany had never before seen. He did not say a word about a match for Hindele, and she left his house on wings, wiping the tears from her eyes. Soon she would be leading one of her children to the wedding canopy for the first time. It would not be much longer before they were all out from under her wing. She trembled over their fate and prayed that they would be fortunate, healthy, and happy.

Indeed it did not take long for Reb Menashele to start proposing candidates for Shalom, every one of them a jewel. Surprisingly, however, Shalom frowned every time Hindele returned in great excitement from Reb Menashele with a description of a prospective bride who had all the necessary qualities, as well as beauty. Shalom would flush red to the ears and run out of the room. Finally Hindele pressed him, insisting that he tell her what was wrong with the proposed match.

He always gave the same answer, "She's a good match, but not for me."

"Why not for you? She's a relation of Simchele the Wood Merchant and that's no small thing."

Shalom gave her one of his blunt, open looks, which went straight to her heart, and said in a voice clear and frank, "To me, she is as ugly as death."

Hindele was stunned. "Reb Menashele is moving heaven and earth for your sake. He's proposed the most beautiful and wealthy girls in Bociany for you, and to you they are as ugly as death?"

"I can't help it," Shalom shook his head and turned his eyes away from his mother.

"So perhaps you only imagine that you want to get married?" Hindele could not understand what had happened to this most reasonable son of hers.

On Friday evening, after the Sabbath meal, they sat at the table singing Sabbath songs, while the two girls played in the yard. Shalom took advantage of the silence between the end of one song and the beginning of another. "Mameshie," he spoke up. "I want a girl . . . "

"I know," Hindele responded with her usual radiant Sabbath smile, although it was followed by a sad glance from her dark, plum-shaped eyes. She consoled both him and herself, "Don't be upset about it, Shalom. Sooner or later we'll find what you're looking for."

"I've found her already!" he burst out and turned red as a beet.

"What do you mean you found her? Suddenly? Out of the blue moon?"

"Not suddenly, Mameshie. I've loved her a long time. I want Dinele, Shayele the Tinker's daughter."

"Loved her!" Hindele exclaimed.

"But she doesn't have a kopeck in her dowry!" Yacov jumped from his seat.

A confused silence followed. Hindele shook her head in bewilderment. How imperceptibly the times had changed! It had never occurred to her that a son of hers would find himself a bride without the help of a matchmaker. She groaned resentfully. "Yacov is right," she said. "Love may be sweet, but it tastes better with bread." She sat quietly for a very long while, adjusting her wig, wiping her nose, and sighing. But gradually her face began to clear. Finally she said, "So be it, if this is what the Almighty wills. Because if a wife is not pleasing to your eyes, you yourself may end up pleasing the eye of Asmodeus. I will, with God's help, send Reb Menashele to Reb Shayele the Tinker with the proposal."

She was starting to feel more cheerful and called on her sons to continue with the singing. When her two daughters returned to the room, she could not restrain herself and excitedly told them the good news.

Within the month Shalom was married to the girl he desired. It was a simple wedding ceremony, but pleasant and serene. The celebration took place in the house of Nechele the Pockmarked and her husband, Reb Laibele the Sexton. Nechele could not carry a grudge for very long, especially against Hindele, and once she heard the news of the forthcoming wedding, she climbed up to the loft to make peace with her friend and wish her *mazel-tov.* She also proposed that for the sake of convenience the feast should take place at her house. She even agreed to let Hindele invite whomever she pleased, including Yossele Abedale. Hindele acquiesced. It would be a good deed to enliven Nechele's childless home with a bit of festivity and joy. Shalom's in-laws also agreed to let Nechele and her husband bustle and fuss as if it were one of their own children who was going to the marriage canopy.

During the ceremony, Nechele and Reb Laibele were so moved that they ceaselessly wiped tears from their faces. But Hindele herself did not cry. She looked at her son, the groom, and recalled the night when she had given birth to him. There was pride in the glow of her large black eyes, and after the ceremony she was exactly in the right mood to dance. When the Hasidic band started up a *patcher,* she proudly joined Nechele and the other dancing women.

The day after his wedding, Shalom wound a few layers of rope around his waist and took up a likely spot on the Potcheyov to begin his work as a porter.

As time passed, both Shalom and his mother seemed increasingly content. After all, material things had never played an important part in their lives. As long as there was a slice of bread and herring on the table and no one went to bed on an empty stomach, what cause was there for complaint? And Shalom remained a devout scholar. Even as he stood waiting for customers on the Potcheyov, he kept his eyes buried in the sacred booklet that he held in his hands. Both he and Hindele seemed to agree that it was the Almighty's wish that poverty and learning should go hand-in-hand in their family. Perhaps because of this, both poverty and learning tasted sweeter to them.

Yacov, however, could not swallow either his mother's or his brother's submission to the Almighty's judgment. He was raging inside, and his resentment surfaced in his impatience with his mother and through his squabbles with her. Her outpouring of affection, which had once soothed his heart, now merely irritated him. And he completely lost contact with Shalom. He could not understand how Shalom could be so selfish as to "fall in love" with a pauper's daughter, doing exactly as he pleased without any regard for others. Shalom could have married the richest girl in town, he could have had the most comfortable life in a wealthy father-in-law's house, and could thereby have helped out his family as well.

Yacov decided to return to his studies and become so exceptionally brilliant that all of Bociany would talk about him, and Reb Menashele would be forced to pick the richest bride in Chwosty for him, or perhaps even in Warsaw. He would get ten thousand rubles as dowry, would have room and board at his father-in-law's all his life, and would be supplied by the latter with new clothes, a gold watch, and all the good things that money could buy. His father-in-law would shower these riches not only on him, but also on his mother, his sisters, and even his brother and sister-in-law. In the meantime, he envied Shalom. At least Shalom was no longer a burden to their mother.

It was not long before Yacov achieved the first part of his goal. At home there was talk that soon after his bar mitzvah he would leave for the yeshiva in Chwosty. Hindele looked at him with eyes that overflowed with tenderness and pride. But Yacov himself felt miserable. Was he not going to warm the yeshiva bench for venal and dishonest motives, even if a good match should come out of it some day? Anyway, his good intentions for the future could not calm his conscience in the present; what he was doing now was what counted. He was ashamed of himself, ashamed of applying himself to his studies for such practical and devious reasons, and not for the glory of the Lord. He was like a body without a soul.

## 12

IT WAS A NICE but cold evening. Hindele covered the children tightly and left the window open. She filled the lamp with oil, cleaned the glass, placed the lamp over the stove, and wrapped herself in her plaid shawl. She sat down beside the stove, put a small book on the cold burner, and inhaled deeply before she started to read. She was thinking of Yacov. When she had touched him a while ago to cover him with the feather quilt, she had felt him flinch under her touch, and she knew that he was not yet asleep. This boy of hers had a complicated soul. There was a riddle to his personality that she could not solve. "Between him and myself there used to be music, little fiddles seemed to be playing so simply and warmly between us. I wonder whether they have been silenced forever," she mused with regret. Yet she felt very close to his troubled soul and consoled herself that it was only his growing pains that had temporarily muffled the music. He was as vulnerable as an animal between shedding one coat and growing a new one. She had to be careful and patient with him. "He'll grow out of it," she told herself.

She reached for the booklet and began reading, moving her lips as she followed the lines with her eyes. Her ears, however, were alert, and while she read, her thoughts were only partly on the text. In her mind she was speaking tenderly to the boy, until she heard him breathe deeply, and sighed with relief. Now she could have a little time to herself.

She was reading a book in Yiddish about an orphaned girl who worked as a maid in a rich house in some foreign city. The girl's masters treated her so badly that Hindele could barely contain her tears. There was so much misery in the world, but there was also kindness. The girl was kind, but downtrodden. Kindness seemed to go hand-in-hand with being downtrodden. Kind people were always being taken advantage of. But the master's son was kind as well. Or was he? Why was he turning the poor girl's head with his sweet words? He had no intention of marrying her anyway. Oh, the poor soul! The girl was so starved for a kind word that when she got one, her mind stopped working. She was so very grateful that she would gladly lay down her life at the young master's feet. She obeyed him as if he had hypnotized her. Why else had she followed him to his chamber at night? Hindele thought to herself that she should never have taken a book so full of sinfulness and indecency into her hands. But it was fascinating. What on earth could the young master possibly want of this girl in his chamber at such a late hour? Could he possibly . . . ?

Stricken with horror, Hindele's heart began to pound. Her lips stopped moving, and she devoured the lines only with her eyes. Then she had to stop for a moment to be soothed by the stillness in the room. Suddenly she stirred. She heard the thump of boots coming from below, as if someone were trying to climb the steps to the loft. She stood up, left the book on the cold burner, and letting the plaid shawl fall back on the bench, rushed to the door and opened it a crack. "Who's there?" she called.

There was no answer, but someone's steps made the bottom stairs creak. She repeated the question. The stairs were creaking louder; it seemed as if one of them had collapsed under the weight of a foot. Hindele's first thought was to bolt the door, but then she remembered how loosely the bolt had been screwed on. She rushed out toward the handrail and saw a burly human mass loom up before her. A white hand slowly slid up along the shaky wooden banister, making it creak. A face. Another hand was holding something that gave off a metallic shine; it came from an ax, which the hand swung at its side. Hindele was speechless with fear, as her staring eyes began to make out the form in the darkness. She heard a voice she immediately recognized.

"It's only me, Hindele. Don't be afraid. Hush. I have a secret to tell you."

Vaslav Spokojny was breathing heavily as he mounted the steps. Another step collapsed under his weight, and he fell back to the very bottom of the stairway. He cursed thickly. Hindele stood paralyzed as she heard his hoarse voice and saw the outline of his figure against the background of the sky when he stood up. Still swaying on his feet, he again approached the stairs. Hindele took the key from her apron pocket, locked the door of the garret behind her, and dropped the key inside her bodice. She knew that the best thing to do would be to scream and arouse Manka. But when she opened her mouth only a faint groan came out. Vaslav, shaking clumsily, was climbing the stairs on all fours, his ax hitting against each step.

*"Shma-Yisroel!"* The sound finally broke through Hindele's tight throat, barely reaching her lips. She felt herself no longer where she was, but saw herself inside the locked attic with her sleeping children.

"May the cholera take your stairs, Hindele!" Vaslav called out, as his leg sank into another hole between the broken steps. She saw him sitting spread-legged on the stair beneath it, the ax lying across his knees. He looked up at her, his eyes and teeth glittering in the dark. He was smiling. "Come down here and sit beside me," he invited, with a peculiar twist of the head.

She stood where she was. "God of Avrom, of Itzhak and Yacov . . . " she mumbled without even knowing what she was saying. Every cell of her body was screaming for help.

"I said come and sit with me, " he repeated gently. "Let me see your eyes. I can't see them now. They're one with the dark. Why don't they shine brighter than the dark? Come down, little woman, for Christ's sake, or I will have to come up for you."

"Panie Fire Chief," she forced the words out. "Please, have pity on me."

"Why should I have pity on you? You'd better have pity on me. Come down." He waved the ax playfully in her direction. "Well, what are you waiting for? You're not afraid of me, are you? You know that I'd rather kill myself than harm you. I'm not as rotten as that." He tapped the sharp edge of the ax against his palm. "I have something very important to tell you, Hindele. Be good and come sit by me."

She inhaled deeply and looked desperately at the door of her garret. She knew that she had to do something, so she tried to gather her strength. Taking a step down, she said in a voice that sounded different from her own, "I'm not afraid of you, Panie Fire Chief, but you must not come here." She waited a moment, watching him pat the stair where he wanted her to sit. "Please," she forced her voice to continue, "can you wait a minute? I must get my shawl. It's chilly here."

"Woman, for you I would wait a lifetime. Go, get your shawl." He carelessly waved the arm holding the ax in her direction.

She dashed to the door. Her hands trembled as she retrieved the key from her bosom. As soon as she succeeded in opening the door, she rushed toward Yacov. "Yacov dearest," she shook him and gave him a light slap on the cheek. "Darling Yacovshie . . . " She saw his eyes open. He stared at her through a cloud of sleep. "Listen," she said breathlessly. "Listen well. You must go and climb out the window. Go and wake up Manka. No, better yet, take the ladder leaning against her house and take Gitele and Shaindele down, too. But do it fast. Do it now! Don't ask any questions!" She tugged at both his arms until he was in a sitting position, then she helped him stand on his wobbly feet. "Go! Do it and hide in the shed. Wait for me there. Hurry please, Yacovshie, and bolt the door as soon as I leave the room."

"Where are you going?" he asked, grabbing her dress.

With a jerk she shook away the pressure of his hand. "God help us, Yacovshie. Bolt the door behind me, quickly!" She grabbed her plaid shawl and rushed out, pausing at the door long enough to hear the sound of the bolt. "Here I am, Panie Fire Chief," she said, gasping. "I'm just putting on my shawl." She locked the door from the outside and felt her way down the stairs as fast as she could. She stopped a few steps away from the fire chief.

"Come closer, woman. Here!" He motioned to her with the ax and pointed to the step just above him. "Sit down."

She obeyed and sat down. The sight of him filled her with dread. She shook so violently that the stair on which she sat squeaked with every shudder of her body. Her ears buzzed and roared. Anxiously, she kept them pricked up for any sound coming from the side of the house where her window was. "God! Sweet Father in the Heavens!" Despair pounded at her heart like a drum.

She heard muffled sounds coming from the yard, as if someone were jumping or falling. She must raise her voice quickly now, to drown out the noise from outside. Talk! Pretend to be calm and talk! What to say? But she must. Without listening to her own voice, she began to tell the fire chief the plot of the story she had been reading. He was quiet, so she continued. How well she remembered it, even though her mind barely focused on what she was saying! But her story came to an end; she could not bring herself to tell him the last part, the part about the young master. She stopped and listened. Everything was quiet now outside. Suddenly she felt something warm on her cheek. Skin. Human skin against hers. Vaslav was touching her face with his hand. She gasped and leaned back with such a jerk that the step above cut into her spine.

"Why are you so afraid of me, Hindele? How can you have so much heart for people in a story and none for me? Look at me." He pulled her by the arm, forcing her to straighten up. "That's better. Now your eyes are shining brighter than the night. You think I want to rape you, don't you? You think the worst things about me, don't you? But how can such a good angel as you think so badly of me? You must know that you are stronger than I am. Angels are strong, aren't they?"

"Have pity on me, Panie Fire Chief . . . " The smell of alcohol on his breath made her head reel and finally released a flood of tears from her eyes. She heard the sound of steps in the backyard.

"Jesus Christ, little woman, what are you crying for?" he exclaimed. "Look at me. I'm calm and cool as a cucumber. Happy at last. Yes, because it's all been decided. Vaslav Spokojny has come to ask a big favor of you. You won't refuse me, will you?"

"Of . . . of course not," she stammered, her eyes fixed on the ax.

He followed her gaze, and raising the ax, shook it lightly in front of her face. "Does this frighten you?" he asked playfully. "There is no reason. The ax is my friend. It does a clean job. Nothing false about it. Truth and the ax are brother and sister, just like you and me. We love one another with the purest love, don't we, Hindele?"

"Oh God, help me, please help me!" she whimpered.

"If you must cry, little woman, then cry for me. Weep for me . . . for our sad love," he whispered. "Your tears glitter like diamonds. I want them for myself. Those precious beads of balsam, your jewels, my balm . . . " Suddenly her head was between his hands. Before she realized what he was doing, he stuck out his tongue and licked the tears off her cheeks. He released her and said, "So, I've come to tell you how this ax works. You've seen a fire, haven't you, Hindele? You've seen me at work." She saw him now rise to his knees, swaying and towering over her. "I lift it high, like this," he raised the ax above Hindele's head, "and loose it on the flaming beams." He swung the ax downwards, so that it cut into the step on which Hindele sat. "A man is like a burning beam," he continued. "If you loose an ax on him, the fire goes out on the spot. That's all there is to it, little woman."

She clutched his arm frenziedly." Panie Fire Chief, I beg of you. I can't take it anymore. Please spare me! My children are small. You're a good man, a kind man. I know it, we've spoken together many times. We're good friends. Please, leave me alone!"

He stroked her arm in an effort to comfort her. "I'm a rotten bastard, Hindele, and don't try to talk me out of it. Cry for me some more. I wish I were a Jew, so that I might be nearer to your heart, to that soul of yours that peers at me from out of those bottomless eyes. I wish I could be with you forever. But you're too saintly for me, your tears are too clean, your love too sweet. Please cry for me. Pray to your God for me, my Holy Mary. Holy Mother of Baby Jesus, I'm such a miserable creature."

His hands formed a steeple around the ax's handle as if he were praying. Then he laid the ax down near Hindele and wept as he embraced her legs and tried to nestle his head in her lap. She quickly seized the ax and jumped to her feet. The bulk of his body blocked the stairs to the exit, so she turned and ran upstairs. No longer aware of what she was doing, she pushed the key at the door, unable to find the keyhole, forgetting that the door was bolted from inside.

Vaslav came after her, planted himself beside her, and grabbed her by the wrist. He was swaying, crying, his face lowered to hers, the reek of alcohol all about him. She wrestled with him, trying to escape his embrace, his wet lips slobbering all over her face and neck as he tried to kiss her. She gripped the ax with all her strength, although he made no effort to take it from her.

"Please, little woman," he sputtered, "you must do me this one favor."

"I beg of you . . . Have pity . . . I must live . . . I want to . . . " Her tongue got tangled in her teeth.

He collapsed into a heap beside her and embraced her legs until she fell over and they both ended by sitting on the landing, gasping, weeping. The ax shook in Hindele's trembling lap.

"Will you do it? Promise me. You must." He shook her with both hands as if she were a sheaf of rye.

"I . . . I . . . "

He removed one hand from her body and wiped his face with it, trying to regain control of himself. "I wanted to do it tonight." The words came out slurred.

"Do? Do what?"

"To kill him with this ax."

She composed herself somewhat. "God Almighty! Whom is it that you want to kill?"

"The . . . him, my brother. But as I was on my way to the parsonage, I saw the Virgin Mary. She was crying. She was trembling. She looked like you. She said to me in your voice, 'Don't be like Cain, Panie Fire Chief. Don't kill your brother.' So I turned back to find you, Hindele. Because suddenly I realized what I had to do, and I was happy, so happy! You'll do me this favor, won't you, my angel . . . My Angel of . . . "

"Do what favor?" She allowed herself to relax a little more.

"I'm a weak man, Hindele, wicked and weak. Your merciful innocent hands must help me. You have the strength, I'm sure. The ax is sharpened and I am willing, so you should have no trouble. Just bring it down over my neck." He bared his neck and jerked his head violently in all directions as if he were trying to dislodge it.

"You're crazy!" she cried.

He grabbed her wrist. Suddenly the air around him changed. His face became grim and harsh. His voice grew rough and menacing. "What if I am crazy! You'd better not speak when a man is ready . . . You just do as you're told!" He slapped her across the face. She tried to stand up, but he grabbed at her and pulled her down, pinning her against the floor with the weight of his body. "You bloody Virgin Mary, you cursed Immaculate . . . Damn you!" he roared as he tore at her dress. "I'll drag you down into my pit! I'll make your soul as black as mine . . . " He tore the shawl from her back, cast it aside, and it fell into the hole between the steps.

Her clenched fist still held the ax. She glimpsed the pallor of the uncovered flesh of her thigh, and her face twisted into an expression of horror and revulsion. *"Shma-Yisroel!"* she screamed, but the sound was muffled by the weight of his chest against her face. She felt herself possessed. "I will . . . I will do it!" she yelled, her words catching in her throat.

He covered her mouth with his hand, but released the rest of her, so that he might loosen his belt. She wriggled out from beneath him, jumped to her feet, and with both hands flung the ax above his head. In a flash she saw the faces of her children, saw all of Bociany aflame. She threw the ax at him and rushed to the stairs. She tripped over a hole in the boards and rolled down until she lay at the bottom. There she quickly scrambled back to her feet, and with her blouse and skirt hanging in tatters around her body, dashed toward the shed, wiping the blood from her bruised face and elbows.

"Come!" she called to the children as soon as she reached them, grabbing the two girls by the hand. She could barely move her legs. Releasing Gitele's hand, she leaned on Yacov's shoulder. As they rushed ahead, she told the children to head for Shalom's house. "Knock on the window and get inside." As soon as they reached Shalom's hut, she let go of them. "Get inside and stay there," she repeated as if she were drunk, and hurried on.

Yacov came running after her. "Where are you going? You're all smeared with blood!" He stared at her in blank fear.

"I'll be back soon. Get inside!" she commanded, looking around to see whether Vaslav was pursuing them.

"I don't want to! You can barely walk!" Yacov cried.

"I'm fine. Do as I say, Yacov. Get inside!" As he did not move, she tried to compose her voice a little. "It's all over, Yacovshie. I'll be back shortly."

"Where are you going?"

"Look, Shalom has opened the door. Get in quickly!" She pushed him toward the house.

With her last ounce of strength she hurried on to Yossele Abedale's house at the other end of the shtetl. It was only when she stood in front of his door that she stopped to consider her appearance. She adjusted the blouse around her neck and tried to cover the torn patches in her skirt with her torn apron. "What does it matter anyway?" she thought coldly. "I'm already desecrated. Didn't that monster see my flesh and soil me with his eyes, his hands, his lips? So, I'm nothing but a piece of dirt anyhow, a forsaken, trampled shard. My body will never belong to me again." But another voice inside her called out with pride. "But my soul is safe, my conscience easy!" She was about to knock at Yossele's door when she suddenly sobered up. "What am I doing here?" she asked herself. "How can I bring myself to tell Yossele what happened to me? This shame I must carry in my heart alone to the grave. But, Almighty God, what do I care? What do I care as long as my children are safe and You protect them?"

She turned away then and slowly walked back in the direction of Shalom's house. She was blinded by tears, by her feeling of total desolation on this dark, cold night without stars. A hollow, dark emptiness hovered above her head. Dogs barked. The bare trees sighed as the wind hissed through the empty spaces between the shtetl dwellings. She leaned against a fence, her cheek resting against the cool surface of the boards. She noticed an imprint of blood where her temple had touched them and spat on the edge of her apron to wipe her face with it.

"I must not let myself get carried away by this horror," she muttered to herself. "I need to think, to find some way out of it. Telling Yossele is no good. He is just as helpless as I am, just as much at the mercy of the goyim. So is all of Bociany. Maybe I should take the children and leave for Chwosty? A Jew can always find shelter and something to eat, especially a homeless mother with children. Charitable people will take us in, or we can stay at the poorhouse. Or maybe I should return to my father and sisters? No, that's no good. The poor old man would never survive the shame, and there is no way I can avoid telling him. My sisters will bemoan my fate and make me feel even more helpless. And how can I leave Shalom alone here? There is nothing in the world that would induce him to leave his pregnant wife, and she, for her part, would not leave her family. And what would happen to my shop and my merchandise? Without that, we are all naked and barefoot. Oh God, if You are looking down on me now, give me some sign, help me decide what's best to do, don't punish me any further. Help me protect my children and myself. They need me. And I don't want to die because some wretched goy, some miserable monster, got too drunk to know what he was doing. I ask nothing of You, God in Heaven, but to help me think."

She wiped her face. Her legs were so weak that when she tried to walk, her knees buckled under her. She resigned herself to her weakness and moved over to the front step of a house to sit down in the cool silence of the night. Her face, wet with tears and blood, was raised toward the sky, as if she were awaiting some sign. The air rustled and whispered as if the night itself were full of ghosts. Now, after what she had just lived through, ghosts struck her as rather harmless companions. They would never frighten her again. She took a deep breath and stood up. Then she turned, and once more headed toward Yossele Abedale's house. She knocked gently at the door, first once, then again, waiting and listening between each knock.

The door opened sooner than she had expected, startling her and making her jump back in fear. Yossele's unpleasant growl demanded of the dark, "Who's there?"

"It's me, Reb Yossele," she stammered. "Forgive me for waking you, Reb Yossele." She was sobbing, but tearlessly; she had exhausted the supply of tears. "You must help me. It's a question of . . . of life and death."

He did not answer, but leaving the door open, withdrew inside the hut, to reappear fully dressed. "What happened?" he demanded in the same unfriendly voice, as he stood outside, at a distance from her.

Hindele swallowed hard, stepped closer to him and answered, "Vaslav . . . Vaslav Spokojny. He came with an ax to my door, dead drunk. He told me that he had been on his way to kill his brother, but changed his mind. And, Reb Yossele, I . . . "

As if wishing to prevent her from shaming herself, he waved his arm violently in front of her face. "Where is he?" he demanded. His figure seemed to grow before her eyes, expanding with his anger.

"He's still there, or he was when I took the children to Shalom's house."

Yossele began marching with nervous, quick strides. She tried to keep up with him on her shaky legs, as she talked to his back.

"I'll kill him!" Yossele waved both his fists. "I'll put an end to him once and for all!" It occurred to Yossele that he might be waking the people in the surrounding houses, so he let his arms drop and lowered his voice, "Curse him! How can I kill him without putting us all in danger from the goyim? They might slaughter us all if I did that."

"Yes, they might," she panted, running after him. "I am considering leaving town with the children."

"Leaving town? But Vaslav might take your escape out on the rest of us. All of Bociany will be at his mercy. Let's go to the *rov* and ask his advice."

She clutched Yossele's sleeve. "Heaven forbid, Reb Yossele! I beg of you, not to the *rov,* not to anyone. Don't humiliate me any further. Don't tell anyone, or I'll die of shame."

"All right! All right!" he shouted at her in frustration, then controlled himself and tried to gather the courage to ask, despite his reluctance to shame her, the question that was uppermost in his mind, "Did he . . . touch you?"

For some reason, she felt relieved rather than shamed, almost grateful to Yossele for having asked the question, although her readiness to answer him surprised her greatly. "I fought him off," she said. "He saw the skin under my dress . . . my thigh. And he did touch me . . . with his hands . . . his mouth." Thus she confessed her secret and her humiliation to Yossele. She no longer had to carry the burden alone to her grave. She had entrusted it to him, and with him she now shared it. She watched him again raise his clenched fists in the air.

Suddenly he stopped, planting himself a few feet from her. "Go back to your son's house," he said. "I will take care of this myself. Unless I let you know otherwise, go to the Potcheyov tomorrow and open the shop as if nothing had happened." Abruptly he walked away into the darkness.

Hindele sat in Shalom's dark room, trying to convince her sleepy, confused sons and daughter-in-law that nothing had really happened, that she had only been frightened by some drunken goy who had climbed up to her door by mistake, and that she had fallen down the stairs while trying to chase him away. That was why her clothes were torn and her face and elbows bruised.

Meanwhile, Yossele Abedale had gone looking for Vaslav at Hindele's house. He had found him lying prone in front of the stairs; he was snoring loudly and there was a large bump on his forehead. Yossele noticed the neck of a bottle protruding from Vaslav's pocket and pulled it out. It still contained some vodka. He raised the sleeping man's head and pushedthe tip of the bottle to his mouth. "Here, Vaslav, have a swig!" he said. He shook him, secured the wobbly head in the crook of his arm and turned the bottle up. The fire chief sucked at the bottle like a thirsty baby. Yossele then slid the empty bottle back into Vaslav's pocket and left him. He hurried to wake Fishele the Butcher and then gathered a few Jews of the night guard from their posts at various points in the shtetl. The men prepared one of the fire wagons quietly, drove to Hindele's house, loaded the still-snoring Vaslav onto it and drove off toward the village.

A light was still burning in Vaslav's house. The men had barely entered the courtyard when his wife appeared on the porch, wringing her hands. "What's the wretch been up to now, Jesus Maria?" She shook her head despairingly.

"An ugly thing, woman, a very ugly thing." Yossele suddenly became unusually talkative, and his voice carried a note of threat. "We'd better undress him and put him to bed." As the men carried Vaslav into the house, Yossele turned to the woman and looked sternly at her. "Put a water compress to the bruise on his head, and when he wakes tomorrow, tell him that he spent the entire night sleeping in his own bed like a baby and that he fell off the bed in his sleep. If he starts to tell you where he was, you tell him that he dreamt it." Yossele had no particular scheme in mind, but merely improvised as he talked. On the spur of the moment, he leaned over to the woman's ear and whispered, "He wanted to kill his brother with the ax." And he handed her Vaslav's ax.

"Charitable Jesus!" the woman exclaimed, pulling at her hair. "How can I thank you, good people?" she stammered, then grabbed at Yossele's hand, wishing to kiss it, but he withdrew it instantly, as if he had been burned.

"There is nothing to thank us for," he said, combing his beard with his fingers. "It's better for you and for us that it should all end like this. And don't say a thing about this to anyone."

The woman swore by all the saints that she would not breathe a word of what had happened to a soul. She thanked the men over and over again. On their way back to the shtetl, Yossele made his men, too, swear to keep the matter secret, so as not to frighten the people of Bociany.

The following day, as soon as Hindele appeared on the Potcheyov, Yossele left his own shop and went over to her. Standing much closer to her than usual, he whispered heatedly, "It's all your own fault, silly woman. You've brought this on yourself! I told you before never to have anything to do with that lunatic." She shook like a leaf under his words. She looked terrible, with her swollen face and with tears rolling down her cheeks. Her tears irritated him. He cut off his tirade. "Stop wailing. Pretend nothing happened. We're keeping a lookout." He quickly told her what had happened after he had left her the night before.

Back in his shop, Yossele thought about how much he had come to dislike that woman ever since her husband's death. Her tragedy had not brought them any closer. The opposite was true, despite the attention she continued to show to his children and himself. Whenever she looked in his direction with her perpetually tear-stained black eyes, which had grown even blacker since the death of her eldest son, he turned his head in the opposite direction. Things had not improved recently, when she had again begun to display her silly, wet smile. That smile made the sight of her completely unbearable.

Hindele made an attempt to go about her business as usual, but it did no good. She was absentminded, incapable of calming her trembling hands or holding back her tears. She was relieved that her children were not with her. Only Shalom stood at his post against the wall of the Potcheyov and stared at her from the distance. He was sleepy, anxious; he sensed that something grave had happened to his mother, but he did not know what. Nothing in the world could have persuaded her to tell her children. So she stood with her back turned to her eldest son.

It was midday when Vaslav Spokojny walked out on the Potcheyov and headed straight toward Hindele's shop. She saw him coming and barely managed to call out, "Reb Yossele!"

There was no need to call him. He was on his guard, as were all the men who had helped him the previous night. Fishele the Butcher appeared at the corner, his chopping knife in his hand. Hindele felt a chill go through her. But then she noticed that Vaslav was walking straight, his face looked rested, sober, his fire chief's jacket buttoned to the neck. When he came close, he greeted her with a cheerful, *"Dzien dobry!"* She had neither the courage nor the strength to answer, but managed to respond with a nod to his greeting.

He immediately noticed her bruised face and swollen eyes. "Blazes, Hindele!" he exclaimed. "You look like the Virgin Mary on the day of the crucifixion! What happened to you, woman?" She slumped down onto her stool, her head bent as if she were waiting for him to pull the ax out from behind his buttoned jacket and swing it over her neck. He smiled at her, smoothed his mustache, then fingered the ribbons strewn over the counter shelf. "Do you think this would go well with my Wanda's hair?" he asked, picking up a roll of yellow ribbon.

She forced herself to speak, "Would you like a yard?"

"Give me three yards, Hindele. I have three daughters, as you know. And give me a pair of stockings for the old lady, too, and socks for the boys, four pairs. I have four sons. Did you know that, Hindele?"

She stood up, scarcely aware of what he was telling her. Her trembling hands reached for the things he wanted; they fell from her fingers. She wished that he would disappear, sink into the ground forever.

He drew closer and said in an excited tone of voice. "Imagine, Hindele, last night I had a strange dream about you, and about my brother." He started to tell her the dream in detail. She forced herself to remain calm, to stop the trembling of her hands, of her entire body, lest she betray herself. "I can't get over it," Vaslav concluded. "It all seemed so real. But when I woke up and realized I'd only been dreaming, I actually kissed my old lady, do you believe that? That's how happy I was."

She managed a grimace that resembled a smile, then she heard herself saying, "There is a moral to this dream, Panie Fire Chief. The moral is that you shouldn't drink so much, or one day you may, in fact, kill your brother, and killing a brother is the greatest sin on earth. You're no Cain. No, you certainly aren't, when you stay away from the bottle."

He beamed at her. "I knew you'd say that. And, see, I'm as sober as a cucumber. My lips will never taste that stuff again. And it's all thanks to you."

"Why . . . ?" She started trembling again. "Why thanks to me? I'm nothing but a trampled shard."

"It's thanks to you because you visited me in my dream. You know that I'm not a complete God-forsaken villain, don't you? You're my guardian angel, my Angel of Mercy."

Her feet almost gave way under her. She felt faint and wished that she could slump back onto her stool again. But now he wanted combs and small mirrors for his daughters and then some other things for his wife and sons. It took a while before she could get all the things together. She made mistakes in her addition, forgetting to add this item or that, then counting the lot all over again. He paid her what he owed, down to the last kopeck.

As far as business went, it had been a lucky day.

Another Rosh Hashanah had gone by. Winter had come. Jewish mothers accompanied their young sons who were leaving for the yeshiva on the Wide Poplar Road. They carried the boys' bundles and boxes until a cart or a wagon passed. They offered the drivers a few kopecks, placed the future yeshiva boys on the seats, and took leave of them with tears, last-minute blessings, and moral instructions. This year the mothers were sending their sons off with more trepidation than ever. Rumors continued to persist in Bociany of unrest and pogroms in the outside world.

This particular wintry morning, Yacov rose from his straw mattress for the last time. Yesterday he had taken leave of his friend Ariele who, notwithstanding the fact that he had the head of an *ile,* refused to leave for the yeshiva. He wanted to find his way in the sea of learning by himself, at the *besmedresh.* Yacov also took leave of Reb Senderl the Cabalist and of his brother, Shalom, his wife, and their baby daughter. His heart was heavy; his head was in chaos.

He insisted that his mother and sisters not accompany him. He stubbornly shook his head. "I don't need you to follow after me as if it were my funeral. And I don't want you to carry my things, Mameshie, nor to see you slip and fall before I leave." Although it was still early winter, there had been a fierce snowstorm the night before.

He wanted to part with all of them at home, say good-bye with as little fuss as possible, and get the whole matter over with quickly. His heart was too full of turmoil, his emotions too drained, to give him strength to prolong the painful moments of leave-taking. Hindele made things still harder for him by clinging to him and fussing as if he were going to the other end of the world, instead of merely to Chwosty. And she looked pale and worn, as if she were sick.

"Chwosty is no more than a leap away," she reassured herself, dabbing at her eyes, which wept and smiled at the same time. "Before long you'll be back again for the holidays."

Of course, Chwosty was no more than a leap away, and people might be separated from one another even if they lived in the same town. But who would watch out for his mother as she carried the pails of water up the slippery, winding steps, which had lately broken in a few more places? She had grown more accident-prone recently, more absentminded, and more than once had she nearly killed herself falling down the stairs, which Shalom and Yacov kept trying to repair, to no avail. She still insisted on doing heavy chores in secret, so as not to bother her children. His sisters, Gitele and Shaindele, were still too busy playing to worry about such things. And Shalom was busy all day on the Potcheyov, carrying heavy sacks on his back, and he had a wife and baby to care for.

When Yacov felt that his guilt and anger, his love and frustration were threatening to overwhelm him, he disentangled himself from Hindele's embrace, brushed his sisters aside, grabbed his sack, slung it over his shoulder, and ran out of the room.

The snowstorm had covered the shtetl, the fields, and roads with a spotless white eiderdown. A solitary stork, late in departing, was winging southward above Yacov's head. It flew right above the Wide Poplar Road, heading toward the horizon like a small piece of wind-blown laundry. Yacov marched with his meager sack of belongings dangling from his shoulder. His head raised high, he followed the departing stork with his eyes. "Who knows if he'll come back next spring? Who knows if I will ever come back?" The thought picked like a woodpecker at his mind.

His feet carried him forward, but his heart pulled him back. The longer he marched, the more he realized how attached he was to his mother and to Bociany. Bociany was a shelter, the safest corner in the world. Even one's fears felt safer there. Bociany was beautiful. It was a familiar backyard where everyone was somehow related to everyone else. There were quarrels, of course, even some people who hated each other, but that could happen among relatives, too. They shared each other's joys and sorrows, enhancing the joys and soothing the sorrows. Certainly the distant world was tempting and enticing with its unknowns, but to go out and meet it was fraught with danger. It made him feel helplessly alone.

Some carts and sleighs passed, but he did not feel like asking for a ride yet. He had to walk off his tension, to crush it under his feet. He was in no hurry to be further away from Bociany than his own legs could carry him. He had to break with his childhood and his past gradually, step by step, weaning himself slowly, so that his new life would slip into his awareness smoothly. He needed to feel that his home and his future were not divided abruptly from one another. That was how he wanted it to be.

He stopped noticing the carts and sleighs that passed by, so absorbed did he become in what was going on inside him. He thought of his parents and about how early in his life, he had learned from them that earthly goods were but a tool of the Evil One; that the poor man was fortunate because he never lived in fear of becoming poor; that the comforts and conveniences of life were just a "vanity of vanities"; that the gusts of wind whistling through the holes of his sweet-smelling, shabby home, where the rain dripped through the ceiling, only contributed to the feeling of being free of earthly burdens, so that, light as a bird, one might soar with greater ease toward the lofty realms of the spirit. Indeed, he had absorbed the charm and serenity of his hungry childhood, but now those years spoke a different language. They added fuel to his rage. In his bitterness, he now hated a God who might not even exist, for not existing, or pretending not to exist—the same God whose Torah he, Yacov, was to study further at the yeshiva in Chwosty. For His glory he would be assigned "eating days," getting a meal every night in a different home, sleeping on strange beds, and waiting for a smile or a friendly word just like a beggar.

So perhaps he was not on his way to deepening his faith at the yeshiva, but to becoming a full-fledged nonbeliever, an atheist? Had he not already performed more than one forbidden act and broken The Law? Should he feel guilty now and beg forgiveness before this God—for doubting Him? But the Torah itself demanded that one sharpen the mind and learn to think. How could one put a fence in front of one's thoughts, no matter what direction they took, allowing them to go just so far and no further?

He passed the gentile cemetery, where the crosses of the gravestones protruded from mounds of snow, cutting like daggers into the massive grayness of the air. Despite the upheaval within him as he tramped on, Yacov suddenly grew aware of sleigh bells tinkling in the distance. Without thinking, he looked back and recognized Reb Faivele the Miller on the approaching sleigh. In an instant he found himself calling, "Reb Faivele! Reb Faivele!" and ran to meet the sleigh.

The sleigh slowed down enough for Yacov to grab hold of a side. Reb Faivele motioned to him, and he scrambled onto the sleigh, falling into Reb Faivele's fur covered lap. "What are you up to? Are you out of your mind?" Reb Faivele pushed Yacov off his lap and onto the seat beside him, while he adjusted the furs covering his legs. Reb Faivele was wearing one of the bulky fur coats usually seen on landlords, with a fur hat and ear muffs. The fur seemed like an extension of his dark beard and sideburns and made him look like a bear with a human face.

"Reb Faivele," Yacov blurted out. "Perhaps you have some work that I can do? At the mill maybe? I'll do anything!"

There was something in the expression on Yacov's face that dispersed the clouds on Reb Faivele's forehead. He edged a little closer to the side, giving Yacov more room to sit comfortably. "Why are you slurping your words as if they were noodle soup? What's gotten you so heated up?" He asked, scrutinizing the distraught lad with mischievously sparkling eyes.

Yacov took a gulp of fresh air. His heart pounded like a thief's. "I'm supposed to be on my way to Chwosty, to the yeshiva there, but I'd rather work and earn money. Or even a little food, a bit of flour for my mother for the Sabbath . . . even that would be enough."

"Stop talking through your nose!" Reb Faivele loosened the reins in his hands. The sleigh now plodded ahead slowly. Reb Faivele gave Yacov an appraising glance out of the corner of his eye. "You're Hindele's son, aren't you?"

"You remember me!"

"Of course I do. How long ago did I hear your bar mitzvah speech? And some speech it was, too! I could wish nothing better for my own sons."

"But that was a couple of months ago, Reb Faivele! And you don't remember me from before then? When you saved my life? When gentile boys were chasing me before Passover, to make a Jesus out of me. Don't you remember that?"

"What I remember is your bar mitzvah speech. So why don't you want to study at the yeshiva? Is it too small an honor for you that Bociany sends you away to become a scholar? A head like yours shouldn't be allowed to get rusty. Aye, why are you crying? Your ship of sour milk drowned at sea? What's the matter? It's not becoming for a yeshiva man to cry, so make an end to it." Reb Faivele removed Yacov's hand from his face. "That's better. When I can see your face, I can tell you something. What is your name?"

"Yacov."

"I'll tell you something, Yacov. I'm not really interested in why you don't want to go to yeshiva. That's your problem, not mine. But I've just had a brilliant idea. Don't turn your face away!" Yacov forced his tear-stained face to turn to Reb Faivele. "Now hear me out. Just as you see me here alive and well, a thought has occurred to me that the Almighty Himself might have had a hand in this business. He sent us a good and proper snowstorm last night, so that I should take my sleigh out and ride into Bociany, with the sole intention that I should meet you here, on this road, and take you home with me. It's clear as the day. He's sent me down a gift. Yes, my dear friend, that's how it must have been."

"What do you mean?" Yacov stared at him.

"I mean," Reb Faivele continued, "that I'm hiring you as a tutor for my sons, to teach them the Bible and the Rashi commentaries. I've been looking for months now for a suitable young man. I don't want to hire some sack of old bones, so that the Torah should smell foul for my little boys, you should forgive the language. Because when a person smells something foul, that person runs to the nearest door, which might lead toward evil education. Mind you, I don't have worldly education in mind, but something much worse than that. I want a vivacious young man who will be like an elder brother to my sons; then the studies will be sweeter for them. You know what I'm talking about, don't you? Aye, your bar mitzvah speech! Smooth and sweet like honey." He loudly kissed his gloved fingertips. "Believe me, you have no reason to cry. Never mind, the yeshiva can wait. You'll have enough time to study a page of Gemara at my place, too. And then there are merchants who are great scholars who stay over at my house. You'll learn plenty from them. And you can help me out a bit at the mill. You won't lack work or get bored, I assure you."

Yacov wanted to grab Reb Faivele's hand and kiss it. Truly, it was clear as day that a superior will had been at work here, placing him on the same road, at the same time as Reb Faivele. "We have a great God in Heaven, Reb Faivele," he muttered. "A miracle has occurred. You've saved my life for the second time!"

Reb Faivele beamed, burying his smile in his thick, finely trimmed beard. "How would a Jew survive without a little miracle now and then, tell me?"

That same day, Yacov, still confused and not at all certain where he was in the world, found himself sitting next to Reb Faivele's two small sons at a large oak table in Reb Faivele's dining room. He was teaching them the alphabet from a prayer book. From gilded frames on the walls, the faces of Abraham and Isaac, and Moses with the tablets, stared down at them. It was past sunset, when Yacov, still reeling from the events that had overtaken him, hurried back to Bociany to see his mother.

Hindele was still trying to recover from her experience with Vaslav Spokojny, and so was rarely fully aware of what was going on about her. She fixed her eyes on Yacov as if he were an apparition. In her mind, she had followed him on his way to Chwosty and had calculated that he had already reached his destination. So perhaps she was only dreaming with her eyes open?

She rushed at him and put her arms around him to make sure that he was flesh and blood. Then she patted him all over, making certain that he was in one piece. Then she peered very closely at his radiant face, just in case it indicated that he had escaped some great danger. Finally, she embraced him again as if they had been separated for years. When she had recovered from the shock, he told her what had happened on his way to Chwosty, and with great fervor, he undertook to convince her that the incident had been a sign from heaven.

"You can see for yourself, Mameshie," he said, pretending not to notice how upset his story was making her. "Because of our accursed poverty, Father and Itchele had to leave this world. Heaven forbid that it should happen again. You're always complaining that Gitele and Shaindele are as thin as sticks, and they need to grow . . . "

"Bite your tongue!" she could not listen anymore.

"I am not going to bite my tongue! This is the truth. We must look it straight in the eye. And before you know it, you'll need a dowry for them too."

"Stop talking so much. Here," she placed a mug of chicory coffee in his hands.

But Yacov could not stop talking. He was so taken by the important step that he had taken on his own and so anxious that Hindele approve of it and bless it, that he voiced all the thoughts he had concealed from her before. He felt that he had to breach the wall of silence that had grown between them. He saw tears in her eyes and began to shout, "I don't want to warm some yeshiva bench! It's not fair! It's selfish! The Almighty Himself, if he had our good at heart, would not require such a thing from a son who has passed his bar mitzvah!"

She covered his mouth with her hand. "Shut up once and for all! Have you been drinking windbag water, or what? Why are you sinning with your words?"

He tore her hand from his mouth. "I'd rather sin with my words than with my actions. And if what I'm doing is a sin, then I take it upon myself!"

Slowly she began to stroke his arm. "It's not as simple as that. It's not simple at all . . . " She waited for his anger to subside and added, "Silly child, the pains of poverty are the easiest for us to bear. There are worse things, and we bear them and survive as well. We must not make a great fuss over suffering, Yacov dear. All things in this world were created through suffering. A human being must learn to accept it and transform it so that something good may result. That's how one learns the art of living. And as for warming the yeshiva bench, I don't have to tell you . . . the *Toyre* is the gate through which you peer into the Almighty's endless and timeless universe, Yacovshie. Without the *Toyre* we are nothing but worms creeping in blindness, with no idea what glory there is in being alive. Without the *Toyre,* man is like a prisoner in a dungeon, doomed never to taste freedom. It is when there is no *Toyre* in a person's life that poverty becomes unbearable. Then one suffers tortures that are superfluous and worthless, for nothing good is born of it."

Yacov was forced to smile. He interrupted her, "Well, isn't it selfish that I should have this taste of freedom, studying the *Toyre* day and night, and leave you behind in the dungeon struggling for a slice of bread?"

She half-smiled back at him, the familiar half-smile hidden in the corners of her mouth. "First of all, I'm a woman, and caring for my home is my destiny. Second, it is I who am selfish, my son, because when you study, you take me with you. Through you, I, too, can get out into the Lord's spacious world. You may not be aware of it, but it is so." Yacov was about to interrupt her, but he caught himself. He had to let her speak. She had to clear a path to him with words, expressing her thoughts, so that they could meet again. She struggled to control her voice. "To tell the truth, you're forcing open doors. The yeshiva is not the only place where a young man can follow the ways of the Lord. Shalom didn't leave for the yeshiva either, and yet he keeps up his studies. Sometimes I even wonder whether the erudition of scholars doesn't put itself between man and his God. Perhaps too much learning obscures Him rather than revealing Him a little more. I know that the Bal-Shem Tov himself said that learned men are so engrossed in the *Toyre* that they have no time for the Creator. So, you understand, Yacovshie, the truth of the matter is . . . is that a righteous man will not be harmed by going into a tavern, and an evil one will not be saved by going into a *besmedresh.* Real faith comes from the heart; the heart must study the *Toyre;* the heart ought to teach the mind. If it's the reverse, then it's no good. But, Yacov dear, to be honest, I badly wanted the yeshiva for you. Forgive my words, but you are not Shalom. The yeshiva could hold you . . . "

"Hold me in a tighter harness!" Yacov jumped, stung by her words. His face was aflame, his voice breaking, "You don't trust me, do you?"

She made as if to embrace him, "You don't understand . . . "

"I understand you very well!" He wriggled out of her embrace. He was shocked, painfully jealous of Shalom. She did not have a good opinion of him, did not even trust his faith. It hurt. And yet she was right. He quickly turned his face away lest she read there both his torment and his agreement. She knew him better than he could have imagined. She sensed that he was not like Shalom, that within him all the reins had been loosened, that he no longer saw a straight path before him and could turn as well in one direction as in another. So, after all, there had been contact between him and his mother all the time. Despite their estrangement, the thread holding them together had not been broken. He felt that he owed her an honest answer. "You know, Mameshie," he said softly, turning back to her. "I think I'll never be able to fool you."

They talked for a long time and when Yacov left the loft, it was on wings.

## 13

BINELE WAS NOW almost ten years old. Thanks to the intercession of the *rov* himself, to whom Yossele had gone for advice, Sore-Leyele, the wife of the ritual slaughterer, had taken her on as a servant.

Sore-Leyele was known as the most pious, God-fearing woman in Bociany, from whom even the *rov's* wife learned how to conduct herself. All the women of Bociany took Sore-Leyele as a model and repeated her wise words to their daughters. If they themselves were unable to grab a seat next to her in the women's section of the synagogue, they would try to push their daughters nearer, so that they at least might have the honor. From Sore-Leyele the path ran clear up to the Garden of Eden. The gates of all the seven heavens stood open to her, and that was why she was capable of seeing inside them.

Like all the other shtetl girls, Binele had heard a great deal about Sore-Leyele. Every Friday, when she went to the slaughterer with the chicken that her father had brought home, she pressed her nose against the window of the slaughterer's house and peered inside. There she could see Sore-Leyele preaching to the other women, who had also brought chickens to be killed for the Sabbath.

Binele could not hear the words through the glass, but she could see Sore-Leyele swaying back and forth, while the women, with their dead chickens already in their baskets, swayed with her. Sore-Leyele gestured wildly with her arms and moved her lips, sometimes quickly, sometimes more slowly. In her bonnet with the tiny crown in front, in her Turkish shawl and large shoes, which she wore with black stockings on scrawny legs as thin as sticks, with her pale face and her eyes burning into the distance, she resembled an enormous turkey. Binele did not understand why the women sitting inside did not explode with laughter, but they did not. They rolled their eyes so piously and intently that it was a miracle that their eyeballs did not fall out of their sockets and land on Sore-Leyele's unlaced shoes. At the same time, their lips moved as if they were chewing on every word that came from Sore-Leyele's mouth.

It had been a cold, rainy evening in the middle of the week when Yossele first took Binele to the ritual slaughterer's house. He had been hoping to catch Sore-Leyele alone, so that he might discuss with her the problems that he was having with his youngest daughter. But the house was crowded with visitors, the door was forever opening and closing, and people were crammed inside just like at the *besmedresh*. The women sat in the large room, the men in the kitchen, and all listened in silence.

Sore-Leyele had charisma not only because she conducted herself like the saintly Sarah Bat Tovim, but also because she had great powers of speech, almost as great as those of the *rov*. In a way, it could be said that she surpassed the *rov* because he could only be understood by the learned, whereas Sore-Leyele spoke in such simple language that even a child could grasp her meaning. At the same time, she had the gift of being able to hypnotize with words, to make them penetrate into the deepest recesses of the souls of both men and women.

In fact, the men were as drawn to her preaching as the women. First they would visit the *rov,* who lived in the same house, on the pretext of needing some questions answered or of hearing a clever saying; then they would sneak away into the slaughterer's dwelling. Once there, they would pretend to have dropped in merely for a chat or perhaps to study some Gemara in his company, because the *besmedresh* was so crowded. Sore-Leyele was after all nothing but a sinful female whose stories were only suitable for others of her sex. But one and all considered themselves fortunate if they could secure themselves a place in the slaughterer's kitchen. They would then lean attentively in the direction of the other room, where Sore-Leyele sat preaching in her dramatic voice, surrounded by her female audience.

On entering Sore-Leyele's kitchen with Binele, Yossele first threw a few kopecks into the tin charity boxes that hung by the door. Then he leaned against the bench where the two pails of water stood, and waited for the crowd to leave. After a while, Fishele the Butcher came over to him. Fishele practically lived in this open, hospitable house. He could always be found either here or at the *rov's* house next door. Here he cleansed himself of his ignorance, soaked up wise sayings like a sponge, and later repeated them to his customers and acquaintances like a scholar. Mostly he hoped to forget his sinful temptations here.

Fishele whispered in Yossele's ear, "Too bad you didn't come earlier. You should have heard . . . " Thinking Yossele was about to apologize for having come in late, Fishele put a finger to his lips and solemnly whispered, "Shush."

Yossele joined the others who listened to Sore-Leyele's voice. He realized that Sore-Leyele was about to tell the story of Kailele the Bride, a story that all of Bociany knew by heart. That was no reason not to listen, of course. Every time Sore-Leyele told this story, it seemed like the first time, and the story perfectly suited the miserable winter night outside. Yossele was not certain that the story was suitable for Binele's ears. He looked around for her, thinking to send her out to the antechamber, but could not find her.

"Kailele the Bride, the poor innocent orphan," Yossele heard Sore-

Leyele's lilting voice saying from the other room, "went mad, may Heaven protect us, on the very night of her wedding . . . " Sore-Leyele's words stung Yossele in the heart. He hoped that Binele had gone out on the porch by herself, or that she had sneaked off to the *rebetsin's* kitchen. "Kailele's bridegroom had been handsome . . . " Sore-Leyele continued and Yossele saw his own wedding night in his imagination. "The bridegroom had been too handsome. And that was her tragedy. She fell in love with him on the spot, out there in the cemetery, where the wedding canopy had been set up so as to brighten the hearts of her poor, dead parents, may they rest in peace. So, when the bridegroom tried to touch her on the wedding night, forgive the expression, she fainted. When he, may I be forgiven the word, kissed her, her brain turned upside down. A few minutes later, she went mad. Yes, yes, naked and barefoot as the day her mother bore her, may God preserve us from misfortune, she ran out of the bedroom. It was a cold, frosty night and the moon shone outside. The night was as bright as poor Kailele's fate was dark . . . "

Yossele's heart froze. His own wedding had been on a wintry, moonlit night. As Sore-Leyele talked, he saw his Mariml in the bedchamber, her white face a cool yet burning reflection of the moon. Now, after her death, it often seemed to him that the moon was a part of Mariml's body, sometimes a breast, or a shoulder, or a knee.

"The moon shone and the snow glittered on the ground, and as Kailele ran, she left her bare footprints in the snow. They led as far as the lake. There, God protect us, she threw herself onto the ice. The ice was too thin to hold her. It cracked. She sank, but only a foot or two. So, Kailele drowned in the lake, but did not go under. She remained floating on that bed of ice, may our enemies not know a better bed, and remained lying there neither up nor down." A long silence followed, during which there was much sighing and sniffling.

"Therefore," Sore-Leyele continued, "the bottom of the lake could not get to the bottom of Kailele's madness, could not suck it in, to let the ground absorb it before the soul of the poor child separated from the body. So the poor soul had no choice but to float to the top of the lake in its mad form. That is why the lake looks like a mirror, and when you look into it for a long time, you can see, may the Almighty have mercy on us, you can clearly see Kailele's mad eyes swimming about in the water.

"And that's why when winter comes and the nights are frosty and there is snow on the ground and a moon in the sky, Kailele's soul rises from the surface of the lake and sets out to look for Kailele's footprints in the dark of the night. The ground beneath remembers these footprints every winter and recreates their forms in the snow. These are the footprints that lead Kailele's soul back to the shtetl. And so the soul begins to wander about in Bociany, going from house to house, seeking a companion in madness, because the soul suffers doubly when it must bear its madness alone. So, sooner or later, it finds a little girl in a house, a little girl with a weak mind, and appears to her in a dream over and over again, night after night, until half of Kailele's madness begins to cling to the little girl's soul."

Yossele bit at the tip of his beard. A bitter frost nipped at his heart. He remembered the horrid taste of his own dreams, of which he could recall nothing specific but the mood that pursued him through his waking hours. Perhaps Kailele the Bride had some connection with them? Or perhaps her tortured soul visited his hut every winter's night, seeking a partner among his daughters? Perhaps it clung to Binele's soul? Had not his women neighbors suggested this to him and he had shrugged it off?

"If the little girl's home is more-or-less decent," Sore-Leyele came to the moral conclusion of her story. "If she has God-fearing parents, the madness remains only in the child's dreams. In that case, Kailele's soul wanders off at dawn, taking along the memory of the dream. But if, God forbid, the little girl has no solid ground beneath her feet and lives on this earth as on an ice-floe, just as Kailele lies on an ice-floe in the water—if the little girl has no decent home, you understand?—then there always remains something of Kailele's soul in the little girl's soul during her waking hours as well. Sometimes its influence is stronger, other times it is weaker, but for the duration of her maidenhood, the little girl will never be able to rid herself completely of her madness."

Yossele looked about him in confusion. Where had Binele disappeared to so suddenly? It was clear to him that Binele was the possessed girl that Sore-Leyele had been talking about. Binele had no decent home, and that was his fault. It seemed to him that Sore-Leyele had told this particular story on this night for his ears alone. She had probably been expecting him, or maybe she was simply aware that he was present in the kitchen, listening.

"It's only after her wedding day, if the girl becomes a good, God-fearing woman, that she is completely cured of her madness," Sore-Leyele concluded with an optimistic sigh. It was because of these optimistic endings to her stories that people doubly enjoyed listening to them. For according to Sore-Leyele, all that a Jew had to do in order to save himself from all kinds of trouble and heartbreak was to be kindhearted, pious, and meticulous in the observance of The Law. The reward was then sure to come, if not in this world, then in the next.

Yossele jumped to his feet and ran outside. As soon as he stepped into the street, Fishele the Butcher came running after him and grabbed his arm. "You heard, didn't you?" Fishele panted, deeply shaken. "Do you see now how things can happen in front of our eyes, while we see nothing?"

"Have you seen my little girl?" Yossele asked him. The rain poured down, mixed with hail like icy pearls. Yossele could see nothing in the dizzying darkness.

"What little girl?" Fishele asked back absentmindedly, clinging to Yossele. As they stood in the street, he began feverishly to whisper in Yossele's ear, "I'm on the verge of a precipice, Yossele. It's no good with me, no good at all, do you hear? I've stabbed myself without a knife. I've found myself a . . . a *shikse,* not pretty, not young, and not stupid. Magda the Widow. And now I can't get rid of her. She wants me to marry her, is what she wants. If I don't, she says, she'll go to the *rov* and tell on me. Tell me what to do, Yossele. Save me! I've a brilliant son. Do it for his sake because I'm going out of my mind."

"I told you before," said Yossele, roughly shaking himself free, although Fishele's confession impressed him deeply, "you must fight your own battles." He pushed Fishele away and set off at a run through the downpour. It seemed to him that the eyes of demons blinked at him from the lighted windows on both sides of the street. "Binele! Where are you, snotnose!" he called into the darkness, wiping the sleet from his eyebrows and beard.

Something drew him toward the Wide Poplar Road in the direction of the lake. Perhaps Kailele's ghost had enticed Binele there, hypnotized her in order to punish him? For was not his own sin a thousand times greater than Fishele's? That was why Binele had vanished from his side like a stone under water. He had to hurry with all his strength, as long as there was life in his body, to find her, to save his smallest, his dearest one. He would dive into the lake and retrieve her. And if he did not, then he would drown, too. Let the bottomless pit swallow him, let it suck him into hell; without Binele there was no sense in struggling on.

He raced along the Wide Poplar Road at a frenzied pace. A gust of wind hit him in the chest. His coattails flew up like heavy, wet wings. His ritual undershirt strained toward his back, but his feet carried him forward with determination, until a heavy gush of water cascaded down a poplar branch and splashed onto his wet face. He stopped, blinded and dazed, and wiped his soaking face with his wet hands. Was he out of his mind, he, the usually reasonable Yossele? Granted, in a dream he could commit whatever insanity the dream dictated, but wide awake? Had he suddenly turned into a woman, that he should become so idiotically superstitious? Had he even looked for Binele properly at the slaughterer's house? Perhaps she had fallen asleep in a corner? She might even have snuck into the room where the women sat.

He ran back to the marketplace, trying to recapture his normal rational self. He could not lower himself to the deranged level of a Fishele. Of course, invisible powers, colossal and diabolic, played foul tricks on every human being. But it was also true that, although man was weaker than a fly, he was also stronger than a lion. He, Yossele himself, was stubborn, iron-willed.

Yet he could not rid himself of the feeling that some dreadful retribution hovered over his head. He had sinned and he would be punished for it. He could even see his punishment approaching. His eyesight was gradually failing, as was that other kind of sight, that of his heart. He was barely capable of deciding what was what. More and more often, he felt himself at a loss. And people sensed it. They no longer behaved toward him as they used to. And as for the Almighty, He was certainly there, but seemed further and further away. Even the most deeply felt prayers did not reach Him; Yossele felt that they reached no one. And yet he had to pray, in spite of everything. As it was written, "Despite yourself you are born, despite yourself you live, and despite yourself you die." That was Fate. That was an act of the Creator's power, and an act of faith on the part of the Creator's powerless creation, the human being, who submitted to his fate and tried to live up to it.

Suddenly, Yossele knew that he would not have thrown himself into the lake no matter how prompted he was by despair. The Almighty would have pulled him out, by the beard if need be, and commanded him, "Carry on, drag on to the destiny I have assigned to you, to the very end."

As he ran back, Yossele raised his eyes to the sky to let the sleet wash his face and soak into his eyebrows, sidelocks, and beard. He whispered through dripping lips, "I submit. But do me just this one favor, God Almighty, charitable Father in the Heavens. Let me find the child, and I will quietly accept whatever further torture you have in store for me." He burst into the slaughterer's house and called out to those assembled, "People, have you seen my little girl?"

Before the people in the kitchen had time to raise their heads, he saw Binele crawl out from under the table. "Here I am, Tateshie," she said, as if nothing had happened, walking over to him.

"Shush! Quiet!" Sore-Leyele's listeners scolded.

"What were you doing under the table?" Yossele asked, barely able to contain his emotion.

"Nothing," she replied. "I was playing *strulkes*."

"Quiet!" The hostile crowd glared at them.

Yossele pushed Binele outside, having determined to return the next day to see Sore-Leyele. "Here, hold on to my coat!" he called after her as they waded out into the snow and rain.

"I don't want to!" she called back, running ahead.

"Hold on to my coat, I said! It's pitch dark and hard to see. Come over here!" He could barely see where to put his own feet down. Nervousness, combined with the rain and darkness, blurred his vision.

"I can see where I'm going!" she called back, skipping ahead.

He followed the bright blotches of the rags she wore. "You just wait, you snotnose! Wait till I get you home!" he yelled after her.

But his heart was singing. God had heard him and responded. Binele was found. Now he was certain that Sore-Leyele had been sent down from the heavens. She had such power, this Sore-Leyele, that she was able to hypnotize adults just by the use of her voice! In her hands, a child would be like clay in the hands of a potter. She would make a decent girl of Binele and destroy her appetite for friendship with the goyish riff-raff. She would turn Binele into a proper daughter of Israel, and perhaps one day Binele would even bring a decent son-in-law into the house. Then Yossele would be doubly satisfied and proud of her. She would brighten his heart and ease the burden of his guilt, so that he would have a valid reason for loving her.

Now, as he raced home in the rain, it occurred to Yossele that he loved Binele very much, just as she was, for no good reason at all. He could find no other word for what he felt for her. Perhaps, after all, something existed apart from duty and obligation? If not, he would surely have remarried a long time ago. True, he had not wanted his children to have a stepmother, but he had since come to doubt that his disinclination had done them a great favor. He did love his children, all of them, of course he did. But even more than them, he still loved his deceased Mariml.

He could not overcome his amazement. A man could live with himself for so many years, and still not understand himself, not know himself, as if he were a thousand miles away from his own soul, blind to his innermost feelings. "Creator of the World," he muttered. "Even more than to myself, I am blind to You. Yet I cling to You with a blind love."

The next morning, Yossele once again set out with Binele for Sore-Leyele's house. To his deep regret, Sore-Leyele was already surrounded by a small group of women. He left Binele there anyway, in care of Sore-Leyele's younger daughter, Perele. Perele was married and lived next door, but she took care of her parents' household. Yossele returned to his shop with an easier heart and with great hopes.

Yossele was so fortified with faith in himself after Binele began working at Sore-Leyele's, that he immediately resolved to do two things that he had promised he would attend to after the problem of Binele had been solved. The first of these was long overdue. He had to have a talk with Vaslav Spokojny, to once and for all put an end to the fire chief's visits to Hindele the Scribe's Widow. These visits were driving the poor woman out of her mind with fear, and for some reason, they made Yossele anxious as well.

Vaslav was not a mean man, Yossele knew, but his lack of self-discipline and his drinking made him do cruel things. True, Hindele had never again mentioned that terrible night to Yossele, but he could not rid himself of the thought of that unfortunate, fragile creature, a daughter of Israel after all, in the hands of that ogre, on the dark stairway of her house. He could imagine the skin of her uncovered body lighting up in the darkness, and the agony in her large black eyes screaming through the silence. Granted, she was partly to blame because of the servile attention she had always given to the fire chief's drunken chatter. But she, daughter of Israel that she was, had been shamed by the rough gentile bull. She was so defenseless, and he was so powerful. No wonder the fear was still with her. And it was the more devastating because not a soul knew of it, except Yossele.

He did not know why she had chosen to confess to him, of all people. He resented her giving him the responsibility, and disliked her more than ever. But the burden was now on his shoulders. He had advised her not to leave Bociany, so her safety was now his business, just as the safety of the rest of the shtetl was his business. Who knew what would happen if Vaslav killed his brother, or if Hindele killed or even wounded Vaslav during one of his drunken attacks on her?

Yossele had no particular plan of action. The main thing was to go to Vaslav when he was sober, which was in the morning. So Yossele left his shop in the care of his two older daughters and, with a sack slung over his shoulder, stepped outside. Without thinking, he threw a glance at the place where Hindele sat all huddled up, warming her hands by the firepot. He managed to read in her eyes how unsafe she felt seeing him leave the Potcheyov. That was how he interpreted the looks that she gave him lately.

As he passed the Jewish inn on the Wide Poplar Road, Yossele peeked in to see if Vaslav, who spent most of his days there, had paid a visit yet. Then he headed for the village. When he reached Vaslav's house, he saw Vaslav's daughter standing on the porch. Wanda's long blond hair was disheveled in a coquettish way, revealing the gypsy earrings that dangled from her ears. She was wearing a bulky, hand-knitted sweater, a loose skirt, and large men's boots. She was polishing an apple against her sweater. As soon as Yossele appeared on the porch, she put the apple against her moist, parted lips.

"The Devil in his most dangerous aspect is here to greet me," Yossele thought. Turning his eyes from Wanda's sensuous, tempting face, he asked, "Is your father home?" She shook her long blond mane, cracked open the skin of the apple with her sparkling, sharp teeth and wiped the juice from her face. She gave vent to a juicy, sour-sounding laugh. "He's still asleep!" Yossele was about to open the door, but she continued through a mouth full of apple, "Not in his bed!"

Yossele made an abrupt turn. In the distance he could see Vaslav's wife and two of the younger children shoveling snow off the bridge that spanned the brook. Wanda took another loud bite out of the apple. "I don't think Mother will buy anything from you today," she said, chewing energetically, her breath transformed into a cloud of steam around her face.

"The stupid cow waited up for him all night, so she's not in a buying mood, unless she wants to dig a grave and bury him with burning lime, after he comes home." The grin faded from her face. She flung the apple core over the fence and into the snow with a violent sweep of the arm. "You Jews don't make such rotten husbands and fathers, do you, Yossele?" She approached him, sweeping her hair away from her face with both hands.

Yossele had no intention of getting into a discussion with her. He rushed to the gate, but heard the sound of her boots creaking in the snow behind him. "You're right not to have anything to do with the bastard," he heard her say behind his back. "He's always boasting how you two used to play together in the marshes when both your fathers worked for the Fatherland. What a scoundrel he is! He wants everyone to be his friend, but he doesn't deserve to have any friends. Stay away from him. Let him grow old alone like a dog."

"I must speak to him," Yossele said loudly enough for her to hear him. "Where can I find him?"

She laughed bitterly. "In the whore Magda's bed! Go there, Yossele, go and surprise him!" He heard her run back to the porch.

Yossele's heart stirred. Magda the Widow was the other problem that he had undertaken to solve that day. This was not just for Fishele's sake. Fishele was a weak, tormented soul, a toy in the hands of the Evil One, whose hold Fishele had to break on his own, or be forever doomed. The trouble was, however, that his actions put the rest of Bociany in danger as well. Magda was capable of "cooking up a broth" with all kinds of slander. Fishele, who had once preached to Yossele about being responsible to the community, was so far gone that he was undermining the safety of the community itself. And then, Fishele was one of Bociany's most important citizens, and Bociany needed the self-assured Fishele of bygone days.

Frustrated, unable to decide on a course of action, Yossele began automatically going from door to door, peddling his merchandise. The weight of the sack that was slung over his back gradually diminished, but his heart was not in the selling today. Something drew him back to Bociany. He wanted to be among his own people, in familiar surroundings. "What do I need all these headaches for? What business is it of mine?" he asked himself. Yet he knew well enough that he would have no peace until he went through with what he had undertaken. He was passing the inn on his way back when he saw Vaslav approaching from the other side.

"Hey, Yossele!" Vaslav called joyfully to him, as if they were two friends meeting after a long separation. "Come inside and we'll have a shot!" Vaslav was still sober; all the buttons on his jacket were done up. But the face beneath the mask of cheerfulness was uneasy, the blinking eyes evasive. The exaggerated, lively tone with which Vaslav tried to cover his real state grated on Yossele's ears.

Yossele walked over to him. "Wanda told me that you still want to be friends with me, " he said dryly.

"When did she tell you that?" Vaslav grinned, ill-at-ease. "She's right of course. Let's go inside and drink to our friendship."

"She told me so a few hours ago. I passed by your house with my sack, but you weren't there."

Vaslav's ears turned red. He shook his head nervously. "So what are we standing out here for? Come inside. Let's kill the worm with a little *monopolka*."

Yossele took his arm and tried to pull him away from the entrance to the tavern. "Vodka doesn't kill the worm, it just puts it to sleep. You know that. Let's talk sober."

Vaslav planted his feet squarely in the snowy ground and shook his head defiantly. "I need a drink right now!"

"Then I can't be friends or talk."

"Friends talk best over a glass of *monopolka*."

"And who will earn a few kopecks for me if I sit around drinking? You? Anyway, I don't believe in renewing a friendship under the influence of alcohol. First we must be friends when we are sober, then we'll see."

Vaslav was growing impatient. "Devil take you! A glass of *monopolka* is my best friend anyway!"

Yossele still pulled at his arm. "Do you know what else Wanda told me? She said that one day you'll be as lonely as an old dog."

The redness of Vaslav's ears spread over his entire face. "She talked a lot to you, the bitch!" He spat. "What did she tell you that for?"

"Because she cares about you, while you break her young heart. Such a pretty daughter, with such a great singing voice! And you shame her so that she's afraid to show her face to people, and she might never get married."

"And what dirty business is that of yours, you mongrel?" Vaslav frowned. "What are you butting in for? I can't listen to these idiocies on an empty stomach."

"So it's not true that you want to be friends with me? That makes sense. Why should you bother with a filthy lout like me, and a Jew to boot? It's only when you're drunk and you don't know what you're blubbering about that you say friendly things to me or to . . . Hindele the Scribe's Widow."

"Leave her out of it, or I'll kill you!"

"Certainly. Where is your ax? You've been going around threatening to kill people, your brother, Hindele, and now me."

Vaslav looked at Yossele strangely from under his thick brows. His lips moved, but for a while there was no sound. Then he shrugged and spoke in a voice that struggled to remain cheerful. "I don't mean it. It's just my way of talking, especially on an empty stomach, you know." He tilted his head closer to Yossele's ear. "I'd rather die than hurt that woman, or you, for that matter. As for my brother, I do wish I could kill him, so help me God. But I am not Cain. I'm a good Pole and a good Christian, whatever Stanislav may say to the contrary."

Yossele weighed some thoughts in his mind. Finally he said, "And yet you almost killed your brother the other night. If Hindele hadn't prevented you . . . And you almost killed her, too."

Vaslav stared at him thunderstruck. "You mean that other night?"

"Yes, the other night. It was no dream. You might have committed murder." Now Vaslav allowed himself to be pulled toward a snow-covered tree and positioned so that his face could not be seen from the road. Yossele continued, "The poor woman almost went mad with fright. She knocked at my door after she ran away from you, and a few men helped me take you home in a fire wagon. I made your wife swear that she would make you believe that it was a dream, so you wouldn't be ashamed. Your wife knows that you wanted to kill your brother, but she knows nothing else. Nor do my men know anything, except that you were drunk. So it is only the three of us, Hindele, you, and myself, who know all of it, and no one else will ever find out."

A long silence. Then Vaslav moaned, "I'm such a cursed dog!"

"Remember one thing," Yossele spoke again. "Once you start wielding your ax, you never know where it will land. One thing will lead to another, and there will be a bloody mess. Whereas if you leave things as they are, everything will be forgotten. Just promise me that you'll never speak to Hindele again and never scare her again."

Vaslav began to cry real tears. Yossele combed his fingers through his beard. Suddenly he decided to pull Vaslav back toward the tavern. "Now let me buy you a drink."

Before they had drunk the first glass of *monopolka,* Yossele made the still-sober Vaslav swear by the sacred memory of his heroic father, by the lives of his children, and by the Holy Trinity, that he would never go near Hindele again. Then Yossele swore by the lives of his children that no one else would ever find out about that night. Vaslav, pounding his chest, also swore powerful oaths, without being bidden, that he would just drink these few glasses with Yossele and never touch the bottle again in his life, nor sleep with another woman, so that his Wanda should not be ashamed of him. "And also because . . . " Vaslav added after a moment's hesitation. "Yossele, you can keep a secret, I know that. So I'll tell you, brother. One of our great patriots, Josef Pilsudski, is organizing the Polish legions to fight for the freedom of the Motherland, and a band of our boys here in Bociany is also getting ready. So if I drink and sleep around, I won't be much of a leader, will I?" And he drank with Yossele to friendship and to a free Poland.

An hour or so later, Yossele, fortified with the strong drink, was on his way to have a talk with Magda the Widow.

Magda was dressed in a pair of men's boots, her blouse unbuttoned at the neck. She was standing in her backyard, in the cold, trying to cover her unharnessed mare with a sackcloth. "Ah, Yossele!" she cried. "Will you sell me a pot of lime at a bargain price?"

"Why not?" Yossele patted the horse, averting his eyes from Magda, although he was more than aware of her overpowering presence. She was almost masculine in her robust build, yet full of vulgar, aggressive femininity. "I'll even make you a present of two pots of lime." He stroked the mare's head. "She's still in good shape, isn't she?"

"She's in perfect shape!" Magda said meaningfully, shaking her loose bosom. "And what, for instance, do you want in exchange? You little Jews never really give something for nothing, do you?"

"Some do and some don't." Yossele pretended to be checking a mark on the mare's eyelid. "I do want to give you something for nothing. If you want it, take it. If not, don't."

"And why should you be so kind to me?" Her nostrils and those of the mare flared in unison.

"I'm not trying to be kind to you. But if you do nothing, you deserve something. That's all."

"What do you mean, If I do nothing?"

"If you do nothing about Fishele the Butcher. I mean, if you leave him alone and don't do a dumb thing like going to the *rov* to tell on him. Why do you want to marry a dirty Jew anyway, a father of five little Jews to boot, eh? You might get him to convert, but the Jewish blood in his veins won't change in the least."

Before he could go on, she burst into such loud peals of laughter that it made the air around her and Yossele and the mare echo with the vibrations. She put her hands on her broad hips, and her eyes filled with tears. It was a while before she could manage to speak again. "Oh, Jesus Maria!" she gasped spasmodically. "What a rotten idiot, that Fishele-Pishele! Me? Marry him? That dirty, flabby nothing? Oh, charitable God in the heavens! Oh, Yossele, my treasure, may the Devil take you! I was making fun of him, the dumbbell! I'd rather die like a dog than marry one of your kind, may the plague take you all!" she roared. "He's not even a man! Oh, Holy Sacrament!"

Yossele grew lively with relief. He rubbed his hands together, then rubbed his ears and jumped like a boy into the air, saying, "Thank you very much, Magda. May your God reward you according to your deeds!" He threw the sack over his shoulder and strode out of Magda's yard.

She ran after him, calling, "Hey, Yossele, you filthy bloodsucker! Where are my two pots of lime? You promised something for nothing, didn't you, Jew boy?" She caught at one of his sidelocks and pulled.

Yossele felt a great desire to smack her hand. Instead, he gently brushed it off. "Oh, I forgot. Of course, my pleasure." He trudged back to her house, poured two pots of lime into one of her basins, and then ran home again like a lighthearted youngster. When he reached the center of Bociany, he stopped at the synagogue, entered, and opened a book of psalms. He began to read slowly in order to calm himself and to regain his equilibrium.

Reb Laibele the Sexton noticed him and went over to greet him. Yossele responded with a firm handshake. Reb Laibele sniffed and wrinkled his nose. Suddenly he exclaimed, "You shameless apostate! How dare you come into this holy place dead drunk in the middle of the day? Are you celebrating Simches-Toyre or Purim in the middle of this regular and profane week?"

## 14

BINELE DID NOT SUFFER from overwork at Sore-Leyele's, although with people constantly coming and going, there was plenty to do—if one wanted to do it. Sore-Leyele, who fasted every Monday and Thursday, was not meticulous about the details of housekeeping. She was more preoccupied with the Almighty's housekeeping, which most women left their husbands to worry about. But Sore-Leyele added a feminine touch to the job.

So long as her oats were cooked, the floor was swept, the house was prepared for the Sabbath, and the Sabbath *cholnt* was at the baker's, Sore-Leyele did not waste too much thought on the insignificant details of earthly life. Nor was it expected of her; she had two fine married daughters who were more skilled in day-to-day matters than was their mother. Sore-Leyele was so deeply immersed in her other worlds, and walked around the house so absentmindedly, that all she achieved in the housekeeping domain was to cause constant problems with the dietary laws because she made dishes unkosher by mixing the dairy with the meat.

Sore-Leyele had taken Binele into her home not just because she wanted someone to help her keep the house in order, but for the more important reason that she wanted to make a *mentsh* of her. A *mentsh* was also a house of a sort and deserved as much, if not more, attention to detail, because within the *mentsh* there dwelled a spark of God's emanation, the *Shkhina.* If this human house was not kept in order, the dirt and mud of the evil world might penetrate and ruin it. So Sore-Leyele preferred that Binele sit by her and listen to her stories rather than walk around the house with a broom.

Sore-Leyele's repertoire was not limited to stories about Kailele the Bride, or about the tragedies that had occurred to sinful souls in Bociany and its environs since the beginning of time. These were only embellishments for her main theme, which was the business of heaven and hell. Her expertise on the dark side of the Other World was so distinguished that few people in Bociany could match her.

She knew the geography of hell as she knew her ten fingers, and on Binele's first day of work, she made her listen to descriptions of the various apparatuses to be found in hell that were devoted to the punishment of doomed souls. Sore-Leyele described in detail the huge arenas for torture, which were furnished with burning stakes and boiling cauldrons and were equipped with intricate machinery for skinning, chopping, biting, and generally demolishing sinners. She described the dark corridors through which flowed the steaming, boiling rivers of pitch foaming with blistering bubbles that cascaded down steep canyons into bottomless pits. These horrific rivers carried with them varieties of laughing scorpions and hissing snakes that spoke with human tongues and told each other jokes, while they wrapped their bodies around the helpless victims and crushed them. She also dwelled on the details of the palace built of human skulls, where Small, the Angel of Death, lived with his wife, Lilith, who seduced men and attacked pregnant women, kidnaping and killing their babies. And the same detail that she used to describe Small, the Prince of Darkness, Sore-Leyele also lavished on the other denizens of his kingdom, the imps and demons, the stokers of hell's furnaces, and the entire army of ghosts and spirits. To her these were not disembodied beings, but creatures of flesh and blood, with concrete features and clothing. It was possible to be accosted by one of them on the streets of Bociany, especially on a Wednesday or a Saturday night.

Then Sore-Leyele embarked on a discussion of heaven's penal code. She could list, without hesitation, which trespass earned which punishment. With this intimate knowledge she froze not only the hearts of weak-willed women, but also those of the sturdiest men who listened to her in the kitchen, men like Fishele the Butcher and his gang of butcher boys, even the hearts of the wagon drivers. As for Binele, it was at this point that she grew too sleepy to grasp fully the meaning of Sore-Leyele's words and became totally indifferent to the fate of sinners, no matter of what category. She yawned discreetly once or twice, then once or twice again.

On the following day, Binele's interest in Sore-Leyele's stories was rekindled. On that day Sore-Leyele talked about the storks. She said that the storks on the roofs of Bociany were not just storks but messengers from "above," sent down to eavesdrop on what went on in people's houses and in the soul of every human being, Jew and Gentile alike. But the storks that nested on the gentile roofs, Sore-Leyele explained, were merely decoys, placed there by the Almighty so that the Gentiles would not become jealous of the Jews for being "chosen," and so would not be inspired to torment the Jews. Sore-Leyele said that nowhere else in the entire empire of Tsar Nicholas was there another shtetl where storks, the harbingers of good fortune, lived on every roof. This, in her opinion, was of great significance. It meant that in the eyes of the Almighty, Bociany had risen to second place in the world, Jerusalem being in first place. This honor put a great obligation on the shoulders of the Jews of Bociany. They were required to be better human beings and stricter in the observance of The Law than Jews anywhere else.

"Doesn't my reasoning make sense?" Sore-Leyele asked her listeners rhetorically. "Has not Bociany been designated to become the first locality where the Messiah Ben David will arrive on his white donkey? Do we not feel this most intensely when we pray in Bociany's splendid synagogue, to which there is hardly an equal in the entire Diaspora?"

And so Sore-Leyele began to tell the traditional tale of the arrival of the Messiah. She knew the exact details of his dress, namely, a simple white robe with gold trimming. In height he would be not too tall, not too small, but of a suitable height for the most dignified Jew. The color of his eyes would be blue, not the blue of gentile eyes, heaven forbid, but a heavenly blue, never before seen by man. The length of his beard and sidelocks would be almost the same as those of Reb Senderl the Cabalist, the hair color also similar to his, but more silvery, with sparkling golden reflections, and the strands thinner than cobweb, softer than silk, and permeated with an aroma of heavenly spices. As for the exact description of his face, no one had ever seen anything like it. Such beauty! Such radiance! Such kindness! Its expression would be full of wisdom and devotion, and everyone who saw him would be overcome with awe and a feeling of having found a soul brother. One glance from his eyes would cure all wounds. The light of the *Shkhina* would rest upon whoever lived to see the day of his arrival.

When Sore-Leyele began to describe the days of the Messiah, there was not a dry eye in the room, nor a heart that did not sing with longing, Binele's heart included. The listeners moved their lips as if they were kissing every word that came from Sore-Leyele's mouth. Now she spoke slowly, giving every word time to unfurl its petals like a rose in her audience's imagination. "Then," she chanted, "heaven and earth will become one, and the Garden of Eden will stretch from one end of God's earth to the other. People will have no need to speak to each other because they will be so finely attuned that they will hear each other's thoughts. There will no longer be any need to greet one's neighbors with phrases like 'Good morning' or 'Good year' because it will always be a good morning and a good year."

Sore-Leyele's dry shrunken face began to glow as if the light of the *Shkhina* were already upon it. Her eyes grew large, like two beakers filled with sweet wine, and the people's longing and hope were reflected in her gaze. She spoke like a prophetess and was as beautiful as a queen. Then her eyes lit up with youthful, mischievous sparks as she lightheartedly offered explanations to her public.

"They tell us women," she said, "that we will become our husbands' footstools in the Heavenly Paradise. Do they really mean footstools? Are we children that we should believe that our men will look in Paradise the same as they do now? That they will wear boots on their feet, or shoes, or even slippers? Of course not! Who would have the chutzpah to walk around in shoes in the Heavenly Paradise? That would be showing disrespect, wouldn't it? So how will they walk? Barefoot? Certainly not! May all our enemies walk barefoot! The truth is that they will not walk at all. They will fly, soar through the air and be as light as feathers, as gossamer. Then what use does someone who is as light as gossamer have for a footstool? So there can be no doubt that this is nothing but a saying to make us understand how happy we will be with our husbands in a hundred and twenty years from now. Their soft, feather-light feet will warm our backs better than the best hot-water bottles, so that our backs will never ache again. And just as a man never quarrels with his footstool, so our husbands will never quarrel with us."

It was no wonder, then, that Yossele and his neighbors thought that Binele's employment as a servant girl in Sore-Leyele's house would open the gates of Eden for her as well. As things stood, neither Yossele nor his neighbors were satisfied with the girl, so Binele's education at Sore-

Leyele's house could not help but produce the best results, and she would cease being a burden on her father's heart and would restore it to him whole as one restores a ruin. This result, however, depended on the obvious condition that she learn the right things from Sore-Leyele and her spellbinding stories.

Binele quickly took a liking both to Sore-Leyele and to her spellbinding stories. She could sit beside her and never tire of listening. In general, if anything disturbed her concentration, it was rather the fault of the other women listeners. As soon as they sat down in a corner of the room, near the *piekelik,* Sore-Leyele's dramatic voice seemed to paralyze them, and the strangest expressions would remain frozen on their faces; or they swayed from side to side. This worked on Binele in two ways. Either the sight of the women lulled her to sleep, or she burst out laughing. She did not want to do either because she wanted to remain at Sore-Leyele's, where she led an agreeable life and ate stuffed *kishka* and spleen twice a week; the ritual slaughterer was allowed to keep the large intestine, the *kishka,* and the spleen from each calf that he slaughtered.

Consequently, Binele had to summon all her concentration to keep her mouth shut tight, so as not to burst out laughing, or her eyes open, so as not to fall asleep. The result was that she had little concentration left for Sore-Leyele's stories. Only on Thursdays and Fridays could she solve these problems. On those two days, the ritual slaughterer would be busy killing the animals for the Sabbath. Then Binele could turn to the window and watch him doing his work in an open shed in the yard, and she would immediately lose the urge to fall asleep or to laugh, and Sore-Leyele's stories acquired their true flavor.

On Fridays, Sore-Leyele outdid herself. On the day when the shtetl bustled with preparations for the Sabbath, and the women had barely a moment to spare between rushing to the slaughterer's with their chickens and putting them on the stove to cook as soon as possible, just then Sore-Leyele grew more inspired than ever, and on that day the women, with the slaughtered chickens in baskets near their feet, listened with greater rapture than ever.

On Fridays, Sore-Leyele's stories of the Day of Judgment harmonized with the Day-of-Judgment squawks of the doomed fowl outside. The crowing, the agonized rattling and wheezing, the flutter of wings of the half-dead chickens, geese, and turkeys from the wealthy houses penetrated the room. The sounds made for a shuddering, a trembling, as Binele watched the slaughterer handle his knives. She saw him remove them from their wooden sheaths and check them against the light of the naphtha lamp, which was lit whenever he was at work. Then he would sharpen them against a stone. Sometimes the butcher boys were present outside, their knives tucked between the ropes that wound around their bloodstained aprons. The slaughterer checked and listened to the knives to see that they had no flaw, then slaughtered the calves, geese, and chickens. The butcher boys skinned the animals. The washtub nearby was full of blood.

The slaughterer had a fine, curly beard and sidelocks that were brown but gave off a reddish sheen. He was as tall and strong as the butcher boys, but at home he was completely overshadowed by Sore-Leyele. Binele often wondered how such a strong man could have such a weak voice. At home he was barely heard, much less noticed.

But outside, as he stood in the shed, killing animals, he merged perfectly with Sore-Leyele's description of the Angel of Death. When Binele saw the sharp blade glint, when she saw the stretched-out necks of the animals, her heart contracted. As the slaughterer sawed at the neck of the animal with his knife and a fountain of blood gushed up at him, her breath froze. But instead of looking away, she stared in horror as the shuddering birds swept the ground with their outstretched wings. It was then that Sore-Leyele's voice seemed to issue not from the room, but from the outside. It was the voice of a calf, or of a bird awaiting its turn under the slaughterer's knife. Hell was as near as the reach of one's arm.

Binele was surprised at herself. When she had been younger and had brought a chicken to be slaughtered, she had looked on, hardly minding. Chicken was delicious food. But ever since she had spent time on Yankova's farm, where she had fed the chickens, played with the cats and dogs, and joined Yadwiga in the pasture where the cow grazed and watched a calf being born, the animals had become more human to her. Each had a different look, way of moving, moods even, as well as its own personal characteristics. A leg of chicken was still delicious, but as she watched the slaughterer working outside, she felt compelled to keep swallowing, just to make certain that her own neck was still intact.

If she noticed Abele the Town Fool in the yard, the frost squeezing her heart would spread all over her limbs. Abele would not allow himself to be chased away. He loved to watch the slaughterer at his work, and smiling, would grind his teeth as he looked on. Every time the slaughterer's knife slit a neck, Abele would emit a squeak and shut his eyes tightly.

"I'm not frightened. I'm not frightened at all," Binele would reassure herself. She let the fear sink so deeply inside her that she was aware mainly of her own gruesome yet insatiable curiosity.

Meanwhile, Sore-Leyele, speaking behind Binele's back, would continue to describe the Day of Judgment in such vivid detail that she immediately cut the throats of any sinful thoughts that may have fluttered in the minds of those sinful women who were her listeners. When she concluded her sermon on her usual note of optimism, about the Garden of Eden and the Coming of the Messiah, her images seemed all the more resplendent against the background of the death sounds coming from outside. The women had a good cry and, with light hearts, hurried home to prepare for the Sabbath. Having a light heart on the Sabbath was even more important to the women of Bociany than having enough meat for the Sabbath table.

Of all Sore-Leyele's stories, Binele preferred those about Asmodeus and Lilith, when Sore-Leyele described their lives from their own points of view and not from that of their victims. The demons in general seemed to be an interesting lot. Sore-Leyele said that demons looked and behaved just like people, getting married and having children. Binele often thought that it might be fun to play with demonic children. Lilith especially pleased her. Binele thought that if demons could be just like people, then people could be just like demons, and she wanted to be like Lilith. Lilith was the most powerful woman in the world, getting whatever she wanted without anyone daring to oppose her.

Sore-Leyele had once told the women that one day when she had visited Reb Senderl the Cabalist to have an evil eye exorcised and to be given a remedy for a buzzing in her left ear, she had gotten into a conversation with him about heaven and hell, during which Reb Senderl told her that Lilith had been Adam's first wife. The Almighty had created her, Reb Senderl said, not from Adam's rib, but in the same way that He had created Adam, from the soil of the earth, but in Lilith's case it had been a cheaper kind of soil. Being created equal with Adam gave Lilith a nose that was too refined and that she carried turned up in the air. She considered herself just as important a personality in Paradise as her husband was. The Almighty caught Himself in time and realized that harmony between husband and wife was hanging by a hair. So He dismissed Lilith and created Eve, although that creation was not so successful either. Eve, too, was a woman who kept her nose turned up for no reason at all. And she talked Adam into eating the apple. It was for the sins of these two first women that future generations of women had to pay with their suffering up to this very day, while men still refused to trust them. Therefore a woman had to be doubly careful in her conduct, and had to try to be perfectly honest and perfectly self-sacrificing every minute of the day.

"So you may ask me," Sore-Leyele continued "was it worthwhile for the Almighty to create two such 'treasures' as Lilith and Eve? Why didn't He create one decent woman who might serve as an example? The answer is plain. With these first women He had wanted to test Adam, just as today He uses women to test men. That's why we women are so important—it is because a man is judged by the kind of woman he marries. We can make them or break them. That is, we can either drive our men crazy or we can inspire them. We can bring them down or lift them up. We can make them happy, or we can destroy them. For we weak women are not so weak at all. And all that we do, we do for the benefit of our families."

Binele enjoyed the moral conclusions of Sore-Leyele's stories much less than she enjoyed the stories themselves. She could not understand what Sore-Leyele was driving at. The other women were visibly moved, however, and they began to sway, sigh, and sip at the air with their lips. They spat three times and then again three times. More than once Binele was forced to run out of the room, covering her face with both hands, a sign, the women thought, of the impact that Sore-Leyele's words had upon her. She ran to the privy, and with her hands still covering her mouth, burst into a fit of long-suppressed laughter.

When she had controlled herself again, she let her thoughts run on Lilith, the only character in Sore-Leyele's accounts who, in Binele's opinion, could serve as an example. There was only one obstacle standing in the way of her becoming a Lilith. Lilith was a stunning beauty, while Binele was a "Marzepa." In sum, Binele drew false conclusions from Sore-Leyele's instructive stories.

That Binele did not turn into a respectable girl, was however not her fault alone; Sore-Leyele was partly to blame. True, there was something in Binele's nature that prevented her from grasping coherently the issues of decency and sinfulness. She knew, for instance, that it was a sin to steal, yet she had learned how to extract kopecks from the charity boxes on the wall near the kitchen door by means of a straw that she first dipped in honey. She helped herself to the money whenever she was unable to master her craving for an egg-cookie. She would run with the money to the pastry shop on the Potcheyov, and she did not even feel sinful about the matter. Why should other children be able to afford egg-cookies, and not she? This she did in spite of the fact that Sore-Leyele was very good to her and never grew angry or hit her. She would chat with the girl and, with an absent look in her large black eyes, tell her about all the things that she saw in her imagination, as if Binele were an entire crowd of listeners.

The problem was that Sore-Leyele saw the things in her imagination much more clearly than she did those in front of her nose. It seemed as though she never really saw Binele as Binele. And if she did, she had more important matters to deal with in her mind than to remember why she had taken the girl into her house in the first place. She saw Binele puttering around, sweeping the floor, offering her or her husband a glass of chicory coffee, and listening when spoken to. Sore-Leyele was used to being attended to, to being served and listened to. She knew that her wonderful daughters took good care of everything. Weren't they an example to other women's daughters? If she had not been successful in bringing up her own daughters, would the women of Bociany trust her so much? And Sore-Leyele's daughters did indeed take care of their parents with great love and understanding. It was they who taught Binele how to care for the house and cater to their parents' needs. But they lived lives of their own and had little time to spend at their parents' house, except on the Sabbath. And so Binele could pretty much do as she pleased. And because spring was in the air, she did not feel like doing very much.

Then came the tragedy of Perele, Sore-Leyele's younger daughter, and Binele lost every chance that she might have had of becoming respectable.

Perele was the apple of her parents' eyes. Not only was she a fine, decent woman, but she was almost a saint, a Sarah Bat Tovim, not only to her parents, but to everyone in need, especially pregnant women. She provided them with clean sheets, cooked chicken broth for them, and collected rags to be used as diapers for the newborn. In short, she resembled her mother like one drop of water resembles another. She was pale, with sunken cheeks, a thin, perfectly shaped nose, big black eyes, thick black eyebrows, and a dreamy but serious expression on her face. She also had the kind of husband that she deserved, a young man from Chwosty, God-fearing, a scholar with a delicate soul; he was shy, retiring, he would not chase a fly off the wall. The pair lived as harmoniously as two doves. Moshele, the husband, spent day and night in the *besmedresh,* while Perele sat in the shop on the Potcheyov, selling fabric. There she nursed her babies who, after the fashion of Bociany, arrived regularly one year after the next.

Then, one day at dawn, while Binele was still fast asleep on her straw mat in the hallway, she was suddenly awakened by a pounding on the door. When she opened it, she was surprised to see Perele, still in her night clothes, with her sleeping cap sitting twisted on her head. Perele burst into the kitchen agitated and wailing. Once inside, she began to pace between the stove and the slop pail, as if possessed. She cracked her knuckles, rubbed her tear-stained face and repeated over and over again, "Oy, Mameshie . . . "

Binele offered her a glass of water, which she gulped down with heavy moans. She wet her temples with the last drop at the bottom of the glass, buttoned her nightshirt up to her neck, and dashed into the next room where her parents were sleeping. The next moment mother and daughter were back in the kitchen. Sore-Leyele blinked sleepily. Her face was as white as the whites of her eyes. More dead then alive, she muttered, "Perelshie, what's the matter with you?"

"Help me, Mameshie . . . " Perele gasped.

Sore-Leyele spat three times before she licked her daughter's eyes seven times. "An evil eye. I can see it, poor child." She tugged at her daughter's sleeve, and they seated themselves on the bench near the table, for Sore-Leyele felt so faint that she did not trust her legs to support her. The upper part of her body swayed as she whispered, "For every person who dies of natural causes, ninety-nine die because of an evil eye. Do you hear, my soul? Ninety-nine, sweet Father in the heavens."

They fell into each other's arms, barely able to cry. Binele offered Perele another glass of water. Perele sipped, moaned, wet her fingers, dabbed at her forehead, at her temples and her head under the bonnet. Her voice came out in a croak, "Mameshie, I'm going out of my mind." She waved her hand at Binele in a gesture of dismissal.

Binele went out and shut the door. At first she decided to go back to sleep on her mat because she was still very sleepy. But she was curious as well, so she kneeled down on the floor beside the kitchen door and peered in through the keyhole. Then she put her ear against it.

"So don't drag out my soul, my child," Binele heard Sore-Leyele sigh tearfully. "I must know what kind of evil eye it is, before I can start doing something about it."

"I won't survive it anyway," Perele muttered. "I'm at the end of my rope, you hear, Mameshie, at the very end."

"May I hear better news, my treasure. For heaven's sake, tell me what happened. A human being doesn't come to the end of the rope so quickly. There is, thank heaven, an Almighty to protect us, and there are, thank heaven, excellent means these days for exorcising the worst evil eye. The Lord is a good father."

"He is not!"

"What do you mean, he is not? Spit three times right away! You don't speak like a child of mine, but as if the Devil has entered you, Perelshie dearest."

"He has, Mameshie, he has."

"Who has?"

"The priest, Mother darling."

"What priest? You've gone crazy. Maybe you're running a fever? Of course. You're hot as a baking oven."

"Yes, I'm hot, but if only I were crazy, Mother, I wouldn't feel this torture, this burning hell in my heart, this pain."

"What pain? Show me where it hurts you."

"My whole being hurts me. Moshele called me a whore this morning, he called me . . . he . . . he'll never touch me again, he said. He'll divorce me, he said."

Binele peered through the keyhole and saw Sore-Leyele wringing her hands until the knuckles cracked. "You are out of your mind, Perele, of that there is no doubt." There was a commotion in the kitchen. Binele saw Sore-Leyele exorcising an evil eye and feeding Perele some potion with a small spoon.

Perele patted her mother's arm. "You cannot say, Mameshie," she said in a somewhat drier voice, "that I am a bad wife to my Moshele, may he live in good health. He is almost like a saint to me. And you know, don't you, how careful I am with all my wifely duties, and if you suggest that I've failed sometimes, I couldn't agree with you, although a *mentsh* is only a *mentsh*. And here . . . " she shook with spasms again.

"But what connection does all this have with the priest?" Sore-Leyele asked anxiously.

"It has, Mameshie. And don't get mad at me, because I won't be able to stand it."

"Then talk."

"How can I talk if there are no words to describe it? I love my Moshele so much, may he live in good health, that I even dream about him. Yes, even in my sleep he comes to me, forgive me for saying so. But now, a fortnight ago, right after the first Passover night, while I was dreaming about him again, I saw him stand up from the seder table . . . He looked like a king during the seder, in his white robe, didn't he, Mameshie, you saw him? And that's how he looked when he came to me in my sleep, but then I looked and saw that it was not Moshele at all, but the priest."

"Why the priest?" Sore-Leyele asked. "Where did you see the face of the priest, woe is me?"

"I did not see it, Mameshie. I swear by my children that I didn't. But one day, before the eve of Passover, his housekeeper came into the shop with two altar boys. The priest was standing outside, talking to the peasants and stopping some Jews. You know he doesn't avoid us the way we avoid him, especially lately. The housekeeper greeted me in a quite friendly way and asked me to cut off twelve yards of the best cotton for her, for the white shirts or aprons or whatever it is that they wear during their ceremonies. Secretly, I spat three times, saying to myself, 'As far as I'm concerned, I'd rather you bought the material for shrouds.' And I measured out the twelve yards she wanted. She didn't even bargain with me, just paid me, took the parcel, said *'Dowidzenia,'* and vanished. And then . . . "

"And then?"

"And then there was a great to-do outside. I went to see what was going on, and people told me that the priest was in Yossele Abedale's shop again. Everyone was crowded in front of the shop, and I saw the priest talk to Yossele, and Yossele didn't turn away but looked him straight in the face and answered him angrily—you know the way Yossele Abedale is." Perele lowered her voice, pointing with a finger to the door behind which Binele was crouching. "And I heard the priest ask Yossele . . . "

"So you did see the priest?" Sore-Leyele sighed.

"Only his back, Mameshie, I swear. I kept my eyes on Yossele and I heard the priest, may his name be cursed, asking Yossele why our God is such a strict, vengeful God, while his God is just the opposite, a loving God who says to the people, 'Love one another!' So Yossele shouted right in the priest's face, 'Because you Christians torture and kill and make war and leave all the loving to your God. We Jews don't kill and don't make war, so we leave all the avenging to our God.' After the priest left, people were furious with Yossele for his angry answer, which could, Heaven forbid, bring down a tragedy on our heads, and also because he looked the priest straight in the eye. Then I went back to my shop. All the customers buying cloth for Passover clothing were shaking with fear. You've heard the rumors going around that the priest is up to something, haven't you? That the tsar is about to decree that all Jews, may God preserve us, will have to convert, that there is a rebellion going on and the tsar has said that the Jews started it. You remember how we dreaded that the first Passover seder would be poisoned for us, that the goyim would come for us precisely on that night. And there's nothing else, Mameshie, I swear."

"What do you mean nothing else?" Sore-Leyele grew even more confused.

"Nothing else." Perele continued, "I sat in the shop doing what I had to do, praying to the Almighty in my heart for a peaceful holiday and thanking Him with all my heart for working in such strange ways. For be it as it may, He sent me down so much profit that I could prepare a decent Passover without having to bite my nails off for a kopeck. And I was hopeful, Mameshie, as we all are, that the Almighty will save us as he saved us by taking us out of Egypt." Perele caught her breath and then exploded in a fresh outburst of tears. "And so everything was good and fine, and we had such a beautiful seder, didn't we, Mameshie? But the same night after the seder, I saw in my sleep, not Moshele but him . . . Beelzebub."

"What Beelzebub? The priest?"

"Who else? He was wearing his new white apron made from my material, with lace trimmings. He said to me, 'Love one another,' climbed into my bed and . . . and he took the silver cross off his neck, and I saw that it was not a cross but a knife with a red blade like the one, forgive the comparison, Mameshie, like the one Father uses for slaughtering, and he uncovered me and cut me open under my belly . . . Oh, Mameshie!"

"Oh, in some way you must have sinned. You've done some forbidden thing, and a demon took the opportunity to come and torment you in your sleep, may it not happen as often as it does. We'll exorcise you well. You'll give a bit more charity, buy candles for the synagogue, pay more visits to women in labor, and may the Lord help you and cleanse your tormented soul."

"But Mameshie, you don't understand! I've tried everything already. I didn't want to worry you. I've gone to see Reb Senderl twenty times or more, but . . . "

"But what?"

"But the monster keeps on coming to me every night, every single night, even on the Sabbath and on Sundays, too."

"The priest comes to you every night in your dreams and climbs into your bed and . . . ?"

"And I . . . I told Moshele about it, with all the details, thinking that it might help. That's when the real tragedy befell me. Moshele refused to touch me. He doesn't want to live with a woman who sleeps with the priest in her dreams, he says, no matter that the priest tortures me in my sleep. He says he will divorce me. And today at dawn, I heard someone sighing. I looked and saw Moshele sitting over the *Gemore,* looking like a child lost in the woods. When he saw me, he said, 'You whore, either you leave the house or I do.'"

There was a commotion in the kitchen. Bench and table squeaked and the sound of sobs and moans drowned out spoken words. Binele could now hear the slaughterer's voice added to the confusion. She thought hard about everything that she had heard, but she understood nothing. What had her father said to the priest? Why were people angry at him, and what connection did it all have with the priest's coming to visit Perele in her dreams? And why should a fun-loving demon change into the robes of a boring, skeletal priest who could barely walk? As she sat huddled and sleepy at the door, it occurred to her that the best way to recognize who was just plain human, and who was human but had a demon living inside him, was by the degree of interest a person awoke in her. "Yankova and

Yanek and Yadwiga and her friends," she thought, smiling, "probably have demons living inside them, and that's why I like them all so much." It was her last thought before she fell asleep.

The following day found Bociany buzzing like a beehive. In Bociany there was no such thing as keeping a secret. In no time at all, it escaped through doors and windows and became a public secret. Thus Sore-Leyele and Perele were soon surrounded by attentive care. Both young and old neighbors worried about them. As if Sore-Leyele and Perele had been victims of an attack, they were immediately put to bed by the women of the shtetl, and they lay there amidst mountains of pillows and bedding filled with goose feathers. The townswomen neglected their own households to keep vigil by the beds of mother and daughter. Professional mourners were called in, and the women sighed and wept along with them. They cooked all kinds of herbs into a broth and fed Sore-Leyele and Perele with little spoons. Everyone agreed with Sore-Leyele that she herself had been the cause of Perele's predicament. Asmodeus had decided to weaken Sore-Leyele's powers by victimizing her child. Perhaps he was even out to destroy her completely, for she was a thorn in his side. All possible means had to be found to protect the lives of these two stricken women, in order to counteract the Evil One.

Nor did the men just stand aside and watch. They, however, were sharply divided on the issue. Some of them—the scholars and the *rov*—took the incident very lightly, too lightly, in fact. They refused to take a stand and propose a course of action. They shrugged off all the evidence and repeated after the *rov* that dreams were the games and tricks of people's hidden follies and that as long as one did not act on them, there was no danger.

But the average men, the Hasidim and the poor shopkeepers, held very strong opinions of their own and were very upset that their beloved *rov* was so inexperienced and irresponsible. These men agreed with the women, although they saw the entire issue in much broader perspective. They were also more practical and down-to-earth than the women, and imitated them in only one thing: they stopped all quarrels amongst themselves. They united in an effort to convince the *rov* of the gravity of the situation on the one hand, and to express their hatred of Shmulikl the Doctor on the other. Shmulikl the Doctor visited the priest regularly and assisted this enemy of

Israel in his struggle against consumption, instead of letting him die like a dog. Did one need more proof of Shmulikl's joining hands with the forces of evil? By himself Shmulikl had been helpless in infecting Bociany with his poisonous godlessness. So a couple of times the windows of the barber-surgeon's house were smashed by "accidental" stones.

The most important thing was that all of Bociany should remain united, as it always was in times of danger. Therein lay the strength of Bociany. When it was a matter of trifles, the people quarreled among themselves, and some of them did not refrain from getting the better of others if they could. But when there were truly important matters at stake, the people of Bociany became what they really were—brothers in Israel.

Therefore, they refused to leave the *rov* and his followers in peace because without them, Bociany could not act as one in resisting an attack of the Evil One. They set out en masse to argue with the *rov,* and to convince him of the gravity of the situation. They crowded into the *rov's* chambers, spilling out into the street in front of the house where Sore-Leyele lay in bed surrounded by her faithful women.

Eloquent representatives of the people bombarded the *rov* with every logical argument at their disposal, trying to make him realize that Asmodeus was using a very simple strategy here, namely, that with the help of his demon he was trying to destroy the family life of the Jews of Bociany by breaking into their homes, into their beds, and undermining the sacred union between husband and wife. If such a thing could happen to Sore-Leyele and her husband, through the predicament of their saintly daughter Perele and her husband, people of truly spotless reputation, then could it not also happen in the homes of those of lesser importance, that is, in the homes of the majority of the citizenry of Bociany? And what could a Jew accomplish without a home, with a ruined family life? Was the home not the rock, the supporting pillar of Jewish life? It was impossible to survive the exile without it.

And then, the people's representatives argued, the problem had political overtones as well. Whatever happened in one Jewish community affected all the people in the Diaspora as a whole, especially in Poland and in Russia. The demon that had attacked Perele was no fool. He had taken on the appearance of the local priest, who had set his foolish mind on converting the Jews of Bociany to Catholicism. His brother was none other than the fire chief, Vaslav Spokojny, the all-powerful leader of the peasants, who was an even more important personage than the county officer himself; he was such a Polish patriot that he was instigating an uprising against the tsar, which spelled grave danger for the Jews, who had always served as the scapegoats. Thus it was necessary to act with more diplomacy and tact than if the demon had dressed himself up as some unknown priest.

The first thing to which the *rov* quite easily gave his consent was that the matter should be kept a secret from the Gentiles. The men took it upon themselves to tell their wives, who in this matter could be counted on for their secrecy. The women would see to it that their children did not catch them whispering among themselves, because this was very nearly a question of life and death. If the Gentiles should, heaven forbid, find out what had happened, they would immediately twist the whole story around and say that Jewish women were scheming to get gentile men into their beds in order to make them convert to Judaism. Whether Greek Orthodox or Catholic, all the Christians were the same, only in different dress. Christianity was the religion of Tsar Nicholas, who would immediately send a band of Cossacks down on the shtetl. The local Gentiles would lend them a hand, doing what Gentiles were capable of doing, and there would be a pogrom like the one in Kisheniev.

As soon as the *rov* agreed to the point about secrecy, the representatives showered him with further questions. Should Moshele divorce Perele first, and only then should they take the necessary steps to rid Perele's dreams of the demon? Or should they try to chase the demon out before there was a divorce? This question immediately led to another, namely, if Moshele did not divorce but went on living with Perele, should he still be allowed to sleep with her, even though she was still sleeping with a demon in her dreams, or should he be forbidden to touch her? And there were many other questions of the same urgency.

The *rov* was so frustrated by all these questions that his usually pale face grew red, and his eyes, dark and deep, became two pits of despair.

"People," he groaned as he towered over them like a black pillar of sorrow, his beautiful black beard blending with the blackness of his gabardine. "Don't you have enough real problems to worry about, without worrying about a thing as natural as a woman's bad dream? I've told you before, dreams are nothing but human foibles played out in one's sleep, so that they should not trouble us during the day. Dreams are just like thought-garbage, which our minds discard to be swept away by forgetfulness. Be patient and the woman, Perele, will free herself of her demon on her own, because dreams get tired of repeating themselves. They wear themselves out and evaporate sooner or later." He noticed the impatient expressions on the faces around him and his eyes filled with tears. "I beg of you, people, do not worry," he pleaded with them.

"What do you mean, 'Do not worry,' Rov?" a man called out in desperation. Others joined him. They looked at the *rov* as if he had taken leave of his senses. "Isn't it a *dybbuk* we are dealing with here? The demon has undertaken to erase Bociany from the face of the earth, and who knows who may be helping him, Rov dear. Can't you see that?"

What the *rov* was rather inclined to see was that Perele's dream was a bad omen. Perele and her mother had had a premonition of a catastrophe for which there was as yet no tangible evidence. But he did not want to divulge this fear to the crowd. He shook his head like a bewildered animal, simultaneously stubborn and at a loss.

"First of all," he said, "a demon is not a *dybbuk* and don't get the one mixed up with the other. Second, a demon is not a human being, so he cannot do us as much harm as a human can. To disarm the demons and render them ineffective all we need to do is abide by The Law. We have nothing to fear, I assure you."

"Are you implying, Rov, that Perele did not observe The Law?" someone else asked, and the people shook their heads, outraged.

"She did. Of course she did, and so did her mother," the *rov* conceded. "But . . . perhaps they overdid it. Yes, there is a kind of saintliness that borders on the sinful." He saw that his words hurt the crowd; they seemed not to understand what he meant to say. And as he stood there, surrounded, he felt completely alone, separated from them in their anguish—by his own. With his whole heart he felt this separation to be wrong. He was their *rov*. It was better to blunder, even to sin with the people, than to abandon them in their torment. He tried to smile, and as if relenting, he cried out, "People, be it as it may, a dream has holes in its logic, and that's why we can always outsmart it."

"How, Rov?" a voice asked. "Who can influence people's dreams, especially the dreams of a woman?"

"Don't worry," the *rov* said. "There are ways."

"And what about Moshele?" the people persisted. "Should he divorce Perele?"

"Heaven forbid!" the *rov* cried. He made an effort to join the people in their reasoning. "That would be playing straight into the hands of the Devil. That's what he wants, isn't it? Aren't we all afraid that he will destroy the harmony between us and our wives?"

"But my dear Rov!" This was Reb Laibele the Sexton, normally a rational man, but now beside himself with anxiety. He could not understand how the *rov* could say such silly things when all of Bociany was in danger. He lifted his protruding belly with both hands and continued, "The woman Perele is . . . she is now in the category of a whore, isn't she? So how can Reb Moshele, may he live in good health, breathe the same foul air as she?"

The *rov* smiled sadly. "Don't worry, Reb Laibele. I know The Law. The Maharam of Lublin has stated that a married woman can only be labeled a whore if she lives with a man who is not her husband. A demon, although he may behave like a man, is not a man, especially if he appears in a dream. So the woman Perele doesn't fit the category of 'whore.'"

"So what category does she fit?" someone wanted to know.

"She fits the category of a woman who sleeps with a demon in her dreams," the *rov* answered.

"And what does one do about that, Rov dear?" The people would not allow the issue to fade, and voices were now coming from all sides. "How do we rid ourselves of such a dangerous demon? It's no small thing, a demon-priest. Bociany could, heaven forbid, be erased from the face of the earth, and not just Bociany alone!"

The *rov* repeated that they should not worry. Then, throwing caution to the winds, he decided to share his true opinion with them. He said that although he understood their fears, he did not think that the danger in Perele's case was so great. Massacres were taking place in other Jewish communities without the help of demons or *dybbuks,* and that was the real danger threatening the people of Israel. But the Almighty would help and the people of Israel would soon be delivered from the hands of their enemies; there were mysterious but clear signs that this deliverance would happen soon.

The *rov* got into a debate about these "signs" with the *dian* and the other scholars around him. The people debated noisily among themselves and continued to pull the *rov* by the sleeve, asking questions. The room was so crowded that it was difficult to breathe. In addition, the women keeping vigil at Sore-Leyele's bed filled the hallway, crying and calling for a decision by the *rov.*

At length the *rov* raised his long arms above all the assembled heads and called out, "People, listen to what I have decided!" The crowd grew quiet. "Before we do anything else, we must see to it that the woman Perele gives the priest back all his money, down to the last kopeck, the money his housekeeper paid for the yards of cotton that she bought from Perele on that day before Passover. That will be the first step to helping the stricken woman recover; then she would not feel she owes a debt of gratitude to the priest."

A storm broke out around the *rov.* Where would Perele get the money, if she had used it all up to prepare for Passover? As for her parents, they, too, although they ate *kishka* and spleen, barely had enough money to get through the week. Despite their honesty, piety, and distinguished lineage, they were just as poor as the rest of the Jews of Bociany.

"You'll achieve nothing by screaming and shouting, and you'll certainly not conjure up the money we need!" The *rov* stomped his foot to calm the crowd. "But if you calm down, and we make a collection, as we do for other charitable causes, you won't even feel the holes in your pockets." He attempted a little levity. "Because your pockets are anyway full of holes. Besides that, we have a few wealthy members in our congregation who, with God's help, will also lend a hand, and surely not an empty one. So don't worry, the Almighty, blessed be His name, will not abandon us."

The crowd refused to be encouraged by this. The *rov* was letting them down during these moments of trial, and he even dared to joke about it like a boy in his teens. Only Reb Laibele the Sexton made any sense. True, he was not overly liked, but at least he had a sense of reality, unlike the *rov,* who lived in the clouds and did not even know that the color of borscht is red.

"Easy to say make a collection," Reb Laibele groaned, and the crowd groaned with him. "In these rotten times, half of Bociany is walking around hungry and the other half has barely enough to eat. And the roof of the synagogue needs fixing after the winter storms, and the poorhouse needs help or it will collapse. And how do we know that this colossal monetary sacrifice will help not only the priest—but also Perele?" Reb Laibele's joke was greeted with approval because it was loaded with sufficient bitterness.

But no one came up with a better plan of action, and the people decided that they should at least try the *rov's* proposal. The collection was initiated on the spot. Everyone contributed, adding a kopeck to a kopeck, while the *rov* himself brought the rest of the money from the wealthy houses. A messenger was sent to Chwosty to buy a special envelope.

Later in the day, the *rov* himself paid a visit to the bald "writer," the landlord's bookkeeper, Pan Faifer, who was also called Pumpkinhead by the people. Neither the *rov* nor the people generally had much to do with this Jewish goy, but his services were needed now. The *rov,* without becoming involved in any conversation with him, or mentioning a word about what had happened in the shtetl, asked him merely to write, "black upon white," a letter to the priest in Polish, as follows:

> Honorable Priest of the church by the name of All Saints:
>
> In this envelope you will find the complete sum of money that the Honorable Priest's housekeeper paid for the cotton that she bought at the shop on the Potcheyov belonging to Perele the Ritual Slaughterer's Daughter, who is returning the money.

With this letter in hand the *rov* left the bewildered "writer." Back in his crowded chambers, he put the letter and the money inside the envelope so that all could see, licked the border with his tongue, and sealed it with an energetic pound of his fist on the table. Then he sent for the deaf-and-mute Sabbath-goy, who did all the things around the house that a Jew was forbidden to do on the Sabbath, and with a few signs, dispatched him to the priest with the letter.

The Sabbath-goy returned to Perele's house with a reply, but the women gathered inside refused to let him in. Nothing more terrible could happen to Perele in her present predicament than to take into her hands a letter written in the priest's own hand. But the deaf-and-mute goy was stubborn. The priest had expressly indicated to him to give the letter to Perele and to no one else. The goy was on his way back to the parsonage with the letter, when the *rov* intercepted him. Gesticulating, the *rov* explained that Perele had a bad headache and could not read Polish, that she was so sick that she could not possibly go to the "writer" to have the letter translated to her. So he, the *rov,* would do it himself.

The Sabbath-goy respected the *rov* and did not refuse him. A crowd gathered around the *rov* as he made his way to the "writer's" house. The stupefied "writer" read as follows:

> In the name of the Congregation of the Church of All Saints, we thank you, Jewess Perla, for your kind offer, which we accept as a donation to Christian charities. We shall pray for you with all our hearts to the Lord Jesus Christ, for a quick redemption of your lost soul, so that you may see the light of the true religion very soon.
>
> Signed: Father Stanislav

When they heard the translation of the priest's letter, the people grabbed their heads in dismay. That was all they needed, that the real flesh-and-blood priest should also conspire for Perele's soul.

The *rov,* who had already proved to the people that he did not merit the love and respect they bore him, surprised them further by letting out a sigh of relief. He rubbed his long-fingered hands and shrugged his shoulders. "Never mind, people!" he exclaimed nonchalantly and waved the letter at them. "The Almighty has not abandoned us. What's written here upsets me as much as a speck of dust on my left earlock!" He noticed the silent, hostile faces around him and held his arms out to the crowd. "For heaven's sake!" he called out. "Don't you have enough faith to realize that our prayers outweigh those of the priest a thousand times? Yes, indeed, one stone has fallen from my chest already. Now, let someone go and fetch Reb Moshele, the woman Perele's husband."

Reb Moshele, pale, his eyes lowered, was brought into the *rov's* chamber. The *rov* called in the old *dian,* and all three men shut themselves up in the chamber and remained there for several hours. People milled about in front of the house, peeking in through the window, but saw nothing more than the three men swaying back and forth as they sat at the table with volumes of Scripture open in front of them. But what was discussed between them, between reading one paragraph and another, remained a secret, and even the best brains in the shtetl were not sure that they knew. The people had to be satisfied with assumptions, hypotheses, and hunches. For neither the *rov,* nor the *dian,* nor Moshele himself said a word about it when they parted late in the afternoon.

The next day, news spread all over Bociany that a miracle had happened. Perele had slept through the night without so much as the speck of a dream. A day later, the rumored miracle appeared to be fact. Perele got out of bed, sent candles for the synagogue and a few pails of coal for the poorhouse, and visited a couple of women in labor. Then she set out for the Potcheyov with her baby in her arms, to open the store, for she was left without a kopeck to her name. She looked better than any one remembered. Her face was smooth and rested, her coal-black eyes were lively, and she was in such good spirits, that all the women came running to see for themselves that the miracle had taken place.

A few days later, the priest, on his way from the village, decided to pay Perele a visit and thank her personally for her generous donation. His appearance at the shop was like a thunderbolt. The women in the neighboring shops almost fainted. But Perele remained composed, as if this were an everyday occurrence. "I am a poor woman, Panie Priest," she answered to his thanks. "But I wanted to sacrifice this money to show how much we Jews want to live in peace with your people. And please, Panie Priest, when you give your sermon in church, don't mention the donation, nor my letter, but please tell them not to harm us?"

"We Christians don't want to harm you, my child," the priest replied softly, his eyes glowing with missionary zeal. "It is for your own good that we want you to join the true religion, so that there should be no rift between us. Only faith in Jesus Christ our Lord will bring you peace of mind and true joy." He made the sign of the cross.

Perele did not react. In her heart she laughed at the nightmares that this shadow of a man had brought her. But she knew that he had tremendous power over the goyim, so she nodded respectfully at him and prepared herself, under her plaid shawl, to unbutton her blouse to feed her crying baby.

The priest waited either for a reply from Perele, or for the baby to shut up, or perhaps for a glimpse of her breast. So she stayed her motion while the baby grew increasingly impatient and began to holler. The priest made the sign of the cross for the second time and left.

In no time, Perele's clever answer to the priest was known throughout Bociany. She became the heroine of the day. The entire shtetl grew lively, and rarely were there seen so many smiling faces as now appeared in the streets. People crowded into the Hasidic *shtiblekh,* the *besmedresh,* and the synagogue in the evening, and everyone made it a point of honor to shake the *rov's* hand gratefully and reverently.

Sore-Leyele was again surrounded by listeners, the men gathering in the kitchen. Her voice was now even more dramatic, and her stories took on an even deeper meaning. Bociany as a whole grew more God-fearing after this incident, but more optimistic as well. The Almighty had given a sign. Only one worry remained to gnaw deep at the hearts of the people, namely, what if the Evil One should, heaven forbid, return to harass them by means of a more complex strategy?

## 15

DURING THE TIME that followed Perele's confession to her mother, Binele had been free as a lark. Generally speaking, she had never been as happy as she was when she worked for Sore-Leyele. No one spied on her, and she could come and go as she liked. Yossele and the good women neighbors put all their trust in Sore-Leyele.

So Binele had often run off to visit Yankova. Sometimes Yadwiga and her girlfriends would gather around her, and she told them the stories about hell that she had heard from Sore-Leyele. She copied Sore-Leyele's histrionic tone of voice and dramatic gestures as she told them of Asmodeus and of Lilith, the queen of the female demons, as well as of the appearance and personalities of the other denizens of hell. What she could not remember, she made up, inspired by scenes she had seen in the slaughterer's backyard, with the difference that, in her descriptions, sinful people took the place of animals.

As she talked, she scrutinized the faces of the girls who listened to her and was surprised at the impression she was making. The girls stared at her transfixed, swallowing her words with just as much eagerness as the women swallowed Sore-Leyele's. They would cross themselves and whisper, "Oh, Holy Mary! Oh Jesus darling!" Now and then they, in their turn, would try to scare her with stories of their own, about Beelzebub and werewolves, but more often they would run off with frightened screams. She knew that she had not jeopardized her friendship with them; on the contrary, they would soon be back for more horror stories. The whole thing seemed comical to Binele, although she did not feel like laughing, because she could not understand their fright and was seriously puzzled by it.

Thus she gradually started to realized that she had come into this world with an additional defect. It seemed to her that the kind of fear that she did know was shared by no one in the world, whereas the kind of fear that was experienced by everyone, Jew and Gentile alike, was alien to her. Her kind of fear, the sudden agony, the inner tremors, the inexplicable gnawing at the heart—the ache that was perhaps related to her lone arrival into the world—was so deeply buried within her, so impossible to express, that she could not even call it fright. So it seemed to her that if the things that frightened others did not frighten her, then she had no knowledge of what fear really meant.

She tried to imagine herself frightened of the things that frightened others. She thought of the death of her father. But his death seemed impossible; her father was as eternal as God. She tried to think of her own death, but this seemed even more impossible. She thought of the beatings that her father could give her, or of a day when she would have nothing to eat, but these things did not seem so horrible either. Her father would have to stop beating her sooner or later, because his hand would hurt, and if the day ever came when she did not have even a crust of bread to eat, she could always sneak into somebody's field and dig up a carrot or a beet. Even if it were winter and everything was covered with snow, she could go through the garbage on the Potcheyov or smuggle herself into a barn or stable and grab a fistful of oats. And if worse came to worse, she could stuff herself with chalk or lime in her father's shop.

She stared attentively into the faces of the girls who listened to her, trying to imagine herself into their fright. She also studied the faces of Sore-Leyele's listeners, while controlling her urge to laugh. Perhaps in this manner she would understand what fear really was. But none of these methods had any effect.

On Friday nights when she slept at home, her older sisters would ask her to accompany them to the outhouse because she alone was not afraid of the darkness. She was not afraid of ghosts and demons, nor of cats and dogs, nor of mice and rats. She tried to mimic her sisters' frightened squeals, hoping that by copying them she would become infected by their fears, but then she would be overcome by an urge to have fun at her sisters' expense and would turn her squeals into the howls of a ghost or a werewolf.

"Stop that, Marzepa, right now!" Raisele or Rochele would pinch her arm.

"It's not me," Binele giggled. "It's Berele the Moonwalker!" She meant

Brontchele the Mourner's eldest son, who sleepwalked during the full moon.

On cold, rainy nights, as she made her way home from the slaughterer's house, Binele tried to imagine that the soul of Kailele the Bride attacked her from behind, and that Kailele's ghost tried to choke her with its slimy hands. "Come to the lake! Come to the lake!" Binele whispered to herself, pretending that it was not her own voice, but that of Kailele's crazy soul, that called her. But even so, Binele felt no colder than she really was, walking in the slippery mud of the street, the soles of her wooden clogs split open and her coat full of holes. Anyway, everyone said that Kailele's soul had been dwelling within her now for a long time. So what did she have to fear?

On Sunday mornings all the shops on the Potcheyov were bolted shut, the houses locked tight, shutters closed and crisscrossed with boards and iron bars. The Jews sat in their houses, none venturing into the street except out of absolute necessity. The very small children were kept indoors, and only the most daring heder boys peeked into the street through cracks in the shutters. Still, even they spat three times frequently and fearfully whispered *kri-shma.*

During the great to-do in the shtetl caused by the demon priest, Binele had the brilliant idea of testing herself on Sunday morning to see if she was afraid to venture into the street. She also wanted to find out the truth about the priest. She had seen him many times, both from a distance and from close up, but he had never really attracted her attention because he looked like any other old man and smelled of boredom. But now her curiosity was aroused, and she wanted a really good look at him. So she decided to sneak out of Sore-Leyele's house on a bright Sunday morning when Sore-Leyele was lying on a heap of pillows on her bed. The house was full of women who had risked their lives to come over and tend to Sore-Layele as if she were a stricken queen. Binele's services were not needed, and as no one noticed her when she was around, no one noticed when she was gone.

Making her way through back streets and alleys, Binele reached the side of the marketplace that was near the church. There, she mixed freely with the crowds of peasants in their Sunday best who streamed into the church through the open front door.

She looked with envy at the colorful dresses of the girls and young women of the village choir, among whom she saw Wanda, the fire chief's eldest daughter, walking proudly and voluptuously. Wanda's voice was like the sound of a flute, clear and sweet, soaring above all the other voices. Binele's mouth watered at the sight of the velvet vests that the women wore, embroidered and studded with beads of all colors. The white blouses that they wore were also beaded and embellished with ribbons and baubles. She even admired the nuns, although they were dressed only in "sheets," white on the inside, black outside. From their shoulders the black "sheets" fluttered like wings, as if the nuns were black storks with stiff white bonnets on their heads.

She stared at the priest. He, too, wore a white garment, which was thickly embroidered with lace. A large silver cross dangled from his chest. He marched slowly, hands folded over the cross, lips moving. His lips were the only dark spot on his entire figure; the rest of him was white and silver. His clothing was as white as chalk, his head, his face and his hands as white as soiled lime. His tonsure was rimmed with silvery hair and his eyes, too, were silver. He was tall and thin, and he looked to Binele like a kind of regal corpse, a dead king marching slowly to his grave inside the church, accompanied by a suite of white ghosts. The church, with its gilded copper steeples reflecting the sun's rays, looked to her like a white-washed palace adorned with golden spiderwebs.

Binele could not imagine this skinny, corpse-like priest-king paired with the lively and talkative Perele. How could this strange apparition find its way into Perele's dreams night after night? Binele now found it even harder to believe that a demon would assume this white priest's appearance for the sole purpose of playing a trick. How could a demon survive being so stiff and serious all the time? Demons were frivolous, fun-loving mischiefs. So Binele concluded that the man whom Perele had seen in her sleep was really her husband, Moshele, wearing a white nightshirt that resembled the priest's dress. No sooner had she reached this conclusion than it became obvious to her that not only Perele, but all of Bociany, was out of its mind.

As Binele stared at the priest, it occurred to her that the material from his gown would make a lovely white dress for her for the Sabbath.

Slowly she moved through the crowd, listening to the singing of the choir girls and grinning at the Crucified One on the huge wooden cross that was being carried into the church. He looked familiar to her; in fact he resembled Abele the Fool. She could not understand why the Jews of Bociany feared this Jesus so much—unless they were all fools. In the meantime she pushed slowly ahead, mingling with the procession. Then she noticed Yadwiga and made her way over to her.

"You look very nice," she whispered in Yadwiga's ear.

Yadwiga frowned. "I can't breathe. This dress is from my first communion. If I take a deep breath, the seams will burst."

"I wish I had such a dress for the Sabbath." Binele said.

"I wish I had a nicer dress for Sunday!" Yadwiga giggled. The fact that Binele had suddenly appeared beside her did not surprise her. She took hold of Binele's hand and together they made their way into the church. Binele knew that what she was doing was an unpardonable sin, that if her father found out, he would either faint or beat the life out of her. This awareness made her adventure doubly intriguing, doubly exciting.

Inside the church, everything looked extraordinary and unreal. Far in the distance of the spacious hall stood the altar, decorated with flowers and glittering silver vessels. From above the altar, another wooden Jesus wearing a gilded crown of thorns peered down from a gilded wooden cross. To one side of the altar stood a waxen figure of a weeping Mother Mary with a little Jesus in her arms. Her glass tears shimmered, as did her headdress, which was fringed with silver. Silver fringes also adorned her long blue robe.

Binele stared at the face of the Holy Mary for a long time. What a beautiful mother she was! How sweet and kind her sorrowful face looked! Binele had heard from Yadwiga how much the mother of Jesus had suffered, how she had cried and trembled when her son Jesus was nailed to the cross. "Mameshie!" A voice cried out in Binele's heart. "What did you look like? Were you as good and kind a mother as Jesus' mother? Then why did you leave me? And if you're in heaven, are you still angry at me for having made you suffer so much, for having killed you? I know I am a Marzepa and a bad girl, but aren't I still better than Jesus? He knew that he would break his mother's heart, but I was too small to know that I was hurting you. Mameshie, you can see when you look down from the sky that I manage well. And I will never, never let them nail me to a cross."

Her eyes welled up with tears. She took her gaze off the figure of the Virgin and looked at the other saints who, with their wide eyes fixed on the ceiling, seemed ready to soar out of their niches straight to heaven.

From high up, the sun's rainbow-colored rays filtered through the stained-glass windows of the whitewashed dome, which was painted with flying angels. Vibrating and shimmering, the rays fell upon the head of the

Crucified One and became an extension to his crown of thorns. All along the walls, hundreds of burning candles blinked and flickered, encircling the colorful gathering of singing worshipers, who sat in pews in the middle. The sound of an invisible organ permeated the air.

Binele knelt when the crowd knelt and crossed herself when the others did. Before she knew it, she found herself moving to the front as if hypnotized, and suddenly she stood face-to-face with the priest. He put a wafer on the tip of her tongue as he did on everyone else's, and blessed her. Now she had a chance to look him over more thoroughly. Wrinkles covered his face like a net. He looked as if something pained him very much. Was this expression part of his official costume? She was curious how he looked when he smiled, if he ever did.

All during the ceremony in the church, Binele did not forget for a moment the Jewish God outside, in the shtetl, her father's God, Sore-Leyele's God. She was glad to be where she was, playing a trick on Him, playing hide-and-seek with Him. It would never occur to Him to look for her here. Yet this spiteful thought was mixed with bitterness and resentment. Would the God of Bociany even bother to look for her? Did He even have a clue that she existed? Did He care? Perhaps He cared about her father, her sisters, her brother, the people of the shtetl; didn't they all talk about Him as if He were a friend to each of them individually? But He was no friend to her. He never addressed her, never gave her the slightest hint that He knew her.

She had once even asked her brother, Hershele, "If you talk to the Almighty, does He listen to you?"

"Of course," he replied.

"How do you know? Does He answer you?"

"Of course."

"What kind of voice does He have?"

"He has no voice. He speaks to me in my heart, when I speak to him with mine."

"But how does a heart talk? Does it have a mouth?"

He explained, "It has no mouth but it can speak, it has no ears, but it can hear. When I am alone and think up words to say to the Almighty, they pass through my heart, and through it I can also hear the Almighty answer me."

She had tried a few times to speak to the Almighty with her heart, but He had not answered her. Therefore He was not her God, and she had the right to behave as though He did not exist.

But the goyish God in the church was not her God either. He belonged to Yadwiga and her family and to the peasants of the villages. And though the Holy Mary was a beautiful and a kind mother, she was someone else's mother, not Binele's. And Binele was just as incapable of speaking to the goyish God with her heart as she was of speaking to the Jewish one. Therefore, just as she had no mother, she had no God either. And it was not really because of God that she had entered the church, but because of curiosity, and for her own pleasure. And she would come here again and again. She liked it here. It was a splendid place, breathtaking, enchanting, a joy to look upon. No one pushed her around here, or nagged at her, "Don't stand here, don't sit there," as the women did in the balcony of the synagogue. Here, in the church, she could sit wherever she pleased.

Once she had had her fill of seeing and listening, she started feeling bored. Then the priest appeared on a little balcony at the side, and Yadwiga prodded her with an elbow, "Come, let's go out. I always fall asleep when he starts the sermon."

They sneaked out into the churchyard, where a few boys and girls were already running around. Binele looked stealthily about her, then tugged Yadwiga into a corner formed by the church walls, in case someone might notice her from the distance and tell her father. She was not eager for a beating, and she certainly did not want him to kill her, although she knew that there was no great danger that either event would come to pass. It would be difficult to single out her blond-reddish head from those of the other blond-haired children. Her tattered, dirty-gray dress was the darkest spot on the bright sun-lit churchyard, however, so she preferred to blend into a shady secluded corner, especially since she wanted to talk to Yadwiga privately.

She put her arm around Yadwiga's shoulder and asked in a whisper, "The priest . . . Does he have a home of his own?"

"Of course." Yadwiga stared at her in surprise and pointed to the house beside the church. "That's his home. The parsonage."

"Does he have a wife and children?"

"A priest has no wife. A priest has a housekeeper, and not even one child."

"Well, I know something about your priest that you don't know."

"Like what?"

"I know that he doesn't spend even a single night in his own bed at the housekeeper's." Binele neglected to mention that it was not really the priest but a demon in the image of the priest, and that this happened only in Perele's dreams—she had drawn her own conclusion concerning Perele's "affair" with the priest. For the fun of it, she decided to keep this information to herself.

"Where does he sleep, then?" Yadwiga's eyes grew wide with curiosity.

"He sleeps with Perele, the ritual slaughterer's daughter, who owns the shop with dress material on the Potcheyov."

"You're joking!"

"I'm not. I swear!"

"Then how do you know that the priest is sleeping with her?"

Binele related how she knew. Yadwiga sucked in a long breath of air, exhaled it in a whistle, slapped her cheeks with her hands, then crossed herself. "Jesus Maria!" she exclaimed and began to shower Binele with questions.

Binele decided that it was better not to tell Yadwiga everything at once, but to keep her in suspense for a while. So she quickly said, "I'll tell you the rest next time!" She ran off, making her way out of the churchyard through back alleys and yards.

She was not yet in the mood to return to Sore-Leyele's house, or to her own house, so she sneaked through the gate that led to the yard of the Potcheyov, which was loosely tied with a piece of wire. She made her way to the shed of Abele the Fool.

Abele was sitting on his straw mattress, looking like a heap of bones. He was engrossed in delousing his torn caftan. When he saw Binele, his eyes lit up and the smile that was perpetually glued to his face broadened. She sat down next to him and took hold of his long arms. "Lift them up like this," she ordered and showed him how. Abele obeyed and spread out his arms. She took his head between her hands and bent it toward his shoulder.

"Like this?" Abele asked.

"No," she shook her head. "Get up!" Abele stood up beside her, but had to bend his head since the roof of the shed was too low for him. She pushed him to the open door, turning him so that he touched it with his back. "Like that!" she commanded. "Now imagine that you are . . . that you are . . . " The door was shorter than Abele and his head and shoulders stuck out above it. She helped him spread his arms again across the door's upper rim, his hands dangling over the corners. She pressed his hands to the door's borders. "Imagine," she said, "that you are nailed here to this door. Do you understand? Your hands and your feet are nailed to it." She pushed his bare heels closer to the door.

"Nailed to it," Abele laughed.

She explained, "When someone is nailed to a door, or to a cross, it hurts, so don't laugh. Cry!"

"Abele cry." Abele drooled and kept smiling.

"You're not crying! You're laughing!"

"Abele crying . . . " he repeated, shaking his head.

"Don't move your head!" She was growing impatient and bent his head back onto his shoulder. She looked around. Apart from the straw mat and the mounds of lime and chalk that Yossele stored here, there was nothing else in the shed. She noticed a small stone outside, near the door, and picked it up. She began pounding it against Abele's hands with such fury that her face turned red and tears ran from her eyes. "Cry! Cry, I tell you! Stop laughing and cry!"

"Abele not laughing, Abele crying," he repeated.

She flung away the stone and threw herself on the straw mat, buried her face in her arms, and started to sob. She wondered to herself why she was crying, why she was suddenly so overcome by despair. Something gnawed painfully at her heart, an alien yet familiar ache that brought more and more tears to her eyes. The tears came from somewhere deep inside her body, as if they were rooted in her toes and sprouted through her limbs. After a while, she threw a glance at Abele and saw through her tears that he had not moved from his place. He remained exactly where she had put him and, in truth, he was not smiling, but crying. Otherwise the expression on his face had not changed. She also saw the streams of blood trickling from his hands. The sky behind his bent head resembled the church's ceiling. She wiped her face with the edge of her dress. "Like a Jesus . . . " she whispered with lips still wet from tears. For a moment she remained motionless, then a tearful smile began to play across her wet mouth. "Abele," she called out. "You're a Jesus!"

"A Jesus," he repeated after her. As her smile turned to nervous giggles, he laughed loudly as well, as if they both shared a secret. She darted over to him and wrapped her arms around his legs, nuzzling her face between them. "You're a good soul, Abele. You'll be my own Jesus and I'll pray to you . . . "

"Abele a good soul," he muttered.

She stood up. “Come, I’ll take you off the cross!” She took his hand and seated him beside her on the straw mat. “Next Sunday,” she sniffled elatedly, patting him on the back, “we’ll go to the church together, you and I. We’ll sneak inside. You’ll see the goyish Jesus on the cross. He looks exactly like you. So you two will meet.”

Abele’s smile was still glued to his face, but he shook his head, winced, and fell back on the mat, drawing up his knees. “Abele not go to church,” he whined.

“Not today,” Binele explained. “Next Sunday.”

He crouched even more. “Abele not go!” For some reason Abele seemed more frightened of the church than any other Jew in Bociany. The mere mention of the word “church” made him tremble.

The following Tuesday’s market day was full of the usual noisy bustle. The Jews, however, were more cheerful than ever. Perele, the ritual slaughterer’s daughter, had just had her first few nights without bad dreams. But a week later, when the peasants began to mill about on the Potcheyov, it was clear that this time it was their turn to be boisterous and good-humored.

“Your Perla has fallen in love with our priest, hasn’t she?” the peasant women called out to the shopkeepers. “Makes up stories about sleeping with our priest, doesn’t she?”

“Your Perla must be a real pearl!” the peasants called out to the Jewish men whom they passed.

They were careful not to tease the Jews too much. It was clear to the peasants that this was not a question of love, but rather that their beloved priest’s missionary efforts had begun to pay off. Surely the ritual slaughterer’s daughter was on the way to converting to Christianity. This must be quite a blow, a knife in the hearts of the shtetl’s Jews, and it was not Christian to throw salt on people’s wounds. It was a great enough satisfaction to know that Father Stanislav’s promise that such events would take place very soon was becoming reality. Father Stanislav’s flock was not really surprised. His congregation knew both his powers of persuasion and his love of humanity and of everything living. That was why his congregation worshiped him so. He was the embodiment of Christian virtues, the blessed opposite of his debauched brother, Vaslav Spokojny. It was scarcely credible that both these brothers had sprung from the same womb.

So the lightheartedness of the Jews of Bociany was short-lived. It lasted only one week. After that, general confusion set in. That market day, no one knew what he was selling, what he was earning, or what he was buying. It was clear as day that tragedy hovered over the shtetl, ready to pounce like a bird of prey. Everyone blamed the *rov* for his bright idea of sending a letter to the priest, with money, thus betraying the secret they had all sworn to keep. Reb Laibele the Sexton greeted everyone on the threshold of the synagogue with a trembling hand. "What did I tell you?" He was bitterly jubilant. "We've cooked up a dish that they're now going to shove down our throats."

The first thought was that the priest had spread the story among the peasants of Perele's letter and the returned money, embellishing the story so that it accidentally resembled the actual event, although very vaguely. Then suspicion began to prey on people's minds. Even if the priest imagined he knew why the money was returned, although it had not been written in the letter, it was in his own interest to be discreet about the whole matter, at least for the time being. Therefore there had to be a traitor, an informer, hiding in the folds of the Jewish community, and no one could trust anyone else anymore. So, although the people's love for the *rov* had evaporated, there was no choice but to go to him with the problem, which he took very seriously indeed. He decided that finding the informer among his own people was of the utmost importance, otherwise they would all suspect one another, and the lack of trust would erode the strength of the community even before anything more serious happened.

The people set themselves to sniffing out the stool pigeon, applying every means and looking for any clue. Sometimes their suspicion fell on one man, sometimes on another. People cried and swore by their lives that they were innocent. The days passed and the riddle remained unsolved. The atmosphere grew more oppressive; the situation was dangerous. Then the *rov* had the idea of questioning the peasants themselves.

The moment Reb Laibele the Sexton heard that the *rov* intended to query the peasants, it dawned on him that the informer must be none other than Yossele Abedale, and he rushed to see the *rov*. "It's him! It's Yossele, dear Rov!" he burst out excitedly. "Who else spends so much time among the goyim, tell me? You can tell all the people that I told you so, dear Rov!"

Reb Laibele's outburst in turn inspired the *rov* as well, but in a different way. He stared at Reb Laibele with his usual mocking gaze, or so it seemed to Reb Laibele, and said decisively, "Send him in to see me right away."

When Yossele Abedale arrived, the *rov* told him that the best way of finding out who had revealed the secret of what was going on in the shtetl was to question the peasants themselves, and that he had chosen Yossele to carry out this delicate task. "The peasants respect you," the *rov* said. "You are friendly with them. You can talk to them. So go and talk, and ask and listen, and let us know where we stand."

Yossele had remained aloof from the whole story of Perele and the priest. So, by the way, had his neighbor Hindele, but for different reasons. Hindele's younger daughter, Shaindele, had been sick. She had been running a high fever for weeks, and Hindele was beside herself with worry that her youngest one might also succumb to consumption. Hindele had hardly been aware of what was going on around her, until quite recently, when Shaindele had fought her way to recovery. As for Yossele, the story about Perele struck him as grotesque, like a tasteless joke, and he had listened with only one ear to what people on the Potcheyov or in the street or at the *shtibl* were saying. But he agreed with the *rov* that having an informer in the shtetl was no laughing matter. So he could not refuse the *rov's* request to carry out an investigation for the community, although he did not consider himself well equipped for the job. It was not in his nature to question people.

He set out for the villages, and stopped the first peasant acquaintance that he met. "Hey, Pietrek, tell me," he asked. "How did you know . . . How did you come to know that silly story about your priest and Perele the ritual slaughterer's daughter?"

The peasant laughed, patted Yossele on the back, and answered, "My old lady told me."

Yossele, who sometimes exchanged a few words with the peasants, only spoke to their wives in the case of an emergency. He debated whether to send the peasant to ask his wife how she had found out the story, but decided against it. He overcame his own reluctance and went to look for the woman himself. This was a job for the community, after all, and he wanted to do it well.

The peasant's wife burst into such loud peals of laughter that Yossele could see all her big strong teeth. "A friend told me," she answered Yossele.

"Which friend?" Yossele asked.

The woman gave Yossele the name of the friend, and he went to ask the friend. "My old man told me," the friend replied.

So Yossele was sent around in circles, until he realized that just like Abele the Fool, he was spinning around in the middle of the marketplace, the butt of everyone's jokes. He went back to the *rov* and told him that he was giving up the investigation. Reb Laibele the Sexton beamed triumphantly, and the people of the shtetl began to view Yossele with real suspicion. Some stopped greeting him, and Yossele began to hear the word "Traitor!" called after him.

The first few times he heard this word, Yossele stopped, for he thought that people were asking him where the traitor was and were angry at him for having given up the search. Thus he called back to them enraged, "Go and look for him yourselves!"

"We don't have to go far to find him!" came the reply.

Yossele shrugged and walked on. It was clear as day that because of its fear of a pogrom, the shtetl had lost its mind. As the days passed, however, the attitude of the people toward him began to bother Yossele. He went back to the *rov* to explain why he had given up the search. He also told the *rov* that the peasants were merely jesting, that they would soon forget the whole story, and the congregation would remain as safe or unsafe as before.

The *rov* agreed with Yossele wholeheartedly and thanked him with a sigh. "It's difficult to quiet the hearts of the people, so haunted are we all by fear, eh, Reb Yossele? But if only we trusted the Almighty with all our souls and all our beings, we could save ourselves so much worry, so much heartache. How can people forget that we have survived two thousand years of exile? That's no small thing."

"The Almighty provides us with bitter trials," Yossele remarked.

"But we have faced them successfully, haven't we?"

"And what of those burned at stakes, raped, or murdered?"

"I know, yes. But, Reb Yossele, not a single drop of our blood will go unaccounted for. Who knows? Who can penetrate the ways in which He works on our behalf?"

"But the pogrom in . . . "

The *rov* raised his hand pleadingly. "Yes, the waters have come up to our necks. But don't I know that your faith—our faith—is as deep as the mysteries in which His doings are shrouded? That is the meaning of being a Jew. The trouble is that we sometimes forget to trust ourselves or our faith." Yossele wanted to interrupt, but the *rov* held him back with the sorrowful gaze of his sad, dark eyes. "I know, Reb Yossele, that your hope, like mine, knows no limits. That's what makes us Jews different from other people. Our despair never hits bottom."

The *rov's* voice grew so soft and warm that Yossele was inclined to agree with him. It was true after all—hope was what kept him alive. Still he muttered, "But Rov, sometimes it makes me look like a fool in my own eyes. Abele the Town Fool is the greatest optimist in Bociany."

"So? Aren't we all Abeles when we face the greatness of the Lord? I wish I were as innocent, and of such pure mind and soul, as Abele. Although, mind you, this is a selfish wish, because what our people need is not fools, but leaders of supreme wisdom. My tragedy is that I can by no means count myself as one of those . . . "

Yossele left the *rov,* feeling elated despite himself, and mystified by the fact that he, the ignoramus and practical, down-to-earth man, should find himself so often in agreement with this young Talmudic erudite and absentminded dreamer.

The summer passed and so did the High Holidays. The shtetl, while making ready for the Festival of Tabernacles, was also preparing itself for an attack by the goyim. Nobody doubted that the goyim remembered the story of Perele and the priest and would eventually construe it as some Jewish trick to catch Christian souls and convert them to Judaism. And whom should the Jews wish to convert first but the priest himself? That was how the Jews tried to imagine the matter from a Christian point of view. It was only a question of time, the Jews thought, before the goyim would reach this conclusion.

New locks and bolts were put on doors. People studied the faces of the peasants to see whether their smiles had begun to fade and whether the fury had been ignited in their eyes. In the meantime, the Jews continued erecting the wooden tabernacles in which they would eat during the holiday.

Usually, Yossele gave up his peddling some time before the Holiday of Tabernacles, and instead devoted his time to helping people build the wooden shelters. But this year no one called on him, except Reb Faivele the Miller, the *rov,* and the *dian.* If he offered his assistance, people turned their heads away and murmured, "Not needed." Yossele shrugged. It was a good thing that his patience was as strong as it was. Never mind, he would survive. "They'll get over it," he thought, and waited for the undeserved hostility to pass. "Sometimes a whole community can behave like children. Something flies past their noses and they frown. After it's gone, they forget about it." So he lavished particular care on the construction of his own *sukkah.*

This year he had the help of his son, Hershele, who was now studying on his own at the *besmedresh* and would be leaving for the yeshiva shortly. The girls also helped out. A feeling of deep satisfaction came over Yossele at the pleasure of doing something together with his children. It was a new and delightful experience. He and Hershele dug the pits for the supporting poles, the girls gathered together the boards from the previous year's *sukkah* and handed them up to Yossele and Hershele as they stood on the ladders, fitting, fixing, and fastening with the rusty nails Yossele had collected for the purpose. The *sukkah* was solid and comfortable, swaying just slightly when a strong gust of wind blew in from the fields.

Yossele sent out his entire brood to gather the thatch for the roof of the *sukkah.* As he spread the green covering, he inhaled deeply its forest fragrance. The girls brought out the table and benches. Binele, who had returned home early from Sore-Leyele's so as not to miss the fun of decorating the inside of the *sukkah,* helped her older sister Faigele sprinkle the ground with golden sand, which they scooped up from a shovel.

Suddenly, something hard and heavy fell through the green roof and hit Faigele in the head. She collapsed near the table, and hit her head against the blade of the shovel. Blood oozed from her head. The sisters screamed. Yossele, up on the ladder, turned and saw a gang of heder boys who did not even bother to run away. "You bastards!" he yelled, climbing down the ladder. Now he saw all of them, the entire crowd of his neighbors, men and women, as well as people from the neighboring streets.

"Traitor!" they shouted, raising their fists at him.

Yossele stormed into the *sukkah* and squatted down next to Faigele. Her eyes were shut, and she moaned quietly. He talked to her, shook her, but she did not seem to hear him. Slowly, he picked her up and carried her into the house. The girls and Hershele followed behind, their eyes wide as they stared at the blood that flowed down Yossele's gabardine from Faigele's head and traced a crooked red line on the golden sand of the *sukkah* floor.

"Cold water, quick!" Yossele yelled. Having placed Faigele on a cot, he began searching among the rags that lay in a corner of the room.

Binele rushed over to him. "Tateshie, I'll run for Shmulikl the Doctor, all right?"

"We don't need anybody!" Yossele roared. But when Raisele and Rochele brought a basin of stale yellow water to the cot, he remembered what the barber-surgeon had once told him about cleanliness, and he called out to Hershele to bring a pail of fresh, clean water from the water pump.

Yossele celebrated the Holiday of Tabernacles as he had intended. Faigele, pale and dazed, her head wrapped in layers of bandages made out of rags, served her father, her brother, and Abele the Fool along with her sisters. Yossele was no longer irritated. He did not shout at anyone, and he maintained a festive mood. But he was no longer on speaking terms with his neighbors, nor with many other Jews in Bociany.

The holidays passed. The peasants behaved as usual. The story about Perele seemed to have been forgotten, and the Jews of Bociany began to think that the local goyim were not goyim but angels.

Faigele's wound healed slowly. She often lay on her cot, not running about at every free moment, as she used to. Her cheerfulness and laughter vanished. Instead, she cried often and complained of headaches. Yossele did not take it seriously. Nothing could ever happen to his children. Just like him, they were as strong as iron.

Yossele went to the synagogue as usual. He had never socialized with the people between prayers or after, but he had always felt comfortable there, a member of the congregation. The chatting and the disputes that went on around him were the familiar buzz of life, without which the synagogue would not be a synagogue. Now, however, he was excluded from this atmosphere of companionship, isolated, not because he wished it, but as if he had been spat out by the gathering like an alien object. Every so often, after the service, he would hear a hostile hiss in his ear, "Get out of this sacred place!" or the words, "Traitor!" and "Enemy of Israel!" He pretended not to hear anything, and paced between the walls of the hall with his hands behind his back. Sometimes the *rov* would come over to chat with him. The people frowned, and Yossele winced at this special honor that the *rov* paid him. "He's risking his good name for my sake," he would mutter to himself. "I don't need anyone to sacrifice himself for me." So he would cut short the conversation.

Once in a while, choking on the hatred that surrounded him, Yossele felt the impulse to run up to the dais at the synagogue and call out, "People, what do you want from my life?" But he controlled himself. He would not even ask to be put before a jury. His only judge was the Almighty, no one else. "Damn your reason and your sense of justice!" He ground his teeth. Then he remembered that he was in a holy place, in "his" synagogue, and that he was in the presence of the Almighty. He called on his devotion to Him to emerge from the Holy of Holies of his heart. His inner being responded; words of faith came to his lips and gave him a sense of peace and relaxation, washing away his ill will. He would leave the synagogue fortified and cleansed.

This sense of calm could be attained only at the synagogue. In his day-to-day life, Yossele could perhaps have borne his solitude and his neighbors' hostility more easily if it were not for Faigele. Thoughts of her well-being began to prey on his mind. It seemed to him long past the time when she should have recovered from the wound to her head, yet she was still not her usual self. Her cheeks burned, her eyes had a glassy look, and she spent most of her days on the cot. At first he chided her, commanding her to get up and not be lazy. He could not bear to see her lying so limply, so listlessly on her cot. She obeyed him, weeping. Now it had gotten to the point where she no longer answered him when he scolded her, but stared straight ahead with that glassy look in her eyes. She seemed blind and deaf. He called in the women to exorcise her and brought all kinds of amulets and ointments from Reb Senderl the Cabalist.

One of the women refused to come. "No exorcising will help," she said. "The curse which you deserve has struck your child, poor thing."

Yossele did not mind her not coming. He had little faith in the whole business of exorcism; he allowed it for the sake of tradition and to ease his conscience. But the woman's words haunted him. She was right.

Faigele, his most vivacious, most cheerful daughter, was paying for his sins, whatever they were. There was only one solution: he had to take over the burden she was carrying for him.

For the first time in his life, he was unable to handle his inner perturbation and decided to talk to the *rov.* It was late one evening when he finally managed to find the *rov* alone in his chamber, studying. He approached him, murmuring, "Rov, forgive me for interrupting you . . . "

When the *rov* was engaged in his studies, the rest of the world ceased to exist for him. His mind was so far away that it took a good while before he could bring himself back to the present. As he watched the pale young man who greeted him, shook his fingertips, and asked him to sit down, Yossele knew that he had not yet been noticed by the *rov.* He grew impatient, angry at this bony, absentminded creature who was the leader of the community; but he was so envious of him at the same time that he had to forgive him. If only he could wander off with his mind into such calm, such oblivion for an hour or so, Yossele was certain he would feel much stronger. For all his running lately to the villages, to the freedom of the roads and fields and the birch wood, there was no solace for him. Wherever he went, he took his obsessive worries about Faigele along with him, and these blinded him to his surroundings.

At last the *rov* was back on earth. His face lit up with interest and affection. Now he greeted Yossele again; his eyes, ears, even his mouth seemed ready to participate in reality and absorb what his visitor had to say. "I'm glad that you've come, Reb Yossele," he said. "There are many things I want to talk over with you."

"With me?" Yossele sat down.

"Why are you so surprised, Reb Yossele? Don't you know how much I envy you? Don't you know in your heart of hearts that you are superior to me in a million ways?"

"Please, Rov, I have not come to be mocked by you, too." Annoyed, Yossele waved his hand.

The *rov* put his hand on Yossele's arm. It did not enter his mind that the powerful man sitting opposite him had come to seek his moral support. "Too bad, Reb Yossele," the *rov* smiled shyly, "that you don't hear the ring of truth in my voice. Because, believe me, I need your help. My weakness and my strength lie in the fact that I feel so much at home in the realm of speculation, in the realm of the mind and spirit. Yes, I feel so very comfortable in the eternal presence of the Lord. Yet at the same time I feel very uneasy with day-to-day reality. I don't know people well. I come in touch with the stuff of their souls, yes; I try to reach them there, but the entanglements of daily life—people's behavior, their oddities, and their pettiness frustrate me. I am so often at a loss. I don't know how to deal with these things. And I am their *rov,* I do have the necessary qualifications. But something more is needed. I often feel that despite all my knowledge, despite the correct answers and solutions I give them, I have not responded to . . . to the questions that peer at me from their eyes. Reb Yossele, I'm sure you understand me. You're such a wise and powerful man."

"But Rov!" Yossele could not bear hearing the *rov* praising him, and he burst out, "What nonsense are you telling me? I'm an ignoramus going blind, and not just in my eyes."

The *rov* shook his head stubbornly. "Every word you say confirms what I've just said. I've been watching you. I can see how you act. You, an ignoramus? You are the salt of the earth, Reb Yossele. You're not conceited, yet you are the proudest Jew I've ever met. You carry the essence of Judaism in you. It's only the commentaries, as Rabbi Hillel would say, that you are not familiar with. Oh, Reb Yossele, I really do need your help."

"I need yours!" Yossele cried.

The *rov* was silent for a while, scrutinizing Yossele's face. "Has something happened?" he asked at length.

"It has. My daughter is sick. The day before the Holiday of Tabernacles a boy threw a rock into the *sukkah* and hit her on the head. She fell and hit her head against a shovel. She hasn't recovered yet. That rock was meant for me. As you know, Rov, the people have begun to hate me."

"Hate you? Nonsense!" The *rov* smiled boyishly. "Everyone runs to you for advice. You've settled more arguments in this shtetl than the *dian* or I."

"You really live in the clouds, Rov! I thought that you made a point of talking to me in the synagogue because you knew . . . "

"Knew what?"

"How many times have you heard Reb Laibele the Sexton talk against me?"

"So let him talk. Something is eating him. That's his way of letting off steam. He talks against me too. So what? No one takes him seriously."

"Then pray go out into the streets and ask people's opinion of Yossele Abedale."

"And this really upsets you? Since when?"

"Since the beginning of my girl's illness. They must be right in hating me, too. I must have sinned greatly if I am being punished through my child. That's the worst part of it, do you hear me, Rov? The worst part!"

"Is your child so sick, then?"

"Very sick. My heart tells me ugly tales."

"Courage, Reb Yossele." The *rov* pointed to the ceiling. "There is someone up there who knows you and is only testing how weak a strong man can become and how well he makes use of his faith to bounce back. Don't worry, Reb Yossele, the Almighty will help." He looked at Yossele with infinite compassion in his deep black eyes. Then his tone of voice changed, and he added, "So let's not waste time on other things now. Come, let's read the psalms together and pray for your daughter's quick recovery."

He pushed away the heavy tomes that lay before him and took two books of psalms from the bookstand at the side of the table, handing one to Yossele. Together they read the psalms until very late into the night.

Yossele began to spend a lot of time with the *rov.* But the little peace that he found in the *rov's* presence evaporated the moment he left his chambers. Yossele saw only one way out. He would get up on the dais at the synagogue and admit his guilt, confess to everything, if this would help Faigele. He would take this great shame upon himself with the utmost humility and let Rab Laibele the Sexton have the satisfaction of whipping him in the synagogue's antechamber before the eyes of all. The happier his humiliation made the sexton, the stronger would be Yossele's hope that Faigele would recover.

Having made this decision, Yossele felt fortified, and he was determined to go through with his plan the following day in the synagogue. And, in fact, on the following day he was just about to run up to the dais, when a great commotion broke out among the people. Fishele the Butcher, his clothes in disarray, his beard disheveled, his entire figure completely changed, broke through the ranks of men and climbed up to the very spot where Yossele had intended to stand.

"People!" Fishele roared, pounding both fists against the pulpit. "People, I have sinned! I have given my soul to the Evil One! May a calamity strike me! People, whip me! Have no pity on me, tear me apart, cut me to pieces!" He raised his strong arms to the ceiling and stood as if his hands were tied to the roof by an invisible cord. Then he threw himself to the ground.

"God Almighty! He's out of his mind!" A murmur of dismay swept through the synagogue, and grew into a confused clamor. "Reb Fishele! Reb Fishele!" The people swept forward with hands outstretched, each one trying to touch him. Many arms lifted the heavy body of the man to his feet.

Squeals and wailing could be heard from the women's gallery. One of the women fell forward against the banister. "Believe him! Believe him, people," she moaned and then fainted.

"His wife!" voices shouted.

Deadly pale, Fishele rolled his eyes in the direction of the women's gallery and nodded. The men carried Fishele out to the vestibule as if they were saving him from a burning house. Soon he was tied to a chain and everyone who passed kicked or spat at him. One or two people pounded him with their bare fists. Then Reb Laibele the Sexton stepped up and whipped him.

Yossele plowed through the crowd in the vestibule, not even looking in Fishele's direction. Despite the fact that people were confused and upset, his departure did not go unnoticed.

Someone asked, "What better proof of Yossele's guilt?"

Another one commented, "He probably feels himself so sinful that he doesn't dare approach Fishele."

Yossele left the synagogue devoured by envy. Fishele was fortunate. He was paying for his sins. What had happened at the synagogue that day was proof to Yossele that his readiness to sacrifice himself had not been accepted, and that his child was indeed in great danger.

When he entered his house, he saw Hindele the Scribe's Widow sitting at Faigele's bedside, feeding her broth with a spoon. His other children stood around the cot. For a moment Yossele stood paralyzed. The air in the house was strangely peaceful and quiet, as if the room were a ship in the silent eye of a storm. The shadows on the walls looked like black clouds announcing some terrible happening. Yossele leaped at Hindele with an outstretched arm, as if he were ready to strike her. "Get out!" he roared, pointing to the door.

The woman bit her lip and stood up. She handed Raisele the bowl of soup. As she passed Yossele, she murmured softly, "Send for Shmulikl the Doctor, Reb Yossele. It's a matter of life and . . . " She left without finishing the sentence.

Shmulikl the Doctor! Yes, Yossele had to try the barber-surgeon. There was no other choice. He dashed out of the house, passing Hindele as he ran like a madman to the barber-surgeon's shop. He burst into Shmulikl's dining room, and without giving the barber-surgeon a chance to speak a word, dragged him toward the door like a man possessed. Shmulikl barely managed to free himself and grab his shabby bag of instruments and medicine. On the way home, Yossele tried, between gasps, to tell Shmulikl what had happened to Faigele.

"You see, brother," Shmulikl said when he managed to interpose a few words, "the two of us have more in common than you think. Every now and then they throw rocks into my house, too."

These words did nothing to ease the burden that Yossele felt in his heart. He was not ready to conceive of himself as a brother to Shmulikl, although he needed his help now. He would have accepted the help of the Devil himself, to save Faigele's life. He would willingly have given up even his own life to save her.

As soon as they entered the house, Shmulikl began to examine Faigele. Yossele placed himself at the door so as not to admit the neighbors who had gathered outside. "Of course," he heard Toybe-Kraindele sob. "Whom else should Yossele the *'tsadik'* bring to his sick child, but Shmulikl the Doctor, the enemy of Israel?"

He heard Peshele the Slob murmur dolefully, "The moment he refused to remarry, I knew that something was terribly wrong with him and that a calamity was in the making."

Another woman agreed, "Of course, as you make your bed, so shall you sleep."

Shmulikl's examination of Faigele seemed to take an eternity. At length the barber-surgeon stood up from Faigele's bedside. Yossele barely had strength in his feet to approach and hear what Shmulikl had to tell him. The look that Shmulikl gave him and the expression on his face were enough to make him go lame. Moreover, Shmulikl was in no hurry to say anything. He picked up his bag, slowly closed it, and only when he was near the door and ready to go out, did he whisper, "Blood poisoning." He swallowed, and there was a long silence during which he put down his bag in the doorway, took off his glasses, and wiped them with his handkerchief. Finally he spoke again, and said, "She needs a miracle."

From the moment he heard the words, "She needs a miracle," they began to haunt Yossele's mind, and he could not rid himself of them. When the *rov* and a group of men came to his house in the evening to join him in reciting the psalms, Yossele heard just those words and nothing else. It was the same the next day and the day after that. Whenever he prayed, at home or walking the streets or in his shop or on his cot, those words were the only shape that his prayers took on. He was drunk with them, possessed by them, ridiculed and comforted by them.

The most difficult chore for him was spending the day in his shop. His eldest daughters were at home, tending to Faigele. He could have taken the younger ones to the shop to replace him, but he did not want to be too far from home and went peddling only once a week. Because he could not stay at home either, he preferred the shop, unbearable though it was.

Like a caged animal, he paced back and forth between the white piles of chalk and lime. He felt a kind of spiteful vengeance against himself in staying there, bearing the glances of all who looked in, as if they wanted to measure his pain and soothe their hearts with his despair. At the very moment he felt himself ready to react violently, he would stop pacing, force himself to step outside, and lean against the doorpost. He would sway rhythmically from side to side, as if he were not the father of a dying child, but a man without a worry on his head. He stared at the people, his eyes like daggers, and whispered into his beard, "They'll never break me! Never!"

Hindele the Scribe's Widow had become deeply involved in Yossele's predicament. She had just lived through weeks of tremendous anxiety over a child of her own, and her heart was still sore. She understood so well what Yossele felt that she identified with him. She was not a quarrelsome woman and had always lived in harmony with her neighbors on the Potcheyov, but she took their attitude toward Yossele so personally, and was so dismayed and outraged whenever she heard them call him a traitor, that she would explode into shouts and tears, threatening the others with the Almighty's punishment. They in turn responded with abuse and mocking laughter, dubbing her the Traitor's Bride. As for her bosom friend, Nechele the Pockmarked, Yossele had again become the cause of a fierce quarrel between Hindele and Nechele, and the two were no longer on speaking terms.

But Hindele got on Yossele's nerves in a different way. She refused to leave him alone and was always shoving her stool closer to him and talking as if to herself. This would go on until he could no longer bear it, and he yelled at her to leave him alone. Then she would move her seat back, only to reappear at his side a moment later.

One day she placed herself beside him and leaned against the wall, warming herself in the early winter sun. As if she were addressing the water pump, she said in her soft voice, "I've just read a booklet that says that the Almighty weeps over us, the unhappy creatures he has created. Yes, Reb Yossele, He weeps, too, but in secret. Do you know why in secret, Reb Yossele?" She tilted her head in his direction. "He weeps in secret because it doesn't suit a lion to weep in front of a fox, or a king to weep in front of his subjects. You men, too, feel humiliated if you cry at any other time than Tisha B'Av or Yom Kippur. Be that as it may, you are not lions or kings. Shedding a tear doesn't mean shedding one's pride. Sometimes one must cry. It's a good deed to cry, Reb Yossele."

She was about to elaborate, but Yossele jumped as if her words had burned him. "Will you shut up!" he hissed.

That evening, Yossele ran to Mariml's grave in the cemetery. He embraced the wooden tombstone, which he had cut and engraved with his own hands, and buried his face in the grass. A spasmodic dry sobbing shook his chest. The tears refused to come.

Life in Yossele's house had taken on a rhythm of its own, a rhythm that resembled normality. Binele continued to work at Sore-Leyele's, but every day after work, she would run home to see how Faigele was doing. Faigele was her favorite sister. Neither Faigele nor her twin, Mashele, ever reproached or criticized her, as the two eldest sisters did. The twins easily forgot Binele's misbehavior. Mashele was a sad, serious girl, while Faigele was lively and fun-loving. It was thanks to Faigele that the house resounded with laughter and cheerful chatter; her presence had filled it with brightness. Now the house was dark and unbearably quiet.

Binele could not long bear the stifling gloom and the sight of the motionless Faigele lying on her cot. Every once in a while, she asked Mashele to accompany her to the Wide Poplar road to wait there for the Messiah;

perhaps he would shorten his absence and come to cure Faigele. Binele and Mashele were now old enough to understand that the Messiah was not obliged to arrive exactly when the Jews most wanted him to, and that he certainly would not arrive just for their sister's sake, but the girls had become strangely childish ever since Faigele had become so gravely ill; they again believed in the miracles that they had stopped believing in a long time before.

After they returned home one day, Binele sat down next to Hershele. "Tell me the truth," she said to him. "When will the Messiah come?"

He looked at her with an uncertain glance. Should he give her a learned reply to her question? Would that soothe her heart? Would it soothe his own? No, this was not the moment for such things. "When there are no more sinful Jews," he replied curtly and then added, "and when we no longer have the strength to bear our suffering."

"But we can't bear it any longer," Binele whispered.

"Yes, but we are not yet free from sin," he answered nervously, dissatisfied with himself. To Binele he suddenly seemed to resemble his father. The older Hershele grew, the more often there were moments when he reminded Binele of their father. "Can't you see how Bociany has sinned against Faigele and against Tateshie?" Hershele asked.

"But why should Faigele suffer because of the sins of Bociany?"

"Because that's how God made the world. One person is responsible for the sins of another."

"That's not fair!" Binele exclaimed, running out of the house.

On her way back to Sore-Leyele's, it dawned on Binele that the Messiah would never come because people would never be free of sin; the whole story about the Messiah was a lie. Her heart ached. She had believed in the Messiah even after she had stopped believing that she had a God. The Messiah was a man of flesh and blood, kind and loving, with the tremendous power of healing the sick and reviving the dead, her own mother included. She had believed in the happiness he would bring and had expected him to be her only salvation. She would have recognized him immediately. But now she knew that there was no one to wait for, or to hope for.

She felt herself drawn to the church again. On Sunday morning she sneaked inside, along with the multitude of peasants. She saw Yadwiga at a distance but made no move to approach her. She hid behind a broad-shouldered peasant, so that Yadwiga would not notice her. Then she sat down between two women and gazed on the folds of the Virgin Mary's dress.

"Mameshie," she whispered, shutting her eyes, her hands folded over her chest. "Mameshie dearest, see to it that Faigele recovers. Let Faigele call me Marzepa. Let her tell me a thousand times that you died because of me. Mameshie, please be good to Faigele and cure her." When Binele opened her eyes and looked at the statue, it seemed to her that her weeping mother was nodding, promising. Her heart full of hope, she left the church.

"Now I'll go straight back to Sore-Leyele's," she told herself as she hurried through the back alleys. "And I'll ask her what else I can do to help Faigele get better. And I swear by the name of Mameshie that I will not steal another kopeck from the charity boxes, and I will not sin even once, and Faigele will have to get healthy again." She was sure of that because she was sure that there must be one kind of justice or another in this world, even if there was no God and no Messiah. She had to believe in miracles, at least now that Faigele was so sick.

She entered the slaughterer's yard from the back alley and was about to sneak into the house through the back door, when she heard strange sounds coming from inside. On Sunday mornings, Sore-Leyele's house was usually full of women who had risked venturing outside in order to come and hear her preach. But the lamentations coming from Sore-Leyele's room now were strangely loud; they grated on the ear, sharp, hoarse, and soaked in such despair that it seemed as though the world had come to an end.

Binele could hardly get through the kitchen, packed as it was with weeping men and women. The other room was likewise full of a wailing mass of people. Binele noticed that the mirror on the wall was covered with a black cloth. Then she saw the slaughterer and his daughters doubled up and shaking spasmodically.

Sore-Leyele had had a heart attack in the middle of recounting the story of the Angel of Death. Bociany had lost a powerful fighter against the Evil One. Now it looked as though the coming of the Messiah would indeed be postponed, for who knew how long.

Faigele died a week later.

## 16

WORKING ON REB FAIVELE the Miller's property, Yacov felt like a bird loosed from its cage. Life took on a new flavor, and he was constantly surprised by his feelings of well-being and lightheartedness. He liked Reb Faivele and his tall, beautiful wife, Zirele. Even when the couple shouted and quarreled, he liked them. And he liked their children. He even liked the housekeeper, Fredka, and her husband, who was in charge of the farm. Everything around him became dear to Yacov. His gratitude and pleasure reflected in his face and could be felt in everything he did.

So it was easy for him to adjust to this new world and to win the hearts of the people in it. He felt comfortable and at peace with them, with himself and with the Creator. Yes, here he had made peace with Him, despite his resentment. "The earth and the sky are like a pot with a cover," he thought, recalling the saying he had learned from Reb Senderl the Cabalist years before.

His employer, Reb Faivele, was not a tall man, but he had a massive body tightly packed with strength and energy. His round face was also firm, with wind creases on the forehead and laughter creases at the corners of his eyes. His eyes were lively and restless, and as black as his beard. His gestures betrayed a dynamic temperament; disquiet bubbled within him as if some compressed power was constantly seeking an outlet, and this made those around him feel restless in his presence. Incapable of staying in one place for very long, he was constantly rushing to and fro at a dizzying speed, while his mood changed as often as his movements. Within the space of a minute, he could go from laughing at one of his own jokes to roaring with rage at something that displeased him. Or he would suddenly begin singing in a deep bass, and a moment later start shouting heatedly again.

Reb Faivele came from Galicia. During the week, he wore neither the traditional gabardine nor a Jewish cap with a visor. Instead, he wore a pseudo-modern German coat and a sable hat like those worn by the gentry. His beard was trimmed in the German fashion, the sideburns in the style of the Emperor Franz Joseph. As a young man, he had wandered through southern Poland, building water mills and sawmills for the gentry and for the local millers. That was how the landlord of Bociany had heard of him, and he hired him to construct a water mill on his land by the river that passed some twenty miles outside Bociany. Reb Faivele was well liked by the landlord and his eldest son, who offered him the ruin of the old windmill on the top of the Blue Mountain as a gift, or perhaps merely as a joke.

Reb Faivele was an expert on all kinds of mills, but he had a particular weakness for windmills. So he rebuilt the old mill and took a lease on the entire Blue Mountain and its surroundings. The location pleased him enormously, and so did the wood merchant's young daughter, Long Zirele. She was dubbed "long" by the people of Bociany because of her exceptionally tall figure. He married her, and together they set up a home and a grain business on top of the Blue Mountain. As for the mill, Reb Faivele made it as modern as he could, and both Gentiles and Jews came to admire the wonder.

Reb Faivele was known to all of Bociany. He quickly took to speaking Yiddish with the Bociany accent and won respect for himself by his generous contributions to the local charities and by his handouts to people in need. The result was that the majority of the people of Bociany had some reason to be grateful to him: brides for his contributions to their dowries, young men for helping them leave for the yeshiva, or for saving them from conscription, or widows for giving them the means to prepare a decent Sabbath. He often took in needy men to work on his property for a day or two, and every Monday he drove into Bociany to buy something from the poorest shopkeepers or to give work to the poorest artisans.

After a time, people stopped noticing Reb Faivele's "pagan" way of dressing or his behavior, which was not always one-hundred-percent traditional. Trespasses that could not be forgiven the other "goyish" Jews were forgiven him. Reb Faivele would, after all, not be Reb Faivele if he did not dress as he did or act as he did. Everyone in the shtetl considered him a distant relative. He was invited to births, circumcisions, bar mitzvahs, and weddings, and was informed of the place and time of funerals. And if on Mondays he left the Potcheyov to play a game of chess with the *rov,* this, too, was forgiven him. People followed him with their eyes with great reverence and with a blessing on their lips.

All the peasants who worked on Reb Faivele's property spoke Yiddish, and Fredka, the gentile housekeeper, who had previously been the wet nurse, ate only kosher dishes while she was breast-feeding the master's sons, so that her milk would be kosher. As the boys, who had arrived quite late in their parents' marriage, grew older, she would say the blessing over the food with them and remind them to wash their hands. On Sabbath nights, she would sing the table songs along with the rest of the family. She saw to it that the little boys did not grow up as goyim.

As for Reb Faivele's wife, Long Zirele, she was a "woman with an earring" as they said in Bociany. She, too, had a fiery temper and ruled the big house and property with a firm hand. In this area she had more of a say than did her husband, who, according to her, had "nothing but windmills turning in his head." Indeed, he relied on her completely. Every Thursday she paid the hired help and gave each one a small glass of *monopolka* and a slice of sponge cake to go with their earnings. The workers trembled with fear and adoration before her, bowing deeply after each word she uttered, as did their wives who worked in the kitchen, the yard, and the fields.

Zirele's temper matched her husband's, but of the two she was the more down-to-earth, and she paid more attention to details than Reb Faivele did. She was unlike him also in never entirely losing her head, even when she was fuming with anger. At least once a day husband and wife clashed in angry exchange, and at least once a week they quarreled. Then the word "practical" would bounce between them like a ball. She would reproach him for not being practical, and he would reproach her for being too practical. Mostly she resented his exaggerated involvement with the mill and what she called his childishness in household and family matters. She considered him a scatterbrain and a spendthrift. "Remember," she warned, "if you live now without keeping account, you'll die without shrouds a hundred and twenty years later!"

For his part, Reb Faivele resented his wife's stinginess and her belief in demons and spirits. "You are as superstitious as old Terakh," he bellowed at her. "And on top of that, your stinginess has locked up your womb, that's what it's done! Because you're so stingy, you didn't even have enough milk to nurse your children!"

When Reb Faivele quarreled, his reason took a rest—he aimed directly for the jugular. Not that Zirele's aim was much worse than his. It was only that he did not hear her taunts, while she heard every one of his and stashed them away in her mind to use later, to make him feel guilty after they made up.

They knew one another well and were not at all indifferent to each other. The storms between them, wild as they were, passed quickly.

Zirele's handkerchief served as a peace sign. She would raise it to dab her eyes, although there were seldom any tears in them, and as soon as Reb Faivele saw the handkerchief, his rage would subside. He would embrace her, bury his thick beard in her neck, and kiss her passionately. "I was only joking, silly woman," he would mumble. "You've given me two sons whom I would not exchange for a dozen others!" Still holding her in his strong arms, he would pull her toward the bedroom, behaving not in the least like a respectable member of the Jewish community.

There were never any marital wars on Fridays. On Friday, Reb Faivele finished his business for the week early, both at the mill and at his *kantur,* as he called his office. But he did not stop rushing about from place to place until it was time to prepare himself, body and soul, for the approaching day of peace. Zirele, too, spent the entire day preparing for the Sabbath, supervising the housecleaning and the cooking of the Sabbath meal, as well as attending to the children and herself.

At sunset all the shiny copper chandeliers were lit in the dining room, as were the other lights because the more light there was in the home, the more good fortune the Almighty granted it. Zirele herself was transformed into a different person. From her face there emanated a particular radiance as she moved slowly through the sparkling clean house, dressed in her black silken Sabbath dress, long pearl necklaces hanging around her neck, and peering out from under the white silk scarf she wore draped around her shoulders. She looked like a true Jewish queen, a queen hiding some wonderful secret in the barely discernible smile on her lips, as she solemnly entered the dining room. Adjusting her Sabbath bonnet, which was covered with lace and studded with tiny diamonds, she approached the table, where the challah lay under a napkin embroidered with silver threads. She lit the candles in the silver candelabrum, covered her head with her scarf, and placing her hands on her face, recited the benediction over the lights in a whisper. Peace reigned in the house, and time stood still.

Reb Faivele and the Sabbath guest or guests would return on foot from the synagogue in Bociany. He would sit down at the head of the festive table, across from Zirele; he was dressed in his Sabbath caftan and his sparkling white skullcap and the white shirt contrasted sharply with his black frock and black beard. The smile on his full red lips and the glow in his black eyes caressed Zirele from the distance in an altogether different manner than during the week. Tonight their desire for each other sang softly across the table. It was like an inaudible musical string, washed and purified by the light of the candles, which vibrated delicately, tenderly between them. Yacov, who ate with them on those Friday nights when he did not go home to his mother, thought that there could be no greater beauty than that of a Sabbath meal celebrated by a family complete with a mother, father, and children.

When Yacov was not teaching the two little boys, he helped out at the mill, where he had the opportunity of being near Reb Faivele.

When Reb Faivele was free from dealing with the grain merchants and had nothing urgent to do in his *kantur,* he would throw himself with great enthusiasm into his work at the mill. There he remained even-tempered for long periods of time. He was vivacious, cheerful, and approachable. He never shut his mouth for an instant, and listening to him was mind-provoking. Everything he said was new and different. He was familiar with science and knew much about the world in general and the Austrian Empire in particular. He pointed out the mistakes of Russian strategy in the war with Japan, could hold forth for hours on the causes of the Russian Revolution of 1905, and knew about the politics of Germany, France, and England. Yacov had heard about these countries before, but this was the first time in his life that he learned something about them. Reb Faivele knew how people lived in other countries. He showed off his knowledge before his visitors, mostly merchants whom he often invited to stay the night or stay for the Sabbath, so that he might have "someone to talk to" and play chess with.

The visitors were obliged to stand against the wall of the mill, as Reb Faivele, shirt sleeves rolled up, suspenders dangling over his hips, ritual fringes fully displayed over his belly, busied himself around the noisy millstones, his voice booming so that he could be heard above the clatter. In the middle of his activities he would suddenly stop to draw from his pocket a newspaper clipping from Vienna, Odessa, Krakow, or Warsaw, and point to a passage that confirmed his theories, proving that his assumptions had been correct.

To Yacov, every day spent at Reb Faivele's was like a Sabbath, although he rarely had the luxury of being completely idle during the week. But the elated feeling of learning new things, and his surroundings, which made him feel so very comfortable, body and soul, made every day seem like a holiday.

The landscape that he beheld every day was a feast of beauty. From the Blue Mountain he could see Bociany in the distance, peeking out from a wreath of poplar trees, the glimmering tip of the church's steeple cutting into the expanse of sky. He could also see the White Mountain and the landlord's mansion in the distance, the birch wood, the lake, the fields and the pastures and forests miles away. The light of the sun, or the blue or gray of the sky, which were reflected in the panes of Reb Faivele's whitewashed wooden house, seemed to lift the house off the ground. It appeared to be navigating through the air like Noah's ark, sailing between light and shadow, on the verge of anchoring on Mount Ararat, surrounded by a sea of green, dotted with bluebottles and heather. When Yacov sat in the little alcove that Long Zirele had designated as his room, he would kiss the Scriptures before opening them and murmur, "All my bones say, 'Who is like unto You, my Lord?'"

Reb Faivele's younger son was four years old when Yacov began to study the Pentateuch and Rashi commentaries with him and his elder brother. The little boy's name was Abraham, but Fredka, the nurse maid, who was of Volinian stock, called him Abrashka or Abrasha, and that was how he was generally known.

Abrashka had two mothers, his Mameshie and his Ameshie, the word for wet nurse in Yiddish being *am*. He loved his Ameshie more than his Mameshie, and his Ameshie, in turn, had a particular fondness for him. She spent more time with him than with her own children.

Fredka was a heavyset, broad-boned, and wide-hipped young woman with strong legs and calves like those of a man. She had a moon-shaped face, smooth shiny skin, and a Kosciuszko nose—that is, a nose turned upward. Her gray eyes were kind. She would often stop in the middle of whatever she was doing, playfully gather Abrashka into her arms and press him against her abundant bosom, kissing him loudly. As late as the previous year, when he had already reached the mature age of three, she still offered him her breast to suck on. Until Yacov had entered his life, Abrashka had spent more time in his Ameshie's cabin than in his own home.

Abrashka was a plump little boy, a big eater, and a smiling rogue. He waddled about on short, fat legs, but he was as quick as a rabbit. Dark-haired like his father, whom he resembled, he had a pair of impish, twinkling black eyes, which betrayed his inclination toward mischief. He dismantled whatever came into his hands so that he could see "from where the legs are growing." One had continually to prevent things from attracting his attention and to chase him from one place to another, because he had the habit of showing up where he was least expected and doing his destructive work in the wink of an eye. He ran around barefoot, one pants-leg down, the other up, his face smeared with dirt. With his chubby face and sparkling black eyes, he reminded Yacov of the cherubs that decorated the picture cards that Zirele received by mail and that her older son collected.

Abrashka clung to Yacov from the moment they met. He studied with him in the morning, and every afternoon, when Yacov had finished his work at the mill, he became Abrashka's exclusive possession. As soon as he noticed Yacov leave the mill, Abrashka would dash out to meet him. He would wrap his arms around Yacov's knees and, raising his disheveled head, demand, "Tell me a story, quickly!"

Abrashka swallowed stories with open eyes and ears. It was the only time that he sat still, forgetting where he was and letting his imagination carry him into whatever fictional realm Yacov created. Yacov was infected by the little boy's intensity and was himself drawn into the world he painted with his words. It was like Abrashka held the key to Yacov's imagination. Abrashka could open hidden doors within it, letting out images, scenes of unusual happenings, impossible yet believable adventures. Yacov was amazed by his own words, wondering how the stories could come so easily to him. Abrashka had turned him into a magician whose every wish was a dove floating on air and shaking the dust of dreams off its wings.

A year went by. The winter was gone and the mud had dried. The Christian spring holidays were approaching. After his work at the mill, Yacov lifted Abrashka to his shoulders and, accompanied by the shaggy dog, Bobik, left for the birch wood. Abrashka would not let Yacov interrupt the story he was in the middle of telling, not even as they marched along. They listened to the chirping of the birds and gathered twigs as Yacov talked on and on, spinning out the thread of the story.

While he was talking, thoughts of his own flashed through Yacov's mind. This birch wood had remained fixed in his memory as the place where he had nearly been "crucified" by his gentile friends. When he thought of it now, he still experienced a moment of fear, and had to talk himself out of it by telling himself, "I'm no longer a child. I'm a man now, nearly two years after my bar mitzvah, and a man must go on weaving fascinating tales for his small charge and move ahead without fear." He fortified himself as well with the thought that the gentile boys who had tormented him then were now as old as he was and worked on the landlord's fields; they no longer had time to play games. Then he noticed how his private thoughts discolored the story he was in the middle of telling Abrashka, making it less exciting and rich with adventure, and he tried to forget everything and give himself fully to the play of his imagination.

When they came to the marshes and the lake, they stood watching the storks catching their food or standing on one leg. Here they were so remote from the nearest house that they seemed to be the only human beings in God's world. So to give them company, Yacov humanized the lake, the storks, the trees, shrubs, and birds, and turned them into characters in his story. This made him feel as though part of him were outside himself, watching the two of them—Abrashka and Yacov—through the eyes of the world that surrounded them. They were the same, yet through the magic of the story they both seemed transformed and created anew.

On the way back, they crossed the field. Yacov was still telling his story, "Abrashka and Yacov walked on and on, until they saw herdsmen sitting in the field . . . " Actually there was only one cowherd in the field, Kazimierz, Fredka's old father-in-law, who was watching Reb Faivele's cows and sat leaning against the pine tree that stood in the middle of the field. It was from the boughs of that very same tree that the gentile boys had made Yacov's cross. As they approached the tree, Yacov continued, "And Abrashka and Yacov sat down beside the herdsmen. The herdsmen were messengers from a far-off country and they did not speak the same language as Yacov and Abrashka." Yacov turned to Kazimierz and asked, "Where is your flute?"

Kazimierz smiled broadly, showing his toothless gums. He took a wooden flute from inside his vest and put the flute to his lips.

"The shepherds could not speak Abrashka's language," Yacov continued, "so they played their flutes instead. Then Abrashka could understand them very well."

Abrashka laid his head on Yacov's lap. The tunes that Kazimierz played were plaintive and sad, and it did not take long for the little boy to fall asleep. Yacov gathered him into his arms and carried him home.

The field was covered with the first grass of the year and the first wild flowers. The ground under Yacov's feet felt as soft as a thick carpet. The old fear returned. "I am walking slowly through the field where I once ran for my life," he said to himself. "But if someone were to attack me now, what would I do? I, an adult, carrying a child in my arms? Would I have the strength to protect Abrashka?" The field gave off a faint, delicate fragrance, which seemed to match the increasingly distant sound of Kazimierz's flute. Yacov looked down at the face of the sleeping Abrashka. "When I am with him," he thought, "I don't remember how old he is, or how old I am. When I am with Mother, the same thing happens. I don't remember how old I am or how old she is. Perhaps if a person loves and is not frightened, the years of his life don't count. When people love one another, they become the same age?"

The day before the Christian spring festivities, there was a great to-do in Reb Faivele's mill. Abrashka had been strictly forbidden to enter the mill, and so he waited for Yacov outside in great impatience. He wandered about with Bobik at his side and called out repeatedly, "Yacov, come out already!" The creaking of the mill's flaps, the groan of the millstones, and the sound of raised voices were all that he got in reply. Finally he saw his father rush out, unbuttoned, disheveled, running in the direction of his *kantur,* where a crowd of merchants stood around waiting for him.

"Tateshie, when will Yacov come out already?" Abrashka shouted, running after Reb Faivele.

The *kantur* was full of noise and cigarette smoke. The merchants were heatedly discussing the price of grain and making calculations with chalk all over the furniture as they pushed their unfinished tea cups back and forth. They sampled the wheat, rye, and barley, chewing on the grains and then spitting them out. They puffed on their cigarettes, nodded or shook their heads, and continued with their calculations.

Reb Faivele removed the pencil from behind his ear, pulled the edge of his caftan out of Abrashka's fist, picked him up, and yelled at the merchants, "Will you stop smearing my furniture with chalk, you savages!"

"Tateshie . . . " Abrashka tugged at his father's beard.

Reb Faivele carried Abrashka to the door and set him down on the verandah. "How many times have I told you not to bother me?" he yelled, and vanished inside the *kantur.*

A minute later he ran out again, back to the mill. Abrashka dashed after him, but the noisy mill soon swallowed his father. Abrashka killed time by climbing onto the assembled wagons and talking to the horses as they chewed their oats. Then he took to wandering around the mill, beating his fists on its boards to the rhythmic sound of the sails going round and round. Every few minutes he would cry, "Yacov, come out already!"

One loose board, then another, gave way under the weight of his small fist. He pushed the boards in by pressing the bulk of his chubby body against them, then wriggled in through the opening. He looked around. The sails screeched, the axle groaned, the millstones moaned. His father was busy giving orders and scribbling things on scraps of paper. Other men worked at the scales or at the millstones. Then he saw Yacov, whose ritual garment was hanging over his naked torso like a curtain, while the suspenders dangled down over his hips. He was carrying a sack of flour to the door. His face was red, his skin glistened with sweat, and Abrashka could see the veins on his neck. Yacov was completely engrossed in carrying the sack on his back. He moved ahead with small staccato steps, his eyes fixed on the spot where he would lay down the sack.

Abrashka darted toward him and tugged at his pants. "Hurry up, Yacov, make it quick!" he called.

Yacov swayed, his knees sank, and his legs twisted. The sack on his back moved precariously and finally fell to the ground, carrying Yacov with it. Abrashka screamed. In a second his father was beside him, lifting him into his arms. "Are you all right, Abrashka? You didn't hurt yourself, did you?" Reb Faivele panted and patted the child's body, then he pressed the boy to his chest and covered his face with loud kisses.

Impatiently, Abrashka wriggled in his father's arms. "Yacov is dead! Yacov is dead!" he screamed.

Yacov stood up slowly. He could barely straighten his back. With one hand he rubbed the bruises on his forehead, with the other he rubbed his knee. He stared at the screaming Abrashka with a twisted smile on his face. "Thank Heaven you're not hurt," he muttered.

Abrashka wriggled out of his father's arms and rushed over to Yacov. He had barely managed to embrace Yacov's legs when Reb Faivele snatched his arm and pulled him away. He grabbed Yacov's shoulders and shook him with savage fury. "What are you smiling like that for, you idiot! Don't you realize what might have happened? How many times do I have to tell you that it's dangerous to let the child in here? Remember!" Reb Faivele waved his short hairy finger in front of Yacov's nose. "If anything ever happens to Abrashka, as you see me standing here, I'll crush you between these millstones!"

Abrashka, his eyes full of tears, followed his father's finger in the direction of the millstones. Then Reb Faivele pushed Yacov out of the mill and, with a slap on the behind, made Abrashka follow him. Outside, Yacov stared at the closed door of the mill for a moment, then rolled up his trousers and wet his bleeding knee with saliva. Abrashka stood a few feet away from him. Their eyes met. After a moment, Abrashka threw himself against Yacov and embraced him. "Yacov," he panted, trembling all over. "I won't let Father crush you between the millstones!"

That night Abrashka dreamed that he saw his father crushing Yacov between the millstones, and he woke up screaming. Reb Faivele jumped out of bed and rushed into the boy's room. But at the sound of his father's voice, Abrashka screamed even louder. From then on, he grew afraid of his father and gradually his fear assumed a tinge of hatred.

Abrashka never forgot the incident with his father at the mill, but Yacov forgot it almost immediately. He liked Reb Faivele as much as ever. "Reb Faivele has a quick temper," he thought, "but he has a heart of gold and would readily lay down his life for his children." He had no doubt that Reb Faivele returned his affection. He easily sensed the feelings that people had for him, and he was so happy at Reb Faivele's that he preferred to remember the good things that happened to him rather than the bad. He remembered how at first he had been unable even to move a sack of flour, how he had struggled with the heavy loads, consoling himself by remembering that his brother, Shalom, had not found the work of a porter easy at first, either. Now Yacov had caught up to his brother. And what a good feeling it was to be able to master the heavy sacks, to feel one's body growing strong and firm.

His entire posture had changed. His back had grown straight, his arms and chest were so muscular that he often wondered how his skin found room for the new bulges. No physical effort was too exacting for him now. Meeting the challenge, conquering the obstacles with energy and will power, gave a particular satisfaction. There was pleasure in moving so massively, so assuredly, feeling the ground more firmly under his feet, as if the ground itself acknowledged his newfound powers.

His trousers had become a quarter too short, and the sleeves of his caftan reached just to his elbows; the whole garment was bursting at the seams. Fredka grew tired of patching it up and finally gave Yacov a pair of comfortable peasant pants and a peasant shirt to work in. When he put them on and caught his reflection in the window pane, he saw someone stronger, more vigorous and aggressive than the self he had known before.

It was not long before Fredka was saying, "We'll have to move the buttons again, won't we, Yacov?"

So he began dressing in the used clothes of the farm hands, a peasant cap over his skullcap, his long sidelocks gathered up inside whenever they got in his way. For the Sabbath he wore one of Reb Faivele's used gabardines, which Long Zirele had given him. The gabardine was comfortable but short and fit him like a shirt. It was the outfit he wore when he visited his mother.

He wanted to look well, if only for the pleasure it gave his mother when she saw him. Hindele beamed and could not keep her eyes off him. She was constantly touching his suntanned cheeks as if to convince herself that they were real. She relished the sight of the twinkle in his warm brown eyes and marveled at his finely shaped lips, which had grown redder than the fruits of the *kalina* tree in the nuns' garden. The air about Yacov was filled with the calm and tenderness of times past, and she recognized the reflection of her own smile dreamily playing around the corners of his mouth.

His sister Gitele was also excited by the sight of him. "Look at this handsome Yacov!" she would cry, rushing to meet him and tug at his sidelock. Although she was now in her early teens, she was still lively and fun-loving.

The younger sister, Shaindele, mimicked her. "Give me a kiss, handsome Yacov!" She pulled at his other sidelock and pressed her pouting lips to his cheek.

He began to suspect that he really was handsome. The girls in the shtetl followed him with their eyes and blushed when he passed them on the street. For his part, he followed them with his eyes on Sabbath afternoons, when they all promenaded on one side of the street, while the young men promenaded on the other. In small groups, they all made their way to the fence along the landlord's court, where the shtetl youth liked to gather. The girls' long dresses fluttered lightly in the summer breeze, beckoning to Yacov to follow. He envied his young male friends, who greeted him loudly and invited him to join them. But he was too shy to go along.

One Saturday, as if to spite himself, he went instead into the *besmedresh,* where the men, among them his former heder mates, studied and argued as they sat over the Scriptures. He sat down next to his friend Ariele, from whom he had grown somewhat estranged.

Ariele had grown tall and pale. A sprouting beard encircled his chin and his long sidelocks matched the color of his big black eyes. The intensity of those black eyes was the same as before—they were sharp, fiery, and restless. But the mischievous twinkle was gone. Instead, a strange, shadowy flame lurked in their dark recesses. He was still agile and temperamental, growing as heated as a Hasid over whatever issue was discussed. More than ever, he hated all authority, especially the authority of teachers and rabbis, and he remained adamant in his decision to study on his own.

Ariele greeted Yacov with an unusually strong handshake, resting his other arm on Yacov's shoulder. "You see," he said, "we are still splitting the same hairs. Bociany remains the same, unchanged since the beginning of time." His eyes began to sparkle. Then, as Yacov waved to his other friends and sat down beside Ariele, the latter whispered heatedly in his ear, "But it only seems so, on the surface."

"What do you mean?" Yacov stared at him.

Ariele pressed Yacov's arm. "I've been meaning to visit you on the Blue Mountain, but somehow nothing came of it. I have become a new person. A new man. All thanks to my father's craziness." His face turned purple, his voice hoarse, full of emotion. "You know, don't you, that my father is a crushed man. So listen to this story. Not long ago he left for Chwosty and came back with a visitor, yes, another visitor. Do you still remember the first one? Well, if the first one was a messenger from the Evil One, this one seemed to be the Evil One in person. They locked themselves up in the same chamber, and I listened through the same crack in the wall. Where the first one blasphemed against the Almighty, this one denied His existence altogether. He said that man had invented Him, that no Redeemer, no Messiah would ever come, if man did not become his own Messiah. Not through miracles will the days of deliverance, called *socialismus,* arrive, but only through rebellion against the mighty, against the tsar and his stooges, against the rich and the cruel. Only then would there be paradise on earth, a life of equality, liberty, and fraternity. Do you understand, Yacov?"

Yacov nodded, anxious for Ariele to continue.

"Father wanted to throw the stranger out straight away," Ariele went on, "but then he thought better of it. He was probably afraid that if he threw him out, he would have a human life on his conscience along with all the other things that he has on his conscience. Because this visitor had escaped from Siberia and wanted Father to help him hide from the secret police. Father is so anxious to erase his sins through some good deed that he sat with the man all night and wept like a baby, while I wept on the other side of the wall. Because, Yacov, I knew that this guest was speaking what is on my own mind. He did not need to convince me, because I am one of his kind, heart and soul, since the day I was born, but I realized this fact only that moment. I instantly knew that these were not the words of the Devil, but the words of wisdom spoken by a man who respects himself and, for that matter, respects the entire human race. Because it is man, Yacov, and not God who is the navel of this world. So what do you say to this?"

Yacov stirred, ill-at-ease. "What happened to the visitor?"

"He's all right," Ariele beamed. "Father questioned him all night. After a while he stopped being angry at him and promised that he would help him. He said that what the guest preached was not what he, my father, was looking for, that there was no point in living in a world without a God, nor was it worthwhile to live without the respect of one's own community. You know—the usual litany. I was surprised at the mild language he used at the conclusion of their talk. At dawn he went to get Zelig the Tailor, who took the visitor home with him. The next day people started saying that Zelig had hired a new assistant, someone from Lodz. Yacov, you should hear this fellow speak. It's as if he has removed the stone from the mouth of the well, do you hear? And mind you, we also found out what has been going on under the surface in the shtetl. We found out about Shmulikl the Doctor, too." He prodded Yacov with his elbow, directing his attention to the other young men in the room, who looked meaningfully back at them. "Would you have suspected that they are all full of the same bitterness and rage as you and I are?"

"As I?" Yacov was perplexed.

"Yes, as you! I still remember the things you used to say to me. Do you remember how we discussed the problem of reward and punishment, and how the rich and evil do well in this world, while those who are poor . . . "

"I don't know what you are driving at," Yacov interrupted him.

"Oh, stop pretending! Don't tell me that you don't know what's going on in the world. Reb Faivele the Miller is the source of some of the freshest news in town. In Shmulikl the Doctor's opinion, Reb Faivele is quite an expert on politics."

"You know Shmulikl the Doctor personally?"

"All of us young people know him personally, as do many of those who are at this very moment on their way to the landlord's mansion, the girls included."

"Are you keeping company with girls?"

Ariele laughed proudly. "How can we change the world without the help of women? They make up fifty percent of humanity, after all, and not all of them have sawdust in their heads."

"Change the world, you said?"

"That's what I said. Shmulikl the Doctor thinks that for the time being it is enough to try and change the fate of the Jews, but we have a quarrel with him about that. I don't think he can achieve his aim, until ours is accomplished. If the rest of the world doesn't change, then injustice won't vanish, and we Jews will always be the scapegoat. There are many things that still need to be thought through, but the most important thing right now is to organize a defense unit. The old team is good for nothing, a bunch of old men. We must organize the young." Ariele leaned closer to Yacov. "How about joining?"

"Me?"

Ariele looked at Yacov sternly. "What's the matter with you? You're behaving like an idiot!" He put his hand on Yacov's shoulder. "Do you remember when we were both still snotnoses, how you would tell me with pride that Reb Senderl the Cabalist had said of you that you were not indifferent?"

"You have a good memory," Yacov smiled.

"And who was it who complained nonstop that the world was no good? And who talked me into believing that rebellion in order to change the world would give meaning to our lives? Look at the boys here. Rebellion is no longer a question with them. The question is whether we should join the party of the working class, which calls itself the Bund and wants to stay on in Poland and fight for justice here, or whether we should join the Zionist Party, which is headed by Shmulikl the Doctor. And there are those among us whose only problem is how to reconcile all this with faith. So do me a favor, Yacov, and have a chat with Zelig the Tailor."

"What for?"

"I told you, didn't I? At Zelig's you'll meet this man who pretends to be his apprentice. He has opened the eyes of many. I've gone to a few meetings and listened to his speeches. I never heard anything like it in my life. He is just an ordinary proletarian, but he has the head of a minister. It's from him that I learned about the Bund. The Bund has been in existence since '97, but Bociany knew nothing about it until now." The more Yacov was dazed and shaken by Ariele's words, the more Ariele was carried away by his own eloquence. "It's as simple as adding one and one. Of course, there are those who have brought Talmudic *pilpul* into these matters, but I hate it. They're now squabbling over what will happen when the revolution is won, or when the Jews have retaken Eretz Israel. It's nonsense. For the time being, the revolution of 1905 turned into a fiasco and Palestine is in Turkish hands, while pogroms have broken out all over Russia. In my opinion, the burning issue for the moment is self-defense. And we must all organize together, no matter what our individual ideologies may be."

Yacov noticed the change in Ariele's language, his use of strange foreign words. He was shocked. "You said 'revolution'?" he muttered, hoping that Ariele would elaborate, so that he might better understand what he meant. He had acquired a certain idea of the word from Reb Faivele. He had heard about the strikes, demonstrations, fights with the tsarist police, which had taken place all over Russia and Poland. Reb Faivele cursed the revolution vehemently. According to him, all the pogroms were a result of it.

"Yes, I said revolution. And what's your stand on that?" Ariele asked aggressively.

"My stand? What do you mean by 'stand'?"

"Stop playing cat and mouse with me. Don't be such a coward, for heaven's sake!"

Yacov pretended that he had not heard Ariele's words. "And what . . . well, what about the Almighty?"

"We are better off without Him."

"Without Him? But your father is right. How can we live without a God, Ariele?"

Ariele's face expressed a sadness that was almost grief. "You've changed, brother."

"I probably have." Yacov hung his head as if he were ashamed. "I am so happy living on the Blue Mountain that I've become a dumbbell. I must start from the beginning."

"Yes, you must start," Ariele frowned. "Start with *The Strong Arm*. Yacov knew that Ariele did not mean the book by that name, written by Maimonides.

After he left the *besmedresh,* Yacov circled the house of Zelig the Tailor. The sound of singing reached his ears, subdued voices, Yiddish words, a refrain, "What do we have to lose, brothers? Nothing but our chains." He did not have the courage to go in. On his way back to the Blue Mountain, he heard the refrain over and over again in his head. It mingled with Ariele's words and nagged at him, making him feel restless, excited, and strangely downhearted. This time he did not notice the peasant girls whose eyes followed him as he passed.

When he reached the Blue Mountain, he saw Abrashka running out to greet him. The serenity of these surroundings calmed him. He no longer felt as carefree as he had before, but he laughed and played with the little boy. When evening came, however, his sadness returned like the recurrence of an old illness. "Perhaps I was born like this," he thought. "I've sucked in sadness with my mother's milk. In this new comfortable life, I escaped it for a while, but now it's come back to claim me. So be it."

A sense of disquiet and dissatisfaction with himself began to nag at him. He had learned to ride a horse. The next Sunday afternoon, when Reb Faivele's farm workers had gone to church, he took his favorite horse, Gniady, which he renamed in Hebrew, Sussi, and rode off into the countryside.

From the top of Sussi's back, the entire world looked new. The landscape passed before his eyes, changing colors and shapes and fusing them into one. The contours of trees, shrubs, and houses blurred into a swimming unity as he rode rhythmically on. Even the gravel on the road seemed lighter, rising from the ground and shooting up in various directions. Everything seemed rootless, nothing firmly fastened to the earth. It made him think that the burden that weighed on his own heart was senseless, almost a sin, that he ought to let go of the reins and allow himself, passive and detached, to be carried along by everything that moved.

As he tried to talk himself into surrendering to the lightness and the ease of life, to allow himself a feeling of serenity, he noticed that the world, viewed through the thin veil of sadness, made more of an impression on his consciousness than it did when he had viewed it with pure joy.

Then, at the sight of an isolated barn, a new kind of restlessness came upon him. It was triggered by the fear that someone might throw a rock at him, or run out to block his way and try to unseat him. Just then, near the barn, he discerned a pair of blond braids, and almost lost control of his horse. The breeze played with a girl's skirt, lifting it to reveal the pale skin of a thigh. It hypnotized him. His hands grew clammy; his body shuddered. "Don't look! It's forbidden!" he warned himself and turned the horse to escape from the double danger.

## 17

THE SHTETL OF BOCIANY, with its many moods and caprices, behaved as if it were the Almighty's prima donna. With one body and one soul, it responded to events with either a smile or a tear, and these moods could change faster than the weather. The slightest breeze could cause the shtetl's humor to shift, for it was Bociany's nature to react to events first with its heart, and then with its head.

Take the story of Fishele the Butcher: after the chief of the Jewish fire brigade had confessed to being a follower of the Evil One, the shtetl reversed its opinion of him and began to despise him as an odious creature. The people could not forgive him, and although he was not expelled from the community, he was shunned as if he himself were a demon. He no longer worked at the butcher shop. His wife, who, in contrast, was treated with the greatest kindness, took over the business with the help of the butcher boys. Reb Toviele the Wagon Driver, one of the strongest and bravest of Bociany's men, took over as fire chief. He was a God-fearing man who possessed neither Fishele's charm nor his talents. But this was considered a plus, as it was now obvious where Fishele's charm and talents had led him.

Fishele himself was a ruined man. He was so ashamed in front of his family, especially in front of his beloved son, Ariele, that he no longer opened his mouth at home. And because he was the kind of man who could not live without the love of those around him, or without the praise and recognition of the community, he suffered doubly and turned into a shadow of his former self. His muscles gave way to fat, his belly grew flabby, his cheeks sagged into loose bags, and the light in his eyes was quenched. He now spent more time with Reb Senderl the Cabalist, studying and praying, than he did at home. He followed the injunctions of the *rov* and the *dian's* court to the letter, and took it upon himself to fast twice a week and to bathe in cold water.

Suddenly, almost overnight, the wind changed and a charitable breeze began to blow in Fishele's direction. The women followed him with their eyes when he passed them on the street, his figure shrunken, his head bowed to the ground. Against their will they found themselves wiping away a tear and remembering Fishele's jokes, his friendliness at the butcher shop, his heart of gold. And so a wave of longing for the Fishele of old swept over the shtetl. "Who can say how much of his sin is his own doing, and how much is due to the tricks of the Evil One? Perhaps the same demon that persecuted Perele, the ritual slaughterer's daughter, had gone to work on him as well? Because wasn't Fishele, too, our pillar of support?" This is what people thought. The shtetl doubled its friendliness to Fishele's wife and children, who had been living with the shame for so long. And gradually people began nodding at Fishele as he passed in the street. Eventually, they began greeting him outright. "He has learned his lesson," the women sighed. "Now he will be a warning to his children and his children's children." They followed him with compassionate eyes, shaking their heads sadly.

As soon as Fishele felt this new wind blowing in his direction, his spine grew straighter and his body more upright, like a tree after a long winter. It was not long before he started to resemble his former self, on the surface at least. Having spent so much time with Reb Senderl the Cabalist, he became quite a cabalist himself, and showed off his new vocabulary, just as he had done in happier times. He began to appear in the butcher shop again, and he joked with the women even more than in the past because he was so grateful to them. But he was completely cured of his attraction to them. He did not even go near his wife. The only emotion he now experienced toward the more attractive half of the human race was fear. At the same time, he became more devoted to his family and to people in general. He was the first to volunteer to do a favor and to serve the community and protect it. Reb Toviele the Wagon Driver, a man devoid of any social ambitions, let Fishele resume his former position of fire chief without rancor. And Fishele's past was forgotten and buried like a bad dream.

Bociany displayed a similar change of heart toward Yossele Abedale on the very day that his daughter Faigele died. At that time, the shtetl had not yet fully recovered from the shock of Sore-Leyele's death, and in its bereavement and bewilderment it was particularly susceptible to feelings of guilt. Suddenly people realized the harm that they had inflicted on a man who might, after all, be innocent. And was not the loss of a child the greatest possible punishment for a human being?

Because the community as a whole felt uncomfortable with the thought that it was responsible for the child's death, it began to place most of the blame on Reb Laibele the Sexton's shoulders. It seemed that all the bad stories about Yossele could be traced to him. It was clear that Reb Laibele was jealous of anyone who had children. First resentment, then hostility, began to burn in people's hearts. Now they followed the sexton with poisonous looks. At heart, they had never really liked him.

The community had attended Faigele's funeral en masse. Indeed Faigele had an exceptional funeral, almost as big as the one for Sore-Leyele. But Yossele was not Fishele the Butcher. He could not swallow his hurt and resentment; it stuck like a bone in his throat.

It did not occur to him to compare his tragedy to what had happened to Fishele or to take the latter as an example. He had lost his child, his Faigele. She had expired in his arms, and his gloomy house had become darker and gloomier still—the last bit of light had left it. His grief was so violent that he ground his teeth and clenched his fists as he followed the coffin at her funeral. "What God has given, God taketh away. Blessed be His holy name," he repeated with his mouth, while in his heart he said, "You are just, Father in Heaven, and your judgment is just, but I accept it with bitterness and rage!" He pressed his fists against the hearse as if he wanted to make it go faster. His anger made his feet move quickly. His eyes were dry and wide and seemed to absorb the entire blackness of the hearse. As for the enormous crowd that followed behind, Yossele never noticed it. He remained blind and deaf to all those who approached him with words of consolation.

Now he again left his daughters to manage the shop while he set out wandering the fields, incapable of staying in one place for very long. He grew more pious, more meticulous than before in observing The Law. He wandered through the fields, praying and reciting the psalms continuously, and ran often to the synagogue. There was both despondence and determination in his religious fervor. The Almighty, to whom he addressed his anger and frustration, was the only justification and meaning of life. Only He could keep Yossele from falling apart, from not performing his duty toward his six remaining children, whom he had left motherless. This rigid sense of duty toward the Almighty and toward his children was the salvation of his soul. He forced himself to go back to the shop every afternoon to send his daughters home to prepare a meal. They had to eat; they had to be strong and healthy.

Standing in front of the shop was hell.

One day, while he was puttering about inside, Hindele appeared in front of him. She had never ventured to go into the shop unless it was to bring him a bowl of warm soup. In her soft voice she now whispered to him, "Forgive me, Reb Yossele, but I've been watching you. You are like a furnace, with grief a roaring fire inside you, ready to blow you apart. Reb Yossele, you must let the grief out. You must cry out. In your heart you haven't buried Faigele yet. You must let her float away with a river of tears, so that you can go on."

He trembled violently and pointed to the door, "Get out!"

The woman stood nailed to the spot and did not budge. "Don't you understand, Reb Yossele? I, too, have lost a child." The wig sat askew on her head. Her nose and eyes were moist.

He wanted to leave her where she stood and run away. His ears could not bear her soft voice or her words. He wished he could grab the ax and chop off her head. Why did she not leave him alone? How dare she break into the privacy of his soul and try to make order in it? But the hand he had lifted toward the door fell limply to his side. He turned his face to her and moaned, "Have you never seen a man, neighbor, who has not learned how to cry?"

"Give in," she whispered. "Let go. Surrender and accept without rigidity, not like a rock, but like a leaf driven by the wind. Because that's what we are, driven leaves. Then they will come, the blessed tears. May you never know the taste of sorrow again, Reb Yossele."

She stood as before, but he had the impression that she had moved closer to him. He was overcome, overpowered by his pain. He wanted to bury his head in her fragile arms, felt a violent need to embrace her, to be embraced by her. He turned to the wall and spread his hands over it as if he needed to hold on to it. His shoulders began to shake. Suddenly the tears came. She left the shop.

He composed himself quickly and wiped his face. No, he would not surrender. What had she said? That he must let go, give in? Oh, no! He did not possess the strength to give in and still survive. To him giving in meant collapsing, falling apart and drowning in his grief. She wanted him to find relief, but that was not what he sought. He wanted to carry the wound open and bleeding in his heart. He wanted to carry all his wounds. And to do that, he needed rigidity, self-discipline, obstinacy. It was only the child within him that longed for tears, that wanted to learn the art of weeping from a woman.

Hindele was not the only person who came in with advice on how to ease his heart. His other neighbors on the Potcheyov and on his street went overboard in their worry about him. But they did not have the ability to enrage or move him that Hindele did. He simply ignored them. As time went on, his resentment against the community and his neighbors softened, but he remained indifferent to their expressions of friendship.

He would go eagerly to the bathhouse. There, in the heat and steam rising from the coals, he felt better. Although it was difficult to breathe, he nonetheless did so with greater ease; although his eyes were blurred by vapor and sweat, it seemed to him that he saw more clearly. He patted the benches like a blind man, climbed to the top, where the heat was at its most intense, and let the bath attendant whip him with wet twigs until he had to stop out of sheer exhaustion. Yossele enjoyed the pain, the burns, the boiling water, and the perspiration that drenched his body.

"It's better than weeping like a woman," he groaned as he sat there one day. "And why should I weep? Faigele is dead and buried. The other children, may they live and be healthy, will go on with their lives. Weep for myself? Oh, no! There is no room for self-pity in Yossele's heart. There is still a day waiting for me, the day that will turn into real night, when I go blind completely. True, my fear of it has diminished since Faigele's death, but still I need the courage to face it like a man, for this is God's will."

His tension eased as the steam wound around his body and penetrated its pores, relaxing the knots of pain inside him, anesthetizing them. Now he could think clearly. He thought that he should fortify his patience, that in time his grief would adjust to him, as it had after the loss of Mariml. But in the meantime, he could not just sit back with his arms folded. His days in the valley of tears were not over yet. There were still obligations that must be fulfilled toward his children, toward his community, although it had wronged him, and most of all, toward the Lord of the Universe.

He concentrated his thoughts on his children. The two older girls were accomplished housekeepers and good salesgirls, and the younger ones were coming along as well. Actually the two eldest girls were almost too old for marriage. He had lost count of how old they were. And Hershele? Hershele should have been at the yeshiva a long time ago. Why was he, Yossele, procrastinating? Was he not luxuriating in his mourning as an excuse not to meet his obligations?

After a number of such visits to the bathhouse, Yossele worked out a plan of action—and all of Bociany assisted him in its execution, although this was a fact which Yossele refused to acknowledge. He had an inexplicable aversion to Reb Menashele the Matchmaker, but it was with him that he had to deal first. He was not surprised, or pretended not to be, that Reb Menashele immediately found two names of likely male candidates in his fat black notebook. One was the *dian's* grandson, the other Reb Shapsele the Melamed's eldest son. The first was a fine, soft-spoken young man, a brilliant scholar. The second had a head for both business and studies; he had already taken over the coal business that his mother and sisters had started. He was older than the *dian's* grandson, so it was agreed that he would be best suited to Yossele's eldest daughter, Raisele, and that the *dian's* grandson would be assigned to Rochele.

Soon the date for the double wedding was set. There was only a year's difference in age between the two sisters. They were almost like twins. Neither Yossele nor his future in-laws were rich, and a double wedding saved money.

A few weeks before the wedding, Yossele's household initiated a period of half-fasting. There was no chicken soup or meat for the Sabbath and no cooked meals on weekdays. Yossele worked harder than ever in the villages, selling his merchandise and working at whatever jobs he could find.

Thus he saved enough money to outfit his daughters as befitted brides from an honorable family. He finally got around to whitewashing his house—and wondered to himself how the death of one who was held so dear could transform despair into a zest for living. Yossele not only whitewashed the house but also put up two pasteboard walls inside, thereby dividing the large single room into three rooms because he insisted that his sons-in-law live at his expense, after the fashion of a respectable father of two respectable daughters.

The wedding took place at the *dian's* house, which bordered on the marketplace. All of Bociany attended the celebration. Despite the fact that his heart was against it, Yossele insisted that the Hasidic band be invited. It was a wedding where satin gabardines mingled with the threadbare clothes of the wagon drivers and artisans, where fur-trimmed hats mixed with faded traditional caps. The mothers-in-law dressed themselves in high bonnets encircled with ribbons; they wore their most elegant scarves and shawls on top of their broad, many-layered dresses, which rustled cheerfully. Here and there, a piece of genuine jewelry could be seen decorating the bodice of such a woman guest as Zirele the Miller's Wife or the *rebetsin.*

Yossele himself wore his old Sabbath gabardine and his worn, fur-trimmed hat. But his youngest daughter, Binele, came decked out in her first new dress. It was made of cretonne with a design of tiny pink flowers and large green leaves. A red velvet ribbon lined the neck, cuffs and hem. Binele was certain that hers was the most beautiful dress at the wedding, although she had little time for comparison. She was too busy admiring herself and enjoying the feel of her body in the dress. It was no small thing, this first dress, made to measure and never worn by anyone but herself. To her, the dress was not in honor of the celebration, but rather the reverse: the entire celebration was in honor of her first dress. She had also undone her braids for the occasion, and her long, beautiful hair cascaded luxuriantly over her shoulders. Only the *badkhan,* the master of ceremonies at the wedding, had the power to divert her attention away from her dress. She listened open-mouthed as he sang, addressing himself—as was the custom—to the brides who sat on their bridal armchairs as if enthroned.

Reb Dovtchele the Badkhan was the darling of Bociany. It was he, with the help of Fishele the Butcher, who usually led the crowds in merrymaking at Purim and other happy holidays. Reb Dovtchele could have made the saddest person laugh, were it not for the fact that he himself was the saddest person. Between Purim and the other happy holiday, Simhath Torah, he walked around with a disconsolate expression on his face, as if some great tragedy had befallen him. Only on festive occasions like weddings did he put on a new face and become a changed man.

During the introductory part of his performance, Reb Dovtchele wore his usual expression, but his sadness was definitely mixed with elation. As the women went through the ceremony of veiling the brides, he delivered his speech in a sing-song that came from the bottom of his heart and touched the bottom of theirs. Although he used examples from the Scriptures, his voice was so intimate and sweet, so moving, that it was not necessary to understand the deeper meaning of what he said. The tears flowed like water. When Binele saw that his injunction to the brides, "Weep, brides, weep," caused all the women to cry, she started crying as well, covering her face with her hands so as not to wet her new dress.

The four-pronged wedding canopies were set up in the yard of the synagogue. The guests got into formation for the procession through the marketplace to the synagogue. They pushed each other to get a better glimpse of the two couples as they were led to the canopies. The large braided candles in the guests' hands flickered like hundreds of stars. The young *rebetsin,* a huge braided challah cradled in her arms, danced forward to meet the two young couples. She charmed the onlookers with her grace and agility. Smiling modestly, she shook her handsome head to the rhythm of the band music. The two couples followed with their eyes covered. The mothers-in-law led the brides by the arm, while the fathers-in-law walked at their side. The band continued playing. Someone in the crowd of gentile onlookers joined in with a harmonica. The Hasidim clapped their hands and sang and danced.

After the ceremony, the crowd filled the *dian's* house. Once the guests were all seated at the tables, which were covered with white tablecloths and laid with the finest china that could be borrowed from the neighbors, the grooms gave speeches. They showed off their erudition, quoting from the Gemara and from Maimonides, asking questions and answering them.

They delighted in the facial expressions of the dignified scholars present, who nodded their approbation.

Then it was time for the guests to enjoy themselves. The food and drink stimulated both palates and spirits. The band formed a line at the door, eating, drinking, and playing. Reb Dovtchele entertained the crowd, telling proverbs, funny stories, and jokes. Once again, there was not a dry eye in the room, but this time the tears were tears of laughter.

The doors and windows were thrown open to the outside, where tables and benches for the town's beggars had been set up. There, Reb Faivele the Miller and his gentile servants handed out cake and glasses of *monopolka* to the peasants. Before long, a few musicians from the gentile band appeared in the marketplace with their instruments. Wanda began a whirling dance with a young peasant, and soon others followed suit.

Yossele walked among the crowd that packed the rooms, hands folded behind his back, a father-in-law, yet almost a stranger. He accepted the good wishes of the guests with a growl or a barely perceptible nod. Although there was no smile on his lips, he looked composed, his face clear and unwrinkled. If he experienced any deep emotion, it was that of satisfaction for having fulfilled his duty. "This is how it should be," he murmured to himself. "This is how it is."

He stepped outside for a breath of fresh air and saw the peasants cavorting in the marketplace. It was not long before Vaslav Spokojny came over to him, dragging Abele the Fool by the arm. Like a few of the other peasants, Vaslav was an unofficially invited guest. He was decked out in his new fire chief's uniform, which he only wore on special occasions. Earlier in the day, he and his wife had given Yossele two peasant quilts as wedding gifts for the two couples, along with their best wishes, as true good friends should. Yossele had responded to the gesture with a degree of warmth. His attitude toward the fire chief had recently undergone a change for the better. Although Vaslav had not kept his word about not touching drink again, he seemed to have seen the error of his ways and given up his visits to Hindele. He had become more dignified and reserved. So Yossele now nodded at the fire chief with a certain feeling of camaraderie. "May you soon be celebrating Wanda's wedding," he said to him.

Vaslav was not entirely sober. "Wanda?" he exclaimed "May the devil take her! She's not mad about getting married. Would you believe, Yossele, that she's moved out of my house? Moved in with her grandmother, to be on her own, she says. The truth is, she hates my guts."

Yossele shook his head in disagreement. "What do you mean she hates your guts? You're her father, aren't you? As for her getting married, what do you need her permission for? Marry her off."

Vaslav grinned. "You don't know my Wanda. If you were her father, you'd talk differently." A glass of vodka cupped in his hand, he motioned toward Abele the Fool, who was shaking like a leaf in the grip of the fire chief's hand. "This Abele is worse than me, devil take him! I gave him one sip of vodka and now he's pestering all the women. Peeks under their skirts, is what he does. And do you think he's any better when he's sober? I caught him peeking through the window into my daughters' bedchamber the other night. Nearly scared them to death!"

Yossele knew that Abele had been disappearing from the shtetl for days in a row. When asked where he had been, he would reply, "There." When asked, "Where? There? " he would reply, "Behind the cherries."

"What cherries?"

"Behind the cemeteries."

That was all that could be gotten out of him. He had also taken to wandering about the shtetl on warm nights, frightening any woman who saw his big white head glide past her window.

"What can I do? Tie him up like a dog on a chain?" Yossele was growing irritable. He did not like the way Vaslav was holding Abele's arm. "Don't worry," he said, more to comfort himself than to comfort Vaslav. "He doesn't do any harm."

Abele tugged at Yossele's sleeve, imploring, "Abele go?" He tried to free himself from Vaslav's grip.

Vaslav shook him and grinned. "Why are you so afraid of me, idiot?" He moved his face closer to Abele's and nodded, "I think it's true what my old lady says. He does look like my holy brother Stanislav, doesn't he?" He gulped down the vodka that was left in his glass and coughed. Releasing Abele, he wrapped his arm around Yossele's shoulder. "Do you remember, Yossele," he whispered in his ear. "I told you once about the uprising that the boys are preparing? They may call on me any day now to become their leader. Then there will be no drinking or fooling around for me, no sir. That's serious business." For a while he stared at Yossele in silence, then he grew lively and pulled Yossele to the middle of the marketplace.

"But in the meantime," he called out, "let's dance and be merry. Come on, Yossele, it's your party, after all!" He shouted to the peasants, "Hey, boys, let's dance with Yossele!"

Yossele struggled to free himself of Vaslav's arm. "No dancing!" He shook his head emphatically to the men standing around. "I'm not a dancer."

"Well, tonight you'll become one!" Vaslav thrust his empty glass into his pocket and began to clap his hands. "Go, grab yourself a woman! Go, grab Wanda!" He nudged Yossele with his shoulder. "She'll dance with you. You're the father of the brides! Go on!"

Yossele planted himself firmly on the ground. "No!" He glanced back at the *dian's* house.

Vaslav gave him a strong push forward. "You will dance! Don't be such a spoilsport. Go on!" He waved to the drunken peasants. "Come on boys, let's take him by the arms and teach him to shake a leg in the Polish fashion!"

The peasants tossed their caps into the air, clapped their hands, and took awkward dancing steps towards Yossele. "Lift your legs, Yossele!" They roared with laughter.

Yossele cast another quick glance at the *dian's* house. He could hear loud Hasidic music, a clapping of hands, a stomping of feet. Inside, the men and women were dancing in different sections of the room. That was all that Yossele needed right now—a drunken mob of goyim outside, a crowd of not very sober Jews inside—tonight of all nights, the wedding night of his daughters!

He saw his neighbor Hindele come out of the house. She smiled as she approached him. "Such a beautiful wedding, Reb Yossele," she said, fanning herself with a corner of her plaid shawl. "It gladdens my heart. May we live to see many more such celebrations. It's so hot inside that I had to get out for a minute." Then she noticed Vaslav Spokojny, and the smile faded from her face.

"Don't be afraid of me, little woman!" Vaslav exclaimed enthusiastically. He quickly grabbed hold of her and Yossele by the arms. "Go and dance!" The other peasants pushed them from behind toward the center of the marketplace. The band music was deafening. Young peasant couples were whirling in time to the music. Suddenly Vaslav swept Hindele off her feet. Yossele watched her stumble, then struggle as Vaslav swung her into the air. Yossele saw her twisted legs rise as if blown up by the wind. He saw her body, like that of a rag doll, swing once to the right, once to the left. She nearly fell, but the fire chief's arms caught her.

It took no longer than a second. Yossele rushed toward Vaslav and put his hands on his shoulders with such force that the fire chief stopped moving on the spot. Yossele grabbed Hindele's arm just in time to keep her from falling to the ground in a faint. She was trembling and her face was as white as chalk.

"Bravo!" The peasants clapped. "Dance with her, Yossele!" A circle of peasants surrounded Yossele and Hindele.

Vaslav stood with his arms still stretched out toward Hindele. He was weighing something in his head and finally exclaimed, "Come on, you two! Don't just stand there! Lift a leg!"

"Neighbor," Yossele whispered, facing Hindele. For the first time in his life, he really looked at this black-eyed, frightened woman, on whose face he read trust and faith in him. "A Jew cannot always be stubborn. We must do it, neighbor. The Almighty will forgive us."

Slowly, awkwardly, he took hold of the fringes of Hindele's shawl. The peasant band joined the circle of peasants that surrounded them. A grating of fiddles. Whistling. Hand clapping. Shouts. Laughter. Yossele raised one foot, then the other. Hindele did the same. She grew calmer. They turned round and round, hopping lamely, first slowly, then faster. She seemed to grow, to become stronger. His beard flew up in the air, her plaid shawl rose like a pair of wings. Their eyes met accidentally. They quickly looked away. Their hands touched accidentally. They hurriedly withdrew them.

While the noise around them grew louder, they jumped up and down, round and round. Between pants, he whispered to her, "If a person doesn't dance out of joy, sometimes he must dance out of . . . "

"But Reb Yossele," she shouted back at him before he could finish the sentence, and her face lit up, "if we must dance, let it be for joy. Of course, for joy!"

She seemed as light as a feather, and he held on to her by the fringes of her plaid shawl. Yossele lifted his feet higher, and moving with increasing vigor, began to whirl her around in a dizzying circle. She was right, after all. She was right!

The crowd of strangers around them, the night that threatened yet smelled so sweet, the lights and noises from the *dian's* house, where his family and his people celebrated, the close presence of Vaslav, all this kept alive the fire in Yossele's limbs. But most of all it was she who kept him dancing, this small woman whom he was carrying along, or rather who was carrying him along. He would never let anything happen to her if he could help it. He would not let Vaslav touch her, even if it meant dancing with her forever. Yes, to dance with her forever and to die immediately after would be good! But to go on living beside her would be better!

"The Almighty will forgive us!" he repeated to her. "He will!" he shouted above the noise of the crowd. And so he danced with Hindele on the wedding night of his daughters. And how they danced!

Yossele's son, Hershele, who was already a young man with a sprouting beard, took his first revolutionary step a week before he was supposed to leave for the yeshiva in Chwosty. His father had never allowed him or anyone else to climb onto the roof of their house. The roof was *shpimba-degimba,* by which Yossele meant that it was as flimsy and fragile as a spider web. It was barely supported by the walls and was broken in more than one place, so that it allowed snow and rain to enter the house. Yossele was haunted by the fear that one fine day he would be left literally without a roof over his head. When he had to install the old wheel as a base for the storks' nest, he leaned the ladder against the strongest side of the house and never set his foot on the roof itself. He was afraid to fix it for fear of making it worse, not better. And when he had to call the gentile chimney sweep, he warned him not to climb on the roof but to throw his black broom with the iron ball directly from the ladder down into the chimney. That was why the chimney and the house were always full of soot.

During the weeks before Faigele's death, Yossele was always haunted by a double fear: that he would return from the villages one day to find not just a broken roof, but a child with broken bones as well.

True, Hershele was no longer a child. But perhaps because of this, he could not leave home without at least one glimpse of the storks' nest at close range. His friends had dared to climb their roofs despite paternal warnings; only he had obeyed his father. Usually it made him feel good to obey his father, for obeying a parent was a good deed. But in this case, he equated his obedience with cowardice.

Hershele was certain of one thing, namely, that even if the Almighty forgave him, his father never would. Nevertheless, he decided to take the risk. Because he did not have the courage to do it alone, he enlisted the help of Binele, who had grown into a big, strong girl and who feared their father less than his other sisters, even the married ones. In Binele's company he felt braver. In addition, there was an advantage in the fact that Binele was as curious about the storks as he was.

They left for the marshes together and collected worms, tadpoles, and snails. Then they waited for an opportunity to execute their plan. Such an opportunity did not present itself quickly. The house was seldom empty. Either one or the other of the married sisters, or one or another of the younger ones, was usually at home. Or a brother-in-law would suddenly appear when least expected. The *dian's* grandson was there the most often because he was a fanatical scholar who would sit for hours studying a volume of Scripture without moving.

So there was no choice but to go through with the plan when their father was away and a heated argument was taking place inside the house. Hershele took the ladder into his trembling hands and leaned it against the roof. His heart pounded like that of a thief. Once he had climbed to the fourth rung, he looked back and almost fell off, when he saw Binele climbing up behind him. "Do me a favor," he implored, "don't climb after me." He checked to make sure that no one from the surrounding houses was watching him and added, "If anything happens to you, Tateshie won't let me get out of his hands alive. You can do it another time."

Binele was generally unmoved by requests not to do what she had set her heart on. But she had compassion for Hershele. He was about to leave home, while she would still have many opportunities to climb onto the roof. So, anxious as she was to look into the storks' nest, she climbed down from the ladder and contented herself with urging Hershele on. "Well, why don't you move? Come on, get up there!"

"You keep watch," Hershele whispered, his voice choked with excitement and fear. "Look out for Raisele or Rochele. Make sure Brontchele the Mourner doesn't see me. Do you see Toybe-Kraindele around, or Peshele the Slob?"

Hershele spent more time looking down than up. Children began to gather around the ladder. Their eyes twinkling, they watched Hershele in silence, occasionally whispering to him, "Tell us what you see!"

Hershele had his foot on the highest rung of the ladder, but his eyes looked down on the children below, lest one of them go and tell on him.

Suddenly he noticed a few women appear down the street. "Who's coming?" he called.

"What are the baby storks doing?" Binele asked in a hushed voice.

"They're looking at me!" Hershele croaked.

"The storks?"

"No, the . . . " Hershele's legs trembled so much that the ladder trembled with him. Without thinking, he stretched out the hand that held on to the ladder, to point out the approaching women. He slipped to one side and the ladder slipped to the other. The children shrieked and jumped aside. Hershele landed on the ground in a thick clump of grass.

The screams of the children were deafening. Women ran out of the houses and rushed toward Hershele. His sisters Raisele and Rochele were already there, as if they had not been quarreling inside, but had been waiting on the threshold for just such a mishap to occur. There was a great commotion. Binele was pushed aside, as her sisters and neighbors clustered around Hershele. He moaned through tightly pressed lips. His eyes were shut and his forehead was wrinkled.

The memory of what had happened to Faigele flashed through Binele's mind, and as soon as Hershele had been carried into the house, she ran to fetch Shmulikl the Doctor. She burst into the barber shop with a shout, "Panie Shmulikl the Doctor! Quick, my brother has fallen off the ladder!"

Shmulikl the Doctor did not even turn his head, but continued working on the mouth of the patient who sat in the barber's chair. She dashed up to him, beside herself with impatience, and shook his arm so violently that the peasant in the chair jumped up with a roar. Shmulikl the Doctor, who had the habit of echoing his patients' moans with his own, also roared, "Oh, the Devil!"

"Are you deaf, Panie Shmulikl the Doctor?" Binele was not impressed by the fierceness of the two men's exclamations. "Don't you recognize me? You cured my head of scabs, and you saw to my sister Faigele. Come quickly or my brother will die, too!"

Binele's tugging at Shmulikl's arm evidently had beneficial results because he extracted from the peasant's mouth a pointy, blood-stained tooth, which he held in his pliers. Now he turned to Binele, and as if he were frightened by her warning, he cried, "Let's go!" grabbed his shabby bag of medical instruments, and followed her into the street.

Women and children were gathered in front of Yossele's house. Inside, Raisele and Rochele, Brontchele the Mourner and Toybe-Kraindele were dabbing at the wound on Hershele's forehead with wet rags. Toybe-Kraindele sighed tearfully as she lectured Hershele, "That's what you get when you do something that's forbidden. Pfui, a big yeshiva boy like you, a bridegroom almost, still playing children's games. What a shame!" Hershele answered with a groan and hissed through lips that were tightly pressed together.

"Why does Yossele, poor man, deserve so much trouble in his life, such a bitter fate?" Brontchele the Mourner wailed professionally, inspiring an abundant flow of tears from Yossele's daughters.

Shmulikl the Doctor put his bag down on the clay floor and, with one sweep of his arm, wiped everything from the table. "Put him down over here," he said to the women, and with their help he lifted Hershele.

The women stared at Shmulikl as if they were ready to devour him. How had this heathen appeared so suddenly? But they obeyed him. In this respect Bociany had changed somewhat. Although it never occurred to anyone to relinquish the exorcisms or potions of Reb Senderl the Cabalist, in an emergency people had begun to ask Shmulikl for help. He could, after all, perform wonders with those devilish tools in his bag. So people treated him as if he were a magician, using his services but avoiding his company.

The women continued to apply cold compresses to the bleeding wounds on Hershele's forehead, but they let Shmulikl examine the boy's limbs, which he turned and twisted in all directions. Finally, Brontchele lost her patience. "Why are you playing around with him so much, Panie Shmulikl?" she asked. "Can't you see the poor boy has broken his arms and legs?"

"And all the blood is gushing out of his brain!" added Toybe-Kraindele. "Yossele will not survive this. His only son! His *kaddish!*" She burst into tears over Yossele's bitter fate, and cried even more, with gratitude, because the Almighty had sent her three sons to say *kaddish* after their parents' death in a hundred and twenty years from now.

There was a commotion at the door. "Yossele's coming!" someone shouted.

Hershele grew so pale, so stiff and quiet, that Brontchele was on the point of taking out the goose feather that she always kept in her apron pocket and putting it against Hershele's mouth to check if he was still breathing. Hershele winced and groaned, "He'll kill me!" He looked desperately around the room as if seeking a way to escape.

As soon as Yossele entered the doorway, the weeping women rushed toward him with the news, "The poor thing has broken his arms and legs and the blood is gushing out from his brains!"

Yossele dashed to the table, his face on fire, madness in his eyes. "Is he alive?" he panted.

"He'll live to be a hundred and twenty," Shmulikl replied earnestly.

Yossele raised his eyes to the ceiling, "Blessed be the Almighty!" He inhaled deeply and immediately set his hand in motion to give Hershele an appropriate smack.

Shmulikl stopped Yossele's hand in midflight. "Grab his foot!" he ordered. "He's disjointed his ankle good and proper. We'd better set it right away. Pull when I tell you." He ordered the women to prepare rags for bandages. Then he gave Yossele the command, "One, two, three, pull!"

Yossele pulled his son's foot. As Hershele let out a heartrending scream, Yossele had the feeling that it was his own foot that was broken and twisted. Shmulikl repeated the command to pull, until a loud crack was heard. Then he made a sign to let go.

"Just you wait!" Yossele panted heavily and shook his finger at Hershele's nose. "I'll have my reckoning with you yet, don't you worry!"

*"Molodietz!"* Shmulikl said loudly, it was not clear to whom. He wiped the sweat from his forehead, and sent Yossele to find a piece of board. Then he turned to the women, "Now hand me the bandages!"

"Why don't you put an ointment on his head?" Brontchele the Mourner asked him resentfully as she handed him a wad of torn rags. In her heart, she considered herself more competent in medical matters than Shmulikl the Doctor because she spent her days at the "gates of life and death."

"Yes, what are you waiting for?" Toybe-Kraindele chimed in. "Can't you see that all the blood is running out of his brain?"

"No," Shmulikl smiled bitterly, taking a bottle of iodine from his bag. "All I can see, dear lady, is that all common sense has run out of *your* brain." He poured a bit of iodine on a piece of gauze and dabbed at the cut on Hershele's forehead. Hershele, no longer the stoic, yelled in pain. Shmulikl put Hershele's ankle against the piece of board, which Yossele handed him, and secured it with strips of rag.

When Hershele set out for the yeshiva in Chwosty three months later, he still limped badly on one foot. But it was more than his foot that was limping. His belief in himself was badly shaken. There must be something terribly wrong with him, he decided. He had not seen the little storks in their nest, nor managed to climb onto the roof, but he had paid dearly just for trying. Both the Almighty and his father were angry at him. Why? Why could other boys get away with doing what was forbidden, and not he, who had been more studious than any of them and had obeyed his father more than they had obeyed theirs? Perhaps he was destined never to amount to much?

Binele missed Hershele badly. She felt a certain obligation to him, to complete what he had failed to do, more in order to rectify things than for her own pleasure. Hershele's defeat in climbing the roof did not frighten her. So as soon as a similar situation presented itself, and her sisters were occupied in quarreling with each other in the house, she decided to carry through her plan. She placed the rotting ladder against the roof and without looking right or left, swiftly climbed to the top, grabbed hold of the chimney and straddled the roof as if it were a horse. She watched Mendl and Gnendl, the parent storks, tending to their young in the nest. She did not dare move lest she frighten the birds. "Let them see that I mean no harm," she told herself.

From that day on she frequently visited Mendl and Gnendl. The storks made friends with her and, without fear, snatched the gifts that she placed around the chimney or on the tip of the roof. They fluttered about her with their wings partly spread, fanning her face. She was afraid that their friendliness might attract attention below, so she moved to the rear side of the chimney and, leaning against it, looked out at the gentile houses.

Once she had gotten herself up on the roof, she was reluctant to leave. No one bothered her there. She had the impression of being very far from Bociany. Her gaze sailed across the sky, taking with it her reveries and longings, which were as formless as the clouds above her head. It made her forget how downhearted she had been feeling lately. Her home now was without Faigele and without Hershele. Instead, it was occupied by strangers, her brothers-in-law, and the new way of life was not the same as the old. Moreover, she had nothing to do. Sore-Lyele had been in her grave for quite some time now and her daughters had taken over the care of their father and the house.

Binele got along as best she could. She busied herself at Yankova's house and offered her help to other peasant women in exchange for some cabbage soup or a slice of homemade bread. She stayed away from her father's shop, as she stayed away from home. She went about with the growing feeling of being homeless and abandoned. The storks seemed to be her closest relatives.

When Mendl and Gnendl were not "at home," being out in search of food, Binele would slither along the rooftop to get a better look at the young storks in their nest. Slowly she stretched her palm out to them and let the storklings nibble at the worms that she held out. She talked to them and caressed their chests, trying to guess what it felt like to have Gnendl for a mother. Then, after she had slowly returned to her place and leaned against the chimney, staring at the expanse of sky above her head, at the clouds that swam by, she dreamed of having a mother or of being a mother.

She was not jealous of her sisters for being married, but she was very envious of Raisele, who had recently given birth. Those were extraordinary days, when Raisele's firstborn, a boy, had come into the world. The walls of the house had been cluttered with notes full of magical sayings and blessings, so that the Devil, who could change into a dog or a cat, would not harm the newborn. Heder boys had come every night to read the *kri-shma,* and neighbors came to visit and rejoice with the family. The whole house seemed to have filled with light, with an air of renewal and good cheer. Binele adored her little nephew. She became so attached to him that she considered him her own. But the good feelings did not last long. Although she was a big girl now, almost an adult, she grew jealous of the little one and felt more unwanted and unnoticed than ever. Her father made such a fuss over this first male grandchild of his!

Binele cheered up again when, sometime after her nephew's birth, she found out that Mashele, her third sister, was engaged to be married. Binele looked forward to the wedding. She loved weddings and hoped that she would get another dress. The dress that she had gotten for her eldest sisters' wedding had grown too tight and short on her. It was badly worn because she wore it daily, having nothing else to put on. It no longer resembled the beautiful creation it had been when she first wore it. So she was excited; a change in the order of things was about to take place again. She tried not to think of what would follow that change because she knew that just as she disliked her elder sisters' husbands, she would dislike Mashele's husband. For while it was true that her brothers-in-law were learned men and important people in Bociany, to her they were monsters, strange, unfamiliar creatures who had invaded her home.

Take Raisele's husband, for example. Granted, he was no fool; he had opened a coal shop on the Potcheyov and was an alert man when it came to dealing with business affairs. But he liked to stick his nose in everywhere, and he ordered Binele around as if he were her father. And though he was not a stutterer, he had the irritating habit of getting stuck in the middle of a sentence, sinking into deep thought, and forgetting to finish the sentence. On the other hand, Rochele's husband, the true scholar, was not exactly lame, but he walked about as if one of his legs were shorter than the other. He moved, his body bent to the left, while his head was bent to the right, and so he resembled a crooked hook. Now Mashele was about to marry a man about whom one could not say that he was sick, exactly, but he had such a hollow cough that it could easily wake up the corpses in the cemetery.

It was during Mashele's wedding that Binele discovered that her father already had plans to marry off Dvorele, the fourth sister. The groom was to be none other than Berele the Moonwalker, the apple of Brontchele the Mourner's eye, who was not yet married because the girls of Bociany were afraid of somnambulists. This completely ruined Mashele's wedding for Binele, who did not even get a new dress on this occasion, but had to be content with Mashele's old dress from the previous wedding of the older sisters. During the entire celebration, Binele was obsessed by the thought that a bridegroom undoubtedly awaited her as well. Her father seemed in such a hurry to marry off his daughters.

Despite the jealously that Binele felt toward her sisters for being privileged to have babies, she shuddered at the thought of having to live day and night with some ugly creature whom she would have to call husband. She could not make out why her sisters were so proud and happy with their new status as married women. They were so haughty and self-assured, so full of strength and energy, that one might have thought that their marriages really resembled the paradise that they had dreamed of in their childhoods. Binele was amazed at how married life had made them grow in stature, how wise and skillful they had become. She deplored the fact that they had begun to resemble their father in character, yet had at the same time become more boring and dull than he had ever been.

And that was how one day, as Binele sat on the roof visiting the storks, watching the sky overhead and listening to the quarrels of her sisters below, she came to make the most important decision in her life. Her sisters' wedding celebrations were all very well, their having babies was wonderful, but she herself would never marry, not even if her father presented her with a bridegroom made out of gold. She had not the slightest wish for the happiness that her sisters enjoyed. And from the moment that she had made up her mind to avoid a fate like theirs, she started to think how to go about putting her resolve into action.

Yossele spent most of his time peddling in the villages. This way of life suited him now more than ever. He enjoyed being outdoors, and his conscience now troubled him less. He no longer worried that something might happen to his children while he was away; they now worried more about him than he about them. And although his bitterness had not completely disappeared, he had mellowed considerably, thanks to the good feeling of having accomplished what he had undertaken. One of the greatest obligations of his life, that to his children, was now almost completed, so he walked upon the earth prouder than ever. He became still more meticulous in his observance of the religious laws and now looked even more "biblical" and majestic than in his younger days. His blond beard was fading into white, his steps were heavier, his gaze more severe, the expression on his face sterner because he strained his eyes badly. He was, on the whole, more massive, but his eyesight grew steadily weaker.

Oddly enough, he often felt much the same as Binele did, that he was a stranger in his own home. Sometimes he had the impression that he was entirely alone in the world. He even missed the physical contact of beating his children. It never occurred to him to touch his married daughters, even when they irritated him. His son was at the yeshiva, and the only daughter not yet engaged to be married, Binele, he saw only when she slept because she avoided him; she was never at home and would not set foot in the shop.

On the rare occasions when his eyes met Binele's, remorse swept through his heart. There was nothing that could straighten the twisted thread of the relationship between them. It grew more knotted and entangled as time went on. Moreover, the older he got, the stingier he grew with words. Unlike Hatzkele the Water-Carrier, he had not taken a vow of silence, but he did not see the sense of talking, unless it was absolutely necessary, as in business or community matters, and then he did not need many words. "Mne . . . " and "Nu . . . nu . . . " were generally sufficient.

Nowadays, when he stood on the Potcheyov, and Hindele came over with a bowl of soup, he did not refuse. He did not thank her, but neither did he get angry at her. He behaved no differently toward her since the time they had danced together at his daughters' wedding. But in rare moments, when he dared to face the truth about his feelings, he was aware that she was the only human being in this world whose soul was attuned to his.

## 18

WHEN RAISELE WAS PREGNANT with her second child and Mashele with her first, the sisters began to insist that Binele help them out in the shop. It was not that they had so many customers that they needed an extra pair of hands, but Raisele now had to look after the coal shop as well. She walked around all day covered with black stains from the coals, and white stains from the chalk. Taking care of their own households and standing on their feet at the shop was not easy for the sisters now that they were all pregnant, for Rochele always imagined that she was pregnant, too. And their fourth sister, Dvorele, could not be counted on because she worked as a maid at the lessee's to save money for her dowry.

Binele would not hear of replacing her sisters at the shop. "When aren't you pregnant?" she demanded one day. "When it's not one of you, it's the other. I'm not setting foot in that shop and that's that. If I even put one foot inside, I'll sink into the same pit as you."

"You enjoy seeing us suffer, don't you?" Raisele, who was having a very difficult pregnancy, stared bitterly at Binele.

"And if I suffer, too, would that make you any happier?" Binele stared back at her sister, her slanted eyes full of spite.

"Of course," Rochele sighed. "You'll ease our burden." And she massaged her stomach with both hands. Whenever she thought that she was pregnant, she began to suffer from nausea.

"Let your husbands ease your burdens for you. They're the ones who made you pregnant, not me!" Binele retorted.

"Shut your mouth, Marzepa!" Raisele put her hands over her heart. She knew that there was no sense in saying anything more. Was this not the Binele who had come into this world a stubborn creature, without a drop of human kindness in her heart? Raisele, overcome with pain, shook her head at the other sisters. "What's the use talking? Don't you know the Marzepa yet, or the trouble Tateshie's always having with her?"

"Only Tateshie?" Binele asked, looking at them with poison in her eyes. "And what about Mameshie? Didn't she leave this world because of me?"

But she felt miserable all the same. Something gnawed at her heart. She was ugly in more than looks. She was a Marzepa even in her soul. For one needed a stone in place of a heart not to feel some pity for the pregnant sisters; from morning until night, they never had a moment's rest and hardly knew what was going on around them. But what else could Binele do? She was disgusted at the mere thought of being trapped by the fate of a Bociany woman, a fate she had vowed to escape.

Binele masked her feelings of unease, guilt, and sin by hiding them behind loud, mocking laughter. She ran out, leaving her sisters to their misery, and headed straight for the house of Shmulikl the Doctor, who had cured her of scabs, who had put Hershele back on his feet, and who would have saved Faigele had he been called in time. Binele liked Shmulikl more than she liked anyone else in Bociany, even if he was an eccentric who spoke a German Yiddish at home. His language was difficult to understand, but that only added to his greatness. Shmulikl the Doctor was practically capable of raising the dead. And to Binele, her predicament was a question of life and death. Unworthy though her life might be, it was the most precious thing that she possessed, and she wanted to save it at any price.

Shmulikl, as was his custom in the morning, was pulling teeth in his barber shop. Jews and Gentiles sat in a row along the wall. The Jews had been coming to him ever since the *rov* had stated that no one pulled teeth as well as Shmulikl and that paying him a visit for this purpose did not imply that one had anything to do with him.

At the moment when Binele arrived, Shmulikl was in the middle of pulling the tooth of the landlord's butler. The man sat in the armchair, and Shmulikl held his head under his arm as if it were a spoiled head of cabbage and he was about to cut away the rotten part. He poked his odd instrument inside the man's mouth, from which there issued a throaty gurgling sound that was echoed by Shmulikl, as if the two were singing a duet. When the man changed the tone to a low bass, Shmulikl did the same. Saliva flowed freely from their mouths and sweat from their foreheads. Obviously the man had teeth like a horse.

Binele, unimpressed by the dramatic scene in the barber shop, walked along the row of those who were waiting, passed the armchair and the two groaning men who were fighting with the same stubborn tooth, and headed straight for the "kabinet" at the rear of the shop. There she sat herself down to wait in the same chair, near the same cluttered desk full of the same books, papers, and bottles, as when she had her scabs removed.

It took a while before Shmulikl made his appearance in the "kabinet." He stepped inside, perspiring profusely and looking preoccupied, but obviously satisfied with himself over the job he had just completed. His back to Binele, he mopped his neck with a long white towel. Humming, he moved his glasses up onto his forehead and buried his face, with its neatly trimmed goatee, in the towel. It was only when he turned to reenter the shop that he noticed Binele. He moved the glasses still further up on his forehead, as if he wanted to assure himself that he was not seeing an apparition, and asked, "What are you doing here?"

She gathered her courage and replied, "I'm waiting for you."

"I pull teeth in there," he indicated the shop with his goatee.

"May all my enemies have their teeth pulled," she shot back.

"What's wrong with you, then?" he asked, impatient to get back to work.

"Why should anything be wrong with me?" She smiled apologetically.

"But what hurts you?"

"May all my enemies be hurt."

Shmulikl gave a short laugh. He turned to face her squarely, casting a long glance at the armchair on the other side of his desk, which beckoned with its velour pillow. After a minute's hesitation, he walked around the desk and sank into the seat, his glasses still on his forehead. Binele sighed with relief when she saw him sitting at the desk across from her. Jubilantly, she looked him straight in the eye.

"I don't have much time to entertain you here," he shook his head, both amused and impatient. He pulled his glasses back onto his nose.

"You don't have to entertain me, Panie Shmulikl the Doctor," she said enthusiastically. "And I'm as healthy as an ox and stronger than a bull."

"Then what have you come for?"

"I came to work!"

With his index finger, he pressed the glasses deeper into the hollow between his nose and his eyebrows. "What do you mean 'to work'?"

"What do you mean asking me what I mean 'to work'?" she laughed loudly to cover the sound of her pounding heart. "I want you to hire me for your wife. I'm only asking for food and a spot on the floor to sleep on. I can scrub a floor until it's white as chalk. I can carry water, do laundry, and wash windows. I can take care of a baby and I can cook everything. I can do everything."

"Whose daughter are you?" Shmulikl allowed himself a combination of a smile and a yawn.

"Yossele the Chalk Dealer's," Binele said proudly. "You cured me of scabs, and you put my brother back on his feet," she declared in a tone of voice that seemed to imply that Shmulikl now had an obligation not to leave her in the lurch. She deliberately neglected to mention Faigele to him. "And," she added, "I wash my hair for the Sabbath with soap!" Teasingly, she waved the tips of her long braids at him.

Shmulikl scratched his head with the reverse end of his pen. It was high time for him to return to the waiting patients in the shop. He stood up with a sigh. "My wife doesn't need you. She has a maid," he said.

"Then the maid needs me!" Binele jumped to her feet quickly and blocked Shmulikl's way out. Their eyes met. He buried a smile in his goatee. Binele stood between him and the shop with her arms spread out, so he had no choice but to turn in the opposite direction and vanish into the depths of the house.

Soon he was back. Behind him towered a tall, bony woman, dark-haired, with a mustache shadow around her mouth and an artificial black beauty mark, a "pepper grain," which looked like a black mole on her cheek. She measured Binele with a long gaze from her dark, sad eyes and grabbed her own head with both hands, as if the sight of Binele gave her a headache. "What's your name?" the woman asked.

Binele told the woman her name and tried to cajole her into smiling. "Everyone calls me Marzepa," she added. "Or they call me Thief's Eyes. But that doesn't mean I'm a thief."

"Are you sure?" the woman smiled faintly, rubbing her temples with the tips of her fingers. Shmulikl's wife was considered the most beautiful woman in Bociany, and it was said that Shmulikl had had to move heaven and earth to get her to marry him. But to Binele she looked downright ugly.

"Of course I'm sure!" Binele tossed her braids back proudly. "Yossele Abedale is my father. He would kill me if he discovered that . . . "

That was evidently enough to convince the woman of Binele's honesty. She drew closer, holding a finger to her lips, and from the expression on her face, it appeared that each word that Binele uttered drilled a hole in her head. So Binele bit her lips and refrained from saying more. For her part, she was wondering whether the barber-surgeon's wife, the educated midwife to the rich, the famous beauty, was as smart a woman as Shmulikl deserved to have for a wife. How could this woman have asked her if she was a thief? Would a real thief ever admit to stealing?

Finally the woman sighed and said, "You'll do. You'll be the maid's helper." She waved her hand as if waving Binele out of the room. "Come tomorrow morning." To Binele's astonishment, the woman suddenly came closer, put out her hand, and stroked Binele's hair. "Permission, *mein Schatz,*" she whispered. "This migraine drives me *verruckt.*" And she waited for Binele to leave.

Binele left the barber-surgeon's house steeped in thought. She could still feel the woman's hand on her head. But what did "Permission, *mein Schatz,* this migraine drives me *verruckt*" mean? Who was the monster who was driving the stupid but good woman *verruckt?* Who was this mysterious "migraine"? She would have to find out as soon as possible and see if she could help the unhappy woman. And why did the barber-surgeon and his wife speak Yiddish in such a way that only one or two words in each sentence could be understood? Was this a sign of their high level of education? Probably. The doctor and his wife were the most educated people in Bociany.

Binele did not forget Shmulikl's wife's words, nor her caress when she started to work as "the servant's servant." It was not long, however, before she began taking cachets for headaches and half-empty vials of valerian drops from the drawers, cupboards, and glass shelves in the barber-surgeon's "kabinet." Shmulikl soon began quarreling with his wife, accusing her of not keeping count and trying to destroy her young life and her migraine with too many cachets and drops.

Binele sold the cachets and drops to the peasant women in return for a cup of curds, a piece of butter, or a couple of eggs. She ate the curds herself; they were so delicious she did not want to share them with anyone. The butter and eggs she took home to her pregnant sisters, mostly out of pity for them, but also as an effort to buy their friendship. The more abandoned and alone she felt, the more grateful she became for any sign of affection. A friendly look was enough to satisfy her.

Her sisters' attitude toward Binele's working at Shmulikl's house differed little from that of their father. They had all, in a way, given up on her and thought that, given the choice between spending her days at the Gentiles' homes or working at Shmulikl's, the latter was the lesser of two evils. Shmulikl would in any case never convert her into a *shikse.* So the sisters, stiff and aloof, accepted Binele's gifts indifferently. For Binele it was enough of a reward that they did not ask how she came by these treasures. But on the Sabbath, after Binele had finished serving the traditional *cholnt* at the doctor's house and had gone home to visit, Raisele rewarded her by letting her take her little son for a walk while the family took its traditional Sabbath after-*cholnt* nap, to gather strength for the coming week.

Binele took the little boy to the garden near the marketplace. She lay down on the grass and let him crawl all over her, tug at her clothes with his little fingers, and pull at her braids. She felt the delicate warmth of his soft skin. Saliva dripping from his mouth, he made her giggle with delight. When the little one rode on her back, her face nuzzled the luxuriant grass, and she smelled the intoxicating fragrance of the earth.

At Shmulikl's house, Binele kept her eyes and ears open. From the servant she learned how to prepare the important dishes, how to stew, broil, roast, and fry, how to melt goose fat to spread on bread, how to prepare a borscht, blintzes with cheese, a carrot *tsimmes,* and apple or plum compotes. The food pantry at the doctor's house was filled with all kinds of goods because the peasants often paid with chickens or geese, with potatoes, fruits, and vegetables. Binele also observed her mistress's manners, the manners of an educated person, and she memorized the "educated" words that the mistress often used. Now Binele heard the word "permission" a hundred times a day, especially when the mistress was referring to delicate female matters. For instance she would say, "Binele, wash, permission, my long nightgown today and hand me, permission, the slip from the chair."

Binele came to the conclusion that the word "permission," was not a curse word, as she had originally thought, but was a French and not a German way of saying in Yiddish, "forgive the expression." And she learned to reply, while slightly mispronouncing the learned word, "Do you mean, premission, the cotton slip, or premission, the fustian one?"

In fact, the doctor and his wife knew a few languages, unlike the other Jews of Bociany, who spoke only Yiddish sprinkled with some peasant words. The doctor and his wife spoke German, Russian, Polish, and French, and they had shelves full of books whose pages were filled with alphabets that Binele had never seen before. She looked into these books whenever she was dusting the furniture, which she did once a week. The weekly dusting seemed strange to her, especially because she had to keep the windows open even if she was only sweeping the floor. Why they were so afraid of a speck of dust, she could not understand. And did dusting do any good? Of course not. All of Bociany was drowning in dust, and it harmed no one.

Binele dressed for work in a clean dress that the maid lent her. She had to wash it once a week. Such were the whims of the doctor and his wife. Everything had to sparkle and shine. Binele forgave them this weakness. People had all kinds of strange notions, and it was no use trying to talk them out of them. When Binele, dressed in her ill-fitting frock, served at the table, she kept her ears open, trying to understand what the doctor, his wife, his sons, and his daughter were saying to each other; they spoke of things she had never heard about at home.

Shmulikl spoke, for instance, of Doctor Herzl, whose portrait hung in the "kabinet" draped in black; he had died since the first time Binele had seen the picture. The only problem was that Shmulikl talked to his family in that difficult Yiddish called Deutsch. And just as often as his wife used the word "permission" in the bedroom, Shmulikl used the word *Zionismus* in the dining room. Thanks to the few words that she did manage to understand, Binele came to the conclusion that Doctor Herzl was a brother or a cousin of Shmulikl's, who had left him an inheritance in his will, in Eretz Israel, and had urged him and his family to go to the holy city of

Jerusalem, where this thing called *Zionismus* could be found, a thing that one could not get in Bociany, not even for gold.

Binele took an immediate dislike to Herr Doctor Herzl, even if he had already found peace in the Other World. Whenever she dusted Shmulikl's "kabinet," she tried not to look in the direction of the black-draped portrait of this man with a black beard and black hair, but no skullcap. The man infuriated her. Whenever she could not overcome the temptation to look at him, she widened her eyes with anger and stuck out her tongue at him. "What will I do if I lose this place at Shmulikl the Doctor's, eh?" she hissed at him and even waved her fist. "To hell with you!" she fumed. "What will all of Bociany do without Shmulikl? Shmulikl will not leave Bociany, no sir, not in a hundred years!"

But in her heart of hearts Binele was not so sure. Shmulikl talked about his brother Doctor Herzl as if the latter were a god. So, in order to know where she stood with them, she applied herself even more, making an intense effort to understand all the oddities that she heard and observed in the house.

The doctor and his wife had three children, two boys and a girl whose name was Genia. Genia was about Binele's age, but in Binele's eyes she was a little girl. Yet this little girl studied together with her brothers, who did not attend heder. All three of them took their *Stunden* together from two visiting tutors who dressed like goyim. One of the tutors lived at the lessee's house, and the other lived at the "writer" Pan Feifer's house. Binele often put her eye to the keyhole of the dining room, where the children did their *Stunden.* Flabbergasted, open-mouthed, she listened to Genia talk to the teacher as freely and incomprehensibly as if she were a learned man.

Then there were the late evenings when the *besmedresh* students, many of whom Binele recognized, would sneak in through the back door. Binele was supposed to be upstairs by then, asleep on her straw mat in the corridor, but she was too curious. She waited on her sleeping mat until she no longer heard anyone enter the house and the dining room door was bolted. Then she ran downstairs, barefoot, and peered into the dining room through the keyhole. She saw the doctor and his wife surrounded by the young men from the *besmedresh,* who, in their excitement, seemed to have lost their skullcaps and who gestured wildly. Strange quarrels took place. The people inside never agreed with each other—at least they did not seem to—yet they patted one another on the back, shared cigarettes, drank tea from the samovar, and even laughed together! The doctor's wife looked strangely beautiful and did not seem to be suffering from her usual headache. She looked so young that she seemed to be her own daughter. She could sit with the young men for hours, talking and arguing, supporting her husband so eloquently that she seemed just as clever and educated as he.

Shmulikl kept repeating, "The Zionist congress in Basel . . . " and constantly brought up Doctor Herzl's name.

When they heard this, some of the young men shook their heads vigorously, and disrespectfully attacked their hosts with words such as "Karl Marx," "Bund," or *"socialismus"*. To these speakers, other young men, evidently on the side of Shmulikl and his wife, responded with an equally vigorous shaking of the head. They waved their hands at the first group as if to say that the latter did not know what they were talking about. "*Socialismus* is no salvation for us," they argued.

"*Zionismus* is no salvation for us," the others responded heatedly.

Although the doctor and his wife were Binele's master and mistress, it took her no time to decide which side she was on. She already knew what *Zionismus* meant for her personally. It meant losing her wonderful place in this wonderful house. So she took the side of *socialismus* because she very much wished that her masters would not heed their relative Herzl's advice and leave for Eretz Israel.

Afterwards, Binele would lie on her straw mat upstairs and think deeply about all that had happened in the doctor's house that day. She was in a strange new world right in the middle of Bociany. So she would lie awake musing about this and that, until the doctor's wife came upstairs, bent over Binele, who pretended to be asleep, and whispered, "Binele, *mein Schatz,* are you asleep?" Binele opened her eyes and rubbed them as if she were emerging from a deep sleep, and with sweetness in her heart listened to her mistress's voice. The latter apologized a thousand times for waking her, then asked, "Make me, permission, a cold compress, because the migraine drives me *verruckt.*" Binele wished she understood the other words as well as she had come to understand the meaning of "migraine."

There was only one problem with her job at the doctor's, and that was the maid. She was an orphan, a spinster, whom the doctor had brought up in his house. She was in charge of the entire household, had everything under her control, and was a first-class cook. But for some reason she had a grudge against the mistress of the house and hated her as much as she loved the master. When the doctor appeared in the kitchen, the maid would turn red as a beet; if the doctor's wife appeared, she would turn green as a snake and would hiss when she spoke. Then, as soon as the mistress left the room, she would grab whatever was at hand, a racking iron or a pan, and raise it over her head, as if she were ready to pursue the doctor's wife and hit her. Binele knew that if she wanted to keep her place, she must be on good terms with the maid, so she did not react when the maid mimicked the mistress's expressions when she had a migraine attack, or talked viciously about her. Although Binele's heart ached for the doctor's wife, she did not utter a word in her defense.

When the maid could bear her hostility no longer, she took it out on the cat or on Binele. Although Binele had little tolerance for such things and had learned to avoid her father's beatings, she swallowed her pride and put up with the blows. It was worth the price. She was happy here. Not only was she well fed, but her masters spoke to her respectfully, so respectfully that sometimes she looked over her shoulder to see if they were not really talking to someone standing behind her. No one had ever spoken to her with such civility before, as if she were not a Marzepa with thief's eyes, but the daughter of the *rebetsin* herself.

And she had grown attached to the doctor's wife, although she still did not consider her very beautiful, or very clever, despite her education. Binele made all kinds of excuses for her and found an explanation for the strange things that her mistress sometimes said that made no sense. The doctor's wife, poor soul, suffered from such headaches, such bad migraines, that even her husband, who could practically raise the dead, could not cure her. On the contrary, it seemed to Binele that the headaches got worse in his presence, judging by the mistress's complaints, which doubled when he was around. Binele decided to forego all the good things that she could buy in exchange for the medicines which she took from the doctor's "kabinet," so that the doctor would not suspect his wife of poisoning herself. In this way she might perhaps ease the mistress's suffering.

When Binele wanted to sleep well at night, she would imagine that the doctor's wife was not only Genia's mother, but her own as well, an educated mother who called her "Binele, *mein Schatz*" all the time and allowed her to study with her brothers. She imagined that the mistress would dress her up in fancy clothes even on weekdays and kiss her a few times a day. Binele did not mind that this imaginary mother was not overly pretty or clever or that she had a black mole on her face and had a sick head.

But everything had its limits. Finally, Binele could no longer put up with the maid's treatment, and she complained to the doctor's wife. She showed her the black-and-blue marks on her arms and on her behind. The doctor's wife grabbed hold of her own head and asked Binele to bring her, permission, a compress of cold water. Then she explained to Binele, "It won't do any good telling her off, *mein Schatz*. We are both in her hands, you and I. I am lost without her. And this is her home. How can one throw a human being out of her home, tell me? And unbutton my corset, permission, because my head is, permission, bursting."

Despite her mistress's headache, Binele gathered the courage to ask her, "Why don't you tell your husband about her? Or do you want me to?"

"Heaven forbid, *mein Schatz*. We must not involve him in *diesen Dingen*."

So Binele went on living in the doctor's house, accepting the good and the bad, until one fine Purim day, when she received a couple of good wallops from the maid's broom. It happened right after the preparations for the Purim party, to which Reb Faivele the Miller and his whole family were invited. The whole thing happened as quick as lightning. Without a moment's thought or hesitation, Binele tore off the clean dress that had been lent to her by the maid, scrambled into her rags, and ran out, slamming the door behind her so violently that the windowpanes clattered.

Outside, the holiday celebrations were well under way. Bociany loved the festivities of Purim. The Hasidic band played in front of the *shtibl*. The doors of the houses and the *besmedresh* stood open. Inside, the Hasidim sat at tables, celebrating with food and drink. Here and there, people danced on tables and chairs. Girls with plates full of Purim gifts for their parents' friends crisscrossed the marketplace. The heder boys, who normally had no time to devote to their favorite games, now ran about to their hearts' content, not knowing what to do with their exuberance; they all seemed drunk, though none of them had touched the alcohol that the adult men drank. The marketplace was crowded with young and old. Many had their faces smeared with soot; others wore masks. Men wore their caftans inside out and hopped about in dense circles, singing at the top of their lungs. The Purim players, dressed in funny costumes, performed in many places in the marketplace or went from house to house. Little girls in unbuttoned dresses, their hair disheveled, held each other's shoulders and marched, swaying from side to side, taking up the whole width of the street, as they chanted, "A happy Purim to you all! Wherever I go, I fall."

Excited masses of people moved in all directions, while the Gentiles stood aside in groups, watching the Jews go crazy. The priest's dog, of whom it was said that he possessed a missionary's soul because he seemed drawn to Jews like a magnet, ran about the dancing men, wagging his tail and barking. The children ran away from him screaming, and he dashed after them with a deafening howl.

For a while, Binele wandered about in the merrymaking like a stranger, dazed and lost, but soon she noticed her sisters in the crowd. Raisele held her little boy by the hand and cradled the newborn baby in her arms, while Mashele cradled hers. The sisters' faces were clear and smooth, eyes sparkling with mischief as they watched the goings-on along with the other matrons. As Binele observed them, she thought that their mature faces resembled their girlish faces of long ago. Their wigs had slid down on their foreheads and looked like the fur-edged hats of the Hasidim.

A few small children from her own street surrounded Binele. They tugged at her hands and skirt, pulling her toward the crowds of dancing people. She waded with them into the very center of the marketplace, where Fishele the Butcher and Reb Dovtchele the Badkhan were leading the reveling crowd in song and dance. She flung back her braids, took the little ones by the hand, and forming a small circle, hopped with them in time to the music.

Bociany yearned for a bit of joy. So did Binele.

For some time, there had been a factory under construction at the foot of the White Mountain outside Bociany. People said that a German from Pabianice, near the distant city of Lodz, had gone into partnership with the landlord's son and that the peasants from the district would work in the factory. So the Jews of Bociany paid little attention to it.

When the building was finished, it became known that it would be turned into a plush factory and that its owners were such generous people that they did not differentiate between Jew and Gentile. They were willing to accept anyone who wanted to learn plush weaving, and Jews could still take the Sabbath off. A number of artisans' children and the children of the very poor registered for work. Binele was among them.

She quickly learned the skills of a *shtoperke,* a mender of faults in fabric that was woven by machines. She received a few kopecks a day for her work and felt proud of herself. Now she had a trade, and she only worked twelve hours a day. The rest of the day belonged to her, unlike the times when she had worked as a servant. Then she had had to be at her mistress's disposal even at night. Her only problem was that the time that belonged to her happened to be late in the evening. It was mild and springlike outside, a delightful, cheerful world. The storks were back, and after the long winter, the shtetl had opened all its doors and windows, becoming one with the outdoors. But Binele never caught a glimpse of the sun on weekdays, and in the evenings her eyelids drooped with fatigue and her back hurt.

She fought her lassitude as best she could. On her way home from work down the Narrow Poplar Road, she luxuriated in the fresh breeze from the fields and gardens. The blue evening light, the quiet gray of the houses at the side of the road, the reflection of the dark trees in the windowpanes, the play of colors in the sky where the pink stripes of the vanished sun were still woven into the cottony fuzz of slowly sailing clouds, filled her heart with longing for some place unknown and distant. Sometimes she thought that she heard the wheels of a carriage behind her and imagined that it belonged to the young master from the manor house, who would invite her into his carriage and take her to the places for which her heart longed.

Instead of going home, she would continue down the road, wandering off to the village to visit Yadwiga and her friends. She no longer felt such a strong urge to be with them; they had grown apart from one another. Binele herself did not know how it had happened, but she felt a similar reticence in their attitude toward her. Suddenly she had nothing to say to them. She could barely make out the familiar faces of childhood when she looked at them. But she went to see them for the pleasure of the walk, enjoying the sight of the yellow sand on the road that cut into the evening blue. This isolated country road also seemed to trace her hunger for something that was not of this world.

At Yankova's house, Binele tried to make herself useful, as she had done in the past, by helping to prepare the evening meal. She still liked Yankova and her husband, Yanek, whose uneven mustache had turned gray. But sitting down with the family at the table did not seem as obvious a thing as in the past. Binele told herself that it only seemed to her that the unnatural silence at the table after the meal was due to her presence. She continued to accept the bowl of cabbage soup as if it were charity. It satisfied her hunger, but made her heart feel strangely hollow.

One evening after the meal, she invited Yadwiga to go for a walk. She took hold of Yadwiga's arm as she used to do, trying to find the same easy contact that had once been theirs. "You know," she said giggling somewhat artificially. "I'm still in love with the young master from the manor. What about you?"

"He's gone, silly," Yadwiga grinned. "He left the manor to become a hero."

"What kind of a hero?"

"I can't tell you that, because you are a *Zydovetchka* and I am a Polka."

"And what were you all these times when we were such good friends and you told me all your secrets?"

"I've always been a Polka. Our country is called Polska, you know that."

"Of course I do. I'm a Polka too, although I'm a *Zydovetchka*."

Yadwiga laughed. "No, you cannot be both. You're only a *Zydovetchka*." She leaned closer to Binele and added in a whisper. "I swear that I still like you, so I'll tell you the secret. Many Poles from our village are getting ready to follow the young master and fight the Muscovites."

"Who are the Muscovites?"

"The tsar and his gendarmes, who stole our country for themselves. And you Jews side with the tsar, so I can no longer be real friends with you."

"But I side with no one!" Binele assured her.

"But I do! And that is the difference between us. Besides, I've found out that you Jews catch Polish children. Either you circumcise them to make them belong to your religion, or you kill them and use their blood to make Passover matzos."

"Pha! Who told you that gibberish? Matzos are made of flour and water!" Binele roared with laughter, as the discomfort that she had felt at Yadwiga's home now deepened into hurt. "It's all a bloody lie!"

"No, it's not!" Yadwiga stared at her with hostility in her eyes. "What about Abele the Fool?"

"What about him?"

"He was one of ours!"

"Abele, a goy? Are you out of your mind?"

"You're out of *your* mind! He's the priest's bastard. The priest had him by his first housekeeper, who died."

Binele, her heart sore, went on laughing with rage, a loud, howling laughter, and laughing, she ran away from Yadwiga, feeling dejected as never before. Now more than ever she felt that there was no place for her in Bociany. Up until now, even during her most severe attacks of despondency, Bociany had been the world to her. She rarely wondered about what went on beyond its boundaries. Now she tried to figure out whether there was not some crack through which she could escape from this confining place called home. What was this country called Polska that belonged to Yadwiga and not to her? And what was this country that Yadwiga called Muscovites? Did it belong to her?

Up until now, she had not really known what crying was. Even though she had wailed as her father beat her, the tears had not sprung from that source of anguish and despair hidden deep inside her, of which she had always been aware as the blind are aware of light. It was the same as when she used to cry over a sad story. But at the end of this summer, when the storks rose from the roofs and soared above the golden birch trees, disappearing between the White and Blue Mountains, she found herself face to face with a hollowness inside her that was so deep that she felt lost in its depth.

She wandered for miles and miles with her gaze glued to the crowns of the poplar trees that ran in parallel rows along the roadsides. The double contours of the trees headed somewhere, toward some distant point where they met, as if the poplars were rows of storks fixed in midair, as if some powerful hand held them in the same place. It seemed to her that she was just such a poplar, with arms ready for flight, yet tied by some invisible force to the ground.

She walked from the Narrow Poplar Road to the Wide one, leaving the shtetl behind. She had almost reached the Blue Mountain when the stars came out and she had to turn back. She wept the entire time, so that she barely saw where she was going.

The day before the harvest holiday Dozynki, the factory foreman let the workers go home after the midday bell. It was one of the last splendid summer days. The fields lay quiet in their nakedness, basking in the sun.

The black soil sparkled as if it were studded with diamonds. The bell at the Church of All Saints tolled the Angelus. Somewhere in the distance, the musicians strummed their primitive instruments, rehearsing for the following day. The smell of frying pork fat came from the houses, which were full of the lively voices of adults and children.

Binele did not take the opportunity to enjoy the light of day, which she so rarely saw ever since she had started working at the factory. The excitement coming from the surrounding cottages did nothing to ease her mind. She only felt her isolation and loneliness more strongly than before. She did not go home but wandered off to the birch wood, the marshes, and the lake shore. She stared into the water for so long that she thought she really did see the eyes of Kailele the Bride peering at her from the lake's depth. The eyes beckoned to her. "Come, join me . . . " the birches seemed to whisper in Kailele's voice. She had the impression that Kailele was stretching out her arms to her from under the surface of the water. "-You'll be my sister," she heard her whisper. "We'll lie here together. The water will cover us softly, and we shall never be sad. If you live in the world above, loneliness is more bitter than death, but if you lie down here, loneliness is sweeter than life. Come, sister. Here your heart will not hurt you, and you will feel nothing, absolutely nothing."

Binele shuddered. Startled and confused, she cried out, "You're crazy!" and ran away from the lake and the birch wood. She emerged on the road near the smithy of Yoel the Blacksmith. Peasants were standing next to their carts in front of the smithy. Yoel, husky and swarthy as the devil himself, was busy shoeing their horses. She saw him take a bottle of *monopolka* from a peasant. He threw his head back and poured the liquor down his open mouth. His face, his hands, his shaggy hair were all black. The color of his neck and hairy chest was only a shade lighter. His open, ragged shirt was almost as dark as the rest of him.

The people in the shtetl said that Yoel the Blacksmith had murdered his wife and children during a thunderstorm and that he was a magician, but Binele was not afraid of him. On the contrary, she was drawn to him. He was laughing with the peasants, a heavy, hot laughter. It made her want to join him, despite the heaviness of her heart. Perhaps he had some magic for her? But for that purpose she would have to visit him later, when he was alone. Then she would ask him . . . what would she ask him? How could she tell him what was wrong with her, when she did not know herself? But first she would ask him to laugh again in the same intoxicating way that she heard him laugh now.

It became even more difficult to control her despondency as she walked away from the smithy. She was very far from Bociany. She would not get there before nightfall, if she got there at all. She did not really care.

She found herself at the foot of the Blue Mountain, so she decided to climb to the top to get a drink of water. She kept her eyes on the windmill, whose blades turned slowly, rhythmically, with an occasional squeak. The sun was setting. When she got to the top, she saw it half-sunken into the horizon. The windmill's blades seemed to be erasing it. They blotted it out again and again, allowing a half-face to peer through and then blacking it from view until it reappeared. The sails seemed to be cutting into the last slice of sun, until they cracked it open and it spread across the sky like the yolk of an egg. The sun vanished completely. The western horizon looked like a fiery hoop. These were the fires of hell, the people of Bociany would say. Curiosity, like a fiery hoop, encircled Binele's mind. She wanted to see the fires of hell. She was not the least bit afraid. Her life could not be any worse than it already was. The fires of hell would at least be something new and different.

She entered the miller's yard and looked around for the water pump. She saw the miller's wife, Long Zirele, come out on the porch with a tray full of hot blueberry cakes that she put out to cool. Zirele was wearing a long, full skirt with a white apron. The collar of her blouse was unbuttoned in the front, the sleeves rolled up to the elbow; she was barefoot. Binele's eyes widened in order to take in the sight of this beautiful woman more completely. Zirele, with her voluptuous figure, her chestnut-colored wig pulled into a bun at the back of her long neck, seemed to her the very embodiment of female splendor. The purple light of the expiring day reflected on her glowing face. The sweat made her skin shine like porcelain glazing. Her dark eyes, overhung by long lashes, pierced Binele with a glance that reached straight to her bones. Binele gaped.

"Oh, Mameshie," she sobbed inwardly. "Perhaps you were just as beautiful. And I never saw you." In order not to burst into real tears, she had to turn her glance away from the woman. She ran to the water pump, which was located in the middle of the yard.

"What are you looking for?" Zirele asked her in Polish, from a distance. Binele looked to her like a peasant girl.

Binele did not have the courage to reply. She began turning the wheel quickly, collecting the water in the palms of her hands, and sipping it. The water was reddish blue, full of the light of dusk. She lifted her head up and saw the first faint stars of evening. Now the pale moon bounced on the wings of the windmill like a ball that one sail threw lightly to the other. Binele shook the water off her hands, placed her wet hands against her face, and then dried them off with her hair.

Long Zirele went to the edge of the verandah and beckoned to Binele with an imperious shake of her head. The girl approached her hesitantly, not daring to look at her face. All of a sudden her nostrils were assailed by the enticing smell of the blueberry cakes. "What are you doing here?" Zirele asked in Polish, still taking her for a peasant girl.

Binele swallowed the saliva that had accumulated in her mouth because of Zirele's close presence and the aroma of the fresh blueberry cakes. The cakes and the miller's wife seemed to have the same fragrance. Binele felt that she could swallow both Zirele and the entire tray of cakes. "I wanted a drink of water," she mumbled in Yiddish.

Zirele looked her over carefully. "You've come from the shtetl, now? Whose are you?"

Binele told her whose daughter she was and added, "They call me Marzepa," in order to make Long Zirele smile.

When she heard Yossele Abedale's name, Zirele put her hand to her cheek. "Woe is me," she said. "You passed the inn all alone, today, so late, with all those drunkards around? And passed the goyish cemetery, too? The goyish corpses could have done God knows what to you. Are you out of your mind?"

Binele was about to boast that she had come through the marshes and the birch wood and had even passed close by the smithy, but she quickly realized that such boasting would not win Zirele. So she stammered in reply, "I'm not afraid." Her eyes were glued to the tray of blueberry cakes. It took an effort to tear them away and fix them on Zirele's long skirt. "I'm not a child," she added.

"All the more reason that you should be smarter. A big girl like you ought to be frightened to take such foolish walks. How old are you?"

Binele shrugged. "I don't know." The folds of Zirele's skirt attracted her attention and inspired her to move closer. Then her gaze fell on the cakes again. They hypnotized her. "Give me a blueberry cake, and let me put my arms around the folds of your skirt," she begged Zirele in her heart. She tried to concentrate all her energy on transmitting her thoughts to Zirele. The hollowness within her now tugged at her with such hunger, such craving, that she almost threw herself on the hot tray, and on Zirele.

But neither a mind nor a belly have windows and Long Zirele, notwithstanding her sharp eyes, could not see what was gong on inside Binele. Instead, she turned her head and called into the house, "Yacov, come out here!"

A tall young man appeared on the verandah. He looked suntanned and vigorous. His shirt sleeves and trouser legs were rolled up, and his ritual undergarment lay creased and lopsided under his suspenders. From below the shiny, cracked visor of his peasant cap, a pair of warm brown eyes peered out at Binele; his long sidelocks, which reached almost to his shoulders, swayed in the breeze. Binele recognized him immediately, although she had seen little of him in the last few years. This was Hindele's son, who had never called her Marzepa. But that did not matter now. She was more interested in the black-haired little boy whom he held by the hand. The little boy was devouring a warm blueberry cake with great relish. His chubby face was blue and red and smeared with blueberry dough. His black impish eyes resembled two black blueberries as they sparkled with delight.

"Take the girl back to the shtetl," Zirele said to Yacov, pointing at Binele with her chin. "And sleep over at your mother's," she added. "You might drag along some ghosts from the cemetery if you came back tonight. We have enough trouble with living goyim. Why tease the souls of dead ones as well?" She turned her dark eyes to Binele. "Don't ever come here alone after sunset." As if she read something in the girl's face, she added in a warmer tone of voice, "It's different when you walk with someone."

Binele tore herself away and ran down the hill. She would never come back here, nor did she need anyone to take her past the cemetery, which she had passed more than once after sunset without mishap. If the woman had not been Long Zirele, Faivele the Miller's wife, she would have told her so straight to her face. But she did not have the heart to contradict Long Zirele, who was so breathtakingly beautiful. Besides, Binele's father brought bags of flour for the Sabbath noodles from Zirele's husband.

As she ran down the hill, Binele could hear the little boy crying and the distant sound of Zirele's voice. But as soon as she reached the Wide Poplar

Road, she forgot about them. She was alone again with her strange sadness, which was even more painful now, causing her eyes to swell with tears.

Her heart dissolving in her tears, she unwittingly turned her head to the side and, through the blur before her eyes, made out Yacov walking along the ditch under the poplars across the road. She was not ashamed and she did not stop crying; she did not give a damn whether he was watching her or not. How could she stop crying now when the hollowness inside her ached like a wound, craving for something she had never been given to taste, for a state of grace that had never descended on her. Anyway, she was on her way back to Bociany, the little town steeped in darkness, Bociany without storks. The long winter would soon be upon it, when the cold and the icy mud would seep through the holes in her shoes and make both her toes and her heart freeze.

Kailele the Bride again entered her mind. Soon Kailele's soul would emerge from the lake, looking for her footprints in the snow. It would wander about the shtetl every night, peering into houses through the frozen windowpanes, until it found a girl with whom to sleep. It occurred to Binele that Kailele the Bride and she were indeed one and the same person, that it was her own soul that wandered about in search of a companion to attach itself to, and that she herself lay drowned in the lake. That was why she felt that she had come into the world with something frozen inside her. Even during the worst heat waves, she felt this frost.

She shook off the strange thought. She was not Kailele the Bride. Kailele the Bride had been crazy. She had had a good pair of shoes and yet had run out barefoot in the snow. She had had a warm bed and yet had run out from under a warm eiderdown and away from a handsome bridegroom to throw herself into a frozen lake, killing herself without a slaughterer or a knife. That was the real reason why she was crazy. "And aren't I crazy to compare myself to Kailele?" she chided herself. "Kailele was spoiled, that's what she was. She was so spoiled that she went mad and took her own life. I'm not spoiled. All I want . . . "

"Look what I have here on my hand." She heard a voice breaking through her sobs. She had been aware of Yacov's presence and knew that it was his voice that she heard. Without thinking, she turned her head in his direction and in the dusky light noticed him walking beside her, his hand open in front of her eyes. She saw nothing but the white of his palm. She shrugged. Perhaps he was making fun of her? "Don't you see?" he asked. "Here, on my finger."

She saw it. "A ladybug . . . " she stammered, still sobbing.

"People call it the Almighty's little cow. It helped extinguish the fire in the Holy Temple in Jerusalem. Here, take it." He moved his hand encouragingly. "Maybe it will extinguish the sadness in your heart as well." She did not know what he wanted of her and did not stretch out her hand for the ladybug. He flicked it off his finger and looked at her as if expecting her to speak. At length he asked. "Why are you crying?" When she did not answer, he spoke again, "My mother says that even if you see your own open grave, you must never give up hope." He was certain that he committed no sin in looking at the girl. She was a child in comparison to him. He recalled the times when he had been charmed by her when she was a tiny girl.

She looked at him askance through her tears. In the dim light, she noticed that his gabardine was three-quarter length and his sidelocks dangled like two strips of shadow from under his creased threadbare cap. Because his beard grew unevenly, his face seemed to have two shades of white, one brighter than the other. His eyes were now black. It was difficult to avoid their calm, direct gaze.

Any other time, it would not have occurred to her to let herself be drawn into a conversation with him. What business did she have talking to strange boys? She had nothing in common with them. To her, they were just dark shadows parading about the background of her world in Bociany. All year long they sat stashed away in the corners of the *besmedresh* or the *shtiblekh* or their own dreary huts, and kept their noses buried in books, shaking their bodies over them like puppets. Or they gathered in clusters in the streets, the marketplace, or the garden, heatedly disputing incomprehensible matters, waving their long, bony fingers in each other's face. Only on Simhath Torah or Purim did they actually come to life. As far as Binele was concerned, they definitely belonged to a different race of two-legged creatures. They were awkward, clumsy, and less interesting than four-legged animals. Green, bloodless dummies, that was what they were. The only exception was her brother, Hershele, whom she missed badly now that he was at the yeshiva. Hershele was a different matter altogether.

At the moment, however, she did not care. She would have been ready to open her overflowing heart to a stone. So, stammering and weeping, she began to confess to Yacov how desperate she was, that she saw no reason or purpose to her life in Bociany, that she wanted to run away to wherever her eyes would lead her. After she had said all that she could say with words, she again gave way to tears. But now the weeping was easier, somehow softer. There was even a trace of pleasure in her crying now, as if the frozen hollowness inside her had thawed slightly.

After a long while, she heard Yacov's melodious voice and broken, soft words. She had to lower the sound of her sobs, to make out what he was saying. "Sometimes," he said, "I, too, feel like leaving Bociany."

"You do? Where would you go?" she stared at him tearfully.

"I don't know. I just feel the urge to leave." The moon was high over their heads. The rows of poplars on the side of the road looked like two dark walls between which the moonlight flowed like a river. The shadows of Binele and Yacov swayed over the flowing silver like sails on a waterway headed for some mysterious destination, for which their hearts longed. Their steps resounded lightly in the silence. The air was full of the raw scent of the naked fields. A breeze rustled the poplars. Yacov's voice fluttered past Binele's ear. "I think," he said in a sing-song, "that I'll save up a few rubles and go to Chwosty, where I'll buy a train ticket to Lodz."

"Why Lodz?" she asked.

"Because Lodz is nearer than America."

"America?"

"Yes. You've heard of America? It's a country on the other side of the ocean."

"I've heard of it. Does it belong to the Jews?"

"No, it belongs to the Americans."

"But if America doesn't belong to the Jews and neither does Polska and neither do the Muscovites, then what does belong to the Jews?"

"You don't say Muscovites, you say Russia," he corrected her gently. "And you know very well that the Jews have a country of their own, Eretz Israel. But for now we can't live there because we are in exile. So we have no country until the Messiah comes and takes us all back home."

Yacov was then in the middle of reading his first profane book, which was called *The Love of Zion.* He had borrowed the book from Reb Faivele's library, and he was so in love with the heroine, Tamar, that he dreamed of her in his sleep. Now, as he walked beside Binele, he had the impression of literally walking through the pages of the book. He began to tell her the plot and to paint the landscape of that distant biblical land as if the two of them were actually there. It was such a different country, and yet it was as near and familiar as Bociany.

Binele listened open-mouthed, enchanted by the story. She let Yacov speak without interruption. Finally, her sadness somewhat abated, she asked, "Then why don't you want to go to Eretz Israel, rather than to Lodz or even America?"

"They say that in America you can sweep gold in the streets, and I must help support my mother and sisters. But in order to get to America, you must first sweep up a little gold here, for steamship tickets and all the necessities. That's why I want to go to Lodz first. To go to Lodz all you need is a train ticket."

"Can you sweep gold in the streets of Lodz, too?" Binele asked.

He laughed. "What do you think it means to 'sweep gold in the streets'? That gold is like garbage, and one goes around with a broom, sweeping it up? To 'sweep gold in the streets' means that there are many chances of growing rich. And Lodz is a world-famous city with many factories. It's easy to get work there."

"Not on your life!" Binele called out with bitterness. She frowned as her curiosity evaporated. "I wouldn't work in a factory if they paid me with gold!" She tossed back her braids defiantly.

"Why not?" he asked.

"Because!" She grew angry and sarcastic. "I can just imagine how much fun it would be! If they put you in jail, at least there's a reason for it. But a factory is like a jail, only you've put yourself there on your own and for nothing!" She looked at him stealthily. Why was she taking her anger out on him? What made her want to yell at him? He might abandon her in the middle of the road and turn back. Well, what did she care if he did? Let him! She had to rid herself of the rage that had been pent up in her for so long.

When she had calmed down and was walking in silence again, he took a half-step closer to her and asked in a low voice, "You work at the plush factory, don't you? Perhaps you've heard about a group, a brotherhood of workers called the Bund? My best friend is one of them. He wants me to join, too, but I still have to think it over."

"Who's your best friend?" she asked.

He hesitated before answering, "Ariele, Fishele the Butcher's son. But we are not so close anymore. You see, we've become somewhat estranged."

"Estranged means to be like strangers, doesn't it?" she asked. "I also had a best friend. Yadwiga is her name. Yanek, her father, works for the landlord. But we have also become somewhat estranged, ever since she started to tell me that I am a *Zydovetchka,* and that the Jews are villains who kill Polish boys and use their blood to make matzos. Such idiocies she tells me. I could have killed her for it. I liked her so much! I still do. But I hate her too. She's stupid. Whatever she hears from the goyim she repeats without thinking. I don't think I miss her anymore."

He was about to respond, but changed his mind. "I wonder," he remarked instead, "if childhood friendships can ever continue into adult life."

"Why not?" she asked. "I could have been friends with Yadwiga forever, if it weren't for what she said about Jews."

Now he tried to express what he had refrained from saying before. "Nothing in the world hurts more than to hear such words. I don't think you'll ever be able to forget them, and that's not because you heard them for the first time, or because you heard them from someone you like. You just never get used to them, even if you hear them a thousand times a day. All you can do is pretend that you're used to it. So have you heard of this brotherhood called the Bund?"

"Yes, I've heard of this brotherhood-shmotherhood, whatever you call it." She laughed mockingly, her mind still preoccupied with what Yacov had just said.

"Why are you laughing? Brotherhood is a fine thing. They also call themselves *Achdes,* which means unity. One for all and all for one. They want to overthrow Tsar Nicholas."

"Naturally! No wonder. If you sit in that factory all day, all kinds of stupid notions run through your head. What do they want to overthrow Tsar Nicholas for, tell me?"

"Because he keeps all of Russia and Poland enslaved."

"And whose business is that? You said yourself that neither Russia nor Poland is our country. Let the goyim overthrow him if they want to."

"Poland is our country," he said with feeling. "Your country is the place where you are born and grow up and live and work. And we Jews have lived here for generations. Reb Faivele says almost a thousand years."

"And what about Eretz Israel?"

"That's for when the Messiah comes. For now we are here and we make our living here, so we need to have peace and happiness here."

She wondered what he might mean by peace and happiness, but instead of asking, she broke into nervous laughter. "That's why you want to leave for Lodz and work in a factory? That means peace and happiness to you? Not to have the slightest pleasure from life, that's what you want?" He tried to say something but she would not let him. "I thank you for such a paradise! I want to be a maid, that's what I want to be. I would make an excellent maid, believe me. I can cook and bake and roast and scrub the floor until it's white as chalk. I can clean frying pans and scrub pots and baking dishes until they sparkle. You can ask the maid at the barber-surgeon's, a calamity should strike her, how clean her dishes were. Is there nothing else in Lodz, besides factories?"

"What else do you have in mind? Lodz is a huge city with thousands of people."

"So there might be someone there who needs a maid, too."

"Of course. The factory owners need maids and servants."

"When do you leave?"

"For the time being I'm not leaving. Reb Faivele employs me as tutor for his sons, and I help out at the mill. I get a few kilos of flour per month, and I don't walk around hungry either."

"But you just said that you wanted to leave!" she cried, exasperated. How could she make sense of all these important things, if one minute he said one thing and the next another? This young man walking at her side pleased her less and less. He was a good-for-nothing like all the rest.

"I said that sometimes I feel like leaving, that perhaps one day I will leave . . . but for the time being I've hired myself out."

"So what? Can't you run away? Are you a horse and wagon? A horse and wagon are hired. Until when did you hire yourself out?"

"It depends on Reb Faivele."

"And it doesn't depend on you?"

"No, I'm fine here."

She frowned. A little while ago he had said that he felt like leaving, now he said that he was fine where he was. "How come you're so fine here?" she asked sarcastically.

"Because I am. Take Reb Faivele's boy, Abrashka. Did you hear him crying? That was because I left with you. How could I leave him just like that and go away?"

"Why couldn't you?"

"I'm attached to him. He's like a little brother to me."

"But he's not your brother, so why are you attached to him? I'm not attached to anyone," she said with bitter pride in her voice.

"Not even to your father?" He saw her shrug. "Don't you love your father?"

"Who said I didn't? But I can leave him. Maybe I'm attached to Mendl and Gnendl, but I can leave them, too. So why can't you leave Abrashka?"

"Who are Mendl and Gnendl?"

"My storks."

"That's not the same thing as leaving people."

"No, it isn't," she agreed after some thought. She felt strangely uncomfortable with the subject. People grew attached to one another; that was proof that they loved one another. So she had made another discovery about her character and had found an added deficiency. Not only did she not fear the things that frightened others, but she also could not grasp what was meant by loving, by being attached to someone. In order to shake off these unpleasant thoughts, she announced, "Then I'm going by myself."

"Where will you get the money for a ticket?" Yacov asked.

"I'll go on foot. I can walk for a day and a night and not get tired," she boasted, nervously playing with her braids.

From a nearby field they heard Wanda singing. Her voice rang through the silence of the evening so clearly that they could make out each word:

> You'll go through the mountain,
> go through the mountain,
> and I through the stormy sea.
> You will bloom like a rose,
> bloom like a rose,
> and I like a windswept tree.

They both listened to the song. Yacov could not take his eyes off Binele's braid, which lay folded on her shoulder. "I know Wanda well," he said. "She used to come over to our yard to visit Manka the Washerwoman. Now she doesn't come anymore. They say that she's changed. Fredka, Long Zirele's housekeeper, says she has fallen . . . fallen in love with a Jewish man. She speaks to no one, just haunts the fields and sings."

"I said I was going to Lodz on foot!" Binele grew impatient. "Why are you staring at me?"

"Your braid. It looks like a golden snake."

She jerked the braid to her back as if she were really getting rid of a living creature. "You're crazy!"

"Yes, I suppose I am, walking so close beside you and listening to Wanda singing. It's a sin."

She had to smile at the silly things that he said. "I like sin," she said. "When I worked at Sore-Leyele's, I always wished I could be Lilith."

"Be quiet. What you're saying is a sin, too. Lilith might be walking behind us right here in the dark. She can play tricks on us."

"Like what kind of tricks?"

"I don't want to talk about it."

"I do! Anyway, you don't have to tell me because I already know. She can attach us to one another. Is that what you were thinking of? Don't be afraid. I don't want to be attached to anyone. I was supposed to be attached to my mother, so she died giving birth to me. I was attached to my sister Faigele, so she died, too. I was attached to my brother, Hershele, so he left for the yeshiva. So why should I want to get attached to strangers, especially strange boys? And how is it that someone as old as you should be afraid of Lilith?"

"The older I grow, the more afraid of her I get. I'm glad you don't care for me. You'll protect me from her because she has already made you quite different from the way you looked a while ago. You have no idea what these demons are capable of."

She could not tell whether he was serious or only joking. She laughed. "I'm not afraid of demons!" She felt suddenly playful, so she took hold of both her braids and tied them under her chin. She widened her eyes and spread out her hands so that they would look like claws and moved them toward Yacov. "Look at me!" she exclaimed. "I'm Lilith the Seductress!"

"Do me a favor." He moved away from her, giggling. "Forget about Lilith."

"You started it!"

"I? How?"

"You said that my braid looked like a golden snake. How can a Marzepa like me have a braid like a golden snake, eh?"

"It's not Marzepa but Mazepa. Mazepa was the name of a Cossack hetman who lived long ago. He was so ugly that they began to call any ugly person by his name. But you are not a Mazepa."

"Want to bet? Ask anyone in Bociany and they'll tell you."

"I have my own eyes."

"Your eyes are fooling you because you see Lilith in me." She tried to frighten him again and moved closer.

"I see you, not Lilith." He took a step away from her.

"But do you want to bet that I can get to Lodz on foot? Do you want to bet that I can reach that barn there before you can?"

He surprised her by his laughter, just as before he had surprised her with his soft, lilting voice. Granted he was, like the other boys, far from brilliant, but she had never before heard anyone laugh so warmly. His full voice caressed the ear with a sad aftertone.

They bet two kopecks and raced. Their shadows danced over the silvery light that the moon cast on the road, as if they were two puppets in the hands of an invisible puppeteer. They reached the barn at the same time, but she insisted that she had been first. He reached into his pocket. "Here are your two kopecks."

"I don't need your stupid two kopecks." She pushed away his hand, but immediately changed her mind. "All right. Let me have them." She took the two kopecks out of his palm.

Panting, they continued their walk on the road, keeping a distance between them. Now and again they turned their heads toward each other and each peered at the other's face through the web of darkness and moonlight. In this manner they arrived at the Potcheyov. The lights of the *besmedresh,* the synagogue, and the surrounding houses blinked softly.

"We're back already," Binele remarked with surprise. The walk home had seemed very short to her. Before parting, she to the north, he to the south of the shtetl, they glanced at each other again in the moonlight.

Binele walked slowly through the streets, bumping into passers-by or neighbors who stood chatting in the dark doorways. The moon overhead and the pale light coming from the houses made her reflection on the windowpanes look like a black shadow. It seemed to her that she was not herself, but a ghost, or a demon. "I've become Lilith . . . I've become Lilith . . ." she murmured to herself. "That's why my eyes are dry and I'm feeling happy." She did indeed feel very joyous. Her mood no longer matched the autumnal sadness of Bociany after the storks had left. She looked at the two kopecks in her palm. "I'll attach myself to you," she whispered, half serious, half in jest.

## 19

THAT NIGHT, Binele was unable to fall asleep for a long time. Everything that had taken place between her and Yacov remained as vividly in her mind as if she were living it again. She could not absorb the meaning of it all, but she could remember even that which had been disturbing, or incomprehensible. She remembered the sight of the road as they had walked on it, Yacov's face reflected in the moonlight, the sound of his voice, his laughter, even the silly things that he had said. She would gladly have walked the whole walk with him again. She was amazed at how the world seemed to have changed for no reason at all, and even more at how she herself could have changed so suddenly.

As she lay on her cot in the darkness of the room, she saw a shadow flicker past the window. What was it? Maybe it was Kailele's soul coming to claim her? Or Yacov's soul? Or a ghost? Maybe the Angel of Death had come to punish her for talking Yacov into committing a sinful act by walking so close to her? She smiled to herself. Yacov had done a good deed. He had practically saved her life.

The shadow appeared at the window again. This time it stopped there. A face, large and dark, with a pair of burning eyes, peered into the room through the pane. Binele sat up on the cot and moved closer to the window. She recognized the face of Yoel the Blacksmith. She jumped down from the cot, ran to the door, opened it, and waited for Yoel to approach. This was indeed a strange night. She had never seen Yoel in the shtetl before, let alone at her hut.

"Go wake your father and tell him to come out," he commanded in his deep bass voice.

She went over to Yossele's cot, bent over him, and withdrew. She had never in her life woken her father. And what if this magician, this murderer, Yoel, wanted to lure her father outside to kill him? Then she would be guilty of causing both her parents' deaths. But she could not keep Yoel's presence at the door secret from her father. Let him decide whether or not to go out. She shook Yossele vigorously by the shoulder and whispered, "Yoel the Blacksmith is outside. He told me to wake you."

In a moment, Yossele was sitting up on his cot, his legs touching the floor. All the years of helping the fire brigade and taking command of the night watch had accustomed him to sleeping lightly and to waking at the slightest sound. His first thought was that a fire had broken out. It took a while for Binele's words to penetrate his mind.

"Who did you say? Yoel the Blacksmith?" He rushed into his pants, threw on his gabardine, and went to the door. As soon as he stepped outside, Binele pushed the door open a crack in case anything should happen to him and she would have to yell for help. She could hear Yoel's deep bass whisper clearly; obviously these were the lowest sounds that he was capable of making.

"I've come to tell you," he said, "because I know that you have a cooler head than all the rest of them put together. Besides, you know the peasants as well as I do. So I'm here to warn you. I'm not certain what they're up to, but tomorrow during the holiday celebration—they'll be drunk, and you'd better keep an eye open and be ready. There's been some whispering among them. Something's cooking. A bunch of them have gone into hiding, along with the landlord's sons. They're preparing some kind of uprising. The lessee's children are also involved. The peasants have got wind of the plan, and they're confused."

"What do you mean an uprising?" Binele heard her father's voice.

"Just what I said," Yoel replied. "There is talk of some guy called Josef Pilsudski gathering an army abroad. If there is a war, they want to be prepared to fight for Poland. Others are getting ready to give the Legions support on Polish soil. But the old ones are scared. They're not for the tsar, but neither are they for an upheaval. They're saying that the lessee's sons have talked their boys into joining the fighters. And there is a story circulating about Abele the Fool, too. A rumor's going around that the Jews abducted him or something like that; that they converted and circumcised him. And then there is the story about Vaslav Spokojny. The rebels won't let him join their ranks, let alone name him as their chief. He thought they would receive him with open arms, so he's gone wild. There, now I've told you all that I know."

Binele heard nothing more. A long time passed and Yossele did not return to the house. Quickly she dressed herself and ran outside. The houses shimmered in the darkness; the roofs were awash with moonlight. The black windowpanes reflected the sky, the white clouds, and the stars. Binele, barefoot, rushed through the streets, certain that she was dreaming.

As soon as she came to the gate of the Potcheyov, she saw her father running around inside, calling, "Abele! Abele!" She hid in a dark corner and waited for Yossele to come out and pass her. He did so and then set out at a run across the marketplace. Dogs started to howl as he vanished into the *rov's* house. A light appeared in the *rov's* window, flickering faintly. After a while, she saw her father come out and hurry over to Fishele the Butcher's door, then to Toviele the Wagon Driver's. Soon a group of men were rushing back to the *rov's* house and from there—to Shmulikl the Doctor's!

A wave of anxiety swept over Binele. If they were all running to Shmulikl the Doctor's, then something terrible was about to happen; some great tragedy lurked in the depths of this silvery night. Her father was in danger. Perhaps the whole family was in danger, the entire shtetl—and Yacov! She had to warn him!

As soon as the thought entered her mind, she set out at a run toward the other end of the shtetl. She knew very well where Hindele lived. More than once when she was small, Hindele's daughters had taken her upstairs to show her the inside of the nuns' garden from the window of their garret. Now she scrambled up the crooked broken stairs, feeling her way with her hands. The steps creaked under her weight, and before she had even reached the top, she heard Hindele's trembling voice calling, "Who's there?"

"It's me!" she called back. "Yossele Abedale's daughter. They say that the peasants are up to something. They might beat up Jews tomorrow. Father is running around telling everyone, so you should know, too!" Gingerly, she crawled backwards down the stairs. In the yard, a woman wrapped in a plaid shawl came running toward her.

"Is Hindele awake?" the woman asked Binele in a hoarse whisper.

Binele recognized Nechele the Pockmarked, the wife of the despicable Reb Laibele the Sexton, who had brought about Faigele's death. Neither Binele nor any other member of her family had ever since acknowledged the existence of the couple. Now, without thinking, she answered, "I just woke her," and ran on.

Hindele was also not on speaking terms with Nechele the Pockmarked. Now, however, Nechele climbed up to Hindele's loft, to tell her to go with her children to the synagogue at daybreak. There was a secret cellar there, dug especially as a hiding place for the Holy Scrolls in case of emergencies. A number of people could squeeze into the cellar as well. Nechele had just come from Shalom's place, having told him the same thing. Despite her last fierce quarrel with Hindele, Nechele still nourished maternal feelings toward Hindele's son, whose wedding had taken place at her home. After promising Nechele that he would take his pregnant wife and his two children to the synagogue—he was now the father of two little girls—Shalom had run off to join the men of the night watch. As for Yacov, as soon as he woke and realized what was going on, he dressed and ran off to the Blue Mountain to alert Reb Faivele the Miller. He hoped to be back with his family before daybreak.

When Binele returned to the marketplace, she could not believe her eyes. It was packed with people milling about, just as if it were day. No one said a word, not even the children. A marketplace filled with ghosts! Not even the dogs barked. The silence was deafening. Some people were carrying packs out of their houses, but there were no lights in the windows. Wagons loaded with women and children stood waiting in the marketplace, the horses harnessed. Binele saw the *rov* running from door to door trailed by a group of men whose beards flew up in the air. They tugged at the *rov's* coat, pulling him first one way, then another. Before long, she saw her father emerge from their own street, leading Raisele's little boy by the hand. Her sisters came after him, with the babies in their arms. The brothers-in-law were carrying sacks and bundles. Yossele made room for his daughters on one of the wagons.

"Look up Hershele when you're in Chwosty. Ask him why he doesn't come home for the holidays and doesn't give a sign of life," he said to his sons-in-law, who were to accompany the women. He looked around. "Where's Binele gone to?" he asked.

She pulled his sleeve, "Here I am."

"Climb up!"

She shook her head, "I want to stay with you!" Before she could manage to run away, he grabbed hold of her and lifted her into the wagon. He walked over to the other wagons, his eyes searching for Hindele. Not seeing her, he wondered whether she had been alerted to the danger. The minute he turned away to dispatch one of his men to find Hindele, Binele jumped down from the back of the wagon.

Suddenly, the door of the county officer's cottage opened, and he emerged in his nightclothes, a nightcap on his head and a lighted lantern in his hand. He raised the lantern high above his head, took one look at the marketplace and knocked at the window of the chief gendarme. The county officer's wife came out holding a sheepskin coat, which she threw over her husband's shoulders. Dressed in the sheepskin, the county officer drew near the crowd at the wagons, holding the lantern in his outstretched hand. "What's the matter with you, Jews? Have you all gone mad, turning night into day?" he exclaimed.

Bare-headed gendarmes, their jackets still unbuttoned, came running out, sabers glittering in their hands. Behind them trotted the priest, accompanied by his housekeeper, who also held a lantern in her hand. The county officer took another step toward the crowd. The gendarmes, buttoning their jackets with one hand, waved their sabers with the other and made room for the priest and his housekeeper to pass.

The crowd gasped, holding its breath. The *rov* pulled Yossele's sleeve, "Hurry to Shmulikl the Doctor and beg him by all that's sacred to come right away!" To the Jews standing around him, he said, "The forces of evil have risen to the surface, and we must look them straight in the eye." He stepped out from the middle of the crowd, and approaching the county officer and the priest, said to them in Yiddish, "We are going to visit our rabbi in Chwosty."

The priest, who suffered from a fever, had trouble standing on his weak legs. He shivered in the cold. He understood Yiddish, and smiled feebly at the county officer, as he translated the *rov's* words, "He says they're leaving to visit their rabbi, but you needn't believe them. No Jew leaves to visit the rabbi at night with women and children, especially not on a Wednesday night." He turned to the *rov* and nodded with pretended reverence. "Why are you leaving to visit your rabbi in the middle of the night, as if you were thieves or robbers, pray explain, honorable Rov?"

The *rov* cast a desperate glance at Shmulikl the Doctor's house. Yossele was taking a long time, probably because he was having trouble convincing Shmulikl to come out. The *rov* pretended that he had not understood the priest's words. A few Jews tried to serve as translators, but the *rov* kept on pretending to be deaf and dumb. He turned his head from side to side, yet his eyes were fixed on Shmulikl's house. At last he saw him appear alongside Yossele, and heaved a sigh of relief, but he was still so tense that he could not bring himself to say another word. He pointed in Shmulikl's direction.

The plan of sending the women and children to Chwosty with the excuse of visiting the rabbi had been concocted by the *rov.* The *rov* believed that if a criminal was needed to save lives, it was permissible to take him off the scaffold, and that was why he had insisted on enlisting the help of Shmulikl the Doctor to make the plan work. But Shmulikl had not liked the plan. He held that there was no good in escaping to Chwosty if danger threatened because the peasants had horses and wagons and could pursue them if they wished. Shmulikl's counsel had been that the usual night watch be kept on alert during the day as well, that an additional defense team be quickly organized, and that for the rest, they should wait and see. But the *rov* had stuck to his plan, and now Yossele had to force Shmulikl to come out and do what he could to save the community.

If Shmulikl was nervous, he did not show it. As soon as he approached the crowd near the wagons, he straightened his back, cleaned his glasses, cleared his throat, and with great dignity turned to the county officer and the priest, bowing to them respectfully. "You must forgive us, honorable gentlemen, for disturbing your sleep." he said. His Polish was so perfect, his accent so urbane, that both the county officer and the priest felt themselves at a disadvantage. "Alas," Shmulikl continued, "a terrible epidemic of fever has spread among our infants. It is a disease already well known in antiquity, which only attacks the members of our race, although it can easily contaminate others if there is close contact. There is, I'm sorry to say, no cure for this disease at the moment, so our honorable *rov* has ordered the heartbroken mothers to visit the Holy Rabbi of Chwosty to be consoled by him. We thought it better that they leave with all their children by night, so as to protect you people from catching the disease, and because owing to the children's high fever, they cannot bear the light and are, in general, easier to manage at night. Please, forgive us the inconvenience, honorable gentlemen."

The priest greatly respected Shmulikl the Doctor. He was under his care for the treatment of his consumption and so had had the opportunity to appreciate his intelligence and erudition. But the story that Shmulikl told did not ring true. He walked up to one of the weeping women—all the women were weeping; this they did not have to pretend—and was about to take a look at the child in her arms, when Shmulikl grabbed his hand.

"Heaven forbid," he said, thoroughly distraught. "You, Father? A sick man like you? I told you, Father, you must keep away. The fever is contagious. It would be wise to alert your congregation."

The priest, who was shaking with cold, grew extremely serious. "Tomorrow, during the procession, the town will be full of children. Yes, we must alert the congregation."

The housekeeper grabbed the priest's arm. "We must not delay, Father. We must send someone to warn the mothers to keep their children by their side tomorrow, so that no one will go near a Jew. Oh, Jesus," she burst into tears, "why have you brought this cursed vermin to live among us?"

The priest patted her on the shoulder and made the sign of the cross over her and the county officer's wife.

The county officer wiped his forehead with the sleeve of his coat and said to Shmulikl, "I hold you responsible for the whole thing. Send off your women and children immediately, before there is a plague!"

The *rov* whispered something in Yossele's ear, and Yossele whispered something in Shmulikl's ear. Shmulikl said to the county officer, "How can we send off all our women and children, when we have only these few wagons, honorable sir?"

"You'll get all the wagons that you need, and we'll requisition more from the villages if necessary. I'm declaring martial law. The Jews must stay in their houses until all the sick die and are buried. You, Panie Doctor, are responsible, and you will let us know when Bociany is out of danger. Then the Jews can come out and open their shops. Starting tomorrow, all shops will be closed until further notice!" He moved closer to the priest. The two men whispered nervously to each other.

In the meantime, some of the Jewish mothers were having second thoughts about going to Chwosty, where they would have to stay for who knew how long. But the *rov* kept everything firmly under control. There was no way back. The game had to be played out to the end. And the danger was not yet over, for neither the county officer nor the priest knew what was going on among the peasants.

The county officer issued an order for all the wagons and horses at his disposal to be brought out, while the gendarmes set off for the villages to requisition more wagons and to alert the peasants not to go near the Jews, neither the next day during the festivities nor afterwards, until further notice. In the meantime, the *rov* sent another message to the *rov* in Chwosty—he had dispatched the first as soon as the plan had ripened in his head—and so it was that in the middle of the night, Bociany was illuminated by all the lights in all the houses, both Jewish and gentile. The night was turned into day, and the shtetl was as noisy as on market day. There was confusion everywhere, a clattering of wheels, a stomping of horses' hoofs. In the middle of the night, all the traffic on the Wide Poplar Road moved in the direction of Chwosty.

Before the priest returned to the parsonage, he once again called over Shmulikl the Doctor and asked him, "What is the name of this disease, this Jewish fever, Panie Doctor?"

"Fervor Judaicus," Shmulikl, who in reality hardly knew any Latin, replied calmly. "Please, wash your hands immediately."

On returning to his house after the wagons had departed, Yossele lit a candle, and found Binele fast asleep on her cot, still dressed in her clothes. His first impulse was to drag her out of bed and unload his heavy heart by giving her a good beating. But he checked himself. This was not the right moment to be getting angry at her. He, too, would have liked to throw himself on his cot, dressed though he was, and sleep off the few remaining hours until dawn. But although he was exhausted, he did not have the patience to stay put. He cast another glance on Binele and blew out the candle. He left the house, locking Binele inside, and rushed over to the *rov's* place. The *rov's* dark chamber was packed with worried, nervous men reciting the psalms.

When she woke in the morning and did not find her father on his cot, Binele grew alarmed. Finding the door locked, she jumped out through the window and ran to look for him. A deathly silence hovered over the empty shtetl as it basked in the sunlight. It was a spooky sight. As she was passing through the desolate Potcheyov, she heard someone warning her in a whisper from behind the door of a locked shop, "Go home, quickly!"

She approached the door. "Do you know where Yossele Abedale is?" she asked.

"He's in the synagogue. On guard."

"What are you doing here?"

"I'm on guard too. Go home. The goyim will be coming soon."

She ran back home.

The celebration of the peasant holiday Dozynki started with the usual pomp. It was a beautiful golden autumn day. The peasants from the surrounding villages and those from Bociany approached the marketplace and the churchyard in long processions. They and their children were dressed in their holiday best.

The men wore knee-high boots, embroidered shirts, and baggy pants. Their four-cornered hats were decorated with flowers stuck behind the strap. The women wore loose red skirts that reached below their knees and frilly white embroidered blouses with buffon sleeves, with tight embroidered black vests on top. Many strings of sparkling beads hung from their necks. Long ribbons dangled from their shoulders and hips and from the flower garlands they wore around their heads.

The processions met in the marketplace, and proceeded forward as one river of color. A train of wagons rolled slowly along in the middle of the crowd. The wagons were also decorated with garlands of flowers and with pine and birch boughs. They carried heaps of rye, wheat, and oats, plates and baskets full of vegetables and fruits, beautifully arranged around the statues of saints and of Jesus and the Virgin, which had been removed from the village shrines for the occasion. The statues shook as they were carried over the cobblestones by the wagons, appearing to nod to the words of the hymns that the crowd sang as it moved solemnly, somewhat sleepily, ahead toward the church. As the people marched and sang, they tightly gripped the hands of their children and fixed their eyes on the Jewish houses.

The Jewish houses looked abandoned, as indeed many of them were. The majority of the men were at the synagogue, dressed in their prayer shawls, chanting the psalms. Those houses that contained people were locked and bolted and appeared empty. The young men of the *besmedresh,* the factory workers and artisans belonging to the Bund, who were members of the defense unit, had visited Yoel the Blacksmith during the night and had armed themselves with all the iron bars they could find in the yard. Now they crouched in the lofts and cellars, peering at the crowd through the cracks. The members of the fire brigade headed by Fishele the Butcher and the guard that Yossele had organized at the *rov's* request were arranged into several groups. One group guarded the synagogue, another hid in the sheds on the Potcheyov, and the rest secretly patrolled the alleys and backyards.

The church bells tolled incessantly. Inside the church flickered the lights of hundreds of candles. The front door stood wide open, so that the sound of the singing voices could be heard throughout the marketplace, where it mixed with the faint muffled chant of psalms and laments that emerged from behind the bolted doors and windows of the synagogue. Yossele was inside with the other Jews. He stood guard at the small door in the rear, peering out at the deserted marketplace. Bociany seemed like a ghost town, empty, yet full of sounds.

After mass, the peasants began to pour out of the church in colorful waves that spread in all directions around the marketplace. But their festive attire did not suit the people's mood. There was only an occasional cheerful exclamation or the sound of someone laughing. The crowd seemed confused and undecided, and even the children looked bewildered. The tension in the air was so thick that it could almost be touched.

No one set out to stroll along the streets or in the garden. The women wiped their eyes and crossed themselves frequently. The crowd did not disperse, however. In front of the church stood tables full of all kinds of pies and pastries, which the peasants had brought in their wagons. People began to mill around the tables, mechanically tasting the cakes of their neighbors, and just as mechanically, the village band set itself up near the tables, unloading harmonicas and accordions, tuning fiddles and guitars. Then, the gentile fire brigade's six-man orchestra came marching out from behind the county officer's house. The players wore navy-blue uniforms with brass buttons, gilded tassels dangling from their shoulders and shiny brass helmets gleaming on their heads. The trumpets blew a fanfare. The crowd was taken by surprise. The orchestra lined itself up on the wide front steps of the church.

Bottles of *monopolka* appeared from under the peasants' camisoles or from the pockets of their baggy trousers. A young man, obviously unable to hold his liquor, broke into a wild dance in the middle of the marketplace. Before long he lay prostrate on the cobblestones. The younger people erupted into hoots and catcalls, cheered by the sight of their comrade on the cobblestones. A couple started dancing the Bociany version of the Krakowiak. Two, then three couples joined them, until the entire marketplace was a whirl of twirling skirts and pounding boots. This dance was followed by a series of others, executed in typical Bociany fashion. Slowly, older couples joined in. But the mothers who had brought their children along held them firmly by the hands and stood around with them, just watching. The crowd was lively but something prevented it from becoming truly exuberant. There was an edge of rage to the dancing, a hostility punctuated by laughter and shouting that grew increasingly harsh and jarring. The musicians played the favorite Bociany tunes, increasing the speed as the dancing gained momentum.

So it went until noon, when the fire-brigade orchestra played a patriotic march. At this point, Vaslav Spokojny, dressed in the uniform that he wore on special occasions, sprang onto a table. Already drunk, he raised his bottle of *monopolka* and cried out, "To our Fatherland!"

A few voices responded with a "hurray," but the other peasants, young and old, rushed toward him with raised fists, yelling, "Off the table! Don't spoil the holiday!"

A young man shouted, "We'll kill you if you don't shut up!"

The young peasant who had collapsed on the cobblestones sprang up beside Vaslav on the table. He raised his bottle of *monopolka* in the air. "Down with the Muscovites and the bloody Jews!" he shouted. He pointed at Vaslav, "Here stands the greatest traitor and Jew-lover in Bociany. He drinks with them at the inn! He's our calamity!"

A third, older peasant jumped onto the table and separated Vaslav and the young peasant, who were already at each other's throats. A deafening noise spread over the marketplace as the storm broke among the peasants. The dancing turned into a dance of raised arms and clenched fists. The musicians went on playing loud and fast. Several men were already fighting hand to hand. The camisoles had been quickly thrown off and cast to the ground. The women retrieved them and tried to tear the fighting men apart, themselves getting entangled in the brawl.

"Disperse, people, disperse!" the gendarmes shouted, waving their sabers. No one paid any attention. The musicians of the fire brigade stopped playing and rushed to protect their chief, Vaslav, who was being attacked from all sides. They pounded their brass trumpets over the heads of his assailants.

Another young peasant jumped onto one of the tables and pointing at Vaslav, shouted, "Get him, brothers! Get that filthy bloodsucker!"

The older peasant pushed him off the table with such force that the young man somersaulted in the air before landing on the ground.

"Friends!" the older peasant cried out, "Friends, why kill one another? There!" He pointed to the Jewish houses. "There lies the pestilence! There are our true enemies!"

"He's right! Hear! Hear!" voices responded from all sides. "Let's get rid of the vermin! Burn out the bastards!"

"Vermin! Vermin!" echoed the voices of the drunken and confused men as they turned toward the synagogue and the Jewish houses. But the women, acting as one, ran ahead of them and blocked their way, so that the men could not advance. "Over our dead bodies!" they screamed "Don't move! You'll catch the plague! Think of the children!"

The children screamed. The priest and the county officer appeared from behind the crowd, flanked by the gendarmes brandishing their sabers. The incensed men tried to brush them aside. "Set fire to the houses! Burn them down to the ground!" they roared, their teeth bared, their mouths drooling.

The priest now stood in front, facing the mob. He raised his arms for silence, but he spoke in such a faint voice that no one could hear him. He tried to raise his voice, but he suddenly felt faint. His housekeeper pulled him away. Rubbing his chest with both hands, he allowed himself to be led off.

Vaslav, his nose bleeding, his uniform smeared with mud and blood, was helped to his feet by his wife and children and the members of the fire brigade. He pushed them aside and on shaky legs made his way to the water pump. There he jumped on top of the platform and pointed to the priest, who was slowly walking in the direction of the church. "Ey, holy Father!" he called after him. "Why do you wash your hands of us? Your flock of sheep needs you! So come back and tell them what to do. Go on!"

"Let him go! We don't need him! And we don't need you!" a young man shouted.

"We don't need either of you!" another young voice confirmed.

"People!" Vaslav roared, straining the veins of his neck. "Listen to me, people!" His voice was hoarse, but he sounded completely sober. "Do with me what you please, but remember, it takes only one spark from a match, and we'll be burned down along with the Jews! And they aren't our real enemies. They're too weak and too wretched themselves. It's the Muscovites, brethren, remember that! So let's go home and celebrate the holiday. There is still roast pork to be eaten to fortify our bodies and hearts. Yes, strong and united we must be ready to face our true enemy!"

"Don't you tell us what to do! We don't want you for a leader!" someone yelled.

"We do want him!" some older men and the women countered.

"I am your leader!" the county officer shouted from where he stood, surrounded by the gendarmes. He sounded unsure of himself and appeared to be nervous and frightened. The gendarmes, utterly confused, brandished their sabers.

"Traitor! Muscovite bootlicker!" The crowd turned on the county officer. The young peasants moved forward toward him with raised fists.

"Leave him alone!" Vaslav roared. His nose was still bleeding, his lips were red with blood, but he paid no attention to it. "Remember, the Cossacks will make you pay for every hair he loses from his head!"

"Don't order us around! Shut up!" voices from the crowd yelled at Vaslav.

"Yes!" others joined in. "He acts as if all of Bociany belonged to him, and our women, too!" Uneasy guffaws were heard.

"It's a lie!" the older women exclaimed. "He's an excellent fire chief! He's Father Stanislav's brother, his own flesh and blood!"

"May they both roast in hell!" young voices called amid the general laughter.

"Jesus Maria!" a woman cried, crossing herself. "Our children are possessed by the Devil!" The other women stared at the young men, stupefied.

"It's you, you stupid cows, who are blinded by the Devil!" a young man shouted fiercely. "Did not our saintly Father Stanislav give away his bastard to be raised by the Jews? Didn't Abele the Fool confess it himself?"

A hush fell on the crowd. The subject had never been brought up in public before. The older women, in a fury of frustration, threw themselves on the young man who had spoken, and their husbands followed suit. A fight broke out between the young and the old, fathers against sons. They had been waiting a long time to have it out in the open. But it was not the same kind of fighting as before; it did not lack passion, but it lacked the determination to really hurt one another.

So the day passed, until rage and alcohol made everyone hungry. In groups and families, the young and the old dispersed slowly to their houses to eat the suckling piglets that were roasting in the ovens.

For a few hours, the tension eased among the Jews in the synagogue and in the houses. Intoxicated by drink and with their bellies full, the peasants could be counted on to be quiet, at least for a while. People ventured out of the synagogue, skirted the deserted marketplace and rushed home for a bite to eat to strengthen themselves and see how those hidden in the houses had fared.

Yossele, too, went home. There he found Binele sitting on her cot and looking out through the closed window. Afraid that her father might beat her, she made a dash for the door as soon as he entered.

He called her back, went over to the barrel that stood near the door, washed his hands, and ordered, "Make something to eat." She obeyed. Taking a quarter of a loaf of bread from the cupboard and a jug of cold chicory coffee from the stove, she placed them on the table in front of him. He beckoned her to join him at the table, and have some bread and coffee. The two of them said the benediction over the bread and ate in silence. They avoided each other's glance. When he had finished, Yossele stood up. He waved a finger warningly at Binele, "Don't you dare crawl out through the window."

She rushed toward him, "Tateshie, please take me with you."

"You're staying here."

"Take care, I beg of you," she whispered.

He was gone. She heard him lock the door from outside.

Yossele joined the other members of his guard to discuss strategy. Meanwhile the *rov* called a meeting of his advisors, while Shmulikl gathered with his followers in his dining room, and the members of the Bund assembled in an attic. The lessee's four-wheeler, carrying members of his family, drove past the marketplace in the direction of the landlord's manor, which was the safest place to weather the storm.

After a few hours, melancholy singing could be heard coming from the peasants' huts, mingled with the sound of harmonicas and the cries of children. It was then that Vaslav Spokojny found Yossele Abedale in the backyard of the Potcheyov.

"Have you seen Abele?" Yossele rushed toward him.

Vaslav was haggard and beaten. He stared at Yossele through bloodshot eyes, his face full of blotches and swellings. "You must save my life,

Yossele," he sputtered. "My brothers . . . my own people . . . they spat on me . . . They spat me out from their midst . . . " He himself was spitting blood as he talked. Yossele noticed that two of his front teeth were missing.

Yossele had no patience for him. He had more important things to worry about than Vaslav's condition. "Have you seen Abele?" he repeated.

Vaslav grabbed Yossele by the lapels. "I want to become a Jew, do you hear me, Yossele? I want to become one of your people, so help me God, or I'll kill myself."

Yossele stared at him. Vaslav did not seem drunk now, he seemed deranged. Yossele was unable to suppress a smile. Human beings were capable of surprising one another in the most incredible ways. "Goodthinking!" he replied ironically. "But for that you would have to be circumcised first, and at your age it's a rather uncomfortable procedure. Afterwards, you're more liable to remain prostrate as a corpse than to get up as a Jew, so you won't have to kill yourself."

"Don't mock me or try to frighten me, Yossele. I can accept death as easily as you people. I already have a Jewish soul, anyway."

"You do?" Yossele was still sarcastic. "Then prove it by telling me how great our danger is."

"May the Almighty protect you."

"And how about you? Will you help us?"

"I'll do what I can."

"So where is Abele?"

"He was at the whore Magda's the day before yesterday. Where he is now, I swear I don't know."

"Go and find him for me!" Yossele requested, surprised at his own emphatic tone.

"I'll try. I'll see that nothing happens to him, that nothing happens to you and to Hindele. I'll defend her with my own life. She'll help me to become a Jew."

Yossele squirmed. "Stop that nonsense! And you'd better leave her alone, I'm warning you. If you have her good at heart, then let me know when your people are going to attack us. Now go. We mustn't be seen together. We Jews are contagious, remember?"

Somehow the day passed, but the night did nothing to dissipate the fears of the Jews. On the contrary, the dark increased them. The following day was a weekday. The peasants left for work in the landlord's fields.

They also had much work to do on their own small properties before the autumn rains started. The younger men and women spent the whole day at the factory. There the young Jewish workers who belonged to the Bund approached the peasant youths whom they had been trying to convert to socialism. The real enemy of the Polish peasants, they argued, were not the Russian masses, but Tsar Nicholas, and Tsar Nicholas was the enemy of the Jews as well.

"Then why do you use the blood of our children to make your matzos? And why do you abduct them and circumcise them, forcing them to be Jews?" the peasant boys asked.

The Bundists explained that these were stories made up by Jew-haters; that when the enemies of the people wanted to divert attention from the real culprits, they invented all kinds of stories against the Jews; that as a matter of fact, the Jews never used blood, not even the blood of animals; and that it was very difficult to convert a person to Judaism, even if that person wanted it badly.

"Then what about Abele the Fool?" the peasant boys asked.

"Abele the Fool," the Bundists explained, "was found at the *besmedresh* already circumcised."

"Then the Jews circumcised him somewhere else," the gentile youths insisted. "The priest and his late housekeeper found a way. You told us yourselves that the priests are two-faced and not much better than your rabbis."

"True, the priests and rabbis keep the people in ignorance. They serve the rich and powerful," the Bundists confirmed. "But get it out of your heads that Abele is a Gentile, and the priest's son at that."

"What do you mean, get it out of our heads? Abele said so himself. Ask Magda the Widow and you'll know."

Abele the Fool had recently grown particularly restless and had taken to wandering about Bociany and the villages at night. A couple of nights before the holiday of Dozynki, he had come to the house of Magda the Widow. Magda was a man-hungry woman. She had invited Abele into her house, fed him a good meal, gotten him drunk on *monopolka,* and then taken him to bed with her.

Abele had enjoyed himself tremendously, so he had paid Magda another visit the following night. But that night, a woman neighbor had knocked on

Magda's door before dusk. She had wanted to ask Magda for some herb broth, to ease her husband's indigestion. Magda's hut consisted of one room, with the bed standing near the door, and in that bed lay Abele, naked. It was no use telling him to wake up and dress because he would take so much time that whoever was behind the door would become suspicious. So Magda had another idea. She quickly tied Abele to the bed with a thick rope, and admitting her neighbor, had taken her straight to the bed where Abele's long, naked body lay limply in sweet oblivion.

"You see," she said to her neighbor, "I caught him outside peeking in through the window, and I won't let him go until he tells me who he is and where he came from. If you ask me, his being a fool is nothing but a pretense. He's not stupid, and he understands our language. But the Jews trained him to behave like this."

The neighbor, curious, looked directly at the naked Abele. "Why is he asleep?" she asked and bent over him. "He really looks like the priest," she said.

"He fell asleep because I gave him too much liquor. I was too impatient and wanted him to tell me everything quickly."

"And why is he naked?"

Magda leaned closer to her neighbor. "I wanted to check whether he's really circumcised. I couldn't bring myself to believe that our saintly priest . . . But when I saw that he was circumcised, I realized that what our people are saying is true. We shouldn't fool ourselves. Our saintly Father Stanislav isn't any different from his debauched brother Vaslav, who has forced my door open more than once in the middle of the night. I don't have to tell you about Vaslav, do I? The only difference is that his saintly brother is smarter than he is, so he is more skillful at covering up the traces."

"Don't you think that the Jews circumcised Abele by force?" the neighbor asked, completely forgetting what she had come to Magda for in the first place, so enthralled was she by what she heard and saw.

Magda hated the Jews worse than she hated the priest, but she wanted to display her sense of justice to her neighbor, so she shook her head and said, "Be it as it may, the priest is as guilty as the Jews in this matter. The priest and his former housekeeper, may she rot in the ground for her sins, wanted to keep their bastard nearby, to keep an eye on him. But they didn't want a soul to know about it, so they paid the price of having him circumcised, which, of course, suited the Jews just fine."

"Is that so?" The neighbor shook her head in horror. Then she gave Magda a quick smile. "I'm going to have another good look. I've never seen a circumcised . . . "

"Look as much as you please," Magda waved her hand generously.

The neighbor could not allow herself the luxury of looking for too long, because she suddenly remembered that her husband was in their cottage suffering from cramps. She asked Magda for the bottle of herb broth. At the door, her face all flushed, she whispered, "Keep him here till morning. As soon as my old man gets better, he'll come in to take care of him the way a man should. Don't worry, the truth will rise to the surface like oil on the water."

In the morning, Abele opened his eyes and looked about with a tremendous sense of well-being. Never before had he slept in a bed that was so soft and smooth. But suddenly, he became aware that he was tied with a rope, and that there was a circle of heads, belonging to both men and women, looking down at him. They started yelling at him. One of them smacked his thigh. The slaps followed one another with increasing ferocity. He began to feel sore in every part of his body. His skin felt as if it were cracking open. In the darkness that encompassed him, he slowly realized that they wanted him to say yes to the torrent of incomprehensible questions that they shouted at him.

Wracked by pain, he shouted, "Yes! Yes! Yes!" until he was hoarse. Thus did the truth surface like oil on the water, and he saved his life, having learned that there was no pleasure for which one did not have to pay one way or another. He also realized that if he went back to Yossele's shed on the Potcheyov, Magda or one of the other peasants might find him whenever they felt like beating him up. So he decided to hide in the birch wood.

## 20

TWO DAYS AFTER THE CELEBRATION of Dozynki, a messenger arrived from the Jewish women and children who had left for Chwosty. The messenger told the *rov* that although the women and children had been hospitably received by the congregation of Chwosty and all had found quarters with Jewish families there, they absolutely insisted on returning home to Bociany. Come what may, they wanted to be with their husbands and those children whom they had left behind. Meanwhile, the Jews of Bociany began to worry about how to go about making a living. The shops on the Potcheyov had to be reopened as soon as possible because the danger of starvation was becoming more serious than the danger of an attack by the Gentiles.

For their part, the Gentiles themselves were having a difficult time managing without the Jewish shops. They began plying the county officer with questions about the fever epidemic among the Jews. The county officer went to Shmulikl, and standing at a distance from him, so as not to catch the "plague," inquired about the situation. Shmulikl was in no hurry. He wanted to let the Gentiles see how much they needed the local Jews. He suggested to the *rov* that they wait until after the next market day.

That market day was one of sheer misery for the peasants. Despite their fear of the epidemic, they, too, had to earn a living. So they arrived with their milk products, vegetables, and fruit and stood in the silence of the marketplace the whole day. Not a single Jew came near their carts, and they were forced to return to the villages with all their goods. Then the news was communicated to the county officer and the priest that the Rabbi of Chwosty had performed a miracle and cured the Jewish children of the Jewish disease. Wagons were sent to fetch the women and children. They returned to Bociany the same day to be greeted by great jubilation and excitement. To the families, the five days of separation had seemed like ages, and when they were at last reunited, there was no real need to pretend that Bociany was not overjoyed, although worry still gnawed at people's hearts. As for Yossele Abedale, he also had another reason for contentment. His sons-in-law had brought him the news from Chwosty, that Hershele had left the yeshiva there to continue his Talmudic studies at the world famous yeshiva in Lublin.

The shops on the Potcheyov opened and the peasants came with their carts loaded with goods, even though it was not a market day. Jew and Gentile greeted one another with delight, bought and sold merchandise, while secretly eyeing one another with suspicion.

The priest, on his way home from administering the last rights to a dying man, stopped by Shmulikl the Doctor's shop to express his pleasure that Bociany had regained its equilibrium, although personally he was downhearted. He sensed a drastic change in attitude toward him in the villages. "How is it," he asked Shmulikl, "that the Rabbi of Chwosty was able to cure a disease and you could not?"

Shmulikl responded in his elegant Polish, "The Rabbi of Chwosty can cure only those diseases for which medicine has no cure."

"Then what do we need medicine for, if the rabbis can cure so easily through miracles?"

"Because medicine proceeds down a sure, straight path," said Shmulikl, never at a loss for an answer, "while the rabbis cannot always perform miracles. They need to be blessed with a moment of grace, so that the Almighty's spirit can rest on them. Miracles are in fact rare in these times."

"That's true," the priest shook his head sadly. "The people have allowed the power of faith to weaken. It's my opinion, Panie Doctor, that the reason is that people are confused by too many religions." He smiled wistfully. "It would be a true blessing if the Jews took on the religion of Jesus Christ our Lord. Then they would be rid of all their groundless fears as well."

Shmulikl suspected that the priest had understood the real reason why the Jewish women and children had been sent to Chwosty, but he pretended not to have heard the priest's remark about Jewish fears. Politely, he accompanied the priest to the door. As he did not have much patience for him that day, he replied with a note of barely controlled anger in his voice, "The Jews do not take on the religion of Jesus because Jesus' religion is the religion of the Jews. The Jews simply refuse to accept a religion centered on Jesus."

Shmulikl followed the priest outside. His eyes surveyed the entire marketplace. Life had resumed its normal rhythm, but he felt an undercurrent of tension in the air. The shtetl was like a boiling pot on the verge of explosion. He had known from the start that the *rov's* scheme would accomplish nothing more than to postpone the danger for a while. Something had happened to the peasants. They were like a herd without a shepherd, disillusioned, confused, frustrated, tense, and miserable. Therein lay the danger to the Jews.

The peasants were indeed in an uneasy state of mind. They could not make out what was happening to them. They had lost trust in their priest, whom they had loved like a father. The county officer was an idiot and a

Muscovite bootlicker. Vaslav Spokojny had been the only one among them who knew how to lead both a fire brigade and an entire community, despite the fact that he was also a drunkard and a bed hopper. But something had come between him and the younger men, and now he no longer had the wish to lead anybody. He had even lost his passion for the bottle, and he walked about as if every spark of life had gone out of him. The community needed a leader, especially now, during these unsettled times, when a rift had developed between the young and the old. Fathers and sons no longer saw eye to eye on important matters. There was no longer any obedience. Sons left home without asking permission, and fathers clung more stubbornly to the soil than ever; it seemed to them the only stable thing left to hold on to.

And just as the peasants felt at a loss, having lost trust in their spiritual leader, so Father Stanislav felt dejected and abandoned. Despite his deteriorating physical condition, he started taking long walks on the Narrow Poplar Road every morning, during which he searched his soul and prayed for long periods of time.

It was during one of these walks that Yossele Abedale, who had always avoided him, caught up with the priest. "Please, Panie Priest," Yossele called after him, trying to control his voice. "Please help me. It's a question of a human life!" The priest stopped and Yossele came up to him, still panting and perspiring profusely as he held on to his beard. "It's about Abele the Fool. He has disappeared. I've heard that the peasants are keeping him somewhere. He's a helpless creature, a mute animal. He knows nothing and understands nothing, but he's a good soul who would never raise his hand against anyone. Only you, Panie Priest, can save him."

The priest's silvery eyes widened but he remained silent for a long time. Normally, he liked to look at Yossele's face when they spoke, but now his eyes focused on a spot in the distance. At length he asked, "Why do you think the peasants are hiding him?"

Yossele hesitated a moment, wondering whether he should reveal what he knew. Finally he decided that the time was right, and he blurted out, "Because they think that he is one of yours, a Gentile. That he is your bast— that he is probably your son. And that we Jews . . . "

The priest gulped mouthfuls of air, like a fish suddenly grounded. He began to sway back and forth, mumbled something, and suddenly collapsed on the ground at Yossele's feet. Yossele looked around, bewildered. What should he do now? There was not a soul to be seen on the road, and the village houses were far off, across the field. Yossele bent down and stared at the pale, corpselike face with its closed eyes. Finally, he stretched out his arms, picked up the limp body without difficulty—it weighed no more than that of a child—and took the short cut to the presbytery through the fields.

"God!" he muttered. "The yokes you put on me are so heavy that they've become ludicrous. Here I am, carrying the man whose death I've wished for a thousand times. I must look ridiculous with my beard and sidelocks and my black gabardine, carrying him like a baby, him, dressed in his black soutane, the cross I've cursed a thousand times dangling from his neck. It would have been so easy to leave him here, in the middle of the field. But you, Master of the Universe, never give me an easy way out. Here I am looking at the cross suspended from his neck, the sign of *their* hatred towards us, and I feel no revulsion. I feel nothing but a wish to get this chore over with as quickly as I can, nothing else."

Yossele felt numb. His heart did not beat faster than usual, when for the first time in his life, he crossed the churchyard with the body in his arms. He heard voices behind him. Peasants came running after him from all directions. Someone ran ahead of him to knock on the door of the presbytery. Before the housekeeper could open the door, Yossele transferred the priest's limp body into the arms of some of the men who had run after him. Then he hurriedly went off in the direction of the bathhouse.

Vaslav Spokojny, who had been sent for by the priest's housekeeper, arrived at the presbytery two hours later. Shmulikl the Doctor had already stopped by and he had managed to revive the sick man. Vaslav was greeted by the weeping housekeeper who led him into the priest's room. There he saw his brother lying on a bed of bare boards with a small pillow under his head. It was in this room that the priest had spent many hours of many nights trying to commune with the Crucified One.

Father Stanislav recognized his brother and smiled faintly. He raised his head slightly, and whispered, "Come closer, my son."

Vaslav moved forward, his hair and mustache in disarray, an affectionate twinkle in his bloodshot eyes. "I did not come as a son, Stanislav. I came as your brother. How do you feel?"

The priest seemed not to hear the question and shook his head. "You still don't understand, little Vaslav. First of all, you are my son. Come closer. Kneel down beside me and let me forgive your sins against the Lord and against me, too. Let us pray together."

"Stanislav!" Vaslav whispered passionately and fell to his knees at his brother's bedside. "My end has come. I cannot bear the shame. I want to fight and, if need be, to die for the Fatherland like our father did. The young people are getting ready in secret. But they don't want me to join them, let alone make me their leader. I can't bear it. I, the man who more than once saved their lives and their homes . . . They treat me like a piece of dirt. They say that I'm unreliable. They say . . . " He burst into tears.

"You are unreliable." The priest laid his thin hand on Vaslav's head. "You have betrayed me, but you are not the only one. All my sheep have betrayed me, yet your betrayal hurts more than anyone else's." Vaslav raised his tear-stained eyes and peered into those of his brother. There was much suffering in those silvery eyes, in that skeletal face, but the words spoken in a soft warm tone, coming from those pale lips, cut into Vaslav's heart like daggers. "They're saying that this Jewish fool is my bastard, aren't they?" the priest asked.

"Stanislav, brother," Vaslav moaned. "I'm at the end of my rope, don't you see?"

"Aren't they?" the priest insisted.

Vaslav grew irritable and responded with venom in his voice, "Well, isn't he?"

The priest shut his eyes. Two large tears rolled down his sunken cheeks. "May the Lord forgive you," he whispered. "May the Lord not punish me for these words, but sometimes I think that rather than have such a brother and such a congregation, I would sooner be . . . be a Jew." And he crossed himself.

"That's a good one!" Vaslav exclaimed sarcastically. "On that subject, we at least think like brothers! I want to become a Jew, too. Would you like to know why? Because you are a Christian, you saintly, selfish hypocrite. Because my people are Christians, and no one can hate better than a good Christian. You are ashamed of me, you tell me, brother dear. Well, same here. I am ashamed of you!" The anger left him suddenly, and he hung his head. "The truth is that Father would not have been proud of either of us, eh, Stanislav?"

"I shall leave this congregation, if I don't leave this valley of tears first," the priest moaned.

"Don't worry, Stanislav, I will leave it before you do." Vaslav's eyes were swollen with tears. He grabbed his brother's hand. which was resting on a wooden cross by his side, and pressed it forcefully.

The priest raised his eyes to the ceiling and sighed deeply. "A shepherd who is not trusted by his flock is no shepherd." He slipped the hand holding the wooden cross out of Vaslav's grip and placed the cross on his face. He shut his eyes as if to block out Vaslav's words. But Vaslav sat there talking for a long while. Then he wiped his face with both hands, uttered a curse, and rushed out of the room.

In the evening, a rumor spread among the peasants that the priest had almost died when he found out what they were saying about him, and that he had decided to leave Bociany as soon as he was fit to travel.

Now an even greater confusion set in. Father Stanislav had been like a father to the peasants. They had grown up with the image of his exalted face before their eyes. He was a part of their lives, a part of Bociany. Confessing to him was different than confessing to a stranger. It was from him that they learned kindness and humanity, with him that they studied the gospels. He baptized and blessed the newborn, sanctified the union between man and wife, and administered the last sacrament. So gentile Bociany changed its attitude overnight, just as Jewish Bociany had done before it. People's hearts cried out with guilt and compassion for the priest. Even if what they suspected him of were true, was not the priest also made of flesh and blood? Did not the peasant men know what torture it could be to live without a woman? And had not Lord Jesus said that only those completely free of sin should cast the first stone? So the villagers began sending delegations to the priest with fervent pleas that he not abandon his flock.

At length the priest relented and annulled his decision. Gentile Bociany became more devout than ever. The peasants thronged to the church for each mass. And whenever the pale, weak priest appeared on the rostrum, they had the impression that he was the embodiment of the Heavenly Son himself, who had been mocked and laughed at when he carried his cross and took the world's sins upon himself. People left the church, feeling humbled and deeply moved, their hearts overflowing with loving kindness.

A rumor had spread among the peasants that it was the Jews who had caused the rift between the priest and his congregation, that it was they who had spread the lie that Abele the Fool was the priest's bastard. People remembered the incident with Perele, the ritual slaughterer's daughter, that had occurred several years before. Although no one could exactly remember the details of the story, there was no doubt that the Jews violently disliked the priest and wanted to be rid of him because he was a thorn in their side.

On the surface, life in the shtetl went on as before, and commerce proceeded in a normal manner. Abele the Fool, driven out of the birch wood by hunger, had returned to Yossele's chalk shop and was once again a part of the daily picture of the Potcheyov. But tension among the Jews grew; fear ravaged their hearts. At night they would recite the psalms until very late, and during the day they studied the faces of the peasants, taking note of every facial expression and analyzing every word that was uttered.

Meanwhile, the chief gendarme was not sitting with his arms folded. The recent events in Bociany, and the tension that he sensed in the air, convinced him that something was brewing, and he considered it his duty to investigate the matter thoroughly. Before long, his informants came to him with the hair-raising news that hotheads among the young Jews and Gentiles were meeting in lofts and barns, conspiring to overthrow the tsar. Moreover, he was horrified to discover that young peasants were training in the forests, preparing to stage an uprising, and that some had already left the villages to join Pilsudski's Legions and fight for Poland's independence. The chief gendarme almost fainted when he realized what was going on under his very nose. He immediately sent a report to his superior in Chwosty, giving the names and addresses of the conspirators.

The following day, a market day, two detachments of the mounted police, in gray uniforms, with guns slung across their backs, rode into Bociany. They arrested the leaders of the Bundist group and a few young peasants, Polish patriots. Only Ariele, Fishele the Butcher's son, managed to escape the fate of the other Bundist leaders. As soon as he heard that mounted police had been seen approaching the shtetl, he ran off through the fields and the birch wood to seek help from Yoel the Blacksmith. Yoel hid him in the ditch near the road, built a kind of tent over him out of a heap of scrap metal, and covered it with straw. Then he called Wanda, who, to Ariele's surprise, had evidently been in the vicinity of the smithy, and made her sit on top of the heap.

In the shtetl, Gentiles and Jews gathered around the county officer's house, which was near the quarters of the chief gendarme and the jail. The bound prisoners were seated in peasant wagons, which, flanked by gendarmes on horseback, headed for the Wide Poplar Road. Weeping mothers ran after the wagons until they were out of sight. Ariele heard the riders and the wagons loaded with prisoners pass by on the road, a few feet from where he lay hidden beneath Wanda's skirt. She was singing, but the lyrics were curses at the bloody Muscovites.

The shtetl, bewildered, shocked, settled down again to business; the struggle of daily life resumed. The peasants began to murmur among themselves that the sad state of affairs was the fault of the Jews who supported the tsar. Others countered that it was all the fault of the Jews who agitated against the tsar.

That afternoon the storm broke. Suddenly a swarm of peasants appeared in the marketplace armed with shovels, axes, and wooden bars. The peasants who were already in the marketplace grabbed shafts, whips, and ropes, and descended like an avalanche on the shops in the Potcheyov and the surrounding houses. They spread into the alleys and yards, plundering, breaking, crushing, and demolishing everything that stood in their way. Deafening screams rose from the shtetl. The shopkeepers, if they were quick, grabbed the weights from their scales and iron bolts and attempted to defend themselves. The artisans came out with their hammers. The Jewish wagon drivers rode their horses into the crowd of peasants and slashed them with their whips. The women shopkeepers rushed home, or to the heders to protect their children. From the *shtiblekh* and the *besmedresh,* men rushed home to protect their families. Doors were locked and bolted, windows shuttered by trembling hands. Whoever had a cellar hid inside it with his family, or hid his children there. The sound of breaking glass and smashed furniture filled the air. Legs of broken tables, chairs, and dishes flew through the broken windows. White goose feathers from the featherbeds, stained with red, descended like snow on the streets and alleys.

Reb Laibele the Sexton was left alone in the synagogue. His first impulse was to lock the doors and rush home to fetch his wife, Nechele the Pockmarked, and hide her along with the Holy Scrolls in the secret cellar of the synagogue. But he immediately realized that the mob of peasants was approaching. Moving unsteadily on his legs, almost unconscious with fear, he bolted the outer door of the synagogue from the inside, took the Scrolls out of the Holy Ark and carried them down to the cellar. He had an impulse to hide himself there as well, but a voice in his head said, "You are the guardian of this sacred place. Your name is not Laibele, but Laib, Lion, the Lion of Judah." He grabbed the broom that he used to sweep the floor of the synagogue.

"Forgive me, Almighty, for my fear," He muttered through chattering teeth as he locked the inside door and stationed himself in the dark antechamber, the broom in his trembling hands. Shaking convulsively, he wept, "Forgive me, Nechele my wife, for having abandoned you. My time to be martyred for *Kiddush Hashem* has arrived. I cannot afford to miss it." He waved the broom in the darkness as if he were practicing with a lethal weapon.

There was a deafening noise on the other side of the door. Shouts. Hoots. Then the voice of a woman crying in Yiddish, "Help!"

Reb Laibele screamed with the woman, "Help!"

Heavy blows pounded on the door of the synagogue, the beautifully carved front door. It seemed to Reb Laibele that pieces of his own body were being chopped off. The door swayed. Reb Laibele was blinded by sudden daylight. He swung his broom against the human mass that broke in and surged towards the second door. Reb Laibele swung his broom with the strength that sometimes comes from extreme fear. "Out of this holy place!" he roared. He was no longer the tiny dejected Laibele. He was Laib, a lion!

He lasted only a few seconds. A piece of iron hit him on the head, and he collapsed amid the mass of men who kicked him as he fell. The inner door was forced open. The band of peasants filled the hall, breaking and crushing whatever stood in their way. After a while the attackers grew bored; there was no satisfaction in just breaking wood. They wanted blood. On the way out, they kicked Reb Laibele's limp body until it rolled outside. One man shoved it against the wall. Reb Laibele remained prostrate in a pool of mud and his own blood. His beard and sidelocks were glued by blood to the foundation stone of the synagogue. His big *yaptzok*-belly, covered with the ripped ritual undergarment, was mired in the mud, protruding like a balloon that would not deflate.

Yossele Abedale had been in his shop when the storm broke. He grabbed his ax and hesitated for a moment, undecided whether he should run home or summon the watch guard. He immediately realized that he could do neither. He was the guard's leader even when he was alone. So he shouted to Hindele and his other women neighbors in the shops to take cover, and hurried to the backyard of the Potcheyov, where Abele the Fool lay hiding. He grabbed him by the collar and dragged him out of the shed.

"Look what's going on, look!" he shouted. "But don't be afraid, boy!" Quickly he handed Abele the iron beam he used to bolt his shop. "Here! Get yourself through to my house and let no one inside, but no one!" He pushed Abele forward, and tightening the grip on his ax, swung it right and left to make a way for himself to Fishele the Butcher's shop. He wanted Fishele and his butcher boys to join him in putting together a defense unit now that the mob had lost interest in looting and demolishing the shops on the Potcheyov and was milling about the marketplace and the streets and alleys. But the butcher shop was bolted. For a split second, Yossele thought that he saw Yoel the Blacksmith arriving on horseback from the Wide Poplar Road. He wanted to get himself through to him, but then he saw him no more. In any case, it would have been impossible to reach Yoel.

Screams and wailing could be heard all over the marketplace. The cobblestone pavement was cluttered with broken wood, milk cans, and fruits and vegetables that had spilled from the overturned carts. Here and there, puddles of blood like red mirrors reflected a red sky. There were no Jews in sight, except for the wounded lying amid the broken carts and neighing horses. Yossele tried in vain to reach the wounded. The peasants, madness in their eyes, were running about, trying to decide which house to attack next. It seemed that the only house they did not dare attack was that of Shmulikl the Doctor. Yossele, who ran from one shady corner to another, concluded that the danger was too great and that it made no sense to stay where there was little that he could do by himself. He rushed into the yard of the Potcheyov, crossed it, got out by the rear side, and raced in the direction of his street.

A crowd of peasants was pouring out of his street. "He's coming! He's coming!" they shouted. Yossele hid behind a gate. He saw Abele the Fool running after the mob, roaring with savage laughter. Risen to his full height, he looked like an ax-wielding giant.

Abele had obeyed Yossele's orders not to let anyone cross the threshold of the latter's house. Yossele's daughters, Binele among them, along with his sons-in-law and his grandchildren, were hiding inside. Binele had not gone to work at the factory since the first days of unrest in the shtetl. Peeking through the window, she saw a familiar face flash by among the attackers, who, spurred on by Abele's defense, doubled their efforts to break into the house. The man resembled Yadwiga's father, Yanek, but she was not sure it was he. The peasants knocked the iron beam out of Abele's hands. Abele suddenly remembered the fun he'd had watching the ritual slaughterer at work. He tore an ax out of a peasant's fist and the next moment, laughing joyously, split the heads of the two men nearest him. As they fell to the ground, Abele gave a victorious hoot. He stretched to his full height and again swung the ax above his head. The peasants were paralyzed with fear at the sight of this giant with his laughing, childish face, who seemed to fear nothing.

"He's Beelzebub!" one of them called as the mob turned and fled. Abele ran after them, chopping down a few more with his ax. The peasants ran out into the marketplace. Whooping and laughing, Abele chased them. Suddenly a hail of cobblestones descended on him. One stone hit him on the head. He swayed from side to side until he collapsed. As he fell, his hand knocked against the body of a dead woman, and the ax slipped from his grasp. A peasant picked it up and ran away.

Yossele looked around. The mob had thinned out and was now moving in the opposite direction, southward. He dashed over to Abele and saw that the slain woman was his neighbor Brontchele the Professional Mourner. He dragged first her, and then Abele, into the nearest backyard and rushed home to check on his family. With the help of his sons-in-law he brought Abele back to the house and carried Brontchele's body back to her home. She had been on her way to the *besmedresh* to fetch her youngest son when the mob had attacked and slain her.

Hindele, her daughters, and Shalom with his family were all hiding in Manka the Washerwoman's house. Manka had taken them in on the spur of the moment. But then she began to fear for her visitors' safety. Her daughter Marysia, by now a pretty young woman of marriageable age, grumbled that if any of her suitors found out about her mother hiding Jews in their home, her life would not be worth living. Manka feared that Marysia herself might betray them. Fortunately for Marysia, her "Uncle," Vaslav Spokojny, drove his fire wagon into the yard at the very peak of the upheaval. Vaslav had first climbed the stairs to Hindele's loft. Not finding her there, he burst into Manka's house, bellowing, "Where is Hindele?" He was completely sober, yet seemed intoxicated by something much worse than alcohol. With Manka's help, Hindele and her family climbed onto the fire wagon, and in full view of the oncoming peasants, Vaslav drove off with them toward the Wide Poplar Road, until he brought them safely to the foot of the Blue Mountain. There he let them off, all except Hindele. "Climb to the top, quickly! The miller will give you shelter!" he called out to the bewildered Shalom. "I'm taking your mother to fetch provisions!"

"What?" Shalom stared at savage-looking Vaslav. But before he could utter another word, Vaslav's whip snapped through the air, and the next moment, Shalom saw the figure of his mother bouncing up and down in the rear of the fast-rolling wagon. He saw her turn back her head and could hear her shouting, "Go, Shalom! Quickly! Go!"

Shalom's pregnant wife clung to him as he carried their baby daughter in his arms. His sisters Gitele and Shaindele, trembling with fear, huddled next to him, as they pulled his other weeping daughter by the hands. Mechanically, he pushed them up the hill, urging them on with incomprehensible words, until they arrived at the top, where the house and the mill stood. The house was surrounded and guarded by Reb Faivele's devoted workers and servants. The house itself was silent, doors and windows shut. But the people inside had been peering out through the windows. As soon as the small group appeared on the flat surface of the yard, the dogs raced forth to attack them. Yacov burst through the front door and chased the dogs away. The first thing he asked Shalom, as he helped him get the girls and Shalom's wife and children into the house, was "Where is Mameshie?"

Fredka appeared on the verandah and she, too, helped herd the badly frightened group into the house.

"Vaslav took Mameshie with him to get provisions," Shalom sputtered out.

"Provisions? What do we need provisions for? I don't like it!" Yacov exclaimed. The next moment he was racing in the direction of the stable.

Shalom ran after him. "I'm coming with you!"

"Heaven forbid!" Yacov yelled back. He grabbed a pick that was leaning against a corner of the stable and mounted Sussi. The gentile workers gathered outside called after him not to leave, but he was already out of earshot, riding down the hill at a furious speed. He felt not the least frightened but rather relieved. Worry had preyed on his mind since the news of the pogrom reached the mill. He had felt frustrated at being unable to rush to Bociany to be with his mother and family. Now he felt better, but only for a few minutes. The road was empty. The peasants' houses at the side of the road looked desolate. Only animals roamed in the yards. All the villagers seemed to be in the shtetl, amusing themselves! And where was his mother? He heard the voice of a frightened boy calling within him, "Mameshie, were are you? Mameshie, help!" He was stiff with anguish. He was the small boy escaping from the peasant children who had wanted to crucify him. But it was his mother who was now in danger. It did not matter, she and he were one in that moment of terror. An icy wave surged over his heart and froze it, stopping his thoughts. He was aware of nothing but the desire to catch up with Vaslav and see the face of his mother again.

The noise from the shtetl rang in his ears. Hoots, screams, the sound of wood being broken, of walls collapsing and glass cracking. The road was still empty; no wagons were in sight. Where had Vaslav vanished with the wagon? Had he taken Hindele to his village? No, that was unlikely. Where then could he have gone with her? Perhaps to the birch wood? Of course! He had taken her to the birch wood. Where else? To kill her, perhaps to rape her first and then drown her in the lake! No use asking why Vaslav would do such a thing, despite being on friendly terms with Yacov's mother. He was capable of it. There was no doubt of that. They . . . *they* were capable of anything. An icy fear gripped his ferociously pounding heart. *"Shma Yisroel! Shma Yisroel!"* he mumbled hoarsely to himself.

Suddenly he saw the abandoned fire wagon in the middle of the field; the horse, still harnessed, was peacefully nibbling at the grass. At the edge of the birch wood Yacov dismounted Sussi and tied her to a tree with trembling hands. He waded into the forest, walking quickly but trying not to make any noise. He made straight for the lake, which he could soon see shimmering in the distance, peering at him from between the thick foliage of some massive oak trees. He thought that he heard a voice, the sound of a man's broken whispers. No, there was silence, only the leaves rustling and the birds chirping. If his mother was there, still alive, why didn't she scream? Why didn't she plead with Vaslav and beg him to have pity on her? Where was she? There was only that silence ringing in his ears, heightening his alarm. Again he heard the strange voice, but now it sounded like a child's whine. A child was whining, a baby perhaps?

Suddenly Yacov saw something big and bulky moving up the trunk of an oak tree that stood against the silvery background of the lake. The lake shimmered, full of dancing shadows. Perhaps the thing moving up the tree was nothing but the lake's shadowy reflection? Yacov crept closer, quietly, warily, holding his breath, angry at his heart for beating so loudly. Then he saw the bulk of a man clumsily climbing the tree, and heard him panting and whining, like a bear impatient to get himself to the honey high up in a beehive. It was Vaslav. Now Yacov heard words, hoarse broken words that made no sense.

"Watch me do it! Watch me, little woman! Look at me, look at me, Hindele, my Angel of Mercy!" Then there was a squealing sound. Yacov, frozen in place, watched Vaslav from behind a tree. He could no longer hold back the groans. At the same time, he heard Vaslav call Hindele's name again. Where was she? Where on earth was she?

Then Yacov saw her. She was tied to a birch tree just across from the oak that Vaslav was climbing. Her black-sleeved arms were turned back, embracing the white trunk behind her. Her hands were tied at the wrists with her handkerchief. Her mouth and chin were covered with her head scarf. She had no wig on and the crop of short hair on her skull made her head look like the protruding stump of one of the tree's lopped-off branches. Yacov gripped the pick tightly in his fist. Only a few trees separated him now from Hindele. He pushed forward, cautiously moving from one tree to the next. Vaslav could not see him. He had reached one of the oak's solid, protruding branches and was preoccupied with climbing onto it. He seemed to be attaching something to the branch.

Yacov finally reached the birch to which his mother was tied. Softly he tapped her on the shoulder. "Mameshie," he whispered through his parched throat. "It's me, Yacov." She did not react. Her head hung limply over her shoulder. *"Shma Yisroel!"* Yacov mumbled, feeling faint in all his limbs.

"Look at me, Hindele. Watch me do it, Mother in Heaven! In the name of the Lord, of the Son and the Sacred Spirit!" Vaslav cried out loudly. Then there was a horrendous cracking of boughs. Vaslav threw himself down the large branch, swinging, and swaying in the air, suspended from a rope that was tied around his neck. As if he were mimicking Hindele, his head, too, was bent to the side, while his grizzled mop of hair obscured his face.

Yacov let out a muffled shriek. It took a long while before his clumsy shaking hands managed to untie the handkerchief from around Hindele's wrists and then remove the head scarf from around her mouth.

"Water . . . " she mumbled, and slumped into his arms.

She was alive! He was strong now, very strong. He had carried so many sacks of flour at Reb Faivele's mill in order that he might now carry his mother toward the edge of the wood and lift her onto Sussi's back, as if she were the lightest sack of flour that he had ever carried. He mounted Sussi right behind her and slowly, ever so slowly, agonizingly slowly, and devoid of any fear in his stupor, he brought her to safety on top of the Blue Mountain.

At length, the county officer and the gendarmes appeared in the shtetl's marketplace and yelled at the crowd to disperse. They took up positions in front of the church, and the storm subsided. Peasants emerged from the streets into the marketplace and helped one another right the overturned carts and retrieve as much of their merchandise as they could. Their losses were substantial. Losing their reason and beating up Jews was a luxury they could ill afford in these hard times.

The county officer and the chief of the gendarmes began making order as well. They lifted the *rov,* whom they found badly beaten, lying between the carts. Blood oozed from his black hair and sidelocks as they carried him to his house. During the height of the attack, the *rov* had torn himself out of his wife's and the ritual slaughterer's restraining arms and had run out to help protect his congregation with his bare hands.

As the gendarmes made their way from one ravaged shop to another, they came upon Reb Senderl the Cabalist, safe and sound in his soap shop. He was sitting on his mat with Fishele the Butcher wailing beside him. A miracle had occurred to Reb Senderl. He had been studying the *Book of*

*Creation* to calm himself after the cavalry led off the Jewish prisoners, and he was still studying when the pogrom had begun. At the onset of the general confusion, Hindele the Scribe's Widow had rushed by with her son Shalom and his family on their way to Manka's house, and she had swung shut the door to Reb Senderl's shop. Reb Senderl had blown out the light of his dirty naphtha lamp and sat down on his mat in the darkness. There was nothing else that he could do to save himself, so he had decided to meet his Maker in relative comfort, while chanting the psalms. The peasants had swung the door back and forth as they passed, but never entered the dark shop.

As for Fishele the Butcher, who now sat wailing in Reb Senderl's arms, he had locked himself up in the butcher shop after the butcher boys had run out armed with knives and axes, and had barricaded the door with chopping blocks. He, who had recently shown such heroism and been so ready to sacrifice his life for the community, had abandoned even his wife and children in this hour of trial. In spite of everything, he was no longer the man he had once been. So he now sat beside Reb Senderl, crying with shame.

The chief gendarme sent a report of the events to his superior in Chwosty. The cavalry officers in their gray uniforms again appeared in Bociany and arrested the wounded *rov* and Abele the Fool, whose head had swollen to the size of a watermelon. No peasants were arrested. The *rov* was arrested because he was responsible for the Jewish community, and Abele because he had slain three men and wounded many others. The *rov* was released the following day, but Abele disappeared from Bociany without a trace.

The night after the pogrom, Yossele Abedale and the members of the watch guard went from house to house to see how the families had weathered the storm. He and his men helped Shmulikl the Doctor set up a provisional hospital in the poorhouse. Shmulikl asked for a few girls to help him, and Yossele sent his daughters Dvorele and Binele. As Yossele walked from door to door, checking on who needed to be transported to the hospital, he also recruited girls who were not afraid to go outside and did not mind the sight of blood. He also looked for volunteers among the younger men for his defense group.

He felt guilty about the day before. During the general chaos, none of the defense groups had functioned as they were supposed to, despite the fact that they were all prepared and the attack had been expected. He promised himself never to let such a thing happen again. In the meantime, he considered it his duty to do what he was doing. That night, the shtetl was without a *rov* and the *dian* was an old, broken man. Reb Laibele the Sexton was dead, and Fishele the Butcher had proved to be a coward. The rich Jews had left the shtetl the day before the attack, probably tipped off about the planned police raid on the revolutionaries.

That evening, Yossele climbed the broken stairs leading to Hindele's loft. He found the door locked, and no one answered his knock. When he had descended the stairs, Manka the Washerwoman approached him. "Forgive us," she murmured. "We are not all like that, I swear to you!" When he paid no attention, she ran after him and grabbed his arm. "My cousin Vaslav saved Hindele the Widow's life, did you know that? He took her and the girls and the son with his pregnant wife and children to the miller's farm. He took them in the fire wagon, with all the mad people looking on. He kept them away with the water hose! Did you know that, Yossele?" As Yossele tried to pull away from Manka, she grabbed the tail of his gabardine. "Yossele, you must forgive us. We suffer, too. Suffering doesn't unite people, it divides them. It makes them go out of their minds!"

Yossele pretended not to hear her, although every word that she said penetrated him deeply. In the middle of the attack, as he had stood alone and bewildered in the marketplace, the faces of his children had flashed through his mind and, along with them, Hindele's face. He had suddenly realized how much he cared for her. For a second, he had seen her frail figure as she stood in front of her shelves, defenseless in the middle of the rampage. "Run!" he had called to her as he rushed off to try and protect others. That was the fate of a guardian of the community. He did not guard those who were nearest and dearest to him, and more often than not he could not do anything for the community that he sought to protect. So Vaslav, not he, had been Hindele's savior. But if that was the case, how safe was she? He had to find out! without a moment's hesitation, and despite the late hour, he set out for the Blue Mountain.

There was some mysterious force at work between Yossele and Hindele on the one hand, and Binele and Yacov on the other. It was as if Yossele and his daughter had both sensed that Hindele and her son had lived through some terrible ordeal. When Yossele returned home from the Blue

Mountain in the middle of the night, Binele was waiting up for him. She asked whether he had any news of Hindele and her family. Her question astonished him. Had Binele been aware of what was going on in his heart and mind? His eyes met hers. Obviously, despite their estrangement, there was some mysterious channel of communication still open between his daughter and himself.

"Thank God," he answered, "They are all safe and well." He did not tell her in what condition he had found Hindele and Yacov, nor what had happened to Vaslav.

The next day all the villages were abuzz with the news: Vaslav Spokojny was dead. Yoel the Blacksmith had found him hanging from an oak tree at the edge of the birch wood, near the lake where Kailele the Bride had drowned herself.

## 21

GENTILE BOCIANY grew more peaceful after it had shed the tension that had been pent up for so long. But Jewish Bociany had found no peace yet. Days and weeks passed. The Jewish defense units were on guard night and day, although relations between Jews and Gentiles slowly returned to normal. They could not help it—they needed each other.

When the Jews and the Gentiles first began doing business together after the pogrom, they avoided looking at each other's faces or saying one word more than necessary. But in spite of themselves, the air between them gradually warmed. The Jews, although remaining vigilant and worried, made an effort to push what had happened to the back of their minds and let it sink into a kind of semi-oblivion along with other memories that they preferred to forget—in order to go on with their lives.

The synagogue was restored and already had a new sexton. Nechele the Pockmarked, Reb Laibele's widow, broken and orphaned though she was, took to selling bagels on the Potcheyov. She installed herself and her basket of bagels beside her friend Hindele, and before long she took in two orphaned girls to live with her and raised them as her daughters. Brontchele the Professional Mourner was replaced by another woman, a good, energetic weeper, who was much needed during these days when there was a demand for weepers in almost every house. But Brontchele's home was kept functioning. Yossele's daughters saw to it that life there went on more or less normally. The two families were about to be joined, after all, by the marriage between Dvorele and Brontchele's son, Berele the Moonwalker.

But if the shtetl remembered the victims of the pogrom, like Reb Laibele, the heroic sexton, or Brontchele, or others who had died of their wounds, it completely forgot Abele the Fool. Only Yossele missed him and remembered him, and so for some reason did Hindele. She was recovering quickly from her own ordeal, about which she never spoke.

It was she who once said to Yossele, "You know, Reb Yossele, I always had the suspicion that Abele was not just a human being. That perhaps he was a golem, and that is why, I suppose, he has disappeared from Bociany as mysteriously as he arrived. The way he protected your home and your street makes me think of the Messiah Ben Joseph, who will arrive one day to clear the way for the true savior."

Hindele had returned from the miller's, where she had spent a few days with her family, a changed woman. Yossele could not exactly pinpoint the change. She spoke the way she had always spoken and behaved the way she had always behaved, yet there was a new energy, a new exuberance and love of life radiating from her. She even looked pretty to him sometimes, although her face was now covered with a delicate net of wrinkles and the strands of hair that peeked out from under her wig, which sat lopsided on her head as usual, were as white as chalk. Yossele suspected that the reason for this inexplicable change had something to do with Vaslav's death. Perhaps she felt relieved, having rid herself of a fear that was known only to Yossele, a fear that had haunted her for many years? Yossele was also puzzled by the change that he himself had undergone. He could by no means understand why he had once had such an aversion to the woman.

Binele resumed her long walks on the Wide Poplar Road in the direction of the Blue Mountain. The slaughter in the shtetl, the gory sights she had witnessed from the window of her house and then at the poorhouse, where she was still helping Shmulikl the Doctor, remained vivid in her mind. Every detail was as fresh as if time had no power over it. And yet she tried to convince herself that she did not remember; she refused to remember the pogrom—now or ever.

It was pleasant to walk on the road and allow her gaze to wander ahead to the revolving blades of the windmill in the distance. They looked like ladles stretched out to scoop up the earth from below and to pull down the sky from above. Once on top of the mountain, she did not enter the miller's yard, but sat down on the grass in front of the fence. She picked the bluebottles that surrounded her like a sea and braided them into garlands that she hung around her neck or put on her head. There was a commotion on the other side of the fence. She could hear people talking in peasant language and in Yiddish, but nobody paid any attention to her.

She looked down from the mountain and saw Bociany in the distance, small enough to fit into her palm. A circle of houses with the church at its center, garlanded by the Wide and Narrow Poplar Roads. A sleepy little world, so quiet, calm, like an ants' nest observed from a height. And just as an ants' nest was one with its surroundings, so was Bociany. It was a colorful dot in the middle of a colorful tapestry. Eternal. Life and death, tragedy and joy glided slowly over it like a lazy breeze or swept as violently through it as a hurricane, and yet it remained unchanged.

And beyond Bociany? Beyond it lay the rest of the world. The rest of the world also seemed small from where she was, as though it were possible to walk through it on foot. If the river Sambation flowed along the horizon, where the little red Jews lived in happiness, ignorant of the exile, as her brother Hershele had told her when she was a child—then where on the other side of the ocean was America? She still remembered every word that Yacov had told her, even those words that had made no sense.

One day she saw the boy Abrashka, who had grown considerably since the first time she had seen him. He was playing in the yard when she looked through the fence. She called to him and listened to his chatter. Then she wrestled with him as she did with her nephew. She rolled down the hill with him and then climbed back up on all fours, only to roll down again. As soon as Abrashka saw Yacov come out of the mill, he rushed over to him, waddling like a duckling. Laughing, his black eyes sparkling mischievously, he grabbed Yacov by the sleeve and pulled him outside to Binele. Yacov pretended to be unwilling, but let himself be tugged. He sat down in the grass near a cluster of heather that separated him from Binele.

"How are you?" she asked, squinting against the sun and the radiant light that beamed at her from his eyes. He smiled awkwardly and mumbled something. His gaze fell on the garland of bluebottles she wore on her reddish-yellow head. "Why are you staring at me like that?" she laughed nervously. Nobody had ever looked at her like that before. It was as if he were taking her apart and reassembling her in a different, prettier form. It seemed to her that he could do magic with his eyes, make her feel magnificent, aglow with a particular kind of glamour. But she remembered how ugly she really was. "Are you counting my freckles?" she asked him. "At night they're gone, but they pop out in daylight. How many did you count?"

"I'm not counting your freckles," he said quietly.

"That's because you can't count so many, isn't it? I told you right away that I'm a Marzepa. Now you can see for yourself."

"It's not Marzepa, but Mazepa. And you mustn't call yourself that because it doesn't suit you." He stood up.

Abrashka grabbed him by the trousers. "Don't go yet, Yacov," he begged.

"Will you be coming up here tomorrow, too?" Yacov asked Binele, freeing his trouser leg from Abrashka's hand. "I mean, if all is quiet in the shtetl?"

"Why shouldn't all be quiet?" she stared at him questioningly, although she knew what he meant.

"I mean . . . ever since that day, my mind is always there, at home. My mother is alone with my sisters. Then there is my brother and his pregnant wife and his children. I should have joined the defense unit, even if they didn't do much. It was too unexpected. I think . . . " He did not finish, although he badly wanted to ask how she had weathered the storm, and he wanted to tell her what he himself had gone through on that day. He saw her toss back her braids and he could read in her face that she did not want to talk about these things.

"If I come tomorrow, I'll bring you news of your mother," she said, standing up quickly. She waved at Abrashka rather than at Yacov and strode downhill, the garland around her neck bobbing up and down on her chest.

The next time Binele came up the mountain, she brought Yacov regards from his mother. He summoned his courage to ask Reb Faivele if he could take her inside the mill and show her how it worked. Reb Faivele prodded Yacov with an elbow as if they shared a secret. "By all means," he said. "If I like Yossele Abedale, I see no reason why you shouldn't like his daughter. Why have you turned beet-red? And why are you gaping at me like a golem? Go ahead, call her in."

Yacov escorted Binele inside the mill. Reb Faivele and his helpers pretended not to look in their direction, and Yacov pretended that he did not see their meaningful glances. He showed Binele how the millstones were connected to the axle, which was in turn attached to the blades; he explained how the sails made the millstones work, and showed her the sacks of rye and wheat. He made her compare the rye flour to the wheat flour, and gave her a fistful of rye grains to taste.

Outside, Binele threw back her head to gaze at the squeaking sails. She listened to the flutter of the canvas on the frames. The mill gave off good sounds, pleasant sounds, and the world was full of magic. The young man Yacov was also full of magic. Sometimes he said silly things, but he also knew about things of which she was ignorant. She was not shy and asked him about these things over and over again. He talked to her as if she were the same age as Abrashka, but she did not really mind. She wanted to understand.

"I bet there's no other mill like this one in the whole world!" she cried enthusiastically.

He almost agreed with her. "At least not around here," he said. "The mills in this area are mostly watermills at the tributaries of the Vistula. It's more practical," he inserted this "educated" word, which he had learned from Reb Faivele and his wife.

The language he spoke was too difficult for her. First of all, what were tributaries, and where was the Vistula? And how did a watermill work? Did it have the same kind of sails as a windmill? And what was the meaning of the word "practical," which she had never heard before, not even from the doctor and his wife?

Sometimes Yacov would accompany Binele home, although he tried to make it appear accidental. When Binele reached the end of the hill and started along the road, he would suddenly appear walking along the ditch across from her. "I'm going home to see my mother!" he would call and pretend to pass her. Or he would hold up two rubles and call, "Reb Faivele sent me to the inn for Okevit brandy." Slowly they would each move closer to the center of the road and begin chatting at a distance of two or three feet from each other.

"I've decided to leave Bociany right after Passover," she told him during one such walk. She had actually reached the decision the moment that she mentioned it. The truth was that lately she had been thinking less and less about leaving Bociany. Granted, the shtetl had become more gloomy and boring than ever, but it seemed to her that she had already left it. She felt strangely renewed, despite the fact that she still worked in Shmulikl's makeshift hospital in the poorhouse, where she constantly came in contact with victims of the pogrom. Yet, as she walked beside Yacov, she felt compelled to mention her "decision," to see what his reaction would be.

"Where do you want to go?" he asked in his usual tone of voice, which to Binele now sounded more indifferent than warm.

"You know where, to Lodz," she replied with a touch of irritability. She could not understand how someone who was so much older than she, and who knew so much, could have such a bad memory and be such a blockhead. Did she know of another place to run away to, besides Lodz? He himself had told her that America was on the other side of the ocean and that one needed a steamship ticket to get there. She watched him out of the corner of her eye.

"How do you intend to go there?" he asked.

"With the beggars who come to Bociany every Passover," she had her answer ready. "They set out on the road right after the holidays, don't they? I asked the cook and she told me that the beggars stop in Lodz also."

"Which cook did you ask?"

"What do you mean, which cook?" She was frowning. "The lessee's cook, of course. I'm working for them now. The lessee's wife employed my older sister, but she's getting married, so I'm taking her place. Only part-time for now, to help with the Sabbath preparations, until the sick in the poorhouse can go home. So I'll go along with the beggars to Lodz. That will be practical," she showed off her good memory by using the foreign word. "What the beggars do, I'll do."

"Beg on the road?"

"Why beg on the road?"

"What else do beggars do?"

"I don't beg. They'll beg, and I'll take."

"Steal?"

"What?" She was offended. "I'm Yossele Abedale's daughter!"

"I know."

"So what are you talking about?"

"I don't understand what you mean by taking."

"What's there to understand?" she asked angrily. "I'm talking about food. Taking a piece of bread or a potato is not stealing. Taking money is stealing. Now do you understand?" She bit her lips and broke off the conversation.

He, too, was silent, walking thoughtfully at a distance from her. He wondered about his feelings. What was happening to him? He was regressing to Binele's age, just as when he was with Abrashka and behaved as if he were the little boy's age. And why did the decision of this girl, who was a stranger to him, upset him so much? True, ever since he had read *The Love of Zion,* he saw Binele in his mind, sitting on the Blue Mountain, a garland of bluebottles on her reddish-blond head, and it made him think of Tamar, the heroine of the novel. The Blue Mountain was then transformed in his mind into the Mountains of Judah, and the entire world resembled the world of the Bible. But who was this girl of flesh and blood who walked beside him in her torn dress and disintegrating shoes? He had no idea who she really was, but he felt her presence powerfully. He was very tempted to talk her out of the idea of leaving. But what right did he have to do so?

"So you really want to leave Bociany?" he asked without turning his head, as if he were speaking to himself.

Some question! Hadn't she just told him so? She looked at him disdainfully. "Do I have a choice?"

"You have a good job at the lessee's."

"Sure. I wish it on my enemies."

"What's the matter with it?"

"They are misers, that's the matter! They're bursting with riches, but when I help the cook prepare for the Sabbath, the lessee's wife, may all the teeth fall out of her mouth, counts every slice of fresh bread that I take. I'm only allowed to eat the old bread, she tells me. But a piece of fresh bread tastes better even than an egg cookie, so it tempts me. So if she catches me, she forbids me to take my two lumps of sugar for my tea Friday night. She counts all the lumps of sugar in the sugar dish. Can you believe that? May my father earn as much money in ten years as her husband gives away for charity in one week, while the wife counts the lumps of sugar in the sugar bowl, to make sure the servants don't steal any, Heaven forbid. Can you understand that?"

He did not answer. He seemed to be preoccupied with something else. It occurred to her that perhaps he had been asking her all these questions because he did not want her to leave. He wanted her to keep coming to the Blue Mountain. But she quickly discarded the thought. Why should he care whether she left?

As if he were reading her mind, she heard him say, "Perhaps you ought to try and leave. You can always come back. Won't you miss Bociany?"

"Why should I miss Bociany?"

"Your father and your family are here."

"So what?"

"You don't have any family in Lodz."

"I don't need any."

Passover was still far away. It was autumn and Binele rushed to the Blue Mountain whenever she had a free moment. She did not always get to see Yacov or Abrashka, but the long walk, the time spent looking down on the world and listening to the pleasant squeaking of the windmill did her good. Behind her, on the other side of the fence, was Reb Faivele's yard. There, in the big white house, the beautiful Long Zirele moved about, giving orders. Somewhere inside, Abrashka and his brother were playing or studying. Often she heard Reb Faivele's boisterous voice mixing with the laughter of the workers, or she would hear his angry shouts coming from the *kantur*. There, somewhere on the other side of the fence, Yacov was busy doing something. A peculiar kind of warmth came to her from behind her, making her feel a part of this homestead on the Blue Mountain, as if the pulse of her heart were joined with the pulse of its life.

It was a sultry afternoon. Binele was sitting on the grass on the Blue Mountain, when heavy clouds suddenly appeared in the sky. She could see them arriving from between the blades of the windmill. Down in the valley, gusts of wind rolled out from under the heads of the poplars. The wind raised the dust from the road and rolled it uphill in huge balls. It was going to storm. Binele did not mind. She liked being soaked by rain. But she would have to let her dress dry while wearing it. What else could she do? She did not have another dress. She was wearing Mashele's dress, the one that had been made for Mashele for the occasion of the older sisters' double wedding. Once it had been quite presentable, but now it was too tight in the bosom and too short for Binele. To walk about all day in a wet dress that clung to the body was not very pleasant, so she stood up lazily and with short, slow steps started down the mountain. As soon as she was on the road, she heard steps running behind her and she looked back.

"I'm going home to see Mother," Yacov said as he came abreast of her. "Come, let's run. It's going to pour."

"I bet I'll reach the shtetl before you!" she cried out. They ran as fast as they could, for a long time, sweat streaming down their faces. They panted, each trying to keep up the speed.

The road grew dark. Lightning seemed to split the poplars to the left and to the right. Thunder rumbled like chariots racing through the clouds, rolling across the sky. Then rain descended on the road like beads from God's ripped treasure sacks. Binele and Yacov continued their race for another few minutes. The rain cooled their faces and washed off the sweat, but it was not long before they were both soaked, their shoes so full of water that they could barely lift their feet. Binele slipped in her soaking shoes and fell full-length into a puddle of water. Yacov dashed over and helped her get up. The touch of their hands burned strangely. Their wet fingers were entangled, glued together by water, and it was difficult for them to release the hold they had on each other.

"Devil take my crazy shoes!" Binele fumed, although she felt grateful to the shoes for making her slip and so causing her to feel the touch of Yacov's fingers. That touch was something marvelous beyond words. "I'm going to take them off and walk barefoot," she added, and stepping out of her dripping shoes, lifted them so that they dangled from the fingers of her hand.

Yacov wiped his chin on his sleeve. "Come," he said. "We'll wait under the roof of the stables over there." He, too, removed his shoes, and he and Binele splashed barefoot along the road. Hunched over against the rain, they got to the stables, which they found bolted with beams. Inside, the horses were neighing with fear. A dog whined in the horse-dealer's house. Inside, someone lit a lantern. Binele and Yacov pressed themselves against the wall of the stable to avoid the sheets of rain that cascaded from the narrow strip of roof above their heads. They watched the lightning streak across the sky and waited for the thunder to follow.

Yacov stood at a considerable distance from Binele and wrung out his dripping sidelocks. "Aren't you afraid?" he asked.

"I'm afraid of nothing," she said.

"Don't say that," he waved his finger at her teasingly.

"I'll swear by whatever you like!"

"Weren't you frightened that day?"

"No, I wasn't." She grew thoughtful and added, "There was no time to be frightened anyway. I didn't want them to kill me, nor my father, nor my sisters and their children. But you can try and frighten me with demons or with Asmodeus, or Hell. I don't mind."

"Aren't you afraid of the Almighty either?"

"Why should I be afraid of Him?"

"I'm afraid of Him and of Asmodeus . . . and of you, too."

"Of me? Why?" she laughed. "Because you think I'm stronger then you are, don't you?"

"Yes, maybe that's it."

They stared at each other across the distance. He saw the shape of her body, with its budding breasts vividly outlined by the dress that clung to them. The earth shivered, trembling as if it, too, were a frightened animal. The neighing of the horses and the whining of the dogs made their hearts restless. It seemed as though the neighing and the whining came from inside themselves.

"Look at the lightning!" Binele exclaimed.

"Now comes the thunder. The whole earth is shaking," he said.

"The Almighty is nervous."

"That's what it looks like. It's as if He's tearing His skin off, trying to shed it. Or perhaps His heart is in pain . . . the pain of pleasure."

She did not understand what he meant. "What does the Almighty really do when He sheds His skin? When I feel like shedding my skin in Bociany, I decide to leave and go to Lodz. But where can the Almighty run to?"

"He runs away into Himself."

"Whereto?" She thought that she had not heard him because of the storm, and took a step closer to him. "Why are you standing so far away? Are you afraid I'll eat you?" she giggled uneasily.

"You are a female," he muttered.

"What did you say?" A peal of thunder cracked the air. Binele had a sudden urge to outshout the thunderbolts, so she burst into song at the top of her voice, "'Play, fiddler, play! Melt my sorrow away!'"

He waved his hand at her, "Quiet! I'm not supposed to hear a woman singing."

"I wasn't singing," she roared with laughter. "I was shouting."

He saw her take another step toward him and stretched out his hand to stop her. "We're not supposed to be standing even as close as this. It's a sin."

"I'm not afraid of sin!" she shouted. She did not understand what was happening to her. If Yacov asked her to commit a sin, she would do it. She felt that she wanted to give him everything that she had. She wanted to bare her soul to him with all its secret nooks and crannies, but mainly she longed for another touch of his hand. "If you want me to," she said, "I'll take my dress off for you. Just as on the day my mother bore me, I'll stand before you. If you want me to."

"You're crazy!" he shouted. You're a daughter of Israel, for Heaven's sake, not just . . . "

"Do you want me to?" she laughed.

"Don't you dare!"

She took another big step toward him, until they were standing at arm's length from each other. In another second, she was standing beside him. "Now!" she cried. "Let the Almighty punish me right this minute!" She turned her face up to the sky provokingly and grabbed Yacov's hand. She had to feel the touch of his hand again, to feel again his fingers entangled in hers. A wet, hot touch. Yacov wanted to pull his hand out of hers, but he could not. She held him tightly, as if she did indeed have more power than he.

"Let the Almighty punish me this very minute!" he echoed her. He felt as if lightning had struck him and gone straight through his body, through both their bodies, welding them into one.

They remained standing like that, backs against the stable wall, arms and fingers glued together. Within their hearts, frightened dogs howled and horses neighed. Within their hearts, the Almighty felt like shedding His skin.

On Tuesday, a market day, a circus arrived in Bociany and set up its tents and a carousel behind the churchyard. Binele, who was now employed full-time at the lessee's house, could hardly wait to finish her work so that she could join the excited crowds that streamed from all sides to see the painted clowns, the jugglers, the acrobats, the magicians, and the bear that could dance. That day, she had volunteered to wash the windows of her mistress's bedroom, which faced the marketplace. From there she could hear the organ grinder's music, hear the shouts of the carousel riders, and if she leaned out, she could see the riders soar into the air on their flying seats.

It was cold outside. A bitter wind swept up the loose thatch of the roofs and sprinkled straw and dust on the crowd thronging into the marketplace. The wind undid Binele's braids. Her reddish-yellow hair fluttered through the open window.

She noticed Yacov in the crowd below, and her hand stopped moving on the windowpane. He was trying to make his way through the clusters of peasants and Jews and to navigate between the wagons loaded with vegetables, dairy products, live chickens, geese, and ducks. He almost bumped into a stray goat that was smelling the carts like a customer seeking a bargain. His sidelocks flew up in the air, as if the wind were determined to blow them off. He was rushing, probably eager to see the circus. Binele felt like flying down to him from the window and letting him carry her along. An image flashed through her mind of Yacov soaring up with the wind to greet her in midair, both of them flying off under the wings of his brown sidelocks and her reddish-blond hair.

He drew closer. He must have seen her because his face was raised in her direction. Before long, he was standing at the foot of the wall. "Come to the mill as soon as you can!" he called up at her. Then he turned around and began to make his way back on the same route by which he had come.

Come to the mill! She would have to be out of her mind to go to the mill on this day. She had never seen a carousel before in her life! And yet, if he asked her to come to the mill—she would. She would go there straightaway. She threw away the rag that she was holding, wiped her wet hands on her dress, and jumped down from the chair. In one breath, she raced down the stairs and before long, was bumping into people and carts in the marketplace, pressing herself through the crowd with great force. Then she ran as quickly as she could, hair flying in the wind, until she reached the Wide Poplar Road and caught up with Yacov. Their eyes met, their gazes locked, anxious and questioning.

"Why do you want me to come to the mill today?" she asked, panting. She pushed the strands of hair out of her face.

Before she could tell him about the circus and the carousel, he said, "A flour merchant from Lodz is staying at the inn with his wife and baby. The wife is ill, so he came to ask Long Zirele if she knew of someone who wants to go to Lodz. If you can take care of a baby and are able to help them out on the way, they will take you." He took a deep, deep breath and added, his voice hoarse, "They'll take you in their covered wagon. But . . . there are rumors going around that there will be a war. The Jews of Lodz are buying extra supplies of flour. So do you really want to leave?"

She heard the note of regret in his voice, but she responded angrily, "Of course I do!"

"You don't mind about the war?"

She felt her heart in her mouth. How strange that precisely on this day, when she least felt like going, Yacov himself had come to tell her of the opportunity to leave. "Why should I mind about the war?" she asked, as if to give herself more courage. She tossed back her disheveled hair. "What am I, a soldier or what?" She grasped his sleeve urgently. "Take me to see the flour merchant at the inn!"

They went to the inn. The flour merchant's wife looked very sick. The merchant asked Binele no questions. He assured her that she would have no problem getting back, since the Jews of Lodz were leaving for the shtetlekh by the hundreds, to collect food supplies. He thanked Binele very much for the favor. Evidently the Jews of Lodz were extremely polite people.

When she and Yacov left the inn, Binele had to cool her face with a little water from the well. She was all aflame. Hair and face wet, she looked at Yacov's sad brown eyes without realizing that she was staring. Her heart was still pounding, and something stuck in her throat. Mechanically, she braided and unbraided her hair.

"Are you going back to Bociany now to say good-bye?" Yacov asked, as if he, too, were bewildered.

"Are you out of your mind? My father would lock me up in the shed."

"So you won't take your things?"

"What things?"

"You're going to leave just the way you are?"

"Of course just the way I am." She weighed something in her mind, then added, "After I'm gone, a few hours after, or maybe a day, go to my father and tell him that I told you to say good-bye for me, and to my sisters and the children, too."

"So you really are going to leave right away?"

"Yes, right now. The flour merchant is in a hurry. You heard him. And when you come to Lodz, will you look me up?"

"Of course I will," he said. Already he longed for her, although she still stood beside him. He took two kopecks from his pocket and put them in her hand. "Take them," he said. "They're good-bye money."

"I still have the other kopecks you gave me," she said, reaching into her bodice. She pulled out a knotted piece of rag, undid the knot with her teeth, and let the two kopecks fall into her palm. Then she wrapped all four kopecks in the rag and stuffed it back behind her bodice.

Half an hour later, Yacov found himself staring after the flour merchant's covered wagon as it carried Binele away; he stared after it until it turned into a speck, which soon disappeared from sight. "I miss you so much," he said to the emptiness of the Wide Poplar Road. "I miss you so much that it hurts." As he turned in the direction of the Blue Mountain, he whispered. "I'll look for you. Even if I never find you, I'll go on looking."

The days that followed found Yacov more restless and dissatisfied with himself than ever. He could not rid himself of the hollowness that he felt inside. The world that surrounded him seemed to have changed once again. Right after the pogrom, its beauty had seemed to fade. But now the entire universe had lost its soul; life had completely lost its excitement and attraction. He avoided Abrashka and everyone else, yet he could not stay put in his alcove after work. He would take Sussi for a ride in the evenings, although he often cut the ride short. Riding made him feel worse, perhaps because he could not ride off to the place that his heart longed for. Finally he decided to go to Bociany and look up Ariele.

Ariele had been in hiding in Chwosty ever since the arrest of the Bundist leaders. Finally, Fishele the Butcher, by means of a substantial bribe, succeeded in convincing the chief gendarme of Ariele's innocence. Ariele was taken off the list of suspects to be found and arrested, and he felt free to continue with his illegal Bundist work in Bociany.

The two friends again spent the night in Ariele's little room, where, in their childhood, they had spent so much time together, discussing the great issues concerning the world. Tonight they forgot about the world. They talked about love. Yacov told Ariele about Binele. Ariele told Yacov about Rivkele, Zelig the Tailor's daughter, whom he intended to marry.

As he grew older, Yossele Abedale surrendered to fate more easily. He accepted his failing eyesight with indifference. Even the wounds to his heart and to his soul, which had once made him rage in protest, he now bore in silence, without rebellion. He often thought of Rabbi Mendele Kotzker's saying that silence is the loudest scream in the world, but that there was still a higher degree than silence—song. But Yossele was forced to concede, "To the level of song, I can't rise."

When he heard the news from Yacov that Binele had gone to Lodz, Yossele's first impulse had been to follow her there and find her. But then he gave it up. It made no sense. She was no longer a child. He knew her well enough to realize that he could never force her to stay in Bociany, if she had set her mind on leaving. Pining for her, his heart bleeding, he said to himself, "I did what I could. I can do no more."

At the beginning of winter, not long after Binele had run away, Ariele brought Yossele a letter. The letter was from Lodz. To Yossele's astonishment, it was not from Binele but from his son, Hershele, who was supposed to be at the yeshiva in Lublin. Yossele suddenly grew so nervous that the letter in his hand began to tremble, as if a strong wind were about to blow it away. He was unable to read it. His weak eyes saw nothing but a net of black lines against a white background. Without a moment's hesitation, he walked over to Hindele, who was standing against the wall of the Potcheyov, by her window shop, warming herself in the pale sun. "Read it to me!" he ordered, his voice hoarse with emotion.

She read as follows:

Dear Father,

I am writing this to you from Lodz, where I have been for half a year now. I am writing so that you will not live with any delusions. Your son will not become what you wanted him to become. He will be what he himself wants to be—a free man.

I am writing this to settle accounts with you. You molded me into a person who felt himself to be worth less than a worm or a tick; you molded me into an obedient tool of Him up in Heaven and of you—down on earth. You and my *melamed,* Reb Shapsele, and the entire clerical clique of His representatives belong to a world with which I no longer have anything in common. I don't want to shoulder the burden of meaningless, hollow religious obligations. I no longer want to be the coward I was. I no longer want to sit, hands folded, blood oozing from my limbs and heart, waiting for the Messiah to come. You, all of you, have thought him up, in order to be able to continue with your wretched lives in exile, to stagnate in your passivity, sinking deeper and deeper into the swamp of helplessness.

I want to be my own savior. I want to put an end to the galut right now, an end to everybody's exile. I want to build a new world of free people; people who wear no yoke, no saddle on their backs or on their souls. I still love you, Father. I always will. I respect you and all the suffering that you had to bear in your life. But there is an abyss between us, and who knows whether you will be able to bridge it and catch up with me. The only thread binding us now is the love we bear for each other. It is my hope that you will continue to hold on to your end of that thread, as I will forever hold on to mine.

Hindele sobbed as she read the letter. Yossele's weak eyes were also blurred with tears. He wept spontaneously, the tears rising from the depths of his being, as they never had before. He snatched the letter from Hindele's hands, tore it into tiny pieces, locked up the shop in the middle of the day, and went home. He told his daughters that their brother had died and that his name must never be mentioned in the house again. He tore his clothes as a sign of mourning, said the prayer for the dead, and sat down on a low stool, thus beginning the *shiva,* the seven prescribed days of mourning, for his only son, his *kaddish.*

When the seven days of *shiva* were over, Yossele went back to the Potcheyov and opened his shop. He placed himself at the doorpost, hands behind his back, and began to sway from side to side as he waited for customers. Hindele turned to him from her shelves of petty "vanities," her face radiant.

"Wish me *mazel-tov,* Reb Yossele!" she called out to him both proudly and consolingly. "My Shalom had a boy! My daughter-in-law, that is . . . Yes!"

# Glossary

***Aggadah*** (Yidd. *agode*): Legend, illustrative material in the Talmud.
***Badkhan:*** Entertainer at a wedding.
***Bal-Shem:*** Miracle worker.
***Besmedresh:*** Prayer and study house.
***Bude:*** Doghouse.
***Cholnt:*** Baked dish served on the Sabbath.
***Dian:*** Assistant to a rabbi who decides questions of ritual cleanliness.
***Dowidzenia*** (Pol.): Good-bye.
***Dzien dobry*** (Pol.): Good day.
***Fresser:*** Glutton.
**Galizianer:** Native of Galicia.
**Galut:** Exile of the Jews from Palestine.
***Gehenna:*** Hell.
**Gemara** (Yidd. *Gemore*): That part of the Talmud that comments on the Mishnah.
**Golem:** Dummy; artificial man created by a saintly rabbi.
**Goy** (pl. goyim): Gentile.
***Havdalah:*** Ceremony at the close of the Sabbath.
**Heder:** Religious school.
***Hometz:*** Food unkosher during Passover.
***Ile:*** Child prodigy.
***Kaddish:*** Prayer for the dead; person who says the prayer.
***Kapore:*** Scapegoat in pre-Yom Kippur ceremony.
***Kashrut:*** Jewish dietary laws.
***Kiddush hashem:*** Sanctification of God's name.
***Kri-shma:*** Prayer said upon going to bed; also said by heder boys at ceremony of circumcision.
***Kugl:*** Kind of pudding.
***Lamed Vov:*** The Thirty-Six Good Men.

***Malkes:*** Lashes, whipping.
***Medresh:*** Biblical exegesis.
***Melamed:*** Teacher.
***Mentsh:*** Human being; complete person.
**Mezuzah:** Small tube attached to doorpost, containing inscription on strip of parchment.
***Mishnah***(Yidd. *Mishne*): Part of the Talmud.
***Molodietz*** (Russ.): Clever fellow.
***Palent:*** A ball game.
**Pan** (voc. panie; fem. pani)(Pol.): Form of address: Mister.
***Pashol vont!*** (Russ.): Vanish!
***Patcher:*** Women's dance.
***Prosze*** (Pol.): Please.
**Reb:** Form of address: Mister.
***Rebetsin:*** Rabbi's wife.
***Rov:*** Rabbi.
***Schlimazl:*** Unlucky person.
***Sefirot:*** Fundamental term of the cabala denoting the ten stages of emanation.
***Shikse:*** Gentile girl.
***Shir-hamales:*** Psalm of degrees.
***Shkhina*** (coll. *shkhine*): Divine Emanation.
***Shma-Yisroel:*** The credo: "Hear, O Israel."
***Shofar:*** Ram's horn.
***Shtibl:*** Hasidic prayer room.
***Shtoperke:*** Female factory worker who mends damaged fabrics.
***Sider:*** Daily prayer book.
**Simhath-**Torah (Yidd. *Simches-Toyre*): Holiday following Succoth.
***Strulkes:*** A pebble game.
***Suka*** (Yidd. *suke*): Tabernacle erected in celebration of the Succoth holiday.
***Svolotch*** (Russ.): Scoundrel.
***Tkhines:*** Women's prayers.
**Torah**(Yidd. Toyre): The Pentateuch.
***Tsadik*** (pl. *tsadikim*): Saintly man.
***Tsenerene:*** Women's Yiddish Bible.
***Yaptzok:*** Hash of potatoes and beans.
**Yeshiva:** Institution of higher Talmudic learning.
***Yontev:*** Holiday.
***Yortsait:*** Anniversary of death.
***Zohar:*** Holiest book of the Cabala.
***Zydovetchka*** (Pol. *Zydoweczka*): Diminutive of *Zydowka,* Jewish woman.